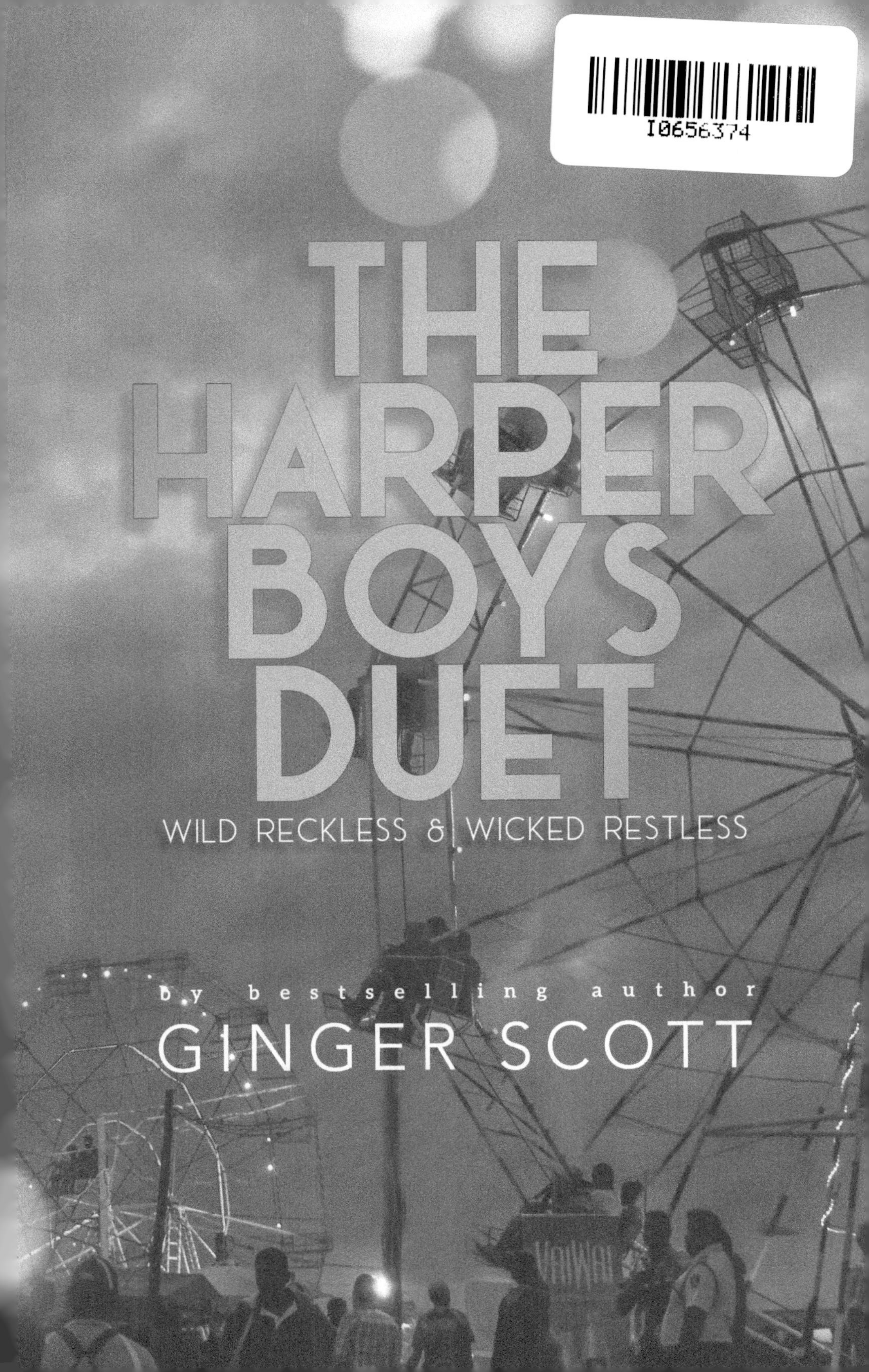
THE
HARPER
BOYS
DUET
WILD RECKLESS & WICKED RESTLESS
by bestselling author
GINGER SCOTT

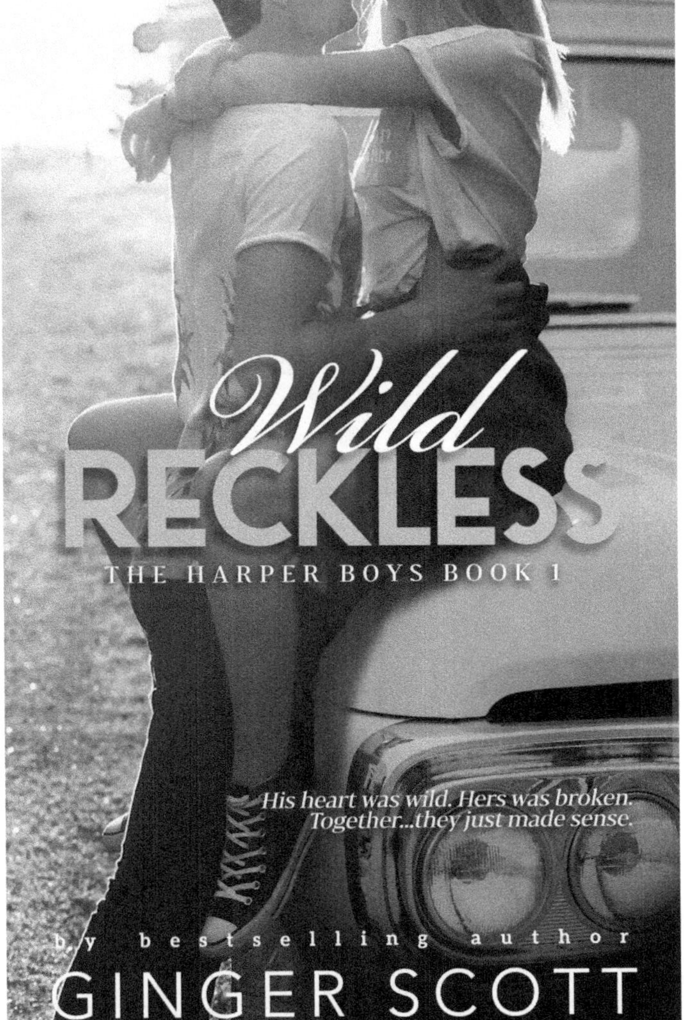
Wild
RECKLESS
THE HARPER BOYS BOOK 1
His heart was wild. Hers was broken.
Together...they just made sense.
by bestselling author
GINGER SCOTT

Wild
RECKLESS
THE HARPER BOYS BOOK 1
by bestselling author
GINGER SCOTT

Ginger Scott

This one's for the girls.

PROLOGUE

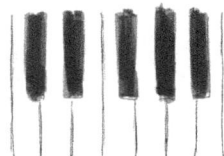

The caramel aroma that scented the air was thick. The smells of the Annual Wilson Orchard Apple Fest always began to permeate the streets the night before. Thin lines of smoke trailed from windows and front porches down residential streets of Woodstock, awakening the noses and stirring hungry bellies one at a time until they found the Harper residence.

This was going to be Owen Harper's first year at the festival. His dad took off special from his job at the warehouse just so he could take his middle son to the hometown tradition where the town's best bakers lined up their pies made of the fruits from Old Man Wilson's trees.

Owen liked the pies. He always ate them when his parents or grandparents brought them home. But what he really wanted to do was go on the Ferris wheel. His older brother James had been to the festival twice. James was ten, and he'd always been tall, so he could pass the height requirement easily and ride alone. But Owen was not yet five, so he would need a chaperone. His mother worked long hours, and his father rarely got a weekend off. But today...today was an exception. And today, Owen Harper would ride the Ferris wheel and look out over the town until he could see the roof of his house.

He promised to bring his younger brother Andrew to the festival one day too. He'd be old enough to walk to the festival on his own then, and tall enough to serve as his brother's chaperone—and together they'd both feel like they could fly.

Owen's dad talked to himself a lot. It wasn't anything unusual to Owen. He'd often watched his father have arguments within his own mind, his lips muttering fragments of words over his cereal. He learned to ignore the nonsensical tirades his dad would have with someone who seemed to be invisible while he drove his son to school. And the long hours on the porch at night, when his dad would stare off at nothing for hours at a time—those were routine, too. Owen loved those nights the best, because he would get to lie in the hammock, and sometimes he'd wake there in the morning.

Bill Harper was talking to himself a lot today. And everyone was staring. But Owen didn't understand why. Nothing was unusual.

His father paid their admission, and his son breathed in deeply, his lungs so full of the caramel, cinnamon, and apple fragrances that he was sure he could actually taste them.

His father's hand was rough from working heavy machines for hours every day, and when he pulled his son's hand into his, his skin felt scratchy. Owen didn't care. His own fingernails were chewed away and his palms were dirty from his morning hunt for worms in his mother's garden. He squeezed his father's hand tightly and let his grin stretch the freckles on his cheeks as he took in the sounds of popcorn popping, kids screaming on the roller coaster and carnival workers yelling out from all directions to win prizes.

Everything about today was perfect—just as Owen had dreamt it would be.

Bill Harper pulled his son up to the ticket booth, and stood him next to a hand-painted post. Owen stood tall, stretching out a little and lifting his heels up just enough that the woman checking his height wouldn't notice he was cheating. He didn't want anything to go wrong, and this would be just a little bit of insurance. In the end, he didn't have a reason to worry. He was forty-four inches—two inches taller than the requirement. Still too short to ride alone, but tall enough to ride. And that was all that mattered.

As his dad handed the tickets to the man wearing overalls and working the controls for the Ferris wheel, Owen noticed the people in line behind him staring again. His dad was talking off to the side, arguing with himself over something. But it was nothing unusual. His dad did this—often. Sometimes Owen did it too, because he wanted to see what it felt like.

Their brows were all pinched, and when one woman pulled her two girls in close to her body, away from him and his father, it made Owen angry. He sneered and actually let out a faint growl, which only made the woman hold on more tightly to her girls, who looked like they were about the same age as Owen. Their blond hair was pulled up on either side in pigtails. They wore matching dresses—pink—and they looked afraid. He had scared them, and eventually they left the line.

Owen was pleased.

He forgot all about the angry and frightened faces as soon as his carriage lifted from the platform and he and his father climbed higher in the air. The wind was colder up there, and everything about the day smelled like Halloween. It was morning, so the lights weren't on for any of the festival rides, but it didn't matter to Owen. The earth looked magical from up above.

While their cart was paused at the top, Owen twisted in his seat, counting rows of trees and buildings until he was sure he had the right road in his view. He counted chimneys to seven. And then he was sure he found it. He turned back around when the wheels started to spin again, satisfied that he could now check off the box in his mind—the one to see his house from up above.

He wanted to show his father. But Bill Harper was talking to himself. His son had learned it was better not to interrupt. He'd wait. His turn to talk would come eventually.

It always did.

After four more pauses, every carriage on the wheel was full, and the ride began its first full circle, the speed faster than Owen had expected. It was a little scary, and he wanted to hold his father's hand, but Bill Harper was still talking, his hands flying in front of him in various directions while he argued with someone—the person Owen could never see.

The air was cold when the wheel hit its top speed, so the young boy pulled the zipper up on his jacket with one hand, his other hand gripping the bar in front of him tightly. As he leaned forward, he noticed the woman with the two blond girls standing below, and he thought about spitting. He didn't, but he chuckled to himself when he pictured it.

His dad would think that was funny. He liked things like that. Bill Harper was very much a boy—he liked dirt, and messes, and swear words and beer. Owen wanted to grow up to be just like him.

By the third pass of the wheel, Owen was no longer nervous, and he loosened his grip on the bar in front of him. He wasn't brave enough yet to stretch his arms out, but he could close his eyes. With his head tilted toward the sky, he smiled big and shut his eyes tightly, letting the crisp air sting his face. With each pass along the ground, he heard the laughing and yelling of more people entering the festival, and the closer his cart climbed to the sky, the fainter those sounds became, until they started up again.

This was going to be the best memory of his life. He knew it.

His car paused at the very top while the riders on the other end of the wheel exited their carts. His ride was over. It was perfect.

When his father reached around and unclipped the latch, Owen didn't flinch. His dad worked with machines all day. He had worked with them for years. He knew what he was doing. He didn't make a sound when his father stood up, reaching for the long support beam above them. He held on tight when the cart swung forward. His father didn't tell him to, he just knew he was supposed to. He wouldn't want Owen to fall out.

It wasn't until his father took his first step out onto the beam below that Owen knew something was wrong. And then he saw the face of the woman below. He heard one of the little girls scream. Owen's world shifted, and everything began happening in slow motion. He slid his body to the place where his father had just been sitting, he reached his tiny hand—the one scuffed with dirt and scratched from trees—out to grip his father's leg, hoping he could just reach the denim of his jeans…reach anything. He reached, and reached, and reached. But no matter what, Owen was too small, his arm not yet long enough.

He tried to scream, but no sound would escape his mouth. His lungs felt flat. His stomach felt sick. This was no longer going to be his favorite day.

His father's boots gripped the beam, and his large hands held on to the large steel bar above him. He was moving slowly down, closer to the center of the Ferris wheel. He was moving down, and that was the only thing that made Owen feel okay.

The words of the carnival worker were a blur. He heard the man who ran the ride speaking over a loudspeaker, but he couldn't quite make out what he was saying.

Owen turned behind him to see if someone was coming to help, but that cart was empty. The one below him was full, and he could see a man with two kids sitting still, watching Owen's father climb out into the center of the wheel, his hands letting go every so often to point while he yelled.

Bill Harper was yelling. He was yelling at someone who was invisible, someone who couldn't be heard yelling back. He was pointing at him, shoving him, laughing wildly, and then crying.

Then he took a step, and Bill Harper fell to the earth.

In the end, all anyone could seem to talk about was how sad it was that Carolyn Potter's apple pie went to waste that year.

Owen never went to the festival again.

And he'd make damn sure his baby brother never went either.

13 YEARS LATER

CHAPTER 1

"Kensington! Come downstairs! Your sandwich is ready!"

We've been in the suburbs—no, *the country!*—for less than six hours, and already my mom has morphed into some form of June Cleaver. I half expect to walk down the steps and see her in one of those poufy A-line dresses with a pretty bow cinched about her waist.

She's been walking on eggshells with me ever since we handed over the keys to our old home. I didn't want to move here. Nothing about this move is about me though. And that's why my mom is playing up the *nice.* Not that she isn't normally nice. Normally, she isn't really there at all. Mom's the head nurse practitioner at a major hospital in Chicago. Dad's a conductor and a music professor in Milwaukee. He was just promoted to the head of the department. So we moved here…to the middle. Woodstock—exactly halfway between the two. "An ideal and convenient location," everyone said.

Convenient.

Far.

Lonely.

My two best girlfriends are starting their first day of senior year at Bryce Academy today. My old school. In the city. I wanted to stay. Mom didn't like me taking the train on my own, though. So I'll have to live vicariously through the pictures and texts they send. This morning's was a shot of Gaby frowning by my old locker. Morgan tried to get her face in the shot too, but all I caught was her ear. She was terrible at taking selfies. I miss them. But there's some strange comfort in visual proof that they miss me too.

It's hot here in the summer—hotter than in the city. There are more bugs, and the grass is itchy. It's green everywhere, and I'm not really used to that either. The houses all seem...*old.* Everyone has a front porch, and driveways that stretch into these enormous garages that sometimes aren't even attached to the houses at all. That's going to suck when it snows.

"Kensington!" Mom yells again, her voice less bubbly than before. The edge in her tone makes my lip tick up into a faint smile; I prefer her being real.

"I'm coming!" I yell, sending a quick heart image message to my two friends, then shoving my phone into my back pocket. I pause at the stairs to look out over the vast emptiness that is my new home. Our things are trickling in, but everything seems swallowed up by this house. It's not like the brownstone we lived in just south of Wrigley. Everything there was tight, and cramped, but it all had its place. Everything was at home. *I* was at home.

And now I'm here.

"Put the piano in the dining room...yes...about there. Perfect. Thank you," my mom says, quickly removing the sheets and pads from my piano. I think she thinks unveiling it quickly will somehow make me happy, like she's just pulled a bouquet or chocolates out of a hat.

"Where are we supposed to eat?" I ask, looking at my piano as it sits squarely under the dated, brass chandelier of our new dining room—like the world's cheapest spotlight. I had a practice room before, in our old house. Nothing fancy, just a door that I could close anytime I wanted.

I miss that door.

"We have a breakfast bar in the kitchen. It's fine. It looks nice there, doesn't it?" she asks without really asking. She walks back to the kitchen, her half-eaten sandwich dangling from her hand.

I think my piano looks stupid there. I think it looks stupid anywhere but in its home back in Chicago. But this isn't really about what I think, so I keep my mouth shut and follow my mom's footsteps into the kitchen where a ham sandwich sits alone on a gigantic white plate. The wastefulness amuses me, and I lift my sandwich, brush away the single crumb, and put the perfectly clean plate in the dishwasher.

"Thanks," I say, holding it up and taking a bite. Mom purses her lips, but she goes back to her lunch in front of her computer at the counter.

My mom finishes her sandwich quickly and without much conversation, then begins carrying boxes from the garage to various rooms around the house. Everything has a label: TOWELS, DISHES, CLEANING SUPPLIES, MOVIES, and KENSI for the few boxes that go to my room. I haven't been called Kensi or Kens out loud in years. I miss that too.

The kitchen has more boxes than I do; most of my things are still in the back of the Honda. My music books were already here and waiting for us when we unlocked the doors this morning. Dad brought them on his way to the office, afraid they'd get misplaced or damaged during the move. I could never say this to him, but there are only a few pages in that box that I really care about—the ones with notes I wrote, for me, for my ears and heart to hear.

I've been playing the piano since I was about three. My grandmother left my mother her old piano when she died, and I somehow knew what to do with it the moment the movers left it in our home. I couldn't reach the pedals, and my fingers barely spread far enough to strike a chord, but I could hear something and instantly mimic the sound. Music came to me before most of my words, and my father was quick to nurture my gift.

Dad plays brass instruments, so he always sought out the help of others to instruct me. My first music teacher was no longer able to teach me after a year, and I outgrew the next by the time I was ten. I've been studying with Chen ever since. He's a music composition professor at the University of Chicago and has scored many of the independent shows that play in the theaters downtown. My father hired him to give me private lessons, to challenge me and make it impossible for the best programs in the country to ignore me and "my gift." But what my father doesn't know is that when Chen comes over—while he's not at home—we play jazz.

Now that we're out of the city, I'll only be able to see Chen once a month, unless I take the train into Chicago on my own. My dad expects me to step up my independent playing. He even went as far as to make sure my extra periods at school were all time in the music room.

I think of everything I miss because of this move, my afternoon jazz with Chen is what I lament the most. It's been replaced by a gilded light fixture and a soaring ceiling that will make my playing echo out into the streets. It will be impossible to run away from the sounds my fingers will be forced to make. But I will practice, and I'll play the Bachs and the Mozarts and the Beethovens—those seemingly impossible songs that have become habits for my hands. I'll practice because that's what my father expects, and if I meet his expectations, he'll support my decision to study in New York or…or Paris or London or Rome. Anywhere…but here.

And then, I'll be free.

Unable to avoid reality any longer, I finally give in and venture to the driveway and the open hatch in the back of the Honda where most of my belongings still rest in taped-up cardboard boxes. My clothes are all stuffed into pillowcases; the wrinkles will have to be dealt with later.

With the last box wedged between my hip and the bumper, I reach up to slam the hatch closed again. The dark pair of eyes staring at me from the other side of the car make me jump—effectively dropping my boxes to the ground, spilling clothes and books and random trinkets from my girlfriends.

On instinct, I bend down to gather everything back into my arms, expecting help with my now disorganized load. Instead, I hear the steady drumming of a basketball along the pavement, and when I bend down just a little lower, I see his gray Converse slide slowly away from me, up our driveway toward the garage.

"Unbelievable," I whisper to myself as I stand with only half of my things, relenting the fact that I'm now going to have to make two trips. My red sweater is barely clinging to my grip, one sleeve dragging along the ground as I cross the driveway to my backdoor. My new neighbor keeps his back to me the entire time, his focus on the slow dribble of his ball. I give him a good long stare as I push my ass into the door a few times, my free fingers fumbling for the handle, desperate to get it open.

"Thanks for helping," I whisper again, following it up with the word *asshole* in my head.

Suddenly, his dark eyes are on mine, and I would swear he heard me with the smug smirk that creeps into one cheek. The ball never stops moving. His hand never stops moving. He's operating completely independent of the hypnosis he's attempting to put me under—the soft squint to his eyes somehow making them more ominous. I'm not quite sure he isn't evil. And I'm also not quite sure that this hypnosis isn't working.

A gift, the door behind me unhinges and I stumble backward inside, somehow catching my balance so I don't make a complete ass out of myself in front of mister darkness.

I race upstairs quickly, tossing my pile of things on my bed without care, hurrying to the window to orient myself with exactly what my view is in relationship to the driveway. With one push of the curtain, I know.

His eyes are right back to me, almost as if he were expecting me to look—expecting me to find him. The damned smirk on his face is still there, and my heart is thumping away at my stomach, not so much from flutters…as panic. The ball is still in motion, and I can't help but beg myself to remember the sight of him, so I can think about it later and decide if he's really as scary as my instincts tell me he is.

His white T-shirt V-necks, and the sleeves hug his biceps. He's wearing long black basketball shorts, and his hair is short, but long enough on top for the strands to twist in various directions. From a distance, he's a really good-looking guy. But I have a feeling—and a fear—that it's his eyes that hold the power. From fifteen feet up and fifty feet away, they literally smolder. If I weren't such a social pariah, I would march back down the stairs and introduce myself. I'd ask him why he's dribbling a ball in my driveway, using the hoop bolted to the eave of *our* garage. But my feet are stuck to the carpet of my new bedroom, and my hands are burning from the roughness of the curtains my hand is now squeezing.

When I think I can't handle much more, his lip twitches, and then he blows me a kiss and turns around to shoot the ball into the hoop.

What. The. Hell. Was. That?

I let go of my grip on the curtain and fall to my knees, wishing there was some way I could erase the last five minutes of my life. Instead, I slide so my back is against the window's wall, so I can't see him, only hear the rhythmic thump of the basketball for the next twenty minutes.

When I feel safe enough to look again, I crawl to my knees and peel the curtain fabric back an inch. The hoop is quiet. The driveway is quiet. Now is my chance.

Racing to the driveway, I scoop up the remaining things that I left there before and close the hatch to the car. I don't glance at his house, and I don't dwell long enough to know anything for certain. But I am positive that the front door was open—the inside of the house barely hidden behind a thin porch screen.

And I'm pretty sure my mystery neighbor from hell was standing there…watching.

CHAPTER 2

Yesterday was registration. I missed it. Too busy with the move for my mom to find the time to drive the two point five miles to Woodstock South. I don't have a car. I barely have a license, so borrowing a car without one of my parents in the passenger seat is out of the picture too. And two point five miles—while not far with wheels—is a hell of a long way by foot.

So I begin Woodstock South High School today—completely and utterly lost.

Dad dropped me off on his way to Milwaukee. It was early enough that I was able to get the printout of my schedule from the front office and find my way to the music room. My first two periods are music—the first one with the band as a whole, and the second one is independent study. This is the only part my father made sure of. The rest, me getting into honors English and math, was all my doing, all the result of my persistent emailing to my guidance counselor to ensure I was not trapped in a public school classroom with burnouts.

This is the first year I've gone to school without a uniform. I know most girls my age would love the rebellion of this, the freedom to choose, to find a *look* all their own.

I miss my uniform.

Uniforms are easy. No decisions to make. Instead, I spent the first half hour of my morning switching from jeans to leggings and back to jeans again. It's fall in Illinois, the leaves are changing, and the winds come and go.

I'm glad I settled on the jeans now as I stand outside the band room door, my knuckles pink and tender from rapping on it repeatedly, hoping someone will let me inside.

"You in, Harper?" I hear a male's voice behind me, rounding the corner. I'm unable to stop myself from turning to see who it is. Soon I'm looking right into the eyes of my mysterious neighbor, the one I named *Demon Spawn* last night as I worked myself up over how cocky and rude he was in the driveway. His lip ticks up, and his eyes squint when he notices me, but he looks away fast.

"You know it! Let me just…make an appearance," he says, pounding his knuckles with the first guy to speak. The group of four guys passes me, and the demon never glances my way again. Once they're a few steps away from entering the main hall doors, I hear them erupt in laughter, drawing my eyes to them again, expecting them to all be looking at me—teasing the new girl.

But they're not. They disappear behind the doors seconds later, and finally the band room door opens and I slip inside.

"Oh my god, how long have you been waiting out here? I'm so sorry; we never hear the door in the morning. It's too loud in here," says a girl with reddish blond hair piled into a bun on top of her head. She's wearing tight black jeans and a black hoodie, and her gloves are missing their fingers. She almost looks tough, except her face is dotted with freckles and her breath smells like strawberry from the giant wad of gum she's popping through her smile.

"Not long. It's okay," I lie. I was out there knocking for a solid five minutes, but this girl seems nice.

"Oh, good. Here, come on in. I'll introduce you to Mr. Brody," she says, waving me forward. I drop my backpack next to the others that are piled by the door. The room is full of noise—saxophones, trombones, flutes—everyone tuning.

"I'm Willow, by the way," she says, reaching out her hand. I shake it and notice how cold her fingertips feel compared to the knitted part of her hand still covered by a glove.

"Nice to meet you. I'm Kensington," I start, but pause, struck instantly by the realization that as much as I don't want to be here, it is a new beginning. And new beginnings do have their perks. "But people call me Kensi."

"Kensi...cool! I like that!" she says, her enthusiasm maybe a little obnoxious. I like her anyway.

"Mr. Brody, I found Kenny," she says, already blowing my new identity, as I trail behind her into a small office to the side of the main band room. A small man stands at my introduction. He's maybe four or five inches shorter than I am, and his glasses are propped on top of his head, which barely has any hair. He's eating a donut, so he finds a tissue on his desk and rests the half-eaten treat on it before dusting his hands for crumbs along his gray pants.

"Kensington Worth, yes. Glad you found the room!" he says, his glasses falling right into place on his nose.

"People call her Kenny," Willow interjects for me. She's assertive, oddly so. I like her a little more, and I'm starting to hope she'll be my friend. I could use a dash of assertive.

"Actually, it's *Kensi,"* I correct.

"Ohhhh, yeah. Sorry, Kensi," Willow says, her face embarrassed at her slip.

"Well, all-righty then. Kensi it is," Mr. Brody says, popping the full other half of his donut in his mouth as he ushers us back into the main room. "So, Kensi...what's your instrument?"

I'm puzzled by his question. This should have been settled. I play the piano. My dad made sure everyone in this entire school system knew I played the piano. And he made sure everyone knew they were to accommodate my need to play, whenever he demanded.

"Piano?" It comes out unsure.

"Right, right. I know that. I mean for band, for marching. You can't really march with a piano." I heard him, but inside I was hoping maybe there was a way I could rewind—reverse myself right back outside the door, back home, back through my boxes, and back to the city.

Marching.

What the hell was I going to do?

"I…I don't know. I don't really *play* anything else. And I don't…march," I say, looking around the room as the hundred or so students begin to file into chairs based on the instruments they play. Yeah…there are no *piano* groups here.

"No problem. We'll make you a pit player," he says, shrugging his head to the left for me to follow him.

"Pit…player?" I ask, but I start to understand the closer we get to the percussion instruments. "Here's a pair of mallets. You'll find your way around the xylophone in no time. You sight read?"

"I do, but…" I start to protest, suddenly aware that he's walking away and mallets are now in my hands.

The xylophone is essentially a piano. The keys are all the same, only you strike them with sticks. I used to love playing on them at my father's office when I was young. But I haven't played one in years.

"Hey, I'm Jess," says one of the guys standing near me. I shake his hand and repeat his name in my head over and over again. *Jess, Jess, Jess. Willow, Willow, Willow.* I know two people here now.

"Hi, I'm Kensi. I guess I'm playing xylophone," I say through a nervous smile.

"Yeah, looks like it," he says, bending over and pulling a harness for a snare drum over his head. "Welcome to the drum line."

"You about ready, babe?" Willow says over my shoulder, causing me to turn and pinch my brow, wondering how I got moved to *babe* so quickly. My question is answered when she brushes by me and pulls Jess's face toward hers and kisses him quickly.

"Sure. Let's get this pep-rally shit over with," Jess says, spinning one of his drumsticks over his head, his eyebrows raised, feigning enthusiasm.

"Pep…rally?" I say, just as Mr. Brody drops a flipbook of music on top of the xylophone. *My* xylophone now, so it would seem.

"Yep, first day of school always starts in the gym. Pep rally. It's our thing," Willow says, pressing a whistle between her lips and blowing hard. "Let's go, peeps. Meet you in the gym in six minutes!"

"She's the drum major. She likes the power trip. Normally she's a flute player. Flutes suck! I get it. And her uniform is pretty hot, so…ya know,"

Jess says, winking at me. He's a typical drummer—shaved head, double piercings in his ears, chain dangling from his back pocket.

Everyone is packing up, lugging their instruments out the door, and I feel like my chest is caving in on me, as if my rib bones are actually cracking into pieces and stabbing my heart and other internal organs. I glance quickly at the booklet of music in front of me. Fight song, national anthem, a bunch of top-forty tunes. Yeah, it's all pretty simple stuff. If I can sight-read Beethoven, I should be able to read this.

"Jess!" I catch him before he steps through the door. "How…how do I get *this* to the gym?"

He grins at me, then slides his sunglasses on. "You push it," he laughs, then lets the door close behind him.

Fucking drummers.

Right. Push it. Okay, I can do this. I tuck the music book under the first layer of keys and then shove the mallets into my back pocket. I slide the wheels back and forth a few times to make sure they're not locked, take a deep breath, and push what is *so very much not a piano* to the doorway.

I'm the last one in the room, so I fling the door open, hold it with my hip and then back the xylophone out, banging nearly every key on the door jam as I do it. Then it hits me. I don't know where the gym is.

I don't know where the gym is!

There's a natural flow of students walking down a hill, so I follow them. And when I start to see instruments in a few hands, I sigh with relief.

The doors to the gym are within sight. Unfortunately, Demon Spawn and his group of friends are also nearby, almost guarding the door. My inner voice is wishing he won't notice me, but the awkward new student is hoping one of them will help me inside and hold open the door.

Neither wish is granted, and his eyes land squarely on me, his lip doing that twitching thing again that lets me know he sees me. It also lets me know he isn't going to be of any help at all.

I'm lifting the front wheels down a level on the sidewalk and am only a dozen or so yards from the entrance when I look at him again to catch him nod a laugh to his friends—just before he kicks his foot toward me, covering my pathway in gravel.

It doesn't take long for one of the tiny stones to wedge itself into one of the wheels, causing a high-pitched screeching sound and leaving a long, chalk-like skid for the few feet I drag my frozen wheel along the walkway. I stop, bend down, and push the rock out with the back of my mallet, my face burning from the attention. When I stand again, he's looking at me —laughing.

"You're an asshole," I say, which only makes his lip twitch again.

"Hey, sorry, this is hard to haul alone," Willow says, opening up the door and staring down Demon Spawn. "Not every guy at this school is a douchebag. Most of them help a girl out when she needs it."

My demon neighbor slowly raises his hand, holding up a middle finger before blowing her a kiss.

"In your dreams, Owen," she fires back.

Willow grabs the front of my keyboard and helps me guide the xylophone inside, all the way to the far end of the gym where the band is now set up.

"Thanks," I say, and I mean it. So far, this first day has sucked epic proportions.

"No sweat," she says, leaning against the wall next to me.

I recognize the principal from my visit to the office this morning to get my schedule. He taps on a microphone a few times and then begins to say a few announcements, something about buses, student parking, lunch hours —none of this applies to me. Of course, an hour ago, a xylophone didn't apply to me either.

When I look to my right, I notice Demon Spawn, who I guess is *really* named Owen, shuffle along the front of the bleachers until he and his friends are almost next to me. He chuckles lightly when he's near me, then turns to climb to the top of the bleachers. Maybe I imagine hearing his arrogant laugh, but I sort of don't think I do.

"What's his story?" I whisper to Willow.

"Who, Owen?" she asks.

"I guess. That's his name?" I respond.

"Yeah. That's Owen Harper. He's...well...he's a dick. Sorry, hope you're not offended by that word," she says, covering her mouth, like she's trying to be demure. I like Willow. She's direct and funny, and she seems like she's fine with who she is. She reminds me of Gaby and Morgan.

"I'm from the city. I've heard worse," I smile, and she leans into me.

"Cool. Okay, well then...he's a major fucking dick!" she laughs, and I join her.

"Right. I think I already had that much figured out. Rocks kicked at me sorta clinched my hunch, but thanks," I whisper to her, trying not to interrupt the rest of the principal's speech.

Willow shrugs, then kicks off from the wall to stand in front of the band after the principal tells everyone to rise and remove their hats. I note the key that they're playing in, and leave my music tucked away. I know the national anthem, so I won't have to read this one. The fight song is going to be a different story though.

Near the end of the song, I allow myself to glance in Owen's direction, and he and his friends are all standing still with their hats against their chest, respectful of this, at the very least. I don't know why, but for some reason I'm relieved that he's not *that* much of an asshole.

We play two or three more songs before the football team is announced, and I manage to figure out the fight song quickly, playing along. My dad would throw a fit if he knew this is how my first period of music was going. I'm kind of having fun, though, so I don't think I'll tell him.

WILLOW HELPED me haul the xylophone back to the band room, and Owen wasn't around to kick any more speed bumps under my legs. In fact, he seemed to disappear entirely after the pep rally this morning.

My second period was blissful, spent alone in one of the music practice rooms. I cheated on my lessons and instead spent the hour playing jazz. My next two classes were less pleasant. Part of being placed in honors math and English meant I could expect homework right out of the gate, which I got—several chapters of reading and a lengthy problem set.

What I didn't expect was to hear the teacher call out "Owen Harper" in both of my classes. Harper—I'm pretty sure that's his last name. That's what that one guy called him when they walked by me early this morning. He didn't strike me as an *honors* kind of anything.

By the time the lunch hour rolls around, my stomach is growling so loudly that I'm sure people near me in the hallway can hear it.

"There you are. How were your morning classes?" Willow asks. She's a junior, so I don't have any classes with her.

"All right, I guess. I have homework already," I say, and she scrunches up her face in disapproval.

"Yeah, me too," she says.

I follow Willow to the cafeteria and mimic everything she does. I grab a tray, shuffle along the counter, and pull the same sandwich, apple, and drink from the coolers that she does. I won't be able to copy her for long; I get a feeling she eats kind of healthy, and I'm going to have to delve into the pizza and fries line one day this week.

We both punch in our numbers for the lunch account and take our trays to a table near the window where Jess is waiting for us along with another couple I recognize from band this morning. Everyone sits—everyone…but me. I'm frozen, locked into where I'm standing, my elbows somehow unable to operate well enough to place the tray on the table in front of me.

On the other side of the glass, Owen Harper is kissing a girl. She seems pretty—her hair a long, dark brown, very different from my wavy blond layers. I try to notice more about her, but I can't take my eyes off the place where his hands are cupped around her face, holding her lips to his with this animalistic sense of ownership. It's almost offensive, but it's also…*something else.*

His right hand slowly slides into her hair, and he tilts her face ever so slightly to one side, giving his mouth a better angle, as his lips grow more aggressive. I'm hypnotized by the power he has over her—over *me.* His lips move over her mouth with a sense of possession, and his grip on her upper lip with his teeth slides away with a slowness that simply oozes sex. I'm blushing—just standing here, a voyeur, and I'm blushing.

I have never been kissed like that. *I have never really been kissed at all.*

He moves down her neck next, his tongue blatantly sliding along the nape then under her jaw. Their friends are all standing nearby, but nobody is looking. I'm stunned no one else is seeing this. His hands are now clutched around her head and body, her shirt twisting up enough to reveal her bare midriff. It's almost a soft porn show in front of the main window for the whole cafeteria to see. Yet, I'm the only one looking.

And then his eyes open, in a purposeful haze, and he looks. Right.

At. Me.

My heart stops. My stomach feels sick, and my lip puffs out with the small gasp that escapes me from the shot of adrenaline now coursing through me from getting caught.

Owen never stops kissing. His eyes toy with me for the brief seconds I stand there in shock. He's laughing with those eyes. He's teasing me—as if he knows that I am so far out of my comfort zone that I may pass out from humiliation at any moment. But I don't. I look right back at him. I can't help myself. And his eyes soften, but not in a gentle way. They become sexier, more daring—he's daring me. *Keep watching; go ahead.* That's what his eyes are saying now. The gray color suddenly looks like a storm brewing, and I'm caught in it, no chance for survival.

"Earth to Kens! We're down here. Tell them to get a room!" Willow says, pulling at the edge of my shirt, yanking me down into my seat, away from the danger tempting me on the other side of the window.

"Sorry, that was…huh…I just guess couples never really did that sort of thing at my old school. You know…so…out in the open?" I say, forcing my eyes onto my tray.

"Oh, they're not a couple. Owen just does that sometimes. And girls keep lining up. Like lemmings," says the small girl sitting with us. Her hair is cut into a sharp bob cut, and her eyes are lined in smoky-gray eye shadow. It's a look I wish I could pull off, just once. "I'm Elise, by the way. I play the flute. And this is Ryan. He doesn't play anything, but I like him anyway."

Ryan shrugs and gives a quick smile before turning his attention back to whatever seems to be interesting him on his phone. Elise ribs him with her elbow, and he rolls his eyes and puts his phone down on the table to give me a proper smile before turning back to her. "There, satisfied?" he says.

She looks at him with wide eyes, then turns back to me. "Ryan is my *ex* boyfriend. I just dumped him because he was rude to my new friend Kensi," she says, and Ryan sighs deeply, this time putting his phone back in his pocket and standing with his hand outstretched.

"Sorry, just stressed. I'm waiting to hear about a college thing. And I'm *not* an asshole, despite what she says," Ryan says, tilting his head toward Elise.

I shake both of their hands across the table, and spare a glance back out the window as I do. The make-out session seems to have ended, but Owen is still looking at me. His arm is slung around the girl's shoulders, and his thumb is caressing her bare skin.

"It's because the Harper brothers have wild hearts," Willow says. For some reason, her statement sparks a collective sigh from her friends. "What? You guys know it's true."

"No, Will. None of us know it's true. We just humor you. And you know I hate it when you start talking this mystical crap," Jess says, standing with his empty tray. "Anyone need anything to drink? I'm not sure I can hear the *wild heart* speech one more time."

Willow pulls a pinch of crust from her sandwich and throws it at Jess before he turns to leave. He catches it at his stomach and throws it back, smirking while he does. "All right, I'll be back in about seven minutes. That's how long this usually takes," he says. Willow squints her eyes at him and shakes her head as he leaves.

"Wild hearts?" I ask, bringing her back to the point. I'll admit, I'm curious.

"Willow thinks because she was *there* when it all happened—that she knows, has some sort of inside knowledge on why the Harper boys are so fucked up," Elise says, pulling open a bag of chips. She offers me one, but I shrug it off. I'm too intrigued by this story now to eat.

"There's more than just Owen?" I ask, wondering why the house next door always seems so quiet.

"Yep, there are three. Owen's the middle brother. His older brother James is a real loser—total druggie. And his younger brother Andrew is a freshman. You'll see him around sometimes," Elise says.

My stomach sinks a little knowing that there are more of them living next door to me, and I turn to look out the window again. Owen's attention is finally on his friends, but his arm is still around that girl, his thumb still stroking her arm like he's keeping her on a leash, reminding her that he's here and he'll get back to her later.

"So drugs…is that what makes them *wild*?" I ask.

"Ohhhhh no," Willow says, piling the remnants of her sandwich and the half-eaten apple up on her tray. "That happened later. And I'm pretty sure it's just James that's a druggie. Their problems started a long time ago, though."

Willow scoots forward, glancing once over her shoulder, and I feel like I'm learning some dark secret. With a slightly lowered voice, she starts to explain. "We were five, maybe not quite. And there used to be this carnival that happened every year—the apple fest. Well, I was there with my cousins, because they usually had cool rides and games and stuff. I was in line waiting for my turn to throw the rings at the bottles when my aunt grabbed ahold of my arm and pulled me close to her body. She was trying to shield my eyes, but she was too caught up in everything happening to do a very good job. I saw everything."

"I'm confused. What to you mean? What did you see?" I ask. Willow's storytelling sucks. I'm starting to understand why Jess left. I'd leave too if I already knew how this ended. But I don't; so I'm glued to my seat.

"Well, Owen's dad was Bill Harper. He was sort of known as the town's crazy man. He talked to himself and did a lot of weird things—like posting strange signs in the back of his car telling people to leave him alone. Anyhow, apparently he finally snapped, and when my aunt pulled me away from the games, I looked up at the Ferris wheel, where everyone else was looking, and I saw Bill Harper standing out on one of the steel beams, about a hundred and fifty feet in the air. He was yelling out these crazy things; none of it made sense."

"What does this have to do with Owen?" I ask, my periphery catching a glimpse of my tall, mysterious neighbor still standing outside.

"He was there. He was on the ride, in the cart, when his dad walked out of it, stepped out to the edge, and jumped. He killed himself right there in front of Owen. And the Harper boys have been ruined ever since," she says, and I can't help but hurt a little thinking of Owen as a little boy. I wonder what he was like then. And I wonder if Willow's right—if he would have been different, wouldn't have kicked rocks at me or would have helped me carry my things inside if he hadn't been damaged.

"They're not *ruined*," Ryan finally says. "Owen's a good guy. He just has to trust you; that's all."

"You're just saying that because he's on the basketball team with you. You have to say that because he's so good," Willow says.

"Yeah, he's good. But honestly? He's always been pretty decent to me. Maybe I've just never labeled him though," Ryan says. I take note of the hint of disappointment in his tone over how Willow is talking about Owen, and it makes me wonder where the truth lies.

"He has an arrest record," Willow says, a little defensively.

"Fuck, Will, so do I! Half this school has some sort of something on their record. We drive too fast, we get caught at parties with beer, we steal shit from the convenience store. It's what we do because there's shit-squat to do out here," Ryan says, standing and kissing Elise on the head. "I'm just saying maybe we're all a little fucked up, and the only difference is the world knows Owen's story, because it happened out in the open. The rest of us…we all just keep our shit private."

Elise doesn't add anything to Ryan's speech, but she looks at her boyfriend with a sort of reverence when he speaks. With trays in their hands, they slide from the table together, leaving just Willow and me now to finish the story.

"I guess Ryan's sort of right," she says, slipping her backpack over her shoulders and nudging me to do the same so we're not late for class. "But… I don't know, Kens. That guy? He has some extra crap going on. He lives on the edge, like he doesn't have fear or something. I've heard he's played that game, Russian roulette…you know, where people take turns holding a gun up to their heads with only one bullet inside? He does that at parties. I don't think that's normal, do you?"

I shake my head *no* when she asks. No, that's not normal. And I think I knew the first time I looked into his eyes that there was nothing normal about Owen Harper. But what scares me is I had this flash of an idea—a fleeting thought—that there was something special about him, too.

When I dump my trash and stack my tray, I hold the door for Willow to walk through. I sneak one final look to the courtyard outside. Owen's hand has finally dropped from the girl's arm, and he and a group of five other guys and girls are walking away—away from the school completely.

He's wearing gray jeans, black Doc Martens, and a tight black, long-sleeved shirt that fits his frame perfectly. From a distance, he's a shadow. I don't know about the *wild* theory. But Owen Harper is definitely dark.

And he sleeps thirty feet away from me.

CHAPTER 3

Why did he bother to show up at all? Why did he leave after lunch? Why did he miss his classes on the first day of school?

Who did that?

I can't quit thinking about what Willow said. Ditching classes, three at least as far as I could tell from his absence during roll call in science, and flaunting his make-out sessions aren't exactly things I would consider *wild.* But that last thing she said—about playing roulette with a loaded gun—I couldn't seem to wrap my mind around that. It frightened me, and it made me dread going home, being *near* someone who could do that.

Mom was working the late shift at the hospital, and Dad wouldn't be home until late in the evening, so I was going to experience my first ride on the country-bumpkin bus. It's really more suburban than that, but compared to the city, where transportation options are waiting around every corner, this feels like I'm waiting for the tractor pull to swing by to give me a lift.

Willow's car slows at the curb next to me, and her honk makes me jump. "Hey, what are you doing?"

She asks a lot of obvious questions.

"Well, maybe my powers of deductive reasoning are flawed, but I was assuming that this was the place where one waited to take the bus home. You see, there's this *sign* here," I say, tapping my fingertips on the metal sign that reads BUS STOP. "Then, there was this gathering of students all in some sort of line-type formation. So I thought..."

"Wow, you're a smart-ass," she says, reaching up on her visor and pulling a pair of sunglasses down to push them on her face. "Good thing I like smart-asses. Wanna ride?"

I wasn't really looking forward to what was shaping up to be a pretty packed bus, so I shrug on the outside and open the passenger door. Inside, I do a dorky happy dance over the fact that I have a friend...with a car...who is willing to take me home. Now, just to convince her to pick me up in the mornings.

"So, where do you live?" she asks, and my mind jumps forward to thoughts of my neighbor.

"About six blocks that way, right off of Eighty-seventh and Canterbury," I say, waiting for her to realize where I live—*who* I live by—but she doesn't seem to put it together. She turns her radio up and starts singing along with one of the hit songs on the pop station. That seems to be the most popular station around here. Not a lot of alt-rock listeners, it seems. That's okay, though—I'm sort of good with all music. Habit of my passion, I suppose.

"So, how do you like Woodstock, so far?" Willow asks. I look around at the brick and stone houses, the rows of trees and colorful leaves dusting the streets. Honestly, it's beautiful here. But it's still not the city, and I don't know how to explain that to someone.

"It's nice here," I say, inciting a quick laugh from my new friend. "What? I mean it. It's nice."

"Right—*nice,*" she says. "You mean...*boring.*"

"Oh, no. I mean, well...yeah. Maybe a little boring. But that's okay. I'm not really into crazy parties and nightlife. It's just, in the city there's always something going on, all the time. I guess I got kind of used to the noise. At night, it just gets so quiet here. That's...that's a little strange," I explain, pointing to the street to make sure Willow makes the turn.

The conversation is about to make a shift, because I can tell by the look on her face that she realizes who my neighbor is now.

"Well it looks like you can kiss that quiet goodbye," she says, nodding forward to Owen's driveway. He's climbing into a beat-up old pick-up, and the girl from earlier is sitting next to him, riding in the middle of the cab between Owen and another guy. He peels out of the driveway, his tires leaving a tuft of smoke and the smell of burnt rubber in the air. The girl screams something as they speed by us, Owen never once glancing our way.

"Yeah..." I start. I unbuckle my seat and pull my bag to my lap from the car floor. "That's sort of why I had those questions. I haven't really officially met him yet, I mean...other than the rock kicking thing. He's just kind of quiet...and, I don't know, mysterious maybe?"

"Kens, trust me on this one. Owen Harper isn't quiet. You just haven't given him a reason to be loud yet. That's probably a good thing," she says. "Just keep your eyes open, and watch out for James. He's the one you need to worry about. That boy's nothing but trouble."

"Great. Nothing like living next door to *trouble*," I say with a deep breath. "Hey, thanks for the ride."

"Sure, I'll be here at six-thirty or so to give you a ride in the morning. Be ready, though. I hate being late," she says, reaching over to turn the radio back up to DEFCON levels. I can barely hear her singing along with the music as she backs out of my driveway and heads for the corner.

The Harper driveway parallels ours, and I spend a few minutes looking at the dark black lines Owen left in his wake. There are fainter ones surrounding it, which means he must peel out often.

Typical boy.

The house is empty—every room is mine alone until at least midnight. I spend the first hour munching on peanut butter cereal and watching people reveal the real father of their baby on one of those talk shows. It's an embarrassing obsession of mine, but watching shows like this is my greatest relaxation. There's something about the circus of absurdity—I find it calming. Helps me put all of the drama I think I have in perspective.

My reading and math homework is a breeze compared to my nightly assignments from Bryce. I feel like I'm learning things I was taught last year at the Academy, and if I were a better student, one who was more driven by academia, I might care that I'm not being challenged. But as long as I get to play the piano every day, I really don't care that my math and science and literature are simple. There's nothing wrong with easy. And I think I've earned easy. Besides, I know all my parents will ask about is music anyhow.

The sun sets around six, and unlike in the city, things actually get dark here. I almost find it charming—the soft rustling sound of the dried leaves being blown along the porch and driveway is strangely comforting.

I leave the front door open, the porch screen closed to let in the chilled air. It's making the house cold, but I like the cold. It justifies pulling on my sweatpants and long-sleeved shirt. If I knew how to light the fire, I'd do that, too. Summer is leaving, making room for fall. I spend a few minutes dumping a pack of powdered cocoa into hot water, then stirring, and I blow on my cup as I walk to the piano. I take a sip too soon, and the liquid burns the tip of my tongue.

Once I set my cup down on the piano bench next to me, I pull out my sheet music from my boxes. There's something that just isn't right, and I've been dying to play through these lines—alone, without the critical ear of my father nearby to offer his opinion, or rather to point out that I should be perfecting my classics training instead of spending time doing the part I actually love.

My eyes closed, I let my fingers find their home. It's natural. It always is, the way the polished slivers of black and white feel slick to my touch.

I crack an eyelid open and relent a smirk at my strange surroundings. This is not where I want to be, not where I want to play, so I close the eye again and pretend I am back in my practice room, my door closed and my sounds for nobody's ears but mine. The rest just happens—fingers flying, pounding, stopping abruptly, and shifting from soft to quiet.

I like the change in music—to move from smooth to staccato, sometimes no transition at all. My father hates it, so I save these moments for nights like this. And before I know it, I fall into my routine, the blues rhythms coming through, taking over. My eyes open because this sound—the sound of my heart—has made me feel at home.

Without warning, though, my bliss is interrupted.

Thud.

Thud.

Thud.

The sound is constant, halted only by the loud clanking of a ball shanking off of the metal hoop outside. The shadows of the trees are sharp and dark against my curtains, and I can tell someone has turned the driveway floodlights on. *My* floodlights. The ones attached to *my* home. Where the basketball hoop is also located.

After what feels like a full minute of deep breathing, I find a fraction of my calmness from before and let my fingers glide back into their position. With my eyes closed, I do my best to tune out the continual barrage of noise taking over outside, and I almost get back into my groove, when the *thud* from before ricochets off of the side of my house.

"Oh, come on!" I shout, standing quickly from my bench and spilling the hot chocolate onto the floor. "Damn it!"

Changing direction, I head into the kitchen first and grab the towel folded over the cabinet under the sink and race back to the spilled drink, doing my best to soak it up from the wood floor.

Thud. Thud. Thud.

Maybe it's the sound—the fact that it still continues—or maybe it's the fact that I'm now on my knees cleaning up my spilled drink, my little night of happiness suddenly ruined.

Maybe it's him.

Something pushes me, just enough, and I toss the towel back into the kitchen and pull my hoodie tight around my body, flinging the screen door open in front of me and leaping from the porch stairs. By the time I round the front of the house and start my way up the driveway along the side, I'm full of adrenaline, not even affected by the sting of the cold, and I ride the wave of bravery right into Owen Harper's face.

"Uhhhhh, do you mind?" I say, grabbing the ball quickly and clutching it to my body, both arms wrapped around it tightly like I'm hugging a teddy bear.

Owen stares at the ground where the ball was bouncing just seconds before, his posture frozen and his face almost surprised. With a tiny jerk, he tilts his head up until his focus is on the ball in my arms, his gaze never quite making it all the way to my eyes.

"I never mind. Can I have my ball back now?" he says, the devil's smirk creeping slowly on one side of his lips until the smallest dimple forms.

Asshole.

When he reaches his hand toward me, I shuffle backward quickly, squeezing the ball even tighter, and for a flash second, something happens to his eyes—they grow dark.

"Careful," he says, his smirk curling slightly, like a fisherman's hook waiting to catch me.

I've spent three years going to one of Chicago's most elite private schools, which left me with some pretty solid experience when it came to navigating high school factions. I avoided the rich kids, and they avoided me right back, so that one was easy. I was friendly to the pot smokers, because those kids threw the best parties, but not friendly enough that I was ever guilty by association. I led among my circle—popular with the music students, crossing over to mingle with the drama crowd and the artists.

Owen—he didn't fit any of those boxes. But I'd force him in one if I had to. I've already lost my practice room, my sanctuary. He wouldn't take away my quiet moments alone with my piano too.

I match the dare in his eyes, take one step back, and drop the ball down to my foot. My kick is swift and purposeful, and despite my lack of any athletic ability at all, the ball flies down the street, into the darkness, the only proof of its existence the sound of its bounce growing fainter with every few feet.

"You're in my driveway. Get your own hoop," I say, folding my arms up in an act of defiance. Only then do I realize how hard my heart is pounding. I don't know if it's the adrenaline still working its way through my arms and chest, or if I'm scared.

Owen's gaze is still over my shoulder, out into the street where I sent his ball. He's slow and resolute with every movement, and the longer it takes him to speak the more aware I am of what I've done.

I woke the tiger.

His soft chuckle isn't friendly at all. Neither is his movement—the way he leans forward and spits on the ground, like a man does just after he's thrown a punch. But Owen doesn't make a move toward me, and he doesn't say a word. He only backs away slowly, raising his hand as he nears his front steps, small puffs of fog coming from his mouth and nose—his breath like a dragon's.

I should walk away. I know I should walk away. If I walk away now, he has no power over me. But I. Can't. Move.

With every step up his porch, his arm raises higher, until finally, at his door, he's pointing at me. He's pointing, and he's smirking. And then he pulls the trigger before winking and blowing the imaginary smoke from his finger.

With the slam of his door closed behind him, I fall to the ground.

CHAPTER 4

Sleep isn't coming. I have been in my bed all night with the lights off, but my curtains open. I sent messages to Morgan and Gaby earlier in the evening, thanking them for the pictures they sent from the first few days at Bryce. I felt so connected to them still, and it broke my heart to see everyone in those images smiling, living—without me.

I did my best to fill them in on my mystery neighbor. Morgan summed him up quickly, texting that he was a "loser," but Gaby seemed to think there was something else to him. She always understands me, and I knew she'd have a different take on things. Of course, she asked if he was hot; she always asks if the guy is hot. But she also asked if he looked sad, or just angry, trying to get at what it was I found so threatening—and appealing. I didn't have to tell her I was attracted to him, which meant I didn't have to admit it to myself. I didn't have to tell her because she already knew. She always knows.

When my phone buzzes, vibrating my pillow, I smile, and my mood lifts for the first time in days. It's late—almost two in the morning. Gaby's been working on her winter ensemble performance, and it's been keeping her at the school studio all night for weeks. She got permission to use the practice rooms and the recording equipment over the summer, when she began writing the arrangements. I admired her balls for even asking the dean, but of course he said yes. Everyone says yes to her. They say yes because she has a fierce determination that comes through in everything she does, and people can't help but want to nurture it, to love it.

Despite how exhausted I knew she must be, she still called.

"Hey," I answer, fighting through my own yawn.

"Sorry, did I wake you?" she asks. "We texted an hour ago, so I thought you might still be awake." She's fighting through her own yawn now, too.

"I'm up. It's not a sleeping kind of night," I admit.

"I had a feeling," she says. She could always sense when something was wrong. It was her gift, her duty as my best friend. And hearing her voice now makes me cry, but I keep my tears silent, because I like hearing Gaby happy.

"This isn't about the mystery neighbor, is it?" she asks, her question a formality. Gaby knows why I'm really sad. I'm homesick—desperate for anything familiar. And she's my one thing—like a dash of medicine—that can make my new life survivable.

"No, it isn't," I say, breathing a heavy sigh and flipping through the pictures I have on my phone, on my Facebook page, and in the box I pulled out from under my bed. These pictures are both blessings and curses. I cherish them because they remind me that my life before was real. But they also remind me it's gone.

"Does it help that I miss you just as much as you miss me?" she asks.

"A little," I say, laughing, my heart slightly lighter than it was five minutes ago. "Okay, a lot."

"Good, well I miss you more. So that should help with that non-sleeping thing," she says, unable to stave off the yawn that trails at the end. "Wanna talk about how sucky this is?"

It's sweet she even asks. It's sweet, because she's heard me gripe and complain non-stop for weeks about this move and how unfair it is. She's helped me try and decipher why it's so important that we live closer to Wisconsin, why my dad always wins the decision-making game in our family. There's nothing new to say, though. And I know she's exhausted. So tonight I let her off the hook.

"Nah, I think I'll just hang up and dream sweetly over the fact that you miss me more. That should do for tonight," I say, and I swear I can hear her smile.

"Okay. I'll send more pictures tomorrow. And maybe snap a shot of mystery neighbor for me," she chuckles.

"Yeah, uh…no. I'm not coming near him. I'm afraid you'll have to stick with your imagination," I say.

When she says "Goodbye," and hangs up, I let one more tear fall.

I carry feeling pitiful right through sunrise, which is partly to blame for my insomnia. The rest was the strange sensation that Owen Harper was lying on his bed, across our driveways and lawns, staring right back at me.

"HONEY, take your breakfast to go. You'll be late for the bus," Mom says, folding the toasted Pop Tarts up in a napkin and handing them to me.

"Actually, I have a ride," I say, sliding into one of the stools at the breakfast bar and breaking one of the pastries in half. The goo that oozes out the side is hot, and it burns my fingertips. "Damn!"

"Careful," my mom says. Such a harmless word—one she's said to me a million times, a million more as a nurse.

But hearing it this morning throws me back into a nightmare, and all I can hear in my head is Owen's voice—the way he said "Careful," and the sinister, barely-there grin that glowed as he walked away.

"Ken…did you hear me?" Mom is waving in front of me now.

"Oh, no…sorry, burned my hand a little," I say, not feeling the burn at all anymore, at least not the one on my hand.

"Who is giving you a ride?" She has her hand on one hip, as if she's concerned about me with someone she doesn't know. I've been walking to school on my own in the city for three years, but a ride from a *very* harmless girl at my new high school is really giving her cause for worry?

"Oh…I made a friend," I say, smiling as I take a bite. This will make her happy, because this will help abide some of the guilt she feels for moving me out here. "Her name's Willow. She's in band. Drum major, actually."

"Drum major, eh?" Mom says, holding her hand out for my napkin, clearly irritated at the crumbs I'm spilling all over the floor. "The band marches out here, huh? Your father is going to HATE that." She flashes her eyes wide when she says the word *hate*.

"So let's not tell him. He's never home on Friday nights," I say, holding my mom's sightline while she considers this. It's true; my father will hate it. He's a purist, thinks I should be practicing orchestra and classical and piano—nothing but technical-music-skills work, twenty-four-seven. But it's also true that he is *never* home on Friday nights. Friday *and* Saturday, to be more accurate. Those are performance nights, and the full orchestra doesn't leave the building until well after midnight. My dad is rarely home before two or three in the morning, and sometimes he stays there on Friday nights, like he did last night. He's been putting in long hours setting up his new office.

"Depends," Mom says, pausing at the garbage can before throwing my napkin away. She chews at the inside of her cheek for a minute, and then she flips her gaze to me. "Do I get to come watch?"

The giggle escapes my mouth quickly, and I slide over and give her a hug, playing the role of good daughter—something we both need a little of. "Yes, you can come watch. But no going overboard."

"So, I can't become a booster or anything like that?" she teases.

"Oh god, no. You can come to one, two shows tops," I say, holding out a hand for her to shake on our deal, knowing that's all her schedule would allow her to attend anyhow.

"Two, with an option for a third—especially if you're playing for homecoming and riding on one of those float things," she says, and I laugh. My mom grew up in rural Illinois, and Bryce never had anything like she had in high school. She grew up with football games and bonfires. Instead, my old school was all about performance, with fall and winter and spring showcases. My mom's been regaling me with tales of life at a normal, public high school for the last three years.

"Fine," I say, giving her hand a firm shake. "If there is ever a float involved, you can be there."

Willow's honking outside ends our conversation, and my mom waves goodbye, grabbing her ringing cellphone and tucking it in the crook of her neck while she grabs a pile of magazines to head upstairs to nap before her next shift.

The music blaring from Willow's car is just as loud as it was yesterday when she drove away, and as I climb in, I spare a glance to the Harper house and note that Owen's truck isn't in the driveway.

"Think he'll bother to attend any classes today?" I ask, my stomach twisted because I know how many of those classes are with me.

"Hard to say. That boy…he does what he wants," she says, backing out of my driveway. "Nobody questions him."

No, I suppose they don't. Why would they?

His truck is parked near the exit. I spot it the second we pull into the parking lot, but after a quick scan around us, I don't see him anywhere.

"You're looking for him," Willow says, her voice startling me a little. She's standing at my passenger door, holding it open for me. I didn't even hear her exit.

"He just…I don't know. He makes me nervous." My explanation is met with an intense stare, and Willow drops her brow then quirks an eyebrow up at me. "We had an incident," I confess.

"As in what? You bumped into his truck? Accidentally opened a piece of his mail?" she says, holding the door wide for me as I climb out and sling my bag over my shoulder.

"As in I drop-kicked his basketball out into the darkness of night because he was making too much noise," I say, wincing now that I realize just how bold I was, and how stupid it sounds out loud.

"Oh my god, you went all *cranky old neighbor* on him?" she pauses, then her face gives in to laughter. I hit her arm, willing her to stop before Jess gets close enough to hear.

"You have a cranky old neighbor?" Jess asks, putting his arm around Willow and kissing the side of her neck.

"Oh, she has a cranky neighbor all right. But he ain't old," Willow teases, and I shove her again. "She lives next door to the Harpers."

"Ha. You're fucking kidding me, right?" Jess asks, leaning forward to check my facial expression for confirmation.

"Afraid not. And I doubt I'll be going over there for a cup of sugar anytime soon," I say. As we round the corner of the building, I notice a few boys all wearing beanie caps and hoodies sitting on a set of picnic tables down the hill. They're smoking—blatantly smoking on campus—and one of them turns around to catch me staring, and smirks as he grinds his shoe over his cigarette butt on the walkway. He nods in my direction, and the guy sitting next to him turns around.

Owen turns around.

His eyes lock on mine fast, and even without words I can hear everything he's thinking—I see my entire evening replay in the reflection of his eyes, the smallest twitch sending the corner of his lip up, and shivers travel down my spine.

One of his friends distracts him, and for once, I'm aware enough to take advantage, slipping into the music room before he can look back. But that look on his face stays with me, follows me for the rest of the hour, and I think it may also be there tonight, in my dreams.

My father would find my entire first period of school to be a tremendous waste of time. Today's first half hour was spent on the school's fight song—something that sounds pretty elementary, and the same every single time we play it. The second half of class was spent learning how to snap to attention on Willow's direction. It was all so military; so very...unmusical.

So purposeless.

So...fun.

My first two days of band practice have been a break for me, a breather from the constant pounding of my fingers up and down the keys. I've lived my entire life with the constant drive to move my hands faster, make things louder, create fuller chords and stretch my fingers so far that they actually ache at the end of the day. But in here, in this room, with these new friends —*could I call them that yet?*—there was absolutely no pressure.

The second hour was mine, and I relished every second that ticked by, making up for my failed night of playing at home. I brought my music book with me, and spent the time working on that one line of notes, leaving the room almost happy with it.

I'm still humming the passage on my way to English, enjoying this little personal celebration of satisfaction, when my happiness gives way rapidly to tension, the kind that drowns.

It's as if Owen was waiting for me to come, his feet perched up on the back corner of the only other open desk in the room. It was my seat yesterday, near the front, and surrounded by other students—other students who clearly moved out of the way for Owen Harper.

I take my last deep breath at the door and promise myself to not be intimidated, at least not on the outside.

"Excuse me," I say, dropping my heavy backpack to the ground next to my seat and resting my eyes on his gray Converse. I will myself not to look at him, and it's harder than I thought it would be. The challenge only grows the longer I stand there and wait for him to move his feet, finally realizing he has no intention of doing so.

I haven't made any friends in this class yet. Willow and Jess are a year younger, and Elise is only in science with me. It seems academically, I'm destined to be paired with Owen.

"Wow, so it's true what they say about you," I say, pushing at the sole of his right shoe with the tip of my finger. It slides a few inches to the right along my desktop, but he quickly flexes and puts up resistance.

"Your little band geek friends been telling you stories, Ken Doll?" he says, and his voice has that same edge it did last night. It's raspy, and tired—as if he doesn't sleep at all. But it's also deep, and I'll admit, it's a little tempting, like something you know you shouldn't like, but crave hearing again.

"It's Kensington, because you and I…we aren't friends. And yes, they've shared a few important facts with me," I say, catching the teacher walking in from the corner of my eye. I give Owen's foot a hard shove, and his weight is finally knocked off balance.

I do my best to ignore him throughout the rest of the class, focusing on the reading questions and discussion points for *Death of a Salesman.* But I feel him behind me the entire time, the small hairs on the back of my neck standing to attention, anticipating his breath—his breath that never comes.

When the bell finally rings, I drop my pen flat on my paper and note how white my knuckles are from my grip. I shove my things back in my bag and close my eyes before standing to leave, every bit of me expecting Owen to be waiting right behind me to continue our face-off.

But he's gone—the only trace is the trailing fabric of his black hoodie wrapped around his waist as the door swings closed behind him.

The pattern repeats in math, Owen's feet back on the only open desk in the room, my desk. And like a fool, I do the same thing and expect a different result.

"Excuse me," I say, like an echo from an hour before.

"You're excused," he smirks, clicking the top of his pen and chewing on the clip part while his eyes dance over me slowly.

The math teacher is less punctual, the bell ringing without much fanfare as students continue to talk to one another, text their friends, and keep their headphones pushed in their ears. Owen continues to stare.

"Whatever," I say, shoving my back hard into his feet as I sit down in my desk.

After two or three minutes, he finally gives in, letting his feet slide away until they're finally under his desk behind me. I catch the tips of his shoes with my glance downward for confirmation.

The principal walks in a minute or two after, and everyone finally slides into their seats, the chatter subsiding.

"Okay, ladies and gentlemen. I'm afraid you're stuck with me for today. Mrs. Carrol had an emergency, and she's not going to make it in today. So pull out your last assignment and turn to the next set of problems in your book," he says. We all obey, even Owen, who I notice has a full page of math problems noted on his pad.

"Eyes forward there, Kensington. No cheating," he says, careful to say my full name slowly—condescendingly. It pisses me off.

"Oh, don't you know? You and I have different assignments. You see, I work out of the calculus book, not the book with pictures of apples asking you how many nickels Peggy spent at the grocery store," I say back quickly, some strange sensation also working down my arm. I think…I think I actually want to punch someone.

A deep chuckle vibrates in Owen's chest, and I force my glance away from him, back in my lap and at my paper on my desk. I force my focus on the next twenty problems, completing them with time to spare, so I continue to the next set until the bell rings.

Just as before, Owen is gone when I turn around. And just like the day before, he's making out with the same dark-haired girl outside the window when I slide my lunch tray on the table.

Today, though, I ignore him. Or at least, I pretend to. I won't give him the satisfaction. Owen Harper may get his way with everything in this school and town and life. But he won't get his way with me.

"Looks like he's sticking with Kiera this week, huh?" Elise says to Willow as she drops her tray down to join us at our table.

"Yeah, it's rare for the flavor of the week to last an actual week," Willow responds. I assume they're talking about Owen, so I don't even ask.

Jess takes over the conversation when he joins us, talking about some concert coming to Chicago in a few weeks, some band they all seem excited about. I've never heard of Phantom Ant, but when Elise urges me to go with them, I shrug and nod *yes*. I've been to concerts in the city before. Granted, most of them have been classical, but I don't think my parents will have a problem with me going.

I'm doing my best to remember the names of songs they're saying so I can look them up later when the tapping on the window behind me becomes impossible to ignore.

"Uh, Kens?" Willow says, gesturing over my shoulder.

I know I shouldn't, but I turn around anyway, and I give Owen my full, undivided attention. His friends have already left, and he's slowly walking backward, showing me his middle finger and smiling with that faint half-grin I've seen far too often over the last three days.

I don't know what makes me do it. In fact, I don't know why I am the way I am with Owen. I've been careful and timid and obedient my entire life, my only mission to please everyone—please my father, Chen, my mother, my friends, my teachers. Please, please, please, please, please. That's all I do. And all it's done for me is land me in Woodstock, away from my friends and the senior year I was expecting to have. I'm not pleasing Owen Harper, too. So I stand with my tray and raise my arm slowly by my side, my eyes zeroed in on his until I'm pointing at him. I close one eye and cock my head slightly to the right, like I'm making sure I have him in my sights—and then I pull the trigger.

"Jesus H Christ, Kensi! What's wrong with you?" Willow asks. She pulls my arm back down, but I keep my eyes on Owen, staring into his gray-blue eyes—eyes that look like a wolf's. "What are you doing?"

"I'm starting a war, Willow," I say, my heart speeding up and my breath growing more ragged as reality catches up with me.

I'm starting a war with a guy who doesn't lose—a guy who doesn't play by the rules.

A guy who scares me, and who knows where I sleep at night.

CHAPTER 5

Each day happens exactly the same. Owen sits behind me, lounging his feet on my desk until I make him move. He makes out with the dark-haired girl named Kiera—practically putting on a show for me at lunch—then he taps on the window and sends me off with a message. One day it was a kiss to the glass, the other, he threw a dollar on the ground. I went outside when he walked away and put it in my pocket, and when I got home, I pinned it to my wall.

Despite the stories and rumors, Owen Harper didn't scare me. Everything he did was predictable; all show with no real threat, and nothing I couldn't easily ignore. I had my circle of friends, and I wasn't interested in winning a popularity contest, so I was fine not being a part of Owen Harper's *cool crowd.*

I'd endured bigger threats than he could offer—threats my father dealt out any time I talked about the idea of maybe not going to college at all, maybe studying jazz or just performing on the road, period. He was quick to poison those dreams, stopping short of disowning me. I was more than welcome to walk my own path in life; I'd just have to pay for it all myself, and not expect to live under his roof ever again.

What hurts more is how my mom always supports him. I'm not the same naïve girl I was a few years ago. I understand the economic dynamics of my family now, and I know my mom earns at least twice my father's salary. But he has this hold on her, and she puts him on a pedestal. My father, Dean Worth, is a talented musician, and when he commands the orchestra, it's impossible not to feel prideful watching him work. But my mother has let that pride take all of the power—and somehow, power over me, and my life, was bargained away with it.

The first football game was at a school only a town or two over, so the bus trip was just long enough to be an adventure. Our team lost, but the band sounded good, so I celebrated with Willow, Elise, and Jess afterward at the ice cream parlor in the old part of town.

Normal teenagers would want to keep the party going, to stay out with their friends until the sun threatens to rise. But I know there's an empty house waiting for me at home, and I'm desperate to touch my piano. What I want and reality, though, are two very different dimensions. I know something is off the second we turn the corner to my street.

There are cars packed in both my and Owen's driveway, many with lights on, pointed directly at the hoop anchored to my garage. There are about a dozen guys all playing ball and crushing beer cans right below my bedroom window, *my bedroom window* that I can see plainly through the thin veil of curtains thanks to the flooding lights.

"You wanted war," Willow says, shaking her head at the scene.

"Yeah…" I say, grabbing my heavy bag and pulling it over my shoulder as I step out of her car. "I guess I did."

"You want me to stay? Come in for a while?" She's asking to be nice, but I can tell she doesn't really want to be a part of whatever the hell this is that I started.

"No, it's all right. I'm just going to put some music on and go to bed. Really, let them do whatever out here. I don't care," I lie.

I wait at the front door until Willow pulls away, then push my key in and quickly shut the door behind me.

"What are you doing?" I whisper to myself, letting my bag, coat, scarf and sweatshirt all fall into one pile by the front door. I pull my boots from my feet and slide along the wood floor in my socks toward the kitchen, stroking my hand along the smoothness of the piano top as I pass it. I could still play, but for some reason, playing while there's practically a party happening on the other side of the wall is far less appealing. It's not so much their disruption and the noise as it is my fear of them hearing me—of them stopping and listening. Maybe a fear of them mocking me and taking away something that's *mine*.

I grab a Coke from the fridge and climb the steps, careful not to turn on my light. I don't need to give them a reason to look up. On all fours, I crawl to the window and lean my back against the side of my bed, cracking the tab on my soda.

Someone's radio is blaring rap music. Not the radio-edited version, but the kind with full swearwords and demeaning lyrics. Kiera is out there, sitting on the hood of Owen's truck, and she's taking long drags from a joint, her head swaying side-to-side, not even remotely in sync with the beat. She's ridiculous, and watching her gives me a thrill for about five minutes.

Owen doesn't seem to be aware of her at all, which she doesn't seem to care about because I'm pretty sure she's high off her ass. He's busy playing basketball. It's barely in the fifties outside, but he's not wearing a shirt. There's a white T-shirt tucked into the back of his black jeans, hanging from the waistband like a rag, and his chest is dripping with sweat. They must have been playing all night.

Sliding against the wall, I let my head come to rest on the frame of the window, my hand tucked under my chin, and I watch. Owen is so focused out there playing this game of pick-up ball—this game that doesn't matter anywhere but in his head. At one point, he's arguing a call, shoving his friend in the chest and threatening him. They're both tall, but Owen's more muscular, his frame that of someone who looks as if he's been in a street fight or two.

Their language gets more vulgar as the hour goes on, as more beer cans get crushed into a pile in my driveway. I wouldn't be able to sleep through this even if I wanted to. I know if my father were home, he'd have the police here to haul everyone away. No one is older than eighteen out there, and I've seen at least three cases of beer go down, as well as two or three joints.

It's one in the morning, and I hear one of the guys call out for the last game. Everyone pulls money from their wallets, handing it to Kiera, who stuffs it in her bra, and they pass the ball to Owen for the final game. He's dribbling it, each bounce slower than the first as he points to guys and splits them up on a team, then he throws the ball to someone and jogs over to his truck, pulling a ringing phone from inside the cab.

There's something about the way he's pacing—the way his hand is on his neck and his eyes are down at his feet—something is wrong. For him to be agitated, it must be *really* wrong, like as in a kind of wrong I can't even fathom.

"Yo, O! We doin' this or what?" one of the guys yells out at him. Owen raises a hand, crouching down and pushing the phone more tightly to his ear. "O! Come on, man. Are you pussying out because you're out two hunny?"

Two hunny...as in two hundred dollars? Owen stands up from his crouch, the phone still pressed to his ear, and he stares long and hard at the guy giving him a hard time. He doesn't say anything to his friend—if that guy is even a friend—but something is communicated between them just from one look.

"Yeah, whatever man. We gotta go anyhow. Hey, Chris, grab my shit and let's get out of here," the guy yells over his shoulder.

Within minutes, Owen's driveway is empty, and soon he's racing down his front porch, dressed in a dark button-down shirt and a pair of gray jeans. His hair is wet; he must have raced through a shower. His keys jingle in his hands as he jogs to his truck and climbs inside, his engine roaring and his tires squealing from their rest.

It's almost two, and my father will be pulling into the driveway any moment. He said he'd be home tonight, and I'm not so sure I want him to see the mess our neighbor left behind. I walk down the stairs to the kitchen and grab a large trash bag, pausing at the back door to gaze out at the shadows cast over my driveway by the bright floodlight. The ground is strewn with trash, piles of lazily crushed beer cans, and cigarette and pot butts. I can't let my dad see this, and not because I care about Owen Harper getting in trouble, but because I don't want to hear my father's lecture about drugs, drinking, being out late—being a real teenager in general.

When I finally push through the back door, I'm too late, though, the headlights are sending new shadows over the drive as my dad pulls in. I'm already standing in the middle of the mess, so I bend down and start putting cans in the bag, my brain working fast at answers for the questions I know will come.

"Kensington?" So very many of our conversations begin with my name. And it's never Kensi or Kens. It hasn't been anything less than formal since the day I started playing the piano.

"Hey, how was the show?" I ask, buying myself time.

"Performance. Concert. Not *show.* This isn't Broadway," my dad says.

"Sorry, I meant concert," I say, careful not to roll my eyes.

"It was good. We're still having some trouble with the cellos. The replacements aren't nearly as good," he says, his voice growing fainter as he paces out into the middle of the mess. I'm done distracting now. "Kensington, what…is this?"

The funny thing is I know my father knows that this mess isn't my fault. I don't do anything wrong, and I've never been in any *real* trouble. I've been scolded, chastised for dreaming, for playing jazz during a practice session, for skipping a lesson, for not getting a scale just right, but serious trouble—like the kind you get from surmising the state of my driveway—that doesn't mesh with me, and my father knows this.

"Yeah, well…" I say, looking over at the dark Harper house. "Our new neighbors…they kind of like to party? Well, or…at least one of them does."

"I see that," my dad says, kicking one of the crushed cans over into the Harper lawn. "But why am *I* dealing with the leftovers?"

"I don't really know. I think it's the basketball hoop," I say, looking over my dad's head at the rusted hoop and rotting wood backboard hung above our garage.

"I see," my dad says, his hand rubbing the beard on his chin as he steps closer to the front of our garage. "This neighbor…the one that likes the hoop—is it a *he?*"

"Yeah," I say, my voice a little hesitant, causing my dad to turn and look at me. "I mean, girls don't really do *this.*"

"No…they don't, do they?" my father responds, turning back to face the hoop. Almost a full minute passes, and I begin cleaning up the mess until I'm distracted by the sound of our garage door opening. My father slides out a ladder, and then goes to a stack of boxes in the back of the garage, searching through three of them before finding what looks like a ratchet set.

He brings the slender toolbox out to the driveway and picks out three or four sizes, then climbs to the top of the ladder, reaching up to loosen the bolts on the basketball hoop.

He's taking it down. I think I knew he would, and I know deep down that's why I told him—why I said everything just as I said it. It was all a delicate game of chess that I mastered for this very moment. Only I didn't expect to feel nervous that Owen would come home suddenly. Worried that we would be caught.

And I certainly didn't expect to feel regret.

That's the emotion tripping me up most. Regret—is that even an emotion? Or is it just a result? I'm not sure, but I know my stomach is sick with it as my father finds the perfect fit, his arm pulling one side of the hoop loose from the backboard while he goes to work on the last bolt, the ache in my stomach traveling to my chest when the rusted ring finally falls to the ground. My dad steps from the ladder, folds it back up and puts it in its place along the garage wall. Then he picks up the hoop, carries it to the end of our driveway and throws it on top of the morning's trash. In the morning, the garbage truck will haul it away forever.

"Pick up the rest of this mess," he says, not bothering to look my way, instead pulling his phone from his pocket to answer a call—probably from my mother—the back door slamming to a close behind him.

It takes me nearly an hour to gather the rest of the debris in our driveway, and I pick up the can my father kicked onto the Harper lawn, the bottoms of my sweatpants getting soaked from the frosty dew covering their long grass. It looks like it hasn't been mowed in weeks, though it will be dead and covered in snow soon, so I suppose there's no reason.

Our lawn is small—most of our front yard made of small plants, wood bark, and bricked walkway. The rest is just a long driveway—Owen's basketball court.

The air is growing frostier, and my breath comes out in a thick fog as I drag the heavy bag of trash to our can near the street. I flip the lid over and hoist the bag up, stopping it right on the edge, pausing to look at the large metal ring weighing down everything inside. The paint is worn from most of it, and at least two of the bolts look to be stripped. It's trash, and it has no business hanging on my house. No one in our family will ever throw a ball through it.

But Owen will. He did. And he will again.

Only, now he won't.

"Damn it!" I yell, my voice echoing in the emptiness of our quiet neighborhood street. I kick the bottom of the large, black, plastic canister, then I pull the bag from the edge and drop it to the ground. I have to stand on one of the can wheels to reach the hoop inside, and its brackets make it heavy and hard to bring back over the edge, but I manage to. I slide it down the side of the can, leaning it against the can while I throw my trash inside and shut the lid.

Holding my breath, I take a few steps closer to my house, looking to see if my father is still inside, still talking to my mom on the phone, but the lights are all off. It's quiet, and I'm pretty sure he's gone to bed. The metal is heavy, but I'm able to loop my arms inside the hoop and carry it to the garage that my father left open. I put his tools away first, knowing he probably won't need them again for quite some time, if ever. He isn't really *handy*; he's more the type of man who likes to be prepared. Then, I slide the hoop behind the stack of boxes to keep it safe.

I'm saving it. I just saved Owen Harper's basketball hoop. *No*...I saved my hoop, at my new home—the hoop Owen Harper uses, at my new home. And I have no idea why he uses it, why he steps foot night after night on my driveway, below my window. I have no clue why he pushes my buttons, or why I let him.

I saved his hoop, and I don't really know why I did it. But I had to.

Goddamn it. I had to.

CHAPTER 6

I spend the rest of my weekend practicing until my mom gets home, going into quiet mode when she needs to catch up on sleep. When she wakes on Sunday, we find the box labeled BLANKETS and make a large bowl of popcorn, settling in for a binge on home improvement shows. My mom has these fantasies of home construction…not necessarily building a home from scratch, but taking a sledgehammer to something—something like a wall.

She would be good at it. I could even see her having her own show —*Home Surgery with Karen Worth.* She did a lot of painting in our row home in the city. She'd change entire rooms on her week off, even if they didn't need new paint. She always said she was addicted to change, but I kind of think change terrifies her, and making those small changes, the superficial kinds, was her way of being brave.

"We should make a fire," my mom says. "Your dad said he got some wood during the week. Go check on the side of the house."

I haven't been outside once this weekend, not since the clean up. Owen's truck came home sometime after I fell asleep Saturday morning, and it hasn't moved from its spot. I would have heard him.

Slipping my feet into my warm boots, I wrap my scarf around my neck twice and push through the front door, letting the screen slam behind me. I follow the small woodchip path along the side of the house, along the driveway, noting Owen's tires still at rest at the end of their skid marks.

My neck is still craned to the side when I hear the sound. He's standing right in front of my mom's car, his ball dropping every few seconds to the pavement, then bouncing back up into his hands. I could run, but he'd hear me, so I keep my eyes down at my feet as I walk past him to the wood stacked in the corner.

"You really had to take the fucking hoop down?" he asks. He bounces the ball two more times while I look at the pile of wood, deciding I can carry two logs at once.

"It didn't do it," I say, not lying. My inside voice begging my outside voice to tell him I saved it. *I saved your hoop. It's here. I promise.* I don't know why I care so much.

"Right," he says, throwing the ball against our garage door, making it ring out loudly. "Like hell you didn't."

Grunting to myself, I shift the wood in my arms so I can hold it tightly to my chest, and I walk back around the corner of the house until I can see him. His eyes are different now. They're...sad. But they're angry, too. And it's the shades of angry that won't let me trust him.

"Really," I say, coming to a stop a few feet away from him. "Like hell I didn't. It was my dad. You kind of left a *mess*, and my dad doesn't put up with bullshit."

There's stillness in the air after I tell him this, and I'm caught in it, my eyes unable to move away from his. He's chewing at the inside of his cheek. His brow falls a little, and there's a shift in his eyes, the sadness making room for the danger that usually lives there.

Willing myself to walk away, I let my weight shift, and I bring my lips into a tight smile and begin to turn on my heels.

"So who does your dad talk to late at night, out here in the driveway?" he asks, suddenly interested in my family.

"Uh...my mom. She works a lot of overnights. And my dad gets home late," I say, realizing I have yet to see Owen's mom—or *anyone* else in the Harper house.

"Right, that's what I thought," he says, and I turn with a shrug, really missing the warmth and easiness from just a few minutes ago inside. "But I meant the other times."

Something about what he says—the way he says it—slams into my chest, and I halt, hugging the heavy wood even tighter, bits of the bark cutting into the palms of my hand.

"You know..." he continues, my back still to him. "Who does he talk to out here while your mom is asleep in bed? Those times."

The tear surprises me, and my hands are full, so there's no way I can stop it, so I let it slide down my face into the threads of yarn in my scarf.

"I bet it's whoever drives that blue BMW I see parked here when I come home for lunch. I bet that's who it is. Whoever...*she* is," he says, every word purposely hurtful. I hear his feet shuffle toward his ball, and soon, it hits the ground again, only this time it's dropped and discarded, rolling by my feet until it stops at the tire of my mother's car. He's casting one more stone, just to let me know who's in charge. And for the first time since I've met Owen Harper, I'm willing to relent—he's in charge. And his words just broke my tiny shred of happiness like a thin sheet of glass.

My arms ache from flexing with the weight of the wood, so I force my feet to climb the steps inside, and I busy myself with the fire, sparing a quick trip to the restroom to wash my hands, and wash my face of any trace of that one solitary tear.

By the time I come out of the bathroom, my mom has the fire roaring, and she's holding out a mug for me, her smile innocent.

She doesn't know. She can't know.

Owen's words—his hurtful, despicable, mean, purposeful words—are all I can hear through the next two hours of pointless television. I sit there next to my mom and feign our world is fine. If I could only shut off the sounds echoing in my head, I could maybe find a way to forget, to chalk this up to just some cruel prank.

But I can't.

When my mom busies herself with housework, I turn to my piano, pulling out the books of sheet music I'm supposed to be memorizing—only now, it's not just a thing I'm not interested in. Now it's a thing I want to fight against doing with all I have. I open those pages and I see his face—my father's face. I play those notes and I hear his voice, his expectations and condemnations for the music *I* like.

Playing from these books has quickly become a thing that represents something ugly. Something I realize I haven't felt love for in a year, maybe more. Something disappointing. My father.

With a smooth stroke, I take my finger and push the loose sheets of music and the book behind them from the ledge to the floor, leaning to the side to see them slide in various directions. A mess—a beautiful, classical, fake mess.

My hands do as they wish, sliding into place, running smoothly over keys until notes blend into one another, sliding from one note to the next sloppily, while sad-sounding blues chords fill the giant dining room and foyer of my house.

My house. This fake house. This place *he* made me move.

I pound harder, playing runs, pausing to breathe and look out the window. Owen's truck is framed perfectly by the picture window in our living room, the taillight like that of a lighthouse, guiding me to truth.

I play what I want to play, even when my mother warns me that my father will be home soon. I keep going, the sounds only those *I* want to hear, and when his car idles to a stop in our driveway—I play louder.

I play him right through the front door, and I hold my head up high, daring him while he walks closer to me, the stern look on his face no longer holding the value it once did. There's no threat here any more. And I couldn't give a shit if he's disappointed in me now.

"You know I don't like that crap," he says, pushing the lid forward, threatening to close it on my fingers. But I anticipate this, and I stop it as I stand to my feet, letting my fingers tap out one last faint pattern that I know my father will hate.

"Have you practiced your showcase? Or did you just spend the entire day wasting time?" he asks, walking back to the front door to kick off his shoes, loosen his tie, and drop his briefcase full of music—full of *his* music. Probably full of his lies, too.

"Who is she?" I ask, my voice loud enough that my mom hears. I hear her hear, the sounds in the kitchen coming to an abrupt stop.

"Who is she, Dad?" I ask again, my voice wavering with the tears I'm fighting to keep inside. I won't be weak for this. He won't face me, and the longer it takes him to speak, the more I start to feel everything.

"Who is she!" I yell, grabbing the last music book lying on my piano and throwing it at him.

My father turns to face me slowly, and the more his face comes into view, the more I see just how broken everything is—my life, my mom's life, our family—we're broken.

"Dean?" my mom's voice questions from behind me. She walks up to him slowly, her hands clutching a towel from the kitchen. With each step she gets closer, the more honest my father's face becomes, the more the puzzle comes into view.

This house, the move—all of it—it's because of *him*, because he was unfaithful. Because he did something my mom couldn't live with, at least, not in our old house, in my *old* life. She couldn't live with the memories from where we were.

My mom slaps my father so hard that his face jerks harshly to the side, and the bruise is almost immediate. Then she hits him again. And again. My father stands perfectly still, taking every hit.

"You son of a bitch!" she yells. "You promised. You promised that it was done. We'd move here, away from the school, away from *her*. It was over, and we'd start over. I would try to forget, and you would never see her again."

School.

Her.

Blue BMW.

Her!

There are key words that ring through my anger. I think I knew the moment Owen opened this wound. But I just couldn't believe my nightmare was *that* horrifying. I didn't want to believe it.

"Dad?" I whisper behind my mother, everything coming into focus, everything hurting me from all sides all at once. My mother turns to me slowly, her hand covering her mouth, her entire body shaking when she realizes what I've put together.

"Ohhhhhh...." I start to cry hard when I see her, when my nightmare is confirmed. Shaking my head, I rush around them both up the stairs to my room, slamming the door behind me, and logging into my computer to sift through my Facebook posts until I get to it—and it's all right there, staring me in the face.

There I am, standing next to my best friend, Gaby, in front of her 18th birthday present—a brand new, blue BMW. It's this picture, the one my father took, and it's the way Gaby is looking back at him, through the lens.

How could I have been so blind to it all?

I hear Owen's tailgate slam, and I rush to my window to watch him round his truck, his keys in his hand, his step quick and determined. I don't have much time.

I grab my wallet from my nightstand, and push it and my phone into my back pockets before stuffing my feet into my wool boots and throwing a white hoodie over my body. My parents are screaming at each other as I come down the stairs, and I realize my mom has broken a few dishes at my father's feet.

"I'm going out," I say, but really only for her benefit.

"Like hell you are, young lady!" my father yells, his step gaining ground on me as I head down the porch steps.

"You can go to fucking hell!" I scream over my shoulder, my legs picking up into a run as I hear Owen's engine turn over. He's slowly rolling from the driveway when I slam my fist on his hood, positioning myself in his path. My dad is still undeterred, walking right at me, and I'm so ruined that I don't care if Owen runs me over.

"Kensington, you don't understand. And it's a Sunday night. You need to get your ass back in this house," my dad yells. Powerless. He has become powerless. And when I look at him, and he looks back at me, he knows I know it. He knows I know it all.

And he knows I'm not coming back inside that house—not while *he's* in it.

"Get your hand off of my fucking truck!" Owen yells, his head leaning out his window and his arm heavy on his horn.

I rush to the side and pull his passenger door open, climbing in and buckling up, locking the door to keep the other side out.

"Oh, fuck no! Ass out of my car! You heard your dad. Get back in your own goddamned house," he seethes.

My breathing is hard from anger, and I don't know if my body needs to cry or scream. "This is your fault. You started this. *You* pushed over the first goddamned domino! So you get to take me out of here. I don't care where, but I swear to God, Owen, if you don't make those tires squeal in about four seconds—I'm going to shove you out of the way and drive away from this place myself!"

Owen spends the first three seconds trying to decide how serious I am, and when I pound my fist on his dashboard, he decides his life is easier if I stay in the truck. "Fuck!" he yells, shifting into gear and pealing away, his back tires fishtailing in the street and the smell of burnt rubber filling the cab. "I don't need this...this...this family-drama shit, all right? We're driving around the block a few times, and then you're going home."

"No," I say, my jaw tight, my teeth clenched.

"Ooooohhhhh yes we are," he chuckles, and I pound his dashboard again.

"No!" I say forcefully, the tears starting to fill the bottom of my eyes now. "No, no, no, no, no!"

I keep repeating the word, keep pounding my palm against Owen's dash, until his hand finally catches mine, holding it down flat while we sit at a stoplight near the outskirts of the historic downtown.

"All right, I got it. *No*. Just...easy on the truck," he says, his palms rough against my skin. I stare at his hand touching mine, my mind trying to make sense of the way it looks. My perfect fingers, my skilled, trained, long and powerful fingers look like weak flowers, wilting flowers, underneath the weight of his large hands.

"I hate you," I let go from my lips in a whisper.

"Yeah, well...you and everybody else," he says, pressing his foot back on the gas as the light turns green.

Owen drives through the heart of town, then turns down a two-lane highway where we drive for minutes in silence. My passenger window feels cold against my cheek, and the regular in-and-out reflection of the streetlights on the window glass keep me from drifting into crying. I just wait for the next reflection to come, counting in my head to see how long it takes. I count, until we run out of streetlights, and then I hold my breath and try not to think about my best friend sleeping with my father—and ruining my life.

"Where are we going," I say, my voice hoarse. Owen remains silent, and I start to ask again, but then realize I don't care where we're going. I'm just glad we're gone.

There's a rustling sound as he reaches into a pocket on the front of the bench seat, then he tosses two strips of licorice on my lap.

"Hungry? Chicks eat when they're upset, right? Isn't that like a thing?" he says, glancing at me and ripping a bite from the red licorice. I hate red licorice.

"I don't think that's a thing," I say quietly, setting my strips of candy on the dashboard closer to him.

It's quiet for several more minutes until we hit a small convenience store parking lot. There are a few other cars parked out here, and I recognize most of the other people from school. I'm suddenly wishing I jumped into a stranger's car to run away.

"Stay in the car. I don't need anyone asking questions," he says, his voice practically an order.

Owen parks next to another old pick-up truck, and I notice Kiera sitting in it. I wonder if they're still together, or whatever it is they are. Kiera's eyes are on Owen as he steps in front of the truck to talk to another guy, the both of them leaning against the front of his truck. This guy looks a lot like Owen, only his face isn't as handsome. He's hard looking, and he doesn't seem to smile. Not that Owen smiles. The only time I've seen Owen smile was when he was teasing me—and when he delivered the news that ruined my world.

I notice the other guy pull out a pack of cigarettes and offer one to Owen, but he shakes his head. I'm glad he doesn't take it, and I wonder if that means he doesn't smoke. I hope he doesn't smoke.

I don't know why I hope he doesn't smoke.

Owen pulls his phone from his pocket when it rings, and he starts pacing in the middle of the parking lot while he answers the call, his feet kicking at a few rocks and his other hand rubbing the back of his neck. When he gets off the phone, he holds his thumb up to the guy he was talking to and smiles—a real smile—then jogs back to his truck.

He slams the door to a close and buckles his seatbelt, and I test mine to make sure it's tight, somehow hoping that will keep me safe wherever it is we're going. Owen doesn't share our plans; he just pops the truck into drive quickly, the wheels kicking up gravel as we fishtail back onto the highway and head back the way we came.

"Where are we going?" I ask finally. Owen glances up at the rearview mirror, then leans his head out the window slightly and adjusts the mirror on his door. The wind coming in is cold, and I fold my arms tightly around my body, trying to fight the chill.

"Party," he says, a smirk on his lips as he notices something in his mirror.

"Party? But it's...Sunday. We have school tomorrow," I say, and Owen looks at me finally, then laughs. No other response.

Seconds later, the truck with his friend and Kiera race by us, the guy's motor growling so loudly that it almost pops as he speeds by us, dust kicking up in Owen's headlights as his friend passes him and moves back to our lane.

There's no pause in Owen's reaction. His right hand grips his steering wheel and he rolls his window up with his left, and the moment it's closed, he punches the gas with a force that sends my back hard against the seat. My hands grip my seatbelt by instinct, holding onto it to make sure it's tight—to make sure I stay in this vehicle.

"Owen, slow down," I say, my heart starting to make my body shake with its beating.

Owen hears nothing, and he starts rocking forward and back with his eyes intent on the truck in front of us, like laser beams locked on the taillights leading our way.

"Owen," I say, this time a little louder.

The grin on his face is maniacal. It's actually maniacal—I've never seen that expression on someone before. We inch closer and closer to the truck in front of us, and Kiera leans over, draping her arm on the back of the seat in the other truck, her eyes on Owen, her mouth twisted into a tempting smile, urging him to do it, to be dangerous.

There's a fast jerk to the truck as he veers to the other lane, and I hear his friend's truck rev a little faster at the threat of being beaten. Owen leans forward and pushes his pedal to the floor, and after a few seconds, we're dead even with the other truck.

"Owen!" I yell, but he can't hear me. He's somewhere else. His hand is pounding on the steering wheel, and I look at his lips and notice them moving, speaking quietly. "Come on, baby. Come on," he's saying, over and over.

His friend is laughing, his head tilted back, and Kiera is clapping. Everyone here is having fun. This is fun. This is what they do for fun. And I want to throw up. In fact, I might throw up.

"Owen, you're scaring me," I say, my voice coming out in a shrill. But he presses forward.

I have no idea where his other friends are. There were at least three other cars in that parking lot. But no one is near us—not in this race. We move about a quarter length ahead of the other truck, nowhere near enough to pass, and as we top a hill, I notice the lights coming at us in the distance.

"Owen!" I scream, my hands grabbing at the side and front of the seat now. Anything to brace myself. Anything to survive whatever is going to happen.

"Come on, baby. Come on," he's still whispering.

We're racing, our engine fighting to be just a little stronger than the other guy's, and the lights are coming closer to us. The other car is just over this hill, and we're either going to veer off the road, or we're going to die.

I don't want to die.

I don't want to die.

"Owen! Please stop! Owen! The car…that car! Stopppppppppp!" I scream. I'm grabbing his arm, trying to get him to change course, and he punches the gas with one last thrust, and our truck slides past his friend's, only a second before the car coming at us head-on rounds the top of the hill and honks at us—the sound of the horn blaring and lasting for several seconds in the night air.

"Yeahhhhhh baby! Woooooooooooo!" Owen is shouting. He rolls his window down and holds his hand out the window, giving his friend the middle finger, and his friend reciprocates.

"Owen!" I yell, my body plastered to the vinyl seat, my heart stopped now from my near-death experience.

"Did that scare you?" he asks, his voice an odd kind of calm. Unable to speak, I merely nod *yes* to him, my arms still clutched to anything I can grasp, and my body no longer cold, sweat dripping down my back and arms.

"I told you to get out of the truck. You should have listened," he says, his focus more calm now, his eyes back on the road.

A large farmhouse comes into focus, and we pull into the gravel driveway, followed soon after by his friend with the other truck. We sit in the truck cab, waiting for everyone to arrive, and there's an awkward silence. Owen's arm is resting on the window, and he's pulled a bag of sunflower seeds from the front seat pocket. I watch as he spits the shells out the window meticulously, one at a time, like he's aiming for some goal I can't see.

I may as well be invisible. He hasn't looked my direction once, and I'm too afraid to confront him—afraid of what he'll do next. His friends finally pull into the lot around us, and Owen steps out when they do. I notice Kiera kiss the other guy, and I wonder how someone could jump from one boy to another so quickly. I also wonder how Owen can be so flippant about it—his friend is kissing the girl whose lips were on his only two days ago, and he looks as if he couldn't care less.

I don't want to be here. But I don't want to be home, either, so when Owen shrugs over his shoulder for me to join them, I slide from the seat and close the door behind me. Everyone walks to the house, and Owen isn't waiting for me. I linger behind; the temptation to walk back to the truck—to hide there for as long as the night lasts—is strong. I feel foolish suddenly, the adrenaline from what just happened catching up to me, and my body quivers with a rush of tears that I quickly squash with the sleeves of my sweatshirt. When I look up again, Owen is waiting for me at the door.

"You almost killed us!" I yell, stopping in my tracks.

"But I didn't," he says, holding the door open and waiting for me to follow him inside, where everyone else has gone. He waits, his eyes rested on mine for several long seconds, and I notice them shift. In the truck, there was a determination in them, like a warrior—the kind you send in for the toughest kill because you know they won't feel any of it. It was like nothing else existed. But for these few seconds, they soften, and he's actually looking at me. And he looks afraid.

"I'm sorry I scared you," he says, his teeth biting the tip of his tongue as if he wants to say more, but he stops himself. His eyes stay on mine, and my body freezes, my mind not sure what to say. I'm empty. I have nothing—feel nothing. I nod at him, and shuffle my feet closer and step through the door. My back brushes against his chest as I pass him through the small space, and I can't help but notice how warm he feels. Maybe I'm just cold.

"Don't do it again," I whisper, glancing sideways at the nearness of him. I won't look at his eyes; I'm not sure how they'll look, and if I'm going to follow him inside, I need to feel safe—the way his eyes felt seconds ago. Instead, I focus on his chin, and neck and the way his dark shirt hugs his chest. His lip ticks, finding its comfortable place back into that sinister smile, but he doesn't respond, so I step inside.

The house is dark, and I follow Owen to a large, sunken living room where everyone is sitting in front of a television that's barely audible. A joint is already being passed around the room, as is a bottle of clear liquor. I have no idea what it is, but I know the moment it makes its way to me, it's going to start a conversation, because I don't drink. And Owen Harper, he's not the boy who's going to pressure me into something.

"Ahhhh, new girl. Yeah, new girl needs to drink," says the guy from the truck race. He holds the bottle out in front of me, but I nod *no* and shrug it away. "Fuck, O. You brought *this prude* to hang out? What the fuck is wrong with you?"

He takes a big swig from the bottle and runs his sleeve along his mouth when he's done, then hands the bottle to Kiera. She's lightly laughing at my expense, but I don't care.

"I don't drink," I say, standing my ground early. "I like my brain cells."

Kiera spits out a little of the drink at my response, and her *new* boyfriend starts to laugh loudly.

"Dude, O! Seriously, are you like…fucking with us with this chick or something?" he says, his speech already sloppy, proving my point.

"I didn't *bring* anybody. She hijacked my fucking truck and wouldn't get out," Owen says, letting his long body flop into a beanbag across the living room from me, his legs stretched out and a small golden drink in his hands.

"Good thing I did. I'll drive your ass home," I say, letting my eyes zero in on him as he raises his glass to his lips. He holds it there as he leans forward, resting his elbows on his knees, his eyes mocking me.

"Nobody drives my truck. And we're not leaving for hours, so I'll be fine," he says, brow raised before tilting the glass back and letting the amber liquid flow down his throat. He keeps his stare on me as he sets the glass down and settles into his seat.

"We'll see about that," I say.

"Yeah, we'll fucking see about a lot of things," he says, pulling his arms behind his neck and leaning sideways as he stares at me for several long, uncomfortable seconds.

His friend from the truck reaches for Kiera's hand, lifting her to stand, and the two of them leave their seat on the sofa and walk up the stairs. The casualness of it all feels so sad—maybe even a little gross—and I can't help the face I make in reaction to it.

"You have a problem with House hooking up with Kiera?" Owen says, bringing my attention back to him.

"His name is *House?"* I ask, keeping the focus on the easier topic.

"Matt House. We've been friends since kindergarten. I call him House. He calls me Harper. Whatever. And you clearly have issues with people having sex," he says.

"I don't give a shit *who* has sex," I say fast, my response not really a lie. I don't care who does what, but that doesn't mean I understand how little importance people place on something like sex. My face is red; I know because I can feel my cheeks tingling. But the darkness shrouds me.

"You're a virgin," Owen says, his lips taking their time with that word. My cheeks burn stronger, and for the first time, I feel flustered from the embarrassment.

"So." That's all I can think to say. At first, I consider adding more, defending myself, but the more time that passes, the happier I am with that response. I won't make apologies for not being easy.

"Your daddy would be so proud of you, proud of his little girl keeping her snatch all sewn up, waiting for her *prince charming*," Owen says, the cruel look glimmering in his eyes and curling his lips.

His words make me want to cry, and I can feel the pressure building, the water wanting to spill down my cheeks, but I won't let him have this. I breathe long and slow, and I hold his gaze, meeting his challenge, until I know I can speak without my voice wavering.

"Nobody likes you. They all think you're crazy. They feel bad for me, because I have to live next to you," I say back. I'm expecting Owen to wince, to feel my words on some level, but he only leans forward and lets his grin stretch larger across his face.

"Then why, little miss sunshine, are you here?" he asks, resting his chin in the palm of his hand. The two other couples here with us have all left the living room for the kitchen, where they're playing some drinking game. Owen and I are alone, and nobody is interested in our war of words. That means no one will hear the details of my broken life.

"I'm here because you took what was left of my barely-decent life and ripped it to goddamned shreds," I say to him, waiting for him to argue and say he didn't.

"What, the little bit about the affair? I was right, wasn't I? Your dad... he's stepping out on your mom. Who is she? Someone...*younger*?" He's seen Gaby at the house. I can tell he knows it's a younger woman by the way he's looking at me, luring me and taunting me. But he doesn't know *how* young. And I don't plan on giving him anything else he can use to hurt me.

"Why do you play basketball in my driveway?" I ask, taking control of the conversation. Owen keeps his eyes on me, his tongue teasing at the edge of his lips as he decides whether or not he's going to let me.

"The Stratfords used to live there. They sold the house to you. They always let me use the hoop, because we don't really have a place for one. I didn't think you'd be assholes and take it down," he says, and I feel a small pang in my side because Owen actually looks sad. He also looks less like the hardened eighteen-year-old and more like a lost little boy.

"Well, like I said. I didn't take it down. My dad did. And it turns out not only does he have a low tolerance for bullshit, but he's a royal fucking asshole, too," I say, finally letting my eyes move from Owen's face to the front pocket on my sweatshirt. I push my hands inside and focus on the tattered strings from the hoodie lying along the front. I'm startled when Owen is standing in front of me, a small drink in his hand. "I told you, I don't drink."

"Yeah, and I bet a week ago you thought your dad was the greatest man alive," he says, moving the small shot glass closer to me.

I take it in my hand and look at it, smelling the edge of the glass and feeling surprised that the odor isn't strong. It's only a small shot, and I won't drink any more—just this one. The urge to do something wrong—something against my grain—is suddenly overwhelming. I lift the glass to my lips, pausing before I drink to look into Owen's eyes. When I do, they're glowing again, and that same feeling of connection is there—the one from the driveway, the one from when he apologized for scaring me on the highway.

I tilt the glass back, and cough the second the burn hits the back of my throat. Owen chuckles softly, then hands me a bottle of water, and when he takes the glass away, I notice his fingertips tickle against mine, pausing as if they're surprised by our touch.

"Just so you know," I say, waiting for him to look at me to finish the rest, "I never thought my dad was the greatest man alive."

He holds my sightline and his mouth sits in a comfortable, flat line as he steps backward until he's at his beanbag again, and he lowers himself to sit.

"Just so you know," he says, holding a newly filled shot glass in his hand, holding it steady in front of his face, but pausing when it's raised between my gaze and his. I sense he's reading me, but I don't know why. "I always thought my dad was…"

He drinks fast, and his eyes close as he holds the burning sensation in. After a few seconds, he opens his eyes again, and the look, the pained, lost boy, is there now.

"I always thought he was the greatest man alive. All the way until he wasn't," Owen says, and my gut twists with a hurt I've never felt before. Sympathy. That's what I feel for Owen Harper.

Just then, I realize, he's not really wild at all. He's heartbroken. And maybe I don't hate him as much as I thought I did.

CHAPTER 7

Owen didn't talk for the rest of the night. We spent several more hours at that house—the one I found out later belonged to some girl named Sasha. Her family farms, but they have a large staff that really runs most of the business. Sasha is home alone often—alone with Owen and his friends and their…recreational habits.

We didn't talk during the ride home, but Owen drove slowly. I think he did it for me. The ride home felt…different. I didn't fear Owen. I hated him for telling me what he told me. I also hated my father. And Owen missed his. As the sun rose, I spent the miles we drove trying to find a way to make those thoughts match up in my head—find a way to make Owen's pain hurt just a little less. And then I became consumed with the realization that I was caring a little too much about Owen and his feelings.

I'm starting to recognize the town, the trees of my street are familiar, and the closer we get to my house—and Owen's—the more my stomach hurts. I sit up on the edge of the truck seat and push my hands under my legs, worried about what will be waiting for me in my driveway.

My phone doesn't have any messages on it, and I'm grateful for that. My mom let me run away, probably because she needed to be alone too. What worries me is where my father is—and if he's home.

Home. Such a farce. This is nobody's home, and now I hope like hell my mom kicked my dad out of it.

"You're worried about your old man. Worried he's there, huh?" Owen asks, his tone on the verge of caring, as if he's really interested, as if he isn't loving every second of my suffering. I won't look at him, only glancing at his profile, but I notice the tilt of his face toward me. It's just enough to let me know he's looking at me, and it makes me uncomfortable, so I pull my arms around my chest. This is the first time I've heard his voice in hours. He had two or three more shots, long ago, but still I should have driven the truck. I don't like that I let him drive.

Maybe I'm still afraid to confront him.

"Yep," I respond to him, nodding as I let my head slide to the side, my cheek pressed on the passenger window. I let my breath fog it up, blurring out my view, like I'm erasing the parts I don't like outside.

"His car's gone," Owen says, making my heart slow instantly.

"Good," I say, pausing with my lips open, my breath fogging the glass once again, this time making the cloud on the window thicker. "I think that's good. That's...good, isn't it?"

I look at him when I ask this, something pulling me to him, forcing me to look at him. When I'm confronted with his calmness, the serene look on his face, a renewed fire grows in my belly, and it makes me angry again—angry with Owen, angry that he was the one to tell me, angrier that he took pleasure in it. He's barely pushing his shifter in park when I shove him hard against his door.

"You...asshole!" I yell, shoving him again, then leaning back against my door, on the other end of the bench seat. He's staring into my eyes, emotionless, completely unaffected by my outburst. My hands are cold from his poor heating system, and they sting when I slap him with them again, my palms coming to a thud against the layers of clothing covering his body, but I push at him anyway, shoving hard. I want to hurt him.

"You...goddamned...fucking asshole!" I scream, so loudly that I'm sure if anyone were awake and outside, they would hear me.

I shove again, and Owen sits there, bracing himself for the impact, but not stopping me. He doesn't stop me—he doesn't say a word. I hit him a few more times, knowing I'm not hurting him, that I'm not strong enough to come close to hurting him, but I do it anyway. I go until I feel foolish, then I get out of his truck and slam the door closed behind me.

The crunch of the wood chips between our driveways is loud under my feet. I walk quickly, never bothering to turn to face Owen, to see if he's following me, looking at me or stepping out of his truck. I march up the front steps of my house, holding my hand on the knob and breathing deeply. When it's unlocked, my heart breaks a little knowing I'm going to have to face whatever life is left inside.

My mother is sitting at the table when I walk in, my father's belongings strewn around the first floor in piles. Everything looks just as I thought it would, but it doesn't make me sad. What makes me sad is the fact that I'm not sad at all to see traces of my father's disappearance. It's just the opposite—I feel nothing.

"Your dad is at a hotel. He won't be coming back. Not…not for a while," she says, her voice showing how tired she is, how hurt she is.

I don't answer, but I nod just enough for her to recognize a response, then I continue up the stairs to my room, the one that looks nothing like my room at all. I stand in the doorway for a few minutes, surveying my things, mostly still in boxes, and I note the time on my clock—almost six. Willow will be here in thirty minutes, and I know I would never be able to wake up if I actually fell asleep, so I grab my pillow and blanket from my bed, and curl up by my window to wait for the alarm to start my next miserable day.

Owen's room is lit, and every now and then, I notice shadows crossing it. There's another car in his driveway, an older sedan. I wonder if that's his mom's?

From my view, I can see all the way through his door, and he passes his room a few times, like he's pacing out in the hallway, until he finally closes his door shut behind him. He pulls his sweatshirt and the T-shirt that was underneath over his head, and I watch the entire thing, letting myself admit that he's attractive. He's more than attractive. His skin is this warm color that's almost golden, his stomach toned, his arms strong…and I let myself imagine how they would feel holding me.

No one has ever held me. Not a boy, anyhow. I've danced with boys, held hands, kissed—but not *really.*

Owen pulls his phone from his pocket, texting someone before putting it down on a small night table near the wall by the window. Reaching up, he shuts off the lamp that's illuminating his room, and just like that, he disappears.

And I admit to myself that I miss him.

"YOU LOOK LIKE TOTAL SHIT," Willow says as I climb into her car, wearing a change of clothes, but yesterday's hair.

"I feel like shit," I say.

"Yeah? Oh, hey…uh…if you're going to vomit? You need to tell me. I need to know because I'm, like…one of those sympathetic vomiters. I'm serious—if you throw up, I'll throw up. And then we'll both be throwing up…in my car. Yeah, maybe you should stay home?" She's talking so fast that it makes my head hurt. I only drank the one drink, but it was enough to leave me feeling not quite right.

"I'm not sick. I'm just tired. It was a long night," I say, noticing Owen's window is still dark, his truck still in it's place—right where we left it.

My mom was awake still, her body frozen to the same chair it was in when I got home an hour before. I have a feeling she'll be there when I get home.

"Homework?" Willow asks, her car skidding over the curb as she backs out of my driveway.

"Uh…yeah…a lot of homework," I lie. I like Willow, but not enough to relive my nightmare, at least not yet.

School is easy, and I'm grateful for that. Owen misses our morning classes, and his crew is noticeably missing from the window show I've gotten accustomed to during lunch.

The afternoon passes in a blur. Owen never shows up, and nobody looks for him. It's strange how nobody asks why he's missing, and I feel like I'm literally watching him slip through the cracks of the education system.

There's a project assignment in science, and I make plans to start it right away, gathering the requirement sheets and supplies from the classroom before meeting Willow in the parking lot—Owen's truck still nowhere to be found. Elise and Ryan are in Willow's back seat, and I notice how much

Ryan reminds me of Owen. Not so much in the face, but his body—his long legs folded to fit in the tightness of Willow's car, his strong arm draped behind Elise, his eyes dark, clothing dark, his hat pulled low.

I'm thinking about Owen. I'm looking at Ryan, and I'm thinking about Owen, and I'm so aware that I'm doing it that I'm ashamed. But I keep thinking about him. He's a distraction—he's also the reason I need a distraction. And he doesn't have to know I think about him.

"How come Owen misses so much school?" I ask, hoping Ryan will give me a little piece to the puzzle. Willow's gaze falls on me fast, and I realize how jarring my question is. "I just saw him last night, in front of his house," I say, my words coming out rushed and nervous. "And I know he's fine, or not sick or whatever. It was weird he wasn't here. That's all."

I'm overly-justifying my question, and Willow knows it too. She keeps her eyes on me a little longer, until the light flicks to green and she pulls away from our school. Her questions are lining up in her mind, and I know they're coming. I just hope I can avoid them a little longer—until I know how to answer them.

"Owen's grades are fine. That's all that matters. He's never ineligible for basketball; he doesn't miss practice, and his grades are good," Ryan says, following up his explanation with a harsh sigh. He's defensive over Owen, and I sort of wish I had someone like Ryan to be defensive over me. "Seriously, Kensi. Don't believe half of the shit you hear. It pisses me off—how people talk about him? He's a good guy."

Willow lets out a rush of air with a laugh at Ryan's words, and he kicks his leg forward into the back of her seat.

"You hush. You're not qualified to be impartial," Ryan says, and something about the way he says it makes me turn my gaze to Willow.

"Like hell I'm not," she says, her face suddenly less...perky.

"What does that mean?" I ask.

"Willow went out with Owen, freshman year. She's still mad about him breaking up with her," Ryan says, and everything inside of me feels heavy. I'm jealous. *I'm jealous!*

"One..." Willow starts, her eyes on Ryan in the rearview mirror, "I did *not* go out with him. We hooked up, at a party, for like...an hour. And two, I am over him. I just don't agree with the way he used me, then ignored me.

And I don't like the way he continues to do that to girls, over and over again. It's…it's demeaning."

It is demeaning. I can't argue with her there. But…it seems to me that at this point girls know what they're in for with him. I've been here for a few weeks, and I have him figured out.

"Whatever," Ryan says, turning his interest to the window, to Owen's house outside. "He's a good guy, that's all I'm saying. Don't date him if you don't like the way he treats girls. But don't judge him. He'd never hurt anyone."

A small laugh escapes my throat, and I cover it up quickly with a cough. Ryan notices, and our eyes meet. I shake his gaze off and turn my attention to the door, to my house, to my crappy life inside.

"Thanks for the ride. I'll see ya in the morning?" I say, holding the door open and noticing Ryan still studying me.

"Yeah, I'll be here a little earlier. We have extra rehearsals in the morning, okay?" Willow says, and I nod, closing the door behind me and blocking out Ryan's stare.

I'm not sure what I expected when I stepped inside, but it wasn't this. Our house—the one I left this morning—is completely void of my father. The only remnant of him the memories I have trapped in the music boxes stashed in the corner…and my piano. The house smells of Pine-Sol, and my mom is listening to music loudly in the kitchen, her hands covered in rubber gloves.

"I thought you were working?" I ask, scaring her a little with my voice.

"Oh! Sorry, didn't hear you come in. Uh…yeah, work. Seems I'm a little upset, and I might have had a little bit of an issue inserting a catheter? So, I'm taking a week of personal time. The chief sort of insisted," she says, running her arm along her nose. Her eyes are red, and I can tell she's been crying.

"So, you're…cleaning?" I ask, holding up a bag of trash tied and propped in the corner.

"Seems so," she says, going back to scrubbing. "I'm getting rid of… things. Anything we don't need, it's in boxes in the garage."

She didn't say it, but I know she means she's getting rid of my father, of *his* things. She's being a little manic, and when I look around the house, I'm a little frightened by how much she's done in the six or seven hours I've been gone.

"Okay, well...do you want to keep going? Or, I don't know...can I help? I have a project to work on, but it's not due for a while," I say, setting my backpack on the counter and my project supplies down next to it. My mom feels lost, and I'm right there with her.

"There's a lot of trash. There's more on the side of the house. Maybe see what you can fit in the can?" she asks, already back to scrubbing the sink. I notice she's thrown my father's food away, the packets of tuna he likes all bagged up neatly—ready for the trash.

"I can handle trash," I say, watching her wipe her brow with her sleeve, watching her pretend. I pick up the small bag of food and garbage and leave through the back door, ready to pretend right along with her.

I notice the bags stacked along the wall when I step outside, and I recognize my father's dress shoes peaking out of the top of one of them.

"That's a lot of nice stuff. Your mom throwing it all away?" Owen asks. I close my eyes, my back still to him.

"Guess so," I respond.

"You should sell it," he says, and I hear his steps moving away from me. I turn and notice he's taking out a bag of trash too.

I drag our garbage and the first bag of my father's things to our can, which is sitting right next to the Harpers'.

"You take out the trash," I say, not sure why I'm surprised seeing him do such a simple thing. But I am. I'm amazed.

"Yep," he says, flinging his bag into his container and closing the lid. I notice how empty it sounds, and I look over my shoulder at the dozen bags waiting for me.

"Hey," I start, but stop instantly, biting my lip to give myself time to think. I almost asked him for a favor, and I don't think I want to do that.

"If I can have those shoes, you can dump your crap in our trashcan," he says, finishing my thought—almost.

"Really?" I'm flummoxed. He's being nice. Or, I think he's being nice. "And...the shoes?"

He gestures to the bags, to the one on top with my father's dress shoes.

"Oh," I say, feeling a little strange about the thought of Owen wearing my father's shoes. "I...I guess?"

"It's for my grandpa. He needs a new pair," Owen says, somehow becoming a little more human with this revelation. He has a grandpa. I don't know why that strikes me as strange, also.

"Sure, then. That's fine," I say, walking over to grab some of the bags. I pull the shoes out of the first and turn to hand them to Owen, surprised when he's close to me. He's so near me, and his eyes aren't dark. They're bright. He looks...happy. "Does your grandpa live close?"

I hand him the shoes, and for a few seconds, we're both holding them. Owen is looking at the shoes. *I'm* looking at Owen's hands and remembering how he stopped me from beating up the dashboard of his truck. I'm remembering how big his hands were—how they covered mine completely, how they were rough, yet warm and soft all the same.

"He lives in a nursing home, just on the other side of town. That was his truck," he says, nodding over his shoulder.

I don't know Owen's grandfather, but I'm suddenly happy he's getting my father's shoes. I like Owen's truck, and I rationalize that I probably would like his grandpa, too. Maybe a better man will wear those shoes.

"Here, let me help you get these in. I think we can fit them all in both cans," he says, setting the shoes down and picking up three bags at once, lifting them easily and stuffing them in my already-overflowing can. He's pushing with his arms, and I have a flash memory of how they looked when I watched him pull his shirt from his body early this morning.

"You missed school today," I say, waiting to see how he responds. He doesn't, much, only offering a shrug. "You miss a lot?"

"I get good grades. But I have to work, and sometimes I just can't do both things at once," he says, walking back to the side of my house for more bags. I lift one for every three he takes, and in two more trips, we have all traces of my father neatly stowed in the giant green trashcans by the curb.

"Where do you work?" I ask, trying not to overanalyze how civil our conversation is right now.

Owen presses down one more time on the top of my can, then pulls the black hat from his head, running his fingers through his dark hair, smoothing the long strands back so they sit neatly under his hat again.

"It's just some job. Look, thanks for the shoes, but I've gotta go," he says, suddenly short and on the verge of rude.

He pulls his keys from his pocket and heads toward his truck, tossing the shoes in the passenger seat and leaving me behind—feeling stupid for even asking questions about him.

I still watch him pull away, though. I don't even disguise it. And strangely, things feel more right talking with Owen than they do with Willow, or Elise, or Ryan. Owen may be my best friend here in Woodstock, and *that* is pathetic.

I step back inside the house, and the warmth feels good. The air is a constant chill now, and I know real winter is coming. In the city, the buildings hid the snow and grayness of the sky. Everything always felt alive, even when the cold was biting. But you can see it coming out here. The leaves have all fallen, and the trees are sticks. The gray of the clouds, the color of winter is consuming—and it's all around.

My piano looks like the sky. I just don't want to play it.

My mother is still cleaning. She's moved upstairs, working on my bathroom or hers; I can't tell. Our house isn't dirty, but I get what she's doing. She's erasing my father. Unfortunately, I can't drag a thousand-pound piano into the driveway, otherwise I'd erase him, too.

My scarf and beanie are still lying on the sofa near the front door, so I grab them and bundle myself up before heading back outside. My feet carry me to the garage, and I lift the heavy door, having to jump to get it up all the way. I walk to the back, to the boxes of tools that my mom will have a much better chance of using.

There's the hoop. Its rust has left a mark on the wall behind it, and I know it's heavy. I remember from dragging it here in the first place. I move the boxes out of the way first, knocking one over and spilling bolts and drill bits in a thousand different directions. Once I sweep them into a pile, I pour them back in the box, not caring how disorganized I'm leaving it. My dad would hate that, and doing it brings a smile to my face.

Gripping the rim of the hoop with both hands, I drag it back out of the garage, and it scrapes along the pavement, leaving an orange mark behind. That makes me smile, too.

I unfold the ladder and place it under the spot on the eave of the house where the hoop hung only a few days before. The bolts are still there, and if I can just manage to get the hoop to the top of the ladder, I can slide it against the garage until I can lock it in place.

"Honey, careful up there," my mom says, her voice igniting a rapid fire in my chest. I wait for her to question what I'm doing, but she doesn't. She's too lost in her own world to care about this. "I'm running to the store. I'll pick up some things for dinner. Need anything?"

"No, I'm good. Thanks!" I yell, thinking to myself about that word —*need.* A week ago, I needed to move back to the city, needed time alone to play my music…how I wanted to. I needed my friends—the ones I used to trust. But now, all I need to do is get this hoop up on the goddamned garage.

I grunt the entire time, and the metal rim scratches my arm through my sweatshirt in a few places, but after at least twenty minutes, I manage to get the hoop back up on the brackets—the weight of it no longer depending on my strength. It takes several more minutes to find the drill in the garage, but when I do, I'm able to lock the bolts down tight, and I push up on the rim to check that it's stable.

After putting the tools and ladder away, I walk backward, shutting the garage door with a tired leap, and admiring my work. It's almost as if it was never gone. I hope the boy who uses it at night comes back.

The car makes a skidding sound as it pulls up our driveway. I turn around expecting my mom, expecting to help her haul in a few bags of groceries. But I'm met with the dimmed headlights of a blue BMW—freezing me instantly.

She looks so different when she steps out of the car. She seems…*older…* and like a stranger. Her blond hair rings around her face, the curls perfect, and I can tell she spent a lot of time on her appearance. She wanted to look her best for me, for this…whatever *this* is. Ambush, I am guessing.

"Kensington," she says, my full name floating from her breath, soft and airy, like she's trying to seduce me.

"Go home, Gaby," I say, brushing the dirt from my hands and sleeves, my belly quivering with nerves that my mother is going to pull in the driveway behind her and have to see this.

"I just want to talk," she says, her hands stretched out, like she's helpless.

"You could have called. Go home, Gaby. My mom will be home any minute, and she doesn't need to see you here. I don't need to see you here," I say, moving toward my house, toward my door.

"Kens," she says, saying my name the way my new friends do. She hasn't called me Kens since we were little, and she no longer has the right to.

"Gaby, you cannot be serious! Coming here? Right now? I mean, are you serious about this?" I can feel my temper boiling, and I notice Owen's truck pull up behind her, which only makes my nerves fire away more. I don't want him to see this. I don't want to be here. I want to disappear!

"Please, Kens…" she starts, and I interrupt.

"Don't talk to me like that! Don't say my name like that! Like we're… what? Friends? Jesus, Gaby! You slept with my father!" I scream, and I notice another guy standing next to Owen, both of them near the front of the truck, watching me—watching *this.*

"I didn't mean to. It just happened. I fell in love with him, Kensington. I love Dean. And I tried not to, but your dad, he loves me too. We didn't mean to hurt you, hurt your mom." She's saying so much. She's saying *too* much, and I notice Owen ushering whoever is with him toward the house —away from my embarrassing display—and I'm grateful.

The distraction lets Gaby get closer without me realizing, though, and soon her hand is touching my arm, and I recoil quickly.

"Don't you fucking touch me. You…you!" I push her as I let go of myself, let myself feel the rage. "You were my best friend, and you betrayed me. You betrayed my MOM! We took care of you, let you stay in our house. My god! What were you doing in my house? Uhhhhhhggggg! You called him *Dean*! Like he's your boyfriend! Oh…my god!"

"It wasn't like that, Kens. I promise," she starts, but I hold my hands up, then I shove her back on her feet. I move her, and she lets me, until she's at her opened car door.

"Just…go, Gaby. Please…just go," I say, my head shaking, and the tears filling up the corners of my eyes. Gaby's face is a reflection of mine, but I have no sympathy for her. I want her to feel the pain of a million needles—I want her heart to ache and her breath to choke her. I want her to cry and never stop. And I want my mom to feel better. I want to move back to the city, away from this place. But I can't even do that, because that's where Gaby is, where *Dean* is.

She climbs back in the car and slowly moves away. I break, reaching down and filling my hands with small rocks from the side of the yard. "I hate you!" I scream, my voice cracking from the force, and I let the rocks fly at the front of her car, pelting it and leaving small marks behind. I reach down for another handful, and cock my arm, ready to throw.

"Don't," Owen says, his hand wrapped around my small wrist, locking me up, unable to move. I snap to his eyes, and they're no longer void of feeling like they were this morning. There's sympathy in them, and that's the only reason I let my muscles relax. "It won't make you feel better. Let her go."

The stones fall from my fingers, and I bring my hands up to my head, scratching into my hairline with frustration as I pace. "What will?" I ask, and he quirks an eyebrow up. "Make me feel better. What will make me feel better?"

"Nothing," he says, and his answer comes so fast that it makes me sad. I'm sad because I get the sense that Owen is right, and he's speaking from experience.

"I'm. So. Angry," I say between deep breaths, letting my guard down a little more, but tensing when I realize that the guy who was in the truck with him is still here, standing a few feet away. Owen follows my gaze, the corner of his lip raising slightly, then lowering fast.

"That's my brother, Andrew," he says, and the younger version of him nods once in response, stepping forward and reaching out his hand. His manners feel so natural, and strange, given how much he looks like his older brother.

"I'm Kensi," I say, shaking his hand.

"I know," he says, smiling enough to show his teeth. Owen gives him a sharp look, and he scrunches his shoulders up defensively. "What? I know her name. So what?"

Owen keeps his disapproving look on his brother for a few more seconds, and I can sense a silent exchange happening between them.

"You ever hit someone?" Owen asks, making a sharp turn in the conversation, his eyes back on mine. They're still bright, and...gorgeous. But there's also a challenge lingering in them, this flare I see every now and then, when he's confronting me, taunting me—pushing me.

"No," I say back, my response clipped and short on purpose. He doesn't like it when I talk to him this way. I can tell because he stutters on his feet a little, like he's not used to someone being so blunt with him.

"Hit me," he says, and now I'm the one falling on my feet.

"Are you nuts?" I ask, and his brother chuckles behind him.

"Haven't you heard, Kensi? We're all fucking nuts. Harper boys are all fucked up in the head," Andrew says. Owen is quick with his reach, grabbing the sleeve of his shirt and jerking him slightly. Andrew continues to laugh lightly, but he straightens up fast and starts to kick at the driveway, moving toward the truck and away from Owen and me.

"I'm being serious. Hit me. You need to feel something," Owen says, stepping a little closer—a little *too* close—to me.

"Owen, I don't want to hit you," I say, letting out a long breath and feeling my arms tingle in fear at the thought of doing something so... so...violent.

"Yes you do," he says, taking another step, his chest now completely blocking my view of his brother.

"No, I don't," I say, shoving him off balance. He steps back quickly with one foot and looks down to his feet, his lip curling on the corner into that smile again, and soon his feet are back where they were, his eyes wide and intensely looking at my face.

"You sure about that?" he asks, moving an inch or two closer, close enough that I notice the scent of his shampoo, his cologne, and the way I remember the inside of his truck smelling.

"What are you, in fight club or something?" I tease, trying to bring lightness to the most awkward and heavy conversation I've ever had with a boy.

"Something like that," he says, stepping nearer. "Go on, Ken Doll. Hit me. You want to, and it will feel *soooooo good.*"

He's so close that I feel the tickle of his breath now. His brother is still close enough that I know he's watching him lure me, and I wonder how normal this behavior is. His right hand reaches to my shoulder, pulling a wave of my hair into his fingers, and he twists it slowly, his eyes moving from his hands to my lips and back again.

"Come on, Ken Doll. Hit me," he says, practically a whisper. He brings his mouth lower to my neck, his hand pulling the wave of hair back until it falls from his fingers completely.

He reaches in again, sweeping a pile of my hair out of his way, his eyes daring mine, that wicked look growing stronger until I can no longer see them, his mouth and nose lost under my chin, his lips almost touching me. I haven't breathed since he started this game.

"Are you…afraid? I won't hit you back. I don't do that," he says softly against my ear, my body now covered in shivers, but my legs holding strong, fighting against the pounding in my chest. "Or…would you rather I kiss you? Maybe that would be better, help you…forget. I bet you've never been kissed before. Virgin. Ken Doll, *my little virgin.*"

With swift force, I bend my elbow and bring my fist into Owen's lower stomach—close enough to his crotch to make him question everything he thinks he knows about me, to make him second guess his assumption that I'm weak. I'm lost, but I'm not weak. When he starts coughing, backing away from me with his arms wrapped around his stomach, he starts to laugh, and I begin to think that Owen Harper might actually be crazy.

"Thata girl," he says, standing with his hands along his back, bending forward and back, trying to work out the damage I did to him. "You feel better?"

"I feel like you're an asshole," I say, igniting a new round of laughter from Andrew.

"You're right about that, Kensi. My brother's a real asshole," he says, coming closer so he can mock his brother. "Dude, she laid you out. You a'right, man? Swallow a nut?"

Owen pushes his brother back a few steps, then coughs a few more times. "I'm fine, douchebag," he says, then brings his focus back to me. "Let me ask you again. Do you feel better?"

His smile is gone, his mouth tight, in a flat line. His eyes penetrating me completely, and I keep my focus on him as I consider this, think about his words, and ask myself with my inner voice: Do I feel better? Absolutely not.

"No," I say quickly, my eyes drifting to his chin, to his neck, and then his chest. What felt better was having him close, smelling him, thinking he might actually put his lips on mine, that he might touch me. Thinking he might actually *want* me in a way that I've never been wanted is what felt good—more than good.

But hitting him only made me feel bad.

I don't hate Owen Harper. But I want him. Unlike I've ever wanted anyone. And while that takes away the ugly I feel about my father, it also scares the ever-loving crap out of me.

CHAPTER 8

Owen came to school for the rest of the week, and his routine was back to the same—his feet up on my desk, his make-out sessions on display at lunch, this time with a new girl I didn't recognize. His friend he called House started nodding to me in the hall, and by the end of the week, I was nodding back. Owen was still making me the focus of his attention, but it felt less cruel now.

"I've never actually seen him flirt with anyone before," Willow says, throwing a French fry at my plate, drawing my attention from the window where Owen is backing away, nodding his chin at me with a slight acknowledgement and an even slighter grin.

"What, that? Please. He's not flirting. He just helped me out with some crap at my house this weekend, and we talked a little. But he's still an ass. Just less of an ass," I say, trying to convince Willow, but clearly doing a very poor job as she smiles at me like she knows all of my secrets.

"Right, he's an ass. Or…is he dreamy? Which one is it?" she teases, and I pick up her fry and throw it back in her lap.

"He's an ass," I say, standing with my tray and pulling my bag over my shoulder.

"Okay. But, I'm not stupid, you know. I can tell you like him," she says, throwing her trash on top of mine, then passing me to hold open the lunchroom door for me to follow.

I don't answer her, because I don't want to lie. I do like him. I've been dreaming about him, and when I don't dream about him, I pray to dream about him. I wait by my window, hoping to hear the sound of his ball bouncing in my driveway. He hasn't been out there since I've put the hoop back up, though. Most nights, I lay quiet and listen for his truck to leave or pull into the driveway. I wish I had a car, so I could follow him to his work —so I knew where he was when I don't see him.

We get to the spot in the hallway where our paths divide, and Willow tugs on my sleeve, stopping me before I'm about to say goodbye.

"It's okay to like him, you know. I meant what I said the other day. You know, in front of Ryan? I kissed him, like two and a half years ago, at a party. It was *nooooo* big deal. And I love Jess. I don't have a *thing* for Owen Harper. Yes, *I* think he's a jerk. But…" she pauses, looking down and stepping closer to me. "But I don't have to like him. And if you do, I will still like you. And maybe you'll make me think more of Owen, just because you're so awesome."

She smiles when she's done and tugs at my sleeve one more time, a nonverbal queue asking for my acceptance and understanding.

"Okay," I say, sucking in my bottom lip with the weight of everything that small *okay* admits to. Willow doesn't judge, and she doesn't make it more than it is. She just nods and tells me she'll meet me in the parking lot so we can go grab a bite to eat before the football game tonight.

Owen is waiting for me in science class, his feet on my chair this time rather than my tabletop. His hands are folded behind his head, and my heart is literally smacking into my chest bones, rattling my insides to the point that I actually feel dizzy. I'm sure it's in my head, but I swear he heard me say "okay" too.

"This is a record for you, isn't it?" I say, pushing his heavy Converse-covered feet from my seat before sitting down and pulling out my notebook. I can hear Owen leaning forward, and I know his face is close to the back of my head, but I will myself to face my desk and not turn around.

"What's a record?" he asks.

"You've been here every day this week. Seriously, they should give you an award. At least a certificate," I say, not feeling as proud as I usually do when I take digs at him.

"Didn't have to work this week," he says. I can hear him lean back in his seat. "Got fired."

I turn around when he says that, wanting to evaluate the look on his face, make sure he's being *real.* His eyes meet mine the second I lean over the back of my chair, and there's a heavy seriousness to them.

"I'm sorry. That...sucks," I say.

"Yeah, it does," he says, bending forward to pull a pencil from the side of his backpack. He slides a notebook out and flips through the pages, and I can't help but notice that his paper is filled with notes, and his handwriting is actually decent.

"Well, at least now you have time for school," I say, moving my gaze from his hands to his eyes and back again; the intensity of the way he looks at me makes it hard to stare at him long.

"Ha, I guess. I'm getting a new job, though. Have to. We've got bills," he says, and I feel like one more page of his story has turned for me to read. Owen Harper is responsible, more than any teenager should be.

"What about your mom? Or...does she live with you? I'm sorry. I just... honestly, I've only ever seen you and your brother," I say, not wanting to admit how much I know about his personal life, not wanting to give credence to the rumors.

"My mom works nights. She's a security guard at an impound lot. She's taking online classes to be a medical tech, so she usually studies while she's sitting in the booth. Her job pays shit, and with gramps in the nursing home..." he looks up at our teacher as he walks in, then taps his pencil a few times on his notebook and nods forward.

We're dissecting next week—baby sharks. We spent the hour looking at slides of the various parts we'll be required to identify. I didn't write down a single thing. All I could do was listen to the sound of Owen's pencil scratching paper behind me, the sounds of his breath, of his feet sliding along the floor, of the noise his hands make when they scratch at the stubble on his chin and his knuckles crack.

It was a two-minute conversation, but I feel like I know more about

Owen Harper than anyone else in this entire school. And all I want to do is learn more.

When the bell rings, I gather my things quickly and turn to face Owen, hoping he'll pick up where things left off. But he's already gone—vanished.

I spend my last hour in health class doing the same thing I did in science—piecing together sections of Owen's life. I never see his brother Andrew at school, and I have yet to meet James, the one everyone says is *real* trouble. Owen seems to always be alone.

Alone.

When the bell rings, I pack up and pull my phone from my pocket to text my mom and let her know I'll be staying at school and grabbing dinner with Willow. I worry about her eating on her own, spending the night by herself. My mom and I have fallen into a routine the last few days—homework, dinner, and a movie. I think that routine is distracting her from my father. He tried to call last night, and my mom turned her phone off. I hope she's strong enough to do the same when I'm not there watching.

"Hey, so Jess wants burgers. You good with burgers?" Willow asks as she slips her arm through mine while we exit the main hallway out onto the front lawn of the school.

"Sounds good. I'm hungry," I say, my voice trailing off when I notice Owen sitting on the tailgate of his truck, parked next to Willow's car. He's waiting for me, and Willow sees him, too.

"Unless, of course...you'd like to maybe have dinner with someone else?" she teases.

"Stop," I whisper harshly, my face burning. I've never been a fan of being teased about boys. It was something Gaby always did to me. One of many thoughtless things my so-called best friend did to disregard my feelings it seems.

"He's waiting to talk to you. He's never here after school, Kens. There's a reason he's here," she says, and my stomach flutters with the same sensation I get when I'm climbing up in a rollercoaster. I think this is thrill.

As we get closer, Owen swings his long legs outward and stands up, closing the tailgate behind him and leaning his arm over it, his head covered in a dark gray beanie, and the ends of his hair sticking out a little on the front and sides.

"Hey," he says, looking up at me quickly, then back down at his feet. He leans out from the edge of the truck with his arm still holding it while he stretches his long body. He looks nervous and uncomfortable, and it's giving me hope about the reason he's here...waiting for me. I hate that it's giving me hope. I know what that means.

"Hey," I say back, looking to Willow for help, a life raft—anything!

"Wow, well that was deep you two," she says, and my eyes grow wide with embarrassment. Owen laughs lightly and pushes his hands into the pockets of his black jeans before stepping closer to me. Willow glances at me before unlocking her car and tossing her bag inside. Jess is walking up, which now has my heart racing even faster, pulsing harder, and my mouth has forgotten how to work.

"I guess you probably already have a ride, huh?" Owen says, cocking his head to the side to look at me with one eyebrow raised.

"Yeah, uh...I have to be at the game tonight. Band," I say, sucking in my lip and cursing band for the first time.

"Right...right," Owen says, nodding and taking a small step back. "I forgot you do that. That's cool. Just thought I'd see if you needed a ride home, but yeah...so, I'll see ya later."

He pulls his keys from his pocket and tosses them slightly before grabbing them in the air and turning on his heels. I want to jump in the other side of his truck, run away with him, go home with him, go anywhere with him. Hell, I want to sit in the truck and wait while he fills out job applications and does whatever else it is he does when he's gone.

"Hey, Kens?" Willow asks, her arm over the top of her car while she looks at me. Owen pauses at the sound of her voice. "You know, Jess and I were thinking we'd just go grab dinner at his house, since it's so close. We don't have to be back here until six, in case...you know...you wanna do something else?"

My lips actually hurt from the force of wanting to smile, but I keep it hidden, pushing my lips tight and only letting the corners of my mouth curl.

"Could you bring me back here? By six?" I ask Owen, hoping he simply says *yes*, that he doesn't bail on this completely.

"Yeah, that's cool. I've got time. I have to pick up Andrew, so..." his voice fades away, and his attention moves to the cab of his truck. I secretly love that he's so unsure of his words with me. This is different from teasing. This is different from being cruel. And I like it.

"We'll see you at six, Kens," Willow says with a wink. Jess is already in the car with her, looking over his shoulder at Owen and me, and I'm sure she's filling him in on everything she thinks this is about. That's probably for the best, because Willow might understand what's happening better than me.

"You ready?" Owen asks, from the other side of his truck. I didn't really expect him to open my door or anything, but he seems so uncomfortable being alone with me now.

"Oh, uh…yeah. Should I just throw my stuff in the back of the truck then?" I ask. Owen shrugs a nod, so I lift my heavy bag to the back of his truck, securing it between the metal side and a tire, then climb into the cab with him. His truck looks different in the daylight, but it still brings back memories of the last time I was in here with him, when I swore at him and slapped him like a girl. I feel a little ashamed, because I can tell he's remembering that, too.

"So, where's Andrew?" I ask, wanting to start a safe conversation—*any* conversation.

"He's at the community college. He splits his time between here and there, usually doesn't get done until after our school lets out," Owen says, his lips forming a prideful smile. "Andrew's sort of smart."

"Wow, so he's like, what? Taking college classes?" I ask. We had a program like this at Bryce, but the professors came to our school.

"Yeah, he has eight credits or something like that. English and algebra, I think? If he passes with an *A*, he gets full credit toward his diploma. It's free, so I made sure when he was selected he took advantage of it," Owen says, his eyes on the road as we pull away from the school—the opposite direction of everyone else.

"That's amazing. You must be proud of him," I say, knowing he is by the way he talks about his brother.

"Yeah, well…one of us should get a college degree," he says. I can't tell if he's being humble or bitter.

"What about you? Where are you going?" I ask.

"Depends," he says, glancing up at the rearview mirror, then beyond his shoulder, his eyes grazing over me as he does. "I'd like to play ball somewhere. But then...who's gonna pay the bills?"

Owen doesn't add anything after this, and I don't know what to ask, so I reach forward and twist the knob on his old stereo to listen to some music. Nothing comes in very well, the classic rock station sounding the best; I leave the dial there. A few minutes later, we pull up at the front of the community college, and Andrew waves from a bench.

"You're going to need to scoot to the middle," Owen says, looking at the small space next to him, the one with the hump in the middle of the floor.

I unbuckle my belt and slide there, bending my knees in front of me and looking for the seatbelt straps.

"There's no belt here. Sorry...I'll be careful, though. I'll keep you safe," he says, his eyes flashing to mine for a beat before moving back to the steering wheel. I notice the hard swallow in his throat.

"Door's locked," Andrew says, his voice muffled from outside. He's pulling on the handle, but nothing's happening. I start to reach over to pull the lock at the top, but Owen puts his hand on my arm, stopping me.

"I got it. It's broken," he says, careful not to look at me while he leans across my body. I practically suck myself to the seat, holding my breath the entire time his body is stretched across my lap. I can see the bare skin on his side as he reaches over, his shirt pulling from his jeans, and I notice the gray band of his boxers.

I'm noticing things I've never noticed about boys before.

When he straightens up again behind the wheel, he turns his focus to his side window, almost as if he's trying to pretend I'm not here, that my leg isn't touching his. All I can feel is his leg—and when he moves it from the gas to the brake and back again—I take pleasure in the movement.

"Hey, Kens," Andrew says, startling me back to the present.

"Hey. Hope it's okay I tagged along," I say, wondering why Andrew called me *Kens,* if he knew I'd like it, and if Owen was the one to tell him so.

"Oh, it's okay," he says, leaning forward to look at his brother. I'm uncomfortable by his suggestion, and I can tell it's making Owen angry by the way he starts jerking the wheel and driving a bit rougher.

"Kensington has to be back at school for band at six, so I'm going to drop you off at home, we'll eat, and then I'll bring her back," Owen says, suddenly acting formal, like a parent.

"We should go to the game," Andrew adds, still leaning forward with the same grin. I keep my face forward, my eyes focusing on a small chip in Owen's windshield.

"I don't go to football games," Owen says, stopping quickly at a light. His change in speed makes me slide forward a little in my seat, so I flex my legs against the floor to hold myself back.

"You said you'd be careful," I say, interrupting his pissing match with his brother.

"Sorry," he says, taking off again a little slower.

"Well, maybe I want to go. Can I go? I'll hang out near the band, by Kens," Andrew says, smiling at me. I'm not sure if he actually wants to go, or if he's trying to goad his brother—but both thoughts make me smile in return.

"Don't call her Kens, Andrew. You don't know if she likes it," Owen says, jerking the wheel hard again while he turns right to head down our street.

"You know that's not true, asshole. You're the one who told me," his brother says, clearing up that small sliver of doubt I had left that I had an effect on Owen Harper.

We fly into Owen's driveway, but his truck skids to a stop. I feel my legs weaken in their fight to hold me in place, and I shut my eyes tightly and bring my arms up to brace myself. Owen's hold on me is fast as his arm quickly covers my chest, and I grab hold of it on instinct.

A rollercoaster ride.

When my adrenaline rush begins to fade, I loosen my grip and look down at the dark knitted fabric of his shirt and how its contrasts with the paleness of my small fingers.

His arm is warm.

"I'm so sorry," he says, his voice more of a whisper, just for me.

"I'm okay," I say, sparing a look at his face. The pain in his eyes is evident, and even though he scared me, I want to erase his guilt. "Really. Owen...I'm okay."

I squeeze his arm one more time, letting my hands feel how strong his muscles are, feel the heat of his skin, sense the beat of his pulse in his veins.

"That's not what I'm sorry about," he says, his voice cracking a little this time.

When I turn to face the open door Andrew left on the other side, Owen's apology becomes achingly clear. My father's car is in our driveway, and he's standing at our back door, practically lying against it, pounding and begging for my mom to answer.

"Fucking hell," I say, the thrill I felt from that small touch of Owen's arm replaced with feelings of regret, anger, betrayal, and dread.

I slide from the seat and move closer to my driveway, my father still unaware I'm behind him. He's slurring—badly—and within a few more steps I can smell why.

"Dad, you need to leave. I'm calling you a cab," I say, pulling my phone from my back pocket.

"Like hell I do. This is my house, and that bitch is going to let me inside," my father says. Hearing him say those words—*that word*—about my mom makes my arms begin to itch, wanting to swing and hurt something or someone.

"Dad, this is all because of you. You're drunk, and you're being mean. You need to leave!" I yell, stopping when my dad finds his footing and stumbles a few steps in my direction.

"You..." he says, pointing over my shoulder. I turn and see Owen near my side, only a few steps behind me. "You're that kid next door. You're a disruption, and you need to stay the FUCK away from my daughter!"

"Dad! Stop it!" I say, sliding to the right a step as if I can protect Owen—as if Owen needs my protection.

"Sir, I think you've had too much to drink tonight. You really should listen to your daughter. If you don't want a cab, I'll take you somewhere—anywhere," Owen says. I turn to look at him as I feel his hand flatten against my back, and when I do, my dad yanks at my shoulder, sending me to the ground.

"You punk-ass little shit! She has worked too hard for you to screw it all up. If anyone is leaving, it's you...right now!" My father hoists his sloppy arm forward, hitting Owen in the eye, and Owen stumbles back a step, but rights himself quickly. When my dad moves toward him again, I get up and run to my front door to get my mom.

"Mr. Worth, you need to stop. I don't want to hurt you, but I'm not going to let you assault me..." I hear Owen say as I race through my door to find my mom sitting at the bottom of the stairs, crying.

"You have to call the police, Mom. Now! Dad's hurting our neighbor," I say, trying to snap my mom out of this strange trance she seems to be in.

"It's been an hour. He's been out there for an hour. I don't know how to make him leave," she sobs, raising her hand to cover her mouth and mute the sound of her wails.

When I hear the sound of a punch being thrown, I pull my phone from my back pocket and dial 911.

"What's your emergency?" the operator asks.

"There's an assault happening outside, in my driveway. Hurry, fast, please!" I move to the window and see Owen straddling my dad on the ground, trying to hold his arms still, but my dad is fighting. He's fighting so hard. Andrew is moving back inside his house on Owen's urging.

"Ma'am, I am going to need your address..."

I pull a bill from the front counter and read off our address that I have yet to memorize—then sprint back outside to Owen. He looks up when he hears my footsteps, and my father takes advantage of the distraction, punching him hard in the same eye again.

"Mother fuck!" Owen says, wincing, and leaning his face against his shoulder, pushing down on my father's flailing arms again, this time with more strength.

"The police are coming. They'll be here any minute. I'm so sorry, Owen. I'm..." I let out a short cry—mortified that this is my life, that Owen is watching this. The boy who minutes ago had my heart racing is now straddling my dad in a pile of dust, trying to keep him from hurting my mother more than he already has.

"Don't," Owen says, his eyes on me again, his right one already blue and puffy—because of me. "Don't you dare apologize."

I nod, then pull my left arm around myself, squeezing in an attempt to stop the rush of nerves and fear coursing through me. The lights flash in the distance, and soon, I can hear the sirens.

"They're here," I say to the operator, pushing my phone back in my pocket without ending the call, just in case. Two cop cars pull in quickly, and two of the police officers rush to Owen, pulling him away from my dad and pushing him flat along the ground.

"Do not try to fight us!" one of them yells, while the other pulls Owen's arms together behind his back, binding them with a thick plastic tie.

"No! He was helping! Don't hurt him!" I start to protest, but they dismiss me and go to work on my dad, sitting him upright and pulling his arms behind his back as well, though with less force than they used against Owen.

"Oh my god, Owen. Your eye!" I say, moving closer to him.

"Miss," one of the officers says, holding his arm out and barring me from taking one more step in Owen's direction. I look across the lawn and see Andrew standing at the doorway, and he's shaking his head at me, telling me to leave it alone.

"I'm fine, Kens. I'll be okay. Go check on your mom," Owen says, his voice a strange calm. He spits to the side, and it's bloody, which only makes me want to get to him more. "Kens...go!"

My mom. He's right. She'll know what to do. Only, just seconds ago, she was practically a statue—frozen in her depression inside my house. I rush inside and she's moved to the window, standing there swaying, holding the blinds open with her fist.

"I need you, Mom! You have to come out. You have to explain that Owen didn't do any of this," I say, but she doesn't move, and her feet keep rocking. "Mom!"

This time I yank on her arm, and she turns to look at me, her face shaking a little, like I just woke her up. "Mom! Come!"

"Right, yes...okay," she says, looking around the house for a few seconds, like she's missing something. She finally grabs her wallet, and I follow her back outside.

"Ma'am, can you explain what happened here tonight?" the first officer asks. I notice the tag on his uniform reads Blakely.

"My husband...he...he was drinking. We're...separated," my mom says, her words coming out in a stutter as she watches the police officers push my dad's head down as they load him into the back of one of the cars.

"Are you hurt, ma'am?" Blakely asks, and my mom quickly shakes her head *no.*

"The boy—" she says, looking to me and then out to Owen who is being jerked to a stand by Blakely's partner, "he was only helping. Please, he was just protecting my daughter."

Blakely stops his pen on his notepad and looks up at my mom when she says this, then to me, before looking back over his shoulder at Owen who is slowly being led to the other car. "That boy? The one right there?" he asks, motioning to Owen with his pen.

"Yes," my mom says, her eyes fighting against the need to cry.

"I'm afraid we're still going to need to talk to him," he says, nodding his head to his partner to continue.

"Can't you talk to him here? Or just call him or whatever? I mean...he saved me!" I sound like a pathetic little girl, and my stomach is overcome with this sinking feeling that they're not going to listen to me, that they're going to take Owen away, and it will be my fault.

"Miss, if you're lying, you're going to be in a heap of trouble. That kid right there—he's not worth lying for, you understand?" Blakely says, but all I can see is the door closing on Owen behind him, and Owen going peacefully—willingly.

"I understand," I say, my eyes moving back to Blakely. "I'm not lying."

He holds my attention for a few long seconds, the sound of his pen clicking open and shut like a bomb ticking away in my ears. "Mosely, let him go," he says, pushing the button on the radio pinned to his collar.

"You sure about that?" I hear his partner respond.

"Seems so," Blakely says, and within seconds, his partner is stepping back out of the vehicle and opening the door for Owen. I don't breathe until his hands are free. When the car holding my father pulls away, I move closer to him, letting my mom finish her talk with the police officers.

"Come on, you need ice," I say, pulling at the sleeve of his shirt, urging him to follow me inside.

Owen's quiet as we walk up my porch and through the main living room, but he pauses at my piano. I backpedal a few steps, and nod toward the kitchen, and he catches up.

"Let me see," I say, placing my hands on both of his shoulders, gently guiding him to one of our stools. I step closer, until my body is practically between his long, outstretched legs, and I move my hands to his chin, tilting it upward so I can see how bad his bruising is in the light.

"That's going to be really bad. God, Owen…I'm so sorry," I say, but he quiets me fast.

"Shhhhhh," he says, his head tilting back down and his eyes on me. His hair is super messy, the beanie he was wearing lost somewhere in the scuffle with my dad.

"I'm so embarrassed," I say, closing my eyes and letting my head fall forward. I want to cry, but I'm so drained; I can't even do that.

"Don't be. Not with me. Not over this," he says, his hand slowly sweeping a strand of my hair away from my face. His gesture sends a short wave of shivers down my neck and arms, and I hate my father for ruining this moment. I want to enjoy it, but I can't.

I turn to the freezer and fill a small plastic bag with a few ice cubes, then wrap it in a dishtowel. "It's the best we have. Don't get a lot of shiners in our house," I chuckle. My joke is stupid, but Owen smiles at it anyway.

"Thanks," he says, taking it from me, his hand covering mine completely when he does. God how I want him to hold my hand.

I move to the stool next to him and prop my elbows up on the counter, digging my hands into my scalp and massaging my head, like this situation is something I could somehow erase, only keeping the good parts.

Our silence doesn't last long, and Blakely comes in to sit in the third stool to take down our version of the story. Owen lets me do most of the talking, and I notice they don't write down anything he says anyway. Seems the Harper-brother rumors have even tainted the local law enforcement's opinion of him.

By the time the police leave, it's time for Owen to drive me back to school, and the trip back feels shorter…or maybe it doesn't feel long enough.

"Thanks for the ride," I say, laughing slightly when I realize how simplified that sounds. "And saving my mom. And me. And for beating my father's ass." My laughing picks up a little more, but it's a nervous laugh, so I suck it in and try to hold myself together.

"Mind if I tell people my brother James did this?" he says, pointing to the now puffy cheek just below his bruised eye socket. "If people know an old man did this, that won't be good for me."

He doesn't laugh at first, so I just nod yes, and start to say I understand.

"Kens," he says. "I'm kidding. I just meant I won't tell anyone. And Andrew won't either."

"Oh," I say, biting my lip and smiling briefly before sliding a step or two away from his truck.

"I'll see you later. I've got some things, okay?" he says, his brow pinching while he looks down to his lap, the light from his phone illuminating the cab of the truck.

"You shouldn't text and drive," I say, causing a whisper of a laugh to leave his lips, and a smile to creep up the side closest to me.

"I wouldn't do anything dangerous," he says, winking and tossing the phone into the empty seat beside him. His tires kick up gravel as he pulls away, and I wait at the front of the school until his taillights are so far away that I can no longer tell if they're his.

CHAPTER 9

I woke up instantly. That sound—it was better than an alarm. That sound was the one noise my subconscious had been on the lookout for—the one thing my ears have been begging to hear.

The bouncing was methodical, and then the clanging of the metal against the eave of the garage was undeniable.

I speed from my room—dressed in only sweatpants and an extra-large thermal shirt— stuff my feet into my boots and race down through the front door and down the porch stairs. My expectations are stunted the second I see a guy, not quite as tall and not nearly as muscular as Owen, tossing a ball up at the hoop—and missing. Repeatedly.

Andrew.

"Oh, damn. I'm sorry. That's...that's probably loud, huh?" he says, looking at his watch and then to me, realizing I'm in whatever I slept in.

"Yeah, it's...it's okay, though. It's eight. I should be up anyways," I say, pulling my arms close from the chill, also trying to bluff the disappointment no doubt painted all over my face.

"You put the hoop back up?" he asks.

That means he knows it was down.

"Yeah, my dad...he was the one who took it down the first time. I felt bad," I say, but I don't know how to finish, so I leave it at that.

Andrew bounces the ball a few more times, then turns to take another shot, this time the ball ricocheting off the eave of the house, missing all traces of the rim and backboard. "I suck at hoops," he says, his sideways grin matching his brother's. I step closer and pick up the ball. Bending my elbows, I push the ball as hard as I can toward the hoop, and it falls about two feet short, clanging off of the metal of the garage door.

"Me, too," I laugh.

Andrew kicks the ball up gently a few times until he gets it back in his hands. "Soccer," he smirks. "I always played soccer."

"Ah," I say, holding out my fingers and wiggling them. "Piano. I always played the piano."

He nods with a quick smile before looking down, an awkward silence settling over both of us. I shiver once, a breeze rustling the newest bronze and yellow leaves in our driveway.

"He likes you," Andrew says, his words like a blanket of warmth, instantly heating my entire body. My eyes are wide, but I keep my gaze at the ground, away from his.

"Ha," I let out a quick, sharp laugh.

"No, really. He hasn't flat-out said it, but he won't tell me he doesn't," he says, and the chill creeps along my skin again.

"That's nice of you to say, Andrew. But I'm pretty sure your brother would have been happier if this house sat here empty," I say, kicking at the ground, and moving my hands to the inside of the sleeves of my shirt.

"Maybe at first. But not now," he says, tossing the ball in the air a few times, then catching it and setting his sightline on me. "He's heard you play. And he says you don't anymore. Just…he noticed. And he's always leaving his window open and shit, even though it's cold as hell. He listens for you."

I chew at my bottom lip, every muscle in my mouth working to keep myself from smiling.

"Where is he?" I ask, pretending to just now notice his truck is gone. I noticed the instant I recognized Andrew was the one out here. I think I actually *felt* that Owen was gone.

"At work," he says, shrugging and walking backward on his heels, moving to his house.

"I thought he got fired?" I'm suddenly a little suspicious.

"He did. Got a new job, though, at the strip mall. He takes out trash and power washes the sidewalks and crap," he says.

"How's...his eye?" I'm embarrassed to ask this, embarrassed because I know everything Andrew witnessed. And the fact that he has yet to bring any of my drama up means he truly is a good person.

"I didn't get to see him. I'm sure he's fine, though. O can take a punch, trust me," he says with a chuckle, turning to face the steps to his house before pausing and looking at me over his shoulder. "Hey, don't tell him I told you, okay? You know...that he likes you? He'll beat my ass so fucking hard for that."

Andrew laughs when he asks, but I don't think he's kidding either. I cross my heart and chuckle, as if this is all a joke anyhow. But there's also that little part of me that is revving from the faster heartbeat in my chest—the part of me that likes that Owen listens for me. And that part of me wants to play the piano for the first time in days, with the hope that he'll hear it.

It's the first full day my mom's been back at work since everything in our lives changed. I've been thinking, though, how my mom's life changed months before mine. She's been pretending to be fine for a while now, but I don't know how she could have been. And as mad as I am at her for pretending, I keep forgiving her every time I feel the urge to be angry.

I have so many questions. I wonder if it all started on Gaby's birthday at the start of summer, when she spent the weekend at our house. She's always been close with my father—the two of them sharing a love of classical music that makes me roll my eyes. My father constantly compared me to her, wishing I had the same appreciation and respect for his work that she does. He loved her compositions—they were classical, not jazz. Or maybe they were just hers, and that's why he loved them. I wonder if that's how they connected? Was it those times my father helped her at the school, helped her with arrangements?

I wonder if all of those nights he was working late, and Gaby was spending late hours at Bryce, if they weren't really together—somewhere else entirely. I'm pretty sure I know the answer to this one, but maybe, just maybe, *every* word from my best friend's lips wasn't a lie.

I wonder if he waited until she was eighteen. Not that it makes it any better, but…

I've been at the piano for an hour. I keep flexing my fingers, popping knuckles, and running the palms of my hands along the wood above the keys. I can't seem to do much else. Every time I lower my hands to play, I hear my father's voice, looming in my mind, telling me jazz is a waste of time, and that my showcase is garbage—won't be good enough.

"You should probably lock this at night." Owen's voice startles me. I kick away from the piano, knocking over the bench beneath me as I struggle to get to my feet. My back is on the floor quickly, my feet kicking in my fight to stand again.

"Shit, you scared me!" My heart is thumping so loudly, I can hardly hear him talking as he closes my front door behind him and walks closer to me, a bag or something in his hand.

"Here," he says, reaching for my hand, helping me to my feet. His grasp on my wrist is for a purpose, and he lets go quickly, but I still look at that spot he touched on my skin, rubbing my own hand around it, like I'm trying to recover from a burn.

Owen sets my bench upright again, then slides onto the end of the seat, looking over the keys, and the pages spread out on the ledger.

"I'm sorry, you…were practicing?" He's starting to stand; I don't want him to leave. I move closer to the piano, resting my hand along the top, trying to make him more comfortable—and maybe blocking his exit just a little.

"No…I mean, I was thinking about it, but…I'm just not feeling it," I say, watching his finger trace the small layer of dust that's formed along the top of the ledge where my music books sit. He stares at the line he's drawn along the wood for a few seconds before breathing in deeply and pulling the small plastic bag to his lap.

"My mom's out—at work. Andrew's out, too. And I was going to make some grilled cheese for dinner, but then," he says, pausing to pull out a brick of cheddar cheese from the grocery bag and setting it on the bench next to him, "I realized I don't have any bread."

He looks up at me with a sideways grin that's unlike any face I've ever seen him make. There's no taunting to it, no motive or front. And with this one look, everything that's always been so hard and scary about being near him fades away.

"I have bread," I say, motioning for him to follow me to our kitchen. He trails closely behind me, and lightly kicks a box that's taken up a sort of permanent residence next to our kitchen island before he pulls himself into the stool at the counter and sets down his block of cheese.

"You've been here for what…a month?" he asks, looking around at the few boxes still remaining in the kitchen. Some of them have been repacked, and are getting donated or shipped tomorrow.

"Some of this stuff…it's my dad's," I say, my back to him so I can't see his face. It's easier to say the hard things this way.

"Oh," is all he says.

"Hit me with the cheese," I say when I turn around, and he makes that same silly smile again—it's almost…*playful.* He picks up the cheese and tosses it to me, but my fingers fumble the reception, and it slides through my hands, arms, knocks off my knee, and skids along the floor.

"Good thing it's wrapped," he teases.

"Shut up," I sass back, picking it up and squinting at him, like I'm daring him to cross me. He makes the same face back, but it's overly exaggerated, and dare I say *goofy*; it makes me laugh.

Owen is making me laugh. And it feels….

If there is one skill I have in the kitchen, it is making grilled-cheese sandwiches. The secret is not to be stingy with the butter, and I lather our bread well so that way by the time I slide the sandwiches from the pan, both sides are golden brown.

"Here, you can have the one with more cheese," I say, sliding a plate over to him. He picks up his sandwich and inspects it, raising an eyebrow at me before putting the bread almost in his mouth and stopping.

"How do I know you're not poisoning me?" he asks.

"You don't. You're just going to have to trust me," I smile, then take a bite of my sandwich, letting the crunch drag on slowly while I close my eyes and let my lips hum an *mmmmmm* sound.

"Right, trust you," he says, his expression soft and his eyes cautious while he considers me. I was joking about our sandwiches, but I get the feeling Owen is now on a different subject. He's making this heavier than I meant it to be, but I like that he's having such heavy thoughts. I don't think trust is something Owen has done in a long time, and it's a belief I fear lately I may be at risk of losing.

Owen finally gives in, and within five bites, maybe six, his sandwich is gone.

"Look, you're alive," I tease as I take his plate and rinse it in the sink.

"So it seems," he says, patting his chest, then gripping over his heart and making the most ridiculous croaking noise.

"You're so obnoxious," I say, reaching over to him and pushing on the arm that's resting along the counter as he sits. Before my hand slips away, he grabs it with his. It's an action I don't think he meant to do—a move he didn't calculate—and everything feels awkward. Both of us are giggling nervously for a few seconds, our fingers sort of tangled and unsure, until he finally grips my hand tightly, squeezes it once, then pushes it away.

I'm thankful for the bread that's still out on the counter, grateful that I have this distraction to busy myself with now. I twist the bag closed and turn to face our pantry, taking a deep breath and staring intently at the knuckles of my hand, the ones that were just embraced by the roughness and warmth of Owen's. When I turn back to face him, he's no longer sitting, but instead is standing by the kitchen window with his back to me, his hand by his side and his fingers flexing and contracting.

Our touch. He felt it, too.

"Thanks, by the way," he says.

I watch him for a few seconds before responding. "It's just a grilled cheese. I mean, I know mine are, like, practically the best in the Midwest, but…oh all right, yes, you're welcome," I joke. I'm joking because I'm uncomfortable. And I'm uncomfortable because all I can think about is the way his hand just felt wrapped around mine—the way he squeezed and paused, and the way he's still trying to cope with the feeling of it on his own hand.

"I meant the hoop," he says, finally turning and looking at me. His eyes are more serious now, and there's that hint of darkness to them. "Thanks for the hoop. You didn't have to put it back up. I can just shoot at the school."

"I wanted you to play here," I admit, a little too quickly. Owen's lip twitches in response. I train my eyes back on the counter, running the dish towel along the perfectly clean surface, then tucking it in one of the cabinet doors, smoothing out wrinkles and anything else I can think of doing that will keep me from making eye contact with Owen after what I just said.

"We should play," he says. I give in and look up. He's shoving his hands into the front pocket of his dark gray hoodie, his feet sliding closer to the back door. "Come on. Game of HORSE."

"Game of…what?" I ask.

Owen stops at the door, his hand on the knob. "HORSE. You know? I shoot and if I make it, you have to shoot from the same spot and make it. HORSE? You never played HORSE?"

"Never even heard of it," I say. "And that doesn't sound like a game I'd be any good at. You said I shoot and make it, but that...that doesn't happen when I play basketball."

His lips slide into the same sweet grin he wore when he first entered my house, then he gestures over his shoulder and opens the door. "Fine, we'll play PIG instead," he says.

"You're just making shit up now," I say, grabbing the zip jacket from the stool in the kitchen and pushing my arms inside. Owen laughs as we shut the door, and he doesn't stop until we're standing directly under the hoop, his ball in his hands.

"I'm not *making shit up*," he says. "You earn letters when you miss shots. You play PIG to make the game shorter. We'll practice with PIG."

"This sounds…pretty stupid," I say, my brow pinched.

"It's not. It's fun. I promise. Here, you take the ball and go first," he says, pushing the ball into my arms. I'm instantly mortified, because I know he's going to see me shoot and miss—horribly. It was one thing to miss a shot in front of his brother. Andrew sucked as badly as I do. But Owen is good. I've watched him play, with guys taller than him. And he's going to laugh his ass off when he sees me attempt to make a shot.

"Is there a shorter word?" I ask, looking at the ball in my hands and then up at the hoop. Owen laughs lightly.

"No, PIG's as short as it gets. Don't worry; you'll be fine. Go on, take your shot," he says, stepping back a few paces and blowing into his hands to warm them.

I am going to miss. There's no doubt about it in my mind. My only question to answer is how badly do I want to miss? I feel like it would look less awful if at least I attempted a farther shot, so I cross the driveway to a crack that runs down the middle, lining myself up a good eight or nine feet away from the hoop. I prop the ball into my hands, practically balancing it in my fingertips in front of my chest, then with a deep breath, I heave it forward, coming nowhere near the hoop and sending it off a jagged brick on the garage wall, bouncing down the driveway and into the street.

Yep. Mortified.

Owen's hands have stopped moving in front of his face. He's frozen, looking at the space where the ball trailed by him, his eyebrows slightly raised.

"I told you I wouldn't be good at this game!" I say, honestly a little upset. I'm more upset that I'm upset over something so trivial, but I'm embarrassed, and the longer it takes Owen to talk, the worse I feel.

"That wasn't *bad*," he starts, looking out to the roadway where the ball has come to a rest in the gutter. "It wasn't *good*. But it wasn't bad. Here, hang on."

Owen jogs down the driveway to the ball in the road, his long legs moving him quickly. I like watching him move.

I like watching him move!

He dribbles the ball as he jogs back toward me, and a few times, he raises his eyes to look at me, but never for long.

"Okay, so first, hold the ball in front of you—like this," he says, forming my hands around the ball, moving my stiff fingers clumsily into place. I'm more focused on everywhere he's touching me to even understand what he's doing or saying. "Next, take a few steps closer. You need to start somewhere small."

Small. Right. Small. I swallow while he stands behind me and puts his hands on my elbows, pushing me forward, closer to the hoop. His breath is on my neck. There's a ball in my hand, the air is cold, and all I can think about is the fact that when Owen breathes, a light fog comes out, and it passes by my ear and cheek and I want to taste it.

"This isn't going to work," I say, once I realize how far away I still am from the hoop. He's going to make me try, and I'm embarrassed all over again.

"Yes it will. Boy, are you like this with your piano teachers?" he asks, leaning to the side to look me in the eye. Damn. He's really close to me.

"I'm good at the piano. I don't have to be like this with them," I say, somehow keeping my head about me.

"You probably weren't always good, though," he says, his gaze shifting from my eyes to my mouth just long enough for me to notice and flush everywhere. I look at his mouth to reciprocate, and when I look back up, I realize he's watching the movement of my eyes closely. *Shit. He knows I'm looking at his mouth!*

"Actually," I say, swallowing, because damn, my throat is suddenly so dry. "I was…always good? I'm sort of…gifted."

Now I feel really lame. Really, super, fucking, horribly, awful, terribly lame. Lame, lame, lame, lame, lame!

"Yeah, well I'm gifted in this. So trust me; trust that I can teach you," he says. There's that word again.

Trust.

I refocus on the hoop, and I listen to everything he says, bending my elbows, practicing the motion three or four times, lining my aim up with the small square behind the hoop. Then the time comes for me to follow through.

"Come on, Kens. You got this," he says, taking two or three steps back.

Kens. He calls me Kens, and it feels so natural. Like he's always called me Kens. I like it when he says my name. I like how it sounds.

I like Owen Harper.

I bend my knees, close my eyes once, then train all of my focus on the hoop above my head. With a silent countdown, I heave everything forward and upward again, and the ball leaves my hands in the right direction. I don't make the shot. But I come close. The ball actually hits the board, then swirls along the rim before falling away.

"I hit it!" I say, turning to face him with my palms pressed on my cheeks. "Holy smokes! I actually hit it!"

Owen smiles and shakes his head lightly. "You don't actually get any points for hitting it, but yes, you showed improvement," he says, kicking the ball up into his hands and dribbling it a few times.

"Pshaw, says you! Did you see that?" I say, pointing up and spinning around once before reaching for the ball. "I hit it. That's a *P.* I get a *P* for PIG."

Owen's hand is rubbing on his neck, and he's laughing silently, but he gives in eventually, and bounces the ball to me to try again.

"Sure. Whatever you want, Kens. You get a *P.* Good job," he says, the world's greatest smile stretched on his lips. It's my new favorite smile. An entirely new one that I kind of think might just be for me and me alone. I like it, almost as much as I like him.

We shoot the ball a few more times, and Owen lets me continue to make up rules as we go. I know that's not how the game is really played, but I like how he laughs when I joke and celebrate my near shots. I actually make one before we're done, and Owen lifts me in his arms when I do, swinging me around once, but discarding me swiftly. It leaves me with the strangest feeling, as if holding me for too long would hurt him somehow.

"Did I win?" I ask at the end, and he just grins and nods *yes,* his eyebrows high to show his sarcasm. The sounds of the night fade back into focus, and Owen's breath fogs the air between us. I breathe out once, just to see if my breath can catch his.

"I should head in. I've got work early in the morning," he says, his ball tucked under one arm, his other hand stuffed in his jeans pocket. He looks unsure of himself, and I can't help but hope that it has a little to do with me.

"Yeah. I should get some sleep too. I'm studying all day tomorrow for the dissection quiz," I say, and Owen shuts his eyes tightly when I mention our test. "You forgot, didn't you?"

"Yeah," he says, sighing. "I think I'll be okay, though. I got most of it down."

"If you want…" I start, then stop myself, biting the inside of my cheek to give myself a second or two to think. Maybe I'm just trying to talk myself out of taking a risk. And maybe I shouldn't listen to that voice any more. "I can help you," I say again, my voice fast and sharp, getting his attention before he heads inside. "You know, study? When you get home from work. I could maybe just run you through my flashcards or something. Only… only if you think you need to."

Ryan said Owen was smart. He probably doesn't need to study. And now I look desperate, like I'm flirting. And I want to somehow breathe in fast, suck in all of the words I spoke before he can hear them.

"That would be awesome," he says, surprising me. "What's your number? I'll just call you when I get home."

Call me. Owen Harper wants to call me. On my phone. From his phone. He's typing my name with his long thumbs, his hat low over his eyes, but not so low that I can't see the thickness of his lashes and the way they move along the letters of my name. He hands the phone to me to type in my number, and I manage to find enough feeling in my fingers to take it from him without dropping it. I type in my number, and before I pass it back, I notice he's written KENS, and it makes me smile.

"Cool," he says, pushing the phone back in his pocket and backing up a few paces to his door. "So…thanks. Yeah, and…well…call you tomorrow?"

He actually stumbles a little when he hits the first step of his porch, but I pretend not to notice. I walk back to my door, click off the driveway lights, and move inside. The house is warm, and I didn't realize how cold I was until now. I notice Owen's cheese still on my counter, so I put it in the fridge before locking the back door and turning out the lights. I lock up front, and glance briefly at the piano I *almost* play before moving upstairs for bed.

I leave my window closed while I change into a pair of sweatpants and my favorite long-sleeved thermal, then I open the curtains and shut off the light, sliding my back against the edge of my mattress for my nightly ritual of waiting for Owen to shut his light off, too.

He rarely closes his curtains. The first few times, I felt embarrassed over what I saw, his bare chest, his boxers, his skin when he would change from his pants and shirt. I never saw *too* much, but it was more than I was used to seeing. I've always been a prude. Not because of any religious belief or self-promise to be a virgin until I met the right guy—intimacy just scared me. Dating intimidated me at Bryce, probably because most of the boys there were dropped off in Escalades and Audis and Teslas. They all seemed so entitled, and I didn't trust any of them—ever.

Trust. I trust Owen.

When my phone vibrates, my body jolts with adrenaline, my stomach trained to feel sick at seeing Gaby's name. She's sent me several texts, and I've deleted every single one. Morgan has tried to call, too, and honestly, I know she is probably on my side with everything. Her messages relayed how shocked she was over what went on between Gaby and my father. But I haven't been able to call Morgan back either. I'm just not ready to talk about it with anyone, and I know that's *all* Morgan is going to want to talk about.

My thumb grazes over the END CALL button on instinct, but I pause when I realize the number on the screen isn't one I recognize. I look at Owen's window, and his light is now off, and I think maybe—just...*maybe?*

"Hello?" I answer, my thumbnail flying to the edge of my teeth, a bad habit to calm my nerves that I've been doing for as long as I can remember.

"Hey," Owen says, his voice breathy and timid. "Sorry. I probably scared you again."

"No, no!" I respond quickly, and probably a little too excitedly. "I just didn't recognize the number, and most of my calls lately have been from unwelcomed callers."

"Ah, yeah. I get that," he says, and I can actually hear him settle into his covers. He's in bed. I'm talking to him, and he's lying down, probably without a shirt on. My thumbnail flies right back to the place between my teeth.

"Did you...need something?" I ask, sliding down a little lower by the window, low enough to gaze through it and attempt to see Owen in the darkness.

"Well, I'm having trouble sleeping. It's weird. I don't know if you ever get this feeling, but...I feel like somebody's watching me," he says, and I sink completely to the floor, my hand fast to cover my face.

Oh god!

Oh god, oh god, oh god!

"Kensi?" he asks, and I swallow hard.

"Uh huh?" I say, my voice nowhere near as loud as it was seconds ago.

"Look up," he says, and I squeeze my eyes shut tightly, pushing myself up on my elbows until I can see through my window to his. Owen's waving at me, a faint light over his face while he lies with his arms folded around his pillow, his hand pressing his phone to his ear.

"Oh, hey. Yeah...so...hi," I say, scrunching my hand like a two-year-old waves. "So...your bed. It's like...right there, huh?"

Oh god, oh god, oh god.

"Yep," he says, and even though he's far away, I can tell what smile he's wearing. It's the teasing one—the one that used to torture me when he was being mean, or when I *thought* he was being mean. Now, it's just one of Owen's many smiles—and I like this one, too, even though my stomach sinks with embarrassment over the cause.

"It's okay," he whispers, and I slide back along my bed, bringing my knees into my chest.

"What is?" I ask, the rush of heartbeats drumming in my head, drowning me.

"I look at you, too," he says, and now my heart is rushing for an entirely different reason.

Oh my god, oh my god....

"Kens? Relax," he says, and I notice his light flips off. I don't know if he did that to make it easier on me, but somehow, it does. I'm braver without having to face him.

"I'm sorry. I'm...pretty embarrassed," I admit, crawling on my knees first, then lifting myself onto my bed, sliding my feet under my heavy comforter, then pulling it over my head because all I want to do is hide.

"I really called because I can't sleep," he says, completely bypassing my embarrassment. I could kiss him for that.

Kiss him.

Now I'm thinking about kissing him—not that I haven't thought about that before, but now I'm really imagining it, and it makes me want to pull my blankets in closer, press the phone tighter against my ear so I can feel every vibration of his voice.

"Wanna talk? Until you get tired?" I ask, now more awake than I've ever been.

"Sure. I mean, yeah...I guess," he says, and I like that he's flustered now, too. "It's always weird, when Andrew's gone, and the house is empty. It's just sort of lonely."

"I know whatcha mean," I say, thinking about most of my nights—both in the city and out here. My parents were always working, and from the age it became socially acceptable, maybe about twelve or thirteen, my parents frequently left me alone at night. I've grown used to it, but I've never *liked* it.

"I'm sorry about the phone calls. From…from *her,*" he says, and I can tell he's treading lightly at bringing up Gaby.

"It's okay. She'll stop calling soon. Or not. Either way," I say, not really believing the indifference I'm trying to portray, but I try to sell it; I try to sell it hard.

"Yeah, probably," he says, and there's a pause in everything. The house is quiet, and the moon is shrouded by clouds, so the night is darker than normal. It feels like the world is hushed, listening to our conversation. "For the record, what she did? Your friend…" he pauses, waiting to see if it's okay to say more. "That was pretty shitty."

Shitty. Yeah, it was shitty. It also might have been illegal—could probably be constituted as rape in some ways—was morally and ethically flawed, and is going to scar me for life.

Yeah, it was shitty.

"Thanks," is all I say in response. I'm not ready to deal beyond that yet. "How's Andrew?" I ask, desperate to return the focus on Owen.

"He's good. Thanks. My brother likes you, you know? I think he thinks you're cute," he says, and I blush even though I know he's just trying to be funny.

"That's what he said about you," I say, unable to stop the words before I speak them. I start chewing on my nails the instant I realize what I've done, and I hold my breath, waiting for Owen to hang up. But he doesn't. He doesn't respond either. He just lets the silence play out for a really long and uncomfortable amount of time. I think he's torturing me, but I also think just maybe…he's smiling.

"So how was your first day of work?" I ask, leaning over the edge of my bed and peaking out the window one more time, on the off chance that he's looking at me, too. All I see is the blackness filling his window, but I smile softly, in case he's hiding in the shadow.

"It was good, I guess. It's a job, and I don't have to deal with people a lot, so that's sort of a bonus. And I make, like, fifty more cents an hour," he says.

"Do you ever resent it? Having to work so much?" I tread carefully; I've learned when Owen doesn't want to have a conversation, he doesn't, and sometimes his end of it is abrupt.

"Nah," he says, yawning a little. "It helps my family, and it doesn't really get in the way of the important things."

"Like what?" I ask, quickly.

Owen chuckles softly into the phone. "Wow, you're like one of those hard-hitting reporters. Right in there with the next question," he says.

"Sorry," I say in a whisper, my face burning again with that familiar sting of embarrassment.

"It's okay. I haven't really *shared* with someone in a while, that's all. Most my friends either already know my deal or they don't care," he says, and I focus on that one phrase—*his deal.* I want to know his deal; I want to know all about Owen Harper and his life and his past and those rumors. I want his story.

"You don't have to...share? If you don't feel up to it, or if it's personal or...whatever," I say, my hand back in place between my lips. I won't have any fingernails left in the morning.

"Well, you already know I play basketball. And it's stupid, but that's one of those important things. I'm good at it. You know how you said you're gifted? Well, I guess it's my gift, if gifts work like that. I lose myself in it, and I like that I get to be aggressive," he says. I think back to when I watched Owen play in the driveway, how masculine every movement he made was. Aggressive seemed to be in his nature even then.

"Well, clearly, I wouldn't know much about basketball," I say, inciting a raspy laugh from Owen. "But, I would believe that you're good...or gifted. You're fun to watch."

I pull my blanket up over my chin after this, knowing how gushing and flirtatious every word from my mouth sounds. I don't regret them, though. I don't regret a single second of my night so far.

"Thanks," Owen says, and my smile kicks in, my cover now hiding more of my blushing face.

"Does your older brother help out with bills too?" I ask. When Owen's answer doesn't come right away, I close my eyes, wishing I could take my question back, my gut sinking, knowing I asked one question too many.

"James," Owen starts, but then his long pause continues.

"It's…it's okay, I'm getting too personal," I say, grasping at hope that Owen won't hang up, that he'll call me again.

"James is a junkie," he says. There are a million reactions I could have had, but what I didn't expect is how much I want to hug Owen right now. Nothing about his small description of his brother sounded sad or affected or heartbroken, but somehow through it all, I know Owen is. I can just sense it.

"I'm sorry, Owen," I say, careful to say his name—to take care of it and respect it. If he doesn't share with people often, then I'm guessing very few people really know about James.

"Thanks. But it's okay. It is what it is. My mom kicked him out a year ago. He started using meth, and getting into some really hard shit. She didn't want Andrew exposed to that. I didn't either. But he still calls me. You know…when he needs something," he says, a certain amount of disappointment in his tone.

"Like…money? Or drugs?" I say, now sitting up in bed.

"Not really money. But I've bailed him out once or twice. And I got him off the hook with a dealer he owed some serious money to. It's usually a problem when James calls," he sighs.

"But you answer," I say, my words practically filling in the blank space left at the end of his.

"Every. Time," he says.

"When was the last time you saw him?" I ask, hoping, for selfish reasons, that it's been a while. Willow said James was the one to stay away from, and now I'm not sure I want him a house away from me.

"The other night. He didn't come here. But he was fucked up out of his head, and he was in a bad place, with some bad people. I had to leave in the middle of a basketball game to go haul his ass back to his apartment," he says, and I close my eyes, remembering that night I watched him get a call in the middle of playing basketball. I remember how angry he was, how fast he drove away, and how vicious his eyes were when he got back.

"That isn't fair to you," I say, my arms pulling my pillow in close to my chest, my mind imagining Owen's heart beating through it, wishing it were him I was holding.

"Nope," he says.

I hold my pillow for several long seconds, letting my face slide against the coolness of the pillowcase. Ryan is so right about Owen; people don't have him pegged right at all. And as much as I want to tell everyone that, I also want to keep it to myself—keep Owen to myself.

"So, you were thinking about practicing tonight…when I walked in?" Owen finally says, cutting through the silence. I think I may have been drifting off to sleep with him in my fantasy.

"Oh, yeah. I was…sort of, " I say, squeezing my eyes tightly, trying to force a little more awake time from them. "I can't seem to figure out what to play. It probably doesn't make sense to you. But, it's just that I was sort of on this directive, had all of these goals, and they all centered around the things my father wanted me to play. And now that he's out of the picture…"

"Those aren't your goals anymore," Owen finishes for me.

"I don't think they ever really were," I say. I know they weren't, but admitting this out loud, saying it without someone on the other end protesting—it feels nice.

"Do you still like playing?" he asks.

"Yes, of course I do," I say. "But not any of the things *he* would want me to play." Saying that feels good too, and it makes me stretch and move my fingers in anticipation.

"So play for *you*. Tomorrow. Play for Kensington. I'd like to hear you. I mean…if that's something you're okay with. Someone listening to you play?" The nervous, fumbling Owen who's unsure of his words seems rare, but he makes my heart race.

"I could do that. I mean, unless it's not cool for Owen Harper to be hanging out with a band geek," I joke, my palms actually sweating. I can't tell if I'm excited at the thought of playing for Owen or terrified.

"I'll make an exception," he says, his laugh even raspier than before, and his voice saturated with sleepiness.

"Well look at that," I say.

"What?" he asks.

"You're finally tired," I smile, satisfied, as if I actually did something to help Owen find sleep. His effect on me was just the opposite, and now all I want to do is tiptoe downstairs and play my piano.

"Yeah, I think you're right. Hey, thanks," he says.

"For what?" I ask.

"I'm not really sure. But I know I should say it anyway," he says, one final yawn escaping his throat.

"Good night, Owen Harper," I say, loving every syllable of his name on my tongue. Owen drifts off before he can say another word, and I leave my phone on for a few more minutes just to listen to him breathe.

He isn't scary at all.

CHAPTER 10

Owen must have worked all day Sunday because I never saw him again. And I looked—constantly. My mom seems to have found a way to put on her performance face at work, but at home, she's simply... manic. When I woke for school this morning, she had started ripping out pipes from under the sink, and all of the cabinet doors were down. She said something about finally getting her hands into something, making it her own.

If it keeps her from crying on the foot of the stairs, I guess tearing apart our house is a good alternative.

Willow's horn blaring outside saves me from having to help with my mom's latest plumbing emergency, so I yell that I'm leaving, grab my backpack, and rush out the door. Being in band means we always have to get to school early, and though the first few weeks had me grumbling from waking up before the sun, this morning, I'm practically skipping. I'm skipping because Owen's truck is in the driveway, which means he's probably going to school today.

"Wow, look who's all happy this morning," Willow says, snapping the gum in her mouth twice and chomping loudly while she analyzes me and my happiness.

"Had a good weekend," I say, meaning it. True, Friday night was a nightmare, but my short-lived basketball career made up for the unwanted visit from my father and from Gaby the week before.

"Uh huh," Willow says, pulling a thermos from her center console and loudly sipping on what smells like coffee. "So, Owen dropped you off for the game Friday night. You, uh…see him again?"

The blush that radiates all over my face is fast and unexpected, and I know I wouldn't be able to lie now even if I wanted to.

"That's a yes," she says, and her smile is genuine, but there's still a shade of disappointment there, too.

"You sure it's okay, that it doesn't bother you if I'm friends with Owen?" I ask, wondering if Willow was being totally honest about her feelings and being over him.

"Kens, I cross my heart. Just promise me you'll be careful. I know it's been three years since I hooked up with him, and he's probably grown up a lot, but still…just be careful," she says, repeating that word again.

I'm always careful; it's why I did exactly as my father said for most of my life—played things carefully, classical…*perfect*. I hold up my hand in what I think is the scout's honor sign and smile a promise to Willow, but I never say it. And as much as I probably should be careful, I kind of want to be reckless.

We pull into the school lot and park right next to Jess. There are no reserved spots, but everyone sort of has their place. We always park at the bottom of the hill, right by the exit. Jess is swinging his feet, clutching a paper in his hand while he sits on the trunk of his car. He looks like an actual kid in a candy store, his smile large and his cheeks red from the morning air. The vision has Willow and me giggling.

"Who wants Carolyn Potter's famous apple pie?" Jess asks, waving the piece of paper over his head. Whatever is printed on it seems to have Willow in a state of thrill, joy, or frenzy. It's hard to tell amid the dancing and jumping she's doing as she takes the paper from Jess's hands.

"Holy shit! It's back!" she says, pounding on the hood of Elise's car as she pulls into the lot next to our cars.

"What the hell, Will? Let me put it in park before you start going all *morning-person* on me," Elise says, dragging her heavy backpack and flute case from the back seat and finally shutting the door behind her. "Okay, what's got you all...*this way?*" Elise waves her hand in Willow's direction, her face twisted with an annoyance I can truly appreciate. Willow is shot out of a cannon in the mornings, but Elise is more my speed—slow to wake, in need of caffeine, and not much for public happy-dancing at six in the morning.

"I think this will change your mind," Willow says, handing the flyer to Elise. I watch her eyes graze over the words, and the more she reads, the more her lips curve until she's smiling so big she's actually showing teeth.

"No. Way!" she says, shoving the paper into my hands. "We're going, right? We're all totally going. Oh my god, this week cannot end fast enough!"

I straighten the heavy pack on my back and read over the flyer now in my possession.

WILSON ORCHARD APPLE FEST

"Is this that thing? That story you guys told me about?" I ask, my focus solely on the part of that story that had to do with Owen—and how this one event changed his life forever. This festival is like the moment he told me my dad was spending time with another woman, and I can't imagine reliving that moment again—*ever!*

I wonder if Owen's seen a flyer like this one?

"Yes! That's it! Oh my god, Kens. You have to come with us," Willow says, looping her arm in mine as we trek up the hill to the music room. She's only focusing on the festive part, completely missing my point.

"I don't know. I'm not really into carnival games and things like that," I say, still thinking about Owen. I want to find him before he finds out, to take him away until the festival is over and done—so he can never know it came back again in the first place.

"It's not just the games and the rides. Kens, oh my god, the freaking apple pies! You have to come, just for a little while. At least go and eat with us?" Willow is actually making a pouty face, her bottom lip jutted out, and her eyes practically watering with sadness.

"It is a lot of fun," Elise adds, nudging me with her arm as we walk through the band-room door. She starts to walk backward to face me. "Ryan will want to go, so we'll all be there. And he never likes to stay at things long, so we can totally take you home early if you want to leave. Come with us?"

Elise isn't full-on begging; that's not her style. But I can tell she really wants me to join them, and I get the sense this is a meaningful thing for my new group of friends—a part of their past they want to share with me. I need friends, good friends that don't lie to me. So I nod *yes,* and Willow practically squeals in my ear with excitement.

Mr. Brody makes a few attempts to play through some of our songs, but band rehearsals are ultimately cut short, the entire class seemingly abuzz with news that the apple fest is back. And when Mr. Brody announces that the band will actually be playing in a mini parade down the orchard road to open the festival on Saturday morning, you would think we were invited to star in the half-time show for the Super Bowl. Everyone was so excited.

With the band performing, I no longer have an excuse to miss—at least not the opening of the festival—so I resolve myself to the fact that I'm going to at least get a really good slice of pie out of this deal, and then I hold my breath and wait for my next class. I pray somehow word of the festival hasn't made it to him yet.

I'M NOT sure whether it's good news or bad news that Owen missed our morning classes. I'm hoping it was because of work, or something else non-festival related. When I see him climb up to sit on top of one of the outside tables at lunch, I feel the weight rise from my chest.

I position myself so I can glance at him from my periphery out the window while we eat lunch, and my body flushes the few times I catch his gaze on me. Every time I look his direction, he seems to be smiling. I also notice that, unlike other days during the lunch hour, there doesn't seem to be a girl in his arms, no one entertaining his lips, grinding on his lap, or kissing at his neck. And that makes me happy, too.

"Owen Harper alert," Willow says, her eyebrows raised as she stares at me from the other side of the table. I turn to the side and realize Owen is no longer on his table outside, and his friends have all left as well. I somehow missed them leaving, but Willow has spotted him again—right behind me.

"Hey, Kens," he says, his voice sounding calm and comfortable as he seduces me right here in front of my friends. I've become addicted to his voice, so much so that I even considered calling to listen to his voicemail once or twice—fear that he might pick up the only thing stopping me, as silly as that sounds. I swivel in my seat and peer up at him, and my response comes out more like a croak.

"Hey, Owen," I squeak. My palms are sweating, and I'm pretty sure my arms and back are as well. In fact, everything about me feels like it's on fire, never mind the gray skies and cold front threatening to bring a massive chill outside the window. Right now, in my body, it's summer in the desert.

I glance around the table and notice all of my friends suddenly only interested in their trays and food, but their faces are all smirking, and it makes me blush even harder.

"Hey, O. What's up, man?" Ryan says, the last to slide into his seat. Thank god for Ryan, the only one acting normal. "Conditioning starts next week. You coming?"

"You know it. I might miss a few; I've got work. But coach already knows," Owen says, tapping his fist into Ryan's as he sits down next to Elise.

"Good. Oh, hell man, what happened to your eye?" Ryan asks, pointing to the spot on his own face that mirrors the deep blue bruise left on Owen's cheek. It's the last remnant of his run-in with my father, and the very conversation playing out at our lunch table right now has my throat closing and my stomach threatening sickness.

"Oh, you know. Just messin' around with House and the boys, pick up games and shit. Some guy didn't like a call, elbowed me," Owen says with a shrug. He never looks my direction, but as he sits in the seat across from me, I feel his foot slide up next to mine and tap it twice. He lied for me, just like he promised he would.

"Dude, some guys just can't keep their cool on the court. I hate that shit. I don't know why you play those pick-up games anyways," Ryan says, leaning over and kissing Elise on the cheek. She looks up for a brief second, but she puts her head back down quickly, almost like the rest of my friends have some secret pact to give me pretend privacy when Owen comes to the table. Truthfully, it's only making me feel weirder.

"So, Kens. Was wondering," Owen starts, looking around the table at the tops of everyone's heads. He shakes his and pinches his brow at how strange my friends are all being. I kind of want to die.

"I have to work Friday, but I thought maybe, if you're not busy, I could repay you for that grilled cheese emergency this weekend? My mom's going to be home, and she'd like to meet your mom, if she's off Saturday night," Owen says, his eyes focusing solely on his knuckles, which he's cracking nervously, over and over. His foot under the table is now tapping quickly with nerves, and it's starting to make the entire table shake a little.

"Uh, Saturday?" I repeat his question, my mind searching for a way to make Saturday happen twice—one version I can live through with Owen and his mom, and the other where I can go to the festival and perform with the band. I'm about to lie, about to pretend there is nothing else I have to do on Saturday so I can make Owen's leg stop shaking and so I can spend Saturday night with him, meet his mom, when Jess decides now would be a good time to quit looking at his lap and insert himself back into my reality.

"You can't, Kensi. We've got the apple fest," Jess says, and everyone stops breathing simultaneously. He couldn't say I had *a thing,* a *band assignment,* a *performance,* something…*anything*…with them—no, Jess had to go and be specific, painfully specific.

I flash my gaze back to Owen, and now he's the one looking at the top of the table, his hands no longer wringing, his foot no longer jiggling. His face is just pure emptiness—as if he's just had the wind knocked out of him—and the way his lip is hanging open and quivering with the struggle to breathe lets me know that this is the first he's heard of the apple fest. It lets me know that Willow wasn't exaggerating her story about Owen and that day. I know it because the look of absolute pain that's fallen over him, taken over his body completely, isn't one that could come from anything but tragic loss. And Owen's experienced the deepest tragedy of all.

"I'm…I'm sorry. I just found out," I say, reaching toward him, but not quickly enough. He's shoved his hands in his pockets and is already standing and sliding away from me.

"Nah, it's all right. Next time, maybe. Hey…I won't be in class this afternoon, so maybe just hit me up with whatever I missed?" he says, his eyes still low—low and sad. So unbelievably sad.

"Yeah. Sure, I'll just send you a text later," I say, keeping my focus on his face, the voice inside me begging him to look up, begging him to be okay. I feel like I'm holding the paddles to his chest, shouting "clear!" and counting over and over while I watch his life drift away. With his back against the door, Owen finally lifts his chin, and that same ice and hardness that was there the first time he looked at me is back, and he doesn't bother to smile as he turns to leave.

"I'm not hungry," I say, standing with my full tray and rushing to the trash. I follow Owen's footsteps to the doorway, but after I dump my food and step onto the walkway outside, I'm only there in time to see his truck speed around the corner of the lot, out onto the roadway, the motor revving like it does when he races—when he runs away.

"Kens, I'm so sorry," Willow says, her hand on my back feels like a knife.

"Just…don't," I say, jerking away. It's not her fault, and I know that. But I don't want to hear empty apologies. They won't make me feel better. "It's okay. I just didn't want him to find out…like that. I'm just worried about him, that's all."

I turn to her and shrug, taking in a deep breath and exhaling slowly, trying to keep the mist in my eyes from forming full tears.

"You just didn't want him to find out at all," she says. I close my eyes and nod slowly. "It's a small town, Kens. By dinnertime, everyone is going to know. That flyer I showed you this morning? There will be one on every tree in town, every business window, and probably everyone's front door. He was bound to find out. And he'll be okay."

I let out a breathy laugh, my gaze falling to Willow's feet first before shifting up to her eyes. "Owen is so far from okay, Willow," I say, my chest crumbling with my admission, with hearing me talk aloud about Owen—the Owen I think I know—to someone else.

"You can't hold him together," she says, stepping an inch or two closer to me. She stops before she's close enough to touch my hand. I think she can sense how fragile my spirit is right now—how volatile my emotions are—so she doesn't say another word. Instead she goes back into the cafeteria to join our table of friends, where I'm sure they'll analyze everything that just went down.

Ryan will stand up for Owen though. And I'm thankful for that.

. . .

As promised, Owen skipped classes for the rest of the day. He missed the following day as well. I texted him both nights, giving him the basic points he missed and due dates for assignments. But I didn't hear back from him. And his house was dark both nights, his truck never once appearing in the driveway.

I never saw Andrew, but I'm sure Owen stopped in for his brother, somehow getting him to school and bringing him home. But I have no proof. The hoop has been silent out front too. In fact, I wouldn't be shocked if Ryan told me that Owen packed up after our last conversation and skipped town. I think part of me was trying to convince myself of that lie. But now I'm confronted with an entirely different truth—the truth where Owen is back outside on the lunch tables with his friends, and another girl is sitting on his lap, his tongue on her ear.

"I told you he'd be okay," Willow says, and even though she's trying to couch it like she's trying to make me feel better—what she's really doing is saying "I told you so" about Owen being *Owen* and going back to his cruel and hurtful ways.

"Looks like it," I say, not giving her—or Owen—the satisfaction of looking up from my lunch.

I eat slowly, and I turn my profile to the side, keeping Owen just in my sight's reach, but I deny myself every temptation of looking his direction. I know he wants me to see him. I know that's why he's out there, making this spectacle just for me. And I know he's doing it because something else hurts.

But fuck him. I have no role in what happened to him years ago. And he's not going to use it as an excuse for being an asshole.

Jess is talking about the parade Saturday, and Elise keeps switching the conversation to the rides she's seen coming into town. I'm not sure about hooking myself into something that arrives by truck in the middle of the night, and is disassembled minutes after the carnival closes, but I remain rapt in Elise's conversation, pretending I'll ride anything and everything she wants.

Every now and then, I glance next to her, to Ryan, and he's chewing on the end of his straw, listening to his girlfriend talk, but looking from me to Owen and back again. I follow my friends from the table, dumping my trash and pulling my backpack over my shoulder, when Ryan stops me last at the door before we leave.

"I know he makes it hard, Kensi. But that guy out there…that's not really him. O's better than that," Ryan says, and I want to believe him. But I also know that men lie, and break promises, and destroy friendships and marriages—and right now that's the only rationale I can think about.

"Sure he is, Ryan. Sure he is," I say, patting him on the arm as I muscle past him and let the door close behind me.

Elise distracts me during science. I'm careful to avoid any one-on-one time with Owen during dissections—immediately pairing myself with Elise, who is still obsessively talking about the festival. I've never been, and already I hate this festival and what it's done to my routine. It's like it's taken over my friends' bodies and minds, too. But I'm grateful for Elise's constant conversation though, and it makes the forty minutes of class fly by.

My next class isn't going to be so easy. When I enter our English class, Owen is sitting in his seat right behind mine, his smirk in its familiar place.

"Saved your seat for you," he says, barely looking up. Like I believe he hasn't orchestrated everything he's about to do and say.

"Whatever," I respond; glad I don't have to push his feet off my chair. I don't like hot and cold. My dad was always hot and cold, probably because he never really wanted to be there in the first place.

"Wow, someone's moody," he says. I know what he's doing. He's shifting everything he's feeling to me; he's making me the bad guy, because he can't be mad at an entire town—at everyone in Woodstock—for being excited about an event that to him means nothing but nightmares and the stirring up of old gossip and rumors. Thing is, though, that's also not very fair to me.

"Someone else is an asshole, so *touché*," I say, not even bothering to fully turn around in my seat to acknowledge him. He hates that, because he wants more of a reaction. He wants that push and pull. I hate that I'm goading him as much as I am. I wish I could just keep my mouth shut.

"Awwww, are you…jealous, Kensington?" His lips are at my neck, and his breath is making the tiny hairs on my skin stand to attention. I hate that he called me by my full name, hate that he's trying to hurt me. But mostly I hate that *yes,* I'm jealous of some stupid *girl of the moment* he was just locking lips with at lunch.

I can still feel him there, close enough that I know if I jerked my elbow back hard and fast, I would give him a matching bruise on the other eye. But I fight my newfound instinct for violence, and instead do something far worse.

Turning in my seat, I put both of my palms flat on Owen's desk and face him, his eyes piercing mine with their coolness. "I'm very sorry, Owen," I say, and he leans back, folding his arms, his face painted with smugness as he waits for me to take his bait, to go ahead and embarrass myself. No, Owen—not today.

"Did you hear me?" I ask, keeping my voice low, keeping this a conversation for our ears alone. He merely quirks his brow in acknowledgement, but it's enough. "I know that this apple fest—or whatever the hell this event is—is painful for you. And I know that you're worried your dad is all people are going to talk about. And some of them probably will. And those people, Owen? Those people fucking suck. But I'm just trying to make new friends at a school I never wanted to come to. At a school I'm at because guess what? My dad fucked my life up too. And my new friends asked me to go to a carnival and eat some pie that's apparently, like, the greatest goddamned pie on the planet. They want me to stay out late, and ride some questionable rides I probably won't even really like. And you know what? You, your family, your dad—they haven't brought it up once. Not. Once. So I'm going to go with them, try to make a good memory, and then I'm going to come home and fall in my bed from exhaustion. I hope I can bring myself to look out my window once before I shut my eyes, but I'm not so sure I care for the view anymore."

Owen's face didn't flinch a single time, and his expression never changed. But I kept my eyes trained on his, looking deep into them, and I think maybe—just maybe—I saw a little crack or two underneath.

I turn back to face the front, pull my notepad from my book bag and spend the next hour ignoring Owen's breathing. When the bell rings, *I'm* the first to leave, and I don't give him another glance.

CHAPTER 11

I am destined never to sleep in again. It's five in the morning, and Willow is knocking at my door and texting my phone at the same time. I hurry downstairs, and let her in while I finish getting ready.

"Crap, it's cold out there," she says, shutting the door quickly behind her and pulling her other glove from her hand to breathe on her palms to thaw them out.

"Seems like a weird time for apples," I say, rummaging around the downstairs for my other boot. The house is in disarray, my mom's remodeling now spreading to the railings for the stairs and the now knocked-down wall that divides the formal dining room—also known as my dusty piano room—from the kitchen.

"Yeah, but the apples are at their best now, right before winter hits. That's why they always want people to pick the trees bare," Willow says. "Wow, you've got a lot going on in here," she adds, taking careful steps toward the kitchen.

"Yeah, my mom's sort of gone nuts with this remodeling thing," I say, tossing a box of paint tarps out of my way during my search. "Sorry, I'll just be a second. I can't find my boot. And I need to grab my jacket."

"Your dad at work?" Her question is completely innocuous, and a few weeks ago, I would have just answered, "Yes," without a second thought.

But it paralyzes me now, and all I can do is stand in front of her with one boot in my hands, looking around the torn-up shreds of my house—proof that my mom is going through some sort of breakdown.

"My mom kicked him out," I say, nodding and looking around at every little thing left in our house. The only items even remotely my father is the piano that Willow is now leaning on.

"Oh," she says, and I can tell she's not sure where to go from here.

"It's sort of new, and I don't quite know how to talk about it yet. Or…do I talk about it? Maybe I do," I say, my eyes catching a tuft of gray fur in the corner, under a box. My boot!

"I get it," Willow says. "My parents are divorced. They split up four years ago. It got ugly, but it's better now."

"My dad cheated," I say. "I'm not sure it's going to get better."

"Mine too," she says, tapping out a few short notes on the piano. "But eventually my mom met someone else too, and now they sort of get along."

"Yeah, well, my dad had an affair with my best friend, so…" I don't know what makes me just come out and say it like that, but it feels good to say.

"Fuuuuuuuck," Willow says, her eyebrows stretched up into her hairline and her hands gripping the front of the piano bench.

"Yeah, that's sort of the reaction I had," I say, trying to make light of it, as if this will ever be something I can make light of. When she taps out a simple melody on my piano again, it stirs something in me, and I move to sit next to her and splay my fingers out over the keys, pressing down hard to form a minor chord, letting it echo in the empty house.

"I only ever get to hear you play the xylophone. You still practice the piano a lot?" Willow asks, and I press down on the minor chord one more time, this time slowly, so the notes aren't as loud.

"I haven't practiced in a few weeks. It was sort of always that thing my dad made me do, and now…" I say, changing one note and playing the chord again.

"Do you hate it now? The piano?" she asks, trying to match the chord I just played. When she presses her hands down, something's off, so I move one of her fingers and she does it again, this time getting it right.

"No," I breathe, running my hands over the smoothness of the keys, searching for that comfortable place where they feel home. "I don't hate it. I love it. But I hate my dad, so I feel like maybe I should hate this too."

My eyes closed, I let my fingers feel for a few more seconds, and then I slowly let them take over, playing softly at first, but growing stronger and more forceful with every single note—until I'm practically pounding out rhythms, my arms flexed and my fingers typing up and down the keys quickly, running the length of my instrument until I stop abruptly in the middle of the song.

"Well, damn," Willow says, and I pull my hands back into my lap, curling my fingers, perhaps a little from shame for giving in and playing something my father would have liked. "What was that?"

"Rachmaninoff," I say. "And I'm never playing it again."

Willow doesn't question me or ask me to play something else, and she never asks about my father's affair. My awful admission though has somehow made us closer, and I'm actually looking forward to the parade and a night with my new friends.

The parking lot at the school is mostly empty, everyone's car parked along the curb closest to the band room. We're one of the last people to arrive, and I feel bad because I know it's my fault we're late. Willow doesn't seem to care, though; she steps out and walks a few lengths to Jess's car, a small blue hatchback that he's filling with drums and drum carriers.

"Ahhhh there she is," he says when I slide next to Willow.

"Uh...yeah. *Ta da*...here I am," I smile, not quite sure why he's so happy to see me.

"So here's the thing," Jess starts, and I take a small step back on instinct. "You can't really march with a xylophone, and Joe's out of town for the weekend so we're going to need someone to fill in on bass drum...how do you feel about playing bass?"

"I've never played drums in my entire life," I say, shrugging. Before I can get my hands in my pockets, though, Jess is lifting a huge drum harness over my head. "Wait...did you hear me? No, not happening."

"Yeah, actually, this is totally happening," he says, resting the heavy metal over my shoulders and handing me two large mallets. "Lean forward and lock into the drum."

"Jess, I don't know how to do any of this," I start to protest, but Willow is smirking behind him. She just heard me fly through one of the hardest pieces of classical composition—from memory—and the small quirk in her lip is her way of challenging me. I let out a heavy sigh, my breath blowing the stray strands of hair in front of my face. "Fine. Just tape the music to the drum."

"Done," Jess says, his mouth making a clicking sound when he winks at me. "Thanks, Kens. You'll be great."

I lift the heavy drum holster back over my shoulders and set it next to Jess's car. "Bet this would totally piss your old man off," Willow whispers in my ear. I smile at the drum, and then laugh lightly, my head tilting back. She's right. Dean Worth would hate the very idea of this.

"Jess?" I holler out to him, catching him before he's out of range. "Think I can get some bigger mallets?"

I swing one of them around, twirling it in my fingers for emphasis, and Jess's body shirks with his laugh as he shakes his head. "I'll see, Kens. For you? Anything," he shouts.

I keep the mallets with me, and even though Jess wasn't able to find any others, I manage to pound the drum loudly with the padded ones he's given me. For a full mile, our small high school band winds down the dirt road through the orchard, families with strollers and dads with toddlers sitting on their shoulders lining either side. We play the school's fight song seven times, and the crowd around us claps along the entire way.

As much as my father would hate this, my mom would love it, and I'm starting to feel guilty that I didn't tell her about it. She's working all night, but I think she would have taken the night off for a crack at a little campy high school fun with me.

By the time we march to the entrance, the families watching the parade have dispersed, and everyone's crowded around an old barn-turned-ticket booth. I feel my shoulders relax the second Jess lifts the drum harness away from me.

"Not bad for a piano nerd," he says.

"Thanks," I say, hugging myself so I can rub the sore spots on either of my shoulders. "You could probably talk me into doing that again sometime. You know...in a pinch."

"You totally liked it," Jess teases, and I smile because yes...*yes I did.*

Reaching across me for Willow's hand, Jess pulls her into his body, hugging her and leaving his arm slung over her shoulder while we walk to the end of the ticket-booth line.

Despite the complete lack of order, we buzz through the line quickly. At the main gate, we hand our tickets to an old man in overalls, who stuffs them into a dented coffee can. The simplicity of the entire thing amuses me, especially when I turn over my shoulder and watch the man trade his full can for an empty one, handing it to a little girl who takes it back up to the ticket booth to recycle the tickets again.

"We have to wait for Ryan," Elise says, waving us over to join her at a small picnic table near the front of the festival. Until today, I went along with the hype for this event, not really understanding the strange adoration every other person seemed to have for it. But even I can't deny the power of the smell being carried through the trees that surround us. It's not apples, but something entirely...*better*. There's a sweetness and a smokiness as well, and it makes my mouth water, craving the crunch of what in my mind must be the world's most amazing crust and the tartness and sugary goo of apple-pie perfection.

"I told you," Willow whispers in my ear, putting her arm around my shoulder and lying her head on my arm. I breathe it in again, and I swear I can almost taste it. "Best. Pie. Ever."

"I need to have some of that, and soon," I say, leaning my head to the side slowly until it rests on hers. For the first time since I left the city, since I said goodbye to Morgan and Gaby, I feel like I have a real friend.

"Hey...Kens?" The way Elise says my name gets my attention fast, so I lift my head and stand from the bench, brushing the dust and leaves that have fallen onto the table away from my sweater and leggings. She nods her head over my shoulder, and her lip pulls up on one side, a faint smile that makes my belly fill with butterflies and hope.

Turning slowly, I scan the crowd as my eyes pan along the various booths for games and treats, until I see three very out-of-place figures pacing near the front entrance. Owen looks terrified. To anyone else, he probably looks frustrated or irritated—his usual intimidating stance as his feet shuffle in the dirt, his thumb impulsively sliding over the screen of his phone like he's texting or waiting for an important call. But I've learned the subtleties of Owen Harper, and right now, he's nervous—he's afraid of being judged.

I start to move closer to them, but before I get there, Ryan walks up behind them and gestures in our direction. Andrew sees me first, and he smiles and holds up his hand in hello. Owen's eyes don't find me right away, but as he gets closer, his gaze finds mine, and his pace slows down to almost a complete stop. His chest is moving in an out like a panic attack—his brother, House, and Ryan all passing him, leaving him behind. When he's finally close enough for me to truly see the look in his eyes, I can tell he's in hell.

He's come to hell, on purpose—and I think he did that for me.

Willow nudges my shoulder, looking over at Owen, who is dressed in black, from the black cap pulled low to shadow his eyes to the dark jeans and black shoes. He's hiding, but I see him. "He looks like he wants to run," she says.

"That's because he does," I breathe, before pulling my arms around my body tight, covering my hands with my sleeves as I step closer to my lost friend—*friend*.

We meet in the middle, and it seems so appropriate.

"So, did you come for me? Or was it the pie?" I tease, kicking my boot into his Converse. Initiating this touch makes my stomach drop with nerves.

Owen laughs once, breathing in through his nose, a puff of fog escaping with his breath. "It's…it's really good pie," he says, his head cocked to one side, lip curled and one eye squinted while he waits for me to buy his line. He's here for me. And my heart hurts with happiness.

"That's what everyone says, but…I don't know. I've had good pie before," I say, urging us back in the direction of our friends.

"Well, it's been a while," he says, a distinct pause as he looks out at the festival, the lights flashing and families milling around about us. "But I'm pretty sure I'm remembering right, and you're going to be eating your words."

"Yeah, well I'd rather be eating pie," I say, folding my arms, my hip slouched to one side in our playful standoff.

"You want me to buy you pie?" he asks, and something about this simple surrender, this sweet offer from a boy to a girl, has my chest swelling with hope.

"Yeah…I'd like to eat pie with you, Owen Harper," I say, biting the edge of my bottom lip to hold my soft grin in place, to keep the full-on smile from creeping too far. It's my first foray into blatant, forward flirting, and my hands are numb with nerves. I'm pretty sure my mouth no longer works, but the way my stupid little sentence makes Owen's cheeks flush makes my courage worth the effort it took to muster it.

Owen and I trail behind the rest of our group, Andrew and House peeling away to step in line for some ride that looks like it's sole purpose is to induce brain damage and vomiting by the way it flips people around over and over again. Willow keeps glancing over her shoulder; I get the sense she's checking up on me to make sure Owen isn't upsetting me.

We all stop at the largest food booth in the center of the festival grounds, and Owen orders for me, asking a man with a grizzly beard and biker tattoos wrapped around both arms and neck for two slices of "mama's best."

"He's not Mama, right?" I ask, and Owen chuckles.

"No," he says, still laughing a little when the biker man hands him two plates slathered with caramel and large chunks of apple and crust. I follow Owen over to a picnic table, sliding in across from him. "It's Carolyn Potter's recipe, but she died a few years ago. Those are her boys. They look rough, but they're not really. That one?" Owen nods in the direction of a more heavy-set blonde guy who also has a beard and his own impressive set of tattoos.

"Yeah?" I acknowledge, pulling my plate in front of me and smelling the aroma steaming from it.

"He's Santa," Owen says, pushing his fork in and lifting up a hefty bite of pie. "Not like…the *real* Santa. I mean he plays Santa. Every year, at the hospital."

I take a moment to admire the man he pointed out, watching closely as he laughs with his brothers, all of them large and weathered, but wearing smiles that are infectious. *Santa* looks like he's picked up his mother's duties, and at one point, he's actually whistling as he peels a ringlet of skin away from an apple.

"Do you know them well?" I ask, stopping to take my first bite of pie. The second it hits my tongue, I concede, my eyes flipping to Owen's while the flakiness of the crust disintegrates into a perfect buttery blend in my mouth, the caramel coating the crunch of the apple, and the tartness coming through at the end. "Holy shit!"

Owen laughs so hard he has to cover his mouth with his arm, his mouth still full from his bite, he's coughing from almost choking. "I told you. It really is good pie," he says, and I like the way his eyes look right now. This moment. *This* is the Owen Harper I like the very best. "And yeah, I know them pretty well. House's mom is married to the cashier; his name's Dale. And my dad..."

Owen stops there. He's pretending to chew his bite while he looks out at the festival crowd, his thumb rubbing over the handle of his fork. After several long seconds, he brings his eyes back to mine, taps his fork a few times on his plate while his teeth hold the edge of his tongue, almost as if he's deciding how much of himself is safe to reveal. "My dad used to help out at the hospital with him...on the holidays. I remember a little, but I was four or five, so it's all sort of fuzzy, ya know?"

"Yeah, I know fuzzy," I say, thinking about my youth, before my life became all about the piano and concertos and following in my father's footsteps. Owen looks away again, and I can tell he's trying to remember more, feel more—bring his past in line with the present. I study him while he's not looking at me. His eyelashes are long and dark, and his jaw is squared, like a man's. My last boyfriend, if you could call him that, had soft skin, a voice that wasn't fully settled in and he watched cartoons in the afternoons. Jacob was privileged, and drove his father's Infiniti to school every day. But looking at Owen now and holding him up against what I remember of Jacob, I realize just how far away from becoming a man he was.

"Why do people think you're so much trouble?" I blurt out, and Owen laughs through his last bite, holding his hand over his mouth so he doesn't lose it.

"Kens, I mean...*all this?*" he says, waving his hand from the top of his head down to his legs, all the while still chewing and mumbling through his words. "I'm pretty high maintenance."

He reserves his serious face while I stare at him, and eventually I pick up the edge of my crust and throw it at him.

"Hey, that's like a felony, you know—wasting perfectly good crust! Shame on you, pie privileges revoked," he says, stealing my plate away.

"You can have it. Ugggg, I'm so full," I say, hand rubbing my stomach.

Owen doesn't even hesitate, shrugging and piling the remnants of my pie into his mouth in two bites—then carefully dragging his fork over the surface to make sure he's captured every single crumb. It makes him seem like a little boy, and frankly, it melts my heart.

He stands when he's done, carrying both of our plates to the trash, and I take advantage of this moment to admire his body, how tall he is, how broad his shoulders are, how warm everything about him looks. A part of me is aching to touch him.

"Seriously, what's the story behind your story?" I ask again, trying to keep myself focused, hoping I'm not pushing too hard. Owen reaches behind his head, pulling his hood over his hat and zipping the front of his jacket closed while he stuffs his hands inside the pockets. He does this when he's uncomfortable, and I've seen him do it before, but this time his smile doesn't leave his face.

"Yo, Ryan," he says, leading me over to the next table, where the rest of my friends are still finishing their slices. "So Kens wants to know why people think I'm an asshole."

"Hey!" I shout, slapping my hand against his arm. "I did not say that!"

"No, not directly. But, let's face it, Kens. People don't call me trouble; they call me an asshole," he says, his lips pressed together in a tight smile, his shoulders raised.

"I'll tell you why he's an asshole," Ryan says, surprising me since he's always the first to defend Owen to me. "He's an asshole..." he continues, standing and pushing his empty plate in Owen's chest, "because he's a ball hog who doesn't like to pass. Hey, ball hog, go take my shot and throw my plate in the trash, would ya?"

Owen blows a kiss at Ryan, who does it right back, and the two of them laugh, but Owen throws Ryan's plate away anyway. There's a genuine respect between them both, like Owen has with House. I wonder why they aren't closer.

"I could give her a few reasons if you'd like," Willow says, standing to throw her garbage away next.

"Oh, I'm sure she's heard everything you've got to say," Owen says, reaching out and taking Willow's plate from her as well. His gesture surprises her, and I notice her brow pinched as she follows him with her gaze while he does her this small, but in many ways enormous, favor.

"Uh...thanks," she says, and he blows her a kiss next. "And there he is."

"You don't hate me. You hate the me I was when I was fourteen," Owen says, challenging her. Willow pauses at the end of the table, keeping her eyes on him, her eyes squinting while she considers what he said, and she finally sucks in her bottom lip and nods once before responding.

"Okay. Clean slate. But..." she says, coming closer to him, just close enough that I can hear her whisper at his back, "don't give me a *new* reason to hate you, okay heartbreaker?"

Owen's laugh is fast and soft, and more of an acceptance of her warning. He never says anything out loud, and Willow pats his back—with a little extra muscle—while she passes behind him.

"Rides!" Elise finally chants, standing next to Jess, grabbing his trash and practically leaping from the table. "I have waited," she starts, pausing to count on her fingers, "like *way* too many years to get my ass on that rollercoaster. Ryan Barstow, I hope you've got an iron stomach, cuz we're riding that thing a dozen times."

"Yeaaaaah, I got something you can ride," House says, stepping up behind us and grabbing his crotch, literally taking the conversation to the playground.

"Don't do that shit," Ryan says, poking his finger hard in House's chest, then grabbing Elise's hand and kissing the top of it before pulling her into his arm at the side as they walk away. She doesn't seem offended, and she's quick to shrug House's statement off, but I'm a little bothered by it. I'm not sure how I would handle him talking to me like that—well at all, and I wonder what Owen would think.

With a single comment, House has managed to send everyone in various directions; the only people left with him now are Owen, Andrew, and me. I'm starting to understand why Ryan and Owen don't hang out often. I'm pretty sure it's House.

"Dude," Owen says, wincing at his friend.

"Oh, don't give me that shit. You know I only have one level. I don't tone it down for no one," House says, shrugging his shoulders in his giant hoodie, then pulling it up over his head. He's embarrassed, whether he wants to admit it or not.

"I need some cash," Andrew says, holding his hand in front of Owen's chest, twitching the ends of his fingertips, like he's scratching an itch.

"Then I guess you need a job," Owen says, his hands still lodged in his pockets.

"Yeah, I'd get one of those, but I have this super overbearing brother who makes me take double high school, so I'm not really sure when I'll find the time..." Andrew trails off because Owen holds a twenty out for him in the middle of his speech.

"Yeah, yeah. Good point. Just go to college. Now take my money; it's all I'm good for," he teases, and Andrew winks at him once and pats his shoulder before jogging over to some carnival game with House.

And for the first time tonight, Owen and I are completely alone. A group of kids run by waving tickets, and a mom rushes behind Owen with a pile of napkins held fast to her son's bloody nose. There's activity everywhere, yet it feels like Owen and I exist in a bubble.

"I got busted with a gun," Owen says, and his statement is so out-of-the-blue, it makes me shake my head. I'm trying to find the context.

"What?" I finally ask.

"You asked why people think I'm trouble," he says. "That's when it started. I was in sixth grade, and I brought my big brother's gun to school."

"Oh," I say, my chest growing tighter with worry about rumors I fear Owen is about to confirm.

"There was this big kid, his name was Hunter, and his dad was on the town council or something like that. Anyway, Hunter made my life a living hell. He told everyone..." Owen looks away, taking a deep breath, so I reach over and tug on his sleeve to bring him back to me. When he turns, his face tilts to the side, and his lips form a perfectly straight line, not a smile, but not a frown. They are complete nothingness.

"About your dad?" I finish for him.

Owen nods, looking down at his feet. "He would follow me home with his friends, yelling shit like 'your daddy was a crazy man' and 'when are you going to go crazy?'"

"That's not very nice," I say, and inside my head I paint a mental picture where I punch this Hunter kid. Owen smiles at my response.

"Yeah, well, one day I brought James's gun to school, and I told Hunter about it and said I was going to shut him up," Owen says, his eyes drifting into that dark place as he remembers. His confession is scaring me, but I hold my ground and keep the worry away from my face.

"I didn't mean it. I was just *acting* tough. And I didn't know any better. My grandpa practically raised us, and he wasn't very well most of my life. And my mom, she was working, even back then. But Hunter ran to his dad, who called the cops, busted my locker open, and the next thing I know my mom was piecing together every penny in our savings account to bail my ass out of juvie."

"Wow…I gotta be honest. I was expecting you to tell me it was all lies," I say, unable to stop my upper body from convulsing in a shiver as the breeze picks up, dropping the air another ten degrees. Without pause, Owen unzips his jacket and drapes it over my shoulders, still careful not to let his hands touch my skin.

"Thank you," I smile, pulling the sleeves over my arms and wrapping myself with the fabric still carrying the warmth from his body. I imagine for the briefest moment that instead of his jacket, I'm in his arms.

"You want me to be honest?" Owen says, and there's a glimmer in his eyes that worries me, making me wonder, but I nod anyhow, giving a slight tip of my chin, then I wrap my arms and Owen's hoodie around me even tighter. "If there's a rumor you've heard about me…" he says, his head tilting down ever so slightly to make sure my eyes are met by his, "it's probably true."

"You held a gun to your head?" My question is a whisper, my inner voice pleading for him to tell me *everything except that.* Everything. Except that.

Owen stands his ground, his head still tilted so our eyes are locked, and he never flinches. Not. Once.

I wipe the tear away quickly, but not before he sees it, and his mouth falls with his spirit.

"Why?" I ask.

Owen shrugs at first, looking beyond my shoulder. When I turn, I notice our friends are walking toward us, Elise excitedly leading the way. When I turn back, I catch Owen's intense gaze waiting for me.

"I don't really smoke. And if you've ever noticed, I don't do drugs. I never once take that shit my friends pass around. I drink. Yeah, I do drink, but that's it. The rest? The rest are all risks I control. I like to feel that edge, to know where it is," he says, a fire flashing in his eyes.

"But what happens when you lose?" I ask, and his fire fades quickly, and suddenly he's back here with me.

"Then I'll know I'm just like him," he says, and my chest completely slams closed, my heart exploding all at once.

"Ryan's sick. I made him go on the big drop too many times," Elise says, and I breathe in a sharp, quick breath—trying to erase, or at the very least bury, everything I just heard.

"Oh, poor guy. You guys done then?" I ask, trying to ignore the look Willow is giving me over the fact that I'm smothering myself in Owen's jacket. I'm far deeper than she realizes.

"Elise wants to ride the big wheel, then we can go…" Ryan stops himself, looking at his friend and realizing his major slip. Everyone is hit with discomfort simultaneously, and no one wants to be the next to speak.

"It's okay. Really," Owen says, being brave. Perhaps just taking a risk. "I'm here, and that was hard enough. It's just a stupid Ferris wheel."

"Right, it's way different, too," Willow says, but Jess leans into her shoulder hard, stopping her from making this worse. "I just meant…from when we were kids…shit. I'm sorry Owen. Hey, I'm just going to go buy my ticket."

"And I'm going to go with her and make sure she keeps her mouth shut," Jess says as Willow elbows him while they leave. Elise and Ryan follow them, and Ryan mouths a "sorry" as they pass; Owen shrugs it off.

"My brother always wanted to ride this thing," he says, looking up at the flashing lights, the spinning buckets, the massive height.

"I could take him…if you want?" I say, and Owen drops his chin, his eyes softening at the sight of me.

"Take me on what? The wheel? Oh heck yeah, I'm in!" Andrew says as he strides up behind me. I follow him to the ticket line, and he's talking about how one of the games he was trying to win is fixed, something about the bottle tops being too large for the ring.

His voice is muffled in my ears because I'm desperately trying to keep my attention on Owen. When we step up to the window, I make my request for two tickets, ready to pay for Andrew's, but Owen's hand reaches over my shoulder, and he slides a ten through the small slot in the window.

"Make it four," he says. "You can ride with House," he says to Andrew.

"Oh, it's okay. Really, I can just wait on the ground with you. We'll eat more pie," I stammer, trying to give him an out as the woman in the booth takes his money and slides four passes into his hand.

"You couldn't possibly want more pie," he smiles, handing House and Andrew their passes, his eyes having a silent conversation with his brother and friend. "Guys, really…it's just a ride."

Andrew nods and moves to the line for the ride, but House sticks with Owen for a little longer, his eyes telling a different story. "I'm fine," Owen says, he grits through his teeth, his voice almost threatening toward his friend.

"Sure you are, man. But if you suddenly decide you're not, you tap out, got it?" House says, holding up his fist, waiting for Owen to accept. Owen just pushes it away finally, his motion harsh and abrupt as he turns and leaves his friend standing with me while he joins his brother in line.

I walk to join them slowly, and before House and I get too close, I ask: "What is tapping out?"

"It's our safety plan. When we race, there's always a point where we have each other's backs—where it's safe to admit we've had enough. We bail on whatever the situation is, back off the gas, pull over and calm down," House says.

"You ever need the safety plan?" I ask, and he nods *yes.*

"Has he?" I know the answer as soon as I ask, but it's confirmed when House sucks in his bottom lip and raises his brow.

The ride before us goes quickly, and Owen is handing the carnival worker our pair of tickets before I'm ready. Instinctually, I look around us, expecting to see a crowd gather, to see people whispering in horror, amazed at what Owen is about to do. But nobody cares. My friends are all up in cars on the other side of the wheel, their view of this completely obstructed. They have no idea how brave Owen's about to be—and I'm terrified that he's not really being brave at all, that he's only being *wild*, as Willow would say.

"Locked and ready," the carnie man yells, signaling something to the ride operator. With a jerk, we stream upward about twenty feet, halting fast and our gondola swinging back and forth while we wait for the bucket below us to load more riders.

Owen's brow is already beading with sweat, and he pulls his hat from his head and runs his long sleeve over his face, his dark eyes blinking fast.

"We don't have to do this," I say, but he interrupts me.

"Yes. Yes, we do," he says, and suddenly, his hand finds mine. His grip on my fingers is hard, but the way we lock together is almost familiar—right. Owen tugs on the fabric of his left sleeve with his teeth, chewing on the ribbed edge for a few seconds before grasping it with his thumb and holding it to his closed lips, his eyes darting from the safety latch to the pivot wheel to the line of people still waiting to load. With every new thing he notices, his grip on my hand gets tighter, and when we swing up even higher, his breath falters.

"I'm going to ask him to stop the ride. Owen, we're getting off," I say.

"No!" he says, closing his eyes and squeezing them, tucking his chin into his chest, then shaking his head *no*. "No," he whispers. "Please, Kensi. Help me through this."

Without pause, I pull Owen's right hand into my lap, and I cover it even more with my other fingers. His leg starts to bounce, and the rhythm is making the cart swing a little too much, so I lift his hand again, this time bringing it to my chest so I can hold it to me closely.

"Close your eyes, and I'll tell you when they're done loading, when you can just look out at the city, okay?" I say.

"Okay," he whispers, doing as I say.

"One more round, and that's it...almost there...loading. Latching. Waving. Okay," I say, still clutching his hand in mine, his fingers fretting and fighting to find more of my hand to grip any time I threaten to loosen my hold.

"Are we moving? Kensi, I can't tell. Are we moving?" he asks, his voice soft and vulnerable.

"Not yet. Soon, Owen. We'll be moving soon," I say, locking my eyes on his closed lids, watching them twitch with panic.

His breathing starts to stutter even more, and I begin to open my lips to beg him to let me make them stop one more time—when his eyes open, his soul looking right into mine. Then the sky begins to move behind him. I keep his gaze, doing my best not to interrupt, to blink, and I let my mouth form a faint smile. "We're moving," I say, his hand still held to my chest, my heart no doubt pounding against our grasp on one another.

"Owen, you can look out now, look at the town and the stars," I say, glancing over his shoulder as the lights from the festival fade and refocus with every pass we make. Owen keeps his eyes on me, never blinking. But I know he's seeing something. I know he's safe, that he doesn't need to "tap out," because he's smiling, and his eyes are showing traces of something new, like the life of a child lost years ago.

It's joy.

As the ride slows, we pause at the top, still frozen in our pose, our hands tethered to the point where I can no longer feel beyond my first knuckles. But Owen's smile remains, and his breathing starts to even out, his chest rising and falling at a normal pace. I spare a look away as my friends exit below us, and I notice Willow point up to our cart as she reaches her arms around Jess and squeezes him.

"I think they're proud of you," I say, gesturing to the group waiting for us about thirty feet below. Owen doesn't look, and he doesn't break our trance. But he does finally speak.

"You are the most beautiful girl I've ever seen," he says, and all at once, I fall for Owen Harper.

CHAPTER 12

Beautiful.

Owen Harper called me beautiful. And then just as quickly, he was gone. I squeezed his hand tightly while the ride slowly brought us down to the ground to exit. We walked down the long, metal exit ramp, where Willow was waiting for me, her eyes full of questions, and when I turned back to find Owen again—he had disappeared.

Gone.

He does that. Just…goes.

His truck was nowhere to be found when Willow brought me home. His room was empty for the entire night. And he's been away all day.

That's why I practically race down the stairs at the sound of the basketball, and I'm not even disappointed when it's only Andrew and House shooting the ball. They might be able to tell me something…*anything!*

Of course, my boldness stops stone cold as soon as House opens his mouth. "Ken Doll! Looking to *hold hands* with your boyfriend while you both eat cookies and drink milk and watch cartoons?" He's saying everything in this overly-childish teasing voice, and I hate that it's embarrassing me.

"Dude, don't be a dick!" Andrew says, throwing the ball hard into House's chest. I like Andrew more and more.

"What? You saw those two acting all junior high and shit last night. Don't pretend like you weren't making fun of them as much as I was," House says, throwing the ball back at Andrew twice as hard, ricocheting it off his less-coordinated hands. Andrew scrambles to pick the ball back up and looks up at me sheepishly, guilty for enjoying a laugh at my expense. I forgive him because he honestly feels bad. House can eat it, though.

"It's Kensi," I say, looking beyond House's broad body into the open front door and windows of the Harper house, wishing to see someone inside.

"Yeah, I'm not calling you that," he says, spinning the ball on his finger a few times, a cocky smirk smeared across his face. I snatch the ball from his right hand and pull it under my arm. My heart is smacking the insides of my ribs as I realize how ballsy I'm being. I stare him down while he maneuvers a wad of chew in his mouth, spitting obnoxiously, the tobacco staining my driveway. I can't help but revolt when he does it, and I let my disgust show. House isn't any different from the privileged boys in uniform I used to have to deal with at Bryce. Instead of flashing his money around to intimidate me, though, he uses his size and masculinity. I bet it's effective on others, and on girls who probably harbor secret crushes on him.

"Oh, *Kensi.* I'm just messin' with ya," he says, snatching the ball back from me and passing it around his body once or twice, his eyes squinted, waiting for me to react.

"Owen's at work," Andrew says, saving me from *all this.*

"Oh...okay," I say, suddenly feeling awkward, like I no longer have a reason to be outside my house.

"You can hang out with me? I'll show you a good time," House says, sliding his giant arm over my shoulder, the material of his sweatshirt is actually damp with his sweat.

"I'm good...thanks," I say, slinking out of his grip. His laugh is almost demonic as he tosses the ball back to Andrew and pulls his keys from his pocket.

"All right, but you're missin' out," he says, walking to his truck near the curb.

"Am I?" I ask, my heart actually hurting with the anxiety coursing through my chest. House makes me nervous. Owen may think he's harmless, but I'm not convinced.

"You let me know when you're done playing footsies with O, and I'll show you a real man," he says, nodding to Andrew, then stepping up into his truck and roaring his engine loudly.

"He's all talk," Andrew says, bouncing the ball a few times to draw my attention back to him.

"Sure he is," I say back, not believing it for a second. I know House's type, and it's entitled. Money has nothing to do with it. He just needs to know he's not entitled to me.

"You like my brother?" Andrew says, and my throat burns with fear at having to answer that question. I can't look at him, so I keep my attention on House's taillights as he pulls away.

"We've become friends," I say, my voice unsteady, unsure, and my mind flashing through the dozens of nights I've waited to see just a glimpse of Owen outside, my palm burning with the memory of the touch of his hand in mine. "Yeah…" I add, my voice even softer now. "I like him."

"He'll be home late tonight. But…he'd like to see you," Andrew says, his foot kicking into mine, teasing me like a little brother should. I nod once and smile at him, and his smile is broad and satisfied.

I head back into my house and tiptoe up the stairs to my mom's bedroom door. Her shift was late, and she's been sleeping most of the morning, so I don't want to wake her, but when I press my ear to the door, I hear her talking on the phone.

"We can talk, sure…but…not now. I'm not ready to talk now. I think I just need time," she says, her half of the conversation piquing my curiosity about the other end of the line. I'm sure she's talking to my father, and I don't like that she's talking to him. I want to cut him out of our existence, to just take a giant eraser to all he was and all he is, and I want to do that for Gaby, too. But then there are those memories, the few good ones of us as a family, home together, on holidays. And maybe we can only let in those small things, but keep everything else out.

I hear the conversation end, so I step quickly to my room, folding my legs up on my bed and pulling my laptop in front of me, acting busy. My Facebook page is still up. I had been looking for pictures of Owen—

anything about Owen—but he seems to avoid being online. I found a mention of his name in a town newspaper archive; he was named to the state's all-star basketball team. But that was all.

My exploration started with a hunt for pictures because I wanted to see his face. But soon I started looking for the bad things, arrest records and proof that Owen was also all of those things Willow and Jess and Elise say he is. But those records don't exist online. And even though it's probably just because he's a minor, I still like the fact that I can't find the bad things. I'm ashamed I even started looking for them in the first place.

What I settled on, though, was my folder full of photos of Gaby and me. I've dragged them into the trash a dozen times, but I keep pulling them back out. As much as I want to erase my father, I don't want to erase Gaby. I only want to erase what she did. God, how I want to erase that.

"So I was thinking of making pasta for dinner. You know, Grandma's sauce? What do you think?" My mom startles me when she comes in my room, and I snap my laptop to a close. Her eyes linger on it, her head tilting, but she doesn't question. It's almost like she knows enough to know she doesn't *want* to know what I'm looking at.

She doesn't. It would kill her to see these photos—reason enough to delete them all the moment she leaves my room.

"Sure. Pasta's good," I say, holding my hands still on the silver top of my computer, my eyes doing their best to bluff happiness. After a few long seconds, my mom turns to leave.

"Hey, Mom?" I ask; she pauses and looks over her shoulder. "Can we have the neighbors over for dinner with us? It's usually just Owen, and his brother. Their mom works nights, and they've just been good…to us…"

My mom knows what I mean—Owen's been good to me, defended me, defended her, stood up to my dad. She smiles softly before she speaks.

"That sounds like a good idea. I'll try to clean up the kitchen some, enough to have guests," she says.

"They won't mind the mess," I say, the double meaning there for both of us. Owen understands life's messy. She nods and smiles once again before leaving, and the second I hear her feet hit the stairs, I open my laptop and delete the visual reminders of my former best friend.

It's the least I can do.

. . .

MY PIANO HASN'T MADE a sound for days, minus the moment I played it for Willow. And when I played, it felt like a goodbye. But today…

Today I just feel like I need to touch it. I've been sitting at it for more than an hour, my mom clanking around the kitchen, cleaning and cooking. All I can bare to do is run my hand along the cover over the keys, my finger tracing along the fine lines of the wood grain. Something so beautiful is also so ugly.

"Kens, hun? I think your phone is ringing," my mom shouts from the kitchen. I slide from the bench quickly, not wanting her to see where I'm sitting. I think I'm worried she'll encourage me to play.

"Thanks," I say, passing through the kitchen to the small table in the nook where my jacket and backpack are sitting. My phone is sitting on top, and there's a message notification on the screen. I grab all of my things, and head back upstairs as I listen to the message, recognizing that the number was Owen's and not really wanting to listen to his voice while my mother watches the smile form on my face.

"Hey, uhm. Damn. Kens? I really hate to ask for this," his message begins. I pause it, his concerned voice making me nervous. I hurry the rest of the way to my room, toss my belongings to the ground, and move to my bed to listen to the rest, my eyes peering out my window to the spot where I'm wishing for his truck to appear.

"I'm in trouble. Not like…*real* trouble," he says, and a voice near him adds, "this is pretty serious, son."

"No, it's *not* serious. That's what I'm trying to explain to you," he says, the phone muffled while he talks to someone in the room with him. "Look, Kensi, I need you to come down to the shops I work at, they're on Eighth and Central. I need you to get something out of my truck, but I'm being held for…shit, I'm being held for shoplifting. This dickhead cop won't let me go, even though he's wrong!"

"That's enough; time's up, Harper," the voice bellows in.

"Just come, Kens. My mom's not home, and Andrew can't help. Please." It's that last word, the *please,* that breaks me. He doesn't sound like Owen at all, instead more like the frightened ghost of Owen that I got to see terrified dozens of feet in the air on that Ferris wheel.

My feet are wandering my room, carrying my body that's not even caught up with my mind yet. I don't know what to do, and I barely know what Eighth and Central means. Owen needs me, and I *have* to go.

I have to go.

I grab my boots and the heavier coat hanging on the hook behind my door. The sky has been gray for days, threatening to open up. These early storms, they aren't really snow. But they aren't rain either. The air has been frosty, and the cold has been harsh. I'm used to the city, which while the wind cuts to the bone, the buildings offer you the occasional reprieve, making it livable to move around outside. There's nothing to hide behind out here, even the trees have lost most of their leaves and are mere spindles standing on dead, lifeless ground.

I'm down the stairs quickly, my wallet and phone sandwiched in my hands. I need the keys. My mom doesn't let me drive often, and I've never had a car of my own. There's never been a need.

I have to go.

"Mom?" I ask, my lip trembling that she's going to say *no*. For some reason, the more time that passes, the more worried I am that Owen is in big trouble.

"What, babe?" she asks, her eyes watering from the onion she's chopping. She runs her face along the bicep of her sleeve, then looks up at me, and I try my best to look calm.

"It was Owen. He's at work, had some trouble with his truck," I lie. "He needs me to come get him. It's only a few blocks. I won't be gone long; can I borrow the keys?"

"Oh, poor kid. Here, let me just turn the stove off. I'll come with you," she says, my stomach starting to fill with the drumming beats of my heart, the heaviness of stress weighing me down more.

"No, no," I start, and she pauses, tilting her head in that way, the same way she did before when she caught me looking at pictures of Gaby. The face she makes says she knows, just not everything. "You're in the middle of cooking. And I'm really looking forward to tonight. I don't want to stop you, or to mess any of this up," I say, this time not really a lie. "Let me go. Let me do this. Please."

Please.

I say the same word Owen said, hoping it resonates. Something does, but my mom waits for a few long seconds before nodding her head toward the keys on the counter.

"If the speed limit is thirty, you drive twenty, okay?" she says. I smile and cross my heart, trying to keep it light, inside wishing I was a better driver so I could be there as quickly as House would be.

He called me. He didn't call House.

That thought…it feels….

I'm careful as I buckle myself into the car, tossing my wallet and phone into the passenger seat. I maneuver down the driveway, onto the road and to the end of our block, and then I shut my eyes while I sit at the stop sign, not a single car coming in either direction. Which way is Eighth? Which way?

My gut tells me to turn right, so I do. I'm rewarded by street names that count down from Seventeenth to Sixteenth to Thirteenth and soon Tenth. When I find Eighth, I actually laugh out loud with the kind of glee I didn't think was real.

"I'm coming, Owen," I whisper to myself.

I see the main grocery store near the strip mall in the distance, and despite my mother's best warnings, I punch the gas, skipping part of the curb as I pull into the parking lot, and my tires squeal as I move down the main lane through the mall. I can see the small security vehicle and the squad car parked next to it, the lights flashing like there's an emergency.

I park right next to the cars, grab my things, and rush into the small gift shop where Owen is sitting, his hands cuffed.

"Owen! I'm here. What's…" I pause when I see his dejected face. His hands are pulled tightly behind his body, and everything about him looks tired and defeated.

"Miss," the officer says.

"Kensington," I say to him, my full name. This feels like I should be formal.

"You know this young man?" he asks.

"Yes. We're friends. He's my neighbor," I say, not really sure what the right definition is for our relationship. I want to say whatever makes this better for Owen.

"We were sort of expecting a parent," the officer says, tipping his glasses down and looking at Owen with an intense scowl.

"I told you. My mom is *working*. I don't have anyone else. And I didn't do anything wrong!" Owen says, his temper showing its familiar flare.

"I'm sorry. Could someone explain what's going on? How can I help?" I interrupt, my hands shaking while I move to a small folding chair across from Owen and an older man.

"I'll tell you what happened," the man sitting next to him says, his white hair tufting on either side of his head, his eyes framed with thick black-rimmed glasses. "This young…hooligan…tried to pocket this charm bracelet while he was emptying out the trash! That's what's going on."

The man waves a small, silver bracelet toward Owen, and it jangles while he shakes it to emphasize his opinion. I look to Owen, looking for confirmation that this is false. But there's a part of me that wonders, the part that knows how dangerous Owen can be. This…this would be such a small thing for him—not even a thrill from the crime.

I wait while he shuts his eyes and shakes his head, and I'm not sure what he's feeling. "I told you, I bought it this morning, from the girl who was working here," Owen says, and my chest fills with air, my body washed with relief.

"There, see?" I say, standing, practically demanding and proclaiming him innocent.

"Then where's the receipt, you little piece of shit?" the old man yells, standing and smacking his hand down on the seat he just abandoned. I look to the officer, who stands silently, his pen already armed to take down the guilty report.

"We've done this already. I can't find it. But maybe it's in my truck. Just let me look," Owen says, his voice trailing off because he knows the response he'll get.

"Bullshit, you'll just take off," the old man says.

"Where the FUCK am I gonna go?" Owen yells, his eyes simmering now, the shadow closing in over him. "Fuck! You know who I am! You all know my family! This isn't a big town. You seriously think I'm going to shoplift a bracelet for sixty bucks—then leave my home and go off into the sunset? Where the fuck would I go, man? Use some goddamned logic at least if you're going to judge me without any facts or reasons."

"Let me look," I say, my eyes darting between the officer and the shop owner, neither of them paying attention. "Owen, where are your keys?"

"In the back. This prick took them," he says.

"Don't you call me that," the old man says.

I ignore them all, march to the back where Owen's keys are sitting on a stack of notebooks on an old metal desk. I grab them and walk back through the store. "Hey, you can't take those. Those aren't yours!" the old man yells as I pass him.

"Yeah, well they aren't yours either, you prejudiced asshole!" I say as I storm through the door, the small string of bells dangling from the door handle announcing my exit.

I find Owen's truck quickly, parked near the road, away from the shops, in a spot no customers would want. I unlock his door and scan my eyes over his seat, the only thing there an empty licorice wrapper and the paper from a stick of gum. Owen's sunglasses are on the dashboard, as are a few papers. I leaf through them, noting that one of them is a letter from Bradley University, interest in Owen's basketball intentions. The letter looks yellowed, so I look to find the date—two months old.

I toss the stack of papers back to their spot on the dash and pull open the glove box, finding nothing but his insurance and registration card and an envelope with a few dollar bills inside and some gas receipts. It has to be here. I know it in my heart that he isn't lying.

Stepping away from the truck, I look at the long bench seat through the open door, and I pull my hand to my mouth, my teeth working on my short, already chewed down thumbnail while I think. With a small tilt of my head, I notice something different along the floorboard, deep in a corner along the floor of Owen's driver's side. There's a small speck of pink, and when I step closer, I realize it's paper. Scooting forward on my elbows, I move my body under the steering wheel and lift slightly on the gas pedal, sliding the floor mat back a tiny bit.

MOORE'S GIFT HUT is written in large, bold letters along the top, and a handwritten note details a bracelet, today's date, $58.47, and it's signed by the name *Patricia*. I grasp it in my hand, wrinkling it, but more concerned about somehow dropping it, or a gust of wind carrying it away. I slam Owen's door to a close and run back to the store where the officer now has Owen standing, his palm on his back getting ready to guide him through the door.

"It's here! It's here!" I say, pushing the receipt into the officer's hands. He sets his clipboard down, lets his other hand fall away from Owen, then unwrinkles the pink paper for inspection.

"Sir, is this receipt from your store?" he asks, handing the paper to the old man, who scrambles to push his glasses to the tip of his nose, holding the paper up in the light. I'm looking at an entire stack of similar pages stuck through a pin on his counter, and I turn to Owen and wink. But Owen's face still looks sullen.

"Patricia, yeah she was here this morning. And the numbers all match up," he says, standing and walking over to the counter, pulling a few old receipts out just to make sure the handwriting is to his satisfaction. He's putting on a show, because he's embarrassed; he was wrong.

"All right, looks like things worked out this time, Harper," the officer says, pulling a pocket knife from his pocket and cutting the strip of plastic on the disposable cuffs that were holding Owen hostage. He rubs his wrists and stretches his arms across his chest, then turns to look at the old man across the counter.

"Well…you can't be too careful," the old man begins, his voice stuttering, panicked. He can't believe he was wrong. Owen doesn't say a word, only holding out his hand until the old man realizes what he wants, and hands him the bracelet.

"I've been stolen from a lot this year," the old man continues, trying to explain to me now, but I'm no longer interested in anything he has to say either. I follow Owen out the door, and as we pass my mom's car, I expect him to stop, but he keeps walking. After he's several paces ahead of me, I call his name, but he doesn't turn around. His pace is steady, and his shoulders are low, ashamed.

I jog until I'm caught up with him again, and follow his footsteps until we're at the driver's door for his truck. "Owen, wait!" I say, wanting to say something better, something that would show him I didn't doubt him. But then again, there was a moment where I did. I doubted him, for just a fraction of a second—because of everything I've been told.

"Here," he says, tossing the silver chain, heavy with charms, to me. I catch it in both hands, looking down at it with a pinched brow, confused. "I got that for you."

He leaves quickly, never looking me in the eyes. The light is fading as dusk starts to settle in, so I shuffle my feet back to my car, my fingers rubbing obsessively over the metal trinkets in my hand. I flip the dome light on as soon as I'm buckled in the car, then I open my palm and look at my gift from Owen. I fall apart all at once; each charm is thoughtful, precious—one a note, one a piano, one a pick-up truck, and the last one a Ferris wheel.

I dial Owen three times, each call going right to his voicemail. So I give up, slam the car gear into reverse, and speed away from the shopping center. A few times, I convince myself that I can see Owen's lights, that it's his truck I'm following. But it never is, each time the driver turning the wrong way.

When I pull into my driveway, the car skids over the dip in the gutter, grinding metal along pavement, but the noise is just enough to stop Owen as his foot is about to step up his porch.

I push the gear in park, fly from the door and leave the car running in my driveway—my feet skipping carefully over the rocks and dips from the concrete of my driveway to his front yard. Owen doesn't move, but he doesn't leave. He stands there, his hands limp at his sides, his hat pushed low over his eyes, hiding how pathetic he feels—how vulnerable he is. I ignore it all, my hand grasping my bracelet, my gift, so tightly that the metal is leaving an indentation in my palm.

"I love it," I say, walking swiftly up to him, my breathing coming hard. "My bracelet. Owen...thank you. I love it."

He doesn't say a word, but he glances down at my open palm, his eyes twitching with the motion of my hands as I struggle with the clasp and work to wrap the chain around one wrist with my opposite hand. I hold my arm against my chest, keeping the end of the bracelet in place and finally hook it closed.

"It's beautiful, Owen. This…it's beautiful. Thank you," I say, my eyes glossing over with the want to cry. I stand before him, waiting for him to say something, say *anything.* Instead, he's motionless, and I give up. "I just wanted you to know how much I love it. How thankful I am…I'm sorry, Owen," I say, my smile fading fast, my eyes falling low as I turn and walk back to my house, to a kitchen full of pasta and sauce, enough to feed a real family. Only I'm coming back alone….

"You're beautiful. That…it's just a bracelet. But you…" Owen says, and I stop, my throat catching my emotion at the sound of his voice. It's deep and raspy, just like that first night in his truck. His hand is on my shoulder, my feet stopped and my body shivering.

With slow movements, his feet glide closer, an inch at a time, while his hand sweeps my hair around my neck. He slides his touch down my shoulder and arm until his hand is completely wrapped around my wrist. Lifting my arm slowly, Owen slides the edge of my sleeve with his finger, exposing the bracelet along my pale skin, the weight of the charms sliding up as he brings my hand closer to my shoulder, closer to him.

I can feel him breathe along my neck, and when the warmth of his mouth tickles my fingers, then my wrist, my eyes roll to a close—the feeling unlike anything I've ever experienced before. This is the dream I've had in my bed every night since I've met Owen Harper. Only this isn't a dream at all. It's really happening.

Owen loosens his grip on my wrist, letting go completely—then moving his hand to my jaw, pulling my chin up so I look at the dark, cloud-covered sky. When his lips touch the freezing skin along my neck, my knees grow weak, and I nearly slip to the ground.

With a more forceful grip, Owen reaches into my hair and turns me into him quickly, my breath catching when I realize how close I am to him, how much of him I can smell, feel, touch—*taste.* Both of his hands rise to my cheeks, his thumbs giving each one a gentle stroke while he looks at me.

No boy has ever touched me like this. No boy has ever given me a gift. And I've never wanted a boy to kiss me more than I do right now—to kiss me like the way they do in the movies, like a grown woman, like the woman I'm so close to becoming.

Every movement he makes is slow and studied, his eyes watching as his hand works in and out of my hair, then runs along my arm again, feeling the bracelet against my skin. When Owen leans into me, I begin to shut my eyes, my lips quivering, ready to meet his, but his mouth keeps moving, finding my neck and ear first, his tongue taking small strokes along the way. I've watched Owen do this, watched him kiss other girls like this. And as much as I also secretly wanted to be in their place, I now know that I don't want to be them at all.

I want to be more.

"Owen, I'm not Kiera," I breathe, his touch halting with my words. His hands never leave their spot, cradling my head, but Owen's mouth leaves my neck, his eyes serious when they come into view, his mouth a tight, straight line. My hands move to grip his elbows, to steady me in my moment of weakness, my legs threatening to betray me and send me to the ground again.

After several long seconds under his scrutiny, under the power of his gaze, he pulls me even closer, shutting his eyes as his mouth comes within a fraction of an inch of mine, his bottom lip grazing my top lip and sending a lighting bolt into the depths of my belly.

His mouth brushes against mine a few more times, each pass leaving me wanting more, forcing my lips to part, my skin to radiate with need, until finally he speaks. "You're right," he says, holding my head to his, our mouths ready, waiting. "You're so much more."

His mouth covers mine fast, his strong lips working my naïve and novice ones quickly into submission. His hands crawl around my head and body until he's pulling me to him so tightly that it becomes hard to breathe, but air—breathing—it's so unnecessary. I follow his lead, copy his every move, and grip him tightly, my fingers exploring the powerful muscles along his back and sides, feeling all of those physical things I've hungered for, until I'm stretching on my toes to reach him just to keep our lips intact.

With one swift action, Owen's hand slides down the small of my back, to my butt, and he lifts me up against him, carrying me while he takes giant strides to his truck, our lips never once breaking their hold on one another. He sets me on the bed of his truck and shifts his hands up the sides of my body, his finger's pausing at my ribs, his hands flexing with indecision. I can tell he wants to touch me, to feel me, and I love that his hands crave the feel of my breasts. The mere thought of him touching me there—in a place where boys who weren't worthy have barely felt me—makes my mouth hungrier, and I put all of the passion I'm feeling into our kiss.

I don't know when the back light clicked on, and I never heard the door, but when I let my eyes slip open, I notice. My wits are with me enough to realize that my mom is probably still watching this from somewhere inside our house. And while a small part of me doesn't care, there's another part that doesn't want to talk about boys and kissing and what's appropriate and what isn't with my mother. Not that I mind talking to my mom, I just don't want to talk about my beating heart with someone whose heart is broken.

"Dinner," I breathe out one word finally—a word that makes no sense to Owen, and barely registers with me. Our lips part, but Owen's hold on my face remains, his forehead resting against mine while he stands in front of my dangling legs, his feet shuffling with what I think might just be excitement and nerves.

"You want…dinner?" he asks, his lip pulling into a smirk on one side, a deep dimple impressing on one cheek.

"My mom. She said I could invite you for dinner. She's…she's been cooking all day. For you…and Andrew," I say, my cheeks finally finding feeling again after the rush of heat that coursed through them.

"Is she trying to poison me?" he jokes, his lips giving mine one small peck while his forehead sways side-to-side against mine in a way that feels natural and familiar.

"No more than I tried with the grilled cheese. You seem to have a very high tolerance," I smile.

"Well, I've had girls try to poison me before. I guess I'm immune," he jokes, and I can't help the way my lips slide into a frown at the mention of girls—*other* girls.

"Yeah, but I'm smarter than them. So I might be able to get the job done," I say, swinging my legs just enough to lightly kick him in the knee.

"First of all, *ouch!* Don't kick the knees. I've had surgery," he says, as he lifts me from the truck, swinging my body around until I'm resting on his driveway, his arms still looped around my body while my hands are clutched against his chest, searching for warmth. "And second of all, you're not just smarter than other girls. You're…"

He doesn't finish his words, instead sucking in his bottom lip, letting his teeth hold it in place while his head falls to mine one last time.

"So are you," I say, letting myself have something I want, say something I mean—something risky and scary.

When Owen's eyes close completely and his smile slowly pulls his lips loose from his teeth, I understand what the rest of that sentence is.

Everything.

Owen Harper is everything.

CHAPTER 13

“So?” Willow says, her face full of nosey curiosity while she watches me climb into her car.

“So…what?” I respond. I'm not going to make this easy.

“Come on!” she says with a laugh while she backs down my driveway. “You can't text me that you kissed Owen, and then pretend it never happened! You ignored every single follow-up text and my two phone calls after that. You're a bad bomb dropper. No cleanup afterward. Like…at all!”

I giggle, and the sound of happiness coming from my mouth is nice, foreign…but nice. It's a sound I haven't made in a while. “You kissed him. You know what it's like. What's to tell?” I tease, moving my book bag into my lap and pulling my gloves out to slip on my hands.

“Kens, I was fourteen when I kissed him. We were still dancing with bent elbows and rocking back-and-forth in the school gym at that time. I've seen that boy kiss now, and trust me—it's *different!* I want deets,” she says.

“Deets?” I say, slowly, one eyebrow cocked in her direction.

“Gahhhhh! Details. Deets! Don't make fun of my hip language, now spill it!” Willow's gum snaps, and I study her for a few seconds while she signals at the light and turns down the street to our school. She's so different from Morgan and Gaby. They both come from money, lots and lots of money. My family was comfortable middle class, sure. But I also used to have to listen to my mom dodge creditors and argue with my dad over bills. Those conversations never happened in my friends' worlds. And while I always found Morgan and Gaby to be more down-to-earth than the rest of our peers at Bryce, that feeling of not being a *real* member of their club was always there—even with Gaby. Willow looks like someone I'm supposed to know, like the friend that perhaps I was always supposed to have.

Like someone I can trust.

"How long have you been with Jess?" I ask, changing the subject, but with a reason.

"Uhhhh, like, more than a year. Why? Is this still about that thing Ryan said? That I'm into Owen? Kens, you know I'm not..." she says, and I interrupt.

"No, no. I know, I was just curious," I say, leaving my gaze on her. I bite at the inside of my mouth, a little nervous to push our friendship. "Have you and Jess....you know?"

I know she knows what I mean. I can tell by the way her eyebrows flare quickly, and the way she adjusts her grip on the steering wheel.

"Uhm, you did only kiss him, right? I mean...was there...more?" she asks, and I correct this quickly.

"Yeah, I mean no. I mean...yes, just a kiss. We just kissed," I say. My armpits are actually sweating, and my chest is pounding, I'm so uncomfortable. I've only ever talked about things like this with Gaby. She had a lot of...*experience,* clearly more than I was aware of, and now she's gone. And I have so many questions. "It's just...I like him, Will. I like him...a lot. I'm pretty sure I've never liked a boy like this. No...I know I haven't. And he's..."

"You're afraid he's going to try to push you too fast?" she asks, and I feel silly just hearing it out loud.

"Oh wow. I'm seriously living an after-school special, huh? Uhhhhhhg!" I say, throwing my face in my hands. I feel a little ridiculous, and presumptuous that I'm even thinking about things like Owen and sex at all. But I am. I'm thinking about it, about a *me* and *Owen,* down the road, when sex might enter into the picture. And when I think of that, I start to think that for him—a guy like Owen—sex is probably already in the picture. And then

I replay that thing he said, the night at the party, when he accused me of having a problem with people having sex. I'm such a fucking prude!

"I just like him, Will. I like him a lot, and I've never..." All of my attention goes to my lap, to my fingers that I'm picking at, to my knee bouncing up and down.

"This summer," she says, and I stop breathing, waiting for the rest. "Jess and me, our first time was this summer. I wanted to wait. And really?" She pauses, looking to the left at our school while we wait at the light, Jess's car parked in its usual spot. "I wanted to wait more. I mean...I don't regret it. But I wasn't *really* ready."

"Oh," I say, sucking in my lip hard, not sure what to say next.

"It got better. And we're careful, and we...we're, I don't know, active? Boy, that sounds really fucking clinical, doesn't it? We do it, sometimes? And I'm glad it was Jess, that he was my first," she says, her lips curving into a smile when we see him standing at the curb, waiting for her to pull in. "But you don't have to, you know?"

"But there have been so many. Haven't there? I mean, Owen and girls..." I say as she puts the car in park.

"Probably. But, really, what do I know? Maybe he just makes out and kisses, and that's it," she says, pausing in the quiet of her car for a few seconds before we both break into hysterical laughter. "Yeah, probably not!"

We both laugh hard while we gather our things, but my laughter dies down quickly, my thoughts going right back to that kiss, how it felt, and how different a boy like Owen is from the safety of group dates and school functions I was used to before.

I trail behind Willow and Jess along the walkway, and am about to step into the band room, when I notice someone sitting on the tables nearby. Owen's hands are wrapped around a paper cup steaming with coffee, his fingers poking through black cut-off gloves; a beanie is pulled over his dark hair.

"Kinda early today, aren't you?" I ask, my fingers instinctively moving to my hair, tucking it behind my ear—a nervous tick in his company, and my face is blushing at the sight of him. He looks up, his lips puckered while he blows over the top of the hot liquid in his cup, the steam making small swirls in front of his lips. The way they slide so naturally into a smile erases every tiny worry I let in during my car ride with Willow. The way his face lights up when he sees me—*when he sees me*—that's enough.

Right now, the way he looks right now, is enough.

"It was weird, I had these awful stomach pains, like someone…poisoned me," he teases, his eyebrows lowered while he stares at me, his legs stretching out slowly as he stands.

"Damn. You're on to us. My mother and I are black widows, with a trail of high school boys and men buried in yards all over Illinois," I say, finishing my last word just before Owen's arm sweeps me into his chest, the softness of his coat backed by the hardness of his body, every single inch of him warm.

"Kens, trust me, you buried me a long time ago," he says, his lips kissing the top of my head, his arm holding me tight to him. This is where I want to be for the rest of the morning. And I am his just a little more.

"I have to go to band," I groan, and he squeezes one last time before letting me go, the cool air wrapping around me the second his arm leaves my body. "I'm sorry."

"No, it's cool. I figured I'd just come early, see if I could see you," he says, and his cheeks—they actually blush. "I had to drop Andrew off early. He's doing this robotics thing."

"Oh," I say, my smile caught in my teeth, my tummy fluttering. "Will I be seeing you in class today, Mr. Harper?"

"Yes, Miss Worth. I will be attending class this week. In fact, I should be here every day, from now on," he says. "Sort of quit the job that tried to arrest me for paying for something," he says, his eyes gliding down my body, to my wrist, where my gift still circles my arm. I haven't taken it off since he gave it to me, even when my mom raised an eyebrow when I told her it was a gift from Owen.

"Is that going to mess things up for you? I mean, you said you needed the money," I say, worried about him.

"Yeah, we do," he says through a deep breath, cupping the back of my head and kissing my forehead before he begins to slide away from me. "But my mom's taking a break from school, so she's picking up a second job. I don't like it, but she wants me to focus on the rest of my year."

I'm hanging on the open door, Willow just out of view, watching my every move from inside, ready to make fun of me the second I close the door. "So I'll see you in a couple hours," I say, my fingers, my lips, my toes—every part of me tingling just watching Owen's eyes rake over me. His lip quirks on the side, the small dimple, the one I used to think seemed so arrogant, punctuating everything about him that makes me weak. Then he blows me a kiss before pulling his ear buds from his pocket and tucking them into ears and going back to his coffee.

"You...are in trouble, missy," Willow says, her head shaking at me, not quite in disapproval, as I close the door and move to my instrument.

"Yeah, I'm in pretty big trouble," I admit, enjoying every second of it.

We spend our morning band practice marching. Most of my time is spent practicing chords and new sheet music on the xylophone—wheeling it to the field to watch the rest of the band march, wheeling it back when we're done. My shoes are caked with wet, dead grass, so I spend my independent hour—the time I'm supposed to be practicing the piano—digging away the grass and mud. It's an excuse not to play. I don't even pretend it's anything but.

When Owen's feet are waiting on my desk, his pencil eraser pressed in-between his lips, his cocky smile underscoring the intensity of his eyes as they watch me move through the desks between the door and our row, I melt.

I melt.

I melt every time.

I don't bother to move his feet, instead sitting in my seat, resting my arm along the top of his ankle, enjoying the nearness of any part of him. I catch the stares from the others in the class. Most people take us in, dismiss us, and then move on. Others, girls who I've seen in the rotation, whisper and stare a little longer than most. But Owen never moves from our touch, and neither do I.

Every class is the same. And when it's time for lunch, Owen actually waits for me by the classroom door, walking by my side to the cafeteria. Just before I reach to open the door, his pinky grabs mine. I stop to notice, my eyes looking at the way our hands look together, my fingers shaking with nerves, until eventually Owen weaves his entire hand through mine, his grip leaving no doubt that this touch—it's intentional, and it isn't fleeting.

"You wanna skip lunch and head outside to make out in front of Willow and Jess?" I joke, really just a mask for how nervous I still am with him. Owen smiles and laughs once, but then he shakes his head, leans in, and kisses my cheek.

"Nah. I'd rather just *be* with you," he says, his eyes meeting mine, but looking down quickly as he pushes the brim of his hat lower. He's nervous, too.

We both pick out a few small things for lunch, and Owen follows me to the table, my friends all watching him sit next to me, take my tray for me, then open the tab on his soda.

After several long awkward silent seconds, Owen puts his soda back down on the table and wipes his hands along his jeans, drying them from the moisture from the can. He reaches across the table to Jess, his hand out for a shake.

"Hi. I'm Owen," he says, his eyes daring Jess to break, for the table to break and everyone to finally get over whatever it is they all seem to find weird. Jess takes over eventually, smiling back and shaking Owen's hand, laughing at himself.

"Sorry, we're band geeks. We lack social skills," Jess says, and Willow ribs him.

"Speak for yourself," she says.

"Especially this one. She's like *head* band geek, so...*ya know*," he says, grimacing and earning an even harder jab from Willow.

"Owwwww! Hey," he says, rubbing the spot she poked, looking up as Ryan slides behind him to his seat next to Elise.

"Hey, O. What's up?" Ryan says, his eyes setting on Owen's left arm, which is now around my shoulders, his fingers slowly scratching at my shoulder, possessively. "Ahhhh, never mind," Ryan adds, a quick wink before giving the rest of his attention to his lunch.

"You coming to practice today?" Ryan says, his mouth mumbling through a giant bite of his sandwich.

"Yeah, I should make them all now. Quit the job. Mom's getting a second, at least, for a while," Owen says, and I reach down and slide my hand over his knee, just wanting to let him know I know the depth of it all —how much his mom working, him working, is integral to his family.

"Cool. Hey, you should come watch, Kens," Ryan says, his eyes smirking when he mentions the invitation.

"Oh, no. She'd get bored," Owen says, and I can feel him stiffen next to me.

"No, I wouldn't. I love watching you play," I say, a little too quickly, the admission that I've watched him before, ever at all, falling out in front of everyone.

"You love watching me, huh?" he teases, his mouth slowly taking in a chip, crunching leisurely, while his smile slips back into place.

All I can do is stare back into his eyes, his eyes that are daring me to say anything different, to pretend and lie, and try to convince the rest of the table that I don't watch him. His eyebrows raise, and my face burns from the redness.

"Practice is at four," he says, his head falling to the side, and his look growing more adoring.

I melt. Every time.

"I'll take you home," he says. "And maybe tonight you can have dinner at my house."

"Okay," I say, smiling while my lips hug the straw for my juice drink, my body still burning from everyone's attention.

Willow doesn't ask any questions on our way to class, and after school, she only sends me a quick text, reminding me to *have fun but be careful,* and some picture of a basketball and a heart. She follows it up with a graphic of a condom, which mortifies me—so I spend the next five minutes looking for a picture of a middle finger to send to her.

My mom is working her night shift, so I don't even bother to text her, knowing she won't see it for the next several hours anyhow. I wander the empty halls, looking around for Owen or Ryan or even House, but everyone's gone. I give my backpack one final check, then slide it up over my shoulders and exit the main building.

I can hear the squeak of shoes as I near the gym, and when I open the door, I recognize Owen quickly. I slip through the front hallway to the side entrance and take a seat in one of the bleachers, near the end. A few parents are watching too, one of the dads standing at the front of the bleachers, yelling out things every now and then. It makes me chuckle to myself. It's not so different from my father standing behind me, watching my hands move along the piano keys. He used to shout things too.

Owen hasn't seen me yet, and I'm glad. He's being himself, his confidence something I envy. He's leading the other guys through drills, the ball always a little sharper, more controlled, when it's with him. It's strange to see him like this, dressed in shorts and a T-shirt with the sleeves torn away. His arms are more defined than I thought, probably because the last time I watched him play in my driveway, his shirt was off, and the only thing I could stare at was his stomach and chest.

He has a tight, black brace wrapped around one of his knees, and I remember him telling me he had surgery once. It doesn't seem to bother him as he glides effortlessly up and down the court, stopping on a dime, switching direction, moving the ball from one hand to the next and rolling it off his fingers near the rim. His touch is flawless.

The coach whistles, and all of the guys jog over for a water break. Ryan sees me first, and I smile, lifting my hand and waving close to my body, not wanting to be a distraction. He elbows Owen, and he looks over and winks, but his focus goes right back to his team.

For two hours, Owen runs. He never stops running. His body never once looks tired. I could watch him for hours, days maybe. He's clearly the best on the team, Ryan a close second, and the way he controls everything is mesmerizing. He shouts things, pushes other players in their chests, smacks their asses when they do something right and scolds them when they're wrong. And nobody ever questions him. They all want to please him—even the coach.

It's almost like they're afraid...

When practice is over, Ryan runs out from the locker room first, sitting next to me on the front step of the bleacher while he slips on his other shoes.

"Owen will be right out. He wanted me to tell you," he says, a faint smile on his face. Ryan doesn't show a lot of emotion, but I get the feeling he's rooting for Owen and me.

"Thanks," I say.

He nods once, finishes getting his shoes on, then starts to stand, stopping with his elbows on his knees. "You wanna know why I like Owen so much?" he says, his face slightly in my direction, his eyes looking at me from the side.

I nod.

Ryan looks toward the door, which is still closed, and leaves his focus there as he speaks. "Last year, my little brother tried to kill himself," he says, my breath leaves my body. "He's small. Like, really small—opposite of me in every way. It's not his fault. Something he was born with, just a weird mutation of our genes. The whole family is tall, like me. Jake, he's short. He's in eighth grade, and he's maybe four feet tall. Anyhow, some kids in his grade, they thought it'd be funny to nominate him for the king or whatever they call it at his junior high dance. That's the only reason he went, because he was nominated, and thought he might win something. So he goes, and he ends up winning, and he gets to dance with the prettiest girl, have his picture taken, all that shit."

Ryan turns to me for the rest of his story.

"My brother came home on cloud nine, thinking he was finally accepted. Then the next day, he found out that everyone voted for him to make that girl have to dance with him, because she had broken up with her boyfriend, the popular guy, and they wanted her to pay for it. They plastered her locker with pictures of her and Jake—with things written everywhere that said stuff like 'that's the best you can do now, bitch.' The girl was mortified, and she left school for the day, too embarrassed to stay."

"That's awful! Awful that someone would do that to both of them. Did they make fun of Jake, too?" I ask, my hand pressed to my cheek in disbelief.

"Now see, that's the thing. Nobody ever paid attention to him, said anything to him about it, teased him—nothing. It was almost as if he was invisible, just the tool for the prank. And being invisible…well, I guess that was worse. He came home from school, after a full day of being invisible, and then he swallowed a bottle of pills. My mom called me away from practice, and Owen had to drive me to the hospital."

"Owen stayed with me all night, brought my mom a change of clothes from his mom's closet the next day, and when my brother finally got to come home and go back to school, Owen showed up with a few of his friends, hung out on the basketball courts outside the school, made sure nobody said anything about the pills. Then he started taking Jake to school, picking him up with Andrew every morning. He hasn't missed a single day in over a year. Not once. Even when he has to work, and he's running late, and when I know he'd rather give the pretty girl who moved next door a ride. He shows up, at our front door, and my brother loves every fucking second of attention he gives him."

Ryan stands finally, his eyes back on the door, where Owen is finally exiting, talking to the coach, his bag slung over his back, his body dressed in his usual black jeans, black sweatshirt, black shoes—like a superhero in disguise.

"I like Owen so much because that dude has character—more character than any adult I've ever met. And the fact that he can do something like that, for a thirteen-year-old kid he doesn't even know that well, while he's got shit to deal with of his own…he's not what people say he is—but I get the feeling you know that," Ryan says, Owen now within hearing distance of us. Ryan smiles as he nods to Owen, who gives him a suspicious look. "See ya, Kens. I'll say hi to Elise for you."

"Was he hitting on you? Cuz, that shit ain't cool," Owen jokes. I shake my head *no* and stand on my tippy-toes, reaching up to kiss him softly, my entire body tingling with a new feeling for Owen Harper. I'm not sure what it is, but I think it might be pride.

I follow Owen to his truck, toss my bag in the seat between us, and buckle in. When he gets in on his side, he shakes his head and lifts my bag up, tossing it on the floor by my feet. "I love Gramps' truck, but your seat is way too far," he says, patting the seat next to him. I'll have to pull my knees up to my chest because of the hump in the floor, but the ride is short—and the few minutes of discomfort are well worth having Owen inches away.

"House said you were looking for me yesterday?" Owen mentions as he pulls us out of the school's parking lot.

"I was. I…I heard them out front playing basketball, thought it was you," I say, looking down at my knees. I'm not sure why I'm embarrassed, but I am.

"I like that you look for me," he says, leaning into me. I'm tempted to tell him *that's good, because I do it a lot.* But I keep that thought to myself; instead, taking my opportunity to steal glances at him while he drives. It's rare to see him without his head covered; he's always wearing a hat or beanie or his hood from his sweatshirt. I think it's like a blanket to him, gives him comfort. But right now, his hair is tasseled in all different directions, messy from his practice, damp with sweat, and possibly the sexiest thing I've ever seen.

That's the thing with Owen. He's...*sexy!* I've found boys cute before, attractive, and sometimes tall and strong, but never sexy. The thought of Owen running into one of the guys from Bryce makes me giggle—and the small noise I make catches his attention.

"What's funny over there, Ken Doll?" I smack his leg at the use of that nickname. "I'm kidding, kidding! Just wanted to get you back for whatever it is you think is funny about me."

"I don't think you're funny. I was just thinking you were...cute. I think you're cute," I say, keeping it safe, a notch less embarrassing than the truth.

Owen glances at me a few times, biting his lip, his eyes hazed and lowered. He's about to say something back when we pull into his driveway and notice two cars pulled in before him. He pulls the keys out, but holds them in his hand, his eyes on the vehicles in front of us.

"Mom's home," he says, his face oddly unhappy.

"Oh, should I...just go home? Or, is she okay with me coming over? I would love to meet her..." Owen hasn't moved, his posture rigid and his gaze stuck on something out the window. "Owen?"

"Oh, yeah...sorry. You should totally come in. She'd love to meet you. Andrew sort of talked you up, before I could. She'll love you," he says, his smile short of being real. I get the feeling it's masking something.

I pull my bag over my shoulder as I exit the truck and follow Owen up the steps of the front porch. He's about to turn the knob to the front door, when he just leans forward, his forehead resting on it and his sigh the kind that carries the weight of something serious.

"My brother's here, too," he says, and at first I think Andrew. But then I realize—he's talking about James. "I don't know what you're going to get, so just..." Owen rolls his head to the side until his eyes find mine. "Sorry... if this gets weird."

Almost every part of me wants to run, turn on my heels and sprint for the safety of my house. I play tough, and I've walked the line with Owen, but James—what I've imagined about James—scares me. My feet drag when he opens the door, and I consider my moment of hesitation, leaving, running, fleeing…Owen would understand. And then it flashes through my mind all at once—when Owen should have run away from me, when Gaby was confronting me, when my father was in my driveway banging on my door…he stayed.

He stayed.

Owen's house is immaculate. I don't know what I expected, but clean and bright wasn't it. Given that it's mostly Owen and Andrew at home alone, I thought things would be disorganized, maybe a little messy. I expected dark, and masculine.

"O? Is that you?" I hear a voice call from the direction of the kitchen. Owen's house is a mirror of mine, only where I have a piano setting he has an actual dining table.

"It's me, Ma," he yells back, his eyes moving around his house, searching. He's edgy.

"Good! I have a few hours before…" His mother rounds the corner and sees me, her step and speech both stuttering. She's tall, like Owen, and her frame is thin, like a woman who works long hours and never stops to eat. Her dark hair is pulled back into a ponytail, and she's wearing a security uniform, her feet only in socks.

"Mom, this is Kensi. She's our neighbor," Owen says, shrugging at me slightly, I think not wanting to offend me.

"Nice to meet you," I smile, stepping closer to her and reaching out my hand. She rubs both of her palms along her pants, then smiles faintly as she takes my hand in hers.

"Kensi, yes. I've heard about you. So nice to finally meet you. I'm Shannon. Is your family settling in okay?" Her eyes look to Owen for guidance, but he only raises his brows high. There really isn't an easy answer for this one, so I lie.

"Yes, we like it here," I say, leaving words like *parents, father* and *affair* out of the picture.

"I was going to have Kens stay for dinner. She treated me the other night, but I didn't know..." he stops there, letting his eyes speak the rest as they move beyond his mom to the living room where the television is blaring.

"No, please. Please stay, Kensi. We'd love to have you. And I was just ordering a pizza. It's not much, but I don't have a lot of time to cook, so... yes, please—I insist! What do you like? Pepperoni?" His mom is already dialing on her cellphone, her back to me, so I look to Owen, not sure what I should do.

"I can go. Really, it's okay," I whisper to him, and his eyes are telling me it's all right to leave. But then a new voice interrupts everything.

"Haaaaaa, look at you, baby brother. Is this your new girlfriend?" James says, his body filling the entire frame of the doorway between the formal living room and the family area. His hands stretch up to touch the ceiling, causing his shirt to raise and show how thin his stomach is. His hair and eyes are dark like Owen's, and his smile is equally tempting—a trait the Harper boys can use for good or evil at will, it seems. Unlike Owen, though, James seems to lack focus, his eyes wild and everywhere all at once.

"James." Owen's greeting is curt and callus, and I feel as uncomfortable as I knew I would the moment he told me his brother was here. Again, I want to run.

But I don't.

His brother holds Owen's stare, the two of them having a private conversation with their eyes—one I know isn't friendly. Eventually, James shrugs and turns to walk back to the family room and the television he has playing so loudly that the sound is distorting. Owen's mom motions for us to join James in the living room while she moves back into the kitchen, and Owen grabs my hand, stopping me before I take a step.

"You can go home. You don't have to stay here for me. This...this is my life, Kens. And you don't have to be here for this." His hold on my fingers is rough, but purposeful, and he's holding his breath, his nostrils flaring slightly while his pupils dial in on mine, begging me to leave. He thinks he's saving me.

"I'd like to stay," I say quietly, my eyes never flinching or leaving his. I want to run, my stomach sinking when I speak, but I can't leave him. I won't.

Owen swallows, taking a sharp breath in through his nose, then turns his attention back to the next room, his hand still linked with mine as he leads me into an older-looking room with family photos covering the wall. The frames are wooden and tattered, and the pictures of Andrew, Owen, and James seem to span most of their youth—stopping at what I'd guess to be four or five years ago. The back wall is a dark-wood paneling, and the television is propped on top of a coffee table that's pushed against the wall next to the bricked fireplace.

As old and dark as everything in this room seems, it's still clean, and it still feels like a home. James is sitting on a large orange sofa with wooden arms, his legs propped up on another table that's covered in magazines, keys, a wallet, and a gun.

There's a gun.

On the center of the table, an inch away from James's foot, there's a gun. It's black, and slick, and it looks like something a cop should be carrying. My body is reacting, a slow sweat building at the base of my neck, dripping deliberately down my sides, under my arms, my heart thumping wildly.

"Dude, put that away. Mom doesn't need to see that," Owen says, gesturing to the weapon. James studies him for a few seconds, his finger holding the tip of a toothpick that he's chewed into a bend, the other side locked in his mouth, mashed between his back teeth. Owen leans forward, his hand reaching for the gun, about to grab it, when James beats him to it, clutching it, his finger at the trigger. In a blink, the gun is pointed at Owen's neck, his brother standing in front of him, staring him down from inches away, his face threatening.

My breath. Is gone.

I open my mouth to scream, but nothing happens. My pulse is racing, and I'm looking around the room for someone, anyone. We're alone, Owen's mom just a room away.

She's only a room away! I'm trying to move my feet, to do something—anything—but I only end up with my back against the wall.

James's lips curve into a smile, and a slow, insane laugh starts to brew in his chest until it eventually explodes from his mouth. He cocks the gun back, away from Owen, and then tosses it back on the table, as if it were a remote.

"You're sick, and you need to leave," Owen says, his stance never once wavering—the gun having absolutely no effect on him, nor the fact that it was just pointed at his throat.

"Come on," Owen says, grabbing my hand and pulling me back through the house, through his front door, and down his porch steps. My body is shaking by the time we get outside, and I start to cry, cupping my mouth with my hand in an attempt to muffle the sounds.

"Shhhhhh, it's okay," Owen says, pulling me into his chest quickly, his hands wrapping around my head, his lips finding my bare skin along my face, his voice working to soothe me. "He's high. He's always high. And he needs money. That's why he's here. I'm so sorry you had to see that. My mom, she isn't supposed to let him in. But she's weaker than I am. That's why he came now. He knew I was gone."

"Owen, you have to do something. Call the police, something," I say, my suggestion met with a roar of laughter.

"Kens, that's a really good thought. But the cops don't come to my house when I call. They come for other people. The Harpers? They sort of *hope* we kill each other off," he says, and I shake my head in protest the entire time.

"No, they would come. Owen, let them help you," I start, but he pulls me to him tightly again.

"They don't come for things like this. And even if they did…" he says, pulling back to look in my eyes, "there's nothing they could do. He's either going to go away and get help one day, or James is going to die."

"No," I weep, shaking my head.

"Kens, my family's fucked up. I told you. Me? James? Even Andrew? We're all just these time bombs, waiting to see if we turn into our dad. James is just helping it along so he can get to the end faster."

Owen's words hurt. They hurt because I want more for him and Andrew, and they hurt because I know how true they are—I saw it, seconds ago. My chest is tight, and it's becoming harder to breathe.

"Do me a favor," Owen says, his eyes looking up, above my head. I turn to follow his sightline; he's staring at my window. "Go home. Get inside, lock up, and sit by your window."

"No, Owen. Come with me," I say, but he shakes my arm, my hands cupped in his, urging me to listen.

"I'm going to make him leave, Kens. He won't hurt me; I've been here—I've *done* this. And when he's gone, I'll go there," he says, pointing to his window, "and I'll find you."

Every time I shake my head *no,* Owen counters with a *yes,* until finally, I'm walking away from him. I look over my shoulder every few steps, and he doesn't leave his spot until I reach my door.

"Wait for me," he says, and I clutch the strap of my heavy backpack, dragging it inside with me and locking the door behind me immediately. I don't even move it away from the doorway, abandoning it, and racing up my stairs to my window, getting there just in time to see Owen step inside.

I'll wait for you.

I'm waiting for you.

I hold my breath for minutes at a time, my head against the glass of my window, my eyes checking every door and window of the Harper house, waiting for any movement, any sound, or new light or shadows. It stays dark, just as dark as it always is—and nothing happens. Thirty minutes go by, and there isn't a single sound. I text Owen, asking him if he's okay, and I keep my phone close to my chest, waiting for his reply.

Ten more minutes—*nothing.*

Ten more.

Nothing.

My finger hovers over the emergency call button, knowing that if I called—if I said there was trouble at the Harper house—they'd come.

I'm waiting for you, Owen. Please...please come to your window.

The sound of Owen's front door outside scares me, and I bump my head on the glass in my reaction. James is practically jogging down the porch steps, his long strides the same as his brother's, and he pushes his hat low while he swings the door to his small sedan open. Within seconds, he's racing down the road, and my eyes wait for Owen to appear.

When his light flicks on, I let out a small cry from everything I've been holding in, and when he raises the blinds and swings his curtains out of the way completely—I bite my lip and smile. This isn't a flirtatious kind of smile, but rather one of deep relief. Seeing him, after the feeling I got when

I saw his brother push a gun in his face, scratches something new inside me, something deep.

I hold my hand up, pressing it to the glass, and Owen sits down in front of his window, leaning forward, resting his head on his hands along the windowsill. We stare at each other like this for minutes, and I rub away the frost on the glass at least twice.

Keeping my eyes on Owen, I slide my phone into my lap, then look down quickly to type him a message.

Want to talk about it?

His response comes a few seconds later.

I think I just want to look at you for a while.

I put my hand back against the glass, this time Owen doing the same, and I stay there, for an hour, looking at him looking at me. And I'm terrified—afraid of what happened tonight, of everything I saw and of the thought that James might come back.

And I'm afraid I'm losing myself to danger—the worst kind, the kind that rules your heart.

I'm falling for Owen Harper, and I'm afraid he's going to die.

CHAPTER 14

The chatter downstairs stirs me awake. My mom's voice is somewhere between normal and a whisper, which can only mean one thing—my father's here.

I'm awake and sitting up in seconds, but I'm not so sure I want to face that much drama this early in the morning. The moon is out, the sun still a half hour from rising. The sky has seemed darker lately, winter bringing a thick layer of darkness that takes over the starts and ends of every day.

My alarm will sound soon, so I push the clock button to at least spare myself the noise of morning DJs that are far too peppy to be real. I grab my jeans, a long-sleeved undershirt and my favorite T-shirt, a black one that reads Mozart Would Have Loved Miles Davis. It's a test day, and I'm feeling unlucky. Actually, I'm feeling unprepared—so I'm going to need all of the superstitious things in my life to align. And clearly, my morning isn't starting off on the right note.

My shower is hot, but the water runs out far too quickly, so I towel dry before my skin has a chance to get cold, drying my hair and scrunching the curl into it. I pull a knit hat over the crown, keeping the little part of my hair that's still wet warm, then I take a deep breath and force myself to go downstairs.

I'm pleasantly surprised when I'm greeted by Owen's back, his feet propped atop the footrest on the stool by the counter, my mom's coffee mug cradled in his hand. Everything pleasant turns to anxiety, though, when my mom makes an obvious detour in the conversation, coughing to announce my entrance into the room.

"Ohhhh, you're up early. Good morning, Kens. You want some bacon? I made some for Owen, and there's some left; it's still warm." She's already putting it on a plate and pushing buttons on the microwave. Owen smiles at me, leans forward, and presses his lips to my cheek while my mom's back is to us.

She made him…bacon?

"Why are you here?" I whisper, my voice quiet but not quiet enough to keep my mom from craning her neck slightly at my question. She's spying.

"I was awake early; Mom left for work, and I couldn't get back to sleep. Didn't want to wake Andrew up yet, so I was waiting on your porch," he says.

"I found him out there," my mom says, topping off Owen's coffee cup —*her* coffee cup, which she gave to him. This is all so….

"Thanks," he nods, taking another drink. The two of them hold each other's eyes, something strange passing between them, but I can't tell if it feels like bad news.

"Have you heard from your brother?" I ask as soon as my mom is out of earshot. Owen only shakes his head *no.*

"I've gotta get Andrew moving," he says, sliding his half-filled mug over to me to finish. I smell it, and can tell it's strong—I drink my coffee with more milk than coffee. I stand to pour it in the sink, then turn to walk Owen to the door, but my mom is already showing him out, thanking him for something.

When she comes back in, she's humming—*humming.*

"What's going on?" I ask, that uneasy feeling too much to ignore.

"Well, I'm dog tired, and I have forty-eight hours off, so I'm planning on napping until about noon, then I'm in for a marathon of HGTV to see if I can turn this kitchen reno into something other than a condemned piece of property," she says, laughing at her mildly funny joke.

"I meant with Owen. What's going on…with Owen?" I ask, and she purses her lips, tilting her head in that way she does when she's trying to buy herself time. My mother has a hard time being anything but honest, and when I think back on it, I realize she tilted her head when she told me we were moving, when she said she was excited about it, and when she told me I'd love my new school just as much as Bryce.

"You know what, never mind. I don't want to know," I decide. If whatever she's keeping to herself is anything like the crap that's unraveled on me over the last six weeks, then I don't want to know; I'm better off not knowing. She can go back to humming.

What's weird though is how quickly she lets me off the hook, how quickly she actually does go back to humming.

I pull my science book out and spend the next twenty minutes cramming for my test, keeping with my theme of only doing lucky things for the rest of the morning. Studying has to be lucky.

Willow's early; I thank my karma for being able to leave the house of weirdness behind. I kick myself though when I realize I'm only getting into a car with a person who's going to interrogate me for the next ten minutes.

"So, how was practice and dinner with the Harpers? You never called, and I was up all night waiting for that phone to buzz, you bitch," Willow says, pushing her glasses tighter to her face with the tip of her finger.

"You're so bad at playing tough," I say, fighting off laughter at the way she said the word *bitch*.

"Am not! Now, don't disrespect me, or I'll cut you, *bitch*," she says, unable to say it with a straight face a second time.

"Yeah, you're one scary-ass mother," I say, my words dripping with sarcasm. "I think it's the rhinestones on the wings of your designer glasses. Yeah, uhm...I'm pretty sure that's it, the mark of a true bad-ass."

"Shut up, my contact ripped, and these are all I have," she says. "Now, how was dinner?"

"We never really made it to dinner," I say, my throat closing at the memory of the night before. I can tell by the look Willow's making that she thinks we detoured from dinner for a different reason—and as nervous as I am about being intimate with Owen, I would have given anything for that to have been the reason we didn't make it to dinner last night.

"Owen's mom was home," I say, clearing her innuendo out of the way quickly. "And James showed up."

"Oh, shit!" she says, giving me her full attention while we wait at the stoplight in front of the school.

"Yeah, it was...well, let's just say those rumors you mentioned seem to be pretty damned accurate," I say, not sure how much about last night I should share. I think I can trust Willow, but still, it isn't really *my* story to tell. I never liked gossip, and Owen's kept my dad's affair to himself.

When Owen's truck is parked in the lot, waiting in the spot next to Willow's usual one, I'm hit with a smothering sense of relief, and I know it's because of how scared I was the night before.

"Well, it looks like you're doing a pretty good job at turning those Owen Harper rumors around," Willow says, her eyebrows lifted above the dark blue rims of her glasses. I suck in my bottom lip, but I let my smile slip through. If I am somehow this exception to the Owen Harper rule, I'm going to appreciate the role, cherish it, and cling to it.

Owen isn't in his truck, but his long legs come into view at the same table he was waiting at the day before. I admit to myself that I was looking for him—I was anticipating him, even before we pulled into the school's parking lot.

I was wishing for him.

"I feel like maybe we were a little rushed this morning," he says, standing and moving toward me, his thumbs looped in his front pockets, his gray jeans hugging his hips, the material gathering at his shoes.

"Why do you always wear your hoodie or a hat or something? Like you're hiding your identity?" I say, pulling the gray and black striped hood away from his messy hair so I can run my fingers through it. It's something I've been dying to do, and Owen watches my face as I let my hands find their way, feeling the soft waves of his hair, gripping the thickness. He lets his face fall to one side, resting on my arm, his unshaven jaw scratchy, but his lips soft and tender when they kiss my skin.

"Well, if I knew you had a thing for hair, I would have ditched the hat a long time ago," he says, half a smirk underscoring his hooded eyes.

"Just your hair," I say, lifting up on my toes to kiss him good morning in a way I couldn't do in front of my mom.

"People used to look at me...*stare* at me. When I was a kid, after my dad..." he says, hand reaching up and running through his hair once before reaching for the hood to put it back in it's place. "I started covering my head to hide. Sounds stupid, but I felt like people saw a little less of me. And habits stick, I guess."

Owen hides. I can't fault that, especially when I have thought so often of hiding myself lately. I reach under his hood once more, running my fingers through the side of his hair and pulling his cheek to me. "I'm okay with being the only one who gets the boy without the hood," I say.

"Ha..." he laughs, but quickly covers his mouth in apology, rubbing his chin and trying to tamper his grin. "Sorry, it was something about the thought of *you under my hood.* For the record, I still think it's funny when people say *balls* too. Guys are all ten-year-olds at their core."

"Clearly," I say, pushing his chest once before I leave. He falls back on his feet, pretending to stumble, but catches his balance quickly and winks at me before turning to walk away.

"See ya in class, Ken Doll," he says, turning around to stick his tongue out once.

"You are such a ten-year-old," I yell. He turns and walks the long way back around the building, and I watch him until he's out of my sight. I love the way he looks.

I've enjoyed the last few mornings of band practice. Apparently, we compete. And apparently, we also win—our trophy case is twice the size of the football team's. It's just in the music room, where nobody can see it.

We've been practicing our show to make it perfect, and I've added a few more instruments to my duties, offering to play the tympani drums and chimes to really sell our closing song. It gives me more things to practice, more things to distract me from my hour of independent study, more things to keep my hands away from the piano—off the keys that haunt me.

Owen's feet are in their rightful place during English, but his head is covered with a hat, his hood pulled completely over it, only his chin visible —that and the wise smirk on his lips.

"Very funny," I say, shoving his feet to the side. His laugh catches quickly, and when the teacher walks in, he's quick to pull his hood down and toss his hat on the floor underneath his desk. It's strange—at school, Owen is always respectful to the teachers.

We're discussing illusions from our reading today, talking about whether or not the main character of *Crime and Punishment* is actually good or evil, and how to spot the signs that tell us what to think. Everyone in the class is so quick to condemn Raskolnikov—convicting him without any chatter. I plan on playing devil's advocate. I'd like to think that it's my academic need to think deeper that spurs me to speak up, to interrupt the hanging ceremony everyone's so quick to have. But I kind of think it's more than that.

"But what about his intentions?" I ask, only one or two students really hearing my question over the debate. Mr. Chessman hears too, and soon raises his hand to quiet everyone down.

"Miss Worth, what was your point? I think the class needs to hear this," he says, and I can feel everyone turn to stare at me.

"Uhm," I say, adjusting my posture in my seat, wrapping my fingers around the top of my desk. More than the class's attention, I feel Owen's—my stomach pounding to the rhythm of my heart. "I was just thinking, we're not really considering Raskolnikov's intentions. We're prosecuting him based on the rules, based on laws. But is it really that simple?"

"Interesting," Mr. Chessman says, leaning on his desk and holding his hand to his chin. "Class?"

"It doesn't matter what his intentions were, he murdered someone. The rules are black and white, and he knew them. Case done, piece of cake," says Cal Russell, one of the more outspoken guys in our senior class. Cal won homecoming king, and he's had the same girlfriend for two years—she happened to win queen. It was all *so very* surprising when they won, according to Willow.

"That's a very narrow view," I say, my foot bouncing under my desk, my temper—one of the trait's I inherited from my father—trying to find a way out.

"Is it?" Mr. Chessman asks. "Explain, Miss Worth. I'd like the class to hear your thought process on this. I think this is opening up a great discussion."

Awesome. More talking, which is probably going to lead to more arguing. And I can no longer hear Owen's breathing behind me. His shoe is resting against the foot of my seat, though, so I know he's still here.

"Well," I say, taking a deep breath and thumbing through a few pages of my book. "Yes, you can say it's premeditated, or whatever, because we read those chapters where he *thought* about the crime before committing it. But..."

"But what? You just said it right there, he *thought* about it, and still did it!" Cal says.

"Stop interrupting!" I say, too loudly. Temper winning. "Sorry," I say a little more quietly. "Let me finish. He thought about it, and we got to read his thoughts. We know that he found good reason, he put the options on the scale, to see if the world was a better place with or without his crime, and he concluded, after *much thought,* that yes...the world would be better if he committed this crime."

"Murder. Not a crime, but *murder!"* Cal says.

"Yes, murder—in this case. But, I think as readers we need to think of the larger message," I say, my voice gaining strength. I've read this book a dozen times, and I know my argument well. Cal isn't going to break me. "There's a reason that, despite committing murder, the reader still loves the protagonist. What Dostoyevsky did was paint a portrait of the most heinous crime he could think of, yet open our minds to the possibility that perhaps the criminal isn't so black and white, that maybe we judge without really seeing *everything."*

"How can you *possibly* know the facts, know that he murdered someone, and sit there and defend him?" Cal says, turning his feet to face me in his seat, he's trying to intimidate me, and my heart is pounding faster. I think it's working.

"I'm not defending Raskolnikov, I'm defending the idea that we ignore other facts and judge people based on what we think is convenient," I fire back.

"That's ridiculous," he says, rolling his eyes and moving to turn his attention back to our teacher.

"No...it's not," Owen says, his voice behind me that familiar tone, the one he uses when he reveals things. Just the sound of it breaks me a little and fills me with confidence and pride all at once.

"Mr. Harper? Care to expound?" Mr. Chessman says, his eyebrows raised ever so slightly, his mouth a small smirk. He likes Owen; I can tell.

I hear Owen clear his throat and shift in his seat, so I turn my head to the side, letting my eyes see him from a periphery. His head is down, and he's sucking in his top lip while he thinks.

"What Kensi's saying is that we sum people up based on a small set of facts, and we use those facts and apply them to every action, every case, every word a person says," he says. I tuck my chin low, trying to hide the smile he's building on my face. "And when you're so quick to convict someone, you run the risk of ignoring their innocence."

There's a quiet over the room, and Cal spends a few seconds looking at Owen, hard. His focus shifts to me and then to our teacher, then back to Owen, and it's when he's chewing his bottom lip, sawing on it, his thoughts right on the tip of his tongue, that I know he's going to fire a bullet.

"You mean like the way we all just assume you're a piece of shit because you stole a car, robbed a store at gunpoint, and then held that same gun to your own head later that night just to prove you're nuts just like your old man?"

Cal only has enough time to find his balance and get to his feet before Owen is in front of him, his hand gripping the fabric of his shirt collar, his weight pushing him backward until his body hits the wall with a heavy thud. Owen forces him into the wall twice, just to make sure the air completely clears his lungs, then twists his hand around Cal's shirt, choking him before finally releasing.

Mr. Chessman's hand is on Owen's back within seconds, and Owen lets the crumpled shirt fall back in place along Cal's chest. Before he steps away, he stares long and hard, his nose practically touching Cal's, he's so close. "Exactly," he says, his eyes dark, his breathing ragged—and his fingers flexing, wanting to destroy.

"That's enough, Owen. You know where to go," he says, his head tilted slightly to one side, his expression caught somewhere between pride and disappointment.

"Yeah, I know," Owen says, turning to leave the class. As he passes me, he drags one finger along the length of my desk, brushing my fingertips as he passes. But he never looks down at me. The door swings open wildly, banging into the hallway wall.

"Cal?" Mr. Chessman says, his eyes falling on the smug blonde asshole still straightening his shirt at the front of the classroom.

"What, me? Are you serious? He attacked me!" Cal defends.

"Yes, but you also broke the rules...and what was it you said?" Mr. Chessman's smile shows again. "Ah, yes...they're black and white. Case done. Piece. Of. Cake."

He pushes a pink slip into Cal's chest at his last word, then motions for him to leave the room. Cal grumbles a few swear words as he leaves, and when he reaches my desk, he gives me a look that proves he's already summed me up, too, just by my relationship with Owen. I'm pretty sure I can sleep at night knowing I don't have Cal Russell in my corner. Maybe I'm making my own snap judgments, but I'm pretty sure he's the dark side in this one.

"Well..." Mr. Chessman says, leaning back to sit along the edge of his desk. His arms folded in front of him. "Kensi brings up a very good point, despite the debate we had just a few minutes ago. I'd like you all to think about that as you finish the next three chapters, and come prepared to discuss—*without* fisticuffs—tomorrow."

The bell rings only minutes later, and the rest of the class quickly goes back to their routine, everyone chatting about lunch plans, weekend dates, parties. I wait for the classroom to clear before gathering my things and heading for the door.

"For the record, Miss Worth," Mr. Chessman says, stopping me just before I open the door. "I think you made a *very* valid point."

My breathing suddenly feels easier, and I let my smile respond for me, then open the door and move into the crowded hallway. It's lunch, and I know Willow, Jess, Elise and Ryan will be wondering where I am, but I have to make sure Owen is okay. I dodge backpacks and elbows through the busy hallway until I see the glass door of the principal's office swing open, Owen stepping through, his own pink slip crumpled in his hand, his eyes still dark, angry.

"Are you okay?" I ask, walking up to him, my steps coming quicker. He grabs my hand fast, his grip on my fingers tight, almost painful, and pulls me behind him through the thick crowd in the hall until we reach the back door, near the loading zone for the cafeteria. He pushes down hard, forcing the door open, then pulls my arm, leading me around a corner to a line of recycling bins.

"I'm so sorry..." I start, but Owen's hands find me fast, his fingers wrapping around my shoulders, his force moving me back until I'm flush with the wall, and then his lips crash down on me.

His hands slide from my shoulders to my neck and into my hair, his mouth covering mine as if he needs my air to breathe, and he closes the small distance between us, the warmth and hardness of him pressing into my body, my hands operating on their own instinct, finding his sides and back until I'm clinging to him, grabbing bunches of his black sweatshirt all at once.

Owen's hand moves to his head while he's kissing me, and he tosses his hat to the ground to the side of us, and I let my fingers move to his hair, weaving the strands in and out, letting the softness of them curl around me.

This is the best kiss of my life. Every kiss with Owen has been the best kiss of my life. But this one—it's full of something more. His lips work mine for long seconds, his tongue passing over mine slowly, his teeth dragging over my bottom lip, my top lip, tugging on me and pulling me into him even deeper. I can feel his heartbeat through his shirt, and I let my hands roam over his chest and around his back again, the feel of him exactly as it is every time I dream.

He finally pauses, his mouth still resting on mine, his lips barely parted as they struggle for air. Owen's eyes are closed, and his forehead is resting on mine, his thumbs still gently caressing my cheeks.

"I...," he says, his breath stuttering, his lips quivering, his body relaxing into me. His head falls heavier into mine, and I can actually feel his entire body shaking.

Owen doesn't finish the sentence, instead kissing me again with the same intensity as before. For the entire lunch hour, his lips work mine until they're practically raw; when the bell rings to resume class, he pulls my hands up to his lips, clasped tightly within his, and he kisses them once before pressing them to the side of his face, looking at me with eyes that have cleared, eyes that aren't full of rage and hate.

I'M honest with Elise when she asks where I was.

"Making out with Owen," I say, and she laughs, but it soon fades when she realizes I'm serious. Our conversation is short, cut off by the bell to begin class. I notice Owen isn't in here, that he never came after our last kiss behind the school. He said he'd see me later, and I was too stunned to register or even ask what that meant.

Our teacher passes out our tests, and I notice that she sets one aside and write's Owen's name on it. Despite my lack of studying, I finish mine quickly, somehow pulling mostly correct answers from the depths of my brain.

When the ending bell rings, I don't wait for Elise, my mind still reeling from Owen, his kiss, how I felt—how *he* felt. Then it turns to wondering where he is, wondering if he's okay, to Cal—to the things Cal said.

"You look like an actual ghost," Willow says when I meet her at her car.

"Yeah...I feel like one," I say, my eyes not really able to focus on anything, too busy looking for Owen, for answers. I climb into her passenger seat and buckle up, and I feel her gaze on me as she buckles, then starts her engine. We get to the light at the school exit, where we wait for cars to pass so we can pull out on the road, before I'm able to articulate anything.

"Did Owen really commit an armed robbery?" I ask, and Willow takes a deep breath, never really saying anything, but letting her silence answer for her. "And he stole a car?"

I wait while Willow's brow pinches, her lips pursing in thought. "I only know what I heard, Kens. I...I've never been very close to him. But, yeah... that's what I heard."

"And the gun..." I start, and her eyes widen quickly, then just as fast relax again. She's trying to keep her emotions in check, trying to make *this* not a big deal for me.

"Will, did Owen *really* put a loaded gun to his head? Did he really do that?" I ask, my stomach feeling punched, inside and out, at the thought of Owen doing any of those things—mostly the last.

"Again, Kens...I only know what I've heard. I've heard the same things you've heard. But I wasn't there. I don't know for sure. But I bet..." she starts, pausing for a deep breath as we turn down the street to my house. "I bet if you asked him, he'd tell you the truth."

When we pull into my driveway, there's an older-looking Volvo station wagon sitting near the back door of the house, nobody inside.

"Company?" Willow asks.

"I've never seen that car before in my life," I say, my gut feeling sick.

"Want me to, I don't know...wait? Or come in with you? You know, in case it's..." She's worried it's my dad.

"Dean wouldn't drive such a thing," I say, my mouth relishing at calling my father by his given name, forgoing any relationship he has with me.

We both step out of her car and move closer to the Volvo, when my mom and Owen step through the back door of the house, my mom holding a set of keys on her index finger.

"Happy birthday, Kensington. I was thinking maybe we put that license of yours to use," my mom says, and I look to Owen, who's smiling and shrugging behind her, his hands deep in his pockets, his hat turned backward.

"Shut up, it's your birthday?" Willow asks, shoving my shoulder once, kind of hard.

"Not until Saturday," I say, my eyes focused only on Owen's, on the sweetness of them, the love in them.

"On Halloween? That's awesome. Oh my god, we should totally have a party. I mean, like...an appropriate party," Willow says, putting on a fake voice of responsibility for my mom.

"You can all come here. I'm off that day, and I'll make a big dinner. We can carve pumpkins," my mom says, stopping right in front of me and pulling my hand up in hers, transferring the keys. "What do you think, Kens? Sound good?"

I smile and nod. "That sounds great," I say, looking at the small music note key ring in my hand, the lone Volvo key hooked on it. "Thanks, Mom."

I reach for my mom, hugging her tightly, my eyes still finding Owen behind her.

"Thank Owen, too. I couldn't have done this without him," she says, confirming what I'd already figured out on my own. "I didn't want to get ripped off, since I don't know a thing about cars. He went to the dealer with me, made sure everything was working right."

Stepping by my mom, I move closer to Owen, my throat closing up with all of the things I want to say to this boy that I…I love, my god do I love with so much of myself. I'm so afraid of everything, of what people say, of what Cal said, but I also don't care because standing here in front of me, looking at me like he is, I know in my heart that Owen is good.

Owen is *good.*

In front of my mother, in front of my new best friend, I stand on the tips of my toes and kiss him lightly, pulling my face away from his before anyone notices, before anyone sees. And I whisper.

"I see you," I say.

Owen's eyes…they respond.

CHAPTER 15

I honestly think Gaby is trying to make me hate my own birthday. There's no other reason for her to do what she did.

A Facebook message would have been simple—an email, simpler. A text, something I could easily ignore, delete without reading. What Gaby's done is far more about Gaby than about my birthday. This package—the one I've been sitting on my bed with, staring at, since about seven this morning—is a Trojan horse.

The knock on the door was faint, but I heard it. I was awake, listening for the sound of Owen's truck, waiting for him to be awake too. Instead, the only other person awake at this hour near my home was whoever left this package on my doorstep.

I *know* it was Gaby.

There was no return address, only my name and house number. More than suspicious—it was obvious. Yet, I brought it inside with me anyhow. I tried *not* to open it. But I've never been good at ignoring impulses. The pull —it was just too much. I had to know what was inside.

Digging my nails into the taped sides, I pulled the flap of the cardboard free, then pulled out the layers of tissue paper hiding my gift. I recognized the dress as soon as I saw the blue fabric of the sleeve. I've coveted Gaby's blue Alexander McQueen dress since the day her mother bought it for her.

She let me wear it to one of my performances, and it was the one that caught the attention of recruiters from Tisch and Julliard. She never let me borrow it again—and now, part of me thinks she was jealous of the attention I received when I wore it.

Gaby was always in it for our school dances our junior year. And now, sitting here, looking at it resting in crumpled tissue paper—in a nondescript brown box, borrowed from something else—I can't help but wonder if she wore it for my father.

"I'm going to burn you," I say to myself, to the dress, a small smile inching up my lips.

There's a letter in the box—a letter I have no intention of reading. I don't even bother to tear the small seal on the envelope; instead I stuff the letter into the crinkles of the tissue paper surrounding the dress.

The incessant faint knock that's happening at my door again feels different this time, and I welcome being pulled away from Gaby's sad attempt to erase the damage she did to our friendship. I toss the box to the floor, leap to my feet, and patter down the stairs quickly, opening the door to a rush of cool air and faint flakes of snow falling behind Owen.

"Looks like it's a white birthday for you," he says, his hands held behind his back awkwardly. I step up on my toes and kiss his cold lips, then tug him into my house by the collar of his shirt. "So pushy," he teases.

"What's behind your back," I say, pulling on his elbow now.

"Wow, you are like...*all about* the presents, aren't you?" he says, his playful smile curling one end of his mouth as he unwraps his neck from his scarf.

"Maybe," I smirk. "Now, gimme, gimme, gimme!"

I pull the bag from his hand and rush to the kitchen with it, Owen trailing behind me, his feet dragging and his hand running along his chin. "I was kind of hoping you would open it later," he says, his brow pulled in as he looks from me to the front door and back again. "I saw Willow pulling up out front, and now just feels weird..."

He trails off, his shoulders slumped, and his spirit deflated. He's embarrassed, and as much as I'm dying to crack open the bag with his gift, the fact that giving it to me *alone* is important to him means a hell of a lot more.

"Okay, I'll put it in my room. Won't peek; I promise!" I say, crossing my heart and zipping past Owen in my socks, gliding along the floor and up the stairs. When I get to my room, the box with the blue dress immediately confronts me, and its presence pisses me off. I kick it under my bed, and then pull my comforter down on the side, completely hiding it from my view.

The doorbell rings loudly as I set Owen's gift in its rightful spot atop my pillow. I race back downstairs, trying to reach the door before Willow has a chance to push the bell again, but I'm too slow.

"Jesus Christ, you're impatient," I say, flinging the door open to a shivering group of four.

"It's cold. My hand slipped," Willow says, somehow still managing to pop a bubble between her lips despite the rapidly dropping temperature on my porch.

"My mom was sleeping in," I explain, before my mother cuts me off and finishes for me.

"She *was.* She's up now," my mom says through an irritated yawn. "Who wants pancakes?"

"Oh, do you have more of that bacon?" Owen says, surprisingly not shy. I'm a little less upset about the bacon-sharing with my mother now that I know their early morning meeting was all about getting me a set of wheels for my birthday.

"You got it. I'll grill up the rest of it," my mom says, winking at Owen. My belly grows warm seeing her accept him so completely.

Willow, Jess, Elise, and Ryan start slipping out of their coats and hats and gloves in my front room, leaving a pile of winter clothing gathered around our front door, and this scene makes me even happier. I love their mess.

"We're still carving pumpkins, right? We *have* to carve pumpkins! I brought my tools and everything," Elise says, and I can't help but quirk an eyebrow at her odd pumpkin fascination.

"It's her favorite holiday. And she's kind of a bad-ass pumpkin carver," Ryan says, shrugging.

"All right then, pumpkins it is!" I say, looking over Elise's shoulder, out the window that is growing frostier by the second.

"Oh, don't worry about that snow. It's not real snow. It's supposed to stop in an hour or two and clear out until next week," Elise says, very insistent that weather does not detour us from our pumpkin mission.

"It's just going to be freezing-ass cold. Awesome time to walk around a field and pick up wet pumpkins," Jess says, rubbing his eyes as he passes me and heads straight for the pot of coffee brewing on the counter. "Can we stop this mid-cycle so I can get a cup now?"

"Seriously? Can't wait the full minute it takes to drip?" Owen says, sliding into the stool next to the counter, pulling me to him so I'm standing between his long legs.

"I'm not pretty without caffeine, yo," Jess says, causing Ryan and Owen to bust out laughing.

"Dude, don't talk like a gangster. You can't pull it off," Ryan says.

"It's the lack of caffeine. It makes me say crazy shit," Jess says, pulling the pot from the machine the moment it stops dripping, filling his cup and blowing forcefully into his mug, working to cool the liquid fast.

"You talk to anyone about this addiction of yours?" Owen says, smirking at Jess as his jittery hands work to tilt the cup up for his first, sloppy gulp.

"Like you should talk about addiction," Jess mumbles, his eyebrows shooting up as soon as he fully realizes the words that left his lips. Owen's arms grow rigid around me, and I know without looking his expression is cold. "I'm sorry man. That was crappy to say. I'm tired and grumpy. Totally uncalled for," Jess says, pulling one hand away from his mug and reaching to shake Owen's hand. Jess's face looks honest and regretful, but I hope Owen can see it too.

While it only takes him a few seconds to accept Jess's apology and shake his hand, those few seconds feel long and ominous. And even after he tells Jess that it's "no big deal," his arms remain tight and his body on guard. I know that it was a *very* big deal, and that one tiny sentence is going to sit on his conscience for most of the morning.

We all devour our breakfast, soaking our pancakes in butter and syrup and stuffing our cheeks until we're all equally sick from the sweetness of the syrup and the richness of bacon. As Elise promised, the small snow flurries have disappeared by the time we're done helping my mom load the dishwasher, and soon we're all pulling on the mountain of winter clothing we left in the pile by the door.

"Make sure you get one for me," my mom says, handing me a hundred dollar bill, urging me to pay for everyone's pumpkin. My father was always stingy with money, never wanting to pay for things with my friends. He wouldn't even buy Gaby and Morgan's museum tickets the times we went in the city. Just one more thing I think about differently now.

"I'm driving," Willow announces as we all pile onto the porch in our heavy boots and coats.

"I'm out. Who's with me?" Owen says, and Ryan is the first to raise his hand, stepping next to his friend.

"Hey!" Willow protests.

"Will, your driving scares the shit out of me in the summer. If I have a second option when there's a chance for snow, I'm taking it," Ryan says back quickly, and I notice Willow shakes her head, a little stunned by his honesty.

"You know you could drive yourself to school in the morning, asshole," she says, her eyes squinting, trying to mask how upset she really is.

"Oh, it doesn't scare me so much that I want to drive my dad's piece-of-shit car. You're still safer than that," he says, and this seems to make her feel better.

"Well all right then," she says, leading the way as we walk down my front steps and toward the street out front. "You know he's not that safe either, though, right?"

"This guy? Hell, he's never had a crash," Ryan says, pointing to Owen, whose hands are buried in his pockets, his hood pulled up over his head and his arms stiff with the wool material of his black overcoat. Owen only rolls his eyes, then pulls his keys from his pockets, urging me to ride with him as well. I go willingly, but for different reasons.

We pile into Owen's truck, and Elise and Jess climb into Willow's car; we head a few miles to the outskirts of town where one of the farmers still has a stand open for fall goods. The pumpkin selection is a little picked over, but we all settle on a few decent-sized ones, and before anyone can protest, I hand the money to the cashier.

"My mom insisted. Part of my birthday present," I say, smiling and enjoying the feeling of treating friends to something—even though it may be trivial.

By the time we get home, my mom has moved a few of the cardboard boxes out to the kitchen floor, where she's cut them open for our carving mess. When I was little, my mom and I used to make a pumpkin for our balcony every year. But that tradition sort of just faded away—forgotten among the other things in life that got in the way. I picked an extra large pumpkin just so she and I could create something together, and when I nod for her to join me, I notice her eyes tear up a little with her smile.

"So, this is gross," Willow says, pulling the lid from her pumpkin, long, gooey strings trailing from the bottom.

"You know there's more inside, right?" Elise says, reaching into hers with both hands, digging her nails in, and scooping a handful of the pumpkin insides onto the cardboard next to Willow.

"Oh my gaaaaaaah," Willow says, bringing her arm completely around her face, smothering her nose. "It smells…so bad."

"You are such a baby," I say, reaching into Willow's pumpkin and pulling out a scoop for her. I let it plop onto the cardboard, splattering some seeds and strings onto Willow's jeans.

"I think I'm out," she says, standing, her nose still buried in her sleeve.

"I'll clean yours for you," I say, and she lifts her arm up long enough to show me her grin and to raise her thumb in approval.

It doesn't take long to understand why Elise likes carving so much. I've managed to create a pretty spooky-looking set of teeth, and Owen's carved his into a series of triangles to form a face—sort of. Elise's pumpkin, however, is straight out of the set for *Sleepy Hollow,* a headless horseman charging forward through thistle with bats and menacing tree roots tangling around him.

"Okay, I officially give up. That is seriously the best pumpkin I have ever seen," I say, laying my knife down on the cardboard and running my messy hands through a towel.

"You should see the one she made last year," Ryan says, standing up and giving up on his pumpkin, which looks about as intricate as mine. "She made a set of four and turned the whole thing into Mount Rushmore."

"You're an artist!" I say.

"Eh. It only works with pumpkins," Elise says, her tongue stuck out on one side of her mouth—her focus still on perfecting her craft.

"It's still art," I say, stepping back and watching her work.

Elise keeps digging and nipping at pieces of pumpkin for the next hour, and eventually, Ryan, Jess, and Owen move outside to play basketball. House shows up with a few other guys, including Andrew, and pretty soon my driveway is serving as home court.

"You like watching him, don't you," Willow says, nudging into me while we sit on the stoop by my back door, sipping hot chocolate. I bite my lip and shrug, relenting to a small smile. It's a fraction of my feelings, because yes, I love watching him. I love how he moves, how masculine he is when he pushes the other guys, when he dominates them on the court. The way the ball transfers from hand to hand is effortless for him, as is his ability to put up a shot from any distance—and have it find the safety of the rusty hoop and net above my garage.

I'm mesmerized by his skill, but more than that, I'm utterly taken with his form. It's barely forty degrees outside, the sky veiled in a thick layer of cloud, but Owen's shirt is off, his chest and abs and arms glistening with sweat. His hat is backward on his head, so he can see, and his jeans sling low on his hips, the red of his boxers like a target for my eyes. The things passing through my mind about him right now make me blush, and I'm almost worried that Willow can hear my thoughts.

"You...love him?" she asks. I think about pretending I don't hear her question at first. But I know she'll only ask me again. I don't answer, but instead shrug and give the same hinted smile I did to her last question. When she breathes in deeply, I know she knows the truth.

I love him.

I want him.

I need him.

I breathe him.

Since the moment my eyes met Owen Harper's, he has owned me, terrified me, consumed me, and I don't even remember the girl I was before him any more.

"Just promise me you'll still be careful. Just...don't let yourself go, not completely. In case you need to come back from him," she says.

With my eyes closed, I nod, knowing that it's already too late.

"Hey," Owen says, his body suddenly in front of me. My eyes start where they shouldn't, and by the time I meet his, his crooked smile threatens to tease me, but he doesn't.

"Hey," I say back, my voice hoarse and raspy.

"So, House and a few of the guys are heading over to Sasha's house, that place I took you for that party?" Owen's shifting the ball back and forth in his hands, nervously. "Anyhow, we can all go, if you want...or not. I mean, whatever."

My stomach sinks, because I can tell Owen wants to leave with his friends, and I can also see how much they don't blend with mine. Ryan is the only connection; the only one among us who seems to move in and out of cliques seamlessly, unaffected. House is leaning on his truck, spitting sunflower seeds into my yard, and Andrew is caught somewhere between both groups, too young to really belong.

"I was kind of planning on hanging out here, passing out candy with everyone, until—" I say, not wanting to say the rest any longer. Not wanting to say I was planning on staying here until everyone left Owen and me alone—not wanting to say how much I just want to be with Owen, and no one else. In a flash, I feel naïve and stupid, and I think of Willow, and her warning.

"No, that's cool. I'll just tell him we're out," he says, his fingers rapping a few times on the ball, his eyes still on me. He's waiting for something, waiting for what? For me to tell him it's okay?

"Why don't you go? Maybe...just come back, if it's not too late. Maybe I'll be up," I say, throwing the *maybe* in there totally passive aggressively, doing a poor job of masking my disappointment.

Willow stands quickly, slipping through the door with the excuse of helping Elise clean up. And for the first time in hours, I'm left alone with Owen, alone while his friends watch us from House's truck along the roadside, his brother and Jess watching from Owen's front porch, and the rest of my friends eavesdropping from inside my house. I'm alone with him, and embarrassed.

The practice conversation happening in my head starts with me telling Owen to just leave, but it always finishes with me begging him to stay. I keep my eyes on my knees, on the toes of his Converse, while I work out my words. I'm interrupted when Owen's hand finds my chin, and I can feel the pressure of his fingers lifting my gaze upward as he kneels down in front of me.

"I don't go without you. And if you don't want to go, we're staying here," he says, his eyes unflinching, his focus completely on me, drowning out the nosey eyes and ears around us.

"Are you sure?" I ask, and he starts to chuckle lightly, leaning forward and kissing the tip of my nose.

"You know what's hot?" he asks, making a turn in our conversation that throws me a little. I shrug and bunch my brow.

"No, Owen. What's...*hot?*" I respond, not sure where this is going.

"When a girl knows exactly what she wants and just asks for it," he says, his eyes daring me. My mouth is dry, and my heart is beating in my stomach. "What do *you* want, Kensi? I will give you anything. You just have to ask."

Elise's giggle slips out, and I know she and Willow are listening on the other side of the door. I also notice Andrew's stare as well as House's just over Owen's shoulder. So many outside forces at play, my head begins to feel dizzy, until Owen's hand pulls my chin back to him again, our faces inches apart, his bare chest within reach, his face like my dreams.

"I want you to stay here...with me," I say, letting myself fall, letting myself trust that Owen will catch me—love me for my honesty.

"Done," he says, his eyes hanging on mine for a few long seconds, his cocky smile tugging at one side of his mouth before he stands and tosses the ball to Andrew across my driveway.

"Sorry, House. I'm out," he says, waving his hand when his friend flips him off and drives away in his truck with the rest of his friends.

"One more game?" Jess asks, dribbling awkwardly as he and Andrew walk up behind Owen. Owen looks at me, and it takes me a few seconds before I realize he's waiting for my approval—not in a rude way, but in a considerate one. I nod back at him and hug my legs tightly to my body.

"Yeah, one more. Then I think we should put some candles on a cake or something," he smirks, watching me the entire time as he falls back on his feet and joins Jess, Ryan, and Andrew for one final game in my driveway.

"Okay, that was hot," Willow whispers after barely opening the back door behind me. She slips out with Elise this time, and they sit on either side of me.

The boys play at least six more games while the three of us watch, taking turns making commentary on their play, mocking Jess's inability to score, and Ryan's pale white skin when he pulls his shirt off. We laugh when Andrew tries to make a layup six times in a row, failing each and every time, until everyone makes a pact not to guard him, just to watch him miss again.

We laugh. Owen laughs.

And suddenly, there's a moment when he's smiling—his eyes find mine, and the connection tugs on me, on my heart. This is the worst and the best year of my life, all at once, yet this single frame, my eyes on his, his mouth curved just right, the perfect smile, the perfect mix of darkness and light—it's winning.

"Yes, Willow," I say, my voice slight.

"Yes, what?" she asks, still laughing at the last play Jess attempted in front of her.

"That question you asked...*yes,*" I say, just loud enough for her to hear.

"I know," she sighs. "And I know you won't be careful either. Can't say I blame you." She leans into me slowly, putting enough pressure on my side to embrace me, and not alert Elise. I lean back, and I watch Owen while I draw on Willow's strength, hoping like hell I can survive loving him.

As soon as the sun kisses the horizon, tiny ghosts, superheroes, ninjas, and small princesses fill the streets. Every birthday I've celebrated has been in the city, every Halloween in the city. This day, in the city—it's different. People trick-or-treat in buildings, never leaving their hallways or sometimes floors. When I was little, my mom would walk me down our small street, up the two or three flights for the row homes connected to ours. I visited maybe twelve households, rung twelve doorbells, took home a small pillowcase of candy.

My mom was looking forward to tonight. She went to Costco, bought the big candy bars. And as the night wears on, and less kids ring our doorbell, my mom starts giving out two bars at once. After thirty minutes, and several Snickers of our own, the night seems to be done, and my mom sends Willow, Ryan, Jess, and Elise home with a pack of chocolate bars each.

Owen waits behind, heeding my mom's orders that we stay downstairs, and that he goes home before midnight. When her door closes, Owen sweeps me into his arms, lifting my legs from the ground and kissing me as he carries me to my piano. My friends gave me a few new music books for my birthday, not really knowing about my silent protest against this instrument. That's the beauty of independent study—I can pretend I'm actually still practicing, and there's nobody there to witness and counter my lie.

"So, explain these things to me," Owen says, settling on the bench with me still in his lap. He pulls one of the books over and flips through a few pages.

"Well, this line here," I start, pointing to the top ledger for one of the Mozart books, "is for my right hand. The one on the bottom, with this symbol, is for my left."

"And you can read this?" he says, brow pinched, finger tracing the lines of notes while his other hand trails up and down my back.

"Uh huh," I say.

"Prove it," he says, pulling the book forward and placing it on the music stand for my piano. He's trying so hard to be smooth, and part of me wonders if he also planned this out in a conversation with my mother.

"Ohhhhh nooooo," I chuckle, closing the book and sliding it back along the top of the piano. "I know what you're trying to do."

"What?" he asks, his face an expression totally foreign to him. It's fake, and Owen can't pull off fake. He's clear about everything, and I like that he can't pretend with me. "Yeah…all right. You're right," he says finally, pushing the book a few inches more away from me. "But you haven't played, not really, not since—"

"I know," I answer without him finishing. "I can't explain it, but…I just don't want to anymore."

"But you love this. You love music," he says.

"I did," I say, looking down at my keys, my right hand finding familiar—hating it and loving it all at once.

Owen studies me, his left hand still stroking my back, soothing me—lulling me. "Bullshit," he says.

"Owen, it's not bullshit. The piano, me playing, studying it—that was always my dad's dream for me," I say.

"Bullshit," he says again, his eyes a little darker, challenging.

"Stop it," I say, my tone angrier. "Don't say that."

"Because it's true," he says. "You might associate *this* with your dad, but there's a part of you, a part of your heart, that *loves* your talent. I know it."

"Owen, I know you're just trying to be supportive, or whatever, but please don't. You don't understand," I say, and he runs his right hand over mine, pressing my fingers into the keys slowly until they make a sound, a sound that breaks my heart and fills my chest.

"Yes I do," he whispers into my ear. "I understand, Kens. You know how I know?"

"How?" I ask, a breath in response to him.

"Because I heard you," he says, his eyes boring into me, like he's reaching inside me, rattling my heart back to life. His right hand holds my fingers into the valleys of the pressed keys. "Play for me. None of *this,"* he motions to the books spread out on my piano top. "Play what you love, what *you* want to hear. Please, Kens. Just this once, for me, for your birthday."

"Do you know how fucked up it is that you are asking for a present on *my* birthday?" I tease, my heart rapid in my chest, my fingers rigid, not wanting to do this. I'm frightened.

"Not a present," he says, his lips sliding into a smile, a new smile. "A gift."

I roll my eyes, but let them settle on our hands together, mine still resting in their position on the keyboard. Slowly, I slide my hand out from under his and crack my knuckles against my chest. With a deep breath, I nod once to Owen, then move my hands back into a different position—one far away from the usual classics I've been forced to practice. I move them into a loose position, comfortable, barely touching the keys. Eyes closed, I begin to drag them slowly around the middle of the keyboard, my foot pressing the dampening pedal, trying not to play loud enough for my mother to hear. It's pointless, though—the music echoes in the cavern of the tall dining room and front foyer of the house.

Owen's hand stays on my back, his rhythm constant, fingers gliding up and down, until I finally let myself have this small break, allowing my fingers to fly further up the keyboard, breaking rules, changing time, changing speed.

What comes out is completely out of my head, something bluesy, and something that never repeats. I play for maybe a full minute, and somewhere along the way, my mouth curves into a smile, and I don't realize until I open my eyes; Owen is looking back at me. I stop abruptly, my smile collapsing fast.

"What?" I ask, embarrassed, feeling foolish, feeling as though I betrayed myself somehow too, giving in to my protest.

"You're something else, you know that?" he says, his eyes bright, his smile full, and his hand never breaking its soothing touch. "What was that?"

"I don't know," I say, pulling my hands back into my lap, closing them into fists. "I made it up."

"Wow," he says, and when I look at him, he's still smiling.

"Stop it; you're embarrassing me," I say, a small giggle slipping out. I tuck my face into his shoulder.

"All I know is you...you loved that," he says. I look long and hard at the keys, my mouth a faint smile, afraid to give in to Owen's temptation, afraid to admit that I did love it, that I still love music, that I still have this connection to my father.

"Stop thinking it's for him," Owen says, reading my mind. My eyes snap to his. "It never was—your gift? It was never for *him.* So don't go giving it away to him now. He doesn't deserve it."

I lay my head back along his chest, and just breathe. Owen holds me, and we sit still in the silence of the enormous room for almost an hour, my hands never crossing over onto the piano again. I let my eyes take it in, though, mentally playing every sound in my head—my sounds, the songs that were always for me.

Owen is right.

"I never gave you your present," he says finally, snapping me back to the present, bringing me out of the dream I was so happily falling into while resting in his arms. "You think we can make it upstairs?" he asks, nodding up, toward my mother's door, the one that comes before my bedroom.

"You go up first, I'll turn off the lights and lock up," I say, not able to fully look him in the eye. The thought of having Owen in my room, alone with me, has my body feeling alive and warm and electric. I'm also nervous and scared—of being caught, yes, but also of being *that* alone with Owen.

We've never been so alone.

I watch nervously as he glides up the stairs, pulling his shoes off halfway, so he can slip quietly past my mom's room. I wait a few extra seconds, making sure he's in my room, then I lock the back door, walking the length of the house from the back to the front, flipping every light switch off along the way.

I check the front door, bolt it and glance at the clock on the wall. It's already well past midnight, and my mother never once came downstairs. I'm pretty sure she's fallen asleep. She trusts me. And I'm about to take advantage of that—a tinge of guilt squeezing at me from the inside, a tinge that I bury and ignore and replace with anxiety over all the *what ifs* that come along with being alone with Owen.

Holding my breath, I pause at my mom's door, listening for the familiar sounds—the buzz of her humidifier, the dull sound of the low television, the constant stream of infomercials that I know she isn't watching. All signs point to her being asleep, to the risk being minimal, so I continue on into my room. I close the door and turn the light out quickly, surprising Owen.

"Okay, so I know I'm ugly, but really? You have to keep me in the dark, too?" he jokes.

"You're not ugly," I say, reaching to the end of my bed and throwing a pillow at him where he sits. He clutches it in his arms and sets it next to him, on the floor—the space where I usually sit to watch him through the window. I notice his gaze pauses at that window, his smile quirking up. For some reason having him here, knowing I watch him from this room, embarrasses me, so I quickly turn my attention away from that space.

His back rests against the headboard of my bed, his feet stretched out in front of him, the small bag with his gift in his lap. When he pats the space next to him, I swallow loudly, kick off my shoes, and crawl next to him, folding my legs up in front of me. My fidgeting hands and feet create a small barrier between us, a barrier Owen is quick to crash down when he lets his hand graze along the inside of my leg, stopping at my knee.

"Present time?" I ask, my voice a whisper. I'm sure if I speak any louder my mom will crash through the door. I'm not sure what she would do if she caught Owen here. She's not the type to get angry over things like this, and I think a small part of her would be glad to see me do something so typical and teenager. But I also know she wouldn't trust me anymore. And that would make me sad.

Owen holds the bag in his lap for a few seconds, turning it and folding over the top a few times. I can tell whatever is inside is small, but heavy.

"I told you how my grandpa raised us, right?" Owen says finally.

"Yeah," I say back. We're both still whispering, and the fact that Owen is —without me asking him to—fills me with relief.

"He was a fixer," Owen says, and I quirk my head to the side, pinching my brow.

"A…fixer?" I repeat.

"Yeah…I mean that's not like his official title or job or anything. He worked in the warehouse with my dad. That's how my parents met, actually. My dad worked for him," Owen says, his fingers wrestling with the strings on the gift, tucking them in and out of the fold nervously. He doesn't share these stories often, and I don't dare speak or interrupt him.

"When he wasn't working, and even more after he retired, my grandpa did odd jobs for people, fixing things. Not really a handyman, because he didn't go to houses or climb ladders for people. But people brought him things. And sometimes, they'd forget to come back and collect whatever it was he was fixing for them," Owen says, his lips curved into a soft, affectionate smile, his eyes showing nothing but fondness for this memory.

"So…" Owen starts, sliding the bag from his lap onto mine. "This is from my grandpa's collection. He saved a few special things, things that sort of spoke to him. He never really knew why he kept this thing in particular. But then, when I was visiting him at the home the other day, I noticed it again. I've probably stared at this thing for four years, both on the shelf at our house and in his room at the home when we moved him there. It never meant anything…until now. When I asked him if I could give it to you, he lit up. He doesn't light up often anymore."

Owen pauses, his hands folded nervously in his lap, his thumbs tapping one another, his eyes cast down on the gift in my lap. The light through the window is dim, but it's bright enough to see his expression. He's anxious, and maybe also a little happy. I unbend the fold in the top of the bag and untwist the knotted strings, pulling out the crumpled tissue paper from the top. When I reach in, my fingers feel something cold, made of a heavy metal. I pull the object out slowly, holding it in front of my face, resting it on my palm. It stands only a few inches tall, and the shape is similar to a small grandfather's clock, but I know what it is immediately.

My heart knows too, and it kicks—violently.

"My grandpa said the music teacher for the old Woodstock elementary school brought it to him. But then the guy retired and left town, forgetting about it completely. I guess you wind it here," Owen says, his hands gentle along mine as he twists the crank on the back until the small object begins to make the regular ticking sound it's meant for, the sound sweet to my ears. "He said they don't make metronomes like this anymore. One wind lasts about six hours, unless you hold the hand still to make it stop."

"Thank you," I whisper, moving my thumb gently along the sharp edges of the heavy metal. The small object is a dark iron, with small bumps along the edges showing its age. I push my finger against the hand to stop the ticking, then wind it again to listen to it begin, holding it up to my ear to hear the mechanisms move inside. My eyes find Owen's while I listen.

"You like it?" he asks, his bottom lip tucked under his top. I nod *yes*, keeping my eyes locked on his while the ticking sound fills my ear. My chest constricts with an overwhelming love for his gesture, and I stop the ticking once again, placing the metronome back in the tissue paper on the side of my bed, then lean forward on my knees and hold Owen's face in between my hands.

"I love it," I say, the beating inside me so strong it feels as though my gift has been swallowed whole and has begun racing inside my chest. My hands hold still, my eyes on Owens, watching him look over my face, down to my mouth and back to my eyes more than once.

"Happy birthday, Kensington," he whispers, his lips grazing mine as he speaks. His next pass is more forceful, and when I feel his hands slide up my sides and around my back, I give in to my most basic urges, crawling over his lap until I'm straddling him and kissing him as hard as our lips will let us.

His hands slide down my back until they're cupping my butt, the thin cotton of my leggings no match for the heat of his grip. Owen sits tall, and I take his signal and reach down to lift his shirt from his body, pulling the two layers of long-sleeved shirts up and over him, revealing the smooth skin I memorized while watching him play basketball outside. Everything about him is warm—his shoulders, warm, his back, warm—his chest against mine, warm. I can feel him through the fabric of my sweatshirt, but want to feel him more.

Without warning, Owen's hands grip the back of my thighs, lifting me just enough to push me onto my back, and soon he's above me, his knee pushed between my legs, touching me in a place I've never been touched. His kiss is rough and fast, yet somehow not hard enough. When his hands slide my arms up above my head, I let him guide them willingly, his kiss trailing down my neck until his lips stop at the collar of my sweatshirt. His hand trails from my arms, which I leave just as he left them over my head, and the further down my body his hand goes, the less I breathe.

The look in his eyes when his head tilts up to gaze at me is aggressive, almost like an animal, and as much as my hands want to reach down and feel the softness of his hair, I keep them in place, instead watching the dark waves fall into his eyes as he lowers his head again, his hand slowly lifting the bottom of my sweatshirt up my belly.

His lips leave small kisses over my stomach and rib cage as he slowly pulls my shirt up, revealing my skin. His thumb hooks my undershirt next, and soon I'm arching to help him lift both pieces of clothing completely up my body.

I'm terrified that he's seeing me. I'm excited that he's seeing me. My breathing is hard, my lips barely parted as Owen's hand slips the thin pink strap of my bra over my shoulder, kissing my skin where the tension of the strap left a small mark. He does the same on the other side, leaving my bra over my breasts just enough to cover my nipples, which are aching for him to expose them, to feel the cold air of my room.

"You're a virgin, right?" Owen says, his question surprising me, igniting a fire over my face and making me feel sick and fearful and wonderful all at once. His smile is soft, and he's not making fun of me, but I'm somehow ashamed that I don't know what to do, that I'm inexperienced.

"I am. I'm sorry," I say, and he lowers his head with a small laugh. When he lifts to look at me again, he lowers himself, resting the weight of his body on top of mine, the heat of his skin covering me, warming me completely, and all my breasts want is the feeling of his skin against them, no more barriers in between.

"Kens, don't apologize. It makes you beautiful. I just wanted to make sure I didn't make any assumptions, to make sure I treat you…right," he says, his lips kissing me softly, and then gliding down my chin and neck as he raises himself over me again. He pauses when his mouth is right between my breasts, resting his chin on the center clasp of my bra, and he looks up at me, waiting for me to tell him it's okay to move forward.

I nod slightly, biting my lip and closing my eyes, arching my back, wanting to press into him harder. Owen's teeth grip the clasp in the center of my bra, and I don't know if he's torn it open or managed to unhook it, but I feel the lacey material begin to slide open, releasing the tension over my breasts, but keeping my nipples covered. The sensation of his tongue on the curve of my breast drives the arch in my back deeper, causing the material of my bra to completely fall to the sides. The cool rush of air on my nipples leaves them feeling hungrier somehow, and I look down, my eyes meeting Owen's, his sexy smile paused right above one of the peaks. I watch as he leans down, his eyes on mine the entire time, his tongue reaching out and taking a taste of my body, the hardness of my nipple responding with shivers across my skin.

Oh. My. God.

Owen does it again, and the reaction within me is just the same. And when he lets his tongue lave completely over my breast, pulling the pink tip in between both lips, tugging gently with his teeth, I whimper.

"Shhhhhhhh," Owen whispers, blowing cool air over my breasts, which drives me wilder. "You…need to be quiet," he smirks.

He's right. I do. But holy shit do I want to scream and beg and do things that just a minute or two ago I wasn't sure I was ready for. Owen hands me my pillow, and I pull it over my forehead, then over my mouth when his lips find my breasts once again. I let myself have a faint moan, muffled by the cotton and feathers I'm pressing over my mouth, my teeth biting the fabric—until Owen reaches up and removes the pillow, replacing it with his mouth. His lips work mine, his tongue probing deep into my mouth, his teeth grazing my bottom lip, tugging and tasting while his hand cups my breasts. When his thumbs rub over the tips, I can feel the throbbing between my legs grow even stronger, and with every pass, my hips grow bolder, until finally, I roll them into his leg, welcoming the pressure of his thigh and knee.

"You feel that, don't you," Owen whispers in my ear, his leg pushing into me once more.

"Ye....yes..." I stutter, my heartbeat pumping in my stomach, racing with excitement.

"You want me to touch you? There?" Owen asks as he lets his hand run softly down my stomach, down my abdomen, into the center of my legs until I feel his fingers graze over the fabric between my legs.

I nod *yes* quickly, holding my breath. Owen runs his hand over my center again, this time with more pressure, and my center quivers in response. He does this a few more times until I'm unable to control the rolling of my hips, my body wanting more of him. Bringing his hand up my hip, he runs his palm flat against my tummy while his lips kiss me deep and hard. When he pulls his mouth away, he leaves his forehead against mine, taking a long, deep breath through his nose. He's trying to be good, trying to restrain himself—and the good angel on my shoulder is thankful, the bad angel on the other side screaming for him to disobey.

My eyes closed, I run my fingers down his arm until my hand is over his, then I push his fingers lower, until my hand and his both dip under the elastic band of my leggings and panties. Owen's breath comes out fast and hard again, and I can feel the sensation of want in his fingers as they twitch and flex, begging to move faster. Once again, I pull his hand deeper, moving him a fraction of an inch at a time, until I can tell he no longer needs me.

I bring my hand back to his neck, opening my eyes to look into his, and the desire in them is intoxicating—and infectious. I pull him to me, kissing him hard as his hand travels the final inch it needs until his fingers have found my center, his hand plunging forward more, his finger reaching into me, penetrating me in a way that is both painful and amazing all at once. The burn is overcome with my desire the more he does it, until my hips begin to rock once again with the rhythm of his hand.

"So fucking hot," Owen breathes into my ear, his eyes hooded and his smile dark and sexy as he looks over my face. "Tell me what you want."

"Everything," I whimper, my face falling to the side, my hand gripping the corner of the blanket to muffle my sounds as Owen leans down and pulls my nipple into his mouth, sucking it between his teeth to a painful, glorious peak again as his fingers rub over my center, teasing me again and again until plunging back inside. The pressure builds fast, and with every pass of his tongue on my breast and his finger through my core, the risk that I'm going to lose control grows stronger. I feel wet around him, and my hips are no longer able to control themselves, rocking into him, craving him, wanting more than his hand, until I fall over the edge completely.

Owen's other hand cups my mouth, muffling my cries while his eyes watch me, his smile cocky and proud as his right hand continues to work, his finger moving in and out of me until the waves of pleasure become bearable and finally stop. When he pulls his hand out from my pants, he lets his head rest on mine again, and just when I begin to feel embarrassed, he speaks.

"That...was the single sexiest thing I've ever done," he says, running his hand down my stomach and over the sensitive area between my legs again, cupping me hard, gripping me forcefully. "Only for me," he says, looking at me possessively, his hand threatening to push me into orgasm again just by this single touch. I nod *yes*, my lips wanting to smile, but unable to gain control through the trembles I'm still feeling. Owen kisses me again, and I'm grateful for his touch, for the rescue from having to speak.

I'm speechless.

I'm in love.

And I want to do that again.

CHAPTER 16

Nothing changed, yet everything changed. I caught sight of Owen when I drove myself to band practice Monday morning, and I blushed. I also felt my body warm just from looking at him.

I felt like somehow Willow knew everything that we had done. She didn't say anything, but I read something in her smirk—in the way she looked at me, her eyebrows raised—while she directed the morning practice session.

I was the last one off the field for morning practice, lost in my own happy thoughts. The wheels from the xylophone were catching rocks, squealing as they dragged them over the concrete walkway.

"I'm pretty sure we've done this before, haven't we?" Owen says, his voice lifting me out of my daydream, only to put me in my real-life fantasy. He bends down and dislodges the small pebbles from the wheels of my xylophone and begins pushing it back to the band room for me.

"Thank you," I say, smiling as I look up at him, completely smitten. He kisses the top of my head in response.

"Haaaaaa haaaaa, you a band geek now, Harper?" some guy bellows, his laugh that obnoxious kind that makes him sound drunk even though he's completely sober. I think he's sober?

"Fuck off, Cruz," Owen says, staring intensely at his friend, who backs down quickly. Owen is tall, and his body is broad, his muscles cut, but he's not the biggest guy in our school. Yet, when he gives a certain look, one with warning, it's unbelievably effective. His friend walks over with his hand out, reaching for Owen's, and Owen makes him wait a few long, painful seconds before he reaches back, slapping hands and pulling the other guy in to bump chests.

"This your chick?" the guy asks, nodding to me, his eyes flirtatious. I should probably be offended by being claimed and called someone's *chick,* yet hearing it, and seeing Owen's chest lift in response, makes me feel proud of being possessed—by him.

"This is Kensi, and yes, she's *my chick,*" Owen repeats.

"Ahhh right. I feel ya, brother. Kensi, nice to meet you. You coming to our game tonight? You've gotta come see your man in action; he's got skills," Cruz says. I look to Owen as he puts his hands in his pockets and shrugs, forever modest. But he smiles, a smile that makes me think of last night, of his lips on me, his hands on me, and I blush right in front of his friend.

"What time? I'd like to go," I say, looking up at Owen again.

"We play at six," he says, his smile sliding into a pleased look that lets me know he's happy I'm going.

"Sweet. Party at Sasha's after," Cruz says, slapping hands with Owen once more before turning to walk back to the group of guys waiting by the outside stairwell.

Owen starts pushing my instrument again, and I trail behind, now thinking about everything *after* Owen's game—about going to that house again, about the things I saw other couples do there. Not just the sex, but the drugs and drinking. I also can't help but remember how I felt the last time I was there—afraid and angry.

"We can just go home after the game, you know?" Owen says, pausing when we reach the band-room door.

"I know," I say, my lip lodged between my teeth. I never say I don't want to go, because there's a part of me that wants to feel that rush again, of being somewhere that feels dangerous, and somewhere *alone* with Owen.

He sighs deeply and smiles with tight lips, pulling me into his chest, the softness of his black hoodie like heaven against my cheek. I want to do nothing else but stay here for the rest of the day.

Unfortunately, my reality slams into us—Willow opens the door, knocking into my xylophone and ending my hug-fest with Owen, my boyfriend. My. Boyfriend. Owen. I'm his *chick.* I let the silly grin and butterflies in my belly carry me through the rest of the morning, and I even let myself touch the piano a little during my independent study. I wouldn't really call it playing, but it's more than I've done in weeks.

In English, Owen's feet are in their rightful place on my chair again. I reach down and squeeze his ankles, threatening to trap them before he slides them away and I sit in my chair. His breath surprises me when I feel it against my neck, his hand sliding my hair out of the way so he can drop a quick round of tiny kisses on my neck and ear. His desk is propped forward on its front legs just so he can reach me.

He backs away when he hears Mr. Chessman coming, pulling his pencil to his lips, chewing on the eraser, his other hand flipping the edges of his book. We're wrapping up our discussion of *Crime and Punishment* today. Owen's been anxious about it ever since the heated debate that sent him out of our classroom.

"Owen, can you join me in the hall, for just a minute?" Mr. Chessman's voice surprises us both. Owen looks him in the eyes for a few solid seconds, like he's trying to read his mind, before leaning forward and dropping the pencil from his lips.

I watch them both walk from the room, the door swinging open and closed behind them, then I turn my attention to Cal. His smug smile pisses me off, and he nods toward the door, saying something under his breath to the girl sitting next to him, who only giggles. I hate him for judging Owen.

When Owen and Mr. Chessman return to class, there's a long awkward silence, the class watching Owen—waiting for him to pack his things, to leave, or to have some type of reaction. But he doesn't. He simply leans forward again, picking up his pencil, and flipping his book open to the final few chapters, pressing his thumb down the seam to hold his book open.

Disappointed, most of the class turns back to the front, giving their focus over to our teacher. But I notice Owen's hand, the one with the pencil, flexing and twisting and tapping the lead, letting the sharp point leave a red mark on the tip of his thumb. His face is low, his hair pushed forward, and I can tell this is one of those times, one of those moments when Owen wishes he could hide.

I should turn around, give him his privacy, let him cool from whatever it is Mr. Chessman told him. But I can't seem to make my arms, my legs, my shoulders work; I can't leave him. Then, his gaze flicks up, and his eyes find mine, and there's something at work behind them.

Owen looks scared.

I manage to catch him as he rushes out of the classroom, but when I ask him what's wrong, he only bites his lip and tells me "Nothing, really."

But Owen is gone for the rest of the day, missing lunch, missing math, and not there again for science. I slip my phone from my pocket before the final bell of the day and send him another text, only to watch it go unanswered just like my previous six attempts.

I'm racing out to my car when Ryan meets me in the parking lot, and I can tell by the face he's wearing he has news about Owen.

"Hey, Kens. Owen just called, wanted me to come find you, tell you not to worry," Ryan says, his hands waving, his long legs making up quick distance until he's standing at my car with me. "He'll be back for our game, too. He said you should just wait here."

"Where is he? What happened, Ryan?" I ask, having no intention of *not* driving right to Owen—wherever he is. I open the passenger door and toss my backpack inside then move to the driver's side, Ryan following me.

"It's James. He…he came home," Ryan says, his head leaning to one side, expecting me to understand. But I don't.

"He…came…home?" I repeat.

Ryan takes a small step back, letting his bag slide down his arm to the ground next to him. He pulls his hat from his head and runs his other hand through his hair, scratching at his head, his eyes squinting when he looks back at me.

"He does this sometimes. Or, at least, he's done this before. Something must have scared him, or he's broke, or…whatever. He goes a few days without getting high, and then he starts to feel the hell of withdrawals, and then he comes home," Ryan says, his arms slung heavily at his sides, his thumbs looped in his pockets.

"Why doesn't Owen's mom kick him out? Or take him to rehab?" I ask, opening my door and moving one foot inside.

"They can't afford rehab, Kens, come on," he says, and I wince because he's right, I should know better. "And James may be a drug addict, but he's still her son. She loves him."

"Is that where Owen is? Right now? Is he at home?" I ask, and I don't have to wait for his answer, because I know that's where he is.

I leave Ryan with his lips parted, ready to speak, and squeal my tires backing away from my parking spot. I hear the whistle from the teacher on parking-lot duty, but I ignore it, maneuvering my way to the front of the exit line, turning right on a red light, into a rush of traffic.

Somehow sparing my car any new dings or dents, I weave through dirt alongside the road until I get to a street that I know goes to my house. I pull up, and immediately I see Owen's truck, and the car I now know belongs to James. But I also see something else.

My father's car is at the end of the driveway, far enough forward to make room for my car— like he's planning on staying here a while. I slow, quietly turning into my driveway, positioning my car near the edge, out of the way so my father can exit. And, near my own escape—I leave my hand on the keys, not sure I should commit to turning the engine off.

On one side, I have Owen's house, and as I roll down my window and listen, everything seems quiet—as it *always* is. There's silence surrounding my house, too, even though my mom's car is also in the driveway. Both of my parents are in that house. Together.

Waiting for me, I can only presume.

I didn't text my mom that I was planning to stay for Owen's game. I thought she would be gone, and I assumed she wouldn't care. But clearly, her ambush screams otherwise.

The *divorce conversation* was bound to come. At eighteen, I hardly feel I need things explained to me. Given the circumstances, I can't see any other end for this game. The moment my father's face shifted when I asked him about the affair, asked him about some other woman—the first thing that flowed through my head was this very conversation my parents are sitting in there waiting to have. That's actually what sickened me most in that first few minutes. How quickly things changed though when Gaby also became a part of this story. It put things into perspective, made *this* conversation not only unnecessary, but a joke.

I'm not having this talk today. And I'm a little disappointed in my mom for trying to force it on me.

With ease, I push my car door closed, latching it enough to make the dome light flicker off, then I jog to Owen's front porch, and I tap my key ring on his front door, wanting to keep everything quiet. When nobody answers after my second attempt, I try my hand on the doorknob, and when it twists, I push lightly, letting myself inside.

"Hello?" I call out, the downstairs lights dim, only a lamp on in a corner by a reading chair. The living room is dark as is the kitchen, but there's a glow from the rooms upstairs. "Hello? Owen?" I say loudly, my voice directed up the stairs. I hear footsteps coming down the wooden floors of the hallway, and soon I see Andrew's sock-covered feet.

"Hey, Kens," he whispers, gliding down the steps quickly and meeting me on the bottom. "You here for O?"

"Yeah," I whisper back, taking his lead. "He left school, and he has a game today. I…I was worried."

Andrew smiles, his hands hanging in the front pocket of his hoodie, his hair disheveled, like he's been sleeping. "I came home sick today," he says, running his hand a few times through his hair when he notices me looking at it, his smile reflecting his youth. "My mom came to get me, because she didn't want to bother Owen. But when we got home…"

Andrew turns to look over his shoulder, back up the stairs, and Owen is standing at the top, his eyes on mine, his face showing a look of disappointment. "Andrew, go back to bed," he says, sighing. He takes a few steps, and meets Andrew in the middle of the stairs.

"See ya later, Kens," Andrew says, a small wave over his shoulder. Owen keeps his back to me, pointing to his brother's door down the hall, and he watches until his brother is back inside, the door closed, before turning back to face me.

"Kens, what are you doing here?" His sigh is heavy, and he looks like he's been mugged, a small bruise forming on one cheek.

"Owen, what happened?" I say, reaching to touch it. He jerks back, moving up and away from me.

"It's nothing. I'm fine," he says, his eyes rolling a little with his temper. "Didn't Ryan find you? I'm coming back for the game. I was just going to meet you at the gym."

"He found me. He said…" I'm interrupted by the sound of open wailing—heavy cries filled with swear words and a few nonsensical things.

"Owen!" James finally yells, his voice broken, sounding nothing like the intimidating figure from before.

"Just…stay here," Owen says forcefully, his hand held up to my face as he turns quickly and takes the steps two at a time, rushing down the hallway to where I'm assuming his brother is.

At first, I do as he asks, letting my hands grip either side of the banister, my body swaying back and forth with indecision—to go up or down. I hear the sound of scuffling at first, then something heavy knocked to the floor, followed by the sound of running water. It's as if my feet carried me on their own volition, and somehow I find myself standing in front of the bathroom. Owen is kneeling, his body leaning over the bathtub, steam coming from the blast of running hot water, and he's soaking towels. He doesn't notice me until he shuts the water off, and begins to twist one of the towels, wringing it of excess water.

"Kens, I told you to wait there!" he yells, his face angry and his eyes stern. He's trying to use his aggression to dominate me, as I've seen him do to others.

"How can I help?" I ask, taking a step into the bathroom, then stopping dead in my tracks when I realize James is lying naked around the corner, his head resting on the side of the toilet, vomit…everywhere. I cover my mouth and nose, both to hide my shock and to stifle the smell. Owen was trying to keep this from me, but it's becoming apparent that he's also trying to keep it from everyone—leaving no one there for Owen.

James begins weeping the instant he sees me, his eyes not able to focus on me entirely, the puffiness almost swelling them shut. Owen slides back against the side of the tub, his hands dropping the wet towel on the floor, his long legs stretching out as he flips his hat from his head, tossing it out into the hall.

"Shit!" he yells, pushing his head forward into his hands, his fingers digging roughly into his hair, wrapping through strands and pulling until he finally releases and lets his head fall back against the edge of the tub. When he rolls it to the side slightly, his eyes catch mine again, and his strength is gone. Owen isn't falling apart; he was never together.

"Let me help," I say softly, my lips quivering with nervous energy, my mind putting the pieces together while everything before comes into focus. I have options, I have help—and it's going to be painful. But Owen can't do this…whatever *this* is…on his own. Not if he still wants to live his life.

"Where's his room?" I ask.

Owen nods to the right and looks in a direction toward the end of the hall. I move closer to him and lift the wet towel from the floor, then pull my sweatshirt collar up over my nose and mouth, hiding the gagging I can't help but do underneath. I reach for Owen, and he looks at my hand, his eyes blinking slowly. Everything in his expression shows his acceptance of the fact that he has run out of options, that he isn't as strong as he pretends. His eyelids quiver as they close, Owen fighting not to feel the gravity of what is happening any more than he has to. He takes my hand finally, and lifts himself to stand with me, grabbing the towel from my hands and going to work cleaning up the mess from his brother's frail, pale, and thin body.

He tosses it back into the hot water of the bathtub then turns to me. "I'll deal with all of this shit later. Just…help me get him in his room," he says, and I nod.

I won't leave you, Owen.

We each take an arm, and James works to bring his legs under his body, his frame swaying awkwardly, his balance nonexistent. He probably weighs less than I do, his tall body is so thin, but his length makes it hard to direct him and move him the few feet it takes to get him to his room. He slips on the floor three times, each time fighting to grip our arms on the way down, his own swinging wildly. This must be how Owen got that bruise.

Once we get him to his bed, he grips the sheets and claws his way to the middle before finally letting his weak muscles give way to the coolness of the bed, his lips parted and dry. He looks half alive, and he's shivering uncontrollably.

"Make it stop," he says, the dull look on his face slowly melding into sorrow, then torture. Tears stream from his eyes, his nose running into the edge of the pillow, his head never making it to the top of the bed. "Owen, please. Make this stop! I can't, I can't, I can't, I can't..."

He keeps screaming, his hands clutching the fabric beneath him, fists grabbing blankets and pulling them to his chest. Owen fights to cover his body, the entire time James working against him, his arms jutting, his legs kicking.

Then Owen makes it all stop. He kicks his shoes from his feet and climbs into the bed next to his brother, pulling his flailing body into his arms, onto his lap and holding him to his chest, his arms flexing and working so very hard. At first, James pushes from him, fighting to get back to the bed, pulling and asking for the floor, to go outside, to get to his car. Every time he fights, Owen just pulls him to his chest harder, his chin resting on his brother's head. Owen's eyes find mine, locking on me. It feels as if I'm his anchor.

"You can do this, James. This is the hard part. You can do this; I've got you," Owen says, over and over, until his brother's body grows tired, and he starts to stare off into space—not asleep, but no longer fighting against him.

"I need you to call Ryan; I'm going to miss my game," Owen says to me, his eyes full of regret, shame, disappointment—so many familiar emotions.

"What about your mom?" I ask. This isn't fair, and Owen shouldn't have to give up something for this.

It isn't fair.

"She had to work. She'll lose her job if she doesn't show up. She's...she's called in for this before. Last time was *the last time,* according to her boss," Owen says, his eyes starting to show his exhaustion.

"Owen..." I say, my head falling to the side, not wanting to see him lose so much, to hurt so much. His brother's pain is killing him.

"He's in withdrawal. If I leave him, he's just going to do something worse. I...can't..." Owen doesn't finish his words; instead, swallowing hard, fighting to keep the water I see building in his eyes from falling, to make the redness in his eyes go away. He wants to stay strong, to stay hard, to stay *dark.*

"I'll be right back," I say, looking at him long enough for him to believe that I will be right back. But I don't go to his room, to his phone. I don't call

Ryan. Instead, I leave his house and walk into my own hell, to my parents who are sitting in my kitchen at opposite ends of the counter, not speaking, but waiting for me. They've been waiting long enough when I step in the house, the first words from my father's mouth are asking what's taken me so long, followed by accusations that my mother doesn't know how to take care of me. Within seconds, they're bickering with one another, not looking at me at all, and if it were any other moment, I would turn around and leave.

But I can't. I can't, because I need my mom. She is the only person who can help Owen.

"Stop it!" I yell, my hands held above my head, waving to get their attention. When they both snap their gazes to me, I drop my hands to my head. "I'm eighteen. I had a birthday…which *you* didn't acknowledge," I say sternly, pointing to my father who opens his mouth to rebut my accusation, but I keep talking, cutting him off before he can begin a single word. "You don't have any right to say *anything* about me, to me, on my behalf! You gave that all up the moment you fucked my best friend, you piece of shit. You don't get to be my father ever again, and when I think about it, you never really were."

There's a feeling of power that comes over me the longer I talk, the words I'm saying freeing, my voice growing calmer, stronger. There is so much I want to say to this man; so much I want to say to my mom, too, for even letting him in the house. But Owen needs me. Those things are going to have to wait.

"Mom," I speak to her, holding my hand up to my father's face, my gesture cruel and insolent, but I don't give a fuck, because Owen needs me. "I need you. It's personal, and I don't want to talk about this in front of *him*."

I hold her gaze, watching her mind process what she's able to read in mine. Please, Mom. Just this once, stand up to him. Don't let him charm you; make him leave.

"Kens, can we just talk first, then when your dad goes back to his hotel, you and I can talk about anything, whatever you need?" she's trying to make us both happy. That's no longer possible, though—we both don't get to be happy.

"No," I say. Nothing more. I won't talk about Owen in front of him, and I won't sit here and listen to them try to talk about me, their marriage, fake apologies, my dad's rights or wishes for me, his role in my life. I'm not having that conversation—not ever.

"Dean..." my mom sighs, her head leaning to the side, her eyes falling on him. She's exhausted, and I can tell he's probably been here for hours, wearing her down.

"Karen, have you forgotten who the parents are in this house? My god..." my dad says, kicking away from the counter, his stool crashing to the floor with his temper. "Are you pregnant? Did that little thug next door knock you up? That's what this is, isn't it? Jesus, Karen!"

I don't answer. My father couldn't be more off-base, and it takes every breath in my body to stand here and keep my eyes on my mom, not to acknowledge him at all. But he just isn't worth it.

"Dean, I think you need to leave," she says, standing and putting her hand slowly along his shoulder. My dad shrugs her off, his brow low and hard, shirking her touch. "Dean, it's time to go."

"A goddamned mess. You...both of you! You did this to yourself!" My father points his finger back at me as he leaves, his face glowing red, his anger radiating.

When the door slams shut behind him, I turn back to my mom, her eyes wide and staring at the door, her face flushed. She stumbles on her feet, her balance failing her, and then grips behind her for her stool, looking for anything to save her. I wait as long as I can, but time is moving, and Owen needs me.

"Mom, I need your help," I say. She shakes her head, rubbing her temples before nodding a few times and bringing her eyes to me. "It's Owen..."

I can see her face flash with panic, worry that my father's guess was right.

"I'm not *pregnant*!" I blurt out, relief washing over her quickly. "But Owen needs you. It's his brother, James. He came home, and he's..." I don't know how to say this in a way that doesn't shed more negative light on the Harper family. I don't know what my mom has heard, and I don't want to contribute to those terrible rumors, but damn if so many of them aren't true.

"James is an addict, Mom. He's detoxing, and Owen's mom has to work, so Owen's at home, by himself, trying to take care of James. He doesn't want Andrew to see any of it, and it's killing him. Mom…oh god, Mom, it's so bad," I fall apart a little, remembering everything I just saw, knowing how hard it is on Owen. I place my palms flat on the counter and breathe deeply, closing my eyes, finding my strength. "Mom, Owen has a game tonight. It's all he's got, and he has nobody to help him. Can you just, I don't know…come take a look? I don't know what to do, Mom. Please…help."

My mom stares at me for long seconds, the air around us quiet and cold. I can't tell if she's judging Owen and his family, or if she's just disappointed in me, that this is the person I've decided to connect with, the one I've decided to love. And I wonder if she knows I love him? She finally stands, silently, and holds a finger up, leaving the kitchen and moving to the stairs. She climbs them and disappears into her bedroom for a few minutes before coming down with a small bag.

"Let's go," she says, everything about her shifting into professional. This is the person I need right now, but I know this person is only here because my mother loves me.

I lead her out the door, across our driveways, and into Owen's house. It's quiet when we enter, and I'm glad that James isn't making noise. I'm hopeful that he's fallen asleep, but I doubt that's the case.

When we get to the top of the stairs, I hold my hand up, wanting to go in first. My mom stands against the wall, and I look into the room, Owen still cradling his big brother, both of their eyes glazing over, staring into nothingness—each for different reasons.

"Did you get Ryan?" Owen asks, his focus coming back quickly. His arms looking tired.

"No," I say, and his posture deflates immediately. "But I got help. Please, don't be mad. She can help."

His eyes look terrified, and when my mom comes around the corner, Owen actually looks sick with embarrassment. My mom doesn't let him feel it for long, though, moving quickly into her medical-care mode.

"How long?" she asks, and Owen cocks his head, his forehead creasing with his confusion, his desperation and all of the hurt. "How long has he been detoxing?"

"Oh…uh, maybe a day or two? He was here a few days ago, and I gave him money. I just…" Owen swallows, the guilt swallowing him back. "I just wanted him to leave. But it wasn't a lot, and I don't think he bought much."

"Heroin?" my mom asks, Owen nodding as she rolls James's listless arm in her hands. "Looks like he's been getting high for a while."

My mom sees a lot of junkies. Her hospital is in the middle of Chicago, and she used to take a lot of rounds in emergency. Since she's been a practitioner, though, she's seen less, her work more with regular appointments. But addicts come in all shapes and sizes, and she still sees them, at least once a week.

"Can you get to a pharmacy?" she asks, and Owen rubs his fists on his eyes, nodding *yes* and breathing regularly for the first time since I've seen him this afternoon.

"Here, this is for buprenorphine, it will help him through the worst of it," my mom says, tearing a page from her script book and handing it to Owen. He reaches slowly, their hands touching as she passes this gift on to him. When his hand begins to tremble, she brings her other hand up and holds on tightly, squeezing.

"What is she giving you, O? Owen? What did that woman give you?" his brother's face is pushed deep into his pillow, his body barely covered with the sweat-soaked blanket, but he's trying to move. His strength has waned so much that the only thing he seems to be able to control is his neck and mouth. "Owen!"

Owen looks from my mother then to me, finally moving along the floor to kneel in front of James, pressing his hand firmly on his back, like a weighted blanket, his brother's shivers stopping temporarily under his touch. "I'm going to get you medicine. She's giving you medicine that's going to make you feel better. You need to let me go, James. I'll be right back," Owen says, standing slowly.

James's eyes follow every movement as the three of us move out of the room. When we're in the hallway, Owen turns quickly and wraps his arms around my mom, surprising both her and me. She looks at me over his shoulder and brings her hands slowly up his back to embrace him, holding him to her and telling him it will be all right. But I can tell in her eyes that she doesn't believe it.

She's lying.

I wait with my mother in the hallway as Owen leaves, and then when the door closes we both slide down the wall, our legs falling in front of us, on opposite sides, and we look *into* each other.

The light seeping in through the windows is growing dimmer with every passing minute, and more than twenty pass before either of us says a word, my mom the first to break.

"I'm sorry, Kensington," she says, barely a whisper.

"You have nothing to be sorry for," I say back.

"I do. I'm weak," she says, her eyes blinking slowly, her lips parted and waiting to find the courage to say the rest. "He wants to work through it."

My heart is on fire, burning with flames that have engulfed my chest. But this is not the place to yell, to rile up the broken man, Owen's suffering brother, in the room next door. So instead, I stare at her, waiting for her, daring her to finish, to tell me the rest. *Say it!* I'm screaming inside.

"Don't," I finally say back, my voice louder than it should be, so I hold my breath after, listening to the door, hoping James hasn't found the strength to move.

"He's all I know," she says back, her eyes drifting down to the knots in the wood floors, to the glue holding the planks together.

I can't sit here, and I can't understand how this woman who is so brave, so strong, can be so pathetic. Even the thought that my mother is pathetic stings my soul, and it breaks my heart. I stand as the tear finds the corner of my eye and I wipe it quickly with my sleeve, not wanting her to see. All of this—she says all of *this*—and still, I don't want to hurt her with my reactions.

"Learn something else," I whisper. "If he's all you know, learn something else." I can't look at her when I speak, so I move to the top of the stairs and climb down a few to sit in the middle and wait for Owen to return home.

My mother's phone rings, and I can tell it's the pharmacy. She recites several numbers, giving her consent as a nurse practitioner, then responding *yes* to a few questions before hanging up. We don't speak again, for the next twenty minutes, and when Owen joins us again, our interactions are forced and rehearsed.

"I'm sorry it took so long. They don't really trust my family at the pharmacist's," Owen says, his lip curled up on one side, his attempt at a joke. I smile back, to comfort him.

My mom helps coax James into taking the pill, assuring him that it will make him feel better. Within seconds, he looks utterly passed out.

"He's going to sleep for days. He'll wake up here and there, but not a lot. And..." my mom pulls her top lip into her mouth, pausing, "he's probably going to mess himself. You'll want to change the bed every morning and night. I can come back when your mom is home, explain things to her."

"Can he be left alone?" Owen asks, looking down at his hands that are folded in front of him. I can see the guilt taking hold of him.

"Don't think that's selfish...to want to take care of *your* things. It's not. You're allowed to put yourself first," my mom says, the irony of her words to Owen striking me—making me snicker to myself. I cough and do my best to cover up my slip, but she notices anyhow, her eyes sending me apology after apology.

"Andrew is here. But...I don't want this to be his problem. If I have to miss my game..." Owen starts.

"I'll stay. I'll stay until your mom comes home," my mom says. Owen shakes his head *no,* but my mom insists. "I've dealt with far worse. Go...go to your game. Take Andrew. I will stay."

"Andrew's sick. He's probably asleep," Owen says, his body wavering between staying and going.

"Go," my mom says, this time sternly. Owen nods and looks to me, and I nod in response. I take his hand as we walk down the stairs, and I never look back at my mom.

OUR RIDE back to the school is silent, but Owen's hand is in mine the entire time, his thumb wearing a line over my knuckles with the constant rubbing. We get to the school with little time before his game, and when Owen finally looks at his phone, he sees dozens of missed calls from Ryan and House.

I walk with him quickly to the gym, kissing him once hard and fast on the mouth when we reach the locker room entrance, then I move into the gym and take my place in a top corner of the bleachers, hoping that Elise doesn't notice and join me.

I want to be alone.

When I don't see her, I finally let myself relax, my muscles aching from how hard they worked to keep my body moving for the last two hours.

Owen must feel worse than this. I can't imagine. His eye doesn't look good, the bruise turning blue. No one seems to question Owen having a bruise on his face, though. I wonder how many times people assumed his bruises were from a fight when it was really from restraining James.

Through it all, his play—it's flawless. This is Owen's court, and this is the one place he can go and be master—everyone looking to him, every decision his. He commands the court, running effortlessly, his legs never showing fatigue. The way he passes, the way he sees the game, several seconds before his team, before his opponents. He would mock me for making this comparison, but I swear he plays chess out there.

Even when he's not the one scoring, he's the *reason* our team scores. At one point, a guy on the other team pushes him, backing his body into Owen, dribbling into him, trying to dominate him. But less than a second later, the ball is in Owen's hands, and he's breaking to the other end, finding House who takes his pass and slams the ball.

The Owen out here is different from any other Owen I know; yet all of those Owens are still in there. I see them. There's a moment—at halftime—when he's drinking from a water bottle, House's elbow leaning on him, and he spits some of the water out in laughter.

My mom gave him this—a small break from the chaos and nightmare at home.

It makes me forgive her weakness for the moment.

Owen is pulled from the game with five minutes left, the coach opting to sub in other players, thanks to our sizeable lead. And as much as Owen is still invested in the game, this rest—his body being idle—lets the bad start to creep in again.

I wait at the bottom of the bleachers for Owen to walk out, and one-by-one everyone leaves, until there's only me, a few students I don't recognize, and a man in a blue-and-white sweater, an expensive-looking briefcase at his side.

Owen finally exits the locker room, the exhaustion hitting him, his body dragging as he slides his feet to me, his bag with his uniform slung over one shoulder, his hair still wet from his shower. The closer he gets to me, the faster his steps come, and I'm starting to wonder if I'm going to need to catch him when he reaches me.

"Owen Harper?" the sweater man says, stepping out from the edge of the bleachers. Owen shakes his head quickly, his guard up instantly.

"Yes?" Owen says, stepping to the other side of me, pulling me in to him close, his squeeze tight.

"I'm Lon Mathison. We haven't met officially, but I've sent you a few letters," he says, reaching his hand out to Owen. Unlike other times, when Owen hesitates, he doesn't here. Though his body next to me is rigid, and frozen, his arm manages to work, moving out toward our new acquaintance, shaking his hand.

"Right, yes…nice to meet you. Were you…I'm sorry, here for the game tonight? I didn't know you were coming," Owen stammers, looking to me and back to Lon, his brow wrinkled.

"I'm heading to Wisconsin, actually. A few appointments, but I figured… you know, Woodstock was sort of on my way," Lon says, his voice coming out in a singsong way, his head bobbing from side-to-side. "You really handled that team from Union tonight. The Kellis brothers are supposed to be pretty good defenders. Didn't seem to slow you down though, did it?"

Owen blushes from the compliment, pursing his lips in a tight smile. It's the same face he makes anytime someone compliments his play. It's more than humble; it's almost like he's afraid to admit to being good, afraid if he acknowledges it, his talent will disappear.

Or maybe he's afraid people will notice.

"Well, I plan to send a few more letters. So, maybe just hang on to this," Lon says, flipping open his wallet and handing Owen a card. I glance quickly, reading "DePaul University" before Owen slides it into his back pocket.

"Right, well…thanks for coming out," Owen shrugs, his hand back in mine, his thumb tapping over mine, his anxiety absolutely boiling.

Lon nods once, then looks to me, but doesn't bother with introductions. He's out the door and pulling away in his car by the time we exit the building. We make it all the way to Owen's truck without him bringing it up.

"So…DePaul, huh?" I say, trying to get something out of him.

"Yep," he says, his answer short and clipped. Great, I'm getting *this* Owen again. I stare at him, waiting for him to break, to share more. Instead, he stops hard at the light, then turns to me. "Look, Kens. I don't want to talk about it. That guy, he's all dreams and opportunity and shit. And I'm just not feelin' it."

He reaches his hand over to my arm, holding it tightly, his eyes penetrating me.

"That's nothing on you. I just need to get myself ready to go back into war. Please understand," he says, my stomach falling to the floor of his truck, my heart stopping and my mouth watering with dread. I force it all—all of those feelings—down deep, hiding them from him, and I pull my lips in tight, hoping that somehow a smile is produced, and I nod.

"Okay," I say, cupping my hand over his.

His phone buzzes and he pulls it from his pocket, tossing it to me as the light turns to green. "It's a text, from House. Read it to me?" he asks, and I open it and recite House's words.

"You and your chick in for Sasha's? Nick scored some PBR," I read aloud.

"Pabst," Owen says, noticing my eyebrow rise at *PBR*.

"Ah," I say, opening the reply, my thumbs ready to type.

"Just type back 'James.' He'll know what it means," he says, and I do what he asks. Seconds later, House replies:

Sorry bro.

I put Owen's phone away, and grab his hand again, and I hold it until we get home. His mom's car is back in the driveway, and the lights are on in my house. We both have places to go, places with *things* that need to be tended to—things we both would rather ignore. But all I want to do is sit here, in his truck, in the dark driveway under the thin fingers of winter branches of the giant trees in our yards. Owen seems to want the same, because we both remain motionless for minutes, never breathing a word, until the first tiny, white flake hits the glass of his windshield.

"Look," he says. "It's snowing."

Owen's eyes close, and his face is washed in pain. I kiss him and let him go inside, then walk to my own cage, locking the door behind me, dragging my feet past my mother who is asleep on the couch, a book in her lap. I kick off half of my clothes, leaving only my underwear and giant sweatshirt for warmth, then I pull my blanket from my bed and curl up by my window, watching the snow cascade down as I wait for Owen to come to bed.

He never does. And eventually, I succumb to sleep.

CHAPTER 17

My dad is at the house again this morning. He was staying at a hotel in Milwaukee before, but he moved to a bed and breakfast in the center of town. This all feels so weird, like he's…*visiting.*

An unwelcomed visitor.

The first few days this week, I asked my mom what was happening. She said he was just coming over for coffee and breakfast before work, making an effort to be friendly—assuring me that was it. I stayed in my room the entire time. I refuse to acknowledge him. I know he leaves when she does for work, though. I asked Owen to make sure of it for me, and he did, once or twice, driving back by my house while I was at band. My dad's car was always gone.

I heard him pull into the driveway this morning, watched him walk up to the backdoor with a box of donuts in his arms. My father never bought donuts. Not once. Not even when I was a little girl and had slumber parties.

Willow is coming over, helping me pick out something nice to wear for the dance after the final football game. I'm going with her and Jess and Elise. Owen and Ryan both don't want to go. Ryan, because he just doesn't like dances, and Owen because he doesn't seem to like much of anything lately.

His brother has been with him for five days, and yesterday, I saw James come outside. He was wearing a pink pair of sweatpants and a large gray T-shirt, his mom's clothing I think. He rushed to his car, dug around in the backseat, then swore a few times before going back inside.

He looked terrible.

I quit asking Owen about it. His answers are always short, resentful. I don't blame him. I hate his brother for doing this to him, for doing this to his family. Owen's mom was able to fix her schedule at work, and for the last two days, she's been able to be home with James when nobody else is. It's not a permanent thing. I don't know how long it takes someone to get off of heroin, but I'm guessing three days is kind of fast.

When I hear Willow's car skid over the dip in the driveway, I call her.

"Hey, lemme guess, you heard me bust my axle on your stupid driveway," she says, her engine cutting off both over the phone and out my window.

"If you were a cat, that sound would basically be the bell around your neck," I joke.

"Yeah, yeah," she says, her voice muffled as she stuffs her phone in the crook of her neck. I hear the door slam closed in the background.

"So, when you ring the doorbell, I'm not coming down," I say.

"Another fine morning with good ol' Dad, I see," Willow says.

"Yes. And don't get a crush on him," I say quickly. "I like you, and I don't want to make another voodoo doll of a former friend."

"First of all, *gross*! Your dad is okay looking, for fifty, but he's not my bag," she says. "And second, voodoo dolls?"

"No comment," I say back, kicking the cutout photo of Gaby I made the other night under my bed. I poked my red pen through the eyes to make her look like the devil. It made me feel better for about five minutes.

"Okay, hanging up, about to ring the doorbell. See you in a sec," Willow says, ending our call. I crack my door open just enough to hear the drone of the conversation happening downstairs. My father is talking about his latest set, some new cellist playing in their symphony. My mom is pretending to be interested. She's always pretended to be interested. I can envision it, her head propped on her hand, the nodding and the *ohs* and *uh huhs*. I never really stopped to pay attention before, but I'm more aware now, my perspective…different.

I bet he's sleeping with the cellist.

The doorbell rings, and I can hear snippets of my mom's conversation with Willow, when I notice the shadow of two people climbing the stairs, I leap from my door to my bed, crossing my legs and grabbing the closest magazine available. It's the most cliché move possible.

"Thanks, Mrs. Worth," Willow says, her eyes wide at me in apology that she led my mom up here with her. My mom's not the enemy. She's just disappointing.

"Thanks, Mom. You can go now," I say, my tone clipped. I'm being a bitch. I've been one for five days—ever since I found out my father was trying to woo my mother, and she admitted that she was considering it.

My mom lingers at the doorway, her eyes glaring at me. She looks pissed, but her resolve dissipates quickly the longer she stands there. Because *I'm* right.

"Your dad brought donuts…" she starts.

"Not hungry," I say, flipping pages on the dog magazine, pretending to be immersed in the cute puppy faces on the pages. It's something we got free in the mail, from a shelter. If I had access to my father's checking account, I'd send in a donation for ten thousand dollars.

"Right, well…" she says, but I look up at her, my eyes snapping to hers, challenging her. Well *what*? Well, I should really come talk to him and think about forgiving him for the unforgivable, because he brought donuts and that proves he's a good person? I don't know what she's expecting, or what he is for that matter. But I've come to terms with the idea that my father is only my father genetically from now on.

My mom closes the door finally, discouraged.

"So that was awkward," Willow says, flopping on the bed next to me, her arms and legs out in all directions, her reddish-blonde hair loose and wild.

"Sorry," I say.

"I get it," she says, rolling on her side, turning to prop her head on her elbow. "My parents are divorced, too. I have to take turns picking sides. Or at least…I used to. I quit caring about offending one of them, and honestly, now that I don't make it a big deal, they don't seem to use me as a weapon against one another."

I nod in agreement, but stand quickly from the bed, moving to my closet, changing the subject. Divorce doesn't seem to be a topic being discussed by my parents, and I don't want to draw comparisons with Willow. I'd give anything for my mom to tell me she's talking to a lawyer.

"So, how formal is this thing?" I ask, flipping through the things in my closet. I don't have a lot of in-between clothing. Dances at Bryce were always *extremely* formal.

"Just wear leggings and a cute sweater or a dress or something like that. It's cold as hell outside, and it's going to snow all night," she says, moving next to me and flipping through a few things on hangers. She pulls out a long gray sweater and tosses it on my bed. "That works. Wear your Uggs, and I'll help you put your hair up. You'll be cute."

I sigh heavily as I sit down next to the sweater, pulling it onto my lap. "You know, I'm totally okay *not* going," I say, but Willow cuts me off.

"Stop it. Jess doesn't really dance a lot, and I like going. You're coming to dance with Elise and me. It'll be fun," she says, tossing my boots from the box on my closet floor.

"Fine," I huff, but I smile when she turns, softening my tone. I'm actually happy she wants me there. I just wish Owen was up for coming, too. He hasn't been himself lately…or maybe he has. Maybe that's what has me feeling this way; I'm worried that the Owen I had was brief, and he's gone back to dark.

I decide to wear my outfit to school for the day, opting to ride with Willow instead of driving myself. I question that decision every time she slides the wheels several inches into the intersection with each stop. We don't have early-morning practices any longer now that the football season is coming to an end. Our state competition is next weekend, so we spend every band class practicing the music, no longer worrying about marching and formations. Thank God, because it's so cold outside. I don't march, and only end up standing on the sidelines watching my breath create fog circles in front of me.

Willow helps me twist and pin my hair up over my head before the end of class, and I manage not to ruin it during my independent study. I let my hands play a few classical pieces today. I wanted to see how it felt.

It felt…like nothing. But it didn't hurt, either. It didn't make me angry.

And it didn't make me think of my dad. But then I let myself play *my* music, and I feel that all over my body.

That's the difference.

With five minutes left before class ending, I do something that I've never done before—I excuse myself to the bathroom, to touch up makeup, to make sure I look good. I want Owen to notice me.

This is apparently where Kiera and her friends go during second period. The smell of stale smoke is in the air, and I know they flushed something the second they heard me walk in. The scent is sweet, yet pungent—probably marijuana. I smile at Kiera, acknowledging that she and I share something in common. I guess we're acquaintances in some sick, twisted way. She smiles back, but never talks to me directly.

She's sitting on the edge of one of the sinks, her legs propped up on the next one over. There's a run in her black tights, and she's dabbing nail polish on the end, trying to stop it from growing.

I'm even more awkward touching up makeup in front of her, and her friends. I can feel them watching me even though they're pretending I'm invisible. It's like being in a room with ghosts.

"You going to the dance?" one of her friends asks her.

"Fuck no! Sasha's having a party; I'll be there," she says, her eyes flitting to my reflection in the mirror quickly before moving back to the run on her leg. I watch as her friend moves closer to her and whispers something in her ear, something that leaves them both laughing and covering their mouths.

Her friend comes toward me after a few minutes, and I work to pack up my things calmly, pretending I've finished whatever I was doing. I'm mentally forcing myself to slow down, not to look nervous. The girl smiles at me in the mirror—then pulls her purse straps from her shoulder, dropping her heavy bag on the edge of the sink. She pulls out a bottle of pills and pours two small white ones in her hand, reaching her other hand down to cup water from the sink and swallowing the water and pills down quickly.

She leaves her gaze on me, her smile never changing, never growing or shrinking. It's just there—like a dare. Her eyes are just the same—taunting, bait. She's waiting for me to flinch, to be offended or question what she's doing. But I don't. A lot of the girls at Bryce did drugs in the bathroom, usually expensive designer ones. What she's just done isn't shocking to me. What's making me uncomfortable is the amount of lips in this room that have kissed my boyfriend.

I smile back at her reflection, amused internally over how hard she's working to intimidate me, her gaze staying on me, her brow lowering. I pull my things together slowly, and then I take the extra step of pulling a towel from the holder and wiping the few drops I've left behind on the sink. Nobody breathes a word when I leave. But the second the door closes, the room behind me erupts with laughter.

I shake my head and roll my eyes. But I also stand still, letting my back slump against the wall around the corner, letting my breath leave my chest in one long exhale, some of my confidence slipping away with it. Their laughter…it still feels bad. I can convince myself of a lot of things, but I think we all want people to like us—like us, or let us be invisible. Right now, I think I'd be happy to have left that room unnoticed.

The bell rings seconds later. I pull my backpack over my body and make my way to class, blending quickly with the backpacks, hats and chatter, shedding everything that made me feel as if I stood out—not in a good way—seconds ago. I step into our English class where Owen's feet are on my chair—waiting for me. My mouth can't help but smile seeing them there. As quiet as he's been, these small gestures are still there. I'm grateful for them.

They let me breathe again.

"Missed you this morning," I say as I slide into my seat, my hip cozying up next to his ankles, my body wanting any kind of touch. Owen's eyes stay on me as he leans forward, sliding the hood from his head. His feet finally fall to the floor.

He tilts his desk as he leans far enough forward for his lips to reach me, but he passes my mouth, moving right for my neck. "I like your hair," he says, his eyes a little hazy. His hot breath on my neck sends shivers down my arms and back.

"Thanks," I say. "Willow did it. It's for the dance."

He pulls away, but keeps his eyes fixed on me, on my bare neck.

"I'm visiting my grandpa after school," he says. "Wanna come? I'll bring you back before the game."

"I'd love to," I say, my heart thumping so heavy with hope. This is the first time Owen's done something different from the routine of his house, from checking on James, from being short with me. It's the first time in a week he's initiated the conversation, and it's made me feel happy enough to cry. I'm not sure why, but the sensation almost chokes me, suffocating my lungs quickly. I think it's because I've been afraid of losing him.

I'm saved by Mr. Chessman's entrance, and I turn to face the front, keeping my head down until the swell of emotion leaves my chest and I'm able not to act so desperate for his attention.

Owen's quiet for the rest of the day, holding my hand briefly in the hallway—sitting at our table for only part of the lunch period, kissing my cheek and telling me he'll see me after school before joining House outside. For a minute, I think I see him taking a drag from House's cigarette, but I can't tell for sure.

He skips science, and I notice the teacher put a packet to the side for him, his name scribbled on a sticky note slapped to the first page. It looks like notes for everything we've covered. This happens a lot. I wonder who delivers these to him, how his work gets done.

I'm already half expecting his truck to be gone when I walk out at the end of the day, so I move toward Willow's car, meeting up with her in the parking lot. "So what's the plan, chicka? Dinner with me, then the game tonight?" she asks, Jess coming up behind her and wrapping his arms around her body, pulling her close. Everything about them is so easy. I hate them for it right now.

"Uh, I don't know…I was gonna go with Owen somewhere, but…" I stand on my toes, looking around, but I don't see his truck anywhere. I pull my phone from my pocket, hoping there's a message. But there's nothing. "I don't see him, so he must have gotten busy."

I say these words, but what my gut feels is that he forgot. It hurts, but I can't get mad, because I've seen what life is like inside his house.

I follow Willow and Jess to Willow's car, and we all climb inside, me taking the small seat in the back. I pull my phone to my hand and watch the screen, waiting for a message from Owen, for anything.

"Burgers?" she says over her shoulder.

"Yeah…that's fine," I say, not hungry in the least. We head to Joe's Burgers, and as we pull into the parking lot, I swipe my screen and open a message to Owen. I want him to know where I am.

I probably want him to feel badly about it, too. It's selfish.

You weren't here, so I left with Willow. We're grabbing dinner.

I keep the phone clutched in my hand, waiting for it to buzz, and the instant I feel it, I step up out of the line for food.

"It's Owen. I'm not that hungry, so I'll wait for you guys out in the car," I say to Willow, her eyes focusing on me harshly for a few seconds before finally giving me her keys.

"I know. I'm not being careful," I roll my eyes. Willow knows a little about what happened with James, but I would never be able to give her the full picture. You can't understand unless you live through something like that—see it for yourself. I start reading Owen's message before I get to the car.

Shit, so sorry. Time got away from me. I came home to check on James. Mom had an appointment. Can I come get you? Where are you?

I text him back quickly.

I'm at Joe's. I'll wait out front.

I rush back inside and find Willow sitting at one of the window-counter tables, her feet swinging back and forth underneath—so carefree.

"Owen's coming to get me," I say to her, dropping the keys on her tray and moving my phone into the side pocket of my bag.

She grabs the keys and slides them in her jacket pocket, but she keeps her eyes on me the whole time. She hasn't actually said anything. In fact, she's been nothing but supportive. But that look she gives me makes my stomach feel sick, like I'm letting her down, letting myself down, breaking rules meant to be followed.

"What?" I sigh, unable to take it any longer. Willow's lips part, but she doesn't speak, instead her teeth catch the tip of her tongue and her lips roll into a soft smile, one that tries to erase every message her eyes have been giving me.

"Will, come on," I say, sliding into the seat next to her, my eyes shifting between the driveway out front and her. "Tell me now, before Owen gets here."

She breathes in long and slow, through her nose, filling her lungs. I know that breath—it's the one used for courage.

"Jess saw Owen buy drugs from a guy out in front of the movie theater last night," she says, letting her words fall out all in one breath, her body heaving forward with the loss of the weight of this secret. "Owen was with House. Jess said he couldn't tell what it was, but he could tell it wasn't something...well, something normal. It was really weird, and Owen didn't look right, and...he's been smoking. I see him smoking with House in the morning, behind the school. Did you know he smoked? I know...I know; it's not that big of a deal. It's just...I didn't know he smoked, and now I'm wondering what else he does. And his brother..."

She stops there, just short of accusing Owen of being an addict too.

I stare at her with my mouth a little open, my eyes wide, my brain working to find a place to put everything she just said—to file it and make sense out of it. I want to argue with her, tell her she's wrong, what Jess saw is wrong.

But I can't.

Then I see Owen's truck pull up outside behind her.

"I...I have to go," I shake my head, standing and trying to wake myself from the shock. "I...I don't know. I'll see you at the game. But I've gotta go."

She doesn't speak, and I leave before we even have a chance to look at one another again. I carry this new twisted feeling right into the truck cab with Owen, slamming the door closed, shivering from the outside air and the cold feeling still lingering inside his truck.

"I'm so sorry," he says, shifting into drive quickly and peeling out of the lot. I smile and buckle up, then I sniff for any sign of cigarettes, alcohol —*anything.*

"How's James?" I ask.

"Same," he says, his usual, one-word answer. He's chewing gum, and I can't help but overanalyze that now. I've never seen him chew gum—at least, I don't think I have? His mannerisms are nervous, almost jittery, and I find myself noting every single twitch. I'm staring at him, and he keeps glancing with his periphery, never fully giving me his eyes.

"Something wrong?" he asks finally, his arms working to turn his steering wheel onto the highway. The truck swerves with his jerk on the wheel as another car veers into our lane. Owen presses his hand hard on the horn, his fist pounding on the window as we fly by the other car. "Fucking asshole!" he screams.

My pulse is drumming throughout my entire body from adrenaline, and I keep my hands gripped around the material of my seatbelt, my palms sweaty now despite the quickly dropping temperature. Owen seems to have forgotten his question of me—or maybe he no longer cares. I don't dare bring it up, instead holding on for dear life and watching out the front windshield as we pass exit after exit, finally getting to ours.

His grandfather lives in a home that's been converted from one of the old farmhouses on the edge of town. The gravel drive is slushy from the rain and snow. There are two wheelchairs on the front porch as well as a plush seating set and a space heater. The home seems old, but it's painted nicely, and it looks like it's cared for. When we step from the truck, I scurry to the front and reach my hand forward, expecting Owen's to meet mine.

But it doesn't.

He stuffs his hands into his front pockets of his coat and walks up the path to the door, spitting his gum out into the rocks along the way.

My heart aches from his cold shoulder, and I feel the dark shadow overpowering us.

Owen rings a bell, and a woman answers, her hair pulled under a bright orange cloth. Her accent is thick, and it sounds Polish. She welcomes us inside, and hugs Owen, his rigid muscles softening under her touch. I'm grateful for whatever her embrace just did.

She welcomes us in; Owen takes my coat. There's a fire and a few people sitting in chairs watching TV. The room is warm and inviting, but the people in there feel lifeless, their faces lost somewhere in the past, their vision not quite focusing on the screen. Any activity happening around them isn't real to them at all. As homey as this place feels, it feels equally as sad.

I follow Owen to a room down the hall, and he knocks twice before turning the knob.

"Hey, Grandpa," he says, his body puffing up again with stress, his shoulders stiff and his breath held.

"Is that you, Relish?" An old man stands slowly from a sitting chair that's facing the window, leaning forward three times before finally getting enough strength to get to his feet. He reaches for the cane propped up against the table next to him then slides a pair of glasses on his face, his head covered in one of those plaid hats that snap in the front.

"It's me. I brought a friend. I'd like you to meet Kensi, Grandpa," Owen says, his voice no longer hard and angry, everything about him softening, as if his grandfather is a flame to his ice.

"Oh, yes...yes...Kensi. This is the one, the girl you...the metronome, right?" Owen's grandpa says, his feet shuffling forward, his weight being assisted by Owen's hold on him. I meet them in the middle of the room and look to Owen, whose eyes flit to me briefly with a smile. It disappears just as fast.

"Yes, Grandpa. That's the one," Owen says.

I reach my hand out, and Owen's grandpa squeezes it in between both of his. His skin is dry, and his hands are cold. His gray eyes are cloudy, and I wonder how old he is. "Well, aren't you lovely," he says, his smile so much like Owen's that I can't help but giggle a little seeing it.

"Thank you, sir," I say.

"Call me Gus. Tell me, Kensi...do you like Rosemary?" he asks, and I look to Owen for help. He shrugs and steps back as his grandfather hands over his cane and slides toward a small dresser against the far wall.

"I guess so..." I say, wondering what he means. Every step he takes is small and cautious, and his hands hover out in front of him, shaking a little. I slide closer, my hands ready to catch him, but when I look to Owen, he just winks and gives a small shake of his head. Gus pulls a record from a paper sleeve on top of his dresser, then lifts the lid on an old turntable sitting next to it, leaning forward, his hand shaking with the weight of the player's needle and arm. He drops it down with careful precision on the record's edge, and soon, soft music spills out into the room.

It's Rosemary Clooney. I recognize it immediately, and it makes me chuckle. "You know, not many people your age appreciate things like this. But I had a feeling you might. Owen says you're quite the musician," he says, reaching both hands out, his fingers twitching, calling me closer to him.

"*White Christmas* is my favorite," I smile, and Gus pauses, raising his plump chin toward me before turning to glance at his grandson.

"Did you hear that, Relish? This one's got good taste," he says, turning back and taking one of my hands and then the other. He holds my arms out to the sides and begins to sway me slowly from side to side, his chest humming along with the tune crackling from his record player.

"Why do you call him Relish?" I ask, catching a glance of Owen over his grandfather's shoulder. He's standing in the bedroom doorway, his head leaning against the frame, both of our coats draped over his arm while he watches his grandfather dance with me. His chest rises once with a short laugh when I ask about his nickname, his hand rubbing his face, then resting over his mouth, hiding what I think is a smile.

I wish he weren't hiding it. I'd give just about anything to see Owen smile.

"Shall I tell her?" Gus asks.

"I couldn't stop you, could I?" Owen says back.

"Ha…I guess not," he says, letting go of one of my hands and encouraging me to spin out and then back to his arms. "This one summer, when Owen was little, maybe four or five, before Bill died, we went to a lot of ballgames out in Kane County. Owen would beg us to take him. But then he'd get there, and the little bugger couldn't sit still. So…I started making a deal with this kid; I said that any time he could pick the winner in the hotdog, ketchup, and relish race, I'd give him a quarter. He picked *relish* every time. But what's weird, is relish *won*…every single time!"

I look back over my shoulder to Owen. With lips tight, he shrugs, his smile faint, maybe a little sad. Memories seem to do that to him.

"Well, this little son-of-a-gun, he found out that the announcers only had one video to show on the board, with *one* outcome. After about six dollars in quarters, I asked the ticket man about it and he told me. He's been *Relish* ever since," Gus says, a sense of fondness in his voice, despite the way his laugh taunts and teases.

"Yep, that's me. Relish," Owen says, his voice more distant. "Hey, I'll be back in just a minute. Take care of her, okay Gramps?"

Gus spins me away from him one more time, then brings me back, waving his hand to send his grandson off. Owen steps away from the door, back in the direction of the main room. Before he turns, I notice his brow pulled in, a deep wrinkle at the bridge of his nose.

"Have I told you about Grace yet?" Gus says, his gravelly voice so thick he has to pause our dance and reach into his front pocket for his handkerchief to cover his mouth as he coughs.

"I don't believe so," I say, wondering if this is going to spin into another interesting story about Owen's youth. I wish he enjoyed hearing them and sharing them more.

"Ah, Gracie. I met her at the Apple Festival, ya know," he says, and I can't help but smile when I realize he's talking about his wife. "She used to date one of the Wilson boys, the family that owned the orchard?"

I nod.

"Huh," he chuckles. "She would have made a mint in life if she just stayed with that fella. Those boys made millions off that land. Sold hundreds of acres to developers."

"I bet she was happy with her life just as it was," I say, spinning myself out for a turn during our dance now. I've only known him for five minutes, and already I think I would be willing to marry Owen's grandfather.

"Maybe so…maybe so," he says, a shadow of sorrow falling over his eyes, his posture sinking a little. "I spent ten cents on a kissing booth to kiss her. We were schoolmates, and I loved her my entire life. Let's just say when I kissed her, I didn't stop when the guy said time was up. He had to pull me away. But Gracie, she never kissed another man after that. We were married in the spring."

Gus steps back from me, reaching for the edge of his bed, so I move with him to make sure he finds his seat safely. He looks a little uneasy on his legs. "Are you sure you haven't heard this story before?" he asks, his eyes glossier than they were a moment ago. He's fumbling with his hands, his fingers working for his pocket, pulling out his handkerchief again, then reaching for the small glasses hanging from a chain around his neck.

"I'm sure," I say, my voice soft. I'm not positive how best to answer him.

"Oh, baby girl. I miss you," he says, and I can see actual tears forming at the edge of his eyes as he looks at me. Gus is confused. I recognize it. My grandfather had dementia, and often thought I was my mom. I can see what's coming; I am good at this terrible game of pretend. "Did I tell you

Gracie died? Her funeral was so sad. Your mama was the prettiest girl in town."

I hear Owen slip in, and I turn to look at him, unable to mask my concern and sadness.

"This is Kensi, Gramps. You just met her," Owen says. He looks over the few books out on his grandfather's side table, surveying the room without making it look like he's snooping. Sadly, I recognize this too. My mom used to have to search my grandfather's room for stashes of untaken pills.

"Right, sorry. It's getting late. I get confused sometimes. I think maybe it's time for my medicine," he says, trying to stand. Owen puts his hand on his shoulder and smiles.

"I'll get Emma for you," he says, nodding to me to follow. We dip into the hall, and the woman who let us in is coming with a small box and a glass of water. She slips into the room with us and doles out a red pill, carefully handing Gus the glass of water and waiting while he drinks it down.

She smiles at us again, her lips never quite making the full curve though, then she whispers something to Owen, both of them looking at each other with a certain heaviness. When she leaves, Owen reaches for his grandpa's hand, giving it a squeeze. "I'll be back again in a day or two, Gramps. I promise," he says, leaning forward and kissing his grandfather on the forehead. I notice the nice leather shoes in the corner, the ones that used to belong to my father, and it makes me smile. They are in a far more deserving place, being worn by a far more deserving man.

Gus sits perched at the end of his bed, his gaze drifting off to the quiet happening outside his window, and Owen and I move to his door.

"You take care of my baby girl now, you hear Billy?" Gus says, his eyes never veering from the window.

"I promise," Owen says. What seems such a simple gesture, pretending to be someone he's not, is so far from that. Owen stepped into his nightmare just to let his grandfather live in a dream for a minute.

Another glance is exchanged between Emma and Owen as we leave, and when we reach the porch steps, I feel the darkness wrangle a hold of Owen even more. Everything about right now feels cold—more frozen than the ice beginning to frost the ground.

Owen walks to my door first, holding it open for me to climb inside, and he stays there long enough to close the door for me. It's gentlemanly, but it's also very robotic. When he gets to his side, his face is completely void of any emotion—he's wiped himself clean. He fires the engine and pulls away, his tires kicking up rocks as he pulls out of the long drive with too much speed. It makes me nervous, and I reach forward, gripping the dashboard's edge with one hand. Owen's eyes dart to my hand, and he sighs heavily, never really slowing down.

We drive in silence for a few minutes, the only sound the clicking repetition of the blinker while Owen waits to enter the highway.

"I'm sorry," I say softly, wanting to show him how much I understand, how bad I feel, how I know how much it hurts—those memories, his grandfather's illness, being called his *father*.

"Don't," he says quickly. Softly.

Cold.

Everything. Cold.

I keep my mouth shut for the rest of the trip, but my inner voice makes up for everything I don't say. I question it all. Question what Willow told me, what others said about Owen. I think about the warnings. I think about his brother, about his father, about his grandfather.

And I question everything I've felt. I still feel it though. And that's the problem. I want to scream at him, punch him, kick him and hurt him physically. I want him to feel the pain this frustration is causing me. But I love him too. And the only conclusion is that something must be wrong inside of me to feel this way. Loving Owen Harper is dangerous; yet I can't help myself.

"Why did you even ask me to go with you?" I ask finally, my voice shouting from the frustration of being stifled for so long. We're pulling into the school parking lot, and the sun is setting. Owen's mouth is in a hard line, his forearm muscles flexing. His head covered in his black beanie, hiding.

Always. Fucking. Hiding!

"You heard me!" I say, pulling my seatbelt from my chest before the truck comes to a stop near the bottom of the hill. He punches the brake to be cruel, and I fly forward, catching myself with my arms, bruising my elbow against the hard plastic of his dashboard. He never looks at me—not once.

"Why did you ask me to come if you didn't want me here?" I repeat my question, one hand braced on the seat, the other on the door handle. Owen is shaking his head, his eyes staring at the center of his steering wheel.

"I have no idea," he says, his voice an eerie calm, his head shaking with a breathy laugh. When his eyes move back to me, I see everything that's left inside him…and in a flash, it all falls away.

Owen. Is. Gone.

I slam his door shut, and turn, walking fast down the walkway to the band room, willing myself to look ahead. But I'm counting. I count every step I take that I don't hear Owen's truck shift—that I don't hear his engine rev, that I don't hear his tires squeal. I get to seventeen before I hear him disappear. I turn, only to see dust, his taillights faint as he whips around the corner.

"Goddamnit!" I yell, my stupid rebellion echoing off of the concrete walls around me. I yell because I'm alone. And I cry. I cry fast and hard, ducking into the shadows of the small outside stairwell. I hide there until the pressure of everything leaves—or at least until I'm able to hide it. All I'm left with is the sharp pain in my chest.

I avoid Willow and Jess during warm-ups, and I busy myself in a conversation with a freshman in the band, a girl I don't think I've ever talked to before. She's telling me about her dance class, and how she learned some sort of hip-hop move. She's excited to do it with her friends at the dance tonight.

She's so happy. Right now, right this second, I would trade places with her.

I didn't want to go to this dance before, *not really* at least. And now, I *really* don't want to go. But I don't want to go home either. I'm caught in hell.

It's the last game of the year, which means we don't have to wear uniforms. They're all being cleaned for competition next week, so I get to keep my hair up, to stay in my stupid flirty outfit—the one I wore hoping Owen would see me and change his mind, that he'd want to go with me.

Stupid girl. I'm such a stupid girl.

This is the same guy who put on a performance every day at lunch with a different girl, the same guy who provoked me with his flirtatious threats. This is the guy who cheats death, who actually seeks it out so he can laugh at that fine line—crossing it from time to time just to prove he can, other times, erasing it completely. My lips must be moving while I talk to myself, while I laugh silently about how crazy it is to think that Owen Harper wants to go to a school dance.

"You okay?" Jess asks, his voice low. He's trying to hide his question from Willow, and I'm glad.

"Nope," I say honestly, sucking in a deep breath to keep the tears where they belong, the sting coming back to the corners of my eyes.

"Owen?" he asks, tapping his drumsticks along his jean-covered leg.

"Yep," I say, watching him tap out a rhythm.

"Sorry," he says, moving his hands over to my lap and tapping the sticks on my shoes, my feet folded up as we sit on the floor. He plays out an entire song, and it makes me smile. He's distracting me, for a few seconds. I'll take this.

When Willow comes over to hold her hand out and lift me to a stand, I look at Jess, my eyes flashing a warning, and he closes his eyes with a quick smile. I know he won't say anything, and I'm going to pretend I'm fine.

I'm fine. I'm fine. I'm fine.

I walk with Willow to the field, a few of the band parents taking care of our equipment for us tonight, pushing my xylophone down the hill. I listen while she tells me about the dances at this school, how they usually go. I let her fill every second of empty air, and when I feel the conversation start to end, I ask her another question, and she begins again.

Our team is almost winning the game, which helps keep us all excited and invested. More blank space filled. If only I drove myself…I'd shove my hand down my throat right now to make myself throw up so I could go home, play *sick.* But Willow's so damned excited about this dance; I couldn't make her miss it just to take me home.

And again—home isn't much better.

The clock runs out, and our team actually wins. It's our first win, so students rush the field. You would think we just earned a play-off berth rather than a record of one and nine. I turn my attention to my things, to the long dark hill of the parking lot. That's when I notice the souped-up, lifted pickup in the distance. I see the glow of his cigarette in the dark, and the glare is just enough to spotlight the two girls standing with him—one of them leaning into him, hanging on his arm.

I keep sneaking looks at him as we file down the bleachers, and I don't even hear Willow talking to me when she finally yanks on the sleeve of my sweater, jerking my body hard toward her.

"Where the hell are you?" she says, her eyes scrunched, her lips flat in a straight line. She follows my gaze to House in the distance, then turns to me again. "It's just House," she sighs.

"I know," I say back, my eyes still on him, my response barely a response at all. I watch as a few more people join him at the end of the parking lot. It's the regular crew. Everyone. Everyone but...

"Owen," she says, getting my full attention.

"Where?" I ask, looking around the lot, trying to find him.

"This...*you.* How you're acting," she says. "This is about Owen."

I keep my eyes on hers, unable to blink. I don't even know how to articulate what's wrong, but something is just...*wrong.* And it won't feel right again until I see him.

"I have to go," I say, my eyes still wide on hers. I'm begging her with them.

"This is what I meant," she says.

"I know," I say, looking back at the crowd of shadows, the faint sound of roaring laughter and House's voice in the distance. "But it's different, Will. I can't explain it, but I just know it's different."

"Whatever," she says, her eyes rolling as she turns to walk away from me.

"Willow, please..." I start, but she holds up a hand, her pace steady, toward Jess. I feel like a lousy friend. I feel selfish. I am selfish, because all I want is my Owen back, the sweet one—the guy who sat on the piano bench with me and forced me to remember things I loved.

The *Owen* I love.

I pull my arms around my body tightly, my hands nearly numb from the cold. My coat is in the band room. But I can't risk going to get it now. House—he might be gone by then.

He doesn't see me coming at first, and I pick up on hints of their conversation as I approach.

"Sasha is such a fucking skank," one girl says, pulling the cigarette from House's hands and putting it between her lips, dragging in slowly and letting a smooth trail of smoke stream from her lips as her chin tilts up to the sky.

"You're just jealous," says another girl.

"Whatev. I could be like her, totally hold some party so I could fuck Owen Harper," she says, handing the cigarette back to House, leaning forward toward her girlfriend. "But I don't need to...*been there, bitches!*"

The other girl laughs loudly in response. They saw me coming, and that conversation was for my benefit. This morning, it might have been enough. But tonight, my issues with Owen are so much bigger than some girl trying to make me jealous. I'm close enough now that House notices me coming, too.

"Ken Doll," he says loudly, an exaggerated laugh coming from the girl sharing his cigarette. "You ditching the punch bowl in the gym for some real shit?" He holds a bag out toward me, several rolled joints weighing it down. His eyes stay on mine with a heavy stare—he's trying to provoke me. But he has something I need, so I ignore his efforts.

"Where is he?" I ask. He pushes the bag back into the front of his sweatshirt, then drops his cigarette to the ground. The girl sitting next to him pouts, so he leans over and kisses her hard, his hand running up her leg and stomach until he's squeezing her tit in front of everyone.

That was for me, too.

"Get in the truck, baby," he says to the girl, and she slides from his hood, dragging her hand over his crotch while she walks by, her gaze on me the entire time. She thinks she's marking her territory. She can fucking have House.

He steps forward, his heavy black shoes stomping the glowing ash into the pavement, then he spits to the side before bringing his eyes to me.

"He'll be at Sasha's," he says, his smirk lingering. I wait for him to offer more, to say something more. But instead, he smiles—that stupid fucking obnoxious smile that's only halfway really there—his eyes barely slits, sleepy from whatever he's been drinking or smoking. I don't care how long he's known Owen—House is a dick.

"Give me your keys," I say, and he leans back, looking up to the sky, laughing hard once.

"If you wanna ride, get your ass in the truck. But I ain't giving you my fuckin' keys," he says, holding them on his thumb in front of me before clutching them. I stare at him, daring him. But House isn't Owen; he honestly doesn't have a line between right and wrong.

"Fine," I huff, brushing by him, giving his body a hard jab with my elbow as I pass. I climb in through the driver's side and slide to the middle, the girl waiting inside staring at me with a look as though I've just made her drink bleach.

"Who the fuck are you?" she says, her breath practically flammable. I look her right in the eyes, then turn to face the front, my mouth never once breaking its hard line. I just need to survive ten or fifteen miles.

House climbs into the truck and starts the engine quickly, my hands still feeling his seat for a belt as he rounds the corner and peels out of the parking lot.

"I don't have belts. Just hold on and keep your mouth shut," he says, rolling his window down at the stoplight and leaning out yelling something to another car pulling up next to us. The rest of the people that were with their group are packed into an old Bronco, and when one of the guys flips House off and speeds by, he punches the gas fast without even thinking, running the red light right behind his friend, swerving us into the middle lane to regain his lead.

The dodging and darting for position happens between every stoplight until we get to the edge of town, when House finally punches the gas hard, his engine growling as we speed away from his friend, toward Sasha's house, toward darkness. My hands are gripping the undersides of my legs hard, trying to keep my heart from bursting with fear, my stomach sour with adrenaline. I hold my breath for minutes at a time, saying silent prayers to a god I've never talked to before—the pounding in my chest actually painful by the time we slide into the dirt driveway of Sasha's house.

Four or five other cars are out front, and the thumping of the music echoes around us. I don't hear any people, though, which only makes me feel less sure about the place I've stranded myself—about what I'll see when I get inside. House exits the truck first, then holds the door open and nods his head rigidly, urging me to hurry.

I slide out, my hand accidentally pressing on the horn as I pass the steering wheel, and House winces.

"Fuck," he says, pulling my arm, his squeeze on me rough. He slams the door closed once I clear it. He meets the other girl at the front of the truck, reaching his hand into the waistband at the top of her jeans, his hand on her actual ass.

I trail behind everyone, entering the house last. Everything is exactly as I remember it. The lights dim, the drone of music drowns almost everything else. People are gathered around the couch and floor, smoking something from a liter bottle. A few others are pouring drinks at the kitchen counter while others make out in dark corners around the house.

My turn is slow, my eyes careful to catch every face, every outline, weeding out each profile that's not Owen. But I don't have to find him. He finds me, his voice haunting, his words harsh—if not indifferent.

"What are you doing here?" he says, the sound barely audible over the loudness of the music. His tone isn't angry. It isn't curious.

It's nothing.

I step into the sitting room, toward the beanbag chair he's sunken into, the familiar clear glass propped between his fingers on his knee.

"Decided the dance sounded lame," I say, taking the seat across from him, leaning back into the softness, letting my arms fold across my chest, like a shield.

Owen keeps his eyes on me, and I let my mouth relax finally, but I don't smile—and I don't breathe. He pushes the plastic glass to his lips, the space between the vodka and his mouth paper-thin, then pulls it away, instead tossing it into the fire next to us—igniting a short burst within the flames.

"Have enough tonight?" I ask, the tightness in my chest relaxing with every second I'm here with Owen and he's quiet.

"Something like that," he says, his eyes lost somewhere off to the side. I want to get up; I want to move to him, to hold him and kiss him—to make him remember how he felt a week ago. But I'm so afraid of scaring him, of offending him—of the *other* Owen. So I wait, and I stare into the flames, catching glimpses of him from the side, waiting for him to move, to shift his eyes from whatever thought is holding him.

"My brother's gone," he says, his voice monotone, his gaze still on the blankness of the wall beyond me. "When I went home to check on him..." his head finally shifts, just enough, his eyes finding me—*finally*. "He. Was. Gone."

"I'm sorry," I say, still holding myself to my place, fearful of disrupting our connection, afraid he'll close this door right back up. Owen is in a cycle. His family is in a cycle, but Owen more so than anybody else. And it's killing him. I've watched it strip life from him in a matter of weeks.

"I wish he would just O.D. already," he says, his words flowing with a small laugh, one he quickly hides, ashamed of it. But I know that laughter, it's not the happy kind, it's the kind that tries to hide pain, hide the need to cry.

He keeps his eyes fixed on me, but not my face, almost as if he's not strong enough to look me in the eye. He watches my hands as I rub my arms, my body still cold from the ride here in House's truck.

"You're cold," he says, sliding his coat from the floor over to me. I lean forward and grab it, wrapping it around my body. I mouth the words *thank you*, and Owen nods.

"You drive yourself here?" he asks, his eyes coming to mine in fits, dropping away quickly.

I shake my head *no*. "I came with House," I say.

"You shouldn't have," he says, biting his tongue, his lips perched to say more, his mouth working to speak, but no sound coming out for several seconds. "I just meant it wasn't safe...not...not that you shouldn't have come," he says, his eyes coming to mine again, holding longer this time.

"Jess said he saw you smoking," I say, regretting it instantly, Owen's gaze quickly falling away. He shrugs. "You...you smoke?"

He shrugs again, and it feels empty. It makes *me* feel empty. I've never seen him smoke. I've never tasted it on him. He told me his only vice was drinking. Drinking...and death.

"Just a few times..." he says finally, his head to the side. His eyes lost again to the flames. "Only recently. It calms me."

I've seen Owen angry. He embraces it, lets it fuel him and carry him through anything. He's fearless. But this Owen is far from angry. He's beyond sadness.

"He says you bought drugs, too. Was that just about being angry, too?" I say, my hands squeezing my biceps, my arms hugging my chest tighter, my frustration building. This question, it seems to stir something, and Owen leans forward slowly, his eyes dark as his hands meet one another in front of him, his knuckles popping one at a time.

"Is this you trusting me? You get your friends to spy on me, spread rumors and come back to you with dirty little secrets?" he asks, the corner of his mouth twitching as his tongue wets the edges of his lip.

"Is it a lie?" I ask, looking at him with the same strength he's showing, not backing away from his challenge. I wait, and Owen waits to. Never answering.

After what feels like a minute, he leans back, his hands folded behind his neck. "James needed more of that shit your mom gave him. We don't have insurance, so I bought it off the street. House knows a guy," he says, his head leaning to the side again, but his eyes still fixed on me.

His answer stabs me in the heart, and I feel horrible for doubting him. The silence takes over again, choking me, and my chest burns. I don't know how to fix this, how to fix any of this.

"You get what you came for?" he asks finally, and I let the silence take over again, my mouth unable to work, and my mind unable to build words to say. The way Owen's looking at me—it's as though I fit into his collection of disappointments, and I don't know how this happened, and it's breaking me in front of him. The muscles in my legs are firing with the want to move, trying to help my heart escape this place before I show him what he's done, how easily he's destroyed me.

But I can't move.

As much as he's hurting me right now, he also owns me. And I let the tear slide down my face slowly without wiping it away. I let Owen see—I let him see inside.

"Why did you take me to see your grandpa today?" I ask, the same question I asked earlier, the one he never fully answered.

Our eyes lock, and I choke down the desire to blink away the water building in mine, giving Owen everything I have left. I wait. And I wait. The fire snapping, the sound of my breathing heavy in my own ears, the thumping of the music a room away, fading to a dull drumming pattern. I'm in a tunnel, Owen the only thing I see, and inside I'm screaming for him to give in, to feel something, to let himself *feel* anything other than wronged and cursed. Owen shrugs finally, his lip lifting the tiniest hint.

He's mocking me.

With one look, he breaks me, and the tears threatening to fall find the heat of my cheeks. My eyes flutter, almost feeling sleepy from the hammering of emotions tearing into me. I stand to my feet, listening to that voice inside that has been begging me to leave since the moment I slid into House's truck. My feet take three steps away from Owen, pausing while I shut my eyes. I ball my hands into fists and push them against my face. *Stop crying, stop crying, stop crying…* I can hear my own voice in my head, and even in my thoughts, I am torn and in pieces. I turn slowly, filling my lungs with one final inhale. I find Owen's eyes quickly, everything behind them empty—lost.

"And here I thought it was because you loved me," I confess, my chest caving in quickly, threatening to cut me off from saying the rest. I let it tumble out with my last breath. "Just as much as I love you."

I let my words hit him, my body still, my thumbnails digging into the palms of my hands—a subconscious effort to create pain anywhere else, to pull this feeling away from my heart. Owen never even moves.

Before the next wave crashes over me, I turn away, stepping over the sweaters and shoes thrown on the floor. I catch House's eyes on me from the kitchen, his mouth smirking, like he's satisfied at my failure to pull Owen back to the light. I pick up my pace, not wanting anyone else to notice me, to see how pathetic I am.

I barely open the door as I slip outside, and when I do, I'm hit with a wall of wind, air so cold it practically slices through me. I pull Owen's coat tightly around me, hating that it's his, that I need it, but thankful for it. I take lunging steps out into the driveway, through the gravel, past House's truck first, then Owen's, until my feet find the pavement of the small two-lane road that brought me here. I can see my breath, and the threat of more snow is very real. I know I can't walk home. It would very likely kill me. But I can't stay here.

I won't.

I pull my phone from my pocket, the few dollars I folded along with it coming out and falling to the ground. "Shit!" I say to myself, bending down and feeling for them, my hands stinging. I grip them clumsily, but stay low, squatting, while I scroll to Willow's number, knowing there's a really good chance she won't pick up. My thumb hovers over her number for a few seconds before my phone lights up, ringing with a call.

Owen.

I stare at the phone, not knowing what to do, then after three rings, his call disappears. Panic swallows me whole, and I drop my money again, my fingers fumbling to call him back when I look up and see him walking swiftly toward me. It takes him three steps more to reach me, his hands clutching my arms. At first I think he's angry, and I flinch at his touch. But he brings me to his chest, the weight of his body working to shelter me. His hand cradles my head against him, and he only holds me harder when I begin to cry, my body shaking hard with each shudder.

My core is starting to shiver from the cold, and Owen scoops me into his arms, holding me against him as he strides quickly to his truck, opening the passenger side and setting me inside, closing the door quickly, and running to the other side. He gets in fast, starting the engine and moving the heat to high, then slides across the middle of the bench seat toward me, his hands cradling my face, his fingers rough, and cold.

"I brought you because I love you," he says, his words coming out in a rush, his eyes piercing mine, the darkness fighting with the light. "I wanted you to meet him because he's important to me...and so are you...because I love you. I hurt you...because I love you...because I'm fucked up, my family's fucked up, and my problems ruin everyone they touch. I don't know how to stop them, how to separate the good things from all the shit in my life. I ruin everyone I touch. People leave me...they leave me—" Owen's breath catches, stuttering, his eyes turning redder as he talks. "People in my life...they die, and if they aren't dead yet, they look for ways to kill themselves. And all I can do is watch."

"Owen," I whisper, my hands wrapping around his wrists. His head falls forward to mine.

"I love you, Kensi," he says, his lips grazing mine softly, before he pulls his mouth away again, leaving his head against mine. "I love you…but I will suffocate you. Drown you. Loving me…it will kill you."

"No, it won't," I say, my hands shaking his wrists. His fingers are still cupping my face, his thumbs trailing tiny circles along my jaw. He rolls his head side-to-side along mine, his breath coming out in a slow spill, his body full of nothing but fear and doubt.

I slide my hands up his wrists, to his fingers, threading mine through his along my cheeks then bringing them to my lips, kissing them, and letting my lips linger along his knuckles before resting my cheek against his palm. My touch finally opens his eyes, and I look into him, searching for my Owen, making him believe.

"I love you, and I'm not afraid to love you," I say. I can see the worry behind his eyes, the warnings working to remind him that he should run, that he shouldn't feel. I can tell I'm not winning the battle, but I'm fighting the war, and every piece of me I give weakens that fear a little more.

"I shouldn't let you," he says, his bottom lip held under his teeth, his breath a sharp intake. "But I don't care, Kensi. Because I think I need you to survive. I think I need you to love me, because that's literally all I've got."

My hands wrap through his hair, grasping at the back of his head and neck, pulling him to me. Owen's hands are just as needy, our mouths crashing together hard and fast—this kiss, it's more than all others. We both hang onto it, neither one of us ending it.

I kiss Owen until the sun threatens to come up. And after he drives me home, I kiss him again, with the same sense of urgency. My father's car is gone; it's a concert night, so my world in my house is safe until tomorrow. I'd be content to stay here, though—in the driveway, in Owen's truck, kissing him. When my lips are on his, I know he's here.

When I finally steal myself away, the worry creeps in again, so I run up the stairs, into my room, collapsing by my window. Owen's truck is empty outside, and seconds later, his eyes are on me, his body where it should be, his smile finding its way.

Please, God, don't let me lose him again.

CHAPTER 18

I'm not sure whether or not Willow meant to text me the photo of her and Elise, smiling happily under the glow of a plastic disco ball. But I'm glad she did.

Her photo was waiting for me on my phone this morning as I woke up, and I texted back immediately, gushing about how cute they looked, how much fun I bet they had.

I wouldn't have traded my night for theirs for all of the disco balls in the world. I'd even live through the hurt and pain of the beginning again to end up with Owen telling me he loves me.

Yeah, well...the picture would have been cuter if there were three of us in it. Beeyatch.

Her attempt to call me a *bitch* makes me laugh.

You can't even spell it right, that's how I know you're not really mad at me. If you were, that bitch would be full of 'I'.

I hold my phone in my palms, my head under my covers, the morning light fading into afternoon. I slept hard and well, asleep at my window by three, then crawling up to my bed at six with a crick in my neck.

Bitch.

She sends the single word, and at first it shocks me, and I think she might actually be mad. But she writes again quickly.

You're right. That felt dirty. Lose the 'I'.

I laugh to myself, and smile, rolling to my side just enough to peer out the window to see if my mother's car is gone. It is. She has the long shift today, which means I'll be free of my father, too. No homework or projects are on my plate, the school semester winding down as Thanksgiving approaches, and James is gone. I know the worry of where he went is there, but the duty of caring for him isn't. I'm hoping—at least for the day—that Owen will be mine.

Everything...okay?

Willow's text is cautious. She's trying to be supportive, though I know that's not how she really feels.

He said he loves me.

I tell her because I'm happy. And because she's the only person in the world I would want to tell. I think, somehow, telling her this will make her see Owen differently. I know it does when my phone rings a second later.

"You're shitting me," she says. No *hello* or pause to wait for me to answer.

"I'm not really sure how to answer that," I say, "but *no*? I guess? Or *yes*, he loves me?"

There's a pop of her gum over the phone, and I hear her keys jingle in her hand. "I'm at the mall. This is serious, and I'm at the mall. Buying shoes. And there are all these people around talking, and I can't hear you very well," she's speaking a million words a minute. It's funny.

"I will give you a play-by-play later. I promise. Go buy your shoes," I laugh.

"Okay, but first…you said it back, right?" she says with a small pause in the middle. She's still worried about me.

"I did," I say. I said it *first*, not that the order matters.

There's silence on her end, and I can hear her moving through the door to another store, the faint noise of other conversations in the background.

"So listen," she starts, and I wait as the phone shuffles some more, and eventually the background noise fades, and her voice echoes. "I'm sorry I walked away from you. I was being overbearing and protective, and it's not really my place. But…"

"Are you in a bathroom?" I ask, really noticing the echo now.

"Yes, I had to pee. Now don't cut me off," she says, picking right up where she stopped. "Just promise you'll talk to him, about those things I said, what Jess saw."

My lips hover, barely parted, and ready to answer, but instead I close them, nodding. "I will," I say finally. I'm satisfied with the answers Owen gave me. But Willow, she'll be more satisfied if she thinks I had those conversations with him on her urging. She wants to be the *super* friend, and frankly, I've got an opening for one of those. I'd like to give her the job.

I hear the toilet auto flush in the background. "Okay, letting you go now," I say, holding the phone out from my ear.

"'Kay 'kay, call you later," she says, leaving her phone on as she stuffs it in her purse. I laugh to myself and hang up for her, but not after considering listening to her shoe shop for just a little while.

I've slept in, and I'm pretty sure Owen has too. His room looks dark, and his truck is out front. His mom is back on her regular work schedule, so I know the boys are home alone, which gives me an idea.

After a quick shower, I head to the kitchen and fry up the rest of the bacon left in our fridge. I scramble half a dozen eggs, then throw in some cheese and toss it all together in one of my mom's big spaghetti pots. I bundle myself, then bundle the pot in one of my mom's coats to keep it warm during the short walk across the yard. It takes Owen a few minutes to get to the door, and by the time he does, I'm shivering out front, the snow starting to fall with some strength now.

"You brought me...chili?" Owen asks, his eyes on the ridiculous pot I've bundled in a brown, fuzzy coat.

"It's bacon," I smile. "But if you don't want it, I could just..." I start to turn and Owen quickly snatches the pot from me. He teasingly tries to close the door after, but eventually pulls me inside quickly too.

Andrew stumbles down the stairs, his body long and awkward in nothing but a pair of pajama bottoms. He doesn't have his brother's build, and his youth is sweet, his chest a little boney and quite pale. He rubs his eyes, so much of him a little boy. Owen protects that part for him, so Andrew can savor it.

"Kensi brought bacon," Owen says, holding up the pot. The mere mention of the word wakes Andrew up completely, and we all move to the kitchen, where Owen pulls out three bowls and serves up my semi-omelet creation. I'm strangely satisfied watching them both eat.

"So now I owe you, what, like two meals?" Owen asks, his mouth full while he talks, one hand gripping the bowl, the other a spoon.

"You could just make it one *really* nice dinner," I say, folding my arms.

"Good," he smiles. "Done. Tonight, I make you a steak."

I laugh, but he steps to the side, reaching into his freezer and pulling out two frozen pieces of meat, tossing them in the sink to thaw.

"Oh, you were serious," I say, liking the idea of being here for dinner.

"Yep," he says, shoveling another giant forkful of egg and cheese into his mouth. "Andrew, you're going to Matt's house."

"Uh, I am?" Andrew says, and Owen drops his spoon in his bowl, holding both hands on the counter, looking at his brother, giving him *the* look. "Oh, yeah. That's right. I *totally* am. In fact, I'll call him right now, see if his sister can come pick me up. Oh, and in case you wondered, Kensi, yes, I do talk robotic like this sometimes. I'm not pretending at all for the sake of my brother getting you alone."

Owen flings a strip of bacon at his brother, and Andrew grabs it off the counter. "Do not…sacrifice bacon, O. You know better," he jokes, popping the bacon in his mouth before rinsing his bowl quickly and winking at me while he dashes around the corner and back up the stairs.

"I…" Owen starts, sliding his bowl into the sink too, along with mine. He moves closer to me, until he has me caged against the kitchen island, his lips starting at my neck and moving along my face, grazing my lips. "…want to spend the entire day doing nothing, but this."

"Oh…oh," I say, blushing. Owen doesn't stop kissing me, and within minutes, he has me slid up on the counter, his body positioned between my legs and his hands running up my back, under my shirt, pulling me closer to him.

"Ehem." We pause when we hear Andrew cough, and I duck my head into Owen's chest, embarrassed. "Matt's sister is on her way. Do you guys think maybe you could hold that shit off for like, oh, five minutes?"

Owen smirks at me, tipping my chin up to look at him, laughing at my shyness. "Nope," he says as his eyes meet mine. "We'll just take this shit upstairs. And you keep your mouth shut to Ma."

Owen scoops me up against him, carrying me backward piggyback style through the kitchen, past Andrew, and up the stairs. I slap my hand to my face, hiding again as we pass his brother, but I'm glad we're alone the second Owen kicks his door closed.

I love the way his room smells. There's a faint leftover scent from his cologne, and there's a certain smell to his bed and clothes, something in the way he washes things. It's probably just fabric softener, but it's my favorite fabric softener in the world. I want to soak every bit of it up—and remember it forever.

Owen carries me right to his bed, kneeling and laying me down on my back, my head resting on his pillow and my body smothered in his messy blanket and sheets. I crawl underneath quickly, pushing my shoes from my feet and letting them drop off the side of the bed. Owen slips under the cover with me, pulling my body close, running his fingertips through my tangled, damp hair with an amused look on his face.

"I just showered," I smile, realizing I'm not very put together at all, even less than normal.

"I wish I was there when you did," Owen says, his lips finding my neck, teasing me. I cover my face with my hand, fighting against the redness taking over. "You blush so easily," he teases.

"I know," I admit.

Owen slides to his back, smoothing out the blanket over us and pulling me into him, letting me curl up onto his side. I can see the edge of my house through his window, and the thought that I was just sleeping over there, on the other side, strikes me. When Owen rubs along the back of my neck, massaging my sore muscles, I let out a small moan.

"Already, huh?" he teases.

"Nooooooo," I push at his side, but not enough to ruin the hold he has on my neck. It feels glorious. "My neck is killing me. I fell asleep at the window."

"I know," he says, his eyes grazing over my face, moving from my eyes to my mouth to my chin, then… "I watched you."

I love that he watches me.

"I'm so sorry, Kens…about yesterday," he starts, and I slide up his body and kiss him once, hard on the mouth, then press my fingers to his lips.

"Don't be," I say. We look into each other for several long seconds, our eyes skimming across each other's faces. How did I get so lucky? How did I get this boy to fall for me?

"I still love you, by the way," he says, his lip quirking on one side; his silly grin makes me melt. "For the record. Last night and today, still feel the same."

I nuzzle in close, letting my eyes concentrate on our tangled hands, the way they look together. I love watching his thumb run along my fingers, over the back of my hand.

"I really liked your grandpa," I say, wanting to focus on everything good from yesterday. Gus was good, and seeing Owen, his capacity to love—that felt good to see.

"Yeah, he's a lady killer. I was worried there for a minute when I left you alone with him. He's been known to steal a girl away from a guy," he says, his free hand finding my hair, drawing it out in long brushes of his fingers.

"Do you visit him often?" I ask. "I'd love to go again."

I feel Owen's breath let out, then his kiss presses lightly to the top of my head. "Not as often as I should," he says, his voice growing faint. "Might see him a whole lot more, though, real soon."

I pull back to look at him, not sure what he means.

"We're a little behind on our payments," he says, his mouth flat, dejected. Everything that sentence means is conveyed in the look on his face.

"Where will he go?" I ask.

Owen raises his brow high, his eyes get wide and he looks from side-to-side.

"But, who will take care of him?" My heart feels heavy even asking this, because I already know. Owen takes care of *everyone.*

"I let coach know. He said he'll keep me on the roster, but my season's pretty much done," he says, unable to mask the sadness in his eyes. For the first time, I can hear the disappointment in Owen's voice about basketball. We've talked about the unlikelihood of him playing in college, but I think he always counted on having his senior season to remember.

"Can't your mom…?" I stop without finishing, instead feeling the touch of Owen's lips back on the top of my head.

"Her job pays the mortgage. She kind of needs to keep it," he says, a breathy but somber laugh slipping out. "Besides, I think seeing my Gramps like he is makes her really sad. She doesn't visit much. We'll get help, from a home health nurse. His V.A. benefits will pay for that at least."

"I'm sorry," I say softly, wrapping one of my arms around him tightly.

We lie there quietly for several minutes, listening to the front door open and close, to Andrew drive away with his friend, and both of us think of how alone we are. I know he's thinking about it; the rhythmic tickle of his fingers along my arm is almost wearing a line in my skin, and the stare from his eyes on my mouth is making my skin twitch with want.

"You've been playing…piano. Willow said something about it the other day. You…thinking about it more?" Owen asks, his words coming out nervously, distracted. It makes me smile against his chest.

"I have…been playing, that is," I say.

"And college?" he asks, his fingers still trailing along my arm, their pace slowing, but his path moving higher, closer to my shoulder and breasts.

"I don't know. My dad's probably moving back in, so I definitely want to leave. But I just don't *love* the idea of studying music anymore. Besides, my showcase is Saturday. I'm not even ready, so I think I'll just bail," I say, my mind just now wrapping around the fact that Saturday is the day that's been circled on my calendar for nearly a year. Saturday. I'd nearly forgotten.

"You should still go," he says, his hand slowing down, his fingers flirting with the idea of moving more, of touching me intimately.

"I'll think about it," I say, not thinking about the piano now at all. Instead, thinking about where Owen's hand is going, what move it will make next, how alone we are, and how hot my skin feels.

I roll into him more, tilting my chin up slowly, hoping to find him waiting for me. His smile is tight and his eyes are trained on mine, the feel of his muscles beneath me, and around me, growing more rigid.

"Play something for me," he says, and I pull my brow in. "I mean, we don't have to go over to your house, just tap your fingers on me. I love watching your hands when you play."

I think about it for a few seconds, closing one eye and looking at him, judging whether on not he's serious. When I realize he is, his smile on me expectantly, I sit up, pushing off his stomach, and inducing a grunt as I knock the wind from him a little. "Sorry," I wince.

I straddle his upper legs, well aware of how close I am to the rest of him, then lean forward and place my palms on his chest. He's wearing a gray T-shirt that's thinning and has a hole in the center of the chest. The thin, smoothness of the fabric grips at him perfectly, and I force myself to pretend he's my keyboard when all I want to do is roam my hands along his curves in slow, smooth motions.

Closing my eyes, I rap my fingers a few times over his skin, feeling his stomach muscles tighten.

"Sorry," he chuckles. "Tickles."

Opening my eyes again, I smile, then stretch my fingers out, just as I would when presenting to the piano. "Okay, so *if* I were to go to my audition, I'd probably play this, along with one or two other songs. I'm a little rusty, but since you can't really hear the notes…" I stop mid phrase, lowering my gaze to my hands from his eyes, trying to concentrate on nothing but my tapping, the flexing of my fingers. I play Rachmaninoff, the same piece I played for Willow, and I let my fingers dance over Owen's chest, only glancing up once or twice to catch his grin as his eyes follow every movement I make. I swore I'd never play this song again, but this doesn't count—there's no sound.

When I finish, I press my palms flat, then smooth out the tiny dimples left behind in the cotton of his shirt. I feel a little foolish having just played air piano on Owen.

"That was fucking phenomenal," he says, and I laugh instantly.

"Shut up, you couldn't even hear anything," I say, and he reaches to grab my wrists, shaking them against him once or twice.

"Didn't have to. I felt it. How do your hands move that fast? That shit's crazy," he says, rolling his grip down to rub my fingers then back up my arms again, locking me to him.

"Thanks," I say, biting at the corner of my lip.

My breath exhales in a stutter, my palms growing hotter against Owen's chest the longer he holds me to him—the longer I look into his eyes. After a minute, he slides his hand from my arms to my thighs, running up my leggings until his hands cup my ass and he drags me forward.

I lean toward him as I move, coming to rest above him, feeling how hard he is through his flannel pajama bottoms, the heat searing from him and directly into me. His eyes never leave mine, and his hands move in fractions of an inch at a time, slow and calculated, until he pulls me down against him harder, making sure I feel everything he is feeling right now.

There is no mistake about what he wants. And his eyes, his smirk, his face…there is just the right amount of darkness in him. And I want it too.

"Remember when I asked you if you had a problem with sex, Kensi?" he asks, his voice gravely, deeper than normal. His tongue is resting at the edge of his teeth, like a serpent waiting to tempt me into sin, his lip curled just enough.

"Yes," I whisper back, my voice giving out, my breath stopping at the sensation of feeling him throb beneath me, my own body reacting, growing warmer…wetter. The first time we had this talk, it was confrontational. This time is different. This time, it's foreplay.

"You said you didn't care *who* had sex," he says, his tongue wetting his bottom lip before he holds it between his teeth, his eyes seducing me.

"Yes," I breathe again, relaxing into him, my thighs falling farther apart.

"I've had a lot of sex, Kensi," he says, his eyes blinking in slow draws as he peers up at me, his gaze growing more intense, his smirk honest. He owns his reputation, and as much as it bothered me, alone with those girls in the bathroom—right now, it's only making me crave him more. "But I have never wanted to feel what it's like to be inside someone more than I do right now. To feel someone I love. Fuck, Kensi, I want to touch all of you."

His fingers grip against my legs, squeezing my muscles, his hands barely able to contain themselves. I reach down for them, running my hands over his knuckles, then leading the way as I lift my sweatshirt up and over my head, quickly stripping my bra away next, leaving my breasts bare and cold, waiting for Owen.

His touch comes fast and hard as he sits up, his hands clutching at my back and his lips meeting my neck first. I arch as he pulls me into him, his tongue tasting its way down my neck to my nipple. Owen brings it into his teeth, looking up at me as he lets it slide from his grip slowly, his tongue circling the peak as his lips stretch into a satisfied smile.

I slide my hands up Owen, moving his shirt up his frame until he pulls it the rest of the way from his body. He reaches around me, lifting me and rolling me to my back, his mouth back to my breasts, which he sucks and kisses until they feel wonderfully raw.

He begins to kiss lower, hooking his thumbs at the waist of my leggings, dragging them down a few inches before stopping to let his kiss tease along my abdomen, kissing my bare hips as he slides the material further down my body, his fingers tugging at the small lace panties I wore with the hope he might see them.

Owen moves to his knees, pulling the rest of my clothing away completely before running his hands up my legs. He slides lower on the bed, kissing the inside of my knee, and I let my legs fall open, reaching for the pillow above my head to hide the redness building on my cheeks. Owen stops me, though, pulling on the corner of the pillow and moving it to the floor.

"Uh uh," he says, his tongue flicking against my thigh, dangerously close to my center. "I get to watch you. I want to see your face."

"But I'm embarrassed," I admit, squeezing my eyes shut, then letting one slip open. Owen slides up to my neck, kissing my ear.

"You're beautiful," he says. "And I want to watch you come apart for the very first time because of me."

"But you…I've…you made me, last time," I say, stretching my arm over my face, hiding. Owen lifts it and holds it over my head, kissing me lightly, his lips speaking against mine.

"Not like this I haven't," he says, brushing his lips down my body until he stops at my very center, his tongue taking long strokes against me, my legs spreading farther, wanting more with every pass of his mouth.

I grip the sheets and tug at the blankets, wanting to hide my face, but more because I feel like every touch of his tongue against my most sensitive parts is bringing me closer to losing control. Everything feels swollen, as if one more touch anywhere will send me over the edge, then Owen slides a finger into me, and the first wave crashes over me. My body shudders against his hand, and he holds on strong, pushing against me, his movements unrelenting until I feel every sensation stop, every pulse slow within me.

I. Am. Numb.

"That," he says, his mouth grazing against my ear, "was just the beginning."

Warmth rushes down my body, and a small whimper escapes my lips as Owen pulls away, standing in front of me. He removes his pants, and my eyes look, but quickly. There's so much of him—I don't know how it could possibly work. But I want it; my body is yearning for him to be inside of me.

Owen reaches for his dresser, taking a small packet from the top drawer, tearing the package with his teeth. I glance again as he holds himself, sliding the condom on with his other hand, and as nervous as I am about the pain, I'm more hungry to move past it, to feel him.

He kneels between my knees, his finger moving up and down my center, sliding in and out, relaxing me and exciting me all over again.

"I want you, Kensi. Please, I have to have you," he says, and I reach down, gripping his forearm, nodding at him, begging him.

"I want you too. Just…go slow," I say, my heart firing a billion beats per minute in my chest, my body clenching in anticipation of everything.

Owen positions himself between my legs, his forearms holding him above me, then he sweeps my hair to the side and kisses the corner of my mouth softly, letting me feel his smile against me. His hand drops lower so he can guide himself into me, and as the pressure of him pushes into me, his lips find my ear.

"Relax, Kens. I've got you," he says, coaxing my body to obey. He moves beyond the tip, pushing farther inside me, my muscles adjusting, my body stretching to take him—all of him—until Owen gives one final thrust, taking me from innocent to *his* in the flash of a second.

A single tear falls down my cheek, the pain stinging inside, and Owen notices quickly, sliding his thumb up to catch the drop as it falls toward his pillow.

"I've got you, Kens. I love you, and I've got you," he says, sliding back out from me almost completely, pausing to let my body relax again before moving into me slowly. The second time is easier—the stretching less, the sensation more—and soon, my body begins wanting Owen there, wanting to feel full from him, to take more of him, deeper.

"What feels good? Tell, me Kens. What do you want?" he asks, his voice sexier than it's ever been, the darkness there, but also a new kind of hunger. Owen may have the experience, but I have the control.

"Touch me," I pant, my eyes barely able to stay open as he moves slowly in and out from me. I feel his hand glide from my side, his thumb grazing my breast and traveling the length of my stomach until his fingers find my center and begin putting pressure on the rest of me, leaving nothing left untouched. Every bit of me is raw and open and on the verge, every push and stroke nearly ending me, until finally, I'm no longer able to hold on.

"Owen, I'm…I'm…" I say, arching my back and pushing my hips into him, feeling more of him against me with every pulse.

"You're so fucking beautiful," he growls, every push of his body harder, his eyes shutting, his breath stopping and his face growing tighter. Owen pushes into me two more times, his breath leaving his chest in one powerful burst before he pulls out from me and lies flat on his bed next to me, our bodies sweaty and tangled and happy.

We lie there for minutes, our hands linking, and our fingers teasing one another until finally Owen breaks our silence.

"That was easily the very best moment of my whole entire life," he says, his head falling to the side on his pillow, his hair tousled, and his eyes simply sweet.

I let my gaze fall to the side, too, meeting him. "I'm so glad Andrew went to Matt's," I smile, biting my lip and giggling.

"Me too," Owen says, standing and walking to his door, pulling his pajama pants from the floor. "He fucking hates that Matt kid, so he totally did that so his brother could *do it*."

Owen flashes wide eyes, and he mouths *"oh"* as he laughs at me, backing away from his room. I reach to the floor and throw his pillow at him, which he catches at his chest.

"Not funny! Oh my god, I don't want your brother knowing about this, that we…*do it*," I roll into the covers and pull them around my body and face. Owen leaps on me quickly, tugging the material away, pinning me to the bed and holding his mouth an inch away from mine.

"Everybody is going to know that you are mine, and that I am yours. And if I have to *do it* with you all weekend to make sure that look of bliss is permanent on your face—I will. My brother just already knows what everyone else will by the time I'm done with you," Owen says, his tongue teasing my upper lip before he moves away, standing to look down on me again, my body bare and ready to be touched again.

"Mine. All. Day," he says, his hands holding at the frame of the door, his body filling it completely. I watch him walk away, and listen as the shower water turns on. After a few minutes, I step from the bed and open the door Owen left cracked for me to begin with, hoping I'd follow. I step inside the hot water with him and let him tattoo happiness on my face just like he promised.

CHAPTER 19

I don't hear the sound of sirens or squad cars. I'm too caught up in my dream, asleep in Owen's arms, the hour late. We spent the day playing house, Owen burning our steaks on the grill, me burning the macaroni and cheese, melting away the water on his stove while I made out with him.

The entire day and most of the night, a dream—a delicious fantasy that is suddenly crashing down around us in a drowning wave of reality.

Owen wakes first, the sharp movement of his body as he lifts his head stirs me. He's to the window in seconds, then back to the bed, fumbling to put on his shirt and pants, sliding his feet into his shoes.

"What is it?" I ask, mimicking him, dressing myself quickly, my stomach sinking, sickness washing over me that something is wrong.

Something *is* wrong. Something is terribly, terribly wrong.

"Cops. My driveway, the street, it's filled with police. They have lights on my house. I'm not sure what's going on," Owen says, grabbing his phone in his hand, racing through his door, down the stairs.

I trail behind him, barefoot. There's no time for me to find my shoes. He slings the door open, ready to march out in protest, but he's met quickly with force, two large policemen standing guard at his door. One of them catches Owen, pushing him back into the house, knocking his feet off balance.

"What the fuck?" Owen yells, trying to push through the officer again. I reach to grab Owen's arm, to calm him.

"Stay in your house!" the officer yells, his finger pointed at both of us, his voice stern and loud.

"What the hell is going on?" Owen asks, pushing to see outside again.

"Sir, I'm warning you, get inside right now. Close this door, and find a safe place in your house and lie low, on the ground, hands over your head," the officer says, pulling the door closed and barricading it. Owen pulls the door a few times, turning the knob with no luck.

"Owen, what's happening?" I ask, my body tingling with nerves. Owen's pacing, moving through the kitchen to his back door, looking through the window to see more SWAT officers positioned there. He rushes to the living room, to the windows that face the backyard, and spots another pair of officers, weapons drawn.

"What the fuck landed in my front yard?" he says, running his hand through his messy hair, walking quickly from window to window, trying to get a glimpse of something, anything that will give him a clue what's happening outside.

"Drop your weapon!" We both hear a voice yell from outside over a megaphone, this warning followed by an eerie silence. Owen turns to look at me, his face frightened, a look I'm not used to seeing him wear. He rushes toward me, grabbing me by the arm and pulling me with him up the stairs, back to the safety of his room, and he pushes me to the far side, the other side of his bed.

"Kens, please! Get on the floor, under the bed if you have to," he says, pushing me down, pulling blankets and pillows to cover me, as if the cloth could stop anything from harming me.

"Owen, stay with me!" I scream, my hands gripping at his floor, my legs kicking to push my body under his bed, my face flat against the roughness, eyes searching for Owen's feet, to find out where he is. He sits low near me on the other side of the bed, so he can look out his window, out over the driveway.

And all at once, I see it—I see everything that is happening outside reflected in the absolute horror that suddenly paints Owen's face.

"James," he lets out in weak breath, his hand losing its hold on his phone, dropping it to the floor near me, his body growing weak in an instant. His knees fall from under him, and he grasps at the windowsill as he collapses, his arms just strong enough to hold his body to the window, his face pressed against the cold glass. His breath frosts it quickly, and he pulls a fist up, tucking the sleeve of his sweatshirt over it, wiping away the moisture in a manic circle.

"What is it? Owen, what's happening?" I scream, my body working to move closer to him, to hold him, to see what he sees.

"No! James, no!" Owen yells, his fist pounding at his window so hard he breaks it, slicing his hand, blood rushing down the length of his arm instantly. The sound of the glass, of Owen's screams and pounding, is so loud it's all I hear. It's the only sound.

Until it isn't.

The shot fires, but only once. Owen falls to the floor, his body nearly lifeless with pain, with sorrow, with grief, with guilt. Everything hits him all at once. I pull myself the rest of the way out from under his bed, rushing to hold him. I pull him to my lap, wrapping his sheet around his hand, doing my best to slow the bleeding from cuts I know are deep.

Owen lets me, his body weak in my arms, his heart—broken.

"Somebody! I need help, please! He's hurt. Help me!" I scream as loudly as my lungs will let me, my voice growing hoarse, raspier with every shout, until finally two officers and a medic come rushing through Owen's door.

"Please, help him. Please, he hurt himself, on the window. There's glass in his arm; I think some of it's still in there," I plead, my arms not wanting to let go of their hold on Owen. His face is strewn with tears, his gaze lost out the window, to the scene below.

I'm afraid to look.

The medic works to stabilize Owen's bleeding, tearing cloth and rewrapping his arm, removing what glass he can. He speaks into a radio strapped to his shoulder, asking for help transporting Owen, and soon two more firefighters arrive, carefully placing Owen's arm in a splint, urging

Owen to lie on his back, on the stretcher, so they can carry him down the stairs.

Owen fights them, unable to say actual words other than "no" and "leave me alone." He eventually walks with assistance down the steps, to his living room, his mom rushing in the door, meeting him with her own tears.

Horror. Both of their faces…horror.

And I can't help.

JAMES WAS HIGH. He was high, and he was scared. He stole a car from a mall parking lot three towns over, then led police on a chase along the highway, hitting several cars, leaving a trail of injuries and damaged vehicles along the roadway as he exited the wrong way up a ramp. He raced down the two-lane roadway to his home, down the dark stretch of country road Owen had once raced on carelessly with me, down the strip of roadway James had taught Owen to drive fast on as a kid.

He swerved through his mother's front yard, clipping the bumper of Owen's truck, and spinning the stolen car to the side, stopping near the end of the driveway—sideways, the hood bent open and the wheel crushing the brick of the house.

Police had him then. He was circled, the three cars that had followed him collapsed on him, six officers opening their doors quickly, drawing their weapons and ordering James to just. Stay. Put.

But James was high.

And he was scared.

And that gun, the one Owen once held to his own head in a dare, the one that I saw James threaten Owen with only a few weeks ago—it was in James's hand.

The police called for back up, and SWAT came quickly. That's when Owen woke up. James held the gun to his side, his other hand behind his head, scratching at his hair, rubbing his neck vigorously, his brain trying to think under a fog of impairment, his heart desperate for a solution, for a way out of *this* hell.

More guns were drawn. James became agitated, holding the gun up over his head. This is when officers began to order him to drop his weapon, when Owen and I ran up the stairs.

It all happened in seconds, slices of time that felt as though they took hours to pass. Owen saw his brother out that window, he saw how frightened he was, how cornered he was, and he knew there was no way out.

Owen knew.

He saw it coming before James lowered his arm just enough, tilting the gun just right, the barrel pointed to his head. He knew a millisecond before his brother drew his finger back, pulling on the trigger with the right amount of pressure.

Owen knew his brother was dead the minute he came home from school two days ago and saw James was gone. He didn't know how it would happen. But he knew it would.

And he knew he'd feel like it was his fault in the end.

CHAPTER 20

My father hasn't been back to the house, and I haven't asked my mother when or if he's coming. I don't care any more. He can move in here, and my mom can give in, live in her self-made prison. I hope she doesn't, but either way, in six more months, I won't be here to see it.

I haven't resolved myself to college or the road, but whatever it is, it will be my choice—of *my* doing. The only person I care about disappointing is myself.

And Owen.

Owen hasn't been to school, and I've noticed the piles of homework left in Mr. Chessman's class for him. Every day, the pile is gone, so someone is taking Owen his work.

There wasn't a funeral. Funerals are expensive, and no one would show up for James, Owen said. I go over to his house every night, and we sit in his room, perched on the edge of his bed, holding hands, but not talking.

We never look out the window.

His mom is home—time to grieve. But even she doesn't seem broken. They just seem as if they're going through motions, carbon copies of themselves—the same tired and exhausted bodies, but spirits and hopes completely washed away. Owen's taking care of the "paperwork" and filing death certificates; investigating old credit accounts in James's name and calling relatives. His mom began cleaning out his room within a few days.

Neither of them has cried again like they did the night James put the gun to his head. I just don't think they can anymore. They're…empty.

Willow and Jess don't know what to say. Even now, days later, they walk along with me out to the parking lot, making plans, talking in half sentences, afraid everything they say might offend me. Everyone's heard the story. Things like this, they spread quickly in Woodstock.

The Harper boys—they're wild. What James did has only cast more eyes on them; I see them look at Andrew when he comes to our school in the morning, before he takes the bus to his school. I bet they look at him there, too.

I bet they'd look at Owen like this. That's why he doesn't come.

"Are you…still in for the competition Saturday? I think Mr. Brody would understand. You know, if…if you can't perform?" Willow asks. Eggshells—everyone is walking on eggshells.

"I'll be there," I say, smiling, eyes wide.

"Okay, but, if you can't…" she says.

"Ohhhhh my god!" I yell, tossing my bag into my passenger seat. "Please. Not you. Please, Will…just be normal. I need you, *you* out of everyone, to act normal. I'm begging."

She's standing before me, her arms folded in front of her, her fingers picking at her elbows nervously, her eyes searching mine. I know this is awkward for her. It's awkward for me, but I'm not Owen. When she sees him, *then* she can get all uncomfortable and formal and careful. But now, when it's just her and me and Jess and our friends—now is the time to be blunt, to pop her gum, to pretend I don't have other shit happening in my life.

"So I'll pick you up at six?" she asks, a shrug of her shoulder to punctuate her question.

I smile and nod. "Yeah, six. And bring snacks for the road trip," I add. I get in my car and watch as she and Jess get into hers from my rearview mirror. Driving away, I don't look at her again, because that small exchange was normal, and I don't want to ruin it. I hold onto it for the few miles to my house, and then I pull into the driveway and see Owen's truck and forget all about normal.

His house is first, and I leave my backpack in my car and don't bother going to my own home. My mom is home today, but she'll see my car out front. She knows where I am—where I've been *every* day. She's been trying to help with paperwork, answering Owen's questions about where to file things, how to handle closing accounts, who he needs to notify.

James didn't leave a very big mark on this world electronically, and erasing what there was of him wasn't very hard.

I don't bother to knock, instead just stepping inside Owen's home. His mom is labeling boxes at the table, taping things closed, and moving them to the front porch one at a time. She marks FOR DONATION on the last box, and I pull it from her arms and take it to the porch for her. When I come back inside, she's still standing at the table, her hands pressed flat against the now-clear surface, her eyes intent on the center.

When I move closer, she flinches, snapping awake again, and runs her hand once over the smooth tabletop before pushing the chair underneath. "Thank you for helping with things this week, Kensi. O and I...we appreciate everything you and your mom have done," she says, her eyes never able to meet mine completely. "Can I get you something to drink? I think we have..."

She opens her fridge, pausing when she sees it's empty. She starts to laugh lightly, closing it, and backing away until the backs of her legs hit the table. She stumbles a little and catches her balance, then turns to me, a full smile on her face, her laugh coming out harder.

"We have nothing," she says, her lips squeezing tight, trying to hold onto normal. Her body begins to shake with laughter again. "Oh my god, we have...*nothing!*"

As if a switch flips, her laughter shifts into tears and her breath escapes her, her knees buckling again, sending her to the floor.

"Are you okay?" I rush to her, helping her to one of the chairs. "Wait here, I'll get Owen."

"No, it's...it's fine. It just, it gets to me sometimes—all of it. It's all just...

so much," she says, her red eyes peering at me, her face pale, her hair thin and tangled.

"I know," I speak, not sure what else there is to say. I don't *really* know, but I know enough.

Owen's mom takes a full breath, closing her eyes just long enough to clear them of tears and hide the redness, then she stands and pulls a hair tie from her wrist, pulling her hair back into a ponytail. "I'm going to run to the store. Owen's upstairs; he'd love to see you," she says, grabbing her coat from the hook by the door and leaving in a rush.

Everything has to happen fast, and there always has to be something to do. If there isn't, she'll fall apart. That much I understand.

I pull my own coat from my body and leave it on the table, then I climb the stairs, catching the soft sound of Owen's stereo. He's listening to the Black Keys, the same album he's listened to for five days straight. There will come a time, I fear, that he will never be able to hear these songs again.

Knocking softly, I push his door open enough to slip through. He's lying on his side, his arm propped up on an elbow, a pile of homework in front of him. "What's this…Owen Harper studying?" I tease. I've actually never seen him do homework, so the sight of it strikes me.

Owen smiles, the curves never quite making it fully up his cheeks, then tosses his pencil in the crease of his book, closing it, and pushing the papers to the side to make room for me. I crawl into his arms obediently.

"I'm a little behind. Just trying to catch up," he says, his nose cold as he nuzzles against my cheek.

"That's nice that the school got this for you. Nobody's really saying anything. You know, about what happened?" I say. Owen lifts his hand, running it through my hair and stopping at the back of my head to pull me to him for a kiss. He backs away a little after and sighs, his chest rising and falling in a pattern that he's kept up for days. Every breath he takes is heavy, an attempt to cleanse himself from how he feels inside.

"Mr. Chessman brings things over for me every couple days. He lives a block or two away. He's cool like that," Owen says, his eyes sculpting my face, looking at me endearingly. His affection for me has never waned, not once, through this tragedy. I think he's clinging to it. And I'm clinging to him.

"How's my boyfriend, Gus?" I ask. I've been wondering about Owen's grandfather, how his role in their house fits now.

"He's good. He misses you," he smirks.

"Well, he and I…we sort of had a fling. He's a really good dancer," I say, sucking my top lip in. Owen leans forward and gives me a chaste kiss, his lips grazing over mine until I let my lip free.

Owen pushes himself up to sit, and I join him, my hands spreading out a few of the assignments stacked on his bed. I notice Owen's math homework, and I pull it out from a folder, looking at the problems that he's already completed. His homework, it's different from mine. It's more advanced.

"Just one of many," he says quickly, taking the folder from my hand and pushing it back into the pile with everything else. He flips his English book open again, pulling the pencil out and tucking it behind his ear.

"I've gotta stop in at home, check in with Mom. I'll let you get to some of this. Maybe next week, you'll be at school with me?" I ask, standing from his bed. Owen smiles quickly, his eyes full of a fake kind of hope, pretending for my benefit.

"Maybe," he says. "I'll text you later, 'kay?"

"'Kay," I say, my eyes on his for a few extra seconds. Every look feels like he's drowning, and I'm trying to pull him back ashore.

I grab my coat and stop by my car for my backpack on my way back to my house, rushing up to my room before my mom has a chance to stop me. She's on the phone and nods with her finger up as I fly by her on the stairs. She'll come find me soon, but maybe I'll have a few minutes to log onto my computer, to be alone first.

My computer isn't where it should be when I get to my room, which sends me back downstairs, back to my mom, who ends her phone call and turns my computer screen around for me to see when I enter the kitchen.

"Why do you have my computer?" I ask, reaching for it. She snaps the screen shut and slides it back a few inches with her fingertips, just out of my reach.

"Why do you have a listing posted on Craigslist for the piano?" she asks.

Shit! How did she find that?

"It's my piano; I can sell it if I want to," I say, reaching again for my computer. This time she picks it up with both hands and hugs it to her chest. "Mom…"

"That's enough, Kensington. You have been stomping around here, acting like the adult of this house, for weeks. You may be eighteen, but this attitude needs to stop right here. Now tell me, without your new brand of sarcasm, if you don't mind, why the piano is on Craigslist?" She's doing that thing where her eyes blink at me slowly. She's pissed. And I still don't know how she found out about the piano listing.

"How did you find it?" I ask.

"Doesn't matter," she says. Her answer is fast. Too fast.

"Uh, no…I kind of think it matters. I put my phone number on there, and my personal email. So…" I wait for her, my head leaned to the side, my brow pulled in tight. And then it hits me.

Dad.

"He saw it, didn't he? That's what this is about," I say, shaking my hand, my feet shifting and beginning to trail back to my room. Fuck it. She can keep the computer.

"Yes, your father saw it. You know he's always looking for good buys on instruments for the program. He recognized this immediately and called me. Kensington, you cannot sell something that's your father's," she says, and I stop in my tracks, spinning on my heels, my blood boiling.

"His?" I shout. "*His* piano? Mom…are you…are you joking?"

"Kensington, you need to take this down…now," she says, opening the computer and spinning it around for me.

"No," I say, folding my arms. I'm throwing a fit. A staunch, standoff kind of fit—like I did when I was four and didn't want to eat my green beans—but a fit nonetheless. This is ridiculous.

"Yes," she says, the word coming out slowly, her eyes scrunched, wrinkling at the corners. We stare at each other like this for several minutes, and the longer I look at her, the longer I think about what she said, the angrier I get.

"You said it was mine. *Mine!* You said that was my piano. You told me when I was ten, after I won my first competition. Grandma died and left that piano to you—*your* mother, not his! And then *you* said it was mine. You told me that it was always meant for my hands, and you loved the joy it gave me. You don't get to take it back. And if I want to sell it, because it doesn't give me joy any more, then I'm going to! And he doesn't get any say in things! You can sweep those awful things he's done under the rug if you want to, but I will never forget. And I will never forgive him!"

I turn around the second my last word is uttered. With a calm but quick pace, I climb my stairs, turning back only after I've made it up the first few. My mother is frozen in her place, her hand just where it was on the computer, her mouth slightly parted, her eyes wide and on me…almost. I may as well have slapped her.

I get to my room and slam the door, like a child, and move to my window, putting my headphones on and pulling my knees up to my chest while I unzip my backpack and pull out my pile of homework. I look up every few minutes, waiting for Owen to look back, and after an hour, I can't take the waiting any longer, so I send him a text and ask him to come over.

My mom must have let him in, because I never hear the doorbell or knock, just the sound of him slipping through my door moments later.

"Homework done?" I ask, everything inside me still churning, still fuming.

"Uh huh," he says, his head tilted to the side as he moves toward me a little apprehensively. "You're pissed about something. Your dad coming over? Cuz I'm not so sure I'm up for wrestling him again."

"Ha," I let out a short laugh, then let my head fall forward into my hands, rubbing my eyes. "No, you're safe. Just doing that thing where I yell at my mom, but I feel bad about it. Even if I'm right…I feel bad."

Owen slides down on the floor next to me, both of our backs against my bed. He flips through a few of the things I've let fall out of my backpack, looking at the back of one of the books I picked up from the library. "This looks like a chick book," he says, tossing the copy of *Emma* I picked up from the library back onto my stack of notebooks.

"It is. It's one of my favorites," I say, looking at the cover. It's an image of the movie version, a carefree Gwyneth Paltrow holding her bow and arrow. "How come you have advanced calculus homework?" I ask the question quickly, keeping my eyes on the book, not wanting to make a big deal out of it. I sense Owen's pause though. I don't know why this makes him uncomfortable.

"I tested out of freshman algebra. I've always been a year ahead in math. Brain just sort of likes numbers, I guess," he says, his voice trailing off at the end. He reaches his arm to my leg, grabbing my hand and pulling it into his lap, cupping it with both of his and playing with my fingers. "What was this fight about? You know your mom gives me bacon; I hope you didn't mess up my supply," he says, leaning into me.

I smile, my gaze into my lap. Owen's joke is sweet.

"She's letting my dad rule things. She always has, and it just…it makes me so mad," I say, the frown taking over again.

"What's he trying to rule?" Owen asks.

"Her," I say quickly, looking up at him. "And me, by extension."

Owen lifts his hand and tucks a loose strand of hair behind my ear, leaving his hand on my cheek when he's done. "So don't let him," he says. Simple, plain. "Is this about your playing again? Because I thought we had that figured out—you do that for *you,* wasn't that the deal?"

"I thought so," I say, standing up to move to my doorway, checking to see if my mom is still downstairs or up. "But apparently it's not *my* piano."

When I turn back to Owen, his eyebrows are pulled in, one eye closed. "Last I checked, it's not the piano that makes that kick-ass music. It's you," Owen says.

"Exactly, so there's no reason I can't sell it," I say quickly, regretting my words just as fast.

Owen's standing now, his body moving behind me. I turn into him, reaching my arms out to hug him, embrace him, move away from talking—but he greets my hands with his, holding his arms out stiffly, keeping me at a small distance so he can watch my face. "Why would you sell it?" he asks.

He knows.

I shrug, nodding ambivalently, as if I haven't thought this through.

"Kens," he says, his eyes looking over my shoulder, out my door, then back to me. "You're not selling your piano."

I let go of his fingers and lean back against my wall, my arms folded—pouting. Pouting and pissed. Why is everyone insistent that I can't do what I want with *my* piano?

"Kens," he chuckles, moving closer to me, pulling on my arms, which I'm holding together tightly against my body. My stubbornness makes him laugh harder, until he pulls his hat from his head, tosses it on my bed and rubs his eyes. He sits down next to it and calls me over to him. I scoot my feet closer reluctantly, and when I get to him, he loops his fingers into the pocket of my jeans and drags me onto his lap, wrapping his arms around me tightly, his lips at my ear.

"It is so sweet that you want to help my family. But that would pay for what? Another couple months of my Grandpa's expenses? I can't let you do that. The cost is too high," he says. "But I *love* that you're willing to do something like that for me."

"I don't want the piano anymore. And it would help," I say, my eyes growing heavy with tears.

"Yes you do. You don't think you want it…but you do," he says, swaying me side to side in his lap, his cheek against mine. I let my head fall on his arm, running my hands along his, holding his caged arms around me tightly.

I don't want the piano. All I want…is Owen.

SIX IN THE morning arrives way too quickly. Owen stayed late, my mom never coming up to my room and telling him he needed to go home. I left my door open, knowing she would feel more comfortable with him here if I did, and I heard her move to her bedroom hours after our fight downstairs.

I feel worse about it today. She's still asleep when I sneak downstairs to brew a cup of coffee and grab a packet of Pop Tarts from the pantry. Willow texted me when she was leaving her house, which gave me precisely seven minutes to shower and get dressed. I lock our front door behind me and pull my coat around my body, shielding the hot coffee mug from the freezing air.

I'm bundled from head to toe, the only things exposed are my lips and nose and the tips of my fingers through my gloves. Jess leaps from the front seat and holds the door open for me, then moves to the back.

"Thanks for letting me ride shotgun," I say, unwrapping my neck from my scarf, letting the heat from Willow's car penetrate my body.

"Thanks for giving me a sip of your coffee," Jess says, reaching through the center to the cup holder where my mug is steaming.

"Go ahead," I roll my eyes.

"You're too nice. I would have spilled it on him," Willow says, backing out of the driveway with enough speed to make the bump jerk Jess's hand a little, splattering coffee on his chin and cheeks.

"Your such a bitch in the morning," he says, slurping the coffee once more before putting my mug back.

"See, now when he says *bitch* it sounds authentic," Willow says to me.

"That's cuz you are one!" Jess says from the back seat. Willow raises her middle finger and smiles at him in the rearview mirror.

"Are you two going to fight all the way to Champagne? I'm just saying, that's like…three hours of bickering. So if I have a chance to bail out now and drive myself, I'd like to take it," I say, looking to Willow. She smirks at me.

"No, we're just going to bicker for the first ten minutes," Jess says from behind me. "The rest of the time we'll be all shmoopy, making kissy faces at each other, and I'll keep feeling her up from the back seat."

"Uh, that's not happening," Willow says, pointing at him in the mirror.

"Worth a shot," Jess says, settling back in his seat, pulling his coat up over his lap.

It's still dark out when we hit the highway, but by the time we make it to the University of Illinois, three hours later, the sun is shining. It's one of those rare days where there's a tiny bit of leftover snow on the ground, too, so everything feels especially bright. I know it will all melt by the time we take the field for competition, but the early morning sun makes the ground look as if it's covered in jewels.

"We're going to tune in ten minutes, then we go to photos and pre-staging before we compete. You're going to love this, Kensi," Willow says. She's wired on a few energy drinks. I counted three empty cans in her car. I'm pretty sure that isn't safe, but I'm also fairly certain that there's little difference in her personality—wired or not.

Willow walks around each section, listening and adjusting instruments as everyone warms up, her whistle perched at the edge of her lips.

"Just one more reason why drum line is the best," Jess says, rapping out a drumroll on the rim of his snare. "We don't tune."

I laugh and wait at the back of the moving truck for a few of the booster parents to help unload the xylophone, smirking when one of the wheels falls off into my hand as they pull it from the truck. I bend down and lift the leg up so I can work the wheel back in place, and suddenly the weight is lighter.

"I hope you know this is butt-crack early, and I would only show up to something like this for you," Owen says, his head buried in its usual black hoodie.

"You're here!" I squeal, rushing into his arms. He catches me and holds me under the sides of his coat, shielding the cold breeze from my skin. We changed into our uniforms the second we got to the campus, and I haven't been warm since.

Owen rubs his hand on the giant feather on the top of my hat. "You guys look like birds. Why do you have to wear these?" he asks.

"It's so the judges can see us on the field. Willow says it makes the formations *pop* more," I roll my eyes.

"But you don't march..." he says, fluffing my feather once again. I slap his hand away and straighten my hat.

"Yeah, I tried that argument, but here I am, all plumed," I say.

"Well, you're adorable. Go win something. You do get to win something, right?" he says, taking a few steps away, moving backward toward the stadium.

"That's what Willow says. This is like her Super Bowl, you know?" I say, wide eyes.

"Yeah, so I've heard." Owen shields his mouth as he passes Willow, but she hears him anyhow and punches him on the arm. "Owwww!"

I smile as he turns, my heart feeling warm inside. Everything feels right —at least for right now.

Most of the morning is spent standing around, rolling my xylophone from patch of grass to patch of grass, until we're in the tunnel. It's kind of cool being in here, and I look around at the motivational words painted on the wall, the most amusing the threat that any opponent will feel the *Orange Krush.*

Before today, there was no reason I would ever find myself in a sports tunnel at a major university. The whole scene feels silly, and maybe a little pointless, but it also feels...*good.*

As we get ready to take the field, Willow calls us all in for one final huddle, and Jess leads everyone in a chant of *hoorahs,* as if we're actually the university's football team—about to scream through the tunnel to take on Ohio State or Kansas. The longer everyone cheers, the more it makes me giggle, and the louder I'm cheering too.

Once we hit the field, it's just like any other Friday—Willow atop a small ladder, her arms keeping a steady beat that we all seem to be perpetually a hint behind. What's different about today though is how everyone in the stands is paying attention. People are actually cheering—people from other schools, either already having gone or waiting to perform. They're supportive, appreciative, and when they whisper to one another between songs, I can tell they're competitive.

Willow was right—this...feels...*awesome!*

It seems like it takes us only minutes to pack up after the performance, and soon we're in the stands, waiting for the final two schools to perform. Owen stays, sitting behind me, his legs on either side of me, his arms wrapped around my body, keeping me warm. We were allowed to change out of our uniforms after the performance, but most of us left our shirts on, wanting to feel like a team.

The award ceremony drags on, with awards for dozens of categories. Willow is beaming because she received a medal of distinction for drum major.

"She does wave her arms with excellent precision," Owen jokes in my ear. I elbow him because Jess is close, but when I hear Jess laugh, I ease up on Owen.

We're all amused because every time our school is called for an award, Willow has to step forward, saluting, then she walks over to the master of ceremonies to shake his hand and take our trophy. We end up winning six, including Willow's and a third-place overall finish. Jess rushes down to the field to help her carry them all.

"I have to admit, that was kind of cool," Owen says during our walk from the stadium to the parking lot. We stop at Willow's car, and Owen pulls out the bag holding my uniform. "Is it cool if I drive you home? It'll be four or so by the time we get home. I'd like to take you to dinner."

"Dinner's good. I never did get my steak," I tease, standing on the tips of my toes to kiss him.

"I'm pretty sure you made out all right," he says, rolling his hands down my back, to my ass and pulling me to him closely. I blush and look to see who's watching, but the moment his lips hit my neck, I care a whole lot less.

"I don't know, I really wanted a steak," I joke, and Owen spanks me once, squeezing his hand hard on my cheek.

"You sure about that?" he winks. I nod *no,* because…no, I'm not. In fact I might forgo eating for days for more nights with Owen. If only I could erase everything that happened the day after.

Willow packs the trophies in the backseat of her car, promising Mr. Brody that she'll bring them to school on Monday. Owen and I wait for them to drive away before walking to his truck.

"Hey," he says, tugging on my arm, taking a step back before letting me climb inside. "Can I take you somewhere in the city? Like, on a real date? Would that be okay?"

"You sure?" I ask, knowing how expensive places in the city are. Owen doesn't have the money to do something like this, but he's looking at me with such excitement, I can't just outright say no.

"Positive. I have a place in mind," he says, his eyes lowered, giving me that look that would make me follow him anywhere. I nod okay, and Owen opens my door, waiting while I climb in and buckle the seatbelt before closing it for me.

I haven't driven in southern Illinois since I was a kid, so most of the things we pass aren't familiar to me. Most of the state looks the same—lush and green in the summer, and thick of dead leaves and stickily trees in the winter. But there's something beautiful about the usual today, and I let my eyes glaze over as I watch the rays of sunshine flash in and out of the thick branches as we rush by.

The constant hum of his engine draws me in, and somewhere along the way, I slip into a short slumber, not waking up until I feel Owen push the gearshift into park then reach behind his seat, pulling out a heavy plastic bag.

I stretch my arms and look around, doing my best to adjust my body's clock, to recognize my surroundings. The gothic buildings orient me immediately, and I flash to Owen, the look on my face panicked.

It's panic punching me from the inside out right now; I know it is. Why did he bring me here? Why are we here? This isn't a date!

"Owen!" I start unclicking my buckle, even though I have no intention of leaving this truck.

"Hold on! Before you get all…*Kensi* on me. Listen to me. Please, just listen to me. And if I don't make any sense, I promise we will drive right out of this parking lot and I will take you to the best steakhouse in the city," he says, crossing a finger over his chest, his other palm flat toward me, as if warning he comes in peace.

Crap—he's coming in peace!

My body deflates in retaliation, but I lift my chin enough to look at him, to stare him in the eyes while he pleads his case.

"I know you think you don't want this. And…and," he raises his hand to stop me from interrupting, my rebuttal stammering at the tip of my tongue. I let it simmer longer. I owe Owen a listen; he's right. "In the end, you might be right. Maybe…*maybe*…you won't want this. But I kinda think you do, Kensi. And if you don't try, if you don't at least just see this through, look inside that door, you will regret it. You are so gifted, and unlike me, you have options."

"Owen, you have options, too," I start, but he grabs my hand quickly and holds it, shaking it lightly and smiling.

"That's not what I meant," he says, his lips curve into a smile against my wrist as he holds it to him. "I'm good with where I am, Kens. I'm all right with not being able to have everything. When I play ball, it's purely recreation for me. It's not a dream. It's not this thing that I always thought about doing for a living. It's an escape. It's the way I lose myself, take control, be someone else, for just a few hours," he smiles.

His head falls to the side, against his headrest, his leg propped up along the seat. He lowers my hand in his and presses it flat against my leg, resting his palm over mine. "I've seen you. No…not just that…I've heard you,

Kensi. I've *felt* you when you play, when you lose yourself so completely to that piano. For you, it's different. And for you, this is something that could mean the rest of your life. And you might not think you want it now, but Kens, believe me, when something's gone—" he swallows hard, his jaw flexing, his eyes struggling. "When something's gone that you love, and you start thinking about how much you didn't appreciate it when it was here... that shit will poison you. And I'll be damned if I'm not going to try to save you from that."

To my left, out the window, is the main music hall for the University of Chicago. I know those steps. I've climbed them for years. There's a small hallway to the right, as soon as you enter, and it dips down, below ground, to a long line of offices and practice rooms. It's where I play with Chen. It's a place I haven't been in months.

And Owen's right about one thing; not going, missing it—my time with Chen—it gnaws at my insides when I let it in.

I draw in a deep breath, the heat from Owen's truck mixing with the coolness of the glass window by my face. I look back at him, his eyes hopeful. I want to do this, maybe more for him than me. And maybe for me, too.

"I don't have anything to wear," I say, looking down at the silly band shirt and jeans I have on. Owen pulls the plastic bag up to his lap, sliding it over to me, inside a plain black dress and a simple pair of black ballet flats. It's exactly what I would have picked on my own.

"I scoped out your closet before I left your room last night. And yes, I had to tell your mom what I was up to when I stopped by your house this morning to get this. But don't worry; she's not coming. I told her I had to trick you into coming, and her being here would probably scare you away," he says.

He's right. It would have.

"My time's at four o'clock," I say, looking at my watch. It's a little after three thirty.

"I know," he says, his head now resting along his arm, against the back of his seat. His jaw is rough, his beard showing more than it usually does.

"Will you come in with me?" I ask, the bag of clothes held close to my chest.

"Wouldn't miss it," he says, a smile so soft, so honest, it makes me believe that maybe I can do anything.

I lead Owen through the corridor, to the hallway bathroom I'm familiar with, and I change quickly. I'm glad Owen brought what he did. Anything...*more* and I would feel uncomfortable. The only thing I need to work past now is the growing nerves threatening to derail the strength and control in my hands. Owen notices them trembling, reaches down, and threads his fingers slowly through mine as we stand along a sparse hallway, the applicant before me staring at the crack in the auditorium door, waiting for it to open, for someone to welcome her inside.

Once she enters, I squeeze Owen's hand harder, looking to my right, to the long wooden bench, and the two boys who have sat down, each of them dressed in a suit.

I pull my hand from Owen's briefly, blowing on my palms, trying to make the sweat stop. Please, for five minutes, just stop!

"Miss Worth?" There's a young woman standing in front of me now, clipboard in her hand, the list of names on it—long.

I smile and let go of Owen, wiping my hands along the skirt of my dress and passing through the doors with him, watching to see just where he sits. I notice Chen at the main table in the center of the auditorium as I pass through the rows of seats. He doesn't smile at first, but when nobody else is looking, he raises his thumb and winks.

I needed that—more than he'll ever know.

"Miss Worth, what will you be playing today?" a man with a graying beard and glasses pushed to the tip of his nose asks.

Clearing my throat, I flex my fingers, searching for the memory of everything I know. I know this. I *know* I know this.

"*Rachmaninoff Piano Concerto No. 2*," I say, my voice losing its confidence the moment the sound of it hits the airy stage, the vastness around me swallowing me whole.

"Very well. Begin," the main man says. I move to the piano, possibly the nicest one I've ever seen, and smooth the wrinkles on my dress. Looking down, I search for the pedals, placing my feet in familiar positions, finding my comfort. I close my eyes and run my hands once in opposite directions, just as I do every time, until I come back to center, and my hands find their natural groove.

It's there; that sensation, the one that tells my fingers they are home. I don't open my eyes at first, instead just letting my mind take me back to my room in the city, the practice room that used to feel like home. The sound from my hands—it *feels* like that home, like my old life, and the longer I play, the more of the Concerto I complete, the more my mouth tastes funny. I'm hitting the right notes, everything coming out just as it should. But what's missing is the passion.

My stop is abrupt, my fingers recoiling into my fists, my eyes flashing open—thoughts of Owen, of Willow, of my life *now,* the good and the bad, surrounding me.

"Miss Worth?" There's a throat-clearing sound. They aren't happy. I'm pretty sure this is how someone blows an audition. But I can't continue to play something that I just don't feel.

"I…I'm sorry. I've changed my mind," I say, my eyes searching for Owen. He's leaning forward in a far seat, his elbows propped on his legs, his head tilted to the side. He's afraid—worried that I'm quitting, giving up. But I'm not. I'm just doing this on my terms.

"If it's all right, I'd like to begin again?" I ask, my fingers finding one another, fretting…maybe hoping a little too that they will get the chance to show everyone exactly what they can do.

"You may," the speaker says, his tone growing more tired with me.

Deep breath.

"Thank you," I say, retaking my seat and looking at the expanse of keys before me, the pattern, the way the black and white lines dance. I'm going to make them dance. I rest my hands loosely, nothing like this room full of professors would wish me to, but…I. Don't. Care. "This is *C Jam Blues,* written by the great Duke Ellington. I'm going to be playing it as inspired by Oscar Peterson. I hope you enjoy."

When I turn to face the keys again, I smirk, my stomach settling, and my heart soaring. I don't even remember hearing the sounds my hands make. This moment, the five minutes I play and pound, smiling the entire time—it's like recess. I'm on one big life recess, and I never want to come back.

I never bother to look, just playing on, dragging out a few of the jazz riffs, some of the repetitions, a few more times than necessary. I do it because I can tell everyone is hanging on every single note I'm playing. They won't admit it—but I have them. I have them because this...*this* is what my hands were meant to do. What *I'm* meant to do.

When I'm done, I feel euphoric, and I stand, the bench screeching along the floor as I move it out of my way. "Thank you," I say, stepping to the side exit, down the steps to the end of the hallway where Owen is now waiting for me.

I'm worried he's going to be mad, maybe disappointed, but he rushes to me, sweeping me into his arms and twirling me around the tiny hallway, his kiss proof that what I did in there—Owen liked it too.

"That was fucking fantastic. I mean, holy shit, Kens! Did you see those guys? They had no idea what to do with you. I mean, I don't know how they work these things, or how they score that shit, but damn, girl!" His celebration is enough, and I tuck myself along his side, the plastic bag with my jeans and band clothes dangling from Owen's other hand.

We climb the small steps up the narrow hallway, my hand on the door I've pushed through so many times. Chen bursts through the opposite side of the hallway, his eyes finding mine right away, his face proud and beaming.

"Ohhhhhh Kensington," he's nearly weeping, and I can see the surprise in Owen's face as this man, probably in his sixties, brushes Owen aside, hugging me as if I'm his own daughter. "So proud. You make me...so proud," he says, his hands on my cheeks, pushing in tightly. I can see in his eyes that he's genuinely happy for me, and I can also see that I blew any chance I might have of joining their program.

And Chen and I couldn't care less.

I introduce him to Owen quickly, and their handshake is fast and awkward before Chen rushes back inside. I breathe easy for the two hours it takes to drive through the city, to Owen's driveway. Owen asks me questions about Chen along the way, about my lessons with him, about my underground lessons—the times we knew my father wasn't around, wouldn't hear. I talk about how Chen made me love jazz, my chest alive and full and anxious for more.

I want to run through the streets of our neighborhood when I skip from

Owen's truck, making noises in celebration just to hear them echo off of the dark houses around us. The moon is out, and still the stars are bright—a pairing that shouldn't happen. And I want to dance, for hours, out here in the freezing cold in Owen's arms. The way he's looking at me, the wonder in his face, it spurs me on, drawing me to him.

And then there's a crack in his façade. My feet stop before him, his arms catching me, his fingers fumbling for mine, teasing the ends, never quite holding on completely.

"What?" I ask, every drop of elation in my body from before now exchanged for dread.

"I'm moving to Iowa," he says, and all I hear is the humming of the blood passing along my eardrum. The color is gone from my body, and the strength is failing my legs. "I know. God, Kens, I'm so sorry. To tell you now…this way…after your night—"

"Why?" I cry, holding my fist to my mouth. I hold it there for several seconds, my lip quivering underneath, until the tingling in my lip is so strong that I know I won't be able to hide how this is all making me feel.

"Kens…it's all been too much. It's just…it's too much for me, for my mom. And Andrew. We're underwater with the house, but if we sell it, the bank has agreed to wipe the slate clean. My mom is going to look for something cheaper, maybe an apartment. And then the extra money from her check will pay for my grandpa," he's speaking so fast; his words don't even make sense.

"What happens in Iowa? Why can't you stay here?" I take a step back, my feet pounding the pavement like a child. I'm embarrassed how it looks, but I'm so afraid of what this means. I'm losing Owen. I just got him, and already…he's gone.

"My uncle lives there. My dad's brother? He owns a print shop, and I'm going to work for him. I'll be able to send some money to Mom, and I'll be able to save for college. The shop isn't much right now, but he says in a few years, he'll leave it to me, retire. I…I could make that place into something maybe. There's a great school there for Andrew, and he'll be away from this…at least for a little while. When my mom gets settled, maybe if she's able to find a place big enough, he'll move back," Owen says.

He'll move back.

I keep my head to the side, my eyes piercing him, my nostrils flaring. Owen can't say anything to take this feeling away, and the longer he stands there, his arms to his sides, his expression just as broken as my heart, the more I want to cry.

"I have a few weeks," he says. "Tonight, let's celebrate you. I don't want to think about the other stuff anymore." He steps to me in small movements, treating me like a deer caught in the sights of his gun. Owen...he's the hunter. And I am dead, my heart broken and time no longer relevant.

CHAPTER 21

We haven't talked about Iowa again. It's coming. I can tell. Owen's mom had a realtor to the house on Monday after school. I walked by them at the table on my way up to Owen's room. Owen and me—we never mentioned it.

On Tuesday they told Andrew their plan. He's about as happy about it as I am. I came over when they were sitting in the living room, after dinner. Andrew walked out in the middle of their talk saying, "I fucking hate Iowa!"

We passed each other through the doorway; Andrew never looked at me.

I understand. I fucking hate Iowa too.

Today, he's packing his room. He's been working on it a little at a time. Owen stayed late at school for a test, still catching up from the days he didn't go. I've been here at his house…waiting for him. I've been stuck to him like glue, not wanting to miss a single second of the time we have left.

"Hey," I say, leaning on Andrew's doorway. He drops a book in a box and puts a lid on top, sliding it into a corner. "Seems like a waste of space. You should probably pack more in that box than just a book." I'm trying to be light, but neither of us is feeling it.

"I shouldn't be packing at all," Andrew says, his mouth twists into a reluctant smile, his shoulders shrugging. I move into his room and sit down on his bed next to him.

"At least you'll have family there. Owen says the school is really good," I say, picking up one of his sweatshirts and folding it over my lap. I don't believe a word that's coming from my mouth.

"You're such a bad liar," Andrew teases, leaning into me. I put my arm around him and lay my head on his shoulder. "I've never even had a girlfriend. I want one of those...here...in Woodstock. I want to get my license, then pick a girl up and take her to the Miller Movie House. I want to go to the Apple Fest with her, and win one of those big, stupid stuffed bears."

"We love those big, stupid stuffed bears," I sigh. Andrew's shoulder rises with a small laugh. "You'll have all that in Iowa too," I say.

"Yeah..." he says through a heavy sigh. "But it won't be here."

"Owen says you'll get to move back; when your mom finds a place," I say. Andrew leaves his eyes on mine, doubt all over his face.

When I hear the door downstairs, I squeeze Andrew once more and step out of his room. Owen meets me at the top of the stairs, his hand finding its comfortable place on my cheek, his lips finding home on mine.

"How'd you do?" I ask about his science test.

"Good, I think. Seemed easy," he says. "Hey, I have to run up to the home. You want to come with me? I know how you love Grampa."

I do love Gus. But more than that, I'm doing *everything* with Owen, up until the very last second. I don't even care if it's a trip to the grocery store for toothpaste—I'm making it.

I nod *yes* and thread my arm through Owen's as we move back down the stairs. I watch Owen as we drive. I've been watching him a lot, watching how he looks at things. He's been living his life, day-to-day, ever since he told me about his family's plans. His eyes never pause or seem sad when he looks out at stuff; every day passes, just as it always did, as if these days aren't coming to an end. The only times he gets sentimental are at night, when we're alone. For a couple of evenings, he sat in his window, on the phone with me, and we listened to each other breathe. But for the last two nights, he's come over around midnight, letting me sneak him upstairs before my mom gets home. I lock my door, not that she ever checks on me anyway, and he holds me while we both lie awake...not talking about Iowa.

Emma remembers me when we enter the home this time, and she nods toward Gus's room, urging me to go on while she and Owen talk.

"He's expecting you," she says as I pass. We exchange smiles, and I think to myself how much she reminds me of my favorite book by the same name.

Gus is facing the door, his cane in his hand, ready to help him stand as I enter. I can't help but smile at the sight of him, and I get to him quickly, giving him a hand to his feet. He hugs me as if I'm his own, his hardened hands squeezing my shoulder then wrapping around my back, patting.

"How's the metronome, young lady?" he asks. I feel guilty, because I haven't used it yet. But I will.

"It's keeping time," I say, walking with him toward his door.

"Let's bust out of this joint," he teases, winking at me. His heavy eyebrows dip down then up when he winks, like caterpillars exercising. I wonder if Owen will look like this one day?

I hold Gus's arm as we make our way out to the main room, to a small table with a checkerboard on it. Once he's sitting, I take the other chair. Gus begins to put the pieces in place, his hands shaking a little as he drops the checkers onto their squares with careful precision.

"So, what's this business about the boys and Iowa?" I'm surprised when he asks. I wasn't sure how much Owen had shared with him, or how much he'd remember.

"I guess Iowa is the land of opportunity," I jest, my answer laced with sarcasm.

"Horseshit," Gus says, tapping his finger on the board between us, then moving his first piece. "That uncle of his ain't worth a damn, and neither is his business. Now Billy…I always liked Billy. Owen's dad? But Richard, Owen's uncle? Well, let's just say I have a hard time trusting a fella named *Dick* for short."

Gus keeps his eyes trained on the pieces on our game board. I'm glad, because I'm blushing from his bluntness. I'm also feeling more uneasy about Owen leaving.

"I want him to stay." My honesty surprises me. Gus, he has a way of filling me with comfort, and I have to talk to someone about how I feel. I think he might be my only outlet.

He looks up at me before reaching forward to grab a checker, his heavy brow cocked on one end. "You need to convince him it's safe to stay," he says, letting his hand go from the board. Gus leans back in his chair, folding his hands over his chest. He looks around the room, and when he sees Owen and Emma far away, sitting at her desk, he looks back at me.

"Owen's always craved security," he says. I can't help the way I react, flinching in surprise.

"Owen laughs in the face of danger," I say, my mind easily counting a dozen things I know about Owen that defy the very idea of feeling comfortable.

"I didn't say *safe.* I said *secure,*" Gus says, patting his hands once on his belly. "That boy has a nose for danger. He likes thrills. But he also needs to know that when he comes back, after he's done playing stuntman with all of his antics, that there will be something there waiting for him—a *home.*"

"I kind of thought I was his home," I answer, my chest hurting.

"You are," Gus says. "But Owen's used to people leaving. And he's never prepared for it. Billy's death did a number on him. He needs to know he has a place. Right now, he's looking at Iowa, at that numbskull uncle of his, as a security blanket for his future. He'll have somewhere to go, something to do...someone to be."

I'm starting to understand more, and I'm starting to feel more hopeless. I lean forward as Gus does, and I watch him move one of his checkers. He puts it in a place where it's vulnerable, where I have no choice but to jump it and keep it as mine. So I do. He makes the same move again, and I jump again. We play without talking for a few minutes, and I grow a small stack of Gus's checkers, feeling bad that I'm winning, and wondering if I should start making different moves to let him catch up. And then, he moves one more into place, and I see it. He's been baiting me. As I sit back and look at the board, only a few of his red checkers left, the rest of the board covered in my black, I see the trail he's left behind. My mind does the math, and I know instantly there's no way I can win.

"Give him a place," Gus says, picking up one of my pieces and handing it to me before working his way out of the chair to stand. He holds his hand on my shoulder, his eyes penetrating mine, his smirk full of confidence and assurance.

A place.

I think about Gus's words the entire way home, about how nice it feels to know your future, to have a plan before you. I think about the way I felt on that stage, when I quit playing for everyone else—and I played something for me. I found my place that very instant. I don't know where it will take me, what college, if a college at all, where I'll be able to play that kind of music. But I know that I need to be able to do that in life if I want to feel that feeling again, to feel alive.

The thoughts and ideas linger in my head the rest of the day, into the late hours. My mom is home tonight, so Owen stays at his house. We text a few times, and I promise to let him know when my mom heads to bed so he can come over, but by midnight, she's still awake. I hear her on the phone with someone, and she shuffles into the small spare room downstairs for privacy. I think she's talking to my dad. She's been hiding their conversations from me.

Eventually, Owen gives up on our plan, texting me goodnight, looking at me once more through the window before turning out his light. I turn mine out as well, but my conversation with Gus keeps rolling through my head.

There's no way I'm sleeping, so I pull my laptop up from the floor and flip it open. I look at pictures of DePaul. I click through their basketball program until I find the picture of the man I saw with Owen, the one who gave him his card. He's on the coaching staff. Then I type the words: BILL HARPER WOODSTOCK DEATH.

The obituary is the first thing to come up. It's a scan of an old, yellowed clipping from the Woodstock News. I read the list of survivors over and over again—James, Owen, and Andrew. That word…*survivors*…it catches me. Surviving someone—I don't know that there's a better way to describe Owen.

I flip through a few more pages, some of them not the right Bill Harper, some of them stories about the warehouse Bill worked at, condolences from longtime co-workers and friends. I'm about to flip the computer closed when a small photo catches my eye.

Owen's dad is standing in front of a big forklift, his hair hanging heavy over his eyes, his face so much like his son's. But it's the face next to him that stops me. It's familiar, and the name with it can't be a coincidence.

I DON'T SLEEP at all, too anxious to get to the next day. I greet Owen in the driveway in the morning, and he's a little surprised to see me up so early. He's leaving with Andrew, his brother's school bag slumped over his back, his body wearing sadness like a suit.

"Don't you get to sleep in later now?" Owen asks. His hair is still wet, and it smells like his shampoo. I kiss him on the lips quickly, breathing the scent in through my nose to remember it, then run back to my own car.

"I do, but I have to do something for English. It's an extra-credit thing, and I have to get it in this morning," I say. I can tell Owen doesn't believe me, but I keep moving forward, waving at him, closing my door, and driving off without glancing back. I know I'll have a good half-hour at school before he shows up. I just need Mr. Chessman to be there, too.

I'm hopeful when the teachers' lot is halfway full, and when the light is spilling out from Mr. Chessman's classroom, I pick up my step into a light jog. I startle him when I stumble through his door.

"Kensi, good morning! To what do I owe the pleasure?" he says. I notice the stack of homework on his desktop, Owen's name scribbled at the top of a few papers. He pushes them into a pile, moving them to the side, trying to get my attention away from them. But it's the only thing my eyes see. I leave my gaze there as I speak.

"How did you know Bill Harper?" I ask.

I take the silence that greets me as confirmation. I move closer to Mr. Chessman's desk, sliding the printout of the picture I found online in front of him. He picks it up, holding it in both hands, his eyes spending long seconds on every detail. It's more than recognition that shadows his face; it's memories.

"How did you find this?" he asks, his eyes still on the black-and-white page. The photo is a bit fuzzy, but the faces are distinct. It's the eyes. I saw *him* in those eyes.

"At first I wasn't sure why the guy standing with Bill looked so familiar. I thought maybe it was a relative, or that I was remembering a picture I saw at Owen's house. I'm not sure how you flashed into my head. But I'm glad you did," I say.

Mr. Chessman puts the picture down on his desk, the caption below labeling Bill Harper and Dwayne Chessman. His palms are flat along either side of the paper, and he peers up at me slowly.

"How did you know him?" I ask again. I know it isn't a happy memory. Mr. Chessman's eyes are distant. His breathing is slow, and it takes a few seconds before he resolves himself to answering my question.

"Bill and I worked at the warehouse together. For about a year," he says, leaning back in his chair. He folds his arms in front of him, his eyes moving lower, to the space under his desk. "I had just gotten out of the Navy, and I was back home, trying to put myself through school. I took the job at the warehouse because the hours fit my classes. They paired me up with Billy because he'd been there the longest," he says, his eyes coming up to mine briefly before he stands and begins pacing his classroom.

"Bill trained me on the machines, and I liked working with him so much, they let me stay on his team permanently. His wife, Shannon, would bring him lunch every day, and after a few months on the job, she started bringing a lunch for me, too. I spent a year on Bill's team, and for a year I sat outside on the picnic table, next to him and across from his wife, eating sandwiches and talking about my college classes and learning about their kids. Shannon wanted to go to college too, but they never had enough money."

Mr. Chessman's gaze drifts away again, his eyes fixed outside, to the sidewalk along the street. More students are arriving, and I know my time with him alone is growing short.

"Is that why you help Owen? Because you knew Bill?" I say. He turns to me quickly, his brow pinched. I move to his desk and lift the stack of papers, all Owen's. "His homework. His grades. I know you've been collecting things and turning things in for him when he misses other classes."

Mr. Chessman's mouth slides into a smile as he chuckles, moving over to his desk and taking the stack from my hand, spreading it out between us.

"I don't do anything *for* him. I collect his work, check in with his teachers, sure. But Owen...he always does the work himself. He finds a way, finds time. He's always been that way, ahead of the rest of the class," Mr. Chessman says, a proud and satisfied grin showing as he pushes the papers back together before moving them to a wire basket on his back table.

"Ahead?" I question. Mr. Chessman leans against the table, crossing his legs and folding his arms. He's told me so much, more than he probably should. His quiet worries me, and I start to think I've gotten everything I'm going to from him. It's not enough. I need more; I need to find out if there's enough there for him to help me, for him to convince Owen to stay.

"We don't offer classes here for college credit like they do at some other schools," he says, and my lungs fill with relief that he's still sharing. "But we were able to work with the district and the university board so Owen could test at the end of the year, but stay here for basketball. It's basically the same program his brother's in, without going to that school. Hopefully he'll leave here with six or nine credits under his belt already."

I nod, thinking back to how Owen answered me, how he said math is easy for him. I don't know why he didn't tell me he was trying to earn credit, unless he just believed it would never happen. That thought…it doesn't surprise me. Owen doesn't expect anything good in the end.

"Why do you help him?" I ask, and I leave my eyes on Mr. Chessman's. My look, it's pleading with him, begging him to give me an answer. His expression drops before he turns to look out his window again, his hands wrapped around the corners of his table, his forearms flexing and letting go. Of every teacher at this school, Mr. Chessman was always the one to stand up for Owen. He was Owen's advocate, and I need to know why. "Please…" I say, leaning forward, my hands pressed together.

"Bill had these quirks," he begins, his back to me while he speaks. "His face would sometimes tick, and he'd talk to himself. I asked Shannon about it one day when we were eating alone; Bill got called back to repair something. She told me he was bipolar, had hallucinations. His medication took care of it most of the time, but sometimes he'd go a few weeks without taking something. Our insurance at the job was crap, and the pills—they were expensive. The hallucinations would get really bad when he'd go a few weeks."

Mr. Chessman turns to look at me again, his face washed in grief, a look I've only seen one other time—on Owen, the day James killed himself.

"They were laying people off at the warehouse," he says, his lips parted, a small breath escaping, his jaw working side-to-side. The anger from the memory he's sharing is still fresh for him after all theses years. His eyes snap to mine. "It was between Billy and me, and I was a couple years younger…a couple years *cheaper.* So he got the pink slip, sent home early."

Mr. Chessman sucks his top lip in, his eyes squarely on mine as they grow with redness. His jaw muscles are working, still trying to understand the rest. His head slowly starts to nod, and my breath shakes when the rest of the story becomes apparent to me, too.

Bill Harper came home early—fired from a job that didn't pay enough to begin with, his brain already confused from his illness, his pockets too empty to afford the medicine he needs.

And then he took his son to a festival…and stepped away from life.

We sit there in silence, and the sounds of students milling outside grows louder, feet scuffling along the sidewalks just beyond the door, lockers slamming against the nearby walls. I entered this room twenty minutes ago, proof in my hands that there was more to Owen's story, hope in my heart that Mr. Chessman was the key—that he would help me find Owen's *place.* Yet all I feel now is crushed, hopeless and heartsick.

"He's going to leave," I say, my eyes looking to the few minutes I have left, my mind able to draw enough gumption to search for a miracle. "Owen's moving to Iowa, and he's going to turn down an offer from DePaul. He's going to quit school, go work in some print shop with his uncle, so he can send money to his mom to help pay for his grandpa. Mr. Chessman…please. I need your help. He needs to see that none of these things are because of him, that he isn't cursed. He needs to stay."

"Kensi, I don't have a lot of money. Not the kind *they* need. If I did, believe me, I'd find a way to give it to that family," he says.

The door opens behind me, and the sound of students filing in drowns what's left of my hope. I stand my ground, not leaving the desk I'm in and leaving my eyes on Mr. Chessman's for as long as I can, until a girl asks me to get out of her seat. I look at him when I stand, and we continue a silent conversation until I back up to the door—my eyes begging him to find a way, his telling me there isn't one.

CHAPTER 22

The way the sky looks outside—bleak and gray, like a giant blanket over the sun—that's how I feel inside.

Two days go by. Two more days that Owen and I don't talk about Iowa. Two more nights that I sneak Owen into my house at night, that I cling to his arm, forcing myself to keep my eyes open so I can look at his skin, smell him—know he's here.

Mr. Chessman never says anything to me, but there are glances. I stare at him during English class, daring him to break away before me. I always win. There is no prize, though.

The FOR SALE sign shows up while I'm at school, and when I get home, it's standing there in Owen's lawn, the red-and-blue stripe, the bold white letters—a wake-up call that we can't live in pretend much longer. Reality is going to smack us both in the face. Owen sits in his truck, staring at it when I pull into my driveway. I kill the engine and walk over, sliding into the passenger side and into his open arm.

"Well, that sort of makes shit real, doesn't it?" Owen says. I chuckle against him.

"Yep," I say, my eyes on the same letters as his.

This is when I should beg. I could ask him to stay, tell him that we'll come up with a plan, find a way for his family to make money, to pay for his grandfather, to keep Andrew safe. But each time I breathe deep, daring myself to speak, to say something that will make a difference—I can't think of anything at all. Truth of the matter is I can't promise Andrew will be safe, or that Owen's mom will be able to earn enough on her own, without Owen working too.

I think I'm giving up. And it makes me sick to my stomach.

Owen and I sit together, his hand running slowly up and down my arm, our eyes trained out his window, for almost half an hour. Neither of us speaks. And when the cars pull up behind us, we don't notice until there's a loud rap on the passenger window behind me. We both jump, and when my mind realizes who I'm looking at, that sick feeling in my stomach starts to get replaced with something else.

Hope.

"What's Mr. Chessman doing here?" Owen says, moving his arm from around me and opening his door. "What's up?" I hear him ask as I sit in the cab, waiting a few seconds to climb out and join them. Just as I'm pushing my door open, I realize Mr. Chessman isn't alone.

"Owen, I think you've met Mr. Mathison. He's from DePaul?" I hear Mr. Chessman say. My lungs open wider.

"I have," Owen says, shaking the man's hand, just as he did the last time they met, after Owen's game.

"Good to see you, Owen. Sorry for this impromptu visit, but I was hoping maybe we could chat. Just for a few minutes. Your mom home?" Mathison asks. He's carrying the same briefcase he was when we saw him at the game, and I kind of think he's wearing the same DePaul shirt and jacket, too. Owen nods to him and leads him and Mr. Chessman inside.

"I haven't been inside yet, but I think she's here," Owen says, glancing toward his mother's car in the driveway.

I smile at Mr. Chessman as they turn to walk up Owen's driveway. He raises a brow in return, just a small symbol that he's feeling as anxious as I am, that he has the same sliver of hope. I follow them inside, making myself part of whatever conversation is about to occur. I should probably give them privacy, but I'm too invested in the outcome.

Owen's mom is walking from the kitchen, a dishtowel drying her hands, as we walk in, and when she realizes Owen and I aren't alone, her footing stumbles. "Oh, I'm sorry. I…I didn't know we were going to have company. Dwayne…hello…" she says, her face flushed as she looks around the house, a few boxes scattered. "I'm sorry, the place is a bit…out of sorts. We're… we're moving."

She steps nervously over to Mr. Chessman, her hands wringing the towel repeatedly before she stretches a hand out to his. At the same time, he reaches for a hug, and she opens her arms quickly, just as he puts his down, offering a hand instead. "Oh, uh…sorry…" he laughs lightly. There's a quiet between them, it lasts a few seconds, and no one really notices. But I notice. They finally hug, and I watch carefully, Mr. Chessman's hand sliding with a tender touch around Owen's mother's back, his eyes closing when they embrace.

He loves her. I see it.

I stick to Owen's side, our fingers linked under the table as we all gather around. Mr. Mathison pulls his briefcase to the table, flipping the gold latches open quickly, pulling out a thick envelope and sliding it over to Owen. He has a few envelopes in there—at quick glance, I count six.

"Full ride. DePaul. And we won't redshirt you. You might not start…at first. But, I think you'll be a pivotal part of the rotation within the first season. By your sophomore year, you'll be the reason people show up to watch the game," Mr. Mathison says.

Owen's eyes are forward on the envelope, and his mother's mouth is open wide. "I heard you're thinking of going to Iowa," Mr. Mathison continues, and my heartbeat picks up, my eyes looking to Mr. Chessman's. He won't look back at me; he's working too hard to stay in character. "Iowa, they won't treat you right. You'll redshirt, and you won't succeed on their court. They don't play your kind of game. We do."

Holy shit, he thinks Owen's going to college in Iowa. My mouth hurts from the pressure of not laughing. I know if I let it slip, I wouldn't be able to stop. It would be that maniacal kind of laugh, the type filled with nerves and wheezing hiccups and such. And I think it would start a chain—one that moves to Mr. Chessman next, and then Owen. Shannon is looking at everyone around the table, her eyes in shock, not following anything that's happening, but knowing enough to realize that she should play along with this charade as well.

"I've got one more meeting, tomorrow morning. It's in Elgin, and I'll swing back by your school on my way out. I'd love to shake your hand and make it official, but you look these papers over, let me know what you think," he says. As Mathison leaves, he shakes everyone's hands, and Mr. Chessman walks him back outside, both of their cars parked in the road behind Owen's truck.

"What was that all about?" Owen's mom finally says, her voice coming out wavering, a sort of whisper, nervous laughter blending with her words. "That man is offering to give you a scholarship? So you can play basketball? Honey…"

"He's not the only one making offers," Mr. Chessman says, closing the front door behind him, holding his hands together and rubbing them as if to say *jackpot*. He's grinning widely, his feet practically skipping as he joins us at the table. "Can you believe he bought the Iowa thing though?"

We all look at him when he says it.

"Look, I never lied. Someone had to call him to report your grades, send in transcripts. I volunteered, and all I said was that I thought he should know Owen was thinking of going to Iowa. Not a lie," he smirks. I slap his shoulder, then apologize quickly, realizing he's my teacher and I've just punched him in the arm.

"Why did you do that?" Owen asks. His eyes are still on the envelope, and he doesn't seem to be sharing the same thrill of opportunity the rest of us are. "Did you put him up to this?" Owen turns to me, and suddenly I can't breathe.

"O…" I start, not sure how I'm going to defend myself, but desperate for the right words, the ones that will make him understand, and say *yes* to this chance.

"It wasn't her. *I* did this. The school knows you're moving, and I merely asked Kensi if everything was all right. She was honest and said she was worried about you. That's all," Mr. Chessman says. The way he covers for me, the ease with which he spins the story—he's practiced this, thought through everything. He cares…he cares about Owen, and he cares about Owen's mom. His eyes never stay on her long, but they search her out every other minute. A constant system of checks and balances to make sure she's there, in her chair, listening, engaged, happy, safe.

Owen sighs heavily, leaning back in his chair, his hands holding the edge of the table, his thumbs pinning the envelope down. He slides his palms flat toward it, then he picks it up and unfolds the top. He tilts it sideways, sliding out brochures and booklets and a letter, signed by Lon Mathison and another name.

"Owen, if this man is offering you a chance to go to college...you have to take it," his mother says, sliding one of the brochures closer, her fingers running over the glossy photos. There's a certain sense of longing in the way she looks at them.

His head shaking, Owen drops the letter from his hands, then leans forward, rubbing his hands over his eyes before pulling them down over his mouth. He looks to me next, his face every bit of lost and unsure. His eyes stay on mine; they're asking me a question. He's torn by duty. And he doesn't know what to do. His mom and Mr. Chessman are exchanging brochures, each pointing out things for the other to look at—both excited about this opportunity. All Owen sees is how he'll be abandoning his mom, his family, when they need him most.

"How are we going to afford Grampa? You know how much money I'm going to make in Iowa, Mom. That paycheck—it's guaranteed. And it will *save* us. What happens with Andrew? Are you going to send him down to Iowa alone? Or does he stay here, where he has to live under Dad's shadow? And I'm sorry I'm bringing it up, Mom, but you know it's there. Iowa is a chance for him to get away from all those things that—" Owen stops suddenly, swallowing as his eyes close.

"Those things that you think killed James," she finishes for him. Owen's mother's voice is soft, her heart broken for both the son she lost and the one who feels responsible for his death. "You can't spend your life protecting Andrew, Owen. And you deserve things too. Good things. And we'll find a way to make it work."

"I don't know," Owen says, pulling his hat from his head, laying it on the table over the documents that are now overwhelming him, his hands rubbing his head. "I don't know, I don't know, I don't..." His voice dissipates, until it's nothing.

Owen stands and stares at me, then turns to his mom. He reaches forward again, grabbing the letter, carrying it with him as he leaves the room. He pauses at the bottom of the stairs, looking at us all. "Let me think about it, okay? And I will…I promise, tonight."

I stand from the table, too, walking over to Owen, his body leaning heavily on the banister. He looks like he's been in a fight rather than just had a major university drop a pot of gold on his table. I don't know why I thought this would be so easy. I was so sure Mr. Chessman would find a way to tip the scales away from Iowa. What I hadn't counted on was Owen's sense of duty.

"Hey…this…" I say, tapping my finger on the edge of the paper in his hand, "is a good thing. I know you have to think about it, but options… they're always good, right?"

It sounds pathetic. My reasoning, it's flawed. It's hard to see something you want as attainable when so many things need you on the other side.

"It's good," Owen says, his lip pulling up enough to press a small dimple in his cheek. He holds it there as he gazes at me, his eyes holding mine while Mr. Chessman comes over to where we're standing.

"Owen, I know you need to think this over, but it's really a once-in-a-lifetime chance. There's always a way," he says, his hand moving to pat Owen once on the back.

Owen's mom joins us then she walks Mr. Chessman to the door, their farewell exchange just as awkward and brief as their greeting.

"I have to get home. My mom hasn't seen me yet," I say, the voice in my head asking him what he's thinking, what his plans are and begging for an answer—the answer I want. Inside my head—there's a lot of begging.

Owen tips my chin up, kissing my lips lightly at first, then moves his hands to my head, pulling me closer and moving his kiss above my brow. I love when he does this, the sweetness of it all, the affection in every touch. I love it, and I'll miss it if he leaves. He *has* to stay.

I wait while he steps backward a few times, moving up to his room, and I turn after he does and leave his house to enter mine. My mom is sitting in the middle of the floor, right next to my piano, with rolls of holiday paper around her and stacks of framed pictures on my piano.

"Hi, honey," she says, her fingers holding small strips of tape, and a curled ribbon dangling from her teeth.

While I kick away my shoes and dump my coat on the floor, I watch her tape down the edges of bright red paper then tie her ribbon around one of the wrapped pictures, holding it up to show me when she's done.

"That's...awesome. You're wrapping crap we already own," I say, sliding closer to her in my socks, peering over her to the various large paintings and décor still waiting to be wrapped, I presume.

"My mom used to do this, every Thanksgiving. She'd wrap the things hanging in our house like presents, and then we'd have Christmas joy around us all season long," she says, turning her first package to face her. She straightens the ribbon then proudly sets the picture down to the side once she's satisfied with it.

"Yeah...that's not weird at all," I say, counting at least sixteen more things she needs to wrap.

"There's some mail for you in the kitchen," she says as she begins cutting and measuring paper for the next package.

I head to the kitchen and grab a Diet Coke from the fridge before turning to the island counter and sifting through the stack of papers and envelopes, discarding the various advertisements and coupons I know we'll never use. Caught in between two of the bigger mailers is a heavy envelope, with no address. I look over my shoulder, and my mom's still in manic-wrapping mode, a nearly empty glass of wine next to her on the floor, so I pull the papers from inside.

The top of the packet is labeled with an embossed masthead for Walt, Kendall, and Katz law firm, and just below that I catch the word *divorce.* I read on quickly, taking in enough to realize what I'm looking at, then I step into the wrapping fray, dropping the packet in front of my mom—right on top of the package she's taping.

She sighs when it lands in front of her, but instead of speaking right away, she reaches for her drink, taking a long sip until she's tipping the glass upside down.

"I'm sorry, Kens. I didn't mean for you to see that," she says, moving it to the side and continuing to tape gold paper on top of green.

I drop to the floor, sitting next to her, and pick the packet back up, flipping it between my hands a few times, waiting for her to give me more. She pretends I'm invisible.

"Does this mean..." I wait for her to finish my statement for me, but she only nods her head toward the tape, a silent request for me to help with this insane craft project. I rip two pieces off and push them onto the paper where she asks. She turns it over to face me when she's done. It's my baby portrait, wrapped and bowed. I don't know how to respond to seeing it, so I just lift my brow high and smile.

"Well, I like it. I think they look pretty. And your father never let me do campy holiday décor. He said it was junky," she says, moving right along to the next picture in the pile, this one a larger framed painting. "And yes, *this,*" she says, nodding to the packet from the law firm, "means I am filing for divorce."

Wow. I wasn't expecting this, and I'm so overcome with pride for my mom that I rush her, leaping on her lap and tearing the paper she's cutting. I kiss her cheek as I hug her, and she laughs with me, but only for a second or two, her focus quickly going back to her task—her eyes never staying on mine for long. "I'm not quite to celebrating status yet. I'm still sort of in acceptance…if that's okay," she says, curling ribbon.

"Acceptance is good," I say, pulling on one of the curly cues on her completed present, letting it spring back into place. "What made you change your mind…if…that's okay to ask?"

There's a harsh ripping sound as she presses with the scissors firmly, her hand striking against the ribbon grain with more force, each pass growing a little rougher until she finally snares one of the ribbons against the blade, ripping it from the cluster. She sets the scissors down, untangling her legs as she stands, her gait wobbly as she makes her way back to the kitchen, reaching for a half-empty wine bottle. When she comes back to the living room, she pauses before sitting back in her spot, her lips forming a tight line, her smile like the Mona Lisa—only there if you look for it.

"I was cleaning out old boxes a couple days ago from your room, the empties from the move. I thought I found one under your bed, and when I dragged it into view, I saw it had a *pretty* expensive-looking dress in it," she says. I wince knowing what she saw, and I'm angry at myself for being so careless with it and not hiding it better or simply throwing it in the trash like I had planned.

"Curious, I opened the letter that was tucked inside the box," she says, her eyes on mine, her smirk somehow growing more wicked. "She wrote you a lovely letter, full of naïve apologies and half-baked excuses. She explained how broken she was over losing him, how he was re-promising himself to me, and how she let him…ha ha! She *let* him go, because she knew that's what was right. You needed to have a father at home, she said. And that's the statement that made me stop. You need a father? Kens, I look at you and have no idea how you've come out as normal as you have. And when I read that, it hit me…you don't need *that* father. And I don't need that man."

Well, damn. I don't think I've ever been more proud of my mother, and all I want to do is celebrate with her. But she's put a ban on celebrating, so instead, I sit with her on the floor and wrap three more pictures from the collection from our walls, not prying any more, and only taking in the extra information she offers.

"And I hope you didn't want that dress," she says finally, mid-tape.

"Why?" I ask, holding the paper flat for her to fasten.

"Because I threw that damn thing, and her letter, in the fire," she says, her teeth tearing at the ribbon in her mouth, her eyes intent on the project at hand. I smile, and I let it beam, because she's not looking.

"Did you get the rest of your mail?" she asks, clearly done on the subject of my father.

"Oh, no. I'll grab it before I head upstairs. I need to call Owen. He might not be moving after all," I say, my mom smiling softly and glancing my direction, but her thoughts still clearly rooted in her own drama. I look forward to the day this chapter is done, because it would be nice to have my mom guide me through some of this.

I sweep the rest of the pile of mail into my arms and race up the stairs, positioning myself in front of the window. Owen's waiting on the other side; I can see the top of his hat, his back resting against the window's wall. I drop the mail in my lap in front of me and reach for my phone to text him, but before I dial I catch a glimpse of one letter—the address on it familiar, the seal exactly as it always appeared in my dreams.

The envelope is thin, and I'm not sure how to take that, so I slide my finger along the edge, tearing one end carefully, pulling the typed letter from the University of Chicago out and unfolding it slowly.

The first sentence stops my breath.

We are pleased to inform you that you have been selected...

I drop it instantly, exchanging it for my phone, dialing Owen, who picks up in the middle of my first ring.

"Hey," he says, turning to face me, the sight of his eyes on mine like coming home.

"Hey, you're never going to guess what I just opened," I say, waiting for him to actually guess. He starts to laugh after a few long seconds.

"I really have no idea how to answer that…a bank account. You opened a bank account," he says, scratching his head.

I hold the letter up, waggling it.

"I can't read that," he teases.

"I got in," I say, and there's silence for a few seconds until it settles in and he realizes what I mean.

"You're kidding," he says, a small laugh growing into a more powerful one. "Holy shit! You got in…doing it your way! Wow, that's…Kens, that's amazing. I'm so proud of you."

"I'm proud of you too, you know," I say, my compliment greeted quickly by silence on the other end. Owen is struggling, and I'm daft for thinking he's ready to make a decision on this so quickly. Like my mom, he's not in celebration mode either—I just hope he's moving toward acceptance.

"What are you going to do?" Owen asks, focusing on his happiness for me.

"I don't know. I was kind of done with the idea of going there, ya know? But then I got this envelope, and it feels real, and now…" I say, looking back to my lap, to the stamp from the school I've dreamed of for so long.

"You should go, Kens. It's what your heart wants," Owen says.

I slide down against the window, letting my head rest along my hand so I can look at him. Maybe once that is what my heart wanted, but now, all it craves is the boy looking back at me.

We don't talk about my letter any more, and we don't talk at all for long. But we never hang up, keeping our phones next to us until our eyes can no longer stay open, so we can listen to each other dream.

CHAPTER 23

I must have heard him. There must have been some sound, something familiar that stirred my mind just enough to force it to remember that I had something to do in the morning. That's the only explanation for the feeling that sinks my heart into oblivion the very moment my eyes open.

I don't remember leaving my room. I don't remember how I traveled down the stairs. And I don't recall how freezing the air was outside when it blasted its way inside my lungs. All I remember is my heart, how it ripped in half the second I saw the small piece of paper tucked in my car window, Owen's truck…gone.

Even now, two hours later, it's like reading it for the very first time.

I had to leave this way. If I didn't, I would never do the right thing. I will love you...for always.
~ Owen

My eyes are raw from crying, and my mom has given up on trying to help. We've been sitting here in the kitchen, sipping strong coffee and sniffling into tissues from the moment I woke her up with my heavy sobs. I couldn't make it back to my room, collapsing on the door when I stepped back inside the house.

The sun wasn't up yet, the clock reading only four in the morning. And I just knew. What I keep playing over and over in my mind is how close I was to stopping him. He only could have been gone for minutes.

I want to stay home from school, but I also want to talk to Mr. Chessman. I need clues, and I need him to stall Mr. Mathison. I've dialed Owen's number at least sixty times, every single time my call going right to voicemail. I've only left a handful of messages, each time my words come out broken, my sentences only halves.

When it's time for school to begin, I drag my bag along the driveway with me, my eyes on the ground most of the way until I reach my car door. Andrew is standing in his driveway, a heavy coat pulled around his body, his backpack by his feet.

"He's coming back, Kens. He has to," Andrew says, rubbing his hands together and blowing into them for warmth. Andrew's been crying; Owen must not have said goodbye to him either. I wonder if he got a note, too.

"Come on. I'll give you a ride," I say. He tosses his bag in my back seat and slides into my passenger side. Seeing him there hurts. It hurts because he looks like his brother, dresses like him…smells like him. But he *isn't* him.

I take Andrew to his school, then drive the few miles back to my own, pulling in next to Willow's car. I can't bear the thought of seeing my friends right now, talking to Will, so I hide low in my seat until the morning bell rings, then make my way from my car to Mr. Chessman's classroom. He has a class, but when he see's me peering through the small window slit in his door, he excuses himself and meets me in the hall.

He knows the moment he sees my face.

"He's gone," I say, my lip shaking just saying the words. "I can't get him to pick up his phone. He's going to miss that meeting. I…I don't know what to do."

Mr. Chessman pushes his hands into his pockets, looking down at his feet. He kicks at a crack in the hallway floor, his shoe scuffing against the roughness a few times before he nods his head and purses his lips. When he brings his eyes back up to mine, he's resolved in the fact that Owen isn't coming. I wait for him to slip back into his classroom before retreating to the girls' bathroom.

Instead of the one near the band room, I climb the stairs to one on the third floor, where I'm more confident I'll be alone. Once inside, I pull my feet up, hiding them from view while I sit in the stall. I bring my phone to my lap and type a few more texts—I type them because he'll see them, and maybe if I say it enough, he'll come home.

I love you.

I love you.

I love you.

I look at my history and count. I've sent the same message to Owen seventy-four times.

When the bell rings, I wait for everyone to rush by, holding my breath when a few students enter then leave my small restroom. When the bell rings again, I exit my hiding place, opening the band door and putting on my game face just long enough to fool Mr. Brody.

"Sorry, I was sick to my stomach. I feel better now," I say as I pass his office quickly. He nods and holds up a hand before going back to his computer. I continue down the hallway to my practice room, my hands reaching for the surface of the piano and my face collapsing against my arms, the tears coming out in another rush against the raw skin around my eyes.

I give in, and I let myself cry hard for a solid five minutes, and then I cut it off, rubbing my nose along my sleeve, forcing myself to breathe in long, steady inhales and exhales. This is the same way I deal with anxiety over getting shots, and the longer I control my breathing, the funnier the comparison seems to me, and eventually I'm laughing to myself.

With my head slung forward, my fingers travel lightly along the keys, walking a finger at a time and somehow finding all of the sharps and flats. I'm setting the sad notes free.

"It's probably good you didn't audition with that."

My stomach drops the moment the sound of Owen's voice hits my ears. Everything in me falls apart in an instant, the tears running down my cheeks and my body losing strength as I turn and reach for him, clinging around his waist until he's sitting next to me, holding me in his arms, his lips kissing the top of my head.

"I couldn't go. I couldn't do it. I'll find a way to make it work. For my mom, and Gramps. I'll find a way, get a job here," he hums in my ear. "I couldn't go."

I pull away just enough to look at him, and his smile is tight, his eyes on mine, his hand stroking the skin just under my eyes.

"These are puffy," he says, bending down and pressing his lips to my tender skin. "I'm so sorry, Kens. I did that. I was trying to do what was right, but I don't know."

My lips form a sloppy grin and my body shakes with happy tears, and every time I shudder, Owen holds me tighter.

"I made it all the way to the border. Do you know how far the border is? I kept trying to make the hard choice, thinking I had to. But all I wanted to choose was you. And then it hit me," he says, his hands finding my shoulders. He turns to the side, forcing me to face him, my legs lying across his, my fingers gripping the fabric of his shirt, wrapping it tightly within my hands, not wanting him to disappear. "I was running scared, Kens. I've never run scared in my life, even when I should. But I did. I was afraid I would fail, that I would be selfish, and then it would cost those I love."

He leans forward, his forehead on mine, his hands finding mine, which have now become fists stuffed with his shirt. He chuckles when he pries them loose, bringing them into his lap, holding them tightly.

"Losing you, the thought that I could love you and lose you too—that scared me—so I figured what was the point if it was all going to just end up hurting me in the end. And then I realized how much it hurt to give you up," he says, stopping to watch the reaction in my eyes. I suck my bottom lip into my mouth, taking quick shallow breaths through my nose, telling my brain, my body—my heart—that this moment is real. "And those texts… you kept sending those texts," he laughs. "What were there, like…sixty?"

He pulls his phone out and holds it in front of me, his hand on my neck as he leans forward and presses his lips to mine, his smile against my mouth warming my chest, numbing the pain and healing the brokenness.

"I got a ticket. Two hundred and eighty dollars, you believe that shit?" he says, pulling a folded, pink paper from his other pocket, a court appearance date stapled to the top. "I drove so fast. I didn't even see the cop on the side of the road. And I picked right back up after he wrote me this, because I had to get back here…back to you!"

The relief continues to wash over me, every minute a wave crashing and pulling away more of the fear and worry and pain that consumed me when I woke this morning. Owen and I stay here, me in his arms, for the entire period, ignoring the bell when it sounds, and passing on the next one too.

A few students come and go from the band room, the lunch hour now, and some people open the door to our tiny haven, hoping to squeeze in some practice. Everyone leaves us alone, though. They don't know our story, or understand how long it took for us to get here, but they let us have our moment anyway. No comments because it's Owen Harper, no questions over my tears, and no lame jokes about needing to get a room. Our affection is chaste, more of a never-ending embrace, and our love for each other the realest damn thing I've ever known.

We stay here, hidden from Owen's past, for as long as we can, finally slipping back into the masses as the lunch hour ends. Owen walks with me to our algebra class, passing Mr. Chessman's classroom along the way, and he sees us. His chest fills slowly with air, and his hand rubs at his neck as I pause at the doorway to our next class, holding my hands together in front of me, praying a *thank you* to him. He closes his eyes, and I know he's saying it back.

Owen's feet slide into their rightful place, his heavy shoes leaving chunks of dirt and debris next to my leg on my seat. When he threatens to pull his foot away, I cling to it, and he laughs.

"All right. I'll leave it," he says.

After the first few minutes of class, the door opens and one of the student aids passes a note to our teacher, both of them looking to Owen. I'm not surprised when they call him to the office. I look at him as he stands, tugging quickly on his arm before he leaves.

"What are you going to tell him?" I ask, knowing Mr. Mathison is waiting for his answer, wanting Owen's commitment just as much as I do. Owen doesn't answer me, but he bites his lip and lets his smile slide up one side of his mouth, winking as he backs away, turning to take the slip from our teacher then make his way out the door.

He's gone for the rest of the class period, and I waver between believing this time is a good sign and a bad one. I practically race from the classroom when the bell rings, and my eyes begin searching for him as soon as I step into the hallway. He pulls me back against him, his body leaning along the wall just outside the door.

I turn into him, and his hands find their place along my face quickly, his lips on mine within seconds, his mouth consuming me until his smile forces itself to break free. I love the way his smile feels against me.

"Well, does this mean you're going? Did you commit? Everything's... good?" I ask, pressing myself closer to him, students bumping into me as they leave the class and hurry through the halls.

"Everything's...*very* good," Owen says. His eyes look up to the ceiling as his grin takes over again, the smile somehow growing bigger than him. He looks back at me, his tongue caught between his teeth, something important waiting to spill from his lips. He's staying. Owen is staying, and he's going to DePaul and life is going to be amazing. It's in his face. I know it—just looking in his eyes.

"How do you feel about orange?" he asks finally, and the only reaction I have is a firm shake of my head, my eyes closing with confusion. But my heart—it still feels happy.

"Orange. Orange is good...I guess," I say, my eyes on him with playful suspicion.

"I've got an idea to run by you," he says, his hand sliding down my arm until he finds my fingers, threading his with mine and tugging me toward the door. "We should go home to discuss."

My legs follow willingly. But my heart follows first. It can't help itself. Owen—he *owns* it. I gave it to him.

And I will follow him anywhere.

CHAPTER 24

One Year Later

"Leave her drum alone," Willow says, slapping Jess's hand away from the harness and snare drum on my floor at the end of my bed.

My roommate this year has been very tolerant. I knew the second I was accepted to the University of Illinois's jazz program that I would also join the marching band. Turns out, though, that playing the snare drum is harder than it looks. I've had to practice, and my roommate Shay invested in some seriously awesome headphones to block out my constant noise. I think she was excited to meet Willow, mostly because she knows I'll be rooming with her instead next year.

Jess pulls my drum over his head and raps out a quick rhythm. Seconds later, Shay stuffs her books into her backpack leaving us for the library.

"Bye. Nice meeting you!" Willow yells over the loud sounds popping off of the drumhead in front of Jess. As soon as the door closes, she grabs the sticks from Jess's hands and passes them to me. "You ran her off; what's wrong with you?"

Jess shrugs, pulling the harness back over his head and resting it on the floor. "Some chicks don't dig drummers. Not my problem," he says, jumping backward to lie on my bed. Willow tosses his feet to the side when he does.

"You're getting shit all over her bed," she says, rolling her eyes.

"Great to know you two are still getting along so well," I joke, straddling my chair and sitting as Willow moves to sit next to Jess. She pulls her legs up and sticks her tongue out at him. He reacts, grabbing her quickly and pulling her on top of him, tickling her until eventually they're kissing. "Wow. That's my bed you're on," I say, standing and closing the clasps on the sleeves of my uniform.

"I can't believe you're marching. I can't wait to see this," Willow says, beaming with pride, as if she is responsible for me being able to walk and pound a plastic surface at the same time. Actually, that took practice too, but thankfully the instructor and I get along really well. Both of us play the piano and love jazz, which has made him more tolerant of the two left feet I seem to walk on.

My phone buzzes in my pocket, and I pull it out to read a text from Owen.

I'm at the stairs.

"He's here," I say, picking up my drum and ushering my friends out the door. I lock up just in time to see Owen step through the stairwell door and walk toward my room. College has been good to him. I swear he's an inch taller, if that's possible, and his face and body—all of him—more of a man than he was a year before.

More than the physical, though, is the peace that seems to have come to him. It didn't happen all at once, and there were times when I thought this idea—this plan he concocted during a two-hour drive from the Iowa-Illinois state border back to Woodstock—was going to explode and ruin us both forever. But Owen stuck with it. Something changed during that drive, an idea found its way into his head, and it invaded his heart, and he wasn't going to let it go.

I was happy with the thought of him going to DePaul. I would have been happy in the city, studying with Chen. Not *my* music, but music still. And I would have seen Owen, our schools only an hour or so away from each other.

But Owen had a flash during that drive, his mind catching on something Mr. Chessman said the day before. DePaul—it wasn't the only school interested. Owen's always been bold. The only thing that intimidated him was the idea of forgiving himself for not being able to save his father and James. Calling his coach at seven in the morning, asking for names, schools, the list of people who have asked to see his highlight tapes and stats—that was easy. And when his coach mentioned that the University of Illinois had been calling a lot lately, that was all he needed to hear.

He stopped at a diner in Rockford, made a few calls, and mentioned to a certain scout that he was getting some serious offers from DePaul. Then he looked up the University's music program, more specifically the jazz division, and saved it. Thirty minutes—and one speeding ticket—later, he found me.

"I still think the uniform's sexy," he says, making the few final steps to me, pulling both ends of my bright orange jacket into him until I'm fully in his arms. He kisses my neck and tries to work my jacket from my body, but I push him away.

"So, I'm late for warm-ups, and Jess and Will are here," I say, tilting my head toward the end of the hall where my friends both raise a hand to say hello. Owen pulls his hat low on his head, feigning he's embarrassed at being caught. I know he's not—Owen still loves to kiss in public.

He leans forward and whispers in my ear, "Okay, but we're ditching them after the game, just for a little while."

"Bright orange jacket just does it for you, huh?" I joke, spinning in my obnoxiously florescent uniform. He stops me mid-spin, wrapping his arms around me and pulling my back into his chest.

"You do it for me," he says, his words always perfect.

We walk to the game, and I join the band while Owen guides Will and Jess over to the student section. He sits with the other guys on the basketball team, and they usually get shown on TV once or twice. I mentioned this to Willow, and I noticed she was wearing a lot more makeup tonight than she normally does.

We've performed for six home games, and every time, the thrill of being out here, of being a part of something like this, gets to me. I think I fell in love with this school the moment I stepped through the tunnel with Will and Jess—and Owen remembered. His season started a few weeks ago. I volunteered to play in the rally band for basketball games too, just so I could watch him. Last week, the crowd started chanting *Harper.* Owen says he didn't hear it, but I know he did. I know because I saw it in his smile—the cocky smirk I fell in love with a year ago.

Much like in high school, our football team is only average, and Owen texts me that Willow and Jess are bored by the third quarter. They only wanted to stay for the band's half-time performance anyhow. Willow's never really been in it for the sports. I text Owen back and tell him to leave with them and head to the pub. I'll meet up with them after. I want to change and clean up anyhow.

The game lasts another hour, and Owen sends me a few texts of pictures of Willow and Jess dancing. Owen snuck them in, like he usually does with me, and I can tell he's also helped them get beer, Willow's craziness amplifying a little more in every picture he sends. By the time I finally get to the bar, my friends are cuddling in a booth looking at stunt videos on YouTube that they for some reason find hilariously funny.

"I left you in charge of them for like, what? An hour?" I say, sliding up behind Owen, my hands moving around his sides over his stomach and up his chest.

"That better be Kensi feelin' me up, otherwise my girlfriend's going to kick your ass," he jokes, pulling me around to face him, his trademark dark jeans and long-sleeved black shirt calling for me to touch him. I move in close, resting my cheek on his chest, his heart beating underneath. I put on his favorite outfit, too—a red shirtdress with black leggings and a pair of brown leather boots. Even now, a year later, I still want to be the only girl he notices.

"Come on," he says, his hand sliding down my arm until his fingers find mine, his eyes drawing a line down my body. He walks toward the dance floor, a small wood-planked square crowded with pretty girls and guys on the prowl, and pulls me into the very middle, holding me against his body. He cups my face, stretching me up to my toes, and dusts his lips over mine, speaking against my mouth. "I want to dance with you," he says, his hands reaching into my hair as he kisses me harder, with enough heat to draw a few whistles from the couples standing next to us. He can feel me blush and start to pull away to hide, so his hands only get firmer, his mouth curving into a smile against mine.

"Don't you go run and hide. They're just whistling at a guy kissing the prettiest girl in the room, wear that crown proudly, princess," he says, his hands growing more bold, sliding over my hips, his thumbs flirting with the waist of my leggings, reminding my body of how quickly he can own me completely.

"I thought you didn't dance," I say, my face tilted up to look at him, his eyes peering down on me, both of us hiding under the shadow of his hat.

"Mmmmm," he hums, pulling me close to him, his chin resting on my head. "This isn't really dancing. It's more like foreplay."

Oh.

"Hey, have you heard from your mom? Did your grandpa get moved in yet?" I ask, and Owen's body slumps in reaction.

"I say foreplay, and you ask about my grandpa," Owen chuckles.

"Well, you always knew he'd steal me away from you. It's kind of your fault when you think about it—you put us together," I laugh. Owen shakes his head, then kisses the top of mine as he holds me against his chest.

"Grampa's good. I still can't believe your mom got him into that program near her hospital. Really, that was amazing of her," he says, everything about his body so different from the stress and worry that always lived inside of him before. My mom started working on Gus's case the day his mom sold their house. The Harpers moved into an apartment down the road until school let out, and by the time Owen graduated and the money had run out to pay for his grandfather's current home, my mom had worked him into the program for veteran's through her hospital downtown. Emma agreed to let Gus stay for a fraction of the cost until my mom could finalize his move.

"My mom has good connections, and I think she's finally getting used to the fact that she can make demands for things, and people will listen. Besides, I think she's a little smitten for Gus, too," I say.

Owen squints at me, his lips pursed.

"I'm not sure I'm comfortable with all this obsession with my hot grandpa," he says, unable to contain his smile, a laugh breaking through and ruining his character. I nestle back into his embrace.

"My mom has a date," he says, his chin once again resting on my head, his thumbs caressing small circles along the small of my back.

"Oh yeah?" I say, having a hard time seeing Owen's mom do anything other than work. In the year I lived next to her, I think I saw her ten times, her eyes always heavy, her body always thin and fatigued.

"You'll never guess who with," he says, his tone all I need to know. I can't help but grin against his chest. I told Owen about what I had learned, about how Mr. Chessman knew his family. I wanted him to know how much he loved working with his father, and how much he respected them all. He needed to know that there were people out there that saw past the wild—people who saw the good. I didn't mention my suspicions about how Mr. Chessman felt, the way I saw him look at Owen's mom. But I think that will all work itself out without me.

"You're kidding?" I say, stepping back and looking up at him again. I love how he towers over me.

"Not kidding. I just feel really bad for Andrew. His teacher is dating his mom, I mean…wow, right?" Owen says, his chest raspy with laughter.

"He's only his teacher part of the time," I say, as if that somehow makes it better.

"Yeah, *okay,*" he says, brushing his thumb over my cheek, his eyes doing that thing where they zero in on me and me alone, the rest of the world fading away. We've quit swaying an entire song ago, the pretense of dancing long gone. We're standing in the middle of the crowded dance floor holding each other, and looking at each other wanting more. I can tell by the way Owen's breathing, by the way everything about him, about us, slows. Owen draws his finger down my chin to my neck, looping it under the small key charm resting at the bottom of my necklace between my breasts. He pulls the key up to his mouth, biting it in his teeth, his brow lowering and his lips curling.

"You think those two will notice if we ditch them, head back to my room?" Owen finally says, my body reacting as it always does.

"Willow has a key; I think they'll be fine," I say, glancing over at my friends, who are settled even lower in their booth, content to stay there until the sun rises I'm sure. My response is enough for him, and he sweeps his arm around me, tucking me against his side, guiding me through the crowd of football fans still pouring into the bar.

We walk the few blocks to his dorm, the same chill in the air that was there the first night I kissed him, the night he gave me the bracelet I still wear every day. I love it when he sees me in it, and I love how he kisses my wrist, like he is right now, as he slips it from my skin.

I love how he watches me, how he watches *over* me, fights for me, and makes me a better version of myself.

I love him.

Truth is, Owen Harper shot me through the heart that day he pointed his finger at me and pulled the trigger. I fell for him then, and I've been falling every day since. All I wanted was for him to catch me.

And he did.

THE END

ACKNOWLEDGMENTS

This book. This book!

It was something that grabbed a hold of me, out of nowhere, and wouldn't let me go until I finished. It had me, from the very beginning, and, while a mother shouldn't choose her favorites, for me, this might be it. This one; it's my favorite. If I didn't own up to it being my favorite, I would be cheating it. I love this book and am unbelievably proud of it, and I cannot thank you enough for the time you've given it.

This book scratches the surface of some extremely heavy topics—suicide, addiction and the struggles of living with mental illness. I want you to know that these topics, they matter to me. I put a lot of care in how I handled them, and above all, I wanted to be honest in the portrait I painted. And to those of you who work in a field that supports those suffering, I commend you with the absolute highest honor. You are angels—remarkable humans.

This is my seventh novel. That number astonishes me, and now I'm eager to watch it grow. I would not be here if it weren't for the amazing readers out there who support me and champion me to continue, who lend their time and give me the ultimate gift—reading my stories. I thank you, from the depths of my heart.

I also must thank my amazing support team, starting with my husband

and son, who only think it's slightly weird that I carry my laptop around to baseball practice and make manic plot point notes on my phone in the middle of the Target electronics section. Thank you also to the amazing *Wild Reckless* beta readers: Jennifer, Shelley, Ashley, Debbie and Brigitte. You field my crazy questions when I'm not sure about something, and you push me when I'm afraid to go somewhere I really should—THANK YOU for making me take Owen to such challenging places. He wouldn't be the man he is if I hadn't, and you helped me accept that.

They say your words are only as good as your editors—Tina Scott and Billi Joy Carson, you are the A-Team of editors, so I always feel prepared going into battle. Also, Wordsmith Publicity—a million thanks for helping stretch the spotlight, encouraging it to shine on my stories whenever you can. Your team is mighty, and my thanks to you enormous.

If you enjoyed this book, please consider leaving a review. Your reviews are often the only way small stories like this can be seen, and I for one know the power readers have. I'm so grateful for every post, mention, recommendation, book club, Tweet, pin and more that readers have given to my books. I hope to give you lots to talk about in the future.

Edited to add in November 2020: This book was nominated for a Goodreads Choice Award in 2015. I knew it was special. <3

Wicked
RESTLESS
THE HARPER BOYS BOOK 2
Love is wicked.
But a restless heart
isn't meant to beat alone.
by bestselling author
GINGER SCOTT

Wicked
RESTLESS
THE HARPER BOYS BOOK 2
350
by bestselling author
GINGER SCOTT

Cover design by Ginger Scott

Ginger Scott

For Sadie.

PART ONE

AgI Na_2ZnO_2
$NaI+H$ $FeCl_3$ Al_2O_3 AgBr
Cu_2S $Ca(NO_3)_2$ $AgNO_3$ H_2O ZnO $MgBr_2$ $AgCl$ NH_4Cl
N_2 O_2 $AlCl_3$ Air $AgCl$ NH_3
$NaNO_2$ Au_2O_3 C_2H_5OH $(NH_4)_2SO_4$ $CuSO_4$
$MgCl_2$ $CuCl_2$ $Cu(OH)_2$ CuI
Cu_2S $ZnCl_2$ Cu_5FeS_4 $NaNO_3$ $Cu(NO_3)_2$
$CaCO_3$ SO_3 KOH SO_4 $BaCl_2$ CaF_2
NaI
KCl H_2SO_4 $CuFeS_2$ $MgCl_2$ $TiCl_2$ Xe $Cu(OH)_2$ PbO
He HCl $BaCl_2$ $CaCl_2$ $FeSiO_3$ $Al_2O_3 \cdot 2H_2O$ $Mg(H)_2$ MnO_2
$FeCl_2$ Ag_2S CaI $CaSO_4$ $BaSO_4$ H_2CO_3
KBr MgO $MgCO_3$ $[Al(OH)_4]$ $MgCl_2$
CO_2 $ZnCl_2$
SiO_2 $NaCl$ Cl_2 LiI HBr V_2O_5 FeS
CH_4 $KMnO_4$ NaN $ZnSO_4$ $FeCr_2O_4$ Na_2CO_3
$Al(OH)_3$ CH_3CH_2OH
$CaCl_2$ $PbCO_3$ NH_4NO_2 $PbSO_4$
Ag_2O BaU_4 $FeTiO_3$
Kn

CHAPTER 1

ANDREW HARPER, AGE 16

Normally, I don't care what clothes I wear when I leave for school in the early morning. I spend my days with people I don't really know. Most of my freshman year of high school was on a college campus—my curse for being *smart*.

I say "curse" because unlike my older brother, Owen, I don't have normal friends. I don't get to go to high school dances or hang out at football games. Not that Owen ever did, but he could have if he wanted to. I get to go to what's called the Excel Program. I'm the lucky one learning physics and advanced calculus. The trade-off is I'll probably be accepted into any college I want, get any job I want, and find the entire process to be easy.

The curse—I'm alone.

My friends were Owen's friends: always three years older; always inviting me to things out of pity; always keeping me out of trouble, but just out of its reach. Protecting me. That was the line. My life was on the periphery. I heard it from Owen since the day I started grade school, and my mother echoed those words whenever I would protest I couldn't go to the party with Owen or hang out in the woods with him and his friends.

"He's only protecting you," she'd say.

Protecting me.

Choking me.

When Owen graduated, so did his friends. My small sliver of a social life evaporated piece by piece as people went off to college or to find jobs in some town that wasn't small. Then my mom sold our house to help pay for my grandfather's care, and I moved into a two-bedroom apartment with a vacant unit on one side and neighbors in their sixties on the other.

Sophomore year is shaping up to be more isolating. My only friend my age, a guy I barely tolerated named Matt who I met during a torturous year when both of our mothers decided putting us in Boy Scouts was a good idea, moved to Guam. Not the next town over. Not California. Not any place I could convince my mother was safe enough for me to visit—*escape to.* The fucker moved to Guam.

I used to go to Matt's house and spend hours playing video games. We didn't talk when we played, which is what made my friendship with Matt work. Now, I go to school, then come home. I study and have dinner with my mom and her boyfriend, Dwayne Chessman, a man we've known for years. He teaches at the high school—the one I don't get to go to because I'm *so smart.*

In the evening, I walk to the rink in the middle of Old Town, to a place called the Ice Palace, and I skate until my feet have blisters. I sprint and stop so many times I wear paths in the ice—so deep, they need to fill them with water when I leave. This is the only place I can go to feel something. On weekends, there are enough guys there to get a game going, but during the week, when I can come, it's usually only me. I've always skated, but when my brother Owen left, I became obsessed with hockey. Seems the skills I lack at throwing a ball are made up for in my ability to move a puck. That, and I'm incredibly fast. It's not the competition. I couldn't give a shit about winning something. For me, it's the rawness, the hunt—chasing something, taking something from someone, hurting them to get it, and not caring how they look lying on the ice in my wake. I don't operate under those morals anywhere else. But I think, maybe, there's a dark part of me that needs it. And I *need* to keep it on the ice.

Usually, though, I'm alone out there. So instead, I push myself until I can barely breathe, sometimes until my chest burns and I vomit. I push until Gary, who cleans up the joint, is coughing under his breath, leaning on the exit as he taps on his watch—his subtle hint to me to get my ass off the ice so he can go home.

My feet are sore today, but that's the last thing I'm going to remember. This is the day so many things are going to change—the day I start caring about what I wear when I leave my apartment in the morning. Illinois passed a law that every high school student needs to take PE, even the smart students who don't go to a real high school. I protested at first, dreading the bus ride I'd have to endure, the awkward blue uniform, and my assured complete-lack-of-allies for dodgeball. But those anxieties are escaping me now. The second I broke through the athletic department door, I saw her sitting against the wall of the PE office, her legs outstretched, the blue fabric of her perfect dress tucked underneath her knees. The vision of her hits me harder as my eyes scan their way up. Her hair is the color of mahogany, and it twists in spirals, like a tornado rushing down her shoulders and spine; a dark storm against her cream skin.

I sit opposite her, sliding down against the wall, stretching my legs out until the soles of my shoes tap the bottom of hers. I do this on purpose. I want to see her eyes. Her gaze comes up quickly, and she pulls her feet in fast, careful to tuck the bottom of her dress underneath more tightly, hiding her modesty. Her eyes are gray, a dark gray, like charcoal.

I don't know her name, and I'm not sure I'll like her when she speaks. But I know I'll never forget her. Her smile, however fast it comes and goes in this moment, coincides with the first full breath I've taken in years.

I try to hold her attention, leaving my grin in place, a crooked one, just to let her know I'm sorry I bumped her. Sorry—*not sorry.* I slide the beanie from my head, and I know my hair is probably a mess by the way she lets out a breathy giggle when she sees it. I run my fingers through, but stop quickly. I like the way she giggles, and I don't care how I look. If my messy hair makes her smile, I'll wear it that way every day.

"Are you new, too?" she asks. I nodded *yes* at first, but correct her quickly. Her voice had me in a trance.

"No, I'm just...special," I say.

She sizes my response up for a few seconds, her lip quirked up on one side. "What makes you so special?" she finally asks.

I hold her gaze for a few seconds, liking this feeling of just sitting here looking at her. I stare until she has to look away, her cheeks growing more pink and her eyelashes fluttering as she stares back to her lap, where she's holding a small pink pass with something written from a parent or teacher. She keeps folding and unfolding the corners, wearing the paper out on the edges. She's nervous.

"Nothing makes me special. I'm not very special at all," I say, which only makes her peer back up with a sideways glance. Her lip ticks up again. Her mouth is pink, and tiny, and there are freckles that dot her nose.

"I bet you're special to someone," she says, her smile reaching the other side of her mouth now. She's being nice. No…she's being sweet. Goddamn is she sweet.

"I have an opening for that job…*someone.* Want it?" I tease. I see her eyes flash wider for a second, and I can tell I made her tense, so I tap my toe against hers again. "I was just kidding. But thanks."

"Emma Burke…Andrew Harper?" The voice breaks through our silence, startling us both to our feet. Mr. Crest, the PE teacher, is standing with his clipboard, two uniforms wrapped in plastic tucked under his arm. I bet these come in a big box, on a big truck, from a warehouse filled with ugly blue uniforms. Thank god my shorts aren't as small as hers. Thank god her shorts are that small.

"I'm supposed to give you this," Emma says, stepping closer to the teacher and handing over her paper slip. He reviews it and stuffs it in his back pocket, then marks something on his clipboard.

"You, this way," he says in my direction, shoving a bundle of pale blue material at me while jerking his head toward the boys' locker room. I don't even care that he's talking to me like this, like I'm some slacker he plans to fail. I don't care because she's still biting her lip, trying not to look right at me for too long.

"I'll see ya around, Emma," I say, taking my ugly-ass PE uniform into my arms.

"Bye, Andrew," she says, only letting her lip go from the grip of her teeth long enough to utter my name. Her voice is just over a whisper, and she's timid, and sweet, and I love PE. I want to change my schedule to nothing but PE. All day. Every day—as long as I can have this class with her.

* * *

I MAY HAVE OVERSOLD my enthusiasm for PE. I've been taking a bus here for three weeks, and so far, I've been the first guy out in dodgeball a dozen times, and forced to stand on the free-throw line in basketball for an hour until I could sink a shot. The only saving grace was the day we played field hockey. Of course, I got a warning from Mr. Crest and a lecture that made me miss my bus after I checked a guy on the field. Apparently, there is no contact in PE field hockey. When I told him they shouldn't call it hockey then, he sent me to the principal's office.

The only bonus about today—we don't have to wear our uniforms. We get a break for the entire week, in fact. It's the square-dancing unit. For about ten minutes, we've been sitting in the gym, our backs flush against the wall outside our locker room, while Mr. Crest struggles with an ancient sound system. Based on the few times he was able to get the speakers to make a sound, I'm pretty sure we're not missing anything by not hearing this music. He finally turns a microphone on and sets it next to a tiny speaker he plugs into his phone.

"All right, gentlemen. On your feet, and form a line against the wall," he says. There's a collective grumble as we stand, but that sound stops as soon as the girls' locker-room door swings open and a single-file line that matches ours begins to fill the space along the other wall.

When I see Emma, I start counting. She's in the middle, and I make it to fourteen before the row of girls streaming through the door ends. I count two more times to be sure, then I count my line.

Seventeen.

Three people away.

Our number fourteen is a guy whose pants are rolled up at the bottom. And the dude isn't wearing socks. He isn't worthy of Emma. But he notices her. I watched him count. And I watched him clench his fist in a silent *yes* when he figured it out. There is no way I am letting this asshole swing her around the gym to shitty music for forty-five minutes.

"Dude," I say, leaning forward, watching to make sure Mr. Crest is still facing the front. "Psssst! Dude!"

Fucker's ignoring me.

"Come on, man. Hey!" He finally looks my way. He's wearing a button-down shirt. The collar is wrinkled. "Hey, trade me spots."

"Fuck off," he shrugs.

I blink at him, a little stunned that he was so quick to shut me down. Owen would have punched him, or saved this memory for later and made him suffer through ridicule—or he'd just date the guy's girlfriend. I glance back down to his shoes, and his hairy ankles. I'm pretty sure he doesn't have a girlfriend.

I look at my row again, making sure I didn't mess up on my first count. I'm still seventeen. I glance back at sockless dude, and he's tucking his shirt in and smoothing his hair out on the sides. I can't believe he's going to touch Emma's arm.

Our line moves forward, and couples are pairing off and finding spots on the gym floor marked with tape. When I'm about ten people away, I count again, relieved that at least I have a shy girl who looks just as uncomfortable with this lesson as I do.

The music is mostly fiddle, and there's a male singer giving directions—spinning, two steps in, two steps out, around the barn and *ain't she pretty.* I laugh a little under my breath. It's my turn to pair off when I glance back up and meet Emma's eyes. I don't show my surprise, and I ignore the grunts in protest of the a-hole two people away from me. *Dude, socks. If you just wore socks, this wouldn't have happened.*

Maybe it would have, though. Maybe...maybe Emma was counting too.

I guide her to our tape marks in the far corner, and while everyone else has unlinked arms, I keep my hold on hers—our elbows locked together—the soft tickle of her skin along mine is possibly the best thing that has happened in my life to date.

I lean over and whisper in her ear while we wait for the remaining couples to find their spot. "The dude doesn't wear socks."

She laughs the most perfect, quiet, careful laugh, then glances over her shoulder as sockless guy walks by with his partner.

"Yeah, thanks for saving me from *that,*" she giggles.

I nod and smile, but while we sit down in our square formation I also feel a little smug. *You had to trade spots with three people, Emma. This wasn't just about the socks.*

We're both leaning back on our hands now, listening to Mr. Crest read through a packet on basic square-dancing moves. I don't think anyone is *really* listening though. The guy across from me has slipped his phone from his pocket, and he's playing a game, the girl next to him is mouthing something to her friend across the room, and I'm staring at the small fraction of an inch of space between my pinky finger and Emma's.

With every word Mr. Crest says, I slide it a millimeter more, until finally the tip of my finger is resting against hers. I glance up at her at the feeling of our touch, and she's still staring at our teachers, *listening.* She also lets a smirk take over one side of her mouth.

"All right, on your feet. Let's give this one a try," Mr. Crest says.

I stand at the same time Emma does, and when I reach for her arm and loop it through mine, she doesn't flinch. It's like that's where her arm belongs.

I spend the next hour noticing things. I notice she wears pink Converse, and they look perfect next to my black ones that are twice the size. I notice her black leggings tuck into her shoes, and her legs are long with perfect curves for every muscle. I memorize where the tip of her hair stops when she brushes it over one shoulder—grazing her shoulder blades in the back and the small swell of her breasts in the front.

When I get to look into her eyes, I memorize everything they hold. The gray is caught somewhere between silver and black, and the longer I look, the more convinced I am she's the perfect storm and I'm lost at sea.

I spend so much time looking at the details, I'm surprised when the bell rings to signal the end of class. When she unhooks her arm from mine, she lets her fingertips slide along my skin, and I memorize that, too.

Square dancing for an hour with Emma Burke is worth being pummeled in a thousand dodgeball games.

CHAPTER 2

ANDREW

Square dancing lasted a week. For five days, Emma Burke and I counted lines of teenagers to make sure we both met in the middle. We never talked about it. There was never a formal plan. It was just something we both did—a silent commitment.

Then Monday came, and we started weightlifting for two weeks. I only saw Emma in brief trips to the drinking fountain while the girls were in the other wing of the gym, tumbling.

I'm pretty sure Mr. Crest thinks I'm diabetic, because I'm thirsty all the time.

I don't have afternoon classes today. There's an event at the college, so the Excel Program is getting the afternoon off. I intend on spending those extra hours learning about Emma.

Dwayne said I could sit in his classroom, since he has a prep hour for the last hour of the day. But I don't know where Emma is, and part of me wants to stand outside to look for her. I don't have my own car yet, just my mom's or Dwayne's when they let me borrow it—so I can't even hang out in the parking lot and offer her a ride home.

I keep glancing through the sliver of a window on Dwayne's door. Every noise I hear in the hall draws my attention.

"What has you so jumpy?" he asks after my twentieth peek through the glass.

I look at him, my heart a little stuck, my chest tight. This is awkward, and I feel edgy—like I'm caught doing something I shouldn't. We don't talk much—Dwayne and me. He was always closer with Owen. I think because Owen had so many struggles. I'm just the smart, quiet one.

"Do you know Emma Burke?" I ask, finally. I want to vomit. I don't talk about girls. Not to Dwayne. Not to anyone really. There's never been a girl to talk about.

Dwayne tosses the marker onto the ledge of his whiteboard then kicks his desk chair around until it's facing him so he can sit. He glides in it to his desk in small scoots, laughing under his breath. He's laughing at me. Because I'm ridiculous.

"Yeah, I know Emma," he says.

I nod at him, my lips tight, then I glance back out the window, figuring now that I'm good and mortified, I'm sure to see her. When I look back at Dwayne, he's still smiling, but he's looking at his grade book and tapping his marker on his desk, not wanting to make me feel any more embarrassed. We both drift back to the silence of before, except now there's a ginormous cloud of *Andrew likes Emma* floating in the fucking air. I'm sure this will be a late-night chat topic for him and my mom.

Awesome. Fucking…awesome.

The tick of the seconds on the clock above his desk is loud, and I start counting with it rather than checking the actual time—testing myself to see how close I come to being right. With two minutes left before the end of the day, Dwayne slides his chair out, letting the rollers carry it to the wall behind him when he stands, and he walks over to the desk I've commandeered by the door.

"Here," he says, dropping his keys in front of me.

I slide them in a circle with my finger, then gaze up at him.

"Your mom will come pick me up on her way home. I have grading to do, and I don't want you to have to stay here. Besides…don't you need to give *someone* a ride home?" He's teasing me a little, and I kind of hate it. But,

I also want to hug this man who is sort of the only father figure I have. Because yeah…there's someone I need to give a ride home to.

I stand, untangling my long legs from the small desk that doesn't suit me, and pull my gray beanie back on my head.

"She's in room one-twenty-seven," he says, smirking, but only for a second, never fully looking at me. He turns around, and I slip out his door just before the bell sounds, hauling ass to her room on the other end of the hall.

I get to her door seconds before she steps through it, and I lean against the wall on the other side, bending my knee and looking natural. Natural; I look like a fucking creeper. I'm rethinking my pose when she surprises me, kicking her foot into mine. This is our thing, it seems.

"What are you doing here, Harper?"

I wince when she asks that way. People call us *Harper,* and it's not usually a good thing. If she's calling me that, it means people have been talking to her about me—about Owen. About my father's mental illness, probably his suicide, and maybe James's drug habits and the way he died last year. The town has been more respectful over James, and I think the fact that Owen landed a basketball scholarship shut them up a little too. But rumors and gossip are hard to kill completely. And us Harper boys—we make headline-worthy gossip. Owen may be the golden college boy now, but he's also the troublemaker with a rap sheet.

"Thought you might want a ride," I say. The confidence I had when I darted to her classroom is gone. I'm pretty sure there's no way this girl is getting in a car with me. I just hope she doesn't laugh out loud.

The look she gives to the blonde walking up behind her confirms my suspicions. Her friend, I've seen her around. I think she might be the sister of one of Owen's exes, or maybe related to someone my brother's friends know. She knows me, and that's enough; her eyebrows are high on her forehead when she looks at Emma. That expression is all about warning her to stay away.

"Oh, I was…I was going home with Melody. We were going to get ready…there's…there's a dance here tonight," she says, delivering the news in fits and starts.

It's cute the way she takes her time with every word, not sure which thing will hurt my feelings more. I'm use to it all, though. I didn't know about a dance, because I don't *really* go here. And yeah, it's probably better she rides home with Melody…

"But if you can wait a few minutes, I'd…I'd love a ride," she says, surprising me enough I falter on my feet. I catch myself quickly, pushing my hands in my pockets and leaning against the wall.

Her friend tugs on one of the straps of her backpack, but she ignores it, shirking away.

"Is that heavy? I could carry it for you," I say, reaching for her backpack. I glance at her friend when I do, letting her know I saw her tug the strap, and I know what she meant by it—*don't go, Emma, not with him.* She sneers at me; I know we have an understanding—an agreement to disagree.

"Sure," Emma says, letting me slide her heavy pack from her shoulder. I layer it over my own backpack, slinging it over my arm, and I wait while she has a whispered conversation with her friend a few feet away from me.

"I just need to get some things from the office. I missed a few classes this morning," she says.

"Sure," I say, following her down the hall. I smile when I see her step carefully with her Converse; she's placing one foot inside every square, alternating from black to white. I do that sometimes.

"Step on a crack, you'll break your mother's back," I mutter. I'm laughing to myself when she halts instantly, spinning to face me, her face serious.

"My mom broke her back last year…" she says, and I look to both sides, feeling like an asshole. When I glance back at her, a grin starts to crawl along her lips. "I'm just fuckin' with ya," she winks.

"Oh my god, that was the funniest *not-funny* thing anyone's ever done to me," I say, pulling my knit cap over my face and rubbing my eyes before sliding it back on.

"Sorry," she smiles, sheepishly.

I hold her stare for a few seconds, until she looks away blushing again. I love that she blushes. And I love that half smile she gives me. It's unsure, cautious. She starts to move toward the office again, and I follow a few steps behind.

"It was more funny than not funny," I say, not wanting her to feel bad.

Honestly, that little stunt just gave me one more thing to be infatuated with when it comes to Emma Burke.

I follow her through the office doors, and Margot, the main secretary, lights up when she sees me. I don't know many of the teachers here, but the office staff knows me well. They helped process the transfers and paperwork for the Excel Program, and I spent a lot of time waiting in the office for Owen my freshman year on days I didn't have a full schedule.

"Andrew Harper, how's that brother of yours?" Margot asks, leaning over the wraparound counter by the secretaries' station.

"He's good," I smile. "I'm driving up with mom and Dwayne…I mean…Mr. Chessman…to watch his game this weekend. He's starting." I'm genuinely proud of Owen. In many ways, my brother was my hero. I think that's why life sucks so much now that he's gone. Of course, Emma is making things suck just a little less.

"You can call him Dwayne, sweetie. That's what we call him, too," Margot winks. She moves to a file at her desk, pulling papers together for Emma while continuing to talk to me. "And I hear you're pretty damn good on skates, so maybe we see you starting for some university too in a few years?"

"Yeah, I don't know…maybe. It's more of a hobby," I shrug. I'm not great at compliments, or attention, or…praise. Margot's husband is one of the guys who shows up at the rink on weekends, and we usually play on the same squad. He's a good guy, and a hell of a goalie for a forty-five-year-old. Their son plays for Northwestern's club team.

"Right, well…as long as you're having fun," she smirks, reaching over the counter to hand Emma a folder of assignments. "That's what I tell Robbie. Lord knows that man better be having fun, considering how little he can walk the day after one of your games."

I chuckle as I tap the tabletop and offer a small wave when we leave. I feel Emma's eyes on me as I hold the door open for her and lead her out to the parking lot. I open up the trunk of Dwayne's car, a decade-old Buick, and slide my skates and stick to the back to make room for our bags. I could have thrown our things in the back seat—there's plenty of room—but I wanted her to see the skates, because I kind of like the sideways glances she gave me when she found out I play hockey. And if she thinks that's even remotely hot, I'm going to run with it.

I slam the trunk closed and look up to meet her eyes.

"Why do you have holes in your ears?" she asks, swiftly deflating my miniscule ego. She could care less about the skates and stick in the back of the car.

I chew at the side of my mouth, smiling through it, then turn from her and walk to the driver's side while she moves to the passenger door. We both climb in at the same time, and before I put the keys in the ignition, I slide my hat back enough to see my ears as I look at them in the rearview mirror. I have small gauges in my ears. I got them because my brother's friend House talked me into them a year ago. I thought they were cool…all the way up until now.

"I mean, what happens when you don't want a hole in your ear anymore?" I let out a short laugh and run my hand over my face before turning to look at her.

"Did my mom send you here? Is that why you've come? Because, I swear to god, you sound just like her," I laugh.

"Hmmmmm," she says, her lips in a tight line, her eyes focused on my right ear for several seconds before they slide over to meet my gaze. We're maybe a foot away from each other, and when she looks at me, the gray around her pupils is all I see. "I guess I'm curious how you can make such a huge decision about your body at sixteen."

"It's just an ear. Now, putting a hole in *other* parts?" She blushes at my innuendo and turns from me to face the front again. I let her off the hook and start the car, but just before the motor kicks in, she speaks.

"I like them…the holes, that is," she says, blush growing and her lip back in her teeth.

"Thanks," I say with a shake of my head as I shift the gear and back out from the parking space. "Where do you live?"

"Fireside and Barrel…do you know where that is?"

I know where it is. It's *the* house—the big one everyone in town knows. There's really only *one.* When I was a kid, Owen had me convinced it was haunted. For a while, I thought it was a museum. Then, one day, it went up for sale. It's been for sale for about six years. I guess it's not for sale anymore.

"Yeah, I know where that is," I say, not looking at her or making a big deal out of it. I can tell she's embarrassed about living in the town landmark. It's not a mansion or anything, but it *is* incredibly old, one of those big houses that could be for rich people if only it hadn't been forgotten. Now, it's falling apart.

It's silent for the first few blocks we travel—the only sounds, her shuffling her feet along the floor and messing with the heater vents, trying to make the air come out stronger.

"That's as high as it goes," I say after watching her shift her vent and flick the button a few more times. "Dwayne's car...it's pretty crappy."

"It's okay," she says, slouching back in her seat. She fidgets for a few minutes, running fingers through her hair a few times, then scratching at her nose and arms while she looks out her window. "So...you play hockey?" she finally asks.

Finally.

I grin.

"Yeah, I play," I say, once again glad I opened the trunk. Pretty sad when your big pick-up move is showing off your used hockey equipment.

"That's cool. I always wanted to skate," she says.

I make the turn on Fireside and the large bay windows and red brick of her house come into view. An older car—a lot like the one I'm driving—sits parked in the street, and a newer compact car is in the driveway. A little boy is kicking a ball in the front yard, and a woman sits on the front steps watching him. She stands as I slow along the curb.

"That's my mom," Emma says softly.

"Little brother?" I nod out the window toward the toddler rushing back and forth around the front yard.

She nods *yes* and smiles. I push the gear into park and step out with her to open the trunk. I lift her bag for her, and purposely touch her hand on the exchange, noting the small twitch her fingers make when I do.

"Have a good time," I say, and she looks up at me, pulling both straps of her bag over her shoulders, her face bunched, not sure what I mean. "The dance...have a good time at the dance tonight."

The scheming part of my brain is already playing out the conversation with Dwayne to help him chaperone—or to see if there's anything I can do to be there in that gym tonight. I wouldn't know a soul, other than the couple guys I've gotten to know in PE. But I'd know Emma.

"Oh…yeah...thanks. I might not go, though," she says, glancing over her shoulder to give her mom a sign that she's coming. Her mom waves, and I lift a hand to wave back. I hope she doesn't know about the Harpers.

I stand there a bit frozen while Emma steps up on the curb, thanking me for the ride. When I move to close the trunk, I glance at my skates again, and take a deep breath before shutting my eyes and blurting something out.

"I could teach you to skate. If…if you want. Sometime. Not tonight, but I was just thinking…I could teach you," I stammer. I feel like an idiot, and I'm already working out a way to backtrack my words and give her an out when she interrupts my self-doubt.

"Why not tonight?" I look up to meet the silver of her eyes, the small curve of her lips, the smile, the flirting.

"Tonight works too," I say. "I can pick you up. Say…six?"

"Yeah…" she turns and takes a few more steps toward her house, before glancing back at me over her shoulder. "Six. I'll be ready."

With her back to me, I push down to make sure the trunk is latched, then move toward the open driver's door, watching her meet her mom and little brother at the front of her steps and head inside. I pull away from her house slowly, careful not to stare at the ornate window trim and the many other things that make this house stand out above every other home in Woodstock. It's sort of fitting that Emma lives there, though. She's the kind of girl who gets noticed.

It only takes a few minutes to get to our street, and I mentally calculate how easy it would be to bike to her house or to walk or jog. I call Dwayne as soon as I get into our apartment, asking him to use his car again tonight to go to the rink. He doesn't ask how the ride home went or for any details about my sudden need to play hockey on a Friday night. I think part of him thinks that we're bonding over this. Maybe we are.

Dwayne was always closer with Owen, but he didn't start dating my mom until Owen left for college. I was left with the awkward shit.

Dwayne's come to a few of the hockey scrimmages with me, and he's helped with a few assignments, but other than that, our conversations have been limited to grocery lists and my mother's work schedule. Of course, now we can add Emma Burke to the small catalogue of conversation items, too.

I spend most of the time at home alone pacing my room before leaving to pick up Emma, switching out my dark gray T-shirt for a long-sleeved black one and slipping on my gray jeans. I look like Owen when I wear this, and I think there's a part of me that feels his confidence in my veins when I resemble him.

I leave a note letting Dwayne and my mom know I went to the rink, propping it up in the small bowl for keys and mail that my mom has by the front door, then lock up fast and jog to Dwayne's car. Within minutes, I'm back in front of her house, the motor idling while I try to find the right thing to say for each possible person who might answer the doorbell once I ring it.

Pulling the keys from the ignition, I push open my door with my foot and step onto the roadway just as Emma is skipping down the front walkway of her house.

"I saw you drive up," she says, working a large sweatshirt over her hips and slipping her hair through the hoodie on the top. She's wearing black leggings and a purple sweatshirt, and she looks like a damned princess.

"Wow, I had a whole speech prepared for your parents and everything," I smirk, opening the door while she slides inside.

"They're not home," she says quickly.

I close the door and step around the front of the car. As I open my door, I notice a figure looking out the window at the front of her house, the shadow lingering long enough to let me know that someone's watching us leave.

I slide into the driver's seat and start the car again, looking beyond Emma and out her window before shifting the car into drive. She follows my gaze, then looks back to her lap quickly, focusing on her seatbelt and the small purse she's brought with her. I wait a few extra seconds, hoping she'll look at me. When she's still focused on the zipper of her purse, I relent and pull away from her house.

My excitement from a few minutes before was swallowed up by the lie I know she just told. The only thing that makes it okay is I know exactly why she told it. I'm a Harper, and her parents—they don't like that she's going out with me tonight. She lied because she doesn't want to hurt my feelings. Wrong or right, the fact that she cares about my feelings sorta makes it okay.

"I'm sorry," she mumbles. She knows I know.

"It's okay. I get it," I say.

We don't talk about it any more. I've heard the stories her family has probably heard, and when she's ready, she'll ask me for the truth, which is somewhere closer to the middle—between rumor and gruesome fact. Of all of us, I'm the one who was probably the most sheltered. Yet, I still get the same rep as the rest of us, buried by the same fallout.

"Hey, we didn't get to talk much in PE. But…you're new here, yeah?" I ask, glancing from her to the road and back again. I threw a shitload of gum in my mouth before I left my room, because I didn't want to have bad breath, and when I'm nervous, I chew gum. Now the chomping is the only fucking thing I can hear, though. I roll down the window and spit the wad out onto the street. When I look back at her, her brow is pinched and her arms are folded.

"Uh, that's still littering, you know?" she says.

I stare at her trying to decide if she's fucking with me again, but after a few seconds, I decide she's serious. I swallow hard and look back to the four-way stop I've been sitting at for a solid twenty seconds. "I'm pretty sure I will never spit my gum out again," I say, thoroughly scolded by the girl who is in *no way* going to kiss me tonight now that I'm a litterer.

"You can spit it out, just not where people step. It's gross," she says, her voice growing a little softer.

"No…you're right," I say, glancing at her again.

"I…I didn't mean to sound bossy. I'm bossy sometimes, but I don't mean…" She's shaking her head while she's babbling, and it's adorable. I reach over and touch her knee with the back of my hand, which has the effect of electroshock therapy on both of us. We straighten in our seats. She tugs at her seatbelt and slides closer to her door as I pick my hand up and promptly put it on the *two* of the *ten and two* of the steering wheel.

A few long seconds pass in silence, and ironically I wish like hell I had my gum back in my mouth to give it something to do. "You're not bossy," I say, smiling as I glance at her sideways. "You were right. It's gross."

"Delaware," she blurts out, and I shrug my shoulders, shaking my head as I squeeze the back of my neck with my left hand.

"Yeah, you lost me. I think I missed the transition," I chuckle.

"Sorry," she says. "That's where I moved here from. I'm from Delaware."

"Delaware." I repeat the state, loving that she's just as damned uncomfortable and awkward as I am now. "That's my favorite colony."

I can feel her looking at me, and I notice her start to laugh lightly out of the corner of my eye as I pull into the parking lot of the Ice Palace.

"You're strange, Andrew Harper. Very strange," she says through the end of her laugh as we both step from the car.

I move to the trunk, open it, and lift out my skates. "I'm not quite sure what makes me strange, but...I'll take strange from you." I grin as I motion toward the front doors to the rink, urging her to walk next to me.

There's a peewee team on the ice when we enter; a group of maybe fifteen kids puffed up with hockey gear and pads and barely balancing on their skates. I nod to Chad, the guy coaching them. He plays with me on the weekends, and he's been coaching here for years.

"Oh my god, they're so cute," Emma says, stepping close enough to put her hand flat along the glass. She watches as each kid takes a turn skating toward the goal, the only mission stopping before running into the metal. It's harder than it looks, especially when you're six. "Was that you when you were little? One of those little round kids wobbling on the ice?"

"No," I say with a shake of my head. I lead her over to the skate rental counter. "My brothers taught me how to skate by throwing me out on a frozen lake. And we played our own brand of hockey, I guess. Or, they hit me hard and laughed when I fell on my ass..."

"That's so mean!" Her eyes show genuine sympathy, and it's sweet as hell.

"Yeah...and no. I mean, they were my older brothers. It's like...a thing, ya know? And I was the little runt. I loved it as much as I hated it. Size?" I look down at her feet.

"Oh, uhm, sevens probably," she responds.

"Sevens," I say to Gary. He pulls out a pair of white blades and slides them along the counter to me, quirking one eyebrow up, his subtle way of giving me shit for being on a date. Am I on a date? I think this is a date.

We both sit on a nearby bench and unlace our shoes, then slip our feet into our skates. I get mine on quickly, then kneel in front of her to help her tie hers tight. Our fingers tangle for a brief second in the laces, and it makes my lip curve up on one side. I keep my gaze low, hiding it.

"So you just played with your brothers. No team or anything?" she says, leaning back and letting me finish working out the knot on her skates.

"Just my brothers," I say as I take her hand and help her to her feet. She lets go of me as soon as she finds her balance, and I exhale my disappointment. With one step, though, she loses her center and grabs hold of my arm, clutching it with both hands.

"I got you," I say, careful as I slide one arm around her back, noticing the feel of the curve of her body on my way. Her fingers dig into the fabric of my shirt on my shoulder, and her grip hurts a little, but I don't care.

"I don't think I can do this." Her words come out in a quiet, nervous laugh.

"Sure you can," I smile. "Look…it's just ice. And it doesn't hurt any more than falling on the ground. I promise. We won't go fast, and I'll hold you the entire time."

I will hold you. Please don't find your balance ever, because I will hold you. This is my job, holding you.

I lead Emma to the edge of the ice, and we pause while the group of young hockey players race up and off the ice, a few of them stumbling onto the carpet, others showing off how comfortable they are on their skates, sliding in sideways just before the wall. Chad nods at me as he follows behind the group of kids.

"See you tomorrow, Drew?" he asks, glancing quickly to Emma.

"Yup," I nod. "Hey, you think maybe you let me score this time?"

Chad glances back to Emma, whose only focus is on her quivering ankles, then he looks back to me. "Only if you earn it, big man. Only if you earn it," he chuckles as he glides past me.

Chad's the same age my father would have been if he were still alive. I have a feeling that he and my father knew each other. I've never asked, and he's never said anything, but there's just this vibe I get from him. I can't explain it, only that when most people know my family's story, they start to treat me with either pity or fear. Chad does neither.

"Okay, are you ready?" I ask, tightening my hold on Emma, bringing her closer to my side. I tell myself it's to give her confidence, but it's really just so I can feel her close to me.

"Ready," she stutters, her eyes still down on her feet.

"Okay, that's good; look at your feet, and keep your weight forward. You get into trouble when the skates move ahead of you. Falling back—that's what sucks," I instruct.

Emma bites her lip and nods quickly.

"Got it, backward sucks," she says. I laugh.

"Not quite what I said, but that's okay," I chuckle. "Okay, you're just going to glide between me and the wall. No steps, just get used to the feeling of this."

I push her, but stay at her side, and we move around one end of the rink inches at a time. After a few minutes, I convince her to bend her knees, and when she finally moves one leg, her feet slide around in a panic as she collapses on the ice, taking me with her.

"Damn, I'm sorry. I'm going to end up hurting you. It's okay. I don't need to learn this," she says, looking around for a way to get up, her face painted with disappointment and frustration.

"Stop it. You can't hurt me," I say, pulling myself up and holding the wall so I can lift her back to her feet. "The average number of falls for a first timer is something like eight," I say, completely making up a statistic. "That was just number one, so we've got a long way to go."

When I raise her to her feet, I circle my arms around her, and her eyes are only inches from mine. Her pupils flare with a short-lived rush. If I were Owen, I'd kiss her—*right now.*

Instead, I look down, dust off some of the ice crystals from her sleeves, and link my fingers through hers. "Come on, let's finish our lap," I say, still wishing I had the guts to kiss her.

I lead her a few more feet at a time around the rink, and we fall, me falling with her, at least a dozen more times. By the time we finish one full lap, though, she's grown steadier, her ankles finding their strength, and when she feels brave, she lets go of my hand and glides a few feet at a time on her own.

This is when her smile takes over ruling every single thing I do.

"Oh my god, Andrew..." she says, a little breathless and excited. "Oh my god! Look!" She moves one foot slowly, and her steps are choppy and awkward, but with me within an arm's reach, she manages to scoot her way around a quarter of the rink, leaning forward when we finally make it to the entrance, clutching the gate and collapsing over the side, exhausted.

"Well?" she asks, twisting her body around to face me. "How'd I do?" she asks.

"Better than average," I smirk, my eyes flitting to her hand, wanting to hold it again. She reaches up and smacks my chest once, but quickly grips the wall again when she feels her balance start to give out.

"You said average was eight falls. I'm pretty sure I fell way more than eight times," she laughs, holding herself along the railing until she finds a bench to sit at.

"Yeah, but you fell...like...*way* better than most people," I joke. She tosses her hair over her shoulder as she raises one leg to unlace her skate, and I get a little lost in watching her move. She leans forward to catch the line of my eyesight to bring me back.

"Show me what you can do," she says. I bunch my brow, not sure what she means. "Out there. Just...I don't know. Skate a lap or something? I want to see if my teacher is all talk."

I laugh and shake my head, a little embarrassed by her attention, maybe a little nervous about flirting, too. When my eyes meet hers, she raises her eyebrows in expectation.

"Yeah?" I ask, not sure if showing off is a good thing.

"Please? Just one lap," she says, and I'm struck by the word *please*. I'm pretty sure that's all it would take for me to do anything for her—anything at all...ever.

"A'right," I say, bending forward and pulling my laces a little tighter. A few girls have entered the rink, and they're spinning in the middle, tracing lines and working on footwork. I've always been more impressed with what they can do. Me—I'm just fast. Those girls—they're full of grace and beauty. Nothing beautiful about what I do at all.

I skate backward, watching Emma as she tiptoes to the glass to watch me more closely. My heart begins to race knowing her eyes are on me. I move to one corner and skid to a stop before shrugging my shoulders at her. This isn't very impressive, but it's what I've got, so I take off quickly to the other end of the rink, stopping fast and sprinting back to where I started, repeating the move again, then pausing at the other end. I wait a few seconds to catch my breath, then glide toward and away from her in circles, like I do when I'm playing defense, and eventually end back at the exit gate where she's clapping.

"Okay," she laughs. "That…was skating. I see the difference now. I was falling. You…you were skating."

I laugh with her, sliding into the bench to pull off my skates. "My brothers were good teachers," I say. There's a simple smile spanning the space between the pink of her cheeks. It's not fake or uncomfortable, but rather exactly the opposite—like the kind of smile you give someone who gets you and your story without even asking. I stare at it a little too long, though, and she starts to let her hands twist in her lap again, nerves creeping back in. It gets quiet when I slide my feet from my skates, and when I grab her blades to return them to the rental counter, she waits for me by the door.

I've only had her for an hour, and I'm not ready to give her up yet.

"You know, Illinois is way different from Delaware," I say when I meet up to her again, holding the door open and fighting the instinct to put my arm around her as I did on the ice. "You should probably get the full tour of Woodstock from a local."

"I was thinking the same thing. I wouldn't want to wander into the wrong woods or something like that," she grins at me from one side of her mouth.

"Precisely," I mimic, holding the car door open, the muscles in my cheeks working hard to keep the excitement I feel—over the fact that she wants more time with me—from fully taking over my face. If I gave in, I'm pretty sure my feet would dance with anticipation.

I pull out from the rink's parking lot in the opposite direction from the one we came, and I take us to the outskirts of town first, pointing out the lake that sometimes freezes over, the homes that are older than hers, if not quite as big, and the Old Town shops around the main square. After we hit the touristy stuff, I drive through a few of the woodsy areas, along the edge of the industrial strip and past the warehouse where my father worked. I don't tell her about him then, but when I pull up to the edge of the Wilson Apple Orchard about ten minutes later, she asks.

"Is it true?"

Everyone has their own way of asking about our story. Some people gossip and whisper, others are more direct—hugging me, touching my arm, offering sympathy and grief counseling even if it's fifteen years later than I really need it. The funny thing is, though, that few people actually really *ask* for the story. Most assume.

I shift the gear into park just outside the orchard driveway gates, the festival season long past and most of the trees starting to show their winter branches. My fingers grip over the top of the steering wheel as I breathe in slowly, then exhale, noticing the slight trail of fog my breath creates as it threatens to leave a steamy circle on the window. I push the heater up one level before resting my arms over the steering wheel, laying my head flat against them and looking at her next to me.

She's beautiful. And I want this one to be the girl—the one I remember. And my sad family history is going to ruin it. But she asked. So I'm going to tell her.

My lips tight, I force a smile, not wanting to make anything about this moment sad, despite the history I'm going to share. She twists in her seat to face me slightly, unbuckling her seatbelt so she can bring her knee up to her chest.

"I've only ever heard the stories, too. I was one, maybe, when my dad died. He was sick. He had bipolar disorder, and his brain—it made a lot of things up. He wasn't taking his medicine, and nobody knows exactly why he stepped from the Ferris-wheel carriage. But he wasn't well when it happened. That's the one truth I know for certain. My brother and mom, they don't talk about him much," I say, turning my head to look down at my lap. "I think what really happened is a secret that will forever be kept between my father's ghost and a five-year-old Owen."

"You said brother. But before...you said you learned to skate from your *brothers.* So that's...that's also true?" Her voice breaks slightly when she asks. I lean back into my seat and stretch my arms forward to flex my muscles before letting my hands fall to my knees.

"Yeah. That one...I have more of a memory of. But..." I stop, holding my breath.

"But it's not a memory you want to share," she finishes for me.

I nod slowly, then look up to her waiting gaze, her stormy eyes lit by the moon. If she was the ocean, I would be happy to be lost at sea. "If that's okay, I think I'll just let the rumors fill that one in for you," I exhale.

Her freckles. Her small nose. The waves of brown of her hair. Her long lashes, and the way her fingers search for something to do when she's nervous. I watch it all; I savor it. "I'd rather just leave it blank...until you want to share," she says, her lip curling briefly on one side. I take that small movement in too. "I don't much care for rumors," she says, her grin stretching just a hint wider.

The radio is barely audible in the car, and part of me wants to turn the music louder to fill the silence taking up too much space between us. Another part of me, though, wants to leave the silence alone, because when it's quiet like this, and she's close, I can hear every breath she takes.

Her phone steals away my choice, buzzing regularly in her pocket until she pulls it out and answers a call from her dad. I only hear her end of the conversation, but her answers are clipped, relegated to single words. Without asking, I shift the car into reverse and back away from the orchard and onto the road. Emma needs to go home; this much I'm sure of.

"Sorry, my dad doesn't like me out late," she says as she puts her phone into the side pocket of her purse, not adding the part where I'm sure her father said he didn't like his daughter out late *with me.*

"It's okay. I'm getting up early to drive to Champaign with my mom and her boyfriend. I should get home too. He'll want me to gas up the car," I say, not wanting her to feel guilty about her parents' opinion of me.

It takes us twenty minutes to get back to our neighborhood, and instead of finding out more about her, I give into my insecurities and turn the music up loud enough to give both of our minds something else to play with. There are a few times, though, where I catch her lips moving with the lyrics of one of the songs, and I tell myself that visual is almost as good as finding out more of her story.

As I sit in the car next to her in front of her ornate, giant house, I know that there's no way I'm going to sleep tonight. There's no guarantee that if I dream, I'll dream of her.

"Thank you for teaching me to skate," she says, pausing with one leg out of the car, the other still here with me.

"I'm not sure we can call it skating yet, but..." I tease, and she pushes my arm with a tiny grunt in dissent. Yeah, I lock that touch away, too. "I'm joking. You did great."

"Well...I'm no hockey phenom," she says, her voice dragging out that last word.

"Neither am I," I sigh. I don't know why it makes me uncomfortable, but I just don't want her thinking I'm more special than I am.

Our silence is drowned out by the ad for legal advice blaring through Dwayne's car speakers, and I watch, helplessly, as she finally steps from my car. There are so many things that I *could* do right now. But just beyond her, the front door to her house has cracked open, and the porch light has flipped on, the blinds to the front window wide as well.

"I hope this was as good as some school dance," I say, every drum of my heart rattling my insides. I'm not sure how I'm going to drive home unable to feel my feet and fingers.

Her feet on the curb, and her purse pulled across her body, Emma stops just before closing the car door, leaning in just enough so I can hear her, and whoever is standing at the doorway behind her can't.

"I'm not sure," she says, squinting one eye as a smile breaks through slowly. "I think we're going to need to try it again so I can be sure. Skating or dancing...it's a tough one."

"You're on. I play Sunday morning, and I'm all yours after noon." When I realize how my words sound, my stomach drops. Emma's smile pushes further into her cheeks, though, and suddenly I don't care so much about sounding desperate for her. I am desperate, and I want nothing but more seconds with her.

"I'll meet you at the rink. I'll come watch you play," she says, winking as she shuts the door finally and skips up her walkway. She quickly passes a man I assume is her father, and he lingers in the light of the porch, his arms crossed in front of his body, until I pull completely out of view.

When I get home, Dwayne and my mom are both up and at the kitchen table eating bowls of cereal. I can sense my mom's desire to ask me a million questions as I grab a soda from the refrigerator and move down the hallway, but I catch the subtle look from Dwayne telling her not to pry, and I'm grateful for him.

With my lights off, I crawl into bed, kicking off my jeans and shoes, and pulling my pillow over my eyes so I can imagine Emma in my mind. Eventually, I fall asleep, but not before I make a list of the million things I need to learn about her—top of that list: what her lips taste like.

CHAPTER 3

EMMA

"All I'm saying, Em, is that you can't take any risks right now. I'm not saying that you can't have a life. *Of course* you can have a life. It's just…for now…for the next little while, however long that is, you have to take life slow."

My mom has been sitting on the foot of my bed, explaining her decision to me for at least an hour. I quit listening five minutes in, when she finally choked out the part where I have to stay home today instead of going to the hockey rink to watch Andrew. Correction: she didn't say I had to stay home, she said she wouldn't give me a ride.

My dad took my little brother, Cole, to this Tiny Tikes soccer program, something they do at this indoor gym by the mall. Not that it matters, because I know he wouldn't take me either. It's part of their concerted effort to make decisions about my life while they whisper behind their bedroom door at night—decisions that I am not a part of making.

"Em, you do understand, don't you honey?"

My mom has asked this question at least six times. Each time, I say *no*. I say it again.

"I'm never going to agree with you. It's ice-skating. I'm not going to get hurt. Nothing is going to happen. It's only slightly riskier than walking," I roll my eyes.

"Honey, you know that's not true. You could fall and break something, and the time it would take you to heal, it all plays into everything," she says. She's making things up at this point, but I don't argue. There isn't a point.

I was standing out in the front yard with her and my father, watching my brother race around the dying grass, when the woman who lives across the street came over. Mom mentioned I was a sophomore, and the woman asked if I'd met anyone nice yet. I said I square danced with Andrew Harper.

I said too much.

After an hour of hearing this woman expose every wound and skeleton that exists in the Harper home, two things became certain—my parents would never approve of Andrew, and I would never be able to forget him.

They won't say it. They won't, because they know how it will sound—bad. It will sound bad because it *is* bad to sum Andrew up based on a nosey neighbor's opinion, and to assume because bad things have followed him through life, he'll do nothing but bring them to me too.

So instead, my parents talk about how careful I need to be—reminding me why we moved to Illinois in the first place, and the promise that is now only weeks away.

I keep my attention on my phone, wishing like hell I were brave enough to ask him for his number so I could text him right now, let him know I won't be there. I hate that he's expecting me, and I'm going to disappoint him.

"What if I promise not to skate?" I ask, surprising myself. I'm putting a foot down, something I haven't been very good at lately. But I'm doing it.

My mom doesn't answer, and for a brief second or two I think she might pretend she didn't hear me. She finally looks at me, and I can see her trying to work out a new reason I can't go. There's a lot of work happening behind her eyes—but unless she's willing to say she doesn't want me hanging out with Andrew, she's got nothing.

"No skating," she repeats, standing and holding a finger up at me, as if I've done something wrong.

"No skating," I say, my stomach sinking a little, knowing I might be lying, because skating with Andrew was so…

"I want you home by noon," she says, her finger still pointing. Why is she pointing? I want to snap it off; it's infuriating me so.

"His game isn't done until noon. I won't get to talk to him at all," I say, standing and getting my shoes on, not bothering to pause while I speak for fear she'll reverse the direction we're moving. I am getting progress for the first time all morning; I'm not halting it.

"Were you planning on spending the whole day with him?" she asks, and I can sense that small hint of distaste in her tone. I stare her down until she looks away.

That's the other part about moving here. We had a long conversation about giving me some freedom, within reason. I am what everyone in my high school would call a *goody-goody.* I call my parents. I come home on time. I don't sneak around—though, I'm pretty sure I'm going back on that whole *no skating* promise. I've never given my parents a reason not to trust me, and if I'm going to go through with the things on my plate over the next few months, then I'm owed a little slack when it comes to the social things that are supposed to define this time of my life.

"We might have lunch. I'll be home before the sun sets. My homework is done, and I won't do anything that will result in a trip to the hospital or casts or…or even a Band Aid," I plead. Dragging my finger over my chest in a crisscross pattern, I stare into my mom's eyes, hoping to hear the sound of her keys jingling in her hand. She reaches into her purse, and I hug her.

"Home by six," she says, one more point with her finger. I don't even mind it this time—I'm so happy.

Andrew's game is halfway over by the time my mom gets me to the rink. She wanted to come in and watch with me, but I begged her not to. She compromised by waiting at the curb by the front doors until I was completely inside. There's a part of me that thinks she might still be out in the parking lot now.

There are a few people sitting sporadically in the bleachers around the rink, mostly wives and family members I think. I first notice the coach who was working with the kids on the ice yesterday. He has a thick beard, which makes him hard to miss. He's waiting on one of the benches; sweat is running down his face, and when one of the other players offers to trade out with him, he waves a hand signaling he's not quite ready to go back in.

I follow the various players gliding around the ice, watching their feet stop and skid. A few of them trip up a little when they have to change direction, but not Andrew. I recognize his feet quickly—smooth, fast. He doesn't control the game, but he changes it, darting in and out of plays before the others can catch up. Andrew isn't the youngest out there—most of the guys are his age. But the older ones *really* can't handle him. He's disruptive.

When he slides from the ice onto the bench, he pulls a helmet off and looks around the glass until he spots me. He smiles on one side of his mouth—he smiles for me. I raise a hand and scratch at the glass, trying to be cute with my hello. He scrunches his hand back at me.

His hair is floppy and lying in all directions; I'm hoping he's almost done with his game, because I don't want him to put his helmet back on. I want to watch him like this. I like looking on while he laughs and talks to his friends, while he yells things and points to other guys—while he's happy. Andrew might be the most beautiful portrait of happiness I've ever seen, and he comes from so much sadness.

He thunders out a "Booooooom!" as one of his teammates scores, and when he comes out on the ice to congratulate him, he hugs him around the neck, mussing the younger guy's hair. Andrew would have been an amazing older brother, and I have a feeling his brothers, at least Owen, were like this with him. It makes me smile, and I wear it bright and wide while he skates around the edge of the ice until he's facing me on the other side of the glass.

He starts moving his lips, saying something, but I can't hear him, so I shrug. He nods, then pulls his glove from his right hand and presses his finger against the glass, writing the word HUNGRY in the frost, followed by a question mark.

I nod *yes*, and he holds his hand by his ear, joking that he can't hear me. I laugh and nod bigger. He races around the other edge of the glass, walking carefully on his skates along the carpet toward me.

"Why are you nodding like that? You look ridiculous," he teases.

"Shut up," I say through nervous laughter.

Andrew is probably the only real friend I've made here, and I only see him at our school for an hour a day, sometimes only entering and exiting the locker room. I don't even know him that well, but I know I would rather get to know him than waste time getting to know anyone else. There are girls I've met here, like Melody. She's in most of my classes, and we like the same TV shows and music. I guess we're friends, too. We call each other, which is more than I do with Andrew. But I would…call Andrew. If I could.

"So, are you ready for lesson number two? Or do you want to eat something first?" he asks, pulling off various pads, but leaving his skates on his feet. I breathe slowly, blinking at them, not sure if I should break that promise to my mom or not. Of course, skating wasn't her real concern anyhow.

"My feet are kind of sore…" I begin my excuse.

"That's okay. Let's just eat, and maybe I'll show you a few more things around town," Andrew says, slipping his feet into his shoes. He almost looks relieved we're not skating. I smile and let myself relax into the bench while he packs his things into a large bag, then carries it over to the rental counter.

"You keep your stuff here?" I ask, noticing him startle when I speak behind him. I put my hand on his shoulder to reassure him, almost out of habit—a habit that doesn't exist, but feels like it should. When I touch him, his shoulders rise with his long breath, almost as if I've healed something.

"Oh, I borrow pads. They're expensive, and these fit fine." He pauses, almost like he wants to say more, but stops with his feet square to mine, his hands looped in his pockets, his eyes staring just above my own. He takes another deep breath, like the one he took when I touched his shoulder, then raises his right hand and sweeps a lock of hair from my forehead over my shoulder. When his eyes meet mine, he looks surprised that I'm watching, and he falters a step backward and rushes his hand back to his pocket before looking down and shuffling a few more steps away.

"So, lunch then? Yeah?" he asks.

"Sounds good. Do you…what…just eat here?" I look over at the menu on the wall of peanuts, fries, and soft pretzels.

Andrew lets out a short breath of a laugh. "No, I was thinking somewhere *a little* nicer than this. Come with me; I wanna show you something," he nods toward the door. We stop back by the bench where his stick and skates are and he carries them through the door, holding it open for me as I pass closely by him. I watch his chest as I do to see if he breathes deeply again, but he seems to be used to me. I'm the one who releases a sharp breath this round.

I follow Andrew into the parking lot, and he stops at the back of an older sports car, the black paint faded in many places, and the glass missing and replaced with cardboard in one of the side windows. He pops the trunk, tossing his skates and stick in the back, then turns to face me as he shuts it.

"What do you think?" he asks. The trunk creaks as he closes it. As I graze over the body of the car, I notice the various rusty places and a few deep dents. My face must be revealing my reaction. "I know; it needs some work for sure. But…it's all mine."

I follow him around to the passenger door, and he pushes in and up on the handle with both hands so he can open it for me. "The door handle… that's one of the many things that needs work," he shrugs with a semi-proud smile.

When I look down, I notice there are several rips in the seat. Andrew reaches in and drags a towel from his side, smoothing it out for me. I slide inside and let him shut the door for me, noting the loud pop just before it closes. He has to push on the door an extra time to be sure it's latched.

He pulls his handle the same way, and slides into his seat, which is perhaps more torn than my side, and the fact that it was more important to him that I was comfortable isn't lost on me. I reach my hand forward and run it along the dashboard, which is slick and black and shiny. I bet Andrew makes the rest of the car just as nice one day.

"It's pretty cool," I say, tilting my head to the side just in time to see him exhale and smile proudly.

"Thanks," he grins, turning his focus to his key and the ignition. The engine roars and the entire car rumbles. I look at his face again, and see a flash of thrill ignite his eyes.

"Well it *sounds* like everything's working," I say, not really knowing if the car sounds right at all. I don't know anything about cars, other than where to put the pump for gas. But I know this car sounds fast and loud, and I get a feeling Andrew likes that.

"Yeah, it's working," he chuckles before punching the gas once and squealing the tires while he backs out, kicking ten pounds of gravel up into the air behind us. I grab both sides of my bucket seat on instinct and hear my mother's warning to *be careful* echo in my ears.

"So...driving lessons from your brothers too I'm guessing?" I ask, my hand somehow now clutched to my chest, crinkling the fabric of my shirt. I don't even remember moving it.

"Sorry...I get carried away," he says, wincing.

"No...it's okay. You just surprised me. I wasn't expecting it," I say. He watches me for a few extra seconds, I think to judge whether or not I'm lying. Eventually, his eyes begin to relax, and he shifts the gear, pulling out of the lot slowly.

"Okay, well how about I take it slow and the next time I want to speed things up I give you a sign," he smirks. My body flushes, because I get the sense he might be talking about *other* things.

"Okay," I whisper, forcing my hands to remain still on my legs, not to pick at one another and give away how tense he makes me.

"But to answer your question," he says, pulling my attention to him again. He's looking at the roadway, so I feel safe to stare at him while he talks. "My brothers would never teach me how to drive. Owen wouldn't let me touch his truck. I had to get his friends to teach me. And his best friend was all about drag racing, so when Owen left us alone, he sort of let me go crazy."

"How nice of him," I say, not masking my sarcasm.

Andrew glances at me with a short laugh. "Yeah, I guess it wasn't safe or whatever, but...I don't know...life is what it is, and you can only control like...this much of it," he says, holding his thumb and index finger out toward me measuring less than an inch. "Sometimes I just want to feel a little more of everything, you know?"

He glances at me again, and I can't seem to smile back at him, as much as I want to. I can't because I know *exactly* what he means. I want to feel more, but I'm on pause—not allowed to really feel anything until I'm cleared and told it's okay to do so.

I'm feeling things now. And I intend on keeping all of that secret.

"Maybe that sounds crazy. God, you probably think I'm nuts," he says as he runs his hand over his face and through the blowing wild strands of his hair.

"You're not nuts," I say, and notice his jaw twitch at my response, his lips tight in a straight line. He clears his throat and leans to the side to roll up his window. We stop at a light in the center of town, and the loud clicking of the blinker fills the dead air, and eventually Andrew and I both laugh.

"Goddamn that's loud, right?" he says, leaning toward me and looking at the gear shaft as if somehow he can control the sound from there. He glances back up, now inches closer to me, and his breath falters again. "So maybe that goes on the list of things to fix."

"No, don't," I smile. He flinches and squints, sitting back comfortably as he turns and pulls into a diner parking lot. "If you fix it, then it won't make that sound anymore, and now it's sort of our thing. We'll always be able to laugh at the loud blinker noise."

His bottom lip sucked into his mouth, he nods as he pulls into a spot and shifts into park, tapping both hands along the black rubber of the steering wheel.

"Well then that's settled," he says, grinning as he pulls the keys from the ignition. "The clicking noise stays."

I nod in agreement, then reach to my door handle.

"Hang on, wait for me," Andrew says, springing from his seat and jogging around the front of the car. He's wearing the same gray jeans and black shirt he wore Friday night, and I'm glad. He looks nice like this. With a jerk of the handle, he has my door open, and I step out and make a silent wish to feel his hand along my back, the way a guy walks a girl from the car when they go on a date in the movies. I get to the restaurant door without ever feeling it, though.

Andrew raises two fingers, and a waitress shows us to a booth in the back corner of the restaurant, our feet touching underneath as we climb into our seats. I move my right foot out of the way, but I leave my left foot in place against his, almost like a test to see what he'll do. He doesn't move either.

We both flip open the menu, and I wonder if he's reading without reading like I am. My eyes are passing over the words, but my attention is on the outer edge of my left foot, the one lodged against the inside of his right one. It's such a stupid touch, but in some small way, it feels like I'm holding his hand.

"So it's a...Camaro?" I ask. I looked at the logo on the way into the restaurant.

Andrew chuckles, his eyes still on his menu, his foot still against mine.

"Yeah, it's a seventy-six," he says. I have no idea what that means, but I nod and smile as if I do. He reads me quickly though and laughs again as he flattens his menu. "There's a guy down our old street who has a backyard that's just...like...*filled* with these classic old cars. I used to go visit him with Owen, and we'd sit in them and pretend we were driving around. This one was always my favorite though. Anyhow...he stopped by my apartment just before we left to visit my brother and said he was getting rid of a few. He sold it to my mom for five hundred bucks. I'm getting a job this summer to pay her back."

I might not know anything about cars, but I understand dreams. I get wanting things, and I can imagine how it must feel to finally have something in your hands you want so badly.

"It's a great car," I say, my smile soft. He looks into my eyes for a few seconds before shaking his head and picking his menu back up.

"It's shit right now. But...it will be a great car. I promise," he says, and there isn't a doubt in my mind that it will be.

We both order sandwiches and sodas when the waitress comes, and with our menus gone, I feel a little more exposed—and much more aware of the weird footsie standoff happening under the table.

"Delaware," Andrew finally says, breaking a long rut of silence. "Tell me about it. What's your story, Emma Burke?"

When he says my name, his lips take care of every syllable. I wonder if he says every name like this, or just mine.

"Well..." I start, pausing to tuck my right leg over my left, shifting my weight, but never moving the foot against Andrew's. I glance up to catch his smirk when I do, and I know he's playing the same game I am. "You saw my little brother, right?"

Andrew nods, and I swear his smile has stretched to cover more of his face.

"His name's Cole. He's three. It's just us, and my parents. My mom's a telemarketer..."

"Wait," Andrew interrupts, looking up and holding his question while our waitress delivers our plates and drinks. When she leaves, he leans forward, elbows on either side of his plate. "Your mom is a real-life telemarketer?"

My eyes wide, I nod, not sure what makes that so interesting.

"Man, that's like the suckiest job! Do people hang up on her all day? Oh...I bet she gets cussed out all the time. Or...do people prank her?"

"I have no idea," I giggle.

"Sorry, I just...I've always wondered who does that job. Every time someone calls us, I wonder how bad it is on the other end. I mean, though...I'm sure your mom is a really nice person," he stops abruptly, then sucks in his bottom lip.

"Okay...anyhow..." I start again, but he holds up his hand to stop me.

"One more question, and that's it. I swear," he says, and I laugh. "What does she sell?"

"Uh...she does surveys, I think. For things like commercials people remember and different food chains," I say, realizing I don't really pay attention to the words my mother says when she's on the phone all day. I just know she gets to work at home because of it, and *that*...has come in handy.

"Okay, I don't think I've answered one of those. Just...ya know. Wanted to make sure I didn't get one of her calls," he says, his lip ticked up on one side. "I'm not real nice to telemarketers. But I'll change that; I swear."

He crosses his chest with his finger then picks up a fry from his plate, chewing it whole.

"Okay, well...you'll love this then. My dad's a dogcatcher," I say, covering my eyes with both hands. When I let my fingers fall open so I can peek at him, he's squeezing his eyes shut.

"I know...he's like Cruella de Vil kinda evil. Except he's not," I begin to defend my dad.

"Uhm...dogcatcher . I saw *Lady and the Tramp* when I was a kid. That shit messed me up, and it's the reason we still don't have a dog. If I accidentally let it loose, your meanie dad will haul it away and lock it up in the rain somewhere," he says, shaking his head.

"So…that's not how it works—and *dogcatcher* really is more like *stray-dog finder.* He always finds a home for animals, and usually he gets called on to deal with strange animal situations for animal control," I explain. Andrew keeps staring at me with one brow quirked.

"Hmmmm, okay, but I'm starting to wonder about you, Delaware. You better want to be something happy when you grow up," he says through a full mouth.

"Surgeon." My answer is one word, and it's definitive. I've known what I want to be since the day I understood who the person was that did that job. I want to save people. I want to be their last hope. Because I will never quit.

"Oh yeah sure, surgeon. Like *those* are good people," Andrew kids. I pick up one of my fries and throw it at him. He catches it against his chest and drops it on his plate, then taps his foot into mine twice, reminding me it's there.

He doesn't move it, though.

We're quiet while we're eating. A group of seniors I recognize from my school spill into the diner loudly, interrupting the awkward quiet. It distracts both of us, and we smirk at each other when one of the girls laughs—her cackle comes out almost sounding like a dolphin's call. I hold a fist to my mouth to keep myself from laughing; Andrew stuffs more fries in his and looks out the window, knowing if we make eye contact again, we'll both lose it.

After a few seconds, we glance at each other, exchanging a silent look that says we both think that chick should do her best not to laugh out loud —ever again.

The group settles down, but after a few minutes, their whispers are what catch our attention the second time. I notice Andrew glancing up from his plate, beyond my shoulder, then back down to his food. His movement is repetitive, and each time he looks at the group behind me, his scowl grows a little.

His reaction forces me to pay attention, too. Eventually, I hear one of the girls speak a little too loudly, mentioning James and Owen, and then I hear one of the guys in the group say something about betting "he'll end up shooting himself just like his brother did or becoming some hardcore junkie."

They're talking about Andrew—or his brother, Owen. It doesn't matter which one, because I get the sense that Andrew and his brother are so close that if you cut one the other bleeds.

Everything that follows happens in milliseconds—my eyes zero in on Andrew's hand, the contraction of his muscles as he grips his fork. Then, I see the flex of his jaw and the strain in his neck followed by the cold shadow consuming his eyes. The hurt he's feeling is there—I see it—but there's anger and hate brewing, too.

I sense his conflict—ignore the wave of familiar ridicule being spun behind me or stand up to it and become one more reason for people to talk. His eyes watering, Andrew has been at this crossroads before. I have a feeling he's been here a lot. And I also think I'm the thing keeping his feet tethered to this side of the line this time.

When our eyes finally meet, Andrew almost looks as if he's apologizing to me, sorry that I am witnessing any of this. It's more than being embarrassed; it's being ashamed. That one look from him breaks me and resolves me all at once.

I smile and hold up a finger, my shift in mood halting him for long enough—the few seconds I need to slide out of our booth. I hear his feet shuffle behind me, and I turn to see him starting to step out behind me, but I smile bigger and hold a hand up with a wink. "Just give me a sec," I say.

Andrew looks uneasy. I feel uneasy. But I also feel right about this, so I keep walking toward the group of seven strangers until I'm leaning over the counter next to the stools they're gathered around at the other end of the restaurant. I purposely brush the arm of one of the girls to get her attention, and she apologizes and steps from her seat to give me room, assuming I'm trying to reach for salt, or napkins, or any of the other tiny things piled in a basket near them.

"Oh, no. I just heard you all and thought I'd come over to join in. You're talking about the Harpers, right?" I say, glancing from one set of eyes to another, an interested smile on my face feigning that I also want in on this *oh-so-fun* gossip fest. They all look uncomfortable, and the girl closest to me—the one who moved out of my way—keeps looking over my shoulder toward Andrew, as if she's trying to clue me in that I should keep my voice down.

"Oh, I know, you're totally right. I should be quiet, huh?" I whisper. "I bet he can hear me."

I leave my eyes on hers for an uncomfortable amount of time. There's a flash of guilt in them when I say it out loud, publicly acknowledging that we heard everything. And normally, I'd stop there; she'll learn a lesson from this, and probably not gossip about the Harpers except in the privacy of her own home for at least a month. But that look on Andrew's face sticks with me, so I take things just a little farther.

"You know, I hear there's a foster home around here that takes care of kids who lost their parents to horrible accidents or illness. Maybe when we're done here, we can go make fun of them for a while, tease them about how they're going to die in car crashes too one day. Or…or…wait! Even better…let's make one of those viral videos where we wake people up in the middle of the night and remind them that their loved one is dead. That would be awesome…no?"

A can see a chill fall over them all, and the guy who was talking the most five minutes before, swallows hard. We all hear it. I step closer to him, letting my fake smile fall back into the hard line my mouth wants to make. "Or, if you'd rather, you can just keep being assholes over here, and I'll go back over there and try and ignore you," I say, pleased at the regretful feelings I've nurtured. "Your call."

I reach to the counter, grabbing a bottle of ketchup, then spin on my heels and walk back to Andrew, who's still sitting with his legs stretched out underneath the booth, munching on his fries one at a time. He doesn't look up at me when I sit back into the booth, and he never glances up when I twist the cap off the ketchup, pouring a small amount on the corner of my plate.

When I'm done, I move the bottle on the table until it clinks against his plate, and I let my hand rest flat on the space between us. After a few seconds, the group I'd just left leaves the restaurant. Neither of us turns to look—the only confirmation, the small chime of the cluster of bells tethered to the door. Once we hear the sound of their cars pulling from the lot just outside, Andrew reaches up, sliding the bottle out of the way, and takes my fingers into his hand, squeezing just hard and long enough to let me feel him.

That's when I finally smile for real.

We finish our meals, and Andrew pulls a twenty from his wallet, not letting me chip in for my half. I follow him to his car and wait while he lifts the handle, then move into my seat.

He attempts to slide over the hood of his car, but his skid stops midway, so he pushes down the front and walks to his door, reaching into the backseat to grab a beanie for his head, sliding it on and pulling it over his eyes, playing up his humiliation.

"Massive fail," he says, poking fun of his bombed attempt on the hood.

"Oh, I just assumed that's how that was supposed to go," I say, pretending to be impressed.

"Uh yeah…I mean, bitchin'…" he says, puffing out the collar of his shirt and shrugging with a sniff before breaking into a short laugh.

"Wow, I was willing to fake it until you said *bitchin'*," I say, unable to help but smile so hard my cheeks hurt.

"Fuck," he says, his head slung forward, his eyes down. "Ruined by my own lame vernacular."

"*Bitchin'* will kill you every time," I say with a short tisk and headshake.

He turns the engine over, but looks at me from the side, his eyes moving in quick motions from mine to my mouth and back again. He chuckles to himself before looking up into the rearview mirror and shifting the car into reverse. "I'm pretty sure you can say anything and own it," he says.

I don't answer, and I watch his cheeks turn just a little redder. I fight grinning at his compliment, pushing my lips together tight, but losing the battle and smiling anyhow.

Andrew picks up where our tour left off the time before, driving me through various neighborhoods and streets, pointing out places he and his brothers used to sled, places where he got into fights, and then down his street, stopping in front of his old house.

It's a simple two story, the color dark brown with brick, the yard neat but simple, and a few trees towering in the front, their branches growing bare for the winter.

"You miss living here?" I ask.

He leans forward on his steering wheel, folding his arms and resting his head on top. "Sometimes," he sighs. "But…I don't know. Never mind."

"No, tell me," I say, for some reason not wanting him to feel he can't tell me things.

He leans back in his seat, his gaze still out the window, on the dull porch light shining in the front. "This house wasn't full of happy memories. At least, not for me," he says, his eyes lost to the light now, and I can tell he's letting it pop in and out of focus.

"Your brother James?" I ask. I pull my sleeves down over my knuckles and bite on the fabric, hoping that question was okay to ask.

"Yeah, that's most of it," he says. "James died here."

I heard the story—both from the gossipy tale my neighbor told my parents and through the whispers spoken in the diner tonight—but hearing Andrew say the words, even though he didn't offer any details, made the pain of it all palpable. His brother was an addict, and when he got caught up in something with the police, he ended up shooting himself in the driveway. When I heard the story, I couldn't imagine it was true. But as Andrew mentions James now, I can tell just by the look in his eyes that it is. And it's awful. And I wish I'd done more to those assholes in the restaurant who thought his pain was funny.

"But I didn't really have much of a life here. I mean…I had my brother's life, my brother's friends. And we lived next door to Owen's girlfriend. But, it was all Owen. None of it was really *me*." His head falls to the side, and I reach up cautiously and let my finger run along the ridge of one of the gauges in his ear. It's not very big, but it's edgier than anything I would ever have the courage to do. I envy him for it.

"I met you while I lived in my apartment," he says, his eyes still on my hand next to his face. I pull it away, back into my lap, nervous about what he may say next. Everything inside of me wants Andrew Harper to like me —*like that.* Everything inside wants him to kiss me—*like that.* And it's also the last thing I want, because then my parents will freak out, and they'll ruin this perfect friendship. I think I might like kissing him. But *I know* I like sitting next to him in his car.

"So being my friend is a good memory?" I say, leading him, and regretting it the second a shade of disappointment paints his eyes. He hides it as best he can, breathing deeply and adjusting his posture in his seat before shifting the car and pulling back out on the roadway.

"Yeah, Delaware. Being your friend is a pretty damn great memory," he says.

Before the sun kisses the horizon, Andrew pulls up in front of my house, and as I expected, both of my parents are waiting on the front porch for me to come home. Andrew puts the car in park, and skips around to my side to open the door for me. I silently curse his broken door, because now that he's out of the car, my parents are going to want to meet him. They're already walking toward us when I step up to the curb.

"Home before sunset, just like I promised," I say through gritted teeth only my mom can see. She ignores my nonverbal plea, though, and shifts her focus right to Andrew.

"Yes, I see. Thank you, Andrew, for bringing Emma home," my mom says, reaching out a hand for him to take. This is a test, to see what he does. But Andrew does nothing but act like himself. He stutters a bit, then responds with a few *of courses* while he repeatedly shakes my mother's hand before awkwardly reaching for my father's.

He calls them both Mr. and Mrs. Burke, saying their names at least a dozen times, and when he's not looking, they're taking turns surveying his car for danger, then memorizing his piercings and the way he's dressed. I'm sure in their mind he looks to be everything the nosey neighbor warned about—the youngest in a brood of hoodlum troublemakers—but I'm hopeful that his bumbling speech and clumsiness in front of them cancels most of it out.

Before I realize it, he's made his way back to the driver's side, and when he gets in the car and revs the engine, I realize I've managed not to get his number for a second time. I regret that the moment he drives away.

I regret it more when my parents begin to pick him apart as we walk back up to the house.

I regret it most, though, when I shut my bedroom door on them and curl up in front of my window and wait for the sun to go down—for one more day to tick off my calendar, for the waiting to be over.

I should tell him. It would be nice to tell someone.

Maybe after our trip to Chicago.

CHAPTER 4

ANDREW

I'm pretty sure Emma's parents don't like me. I don't think they dislike me, but I got the strong sense they were working through a lot of Harper-shit to drill down to the real me. And I think they still think the real me isn't far off from the stories they've heard.

I didn't help things by acting like an idiot. At least I wasn't threatening.

Of course, now I can't find Emma. I drove by her house every morning this week, and their cars were always gone. I looked for her in PE every day, but she was missing from the line of girls racing up the steps or out from the locker room. After my morning drive-by on Friday, when I got a strange look from the woman who lives across the street, I finally broke down and asked Dwayne where Emma was. He checked with the office for me and said her parents signed her out for the week.

I know she isn't gone because of me. But there's also that fucked-up little voice in the back of my head that's working real hard at convincing me that *yeah,* she's gone because of me. I creeped her out. Her parents hate me. She's moved back to Delaware—fleeing the entire state of Illinois because Andrew Harper is bad news.

The only thing that's made me feel better is skating, and I've been extra rough with the guys who've shown up to scrimmage this week. One of them finally had enough, and checked me back, then took his elbow to my chin hard, cracking my lip open.

I've been sitting on the other side of the glass, spitting, for the last fifteen minutes. Chris, the dude who popped me in the face, stopped by to apologize. I flipped him off.

"Look at baby Harper," a voice calls from behind me. I twist in my seat, wincing at the deep bruise Chris apparently left on my ribs. I'm able to shift enough to see my brother's friend House in my periphery. House is kind of an asshole, but he's harmless. And he was glued to Owen for most of my life; when he moved away, it was kind of like losing another brother.

"Dude, what are you doing in town?" I say, standing, but holding the washcloth to my mouth while I slap House's hand with my free one.

"Yo, Indiana sucks worse than this shithole," he says, spitting his tobacco into a cup he's carrying. That cup—it's fuckin' disgusting.

"Yeah, well, I could have told you that. If you want change, you need to go to the city, or some place like Vegas or California, man," I say, testing the bloodstain on the rag I've been holding to my mouth. The blood is less, so I toss the cloth on top of my borrowed equipment on the floor.

"Your lip's all fucked up, dude. What happened?" he says, reaching his hand toward my face as if to touch it. I smack his hand away, but he does it again. He keeps doing it until I punch his arm. "Look at that, baby Harper's growing up, and he's feisty."

"Dude, whatever," I roll my eyes and bend down to pick up my things to return to the counter. "It's nothing. I just took a jab to the face."

"You Harpers, always getting hit in your pretty-boy faces," he says, pulling himself up to sit on the counter while I hand my things over to Gary and toss the bloody cloth into the trash.

"Whatever, man," I say, stepping toward the door and encouraging House to follow. He isn't quiet, and people are already starting to watch us suspiciously. House—he's like a warning siren for a shit-storm of trouble.

He follows me out to the parking lot, to my car, and when he whistles, my chest feels a little fuller. There are few people who will recognize this car—my brother and House are at the top of that list.

"Damn, that old man finally sold it. Or...wait, did you lift this shit?" he says, stepping back with his hands in the air.

"Fuck off. Mom bought it, but I have to pay her back," I say, cracking open the door, not even minding the sound it makes.

"You are the good son," he teases, pushing me out of the way and sitting in the driver's seat. "Ohhhhhh, baby Harp. This shit is fast, yo? Hey...you got time? I'm dying to see it open up."

I glance at my phone as if I have anywhere to be. It's not quite lunchtime on Saturday, and the girl I'm stalking is nowhere to be found, so I look back up at him and let my grin grow slowly.

"Yeah haaa haaa," he says, slapping at the top of the steering wheel. He reaches for the keys, but I only open the door as wide as it will go. He gets out with a chuckle, then jukes toward me like he wants to grab my keys. I don't flinch, because House has been doing shit like that to me for years. Maybe I see him coming now, or maybe I'm just so used to it I don't juke for anyone any more. I think the latter might be the case, and I also think that's maybe why I let Chris punch me with his elbow about twenty minutes ago.

House gets into the passenger side, and I buckle up and wait for him to do the same. He rolls his eyes at me, but he does it anyhow. I look around the lot, and when I confirm it's empty, I fishtail backward from my spot until I hit the roadway, then I punch it and feel the tires grip after a few seconds of burnt rubber and smoke. The back end slides for the first hundred yards, but I straighten everything out—careful not to punch the gas until we hit the edge of town.

House leans forward, and we both glance in all directions, checking for cops. It's winter, so the landscape is pretty clear. In the summer, the asshole cops hide behind the corn. I crack my knuckles as a joke, and House laughs, his cackle growing more maniacal as I hit the gas hard and climb the car up to ninety in a few seconds. The roar echoes everywhere; I try to take the car up over a hundred, but it starts to feel loose, so I back off.

I flip around at the edge of the woods and push it just as fast on the way back toward town, slowing down to the speed limit when we start to see other cars. House has turned the radio up, and he's rolled down his window. I can tell he's happy. It's nice having him here, too. He and I—we used to do this a lot.

I drive him back to the Ice Palace lot and pull up next to his truck. He gets out, but pauses at my door, knocking on the window. I roll it down.

"Hey, a few of us are getting together for a little party at Sasha's. Mostly guys you know. Anyhow, if you wanna come, just hit me up," he says. I nod, and think about forgetting his invitation immediately—just like I used to. But then I realize, Owen's gone. And I was invited.

"Hey! House!" I shout out the window just before he climbs into his pickup. He turns and flips me off, because that's his thing. "I'm in. What time?"

"Show up around five. And bring fuckin' pizza!" he yells, half chuckling.

Maybe I'm the guy bringing the pizza, but House wouldn't invite me if he didn't want me there. He's always been an extension of Owen, and I think I'll always be a kid brother in his eyes because of that closeness.

One fucked up family. But it's mine.

* * *

I SPEND a few hours wrapping up some reading on existentialism for an essay due next week, then I rush out of the apartment around four, giving myself enough time to pick up pizza and avoid my mom coming home from work. I leave a note for her and Dwayne that I'll be out late, knowing if I say I'm with House that she will call. I just say I'm meeting with a few of the hockey guys instead.

On my way to pick up food, I swing by Emma's house, and everything about it is as quiet and shut down as it has been all week. Her family has disappeared, but there are a few lights on inside. It's always the same ones, which makes me think maybe they've just taken off for a family trip or a vacation. A little weird in early October, but maybe that's a thing normal families do. I wouldn't know. We've never taken a trip anywhere, other than a drive for the day up to Wisconsin for some water slides. And that trip was all Owen's doing.

I stop by the pizza joint next, pick up the four large ones House ordered, and head to Sasha's.

I've been here a few times, but never for long. Usually, I was tagging along with Owen while he talked to someone about something or made plans with House. He never let me stay. But tonight, I pull up on my own, in my own car—invited.

"Douchebag!" House shouts the second I walk through the door.

"You owe me fuckin' money, yo!" I say, sliding the pizzas on the counter seconds before a dozen people I don't recognize flip open the lids and start taking away slices. House walks into the kitchen and throws a wadded up ten-dollar bill at me. I look at it in my hand and then furrow my brow at him.

"It's all I got now. I'll hit you up with the rest later," he says, already devouring a slice.

"Right you will," I say, stuffing the money into my wallet and knowing it's all I'm going to get. House confirms it with his full-mouthed laugh.

I grab a slice and follow him to the sunken living room, taking a seat in one of the large beanbag chairs. The lights are low, and there's a group of people playing pool at a table in a room near the back of the house.

Everything in here is either really expensive or a piece of trash. It's weird. I know Sasha's parents have money—they own a lot of land, and they've sold most of it. They farm this small plot, and they don't even do their own farming.

They're never around, but I heard Sasha and her friends are staying here for college, driving to Northwestern for school. The result—this farmhouse has become a five-bedroom dorm without any supervision.

"Hey, baby Harp..." House nudges me with a red plastic cup in his hand. I take it from him and smell it; it isn't beer. "Just drink it."

I take a small sip and start to cough instantly while House leans forward and lets out a belly laugh. "Welcome to your first taste of Jack, baby Harp. Don't tell your brother I gave it to you; he'll kick my ass," he says, holding his cup out to click cheers with mine, urging me to drink the rest along with him.

I do.

And I drink one more after that.

I've been drunk on beer before. Owen was always more lenient about that. But never the hard stuff. This buzz...it's different.

I like it.

I stop after two, though, and manage to discard a third shot of whiskey, knowing any more will probably have me throwing up. The living room has become the hub for the party, and Sasha has set herself next to me, her legs draped across my lap from one side of the beanbag to the other. I can tell she's lit, and House keeps raising an eyebrow at me.

"You look a lot like your brother, you know?" she says, taking a long, slow drink of whatever's in her cup. Sasha was always *the* girl—the red-hot one who every guy wanted to sleep with and many had. She always liked Owen, though. They had a fling, but I don't think she could ever call my brother hers.

Right now, she's looking at me with eyes that say she's willing to accept the consolation—even if it's three years younger.

"Well, we're related," I say, laying my hands on her knees, feeling the temptation of how smooth they are sting my fingertips. I leave them there for a few seconds and slide them out an inch at a time, moving up her thigh and down her shin simultaneously, like I'm playing an instrument. She bites her bottom lip when I do, letting it slowly slide from her teeth, and I can completely understand why every other dude in the room wants to trade spots with me right now.

"You're the cuter one," she teases me. I keep my eyes on her legs, knowing if I look to the right, into her eyes, they'll be waiting to seduce me. But then…

Sasha isn't Emma.

I'm buzzed, but that thought floats on repeat in my head. Emma. I can't stop thinking about Emma.

"Well, I'm younger, so I guess that makes me cuter," I say, lips tight in a semi-smile, hiding my inner struggle to do the right thing. Sliding my hands under her legs gingerly, I let myself hesitate for one extra second before lifting her legs from my lap and pushing myself to my feet.

I move to the stools on the other side of the room, taking a seat next to House, who is shaking his head at me.

"Dude, you might be the first virgin I've ever seen say no to that," he laughs lightly.

"Yeah," I sigh.

"Here," he says, handing me a joint he's been smoking for the last few minutes. I look at it in his hand, then look to Sasha who has now let her legs fall open; I can see the black lace of her underwear peaking out through the middle. I turn back to the joint and pinch it between my fingers, bringing it to my lips. Drunk and high is still probably a better choice. Of course, the smart thing probably would have been to choose neither, but I blew that with the second shot of whiskey.

I spend the next three hours intensely watching two guys play a made-up game on the pool table—rolling the striped balls at the solids. There don't seem to be any rules, or fuck—maybe there are rules. Whatever, it's fascinating. I watch it until I realize exactly how boring it is, and when I glance at my watch, it's ten o'clock at night and somehow five hours of my life have passed and I missed it.

I walk through the house to find a bathroom and stumble into a room where House seems to have filled whatever need Sasha had, and I feel a little tinge of regret that I didn't give in. Her shirt is off, and her bare tits are staring at me. She's clearly comfortable with her body, because she stands up from her straddling position on House, her lace underwear the only thing on, and steps toward me. House slaps her ass as she walks away, his drunken laugh a soundtrack to her strut.

"Bathroom," I stutter, somehow. She giggles and moves close enough to touch my chest with her index finger, dragging it slowly down my T-shirt and stomach until she runs it along my now-hard cock.

"Down the hall one more door," she smiles, pressing her palm flat against my jeans and pausing as I pulse. "Or you can stay…"

"I'm good," I breathe, aware of every sensation happening under the zipper of my jeans. I leave the room and hear her laughter briefly behind the door, but I keep my resolve, putting one foot in front of the next until I get to the bathroom where I take the most painful piss of my entire life—then spend about five minutes running water over my face.

I quickly pass the room on my way back down the hall, not wanting to hear any sounds that might act as a siren and call me in.

Grabbing a bottle of water from the fridge, I twist the cap and drink about half of it before fishing my keys from my pocket. In a house full of people, I'm still alone, and I wonder if this is how Owen felt when he would come to these parties.

I step out front and spend a half an hour throwing rocks from Sasha's driveway into the thick forest abutting her property—listening to each rock fall through the cracked branches and onto the bed of dried brush and leaves. The first snow hasn't happened yet, but it's coming. I can see my breath.

My breath.

I cup my hands and smell as best I can. I'm sure I stink of whiskey. Or maybe not. I only had a couple shots hours ago, though, and I feel fine. Maybe a little bit of a headache, but fine otherwise.

I climb into my car and turn the engine on, letting the heat seep into my sweatshirt and reach my skin. My knuckles are red from being cold, so I hold my hands over the vent for a few minutes, letting my bones thaw.

When I glance to the empty seat next to me, I think of Emma. Shutting my eyes, I let my head fall back against the seat and imagine her there. I'm interrupted by the sound of my car door flying open, and I'm startled when House climbs in, laughing hysterically and talking a million-words-a-minute.

"Fucker, get out of my car," I push at him.

"Yo…yo…no, listen," he says, speaking through laughter. He's drunk. And stoned. I've seen him like this a hundred times, and it's always a pain in the ass. "I'm hungry. Like, really hungry. Take me to get a burger, dude. Come on."

"Go make a sandwich, and get the fuck out of my car," I say, gripping the wheel, intent on not taking House *anywhere*.

"Awwww, come on man. Here, here…I'll give you some shit," he says, pulling a sad-ass bag of weed from his pocket, giggling as he fumbles with it.

"Dude!" I roll my eyes.

"Fucker. You suck," he says, reaching over the console and smacking my face hard enough that it stings and I'm sure it's pink.

I lunge at him, but he's too fast, and is already out of the car walking back toward the house. I am pretty sure I'm okay not getting invited to another one of these parties.

With a deep breath, I look back at the wheel and then to the once-again empty seat, trying to get back to the place I was—imagining Emma there. When it doesn't work, I push the car into drive and do the next best thing, heading to her house.

I expect the same empty driveway, the lack of cars in the street, the single light shining through the upstairs window. But when I pull around the corner, everything about the Burke house is full and lived in. I'm fumbling with my seatbelt before I even stop the car; I shove the gear into park, and turn the engine off the second I pull behind the small car along the street.

I get to the middle of the brick walkway when I realize I have no clue what I'm doing. It's almost midnight, and I'm sure everyone in the house is asleep, and I barely know Emma—let alone her family, but she's in there.

Knowing I can't knock on the door, I step backward along the walkway and look up to the brightly lit windows over the front door. I make my way to the other side of the street, my eyes straining to figure out what room I'm looking at. I can see two ceiling fans spinning, and the tops of some bookcases, and I'm sure I'm looking at a loft space.

Jogging back across the street, I slow when I come to the corner of the house, and I walk cautiously over the wood chips and mulch along the trail in the side yard. There's another light on near the rear of her home, so I move to that area, stepping back just enough to let me see pink drapes along either side of a small bay window and then a knee.

Her knee.

I know it's her leg. I've stared at it in PE shorts and pretended to grip it with my hand in my car. I've memorized the fantasy of that leg, and I would know it anywhere. She's sitting in her window, and I'm overcome with a sense of urgency to talk to her.

Looking around the ground in front of me, I bend to pick up a few wood chips then toss them at the base of her window. They're not heavy enough, and they fall back to the ground after a few feet. I move a little farther away from her window, and finally find some stones nestled in the tufts of dead grass around her lawn. I toss my first one gently, not wanting to make too loud of a noise, but it barely grazes the side of the house. I wait, and her leg doesn't move.

Fuck.

I hold my arm up and take a deep breath before launching my second attempt. This one pings directly off her window, and her leg jumps back fast. I scared her. Shit! I scared her. I hold my breath, waiting for her face to appear. But it doesn't. She's not looking for the noise. I panic and look for another rock, finding a small one and throwing it quickly without much aim. It ricochets off the side of the house, but close enough to her window that she has to know.

Come on, Emma. Look out your goddamned window.

I look for another rock, but hear the sound of her window sliding open.

"Andrew?" she says in a loud whisper. "What the hell are you doing?"

I smile and let the small stones I've just found fall from my fingers. I stretch my arms to either side of me and almost laugh.

"I have no idea," I grin. "Come down."

She pauses and looks at me for a few seconds, her hair blowing along either side of her face as she leans out the window. I am kissing this girl tonight. I am kissing her, and I don't care if she hits me because of it. I'm tasting those lips, and I will savor every second I get of it before she smacks me across the face.

"Hang on," she says, pulling her window shut again. Her light stays on, so I'm not sure whether to look at her window or wait for her at the front door. Finally, I hear the sound of her door opening, so I jog over to her the porch. She locks the door behind her and ushers me to follow her closer to my car along the street.

"Oh my god, what are you doing here?" she asks, her eyes lit up, glowing silver. She's smiling. She's smiling because she's happy to see me.

I...make her happy.

"I missed you," I admit. Those words hit my chest the second they leave my lips, and I feel both free and terrified at the same time. My hands go deep into my pockets on instinct, and my legs feel numb.

And then her lip ticks up on one side.

"I missed you, too," she says, her voice soft, not wanting to wake anyone. "Let's get out of here."

I don't hesitate, running to the passenger door and working it open so she can get inside. The sight of her *actually* in my passenger seat is so much better than the version I had going on in my head. I close the door and run to my side, getting in quickly and shutting the door carefully. I know the engine is going to make a loud sound, so I wince when I crank it, but pull away slowly, hoping I didn't disturb her parents.

"I hope I don't get you in any trouble," I say, looking in the rearview mirror, as if I could tell by looking in the one-inch reflection if her parents were awake and catching her escape.

"Me too," she giggles.

She's wearing this plaid shirt with long sleeves, and it's big on her, like it's her father's. Her legs are in a pair of tight black jeans, her feet wearing the pink Converse that I use to track her in PE. She's holding her hands over the vent in front of her, warming them, and I wish I didn't have to drive this car so I could reach over and warm them within my own.

I drive until we get to a forest preserve, pulling off into the parking lot, not really knowing what I'm doing. I have no plan. I just had to see her. And when she told me to go, I went.

"So..." I say, then let my breath fall into a nervous laugh. I'm gripping the steering wheel for strength, knowing I can't just kiss her now, but god do I want to.

"So," she says, pulling her seatbelt off and turning sideways in her seat. She pulls her knees up into her body, her feet flat along the center console. She looks cramped and uncomfortable.

I stare at her shoes for a few seconds, thinking of my life a few hours ago, when an older girl wanted to hook up with me and draped her legs over my lap without invitation. This scene—it's a million times sexier, maybe because I have to work for it.

With timid hands, I reach to the heel of one shoe, my eyes moving to hers briefly before coming back to her foot. She's watching me, but she isn't stopping me. I cup the back of one shoe in my hand and lift her foot from the console and pull it toward me. I let my hand move from her shoe to the back of her leg, my fingers shaking nervously, as if I could break her leg if I were to drop it.

Emma gives in easily, giving me complete control, her muscles relaxing, and I move first one leg then the other to my lap. She eases into the side of her door slowly, her hands clinging to one another in her own lap. I let out a short breath when the weight of her sinks into me, and I rest my hands along the soft denim over her legs, sliding them up and stopping at her knee. That knee. I squeeze it once, and she twitches with a giggle.

"Ticklish," she smirks.

"Good to know," I say, my head tilted to the side, my eyes unable to look away from her.

There are so many things I want to know, so many little facts I need to memorize about this girl. But I can't take my eyes from her lips; I know I can't kiss them yet, so I look back down at my hands, letting them run down the length of her leg to her ankles. Her ankles to her knees—that's my line.

"What brought you to Woodstock?" I ask, rapping my fingers a few times along her legs to work out more of my nerves. "I hear it's the hot bed for dog-catching and telemarketing careers, but..."

She lets out a breathy laugh, then stretches her hands out flat along her thighs. I watch her move, wishing I could touch her there.

"Sort of a family thing. We...we needed to be closer to Chicago," she says with a lopsided smile and a shrug.

"Woodstock is so not Chicago," I chuckle, thinking about the ways my hometown is so small compared to the city. There are things I love about being here. The smallness is comforting at times. But the older I get, the more I sense how suffocating it is too.

"No," she laughs. "But it's also not Delaware."

"Good point," I say.

"What's your favorite food?" I ask. She tilts her head and offers a suspicious smile.

"Pancakes."

I nod, then look out to the blackness in front of me to think of another question.

"Have you ever had a pet?" I ask after a few seconds of silence.

"Lots of them. But never very long. I told you...my dad is always rescuing things," she laughs.

"I've never had a pet. I always wanted a dog," I say, leaning my head back again and looking at her.

"They're a lot of work," she shrugs.

"Yeah, but I think I'd be okay with that. I'm good at working hard. And I don't want a small one; I want one of those big breeds, like a mastiff," I say, lifting my hands and measuring a wide distance with my arms in front of me.

"You know that means their poop is bigger."

"The bigger the better, baby," I joke.

It grows silent again, and I flit my gaze from her to my hands a few times, my stomach twitching nervously.

"Do you like the Excel Program?" she asks.

I suck in my bottom lip and shrug. I never know how to answer that question. It's like asking someone if they like being really smart. "It's all right," I say.

"I bet it's amazing," she says, looking to the side, her hair falling over her shoulder slowly, like an avalanche. "You get to go to a college, hang out with professors and learn things like philosophy and culture."

"It's not *that* amazing," I say. "And I still have to do calculus, and language arts and shit."

"Whatever. It's amazing, and you know it," she says, lifting her foot and nudging my chest with it. I grab hold of her leg and hug it. It seemed like a good idea when I spontaneously did it, but then it got weird instantly.

I made it weird.

We're both quiet and staring at her leg that I'm now hugging, and I start to laugh at the absurdity. I rock it side to side, like it's an infant, and she gives into laughter too. She kicks at me with her other leg, so I tug on her and pull her closer to me, holding on tight and moving her into me as if I'm pulling in the length of a rope—until she's in my lap. Her legs curled up against my door, her body in front of me, and her hands pressed on the ceiling, her laughter fills ever inch of space inside my car.

Her sound fades as her eyes open and her gaze meets mine.

Inches. There are inches in life. Inches that make the difference between a race, that determine your height or pants size, that might mean you make it to the train on time.

I'm living in inches right now, inches and breaths.

Beautiful inches.

"I like you, Emma," I say. My heartbeat fills my throat; I swallow and feel the heat take over my chest and arms and hands.

She doesn't answer with words, instead letting her lashes sweep shut while I take in the dusting of freckles along her cheeks. Her lips part with a shallow breath, her bottom one trembling.

"Andrew," she breathes out my name. It's a whisper. Like I'm a secret.

Maybe I am.

I move my hand to her cheek, and she lets her weight fall into my palm, her eyes closing again briefly.

"I want to know everything about you, Emma Burke," I say, sweeping hair away from the one side of her face, leaving my other hand flush against her cheek, my thumbs over those very mesmerizing freckles.

"I'm not very interesting," she says, her voice tiny and unsure. I can see so much of her nerves in the slight tremors on her lips, the way her hands are now quaking with her grip on my sleeves along my biceps. Her eyes, they tell me so much of her story too.

"You liar," I smirk. She flinches at first, looking hurt. "You are incredibly interesting."

I let my head fall forward to meet hers, and her eyes close as she hums.

"You're a lot of other things, too. Like beautiful, and spirited, and funny, and smart," I say.

"You don't know that I'm smart," she lets out with a laugh, her lips almost brushing mine when she speaks.

"Yeah, I kinda do. I saw your transcripts," I admit.

She slaps her hands flat against my chest and leans back, trying to decide if I'm kidding. I grin with half my mouth and shrug.

"I'm tight with the front office, and I was worried about you missing class last week. I was going to get your work for you," I say, now my own nerves kicking in. I sound like a lunatic stalker.

Thankfully, Emma thinks differently, her head falling to the side again, her hands retracing their path along my arms.

"That's sweet," she sighs. "I got my work. It was a planned trip. With my family."

"I figured," I say, not able to pull my eyes away from hers. "You have really pretty eyes."

She lets her head fall forward against mine as she lets out an embarrassed laugh.

"I'm serious," I say. "Don't let that make you uncomfortable. I mean...it's almost selfish not to take that compliment. Think of all the people walking around with really hideous eyes."

She laughs harder, and her grip on my arms gets tighter.

"You're really funny, Andrew," she says. I move my hands back to their rightful spot on either side of her face.

"And maybe a little cute? Maybe...just a little?" I squint. I'm teasing her, and I'm begging her. I want this girl to be *the* girl—my girl. The one I take to things and experience everything with.

"I'd have to say...." She pauses, her eyes taking in various features along my face, like she's evaluating me, but her grin betrays her, breaking into her cheeks until we're staring into each other's eyes again. "Yeah...you're pretty cute, Andrew."

I blush. I can feel it, my cheeks warming, my mouth unable to keep a straight face. Every part of me is smiling.

"I'm gonna go ahead and kiss you now," I say, my lips practically tingling to the point they almost feel numb.

Emma pinches her lips closed tight in a tiny smile, as her eyes close again. Her head held in my hands, I move her the few fractions of an inch left between us until I feel the tickle of her breath and her bottom lip between mine. She lets out another breath, and I suck her lip, tasting it with my tongue, holding her here, in this perfect place, this perfect moment, until I'm sure I'll never forget it.

Then I move to her top lip, doing just the same. Tugging it into my mouth and holding it lightly with my teeth until she whimpers. My hands find their way into her hair, and she turns so more of her body is facing me, her hands sliding around my neck and back, pulling our bodies closer together.

When her tongue finally brushes against my lower lip, I know that I'm gone. I will never be the same after tonight. I've kissed girls, been fixed up on dates of younger siblings of people my brother knew, and I've had crushes.

Emma Burke is different from anything else.

She's what I'm supposed to have. She's what my first kiss should have been. And she's the only kiss I ever want to remember. I kiss her harder, letting my tongue explore the inside of her mouth, letting my hands move down her back until I grab her hips and ass, pulling her into my lap to straddle me. I kiss her and touch her and memorize every frame of us, erasing everything that I ever knew of what a girl was supposed to feel like before.

We kiss like this for nearly an hour, the windows of my car frosting up with our breath. I touch her skin, letting my hands roam under her shirt, feeling her back and shoulders until I know it's okay to feel more.

I touch her breasts, letting my fingers find every curve, my thumbs grazing her nipples and my mouth watering with the want for more. But I know that this is as far as Emma Burke wants me to go. And I'm okay with that, because this girl has me, every part of me. She owns it all, and I am willing to wait for every new touch, knowing that it will feel just the same, just as perfect as this one does.

She is what I will look forward to.

When I look at the dashboard finally, I realize it's nearly two in the morning, and at some point, both Emma and I need to return home. I don't want her parents to worry, so I sigh as I stare into her eyes one last time.

I reach into my pocket finally, looking for my keys, but don't feel them. I check the other pocket and then let my hands start to search the sides of the seat when I don't feel them there either. I'm about to slide my hand between the seat and the console when Emma starts to giggle.

"You," I point at her. She dangles my keys from her thumb, fumbling with the door handle and finally racing from my car as I lunge at her. I get out of my side and race after her, catching her only a few steps away, pulling her into my arms and lifting her in front of me. She kicks her feet up into the air as I raise her, her entire body rumbling with the vibration of her laugh.

"Girl, you are going to make your parents hate me if I don't get you home before they notice you're gone," I say, reaching for the keys as she pulls them into her chest.

"I know. We can go, but…" she looks at the keys in her hand then up to me. "Can I drive? I know, I know…it's your car and she's some Camaro or something, but…"

"I don't know," I say, feeling a little bit like an asshole over the fact that I don't want her to drive my car.

"It's…it's okay. It was a dumb idea, never mind," she says, handing my keys back to me. I take them and follow her back to the car, but I grab her fingertips just as we get to the front of the car, pulling her into me.

"Here," I say, closing her hand around the keys while I kiss her one last time.

"Really?" Her voice is almost a squeal, and I can tell how excited she is. I nod *yes*, then move to the passenger door, climbing inside. Emma slides in excitedly next to me, pushing the key in quickly and turning the engine before we've even buckled up.

"Whoa," I say, grabbing my belt and buckling fast.

"Oh, right. Sorry…" she says, biting her lip. "I was anxious, and I didn't want you to change your mind."

"It's okay, just…take it easy. This car has some kick, all right?"

She nods and buckles her belt, checking all of the mirrors and turning on the lights before moving the shift into reverse. The car rumbles as she backs out slowly, her lip firmly planted in her teeth now. I don't think she's letting go, and her concentration is my second-favorite expression she makes. My first, the one she makes right before I kiss her. She idles her way to the exit, turning slowly onto the main roadway, and she glances at me before she looks back to the road, scooting forward in her seat, clutching the wheel, and pressing on the gas.

We travel for about a mile, going maybe thirty miles per hour, and eventually I start to laugh.

"Don't make fun of me," she chides, reaching at me with one hand, but only for a second, returning her grip to the wheel.

"I'm sorry, you're just so damn cute," I say. "You're so nervous. It's a car, you just drive it."

"I drive my mom's Honda Civic. It's…like…*way* different. Trust me," she laughs nervously. She's constantly looking over her shoulder, then in both mirrors. We've made it maybe two of the ten miles we need to travel.

"I know, trust me. I drove my mom's boyfriend's Buick, remember?"

She glances at me and smiles, then looks back to the road, relaxing a little more into her seat, the gas flowing a little heavier as our speed finally climbs up to forty-five.

"I loved that car, too," she says, blushing for a different reason now.

"You know I tried to be your partner for square dancing first, right?" I say, taking in her profile. I love the slope of her nose and the high roundness of her cheeks.

"You faker. I'm the one who picked you!" she huffs. It's cute that she wants credit for such a simple thing.

"Yeah…you did," I say, knowing the truth. I picked her the second I saw her legs stretched out in the hallway. I think maybe I chose her once in one of my dreams.

Our calm shifts into chaos in a blink.

Emma screams as she jerks the wheel to the right, sliding the car into the rough brush along the side of the road. We skid, fishtailing a few times before coming to a hard stop that sends both of us forward, our bodies held fast by the pull of our safety belts. Her forehead slams into the steering column, cutting her just above her eyebrow.

"Emma, Emma," I say her name over and over, my veins coursing with adrenaline, my body numb with panic and fear. She looks at me, and blinks; her tears are instant.

"Oh my god, Andrew! Oh my god, oh my god, oh my god!"

She's panting; she's breathing so hard. She's fighting to free herself from her seatbelt, and I'm only making it worse by getting my hands tangled with hers. I finally hold her hands still, and my other hand rushes to her face, moving her hair to the side.

"Emma, you're bleeding," I say, trying to keep my voice calm.

She touches her fingers to the place on her head where mine are, then pulls them in front of her to see the red on her hand.

This only makes her cry harder and begin to shake.

"I hit something. Andrew, I hit someone," she shouts. Her body is shaking, and her eyes look terrified.

I felt it too. Just before she jerked the wheel, something hit the front of the car. I wasn't watching the road. I was watching Emma.

Emma was watching me.

We didn't see it.

"It's okay," I say. "You hear me? It's okay."

I reach for the passenger door and she grabs for me.

"No, Andrew. No! Don't leave!"

I hold her hand, bringing her fingers to my mouth. Her cut is dripping blood into her eye now, so I reach into the glove box for a napkin and put it in her hand.

"Hold this right here," I say, guiding her hand and pressing firmly on her gash. "Leave it there, and keep the pressure on. I'll be right back."

She nods, but I can already see her hand starting to slide down and grow weaker. I push on it again, and she follows my lead, pressing harder.

I step from the door and move to the front, seeing the large dent in the bumper. The headlight is busted too, and there's blood on the glass. My stomach drops, but I don't let my face show any of it.

Watching her watch me through the back window, I hold up a finger, signaling I'll be right back. I step into the roadway, keeping my face still, no sign of the terror ruling my body. When I turn back to the road, I see a large mass lying on the asphalt—my only relief, it's moving.

The moaning hits my ears when I'm ten feet away; I realize it's an older man and his dog. I rush to his side—his head is bleeding onto the pavement.

"Sir, can you hear me. Sir?" I shout. I touch his neck, looking over him again, and he rolls to his side and the extent of the cuts and injuries to his abdomen and face hits me.

"Sir, I'm going to call for help," I say, standing and fumbling my phone from my pocket. My eyes are seeing things in scenes—in flashes, really. This man lying on the ground, his injuries, his dog whimpering at his side flat against the road—they are all scenes from a nightmare—then I look to the car, nearly one hundred yards away, and my eyes lock onto Emma's…I realize this nightmare, it's just beginning.

The emergency operator answers instantly, and I give our approximate location along the dark rural road. The temperature feels about twenty degrees colder than before, my breath thicker, and the air damp with mist.

I pull my sweatshirt from my body, wrapping it around the man's head, resting it easily on the pavement and promising him I'll come back.

He seems to be fading in and out of consciousness. I reach for his small dog, and it growls at me, so I leave it where it is and jog back to the car, where Emma is now rocking in the driver's seat, her eyes wide and full of tears.

"He's going to be okay. Emma, listen to me." I cup her face in my hands, turning her to face me. I feel badly because I'm being a little forceful, but she's slipping into a real state of panic, and I don't think that's going to help.

"Andrew, this is going to ruin everything," she says.

I shake my head *no*. She's just panicking, and I understand that. But the man is going to get help; he'll be okay. My car—it's just a dent. These things, they're not forever nightmares.

No.

"You don't understand," she says, her voice more forceful, her worry showing in her eyes in a different way. There's something about the way she's looking at me that says something more, something she can't seem to verbalize. "Andrew…I can't. This…oh my god. Andrew—"

Her shaking begins again, so I cradle her to my chest tightly, looking out the window that is hazing over with dew from outside.

"They are going to take everything away," she whispers against me, her eyes open, staring into emptiness. Nothing I say seems to bring her out of this trance. I know I need to get back out to the roadway, to the man lying there in far worse shape than either of us, but I can't leave her here, without hope. There's an absolute look of fear on her face, and the more seconds that pass, the more dire her expression becomes.

"Come with me," I say, stepping out of the passenger side and moving quickly to the driver's door, opening it and pulling on her arm. She shakes her head *no*, so I reach in and lift her into my arms, carrying her to the passenger side, where I place her in the seat I just left.

"What are you doing? Andrew…no…"

"Shhhhhhhh," I interrupt her protest, holding her head to mine as I kneel in front of her. "Listen to me. You. Were not driving. Tonight—you never touched the keys. This car, you never drove it. Not once—ever. I was driving. Do you understand?"

"Andrew…I can't let you…" I look up and see lights reflecting in the distance, an ambulance and fire truck on the way. Police will not be far behind.

I leave her in the seat and rush over to the ignition, pulling the key out and wiping it with my shirt then shoving the keys into my pocket. I run back around the front of the car to her, and hold her in place as she tries to step out from the car.

"Emma, I'm going to be fine. He's hurt, and we didn't do anything but have a horrible accident. He was walking on a dark road at night. I didn't see him step into the roadway, and I hit him with the front end of the car. I called for help right away, and you hit your head on the dashboard." I repeat myself three times, and she shakes her head and mutters *no* the entire time. I see the police cars trailing behind the medical help, and I know I only have seconds to get her on board with my story.

"Emma, I drove this car tonight," I say with more force, my teeth gritting. She needs to embrace this—she needs to let me lie. "I'm going to say this to them, and I need you to back up everything I say. I *need* you to!"

She gives me a slight nod, her eyes never once blinking, and her gaze looking over my shoulder at the emergency personnel now rushing in all directions.

"Sir, are you all right?"

There's a flashlight in both of our faces, and I stand to talk to the firefighter at my car.

"She hit her head on the dash. I think there's a cut," I say, and he flashes his light on her immediately. I move out of the way and let him work on cleaning up Emma as I step away to the man on the road. By the time I get there, three men and a woman are working on him, checking vitals and stripping away his bloodied clothing. My sweatshirt has been tossed into a biohazard bag along with the man's shirt. His injuries don't look life threatening, but I can tell he's not fully aware of what's happening.

"Is he going to be okay?" I ask, getting a variety of short responses—the gist always to let them work and they don't know enough yet.

I step away to give them room and move toward my car, where two firefighters are now working on Emma, walking her to the side of the car and checking her for more injuries. Two police officers have also started circling my car, and I notice them ask her a few questions.

Come on, Emma. Lie for me, baby. Please...just this once—tell a lie.

She shakes her head no, then her eyes flit up to me—our gazes lock, and I know she's done as I asked. She looks so ashamed, but I nod and close my eyes, so thankful she followed through. Whatever has her terrified of this—whatever she thinks this will ruin—is in the past with that one little lie.

I walk slowly toward the car, and as I get to the front, where the damage is, the second officer moves from my back seat leaving the door open.

"Is this your car, sir?" he asks.

"Yes," I nod.

"Were you driving this vehicle tonight?"

Yes, this is what I was hoping for. I'll explain everything; there will be some processing. Insurance is going to suck, but the man...he's going to be okay. I know it. I'll be fine. Emma will be fine.

"Yes, I was. It was dark, and he stepped into the roadway after that bend, and—"

"Place your hands on the roof of the car, please," the other officer says. I do as he asks, and open my mouth to finish my version of what happened, when I feel him kick my feet farther apart as his hands pat down the front, sides, and back of my body.

"I'm going to put these cuffs on you, sir, and they're going to feel a little uncomfortable, but if you don't resist, it won't hurt," he says, jerking one arm behind my body, then the second.

The cuffs are more of a giant zip-tie, really, and he pulls them tight, then leads me backward a few steps, pointing me so I'm looking at his partner.

"Is this your marijuana, Andrew?" the officer says. I look at the bag, the same small fucking bag of weed House dangled at me as payment to buy him a cheeseburger, and I feel overwhelmed with the need to throw up.

"That's not mine," I say, realizing how typical every word I just said sounds. That's what everyone says. And it's never the truth—except this once. This isn't the lie I'm telling. But it's the only one they're interested in.

"Have you been drinking or have you taken any drugs tonight?"

Shit.

I glance to Emma, who is now a hundred yards away near the fire truck, and I look back to my officer, knowing I'm fucked. I nod *yes*.

"Andrew, I'm placing you under arrest. You have the right to remain silent. Anything you say, can be..."

I hear his voice. It's a droning sound, and I know every word he's uttering. I know the law, the way it works, what happened, and I can see every single frame of this moment and how the universe has lined up to destroy me. I'll call my mom. She'll find a way to fix this. She'll call Owen.

My heart is beating so fast I think it might stop from exhaustion at any moment—the rhythm hurting my chest from the inside. I look up as the officer presses down on my neck, lowering me into the backseat of the squad car, and Emma's eyes lock on mine.

"No!" she shouts, and I see her pulling away from the medics trying to help her, the woman holding her arm and keeping her still. "No, Andrew!"

I can't hear her second scream, because the door is shut on me. I only see her lips moving, her arms jerking and her legs fighting to get to me. She's trying to get them to stop, and she's probably trying to take my place, but it doesn't matter. I don't want her to, either. She needs to stay with them, to wait for her parents, to go home and to be safe.

She doesn't need to be afraid. She is not going to lose anything. She can't and she won't. And I'll be okay.

I'll be okay.

CHAPTER 5

ONE MONTH LATER

Emma,

I'm sorry that this has to be a letter. It's the only thing I'm allowed to do. I wanted to call you, but there really wasn't an opportunity. I didn't know where to call, either. All this time, and I still never asked you for your phone number. I'm such a jerk.

I'm sure you heard. Dwayne, I mean Mr. Chessman said he would let you know. I hope you didn't get in any trouble. And I hope whatever you were afraid of losing is still with you, or still yours. I hope one day you'll explain.

I'm not proud of some of those things you've probably learned. But I had to explain, and I know you'll believe me. I'm not a druggie. That weed wasn't mine, either. It was my brother's friend's. He was visiting me, and he dropped it. Not that it matters. It sounds so cliché, and I laugh even now about how perfect it all is. Not a funny laugh. Nothing funny about this. But, I'll still be okay.

I did smoke a little. It was a stupid move, I know. But I was trying to feel less alone. Maybe I wanted to fit in. Fuck, if I'm honest, peer pressure is a thing. It's real. And I missed you. You had been gone for a week, and there was a part of me that thought maybe you'd never come back. I think maybe I thought I'd imagined you, too. Only, if I imagined you, I'd close my eyes now and you'd be here. Believe me, I've tried.

Anyhow, none of that matters, and I own that bad decision. I fell to peer pressure, and it kicked my ass. My mom kicked my ass, too. Owen—he won't talk to me. Which hurts. But I know that won't be forever. I'm sending him a letter, too.

They won't let me make any phone calls for at least three months. My schedule here is very...rigid. It's not military school, but I imagine it's not far off. At least my classes aren't boring. They aren't quite college-level, but the work keeps me busy. I have duties every morning until seven, and I'm in class until four. We have counseling at five, and then sometimes they give us recreation. I call this place juvie, but I guess that's not really accurate. It's more of a reform school, part of the bargain I got. Lake Crest Boys Academy.

I should be able to start back with the Excel Program in a few months. This isn't forever, and I'm okay. That's what I'm really writing about. I've been talking about you to someone here. She's a counselor, sort of, though, I'm not really sure how qualified she is. Don't worry, I don't tell her everything. Just...that you were with me, during the accident. She mentioned that you probably feel guilty about this, and I don't want that.

I'm okay, Emma. I'll be okay. And I'll be home soon.

I miss you.

Andrew

TWO MONTHS LATER

Dear Emma,

Did you get your gift? I made you something for Christmas. I get to go home for the holiday, but I don't have a lot of time. It's not even a full day, really. I want to visit. I hope you know that. But, I may not be allowed.

I miss hockey. I know that probably sounds selfish, but I do miss it. I'm honest with you. And as much as I miss my family, my boring routine and that shitty apartment, I miss kicking someone's teeth in on the ice more.

They have basketball here. Owen would love it. Me...not so much. I suck to the point where I'm literally the last one picked during rec time.

A lot of these guys are real assholes. And a lot of them actually did some bad shit, but nothing really bad. Petty theft, fights, drugs—things like that. I mean, it's reform school. They call it boy's academy. I guess that makes it sound better.

Oh hey, I got a letter from Owen, by the way. They let me get mail. I'd love to hear from you. Please write if you have time. I get phone privileges next week for being "good." I've already been offered twenty bucks to make a call for someone who doesn't get them. I'm thinking of taking him up on it.

Anyhow, I guess I just hope you're okay.

Andrew

SEVEN MONTHS LATER

Emma,

I get to come home next week.

I'm not even sure why I'm writing this to you, because I know I will have the choice to see you in person next week.

I say "choice" because...you know why I say choice. I think you know what I'll choose. I'm sure you're hoping for it.

This letter, I think it needs to be the last one I write. I didn't keep track, but I know I sent you more than twenty. Whatever the number is, it's the same number you never sent back.

It's spring, and the weather is warm. I've worked ahead of my class here, which really wasn't very hard. They offered to let me into the Excel Program again, although I'm on probation. My mom has forgiven me, for the most part, and Dwayne comes to visit every weekend. Even Owen came last week.

Owen had a lot of questions about the accident. I think he knows things don't add up. That man on the road, he lives in one of the housing projects on the edge of town. He's in his sixties. My mom said he recovered, though, and they've settled with him. I don't ask for the details, because I'm sure Dwayne had to help with the costs. I don't like that. But I guess that's just money. I'm alive. I'll go back to where I was. And you...you'll be wherever you are.

Oh, and I never told anyone. I never will.

Maybe I'll see you around.

I probably won't.

Andrew

ONE YEAR LATER

Dear Emma,

This letter is for me. It isn't for you.

I resent you.

I blame you.

I hate you.

And when I sat in my car last week, just out of your view, and saw you dressed in that pink homecoming dress, your hair done up, probably from one of those fancy salons in the city, and saw you kiss that guy on your front porch... I thought about going back to that moment and taking it all back—letting you stay in that seat, letting you lose everything important to you.

I thought about it.

I want to want that for you.

But I can't. I'll never want that for you.

I'll always want you to be the one who gets to be okay.

And I hate you for that most of all.

You said that night ruined everything, and you were right. It ruined me. I will never be the same.

It ruined us—as if there ever was an us.

I can't stay here. I can't stay in this town because there's too much of you in it. I've seen you too many times. You never see me, but I see you. I see you fucking everywhere!

And I don't want to see you anymore.

I'm going to live with my uncle in Iowa.

It doesn't matter, because you'll never visit.

I'll never give you this letter.

It wasn't for you anyway.

This letter—it's the only thing I've done in a year for me. Just for me.

I'll never make the mistake of picking someone else again.

I pick me.

Me.

And you can go to hell.

Andrew

PART TWO

CHAPTER 6

ANDREW HARPER, AGE 21

"You're a fucking cocksucker, Harper," Trent says, slapping the back of my head as he passes behind me at the bar. I hit him hard today. He blew it last week, though, and that's my job—to get guys ready to take hits in the real games.

I get to play, but I'm more of an insurance guy—the one they send in to be distracting and cause trouble for the other guys, to shift the game to our advantage. It lands me in the box a lot, but we're surprisingly good at penalty kill. We come out stronger, and sometimes we need to feel the pressure to get things going.

"I wouldn't have to hit you so hard in practice if you weren't such a pussy during games, Metzger," I say, pulling my lips from the rim of my beer bottle just long enough to dish out a quick insult to my best friend.

"Fuck off, you're just bitter that girls like me more 'cuz I'm the sexy captain," he says in this fucking annoying-ass voice while he rubs his chest like he's a stripper. It's creepy.

"Yeah, you got me. Totally jealous of *all that*," I deadpan, gesturing toward him.

I kid with him, but truth is Trenton Metzger is the most talented goddamned hockey player I've ever been on the ice with. He's the only reason people talk about Northern Tech hockey, and it's an honor to be on the roster with him.

Hell, it's an honor to be on any roster at all. I'm a partial-scholarship player; partial lots of things, really. After two years of busting my ass in junior college and proving myself in junior leagues, I managed to pull together enough of an academic and athletic resume to get my ass into Tech. My grades were never the issue. It was my stint at Lake Crest that gave people pause. The list of schools willing to hand out free money just so I would go there dried up fast even though I finished out high school in the Excel Program, my senior year in independent study—graduating early with shining academics. I was still accepted lots of places, I just couldn't pay for them.

What a fucking tease college is. *Hey, come to our university and have this awesome life we're showing you in these glossy pictures. Oh...what? You can't afford it? Here...here's a nice mug and calendar magnet of our football schedule instead.*

Luckily, I'm enough of an asset on the ice for NTU to pay for part of my last two years. Part. I get another small percentage in academic scholarships, but even then there's still a shitload I have to figure out on my own. My mom and step-dad Dwayne help, but they don't have much either. They gave me what little they made from combining households when they got married two years ago, and that little went right to what was left on my tuition tab my first semester. So I work the rest off with odd jobs. Right now, I have two. In the mornings, I work at a nearby elementary school. I get there early for the parents who have to drop their kids off before school actually starts. We play dodgeball for two hours, and the girls sit at the tables and color. It pays shit, but it's better than nothing.

My other gig is…different. But the pay is awesome—when it comes. I'm a fall guy. Basically, I spar with wannabe fighters for this dude Harley who manages up-and-coming boxers. He pays me ten bucks an hour to throw a few punches, but take way more than I throw. It builds up confidence in the guys he wants to move up and it keeps me aggressive on the ice. When he thinks his guys are almost ready, he sets up small fights at a few of the gyms in the city, and my job is to always go down, but not until we've gone at least three or four rounds.

This is where I make my tuition money.

Harley takes bets on the side—rolling money into the thousands with a network of bookies he knows. I get a cut—because *I'm* the one who gives him the lock. He's careful about running me too often, switching me up with two or three other guys who have the same deal, and he always loses a bet when he needs to make it look legit.

The fights are only on Sundays, so it never runs into practice or games. And it's rarely more than one a month. But one fight can land me a few grand in a night. It's money I need, and the first time I did it, I couldn't believe how many of my financial problems it helped make go away. But that's not what made me come back.

That feeling—the one of knowing my arms aren't going to move fast enough, that my instincts are going to be purposely numbed, is a rush. To know the hit is coming, and that I'm going to deny myself protection. When I get hit—gloves to the temple, chest, chin, ribs—it's like getting high. Everything that hurts gets centered on the pain, and my runaway thoughts and fears come to a grinding halt. Regret fades. The only thing that exists is getting my ass kicked, feeling my flesh sting and my body hum with pain.

Sometimes, I think that if I didn't do this—if I hadn't stumbled into Harley's gym one day and found my way into a ring with a boxer twice my size—that I would have turned to something else. My body can take the abuse, and my mind…it craves the distraction. It's the same way on the ice.

"All right, Harper. Who's the target tonight?" Trent leans over me, startling me out of my trance, grabbing my next beer and taking it for his own.

"Hey, dickhead," I say. He holds up a hand and orders another one, sliding it to me. "I'm pretty sure it's your turn this time."

His face falls and his complexion turns green. Trent and I have this game we play with one another. It started as a drunken dare a few months ago, when he goaded me into taking a girl home from Majerle's Pub. I'm not suave; I don't have great pick-up lines. I usually wait for girls to hit on me. I wait for *easy*. When Trent dared me, I came up with my own set-up—I stole a girl's wallet. I returned it to her later, pretending I'd found it. She was so grateful she spent the rest of the night sitting on my lap, her arms looped around my neck, her lips sucking on my skin, her hands soon finding their way in my pants.

That first girl taught me never to bring any of them to our apartment. I go to theirs now. It's easier to leave than it is to kick someone out.

"Fine, I'll go. But next time, I get to pick your girl," I say, tipping my beer back to drink what's left before leaving the bottle on the bar behind me and pointing at my friend.

"Dude, whatever. You know it's your turn anyway," he says.

"My choice next time," I remind him as I walk backward. I know it's his turn, and I also know he doesn't really like taking the dare. Trent's too nice, and he usually ends up dating the girl for weeks after. He doesn't like to be an asshole. Or maybe he just doesn't like people to say bad things about him. Maybe there's no difference between the two.

I couldn't give a shit what people say about me. Let 'em talk.

I make one pass through the crowded bar, letting my eyes roam over the dance floor and the tables that line the back wall on the way to the bathrooms. It's a Friday night, so there are lots of girls here. It's the middle of the semester, too, so they're all ready to party—no finals to worry about. There's one group that seems like an easy target, a blonde on the end who keeps trying to talk the others into dancing. I hover around the restrooms waiting for my shot, and when she finally drags the group of girls with her out to the dance floor, I walk back through the crowd, passing their table.

So easy.

Their wallets and purses are all piled in the center of the table except for a red bag looped over the back of a chair, the ID sticking out of the top. I drag my hand along the bottom of the table, and as I pass the red handbag I grab the small plastic card poking from it, tucking it into the sleeve around my palm. I glance up to make eye contact with Trent, and raise the corner of my mouth in a smirk.

"Dude, you are so slick at this. Seriously, if you flunk out of the engineering program you should just turn to a life of crime."

I slide into my stool and look away from him. I know he was just saying words, but the joke doesn't sit well with me. I have a chip on my shoulder. It's my fucking chip, and I earned it by giving up a year of my life for a series of bad decisions and shitty circumstances. Trent knows my story—

mostly. He knows there was a girl, and he knows I got screwed over by both the girl and the law. But I'm not sure he knows exactly how fucked up it all left me. And he also doesn't know how many nights I walk that line with Harley, fixing bets that are illegal in the first place. Trent just thinks I like the workout boxing gives me.

"Well...let's see it? Who's the lucky lady?"

I pull my sleeve loose from around my wrist and let the card slide out, flipping it over while I drink what's left of my beer, and that's when karma slaps me like a bitch.

She's older. Of course she's older. She's twenty-one, too. But she looks... older. She also looks the same. Nobody looks good in an ID photo. Emma Burke looks like a dream. Her brown hair is just as I remember it, long waves around her bright pink cheeks, lips that stretch into this sensuous smile. I don't know if it's sensuous to anyone else, but to me, it sure as fuck is.

It's also cruel. I swear to god she's mocking me in her picture, her eyes shining through and looking at me, calling me stupid, telling me what a chump I am for thinking I was some sort of hero or something.

She's slapping me in the face for being good and decent to her.

Don't worry, Emma. I won't ever be good and decent to you again.

"Well?" Trent asks. I slide the card toward him, never looking down at it. He picks it up, holding it in his hand and reading her details while I choke down another beer and wonder how the hell I'm going to get out of this.

"Damn, Harp!" he says, his heavy pat on my back almost making my beer spill down into my lungs. I know what has him impressed; it's her eyes. I get it. They worked on me too. That's the first thing I recognized. And *like hell* am I putting myself in a position where I have to stare into them again. She'd probably hypnotize me right into prison—for good this time!

"It was your night anyhow; you take her," I say, letting my gaze drift off to the TV mounted above the bar. It's a commercial for toothpaste, and I'm so interested in it. So very interested. I'm ignoring everything—Trent, the brewing sensation in my gut, the heaviness of knowing Emma is in this room, breathing the same air I am.

I feel the card slide under my elbow, and I close my eyes.

"Awwww no you don't. You're not going to pussy out on me now. You know the deal." He's talking loudly. I know there's no way she can hear me, no way she'd know, but my body heats up at the thought of getting caught.

I take a slow, deep breath so Trent doesn't notice how tense I've become, then slide the card back into my palm, glancing at it before putting it in my back pocket as I stand. I toss a twenty on the bar and put my empty bottle on top of it.

"Whatevs, man. I'll play hero a little later; I've got some shit to take care of," I say, nodding goodbye.

"You're such a prick, making her wait," he chuckles.

If our friendship were a superhero, Trent would be Ironman, and I'd be Tony Stark. I think Trent is amused by my dick moves, because he's the good guy and could never pull them off. I used to be that way, too.

I don't respond. Yeah, I'm a prick. I'm a prick because what I really want to do is toss her ID in the trash on my way out. But I don't do that, because instead I'm the kind of prick that gives up a year of my life and any possible future because of a fucking crush on a high school cock tease. This gift—knowing where she is—feels like something I shouldn't waste, so I'm going to think of the perfect way to play it all.

I hit the exit and glance over to the group of girls on the dance floor again, and I wait for a few seconds until I see her body come into view. She looks like she's having the time of her life, arms over her head, eyes shut, smile on her face, sweat dripping down her body. She's the sexiest thing I've ever seen. There was a time when I imagined her like this, grown up—this is what I saw in my sixteen-year-old fantasies.

That hate I've worked so hard on burying comes right back, and my heart hardens as her eyes drift open and there's a short flash of recognition that crosses them. That's right, Delaware—it's me, and I see you.

I leave quickly, pretending not to notice her, knowing that she's still not sure about what she saw. I don't want to give her enough to be sure. I want to give her doubt and worry, and then I never want to see her again.

* * *

When I left the bar, I headed to the warehouse. Harley wasn't expecting me, but he let me work in, take a few rounds in the ring. Harley's only at the gym at night, and usually only on the weekdays. During the day, he's the perfect law student his rich parents think he is. He manages the warehouse space as a gym; it's in a building his grandfather owns. He told his dad he wanted to learn about running a business. Nobody in his family visits; they just take his word on things.

Harley is the kind of guy people trust.

I've run the numbers in my head, and I'm pretty confident Harley's making out better running his boxing scam. His father's a pretty powerful corporate attorney though, so there's an expectation of his life going one way. If things go south, I guess he'll be able to find his own loopholes and get his ass out of trouble.

The only guy boxing tonight is a dude they call Pitch Black. He got that name because he knocks people out cold. I've never sparred with him before; he's not one of the guys Harley needs to *fake* things with. He took it easy on me; I could tell. But he still fucked my face up pretty good. I've had the ice out for an hour, and I'm just putting it back in the freezer when Trent walks in, sliding his keys on the counter behind me.

"Dude, do not tell me you blew that chick off just to get your fix at the gym." He's leaning back against the counter with his arms crossed.

"I had a guy who wanted to work on some things with me," I lie.

"Yeah, like seeing how many stitches he could rack up on your face?"

"Fuck off; it's not that bad," I say. He reaches at me, poking my tender jaw, and I wince and slap his hand off me in one motion.

"Right…not bad at all," he says, judgment oozing from his tone.

I sigh and open our pantry, grabbing a handful of almonds from an open tin. Then I shut the door and ignore my friend, knowing he's going to ask me about the girl and the ID and my plans. I thought going to the warehouse would help me gain perspective. I was wrong.

"Look," he starts as he kicks his shoes off and empties his pockets onto the counter. He leaves his shit in piles—drives me fucking nuts, and it's not just because I'm in a bad mood.

Maybe it is. Whatever. I stare at his crap until he waves a hand to get my attention back to his face.

"Drew, man...if you weren't really in the mood to hit on some chick, you shouldn't have taken her ID. That girl is going to be freaked out and worried when she can't find it, so at least just get it back to her."

My gaze has drifted away from him again, back to his pile of stuff.

"Why can't you dump your crap in your room? That's what I do when I come home. I go to my room, put my things in there, and *then* I come out here."

Trent cocks an eyebrow at me, staring for a few seconds, then moves back to the kitchen, scooping up his wallet, keys, and change and holds it up so I can see him and acknowledge it.

"Don't forget your shoes," I add.

He laughs once. Not a funny laugh. He's pissed. I'm being an asshole. He can fuck off. He doesn't have *her* ID in his back pocket.

Trent bends down and grabs his shoes, pointing one toward me as he goes to his room.

"Sometimes you're a real dick, Harper," he says. He lets his door slam closed behind him.

I turn my attention to the TV in front of the sofa and hold the remote up, turning on some bad teen soap opera and cranking the volume up to an obnoxious level. Might as well let this being-a-dick thing really run its course.

* * *

TRENT NEVER CAME out of his room, and I finally fell asleep on the couch to some protein-supplement infomercial. I woke up when Trent let the front door slam shut loudly. We have practice in thirty minutes, morning skate before our game tonight. We usually ride together, because Trent has a car. Looks like I'll be walking today.

After a quick shower, I change into sweats and my long-sleeved tee and jog to the arena about two miles away. I shove Trent's pads off the bench when I walk by his locker. He laughs, so I know he's over being pissed at me. I also know that I still have Emma's ID in my wallet.

Pre-game skate only lasts half an hour, so I can't put things off any longer. I want to. I want to be so busy I can never go to 407 Clark Street, which yeah…is less than three miles from my apartment. Usually, I have to look the girl up to find her address—her license normally from another state, but Emma's is right there on her license. She must be planning on living here for a while, or maybe she already has. How the hell I haven't seen her in the year I've attended this school is a miracle.

Then again, I get the feeling Emma and I probably run in different circles. I know her building. It's the big high-rise on Clark. Balconies, windows that look over the lake, a bellman at the front desk—a far cry from the rats and drug deals that go down out on the street in front of our apartment. It's not like *gangland* or anything, just cheap rent and a lot of college kids who like to get high.

When I'm done skating, I rush through changing and just hold up a hand with her license for Trent to see. He smirks, figuring I'm off to make good on my dare. I'm really going to take my penance. Lesson learned—I'm never playing *this* game again.

The wind from the lake has a cold bite to it, so I pull my hoodie from my bag and throw it on over my beanie. Maybe I'm also shielding myself. I get to the front of her building, and my heart starts to race wildly, my throat dry, but somehow my mouth so moist I feel like I'm going to throw up.

The doorman is helping a group of girls when I walk by quickly, and he glances at me, probably memorizing what I'm wearing, but he doesn't stop me when I pass. My hands are shaking in the elevator, and when I press the button for the ninth floor, I hold it down, afraid to fully commit.

Number 907.

I'm nine stories away from the girl who ruined my life.

My plan is pathetic. I'm not going to ring the bell. I'm not going to knock. I'm just going to slide the ID under her door, then get the fuck out of here. I thought about leaving it with the doorman. But I *have* to see. There's something that's pushing me forward, some part of me that just needs to get close, to know exactly where she lives, what her door looks like.

When the elevator dings and the doors slide open, I pause briefly, considering riding it back down and going with the other plan—leaving her license at the front desk. But the hallway is quiet, and that silence coaxes me through the doors that fall closed behind me.

Breath held, I glance back down at her picture in my hand, the sharp edges of her license digging into my skin as my hand closes on it, squeezing it so hard I bend it a little. Signs on the wall guide me down the hallway to the right, so I walk by a few doors until I get to her number, slowing down before I'm fully in front of the frame. I don't want her to see me here—not through a crack in the door, not through a peephole.

There's nothing special about her door at all. There's only the number on the outside. No welcome mats or seasonal décor plastered on the doorknob or frame like a few of her neighbors. It's just a door, and it looks just like any other door.

Emma is just any other girl, I remind myself.

I laugh lightly at how ridiculous I'm being and how nervous I am for no reason. She'll never even know, and I can go back to living a life without her, now knowing a few places to avoid.

Bending down, I slip her license from the pocket in the front of my hoodie, and hold it between my thumb and finger, sliding it along the carpet until it meets the bottom edge of her door. When I see it fits, I flick it hard with my finger, satisfied when it disappears underneath.

"Uhm, excuse me?"

The voice behind me scares me enough that I jump forward and press my hand flat on Emma's door to catch my balance. I know it isn't her; I'm pretty sure I'd still know her voice. But it's someone. And I've now been seen—*here!* When I get to my feet and turn, I'm greeted by a girl with a laundry basket filled with towels, detergent, and fabric softener.

Not Emma.

All that matters.

"Sorry, I…" I stop, realizing I can't really make up an excuse, nor do I need to. "I found someone's license at the bar last night, so thought I'd just drop it off. I…I knew where the building was."

I slide my hood from my head when she starts looking at me suspiciously. I pull my beanie off too and run my hand through my hair, pushing it out of my face. I probably look a little rough, still bruised from a fight and sweaty from practice.

"Oh my god. Emma's!" Her eyes light up with realization. "Thank you so much! Oh my god, she's been totally freaked out over that! She's going to die. I have to call her. Thank you so much!"

"No problem. Really," I say, exchanging places with her in the hallway. Just hearing her say Emma's name does something, twists something deep inside. I was anxious to leave, but it's like there's a part of me that's been asleep for years, and hearing the word *Emma* woke it up. My mind is begging my feet to carry me away, but there's that other thing inside me that suddenly wants to stay.

The girl is balancing her basket and reaching for her keys. She drops them on the floor, and as I see her struggle to kneel down with the basket and pick them up again, an idea strikes me.

"Here, let me hold that," I say, bending and taking the basket from her. She smiles gratefully, fumbling with her keys, sorting through the dozen or so on her ring to find the right one. Why do chicks have so many keys? How many things do you seriously need to keep locked?

Finally finding the door key, her eyes flit up to me a few times as she nervously works it into the lock. The more jumpy she gets, the more I start to like my probably-very-bad idea. I like how it's making me feel.

Her door finally open, I follow her inside, reaching down to pick up Emma's license as we step over the threshold.

"Here, I slid it under the door," I say, stepping in a little closer than I need to. I want to see her reaction. Her mouth twists into the kind of smile she's trying to control. I can tell by the slight shiver in her lips. I step to the side, giving her some space, and notice the deep breath she lets out. I slide her basket onto the table right inside the door, glancing around to take in the full apartment.

So this is where Emma lives now.

"I like your place," I say, noticing she's still looking at me, still trying not to smile. She glances to the side of my face, examining my bruise. "Oh, I…I play hockey here. Game injury," I lie. She likes my excuse though, her smile losing its battle a little more.

When her back is turned, I look down the hallway and out on the patio that seems to run the width of their apartment. There's nothing in here that screams *Emma*—not that I'd know what that would be any more.

It's a nice apartment. Not any bigger than mine, really, but the neighborhood's nicer, everything's newer. It's a good place for two girls to live alone.

"Hockey, huh?" the girl says. Interested. Yeah, that usually works. I nod down at my chest, to my NTU Hockey sweatshirt. "Oh…" she says, blushing when she looks back up and our eyes meet.

"That's where I came from. We had a light practice. There's a game tonight," I say, my pulse kicking in all the right places. It's a mix of adrenaline and fear of being caught. "You ever come out to the games?"

Or maybe you and your roommate? Does she know I'm here? Is she avoiding me? Dozens of questions race through my mind, but I keep everything calm on the outside.

"Oh, no. Emma and me don't get out much. We're both pre-med—total book nerds. Almost scalpel nerds, ha! We just moved in…maybe two months ago," she says. "Last night was rare for us. We hardly ever go out."

She doesn't ask me to leave, instead moving into the kitchen toward the fridge, so I give her a little space before following her steps. I don't want to make her nervous. But I also want to see how far I can go with this—what I can learn.

Scalpel. She's really becoming a surgeon. I almost smile at the thought of her living one of her dreams, but then my other feelings take over.

"So just the girl on that ID and you here?" I'm looking around for a sign of a boyfriend, but I'm not getting the vibe that one exists from this girl, for either of them.

My naïve host is wearing a sweatshirt and leggings, and she's already kicked her feet out of the boots she was wearing which means she's comfortable with me being here in her space. She's cute—short hair, cut to her shoulders, kind of brown, kind of blonde. She's small, like the sort of girl I could pick up easily over my shoulder, and what I can see of her body, looks pretty tight.

"Yeah, just Emma and me," she smirks, sliding an unopened can of cola toward me when she turns back. I pull the tab up, and the carbonation sprays over the counter. Pulling my sleeve forward on my hand, I wipe it away before peering back up at her to catch her lip in her teeth while she watches.

"And *you are?"* I tilt my head to the side, and I know the second her lip slides loose from her teeth that I've got her. She blushes—hard.

"Oh, right. Hi, I'm Lindsey." Her voice comes out in a nervous giggle. I stand and wipe the moisture of the soda from my hand, reaching across the counter to her.

"Nice to meet you. I'm Drew."

Her hand is cold when I shake it, so I bring my other hand up to cup it completely, rubbing them together to warm her up. She likes it. I can tell. Her entire hand is swallowed up between both of mine. It's almost sweet. Yet…I feel nothing.

"Thanks," she sighs, the smile she's been trying to manage growing a little more out of control. She's into me.

"So…I've gotta go, Lindsey…game tonight and all. But I was wondering if maybe you'd let me come back here sometime, say around dinnertime, so I could take you out?"

Her eyes grow wider, and I get the feeling she's not used to guys being so blunt. That's fine, because I'm not used to hitting on girls without some sort of pretense—like a missing phone or wallet. There just happens to be a bigger thirst I'm trying to quench right now, and Lindsey's really the only safe way for me to get at it.

Lindsey isn't really safe at all.

But I can't stop. Whatever I'm doing has my belly warm, and I feel more energized about the next minute, the next hour and the next day than I have in years.

This isn't flirting; it's strategy.

"I'd like that," she says, her eyes flitting once more. I could kiss her right now, and she'd let me. I think about it, letting my tongue lick my bottom lip at the thought. Oh how great it would be if Emma walked in right now, and my lips were on her roommate. My eyes haze a little, and her breath hitches, which gives me a satisfied grin. I don't give her what I know she wants, instead stepping back and watching her smile falter, replaced by disappointment. She stammers to get me to stay longer.

"Here…uhm…what's your number? I'll text you." She's opening her contacts screen on her phone when I take the device from her, letting my hands run into hers during the exchange. She giggles.

"There," I say, handing it back after I've typed my number in and sent myself a message with her name. "How about Wednesday at seven?"

"That's good," she says, following me back to the front door. My pulse is racing with adrenaline. I have no idea if Emma is coming upstairs, or if she's doing laundry too. I know that she's worried about her ID, and I know Lindsey will text her about it the minute I'm gone. She'll tell her all about the guy who brought it here then asked her out. I'll be this cute story they'll share. Then on Wednesday, I'll find out exactly what Emma's doing here, how long she plans to stay, and how long I have to think about her.

"Good. I'll text you, and we'll meet somewhere nearby," I say, stepping through her door, relief washing over me when I find the hallway still empty. There's a slight exhilaration that flies through my veins too. I'm playing with fire, and I like how it feels.

I wink at her before I turn to leave. When her door shuts, I take big strides toward the stairwell, deciding this is probably the best route to be sure I don't run into Emma. There's a part of me that feels lighter now that I don't have her license on me, like I've gotten rid of this massive obligation. Adding the roommate into the equation was a bigger risk—the entire thing completely happening on impulse—but it also excites me. I need to know more about Emma. It's curiosity, probably driven by the desire that she's suffering…in some way.

One date. With a cute girl. Harmless.

I'll learn secrets, get enough to satisfy things, enough to move on. Then, I'll let Lindsey down easy.

I rush by the front desk when I make it to the first floor, but I'm careful enough not to draw any more attention from the doorman, who's still talking with the group of girls from earlier. Once I've made it safely a block or two away, I pull my phone from my pocket and send Lindsey a text.

I'm really glad I found that license and ran into you.

I know exactly what my words are going to do to her. And when she sends me back a gushy smiley-faced emoticon, I know it worked. I send her one more message, just to cement everything in place.

Can't wait for Wednesday.

She writes back quickly that she can't either. Satisfied, and feeling a little proud of myself, I put my phone back in my pocket and decide to jog the rest of the way back to my apartment. I spend those few miles thinking about the perfect way to work in my questions about Emma. I think about that, and I think about how she looked on that dance floor last night, and in that picture on her ID.

I think about her eyes.

The ocean.

Lake Crest.

I think about the fact that her eyes have found their way back into my mind…uninvited.

Then I think about how good it felt asking out her roommate.

CHAPTER 7

EMMA

"So…it's a little weird for you to be giving *my date* a present. I'm just sayin'," Lindsey shouts from the hallway bathroom. I'm in the kitchen, layering the last batch of oatmeal cookies over the sheet of wax paper I've cut to fit perfectly in the tin.

"I know, but seriously, that guy saved me from having to deal with the DMV and lines and mean people," I say, tucking a short thank you note under the lid before closing it. When she steps into the kitchen, I hand her my gift. "Here…you can just tell him your roommate is a nut, but she's grateful. It'll be an icebreaker—seriously, you could spend an hour on the topic of your crazy roommate alone."

"Don't I know it," Lindsey says, her mouth twisted in a one-sided smile.

"You didn't have to agree so quickly," I laugh, turning back to our oven to shut everything off.

I don't have many domestic skills. My laundry remains in the basket when its both dirty and clean, dishes are only done in our apartment because of Lindsey, and forget about vacuuming. I don't really like cooking, either. But baking—that's different. When I bake, I get to eat the ingredients along the way. It's not like I can sample pieces of a casserole while I'm throwing in corn and meat and crap, but chocolate chip cookies? *Oh yeah.* Oatmeal are my favorites though—it's the brown sugar. I could eat that stuff by the spoonful.

"Okay, enough about you. How do I look?" she asks, spinning slowly. She's put a lot of thought into this date—blew out her hair, bought new lip gloss and I'm pretty sure she got a manicure. It's sweet. She doesn't go out much, even less than I do, really. It's part of being a medical student. And I know it's only going to get worse next year. Lindsey's studying general surgery, I'm cardiothoracic. I've only ticked off three years, so only…seven left.

"You look like a total hottie," I smile.

"Eeeek, thank you," she squeals, before running into the bathroom one more time to check her makeup, and dashing out the door in a cloud of Victoria Secret body spray.

I shake my head, smiling at my friend, then move back into the kitchen to finish cleaning up. I run right into my tin of cookies, which stares back at me, forgotten in the midst of my friend's excitement. I snicker quietly to myself, grabbing the tin after I finish mopping up the stray grains of sugar from the counter. I climb into the worn part of the sofa, the spot my roommate and I both refer to as *my corner,* raise the remote, and begin my big night out.

It's the first night in weeks I haven't been swallowed up completely with biology homework. I intend on watching mindless television until I can't keep my eyes open, and it looks like I'll also be making myself sick on oatmeal cookies. Glad I baked my favorites.

I make it twenty minutes into one of those shows where two people take over decorating a couple's house when my phone buzzes with a text from Lindsey. I'm tempted to read it after I watch the big fight—the guy hates everything they're doing to the house, but the wife loves it. But my phone buzzes again right away, so I mute the TV, brush the few oatmeal crumbs from my lap, and lean forward to read my text.

Help! Please.

I panic at her first text, getting to my feet fast and moving to the front door for my shoes as I scroll to her next one.

Sorry. I didn't mean to make that sound that urgent. I just feel like an idiot. I don't think this guy is going to show up. I texted him...twice. Now I just feel stupid, and I'm sitting here at Mello's alone drinking wine like a loser.

I relax a little knowing Lindsey's not in trouble, but I move forward with my shoes, grab my keys, and put the lid back on the cookies so we have something to share when I get to her.

On my way.

She writes back fast: *You're the best!*

Mello's is one of those places we always wanted to try, but just haven't yet. We spent our first three years in the dorms, and decided it was easier to concentrate in a place of our own without freshmen running around screaming and hooking up with each other next door at all hours of the night. Lindsey's parents pay most of the rent, but I chip in with what little I earn in summer jobs and the money I get from home and financial aid.

It takes me five minutes to get to the restaurant, and I find my friend sitting near the wall by the front door the second I step inside. I brush by the host table, beelining toward her and sliding into the other side of the booth quickly so I can tuck my sweatpants and sneakers underneath.

"I didn't really dress for this," I whisper to her, pushing the tin of cookies on the table in front of us.

"I wasn't planning on making you my date," she shrugs, her lips a tight smile that I know is hiding her disappointment. She pops the lid from the tin and laughs to herself when she sees the top layer is missing. "You get hungry?"

"They're my favorite," I smile. "Good thing you forgot them."

"Yeah, sorry. I was just so nervous, I left without my key, too, so I would have had to call you or ring the doorbell like mad anyhow," she says.

Lindsey pushes half a cookie into her mouth before sighing and relaxing into the plush back of her seat.

"So he's a no-show?" I ask, breaking one of the cookies in half to nibble on.

"Looks like it," she sighs. "I texted him about ten minutes ago. And oh my god, Em, I sound like an idiot."

She hands me her phone, and I read her messages that at first asks if maybe she has the day and place wrong, noticing that he texted her right above that with the exact time and place for them to meet on Wednesday —*today*. Then she tried to fix it with a: *duh, I could have just read your last text. Okay, so I'm here. I'll just be here waiting.*

I cringe when I hand it back to her, and tilt the lid on my cookies a little higher, encouraging her to take one more to console herself.

"I know, right? So bad," she sighs, falling back into her cushion. "Do you want some of my wine? I got a whole bottle."

"Sure," I say, reaching for one of the upside down glasses at the end of the table. I pour a small glass, and hold it up to toast when Lindsey grabs my wrist, making me spill a drop or two on the sleeve of my favorite Tech sweatshirt. Damn.

"Oh shit! He's here!" she whispers excitedly, immediately brushing off the front of her dress, wiping the corners of her mouth and fidgeting in her seat. I'm blotting at the now-purple spots on my super-soft, I'll-never-find-one-like-this-again, white sweatshirt when Lindsey drops her uneaten half of a cookie back into the stash to hide what we were doing. She's making me nervous now, too.

"Oh…crap…uh…I'll go," I rush, grabbing my cookies and lid and chugging my glass of wine quickly while I try to exit the booth gracefully. I don't realize what's happening—what has happened, what this would feel like or the fact that I could feel anything like this at all—until I stand and stumble forward, letting my hand land flat in the center of his chest.

I'm sixteen the second our eyes meet.

I'm sixteen again, and I'm right back at the kitchen table with my parents, and they're telling me how right they were, everyone was, about Andrew Harper.

I'm sixteen, and I'm looking at the aftereffect of my lies—my omissions.

I kept my mouth shut.

And Andrew did too.

Now here we are, five years later, in a wine bar where he's meeting my best friend for a date. Their first date. And he's looking at me like I might be the worst human on the planet. But then, he also looks at me like he misses me. And a little like he hates me, then as if he doesn't know me at all. It's all in there, in that space behind his eyes. They're swirling—his emotions.

My heart has never hurt like this. I've thought I saw him so many times. I never thought it was real.

I feel like I've been kicked in the chest, my lungs are burning, and my mouth is trying to remember how to gasp for air, all of me too stunned to actually just breathe. By the time my lungs function again, I suck in air so fast it chokes me, and I start to cough. I realize my hand is still on his chest when he looks down at it, his brows raised. I pull it away quickly, balling it into a fist, because for those few seconds I had my palm on him, I swear I felt his heartbeat. It's like I want to catch it and put it away for later.

"Emma, this is your big hero," my friend says behind me. "Drew, this is Emma."

The irony that she calls him that strikes fast, and I laugh once, but quickly cover my mouth because a part of me also feels like crying. I'm unable to close my mouth under my palm. That anxiety that plagued me for months after our accident comes roaring back into my being. It never truly left. The scar—the memory of that night, of him being driven away from me, the feeling in my gut at what he was doing…for me—it creeps in at night, invades my dreams, and surprises me in quiet moments. That sharp stab—it's always really there.

What can I possibly say to him? That question etches itself into my mind all hours of the night, while I lie in bed and look out my window wishing he'd just show up, stand outside and throw a rock up to wake me. If he did, what would I say?

What can I say now?

Thank you? Thank you for taking the fall for me, for my carelessness? You may have saved my life. But then...why were you high? And...how could you? You drove like that; you could have killed me. Did I ever really know you at all?

Did I?

"It's nice to meet you, Emma. I'm glad I was able to get your license back to you. I bet that had you worried," he says, holding his hand out for me to shake, his eyes directing me toward it, to shake it. It's the same smile from our youth, but…then it's not.

"Yeah, uh…nice to meet you too," I stammer, my voice awkward and meek. I take his lead, playing this as if we're strangers, but I know he recognizes me. I feel my friend's hand on my shoulder, and I jump, turning to her just in time to see her holding the tin of cookies. *Oh god, she's giving him the fucking cookies!*

"She was so grateful, she baked you cookies," Lindsey laughs. I smile at her through gritted teeth, my brow pulled forward and my mouth aching from forcing a smile. She shakes her head at me, unsure why I look so desperate. "We…uh…well, sort of ate a few while I was waiting."

Andrew takes the tin in his hand, and I'm glued to his face again, waiting for his reaction. This whole scene is a morbid type of irony, and I'm not sure I'll ever be able to taste an oatmeal cookie again without associating it with everything I'm experiencing right now.

Here he sacrificed so much, and I'm giving him cookies.

He holds the tip of his tongue between his teeth as his mouth slides into that familiar smile, the one I was so smitten with as a teenager. It dimples his cheeks exactly as it always did, but those cheeks are now covered in stubble, and maybe a small scar on the right side. I bet there's a story that goes along with it. I bet there are a lot of scars and stories we both have to share.

"I love cookies," he says finally, his lips closing into a tight smile. His amber eyes burn through me, into me, and for that brief second, it's like I can see his *him.* "I bet I'll *really* love your cookies, Emma," he smirks, his eyes haze, and I notice a difference in his tone and demeanor. He gives me a look that is meant just for me, and he slips it in right when Lindsey isn't watching.

Andrew Harper has no intention of sharing secrets with me ever again.

I swallow hard enough that I fear the couple sitting at the next table can hear it. I'm showing my nerves, and it makes Andrew chuckle a little. He sets the cookie tin down on the table, then steps closer to Lindsey, tucking her hair behind one ear and kissing her lightly on the cheek.

I hate it.

"I'm sorry I'm late. I just saw your text," he says, giving her all of his attention, along with the gentle smile that still shows up in my memories. He pulls his knitted hat from his head, sliding his other hand through his hair. It's longer, but the same. He's still wearing black gauges, but even those somehow look older—harder. "We weren't supposed to practice today, but this weekend is gonna be tough, so we worked out this afternoon. Set me behind a little, but I thought I'd still be on time."

"Oh, it's okay. Emma came to keep me company," she says, turning the attention back to me. I can't look at either of them. I don't know why he's pretending we don't know each other, yet I'm oddly grateful for it.

"Oh…uhm…yeah," I smile and chew at the inside of my mouth, my face heating up and my legs starting to feel weak. I put my hand flat on the tabletop, knowing it won't do much to keep me from passing out, but maybe it will at least stabilize me long enough for the feeling to pass.

"She was afraid you were going to stand me up," Lindsey blushes.

Andrew chuckles, and I look at my fingers, how they're touching the tabletop, my knuckles turning white. His voice—it's deeper.

"Oh, I always show up when I make a promise to someone. It's kind of a thing with me," he says. That statement—that was for me, and when I glance at him quickly, I feel the burn of it.

"Well, I'll let you two have your night. I've got a couch waiting for me," I say, pulling my purse close around my body and tucking the soiled ends of my sleeve into my hand.

"Thanks, Em," Lindsey calls out as I leave. I wave to the side without turning, but I know they're both watching me leave.

I focus my attention on my feet, my steps, and the stains on my shirt all the way back up to our apartment, and when I get through the door, I rush to the bathroom and throw up.

I slide down to the floor with my back against the wall and tug the towel from the shower bar into my lap, shaking it out to cover my body so I can curl up into the corner. The tears come from a place I never thought I'd see again. All these years, I've always thought of Andrew, but not since those first few months did I cry for him.

I'm not even sure why I'm crying, but every time I convince myself to stop, my breath catches and my lip quivers and I can't hold it together.

He was gone.

Gone!

And now he's here.

After an hour, I manage to calm myself enough to move into my room, to my bed, where I pull my covers up to my chin so I can throw my ruined shirt on the floor. When I squeeze my eyes shut, Andrew is all I see. Sometimes, it's the young version, the innocent one. Other times, it's tonight—the smile, the hard line, his eyes.

My entire body is throbbing with the beat of my heart, and my chest hurts so much I start to count along with every thump.

"Emmmmm? Are you in your room?" Lindsey calls from the doorway. All I can do is leave my arm over my face, blocking my view of anything, while I lie here in bed and pray she's come home alone.

Please have hated him. Please, god. Please, please, please.

"There you are," she says, opening my door completely, but thankfully leaving my light off. "Are you sick?"

"Migraine," I answer. My head hurts like it does when I get them, but this…it's way worse than a migraine. My migraines go away eventually. I fear this is just beginning.

"Oh, damn. You haven't had one of those for a long time. I'm sorry, Em. You need me to get you anything?"

Lindsey is the kindest, sweetest girl I've ever known. She's a true friend, and I'm so lucky that I found her. She's been my rock through pre-med, through mountains of academic stress, through life's growing pains—through my mother's death. And all I can think of is how much I resent her for spending the night getting to know *him.*

"No, I'm okay. Just a little tired. It hit me as soon as I got home," I say, my voice breaking with a cry. I clear my throat to mask it.

"Here, let me get you a washcloth at least," she says, stepping out of my room and into our bathroom. I breathe heavy, trying to clear out everything else while she's gone, and I manage to smile at her when she steps back into my room.

"Thanks," I say as she presses the cool cloth to my forehead. It soothes me some, reminding me that I'm alive, that I'm here where I always wanted to be—reminding me of what's important. I can feel this coldness, and that is a blessing.

"I'm sorry you're sick," she says, and I can sense the girlfriend part of her begging for me. She's happy, and she wants to share.

I slide the rag down to cover my eyes and pinch the bridge of my nose, feeling the force of my grip tighten as I speak.

"Did you have a nice time?" I ask.

Her sigh crushes me. I feel the bed shake as she sits next to me, taking over pressing the cloth on my head, as she shares. "Oh my god, Em. He's like so…gah! I don't even know. He just…he's so fucking sexy!"

She laughs, and I let my mouth smile even though my eyes tear.

"Yes, he's pretty good looking," I swallow, turning from her to roll to my side. When she flinches I hold my hand up. "Just trying a different position, to see if that helps," I say, wanting to hide my face from her, knowing I won't be able to plaster the smile on the entire time.

"He's a hockey player. For Tech? He said he isn't very good, but he gets to play." She sounds so excited when she talks about him. She sounds exactly like I did when I lay in bed next to my mom after skating with Andrew the first time and told her about this cute boy who plays hockey who isn't anything like the neighbor said he was. She sounds so happy.

"That's cool," I manage to eek out.

"I know, isn't it? I'm going to watch him play Friday. They're home. Oh my god, he was just so…so real, you know? Like a normal, real guy," she pauses, pulling her feet up on the bed now and kicking her shoes off. I feel her weight slide down next to me and her arm come up to sweep under her neck on the pillow.

"Yeah…" I start, my eyes fluttering to a close again. "Normal. That's… that's great, Linds."

So terribly, awfully, nightmarishly great.

"You know, it's true what they say," she says through a yawn. I let out a short breath and laugh in response—no clue where she could be taking this conversation. I can't believe this night is happening to me. "You know. About not looking?"

"Sorry, I'm lost," I respond, not able to sound enthused any more. My eyes are staring at the numbers on my clock, watching the dot count seconds, waiting for this to be over.

"The good ones always show up when you stop looking for them," she says, my mind finishing before her words enough to let a single tear slide from my eye to my pillow.

"Yeah," I say, biting my lip and drawing as much air as I can get through my nose. "It's true. They always come…right…when you…stop looking."

"Thanks for losing your license," she says, reaching her hand over to grasp my arm once and give it a squeeze. I want her to leave. I want to be alone. I want to cry.

But I can't do any of that. I'm hell bent on pretending that the past isn't real, just like Andrew. Maybe that's how it hurts him less. And if it works for him, maybe it will work for me, too.

"You're welcome," I whisper, playing the part of a liar. That's what I am, after all—a liar.

Lindsey yawns again, and soon her breathing starts to fall into a regular pattern. She's on her way to dreams, and I'm sure they'll be wonderful. She deserves them, but I'm jealous all the same.

It's nine at night, and we're both usually exhausted. It comes with our schedule, with the amount of extra everything we both put in just to be med students. Lindsey is an amazing friend—an amazing girl.

And she found him.

Maybe...maybe I give him this.

CHAPTER 8

ANDREW

"Kind of an early night for you…for a date night…no?" Trent says to me the second I step through the door. His crap is piled on the counter again. I just laugh this time and ignore it. I'm not in the mood to be pissed off at my friend for no reason. I'm too pissed at myself.

"Yeah, I guess," I shrug, passing through the kitchen and grabbing each of us a beer, then handing him one.

I sit on the opposite end of the couch and kick my feet up on the coffee table. He's watching a bunch of guys debate on ESPN over the latest drug scandal in baseball. Actually, right now he's watching me. I can see his face pointed in my direction, his bottle tipping my way so his eyes stay on me. He's waiting for me to open up. Trent…he's a *feelings* kind of guy. We are one of those sets of opposite-types of friends—his feelings are complimented by my complete lack there of.

"License girl not what you expect?"

I keep my breathing normal, stifling my desire to huff and sigh. I shake my head as if I didn't hear him. "Huh, sorry. Was lost in the show," I say.

There's a commercial on right now, and he looks at me in a way that says *bullshit.*

"License girl?" he asks again, shit-eating grin and all. He senses there's something off with me about this.

I shrug and turn my attention forward again, taking a short drink from my beer. "It was her roommate I went out with. She's the one that answered the door the other day. She's cute. Just…I don't know," I let the rest of my words linger, never finishing.

We watch about ten more minutes of TV. The entire time, all I see are Emma's eyes—her goddamned heartbreaking eyes.

I don't know what I expected, how I thought any of this would go. I know I wasn't expecting to see her though, and maybe that was stupid. It's clear that Lindsey is her best friend. And unless I planned on ditching Lindsey and never calling her again, changing my number and avoiding her at all costs, there wasn't much of a chance that I would never see Emma.

I knew it was her the second I stepped into the restaurant. Her hair color is unmistakable. I'm sure to anyone else, there's nothing about it that's unique or rare. But I can see it. It's familiar. It's part of me.

I know how it feels in my hands.

My first reaction was anger. That's what urged me forward. Something inside got excited at the idea of messing with her, making her feel uncomfortable and out of place. Fuck—if I'm being honest with myself, I *wanted* to see her cry.

And then she looked at me.

I didn't want to make her cry any more. But it was there. She looked sick, and shocked. And the next ten minutes were this pendulum of hate and pity, and I wanted to punish her and save her at the same time. I'm still swaying now.

"Dude, what are these?" Trent gets my attention from the kitchen. I stand up to see him lifting the lid off the cookies.

"Oh, yeah. The chick whose license it was made me cookies. I had one; they're good. Go ahead," I say, walking toward him.

Of course she made cookies. And then I made the cookies into something sinister. I taunted her, twisted the guilt knife I imagined in her gut, and it felt good and terrible all at once. I couldn't stop, though. I just couldn't stop.

"Oh shit, these are good," Trent says, inhaling the rest of the cookie he started and picking up another one. "Oh…hey. I think there's a note in here for you," he adds, crumbs falling from his mouth as he chews and slips a paper from the edge of the tin and begins to open it.

My chest seizes a little, and I reach for it quickly, taking the folded paper from his hand. He looks at me like I'm crazy for a second, but rolls his eyes eventually and just gives over to his second cookie. I unfold it and hold it in my hand in such a way that he can't read it. Trent knows the name Emma. He doesn't know she's *the* girl, but he knows she's one I don't care to see again. Apparently, I got really lit one night at a team party and made up an entire rap about her. It wasn't flattering. Trent isn't stupid, and I know he'd put this moment and that one together quickly. I don't want to have to lie and say it's just a coincidence—so I graze over the words without really reading then shove the note into my pocket.

"What'd it say?"

Nosey fucker.

"Just thanks, you saved me, you're my hero, I want you, take me…" I make a joke out of it, and Trent flips me off then grabs another cookie.

"You going to study hall tomorrow?" he asks, and I'm unusually grateful for the change in subject—even if the new subject is also a pain in my ass. Part of being in the university's athletics department is making mandatory grade checks. It's never a problem for me, but everyone has to log so many hours a week at the study room near the athletic department whether they really need to go or not. I'm always making up my hours at the last minute, and I'm five behind for the month.

I sigh in response, looking up at the ceiling before leveling my gaze back at my friend.

"Dude, don't take it out on me. It's not my fault you're smart and don't need to sit in a library with the rest of us dumbshits," he says. "You better go tomorrow though. You know they're checking hours before the game Friday."

"Yeah, yeah. I'll go," I say over my shoulder. I leave Trent with the rest of the cookies and shut my bedroom door behind me. I pull Emma's note from my pocket the second I'm alone, sitting on my bed and flattening out the paper against my leg. She wrote a lot. Maybe it's a lot. I wouldn't know —this would be the first letter I've ever gotten from her.

Dear Drew,
Thank you for being the kind of guy who pays attention to lost things. You have no idea the trouble you saved me. I made you these cookies because they're my favorite. It was the least I could do. I'm glad you met Lindsey. She's a great girl, and I think you'll like her a lot (do not tell her I said that ;-))
Anyhow. Really, thank you again. I think that's the nicest thing anyone has ever done for me—and here I was a complete stranger.
Enjoy the cookies.
~ Emma

I read the letter six times, each time flipping it over, expecting more, expecting…I don't know…a joke maybe? What the fuck? This…*this* is the nicest thing anyone's ever done for her? A complete stranger?

After my last read, I crumple the note and throw it on my desk, then grab my jacket and keys. I pace a few times, my hand twitching and wanting to hit something, my body craving adrenaline. By the time I step from my room, I must look like an amped up bull given the way Trent reacts to me.

"What the hell's wrong with you?" he asks, sitting up a little straighter on the sofa, squaring his legs as if he's considering tackling me or holding me down.

"Nothing, just…just some shit I found out," I say, not wanting to give him more.

"Owen? Your ma?" he asks, one eyebrow up. Trent hears me argue with my mom over not visiting enough, over making sure I'm following rules, driving safe—she and I argue over everything. She thinks I'm a fuck up and that I'm going to blow it now that I've climbed back this far. And Owen just calls to echo everything she says. I take a deep breath and remind myself to act rational.

"Sort of," I say, simultaneously thinking of the number of lies I've told my friend in the last two days. I'll never be able to keep up, so I stick with half answers that never satisfy, but at least aren't totally wrong.

"Wanna go shoot some pool?" Trent asks. I don't make eye contact and do my best to think if that would help. What I'd really like to do is find Pitch Black and go a few rounds with him, but Harley usually likes to schedule fights on Wednesdays, so I'm pretty sure the gym is closed.

I grip the back of my neck and stare at Trent's feet for a beat before nodding. He doesn't pause at all, just moves to the door, leaving the TV on in the room behind us. He slips on his shoes and the sweatshirt he left hanging on the back of a nearby stool. He locks up as I start down the walkway to the main road.

We live on the first floor of a two-story building. No need for elevators. No doorman greeting me as I come and go. No one doing amazingly nice things for me that would make me want to bake them cookies. I fume over the words in Emma's note the entire way, sometimes talking to myself. Trent can sense I'm pissed, so he doesn't question me. He's used to seeing me get worked up over a bad game or a weekend with my mom and stepdad. Usually, I'm frustrated at having to defend myself, prove that I've grown up. The only sound he makes tonight is the occasional huff of breath in his hands to keep them warm. Winter is coming in Northern Illinois.

Majerle's is warm, and I don't waste any time ordering up two shots of Jack and commandeering a pool table in the back corner. This is a common scene for Trent and me—honestly, this is what we do for dinner most nights during the off-season. Trent is easy going, and I like to look for trouble. He keeps me in line—usually—and Majerle's accommodates us both nicely. I rack quickly and toss a stick to Trent. He grabs it in the air.

"I'll break," I say, positioning myself and bending forward to line up my stick without waiting to hear his answer.

"Do you have to be a bossy fuck, too?"

I lean forward with my hands on the edge of the table, my stick leaning against it too, between my palms. I've gotten myself so worked up that I've lost sight of reason—and being reasonable. I let my head sling forward more as I exhale, then tilt my head up to look at my friend leaning against the wall across from me.

"Sorry," I sigh.

"You know you're miserable when you get like this?" He picks up the white ball in front of me, tossing it in his hand a few times before motioning for me to step to the side.

"I know," I say, taking two steps back.

"Okay, as long as you know," he says, leaving his eyes on mine for a few seconds, like he's waiting to see if I'll explode some more or actually calm the fuck down this time. I hold up a thumb and nod, mouthing *I'm good.*

"You wanna tell me what this is all about?" he says, leaning forward and lining up his break. He slides his stick twice before sending balls in all directions on the table, sinking both a stripe and a solid. He works his second shot, sinking a solid again. "You're stripes."

Our waitress drops off two shots, and I take mine fast, setting the glass back on her tray before she's more than a step away. I hold up my fingers for two more, and Trent tells her to make it only one.

"Pussy," I call him.

"I have a test in the morning. And then we're going to the tutoring lab. You show up hung over, and I guarantee you that'll be worse than telling coach you're two hours short on your time," Trent says.

I keep my eyes level with his, reach for his shot on the tray, and drink it.

"Two more," I tell the girl. She smiles at me uncomfortably and heads back to the bar.

"Fuck," Trent breathes, shaking his head in disappointment.

I sit back on my stool while he works most of his balls from the table, missing with only two left. I take over and sink three before missing—just in time for my next two shots to arrive. Trent reaches for one of them.

"Hey, hands off, bitch!" I say, smacking the top of his hand. He flips me off and drinks it down, leaving me with only one to grab and follow suit. "Two more!" I shout, holding up two fingers.

"What are you doing?"

"Drinking." I don't look at him, instead circling the table like an animal.

Nicest thing anyone has ever done for me.

Is she fucking serious? I bet someone lent her a penny once when she was short. Is that guy higher on the list, too? I guess I shouldn't complain, at least she thanked me for returning her missing ID.

Emma wouldn't have had to go to a place like Lake Crest.

"Are you going to shoot or what?" Trent asks. I'm irritating him. Good. Melissa, our waitress—whose name I got from the nametag pressed against her tits—has brought more Jack. I think I'll drink these two first.

I grip the first glass between my finger and thumb. Trent takes my stick from my hand when I do.

"Andrew," he says, leveling me with the kind of look I should only get from my father. If I had one. I have Dwayne. Fuck Dwayne. And fuck Owen.

I push his chest so hard he stumbles backward, knocking over one of the high-top tables. The bar isn't crowded, but the dozen or so people around us get quiet, and one of the security guys walks over.

"It's fine," I say, raising my hand up. "Go on, get back to the front door with your stupid tight black T-shirt and flashlight, like that really helps you spot fake IDs."

Trent's face falls into a look of disgust, and he sighs, shaking his head and tossing both of our sticks on the pool table before walking away.

"Come on," the bouncer says, his arms folded in front of his body as he steps into my personal space. "You're done for the night, kid."

I hate being called *kid*. I haven't been a kid in years, since I ran after an ice cream truck with a crumpled dollar bill. I spit on the floor, and for a brief second, I consider taking a swing at him. Luckily, I'm not drunk enough for that yet. This place—it's my favorite bar. Trent and I come here after games and tough practices. I'd hate myself more than I already do if I fucked that up, too.

"Yeah, yeah," I say, pulling my beanie from my back pocket and sliding it on my head. I toss two twenties on the pool table, then shove my hands into my jacket pockets when I leave, stopping a few steps from the bar's front door. Trent didn't wait for me; he's already a block away. I let him go, because if I caught up with him I'd only keep being an asshole, and he didn't do anything wrong.

He's right. I don't know what I'm doing. I'm lost. I was barely with it before, but then I saw her. Now I'm done.

I lean to the side and spit again before looking up into the eyes of the dickhead who kicked me out. I thrust my chest toward him, juking him with my arms out wide. He doesn't flinch.

"Fuck this place," I say…to no one.

I walk the long way home, circling through campus, by the lake. A few students are out running, and others are walking quickly from the library in the center of campus out to cars or to their dorms. I bet they're walking fast because they're afraid of me. I pause at a bench that's shadowed by the only tree around that seems to still have its leaves. I sit down and pull my phone out to check the time. I notice a few texts from Owen.

Are you making it to mom's and Dwayne's for dinner Sunday?

He sent it only a few minutes ago, so I respond.

Yeah. I'll be there.

I don't want to go. But I don't want to hear the mountain of shit I'll get for not going more. He writes back a minute later.

Good. Mom's really freaking out because Kens and I are going to Germany. Try not to be an asshole, K?

Yep.

I lean my head forward into my hand, my arm rested on my knee. Owen and his girlfriend are spending a year in Germany thanks to some offer my brother got to play basketball there. His girlfriend Kensi plays…like…a dozen instruments or something. She got into some master's program over there to study with the national symphony. They've lived together in the city since graduation—Owen coaches at some prep school and Kens plays in an orchestra. I think they'll probably end up getting married, which is good because I like Kensi; she's good to my brother and my mom. Better than I am.

Kensi visited me at Lake Crest. I can't even count how many times she came to see me—sometimes with Owen, sometimes on her own. When I got in my first fight there, she was the one I called. I was beaten by a guy twice my size and two years older than me. He was in Lake Crest for committing armed robbery; he drove the getaway car. When he asked me to write his term paper for recent American history, I said *no*. So he fucked me up when I rounded the corner after my shower in gym. My eye was swollen shut, and he cut me on my cheek and arm with a knife he wasn't supposed to have, but no one dared take away from him. I called Kensi so she'd come up with an excuse to keep my mom away for an extra week. She did.

Kensi made a lot of excuses for me.

That right there—that small thing that the girl, who will probably marry my brother, did for me, no questions asked—is *the nicest thing anyone's ever done for me.* Kensi wrote to me, too. She sent me clips from the college paper on Owen's games, and she took pictures and printed them out to make collages of things I missed—my car, my old house, the rink.

I gave up a year and a future, and Emma Burke couldn't be bothered to stamp a goddamned envelope.

Pulling my phone from my pocket, I scroll to the string of texts between Lindsey and me, and I send her one more.

Can't wait for Friday. Can I see you tomorrow? I'll come over. Oh, and don't tell your roommate, but her cookies made me sick. Had to throw them out.

Standing from the bench, I push my phone back into my pocket and stuff my hands into my jacket, walking back to my apartment feeling entitled to lots of things. First on that list is Emma Burke's roommate.

And I intend to have her.

* * *

EMMA

I didn't sleep.

Lindsey did.

She slept right through the sound of her phone buzzing on the bed between us. She'd brought it in with her, never stopping in her happiness to leave things in the kitchen or her room. She came to take care of me, then left her phone there as she fell asleep. I know she didn't do it on purpose; she doesn't have a clue about any of it at all, about who Drew *really* is. But it still all feels so carefully played, as if she's working with him to make sure just the right everything finds my ears and eyes and insides.

...her cookies made me sick.

My body ached reading those words. They weren't for me, but yet... they have to be for me. I lay there and thought about the way he looked at me—and the way he looked.

I let Lindsey stay asleep in my bed. Sneaking out of my room to the shower, I slip into my workout clothes so I could head to the gym before my morning class. I packed a bag with everything I thought I'd need, the plan to stay away until I heard from Lindsey about a date—that he'd come, and they'd both be gone.

But that text never came. Not a word. Nothing—not even an excited text from my friend about how he wants to see her now, because he just can't wait.

I fought the urge to text her leading questions that would prompt answers about Andrew. We only shared labs on Mondays and Wednesdays, so I was on my own today, which made it harder to stretch things like lunch and studying into taking longer than they really needed to. By the time the sun was down, I was exhausted, running on maybe an hour of sleep in total. If they were going out, they'd be gone by now, and Lindsey would have let me know.

My backpack loaded down, I drag my tired legs to our apartment building, through the lobby, and to the elevator where I'm so exhausted I drop my bag from my shoulders during the ride and drag it along the floor as I exit and walk to our door.

It's a weird season here now—not quite the snowy winter I've grown to love, but not warm enough to wear single layers. Every hallway and classroom is pumped with heat, though, which makes me sticky and uncomfortable by the end of the day. I've hit my limit for today.

I listen before putting my key in the lock. It's quiet, which makes me think that maybe Lindsey left without telling me. My mind runs away with this thought, jumping to the conclusion that Andrew mentioned how he knows me—and my friend didn't want to hurt my feelings, so of course now they're off somewhere both talking about how they need to keep this a secret from me. I let these thoughts dance in my head until I open the door and see the both of them laughing, throwing strings of pasta at each other in our kitchen. Confronted with what's real, I actually wish the daydream in my head from seconds before were the truth. At least then, I wouldn't *really* know and see it all.

I'm too noisy, and they both turn to look at me, my clothes disheveled from being stuffed in my bag for the morning, my hair limp and stringy from my rushed shower, my back sweaty from carrying my heavy bag all day. Lindsey covers her mouth, hiding her giggle from whatever they were doing before—whatever was funny—but finally lets it go, laughing without abandon as she walks closer to me.

Andrew isn't laughing at all. She doesn't notice he's stopped. He's behind her, and all he's doing is staring.

"There you are!" she says, rushing at me with a spoon. "Here! Oh my god, taste this."

There's a red sauce in her spoon, but I look at it as if it's poison, my eyes flitting to Andrew for a second, but looking back to the spoon because he's still looking at me, not smiling, and if it is poison, I think it's still my better option.

"What…is it?" I ask, pulling my bag back up to my shoulder and adjusting the weight of it.

"It's marinara. Drew made it, and it's so freakin' good. You have to try." She holds the spoon to my lips, and I lean forward, letting her feed me like a child, my eyes glancing to Andrew—*Drew*—as I taste it. His mouth tugs up on one corner into a smirk, and I can't help but hear his voice in my head.

Her cookies made me sick.

"It's good," I say, my eyes on him the entire time. It's delicious, but *good* is polite. It won't make me sick, and it won't make me well. It's just a taste that somehow feels very much like the boy I knew…know.

"Made it from scratch," he smirks. Lindsey joins him in the kitchen again, and he takes the spoon back from her, but his gaze lingers on me. "Dinner's served in ten minutes," he adds, waiting for me to react. My stomach sinks.

I was gone the entire day. My body hurts, and all I want is a hot shower. I wanted to miss this, yet somehow, I timed it just right.

"Oh…it's okay, I'm not that hungry," I say, looking down to my feet. His stare—it hurts. And he won't stop.

"You sure? We made plenty. We didn't want to leave you out," he adds, turning back to tend to the stove. Lindsey's looking up at him with stars, hearts, and probably rainbow unicorns in her eyes; it makes my breath feel heavy.

"I'm sure, but…thank you," I say. His arm stops moving, no longer stirring the noodles in the water. Lindsey steps away, carrying a pile of bowls and plates to the small kitchen table by our window, and the second she leaves the room, he turns to face me, the mask gone.

"You're welcome, Emma," he says, his mouth a hard, flat line and his eyes cloudy with what I'm pretty sure is regret.

We stand in our little pocket of silence with our eyes locked for a few seconds, and it's like he's memorizing parts of me he's forgotten while I'm counting how many parts of him have changed—nearly all of him has as far as I can tell.

"Please join us," Lindsey startles me, her hands wrapping around my bicep. I jump, and she laughs. "Sorry. Really, though, I was about to text you to tell you he was here, and we made dinner. It'll be fun. We usually eat sandwiches or microwave meals, Drew. This is a big night out for Em and me. Ha...and we didn't even go out."

I manage to keep my attention on her, even though I can see Andrew standing in the same place behind her, his eyes never once leaving their hold on me.

"Please?" she begs, making tiny jumps on her toes as she slides her grip down to my fingertips. This is how a toddler begs for a toy. It's effective.

I breathe in slowly through my nose and nod a few times.

"Sure. I just need a minute," I say. I need several minutes. I need hours, maybe days. But minutes are better than nothing.

I carry my bag to my room and fall into my bed, crawling up to the pillow and pushing my face into the folds of the material. All I want is to stay here. I indulge in the coolness of my bed for a full minute, breathing in and out until I convince myself my anxiety isn't going anywhere.

I sit up and look at my reflection in the mirror above my dresser, my hair now knotted in twists and tufts around my head. Leaning forward, I grab my brush, holding my hair near the base of my head and tugging it through the long strands until I look a little less wild.

I kick off my old clothes, putting on a clean pair of jeans and the purple sweatshirt slung over the end of my bed—throwing it over my head without even thinking until I step back out into the living room and Andrew's eyes fall on me, registering the familiar shirt. His expression tells me he recalls the memory that goes along with it. I usually think of it, too. And I don't know why I didn't tonight. Maybe, my mind wanted to fool me into wearing it just to spite me, my subconscious in cahoots with the boy who built up the memory in the first place. I wore this sweatshirt when Andrew taught me how to ice-skate. It was new then, and I've thought about throwing it away or donating it so many times since. I could never seem to part with it, though.

"You look nice in purple," he says, stepping closer to me on his way to the dining area, his voice low enough Lindsey doesn't hear as she finishes setting the table for our awkward dinner-for-three. He doesn't linger, and he doesn't look at me, not directly anyhow. His eyes hover along my shoulder, tracing a line down to my fingertips, to my hand—the one he held when I was sixteen and unsteady on my feet.

When we were young, and nothing bad had happened.

My fingers tingle as a short burst of adrenaline runs through my body, and I flex my hand wanting to force the feeling away. I remind myself to breathe, repeating a mini version of my useless calming exercise from earlier, and I follow Andrew to the table, noticing his hand down along his side, flexing just as mine did.

Our table is a circle, a small one, the space not made for anything large, meaning we're all technically sitting next to one another. I wish it were bigger. If it was, there would be more too look at. I hyper-focus on my spoonful of noodles, on the sauce I drizzle from the hot pan over them, on the salad I put in the bowl—I spend as many minutes as I can making my plate perfect, ignoring the laughter and banter between Lindsey and Andrew.

"Here, you didn't get enough," Andrew says to me after everyone's plate is full. He stands, and my eyes catch the frame of his body, the tight gray shirt he's wearing, how it clings to his waist, his stomach and the expanse of his chest underneath the thin fabric. I look up to see him watch me take him in, and his cheek dimples as he raises the corner of his lips, careful to keep his attention on my plate the rest of the time.

"Thank you," I say, and he chuckles.

"You're still welcome," he says, this time a little bite to his tone.

I drag my fork through the noodles, wrapping them around the prongs and lean forward to take my bites, doing my best to become small. I'm taking mental measurements of the amount of food on my plate, cross-referencing it with the amount of time it's taking me to swallow each and every forkful, and I grow discouraged. I feel like a child with a bowl of broccoli—no dog to feed it to.

"Oh, you missed it earlier, Em. I was telling Andrew about how we met —me and you?" I choke when Lindsey speaks, reaching for my glass of water while I wave them both off that I'm fine.

I'm fine—only that I met Lindsey in perhaps the worst way possible for this very moment. We met at driving school. It was the summer before our freshman year. I had run a red light near campus, trying to make it to the admissions office before a deadline. When the officer pulled me over, I had a panic attack—to the point that he had to help me lie down on the side of the road so I didn't collapse and crack open my head. He still gave me a ticket. Just the flash of his lights brought so many feelings back, but I never told Lindsey that. And I don't think Andrew's interested in that part now.

Lindsey was in my class for blowing a stop sign. We were the only two people in the class under fifty, and when we both found out we were going to Tech and would be freshmen pre-med, we decided to room together.

"Lemons out of lemonade," Lindsey said at the time.

It goes down like venom now.

"Yeah, Linds tells me you're quite the speed demon," Andrew says through a mouthful of food. He's remaining aloof, but I know better. I can see the truth in his eyes.

I open my mouth, partly to defend myself, and partly to explain, but the way he pauses—leaning with one arm along the back of his chair and his body to the side, so he can hold me hostage with the look on his face—makes me forget the words to say. Not that I had the right words ready. I don't. I never have.

"Hey, I didn't say that," Lindsey says, the laughter escaping her teasingly and sweet as she swats at his thigh with her hand. He catches it and holds it, his lips curling into a grin as he brings her hand up to his face so he can kiss the knuckles, his gaze shifting to me as he lowers her hand back down, never letting go.

I look down at my plate, admonished. I'm struck with an overwhelming sense of shame, but it's more than that, too. I'm hurt, and I'm jealous, and I don't understand what any of this is about. Why are we keeping our history a secret? Why am I allowing it?

"So, Lindsey says you two have lived together for three years now. And you're both...med students?" he asks.

I find myself spending too much time studying him, trying to find the next double meaning so I can be prepared for it. But he doesn't look up again, instead, going back to his dinner plate.

"She's my best friend," I say, smiling at her quickly, genuinely, but returning my attention back to the table in front of me. I don't know why those are the words I say. There's a part of me that wants to make sure he realizes what he's messing with, I guess—that he's being personal. Lindsey is personal.

"Med school is so hard, and it takes so long. It's just kind of nice to have someone by your side who gets it," Lindsey says. I smile at her again, catching Andrew's eyes as I look away. It's like he never really stops watching me.

"You two should open your own practice when you're done," he says, pushing his plate a few inches forward. He's done eating, I guess, though his plate is still full.

"I wish," Lindsey says, picking up a tomato from her salad with her fingers and popping it in her mouth. "But Emma here is all about cardio-thoracic. She was hand-picked by the goddess of surgery herself."

"Linds," I say, my eyes begging her to stop from saying too much. Why I got into Tech, why I'm studying here with Miranda Wheaton, is a story I don't really want getting around. My being here looks like pity to the outsider—a lot of things in my life look like pity and charity. But it's not. I earned my spot here just like every other student.

But Andrew won't see it that way. He'll see it as selfish. He'll see it as selfish because he'll put it all together, see how it fits with that night and what I let him do for me. And then, quite possibly, he'll hate me even more.

Andrew grows quiet, his eyes studying both of us as we have our silent exchange. I can tell he's unsatisfied. To punctuate things, he pulls his hand—the one holding Lindsey's—up to rest on the tabletop, putting on a show of his fingers caressing against hers, his thumb teasing along the top of her hand and then around her wrist. I hate that I'm looking at it, but I can't look away.

I'm weak.

"So you're gonna be a surgeon, huh?"

The way he says it, it's both innocent and dripping with contempt all at once. I smile despite him, and nod *yes*. But my lips can't hold their form for long. I feel his leg slide forward, and I wish for it to be a coincidence, hoping he just doesn't realize how close he is to me. I say it isn't so over and over in my head until his foot comes to rest against the outside of mine, his shoe perfectly matched against my bare foot, my toes recoiling as he taps against them twice, a gentle reminder—a threat.

I back away from the table abruptly, my hands gripping the front of the table hard. Realizing how crazy I look, I tap the tabletop twice and grin at my friend before forcing a pleasant look to remain on my face as I answer Andrew's question.

"I am," I say, standing and pulling my plate into my arms. The food is delicious, but I wasn't hungry when I walked in; I'm certainly not hungry now.

"Is that so you can cut people's hearts out?"

My back is to him when he speaks, and I'm so glad, because I wouldn't be able to hide my reaction to his words. Lindsey has already interrupted, telling him he's being gross. She's laughing, and he laughs with her, apologizing for being graphic. He's playing along with her, like the words he said were just for morbid shock value. And they were—just not for the reason Lindsey thinks. I keep moving forward, one foot in front of the next as the tear falls down my cheek, thinning as it reaches my chin. I lean my head to the side, rubbing it dry along my shoulder.

"I'm still not feeling well, Linds. If it's all right with you, I'm going to lie down for a while," I say from the kitchen, pulling a sheet of foil from a drawer and covering my plate with no intention of eating it later. Two of my favorite things now ruined—pasta and oatmeal cookies.

"Okay," she says between flirtatious whispers and laughter.

I tuck my dish inside the fridge and walk to my room, closing the door behind me, and letting my hand rest on the handle—feeling like I need to hold it to keep the bad stuff out like they do in those zombie movies. After a few seconds, I loosen my grip and backpedal until my legs hit the edge of my bed, forcing me to sit.

I pull my sleeves low into my palm with my thumbs looped on the inside and bring my fists to my face, inhaling the fabric, searching for any trace of a scent from years ago. I know it's futile. I know it's gone; he's gone. I sent him away.

Another tear is threatening to come, so I run my sleeve along my eyes, wiping what's left away with my thumb. I move my thumb over my skin twice, imagining it's Andrew's thumb the second time. I bring my hands to my lap, and lock my fingers together, imagining one is his, before closing my eyes with a single laugh of pain. My hands look nothing like his and Lindsey's, and I'm being foolish.

The sound of the television comes on soon, and I pull my biology book into my lap as I scoot all the way to the back of my bed, sliding my laptop out to review our lab assignment in the morning. I read the same page for an hour, listening for clues on the other side of the door. I've kept the earbuds in my ears the entire time, never once playing any music. When Lindsey raps on my door and opens it, I fake startle, pulling them from my head as if I've been listening to music the entire time.

"Drew go home?" I ask quickly, realizing how anxious I sound about it, so I start to busy myself with papers and my backpack and my computer screen angle.

"Uhm…" Lindsey says.

I know.

I keep my eyes down so she can't see the truth, but I let my sigh fall out in a heavy breath.

"I asked him to stay…but he's such a gentleman, he wanted me to make sure it was okay with you," she says.

My body jerks with a slight laugh. Shaking my head, I lift my gaze to her as I swallow.

"What's that look for?" she asks.

I have a look. Of course I have a look. Why is he doing this?

"Emma Brooklyn Burke, I'm a grown woman; if I want to sleep with a guy after the second date, then I'm going to," she says, stepping to my door, gripping the side of it as she turns to face me. "I'll tell him you said it's fine."

She glares at me as she shuts it behind her hard.

Time stops for a full minute. I don't blink. I don't breathe. There isn't a sound to be heard, until the familiar click of her bedroom door across from mine.

I kick my things from my bed and let out a battle of grunts I try to keep quiet—my papers, computer, pens, and notecards all scattering around the foot of my bed into a mess below. The sensation doesn't satisfy me, so I rip my blankets away too, crawling up on my knees as my fists grab at the sheets, pillows, and mattress pad, tearing the corner as I yank so hard it pulls up the corner of my mattress.

I wad everything into a ball and push it on top of my papers, leaving me in the center of my empty bed, breathing hard and numb, not knowing how to feel. I feel angry—angry with Andrew, and angry that I feel anything at all.

He left. He's the one who left.

And now he's here. And he's gone. The boy he was…he's gone.

I scramble to my feet, cramming my papers and computer back into my bag, shoving and kicking my pile of blankets out of the way. Stuffing my feet into my shoes, I pull the purple sweatshirt from my body, switching it out for a Tech one hanging on a hook behind my door. I grab my headphones, keys, and phone, then grab the purple sweatshirt and carry it with me out the door, pausing in the kitchen to step on the trash lever and throw the fucking sweatshirt away.

I let the main door slam closed behind me, locking up with a hard twist of my wrist as I bang my bag against the hallway wall on my way to the elevator. When I get outside, I look up and see a light still on in Lindsey's window. After a few seconds, it goes out.

And all of my breath escapes me.

CHAPTER 9

ANDREW HARPER, AGE 16

Dear Emma,

I'm losing myself. For the first two months, I swore that wouldn't happen. I said it every night before sleep; I woke up reminding myself of who I was.

I haven't done that in days now...maybe weeks.

I'm letting go, whether I want to or not. I don't care, and that scares me a little. Not caring? It's liberating. It's lonely.

There's a guy here; he's 18. His name's Kingston, but most of the "students" here call him King. They say he was in some gang or something; that he used to sell drugs. He has tats all over his fingers and the rumor is he drove a getaway car for his older brother during some armed robbery over in Rockford. I'm not sure if he was really all that tough before he showed up here, but he sort of took the lead. A lot of the other guys let him. They buy the stories—his self-made hype.

He doesn't like me.

I don't like him.

Apparently, he's not used to people telling him no. I tell him no a lot. Last week, when I told him no, he snuck into my room at night and put a pillow over my face. He's pulled shit with me before, tripping me at lunch and sucker punching me around corners. This time, though...I was ready. I stabbed him with a pen, dug it into his side and held it there. I thought that'd make him stop right away. But he just pushed the pillow into my face harder. The harder I fought, the stronger he was. And for a moment, I was losing.

I almost gave in. Just...let him take me. But something made me keep fighting.

I struggled enough to wake someone across the hall, and then the guard set the alarms off and another person pulled him from me. I lost my phone privileges for an extra month for stabbing him. I got extra therapy sessions too, to talk about my aggression. Fucker tried to kill me; pretty sure aggression was the only way to go with that.

King got a trip to the emergency room and an overnight at the hospital. Funny thing, it was phone day today, and I saw him making his calls. I guess a pen weighs more than a pillow in this fucked-up court of justice I'm stuck in.

I hate them all. They pretend like they're teaching us lessons, reforming us to become better men. We go to these sermons, and there's an old man who gives us these long stories that we're supposed to identify with and recognize our weaknesses so we can improve. Nobody listens. I tried to last week, but the longer he spoke, the more I focused on the lack of passion in his voice, the way he really didn't care if he made a difference, or if we changed—just as long as he got a paycheck.

I looked around at the room of these forgotten kids. That's why we're here, because we're still kids according to the state. Worth saving. Our offenses forgivable. I was a better person three months ago, before I got here. Whatever I am now, I'm not so sure it's good.

I've had a few fights. Nobody knows except my brother's girlfriend. She knows. She visits. She convinced everyone that she's family. She threw around stories about my grandfather. Everyone bought it. I like it when Kensi comes. Sometimes we just sit without talking. It's nice. And when I have things I need to hide, like bruises or...other things...Kensi helps. She doesn't like it; I can tell. But she understands.

I think she tells Owen. But I also don't think she tells him exactly how bad it is. I begged her not to.

My family can't see me this way. They won't like what I am becoming.

At first, the fights came out of nowhere—guys who have been here for months, or almost a year for some, would just kick me and beat the shit out of me to prove they could. The longer I've been here, the less initiating I get.

Thing is, though...the fights...they give me something to do. I've started instigating. I don't mean to, and every night, I tell myself I'm going to stop. But I can't. I don't do it without cause, really. Usually, someone newer than me is getting picked on, so I open my mouth and say shit to get people to stop. And when they turn their attention to me, every other thought and feeling I have goes away. It's nothing but fighting for survival in this place.

I guess I'm surviving.

When I fight, I forget about you. I didn't want to tell you that part, but now that I've written it...I think I'll leave it.

I hope you'll write back.

Andrew

CHAPTER 10

EMMA

"Are you *sure* you can't come…just for the first period. Look…see what I just did there? I called it a period. I'm learning my hockey lingo," Lindsey says, holding her fist out for me to pound. I do it slowly, my lips in a tight smile as we touch. This faking and pretending thing…I'm not sure how long I can keep it up.

"Yeah, they should totally let you in the booth to call the game," I tease, pushing myself to be light and funny despite how sick I really feel. She scrunches her face at me as she continues putting on her boots and wrapping her knit scarf around her neck. I haven't been able to make eye contact with her for longer than a few seconds at a time. Lindsey and I have never been big on swapping stories about our intimate moments. She's only slept with a few guys, and my list is still at *zero,* so I guess there isn't much to share. I hope we don't start with this one.

"Very funny," she says with a grunt as she finally gets her boot snug on her foot. "Seriously, though…I'm going to be sitting there alone. Can't you come for…like…just a little bit?"

I could come. I have some time before Miranda's presentation. But I managed to hide myself in the library on campus until the morning, and I snuck in here at five, exhausted enough that I didn't have to hear Andrew leave for his place. I know he was still here when I came home, because his wallet and keys were on the counter when I came in. I touched them. I wanted to flip his wallet open, look at it. But I didn't. I can't actively go see him play hockey—not now that I've done such a bang-up job of avoiding his face for almost a full afternoon. And seeing him on the ice? I just…I can't do that. I wouldn't be able to pretend anymore.

"I'm just really stressed. I'm introducing her, and they want the usual speech—you know…about *me?* Anyway, I really want to get there early. I'm so sorry; don't hate me," I say, biting my lip, my inner voice begging her not to guilt me anymore. I can't handle any more guilt.

"I get it," she sighs. I sigh in response when I turn away from her, about eleven hundred tons of pressure fleeing my shoulders all at once. "At least…tell me, how do I look?"

"You look nice," I smile at her, taking her full outfit in. She's dressed like she's ready for a ski trip. It's not *that* cold at the rink. But I don't want to burst her bubble. And there's probably also a part of me that likes that she won't have to borrow something warm from Andrew.

When Andrew left, I sort of got into hockey—Blackhawks mostly. My dad had always been a fan and was thrilled, and we went to a lot of games. I learned the basics from watching, and my dad taught me the nuances. It was our thing, even though I went in the beginning because it reminded me of Andrew. When my mom got sick, we had to put a stop to our trips. Neither of us ever wanted to leave her home alone for long—her body was weak, and the chemo…it wasn't working. I think we knew it wasn't working long before a doctor told us. We didn't want to miss any time with her, certainly not so we could sit in nosebleed seats at the United Center.

I haven't been back to a game since. It just doesn't feel right going without my dad. And I don't think going anywhere but to work and home feels right to him. She's been gone for two years, but it still feels like yesterday we put her in the ground and said *goodbye*.

I move to the kitchen while Lindsey finishes getting ready. There's a dinner being served at the presentation tonight. It's fish—salmon—which I guess most people think is delicious. It makes me gag. I pull the peanut butter from our cupboard, scraping it empty so I can overload a slice of bread to tide me over until the presentation's done. I flip open the trash lid to throw the jar away, then go back to spreading the peanut butter when a flash hits me; I flip the lid up again with my pinky finger. No purple. The trash is halfway full. I know it hasn't been taken out.

No purple.

I drop the knife and wipe my hands on a towel, then completely lift the lid, kicking the side of the can to move debris around just enough that I can see if my sweatshirt is buried.

It's not.

"Hey…uhm…Linds?" I call for my friend, prepping myself to ask her if she's seen my sweatshirt—if she's the one who saved it from the county dump or if *someone else* did—when I march by the front door and do a double take at the clothes hanging from the hooks nearby. Her jacket. My jacket from last night, which I know I hung there without seeing anything else. But this afternoon…there *is* something else. My sweatshirt is hung on the last hook.

I pull it free and smell it, noticing it doesn't smell like it's spent the night in the trash. It also doesn't smell like Andrew.

"Yeah?" Lindsey answers behind me. I grip my sweatshirt and take a quick breath before I turn to face her.

"My sweatshirt…" I start, waiting to see if she has a reaction to it, like an *oh yeah, I saved it for you* kind of reaction. She doesn't, which means…

"You know, I heard Andrew say he liked purple. He mentioned it—that it's a nice color—when I wore this. You should wear it," I say, the words just coming out one after the next before that little gatekeeper in my head has time to tell me to stop it, because this is a really bad idea. And it's mean. I'm using Lindsey.

She smiles and takes my sweatshirt into her hands, and my insides rush with conflict. She's taken it, though, so I walk the line on the other side—the one that's not being nice—and keep going.

"You know, I always loved this one. You should wear it more," she says, carrying it back to her room.

I love it too. That's why I wore it the first time I went out with Andrew. It's Roxy, and has little diamonds on the front that are both tough and feminine at the same time. That's what I wanted to be—tough and feminine. Not broken and frail and unable to do things like run, or skate, or date a boy. I should wear it more, especially now that my new go-to sweatshirt is forever ruined with wine stains. Except now, it reminds me of *this* Andrew—*Drew*—which makes me love it less.

I hover in the kitchen, nibbling at my sandwich while Lindsey changes, and when she comes out in my shirt, I compliment her, ignoring the loud voice kicking me from the inside and telling me I shouldn't do this. I'm not being fair to Lindsey, and I'm stooping to Andrew's level. But I let her walk out the door anyway, and I sit quietly in my chair and finish my sandwich, playing out the scene that's about to happen in my head—she'll show up, he'll see her, and he'll think of me.

* * *

PART OF BEING the prized student is being available to shine the spotlight on your benefactor at a moment's notice. Miranda Wheaton is winning an award, and she called me two days ago to ask if I would introduce her before her presentation and speech. She's kind—but there's also a very rigid thread that runs through her that's not to be messed with. When she asks, you say *yes*. That's the unspoken rule, and I learned it quickly when I backed out of something freshman year and found myself fighting to get back into her circle.

I'm special, and I still had to fight. There is no gray with Miranda Wheaton—everything is black and white. You are either *in* or you're *out*.

I need to stay *in*.

I also need to get the projector working. I'm sweating. I sweat when I panic. I'm panicking, too. Even though I'm not the one really getting an award, I *am* the one sitting up here on my knees in front of the small table, unplugging and replugging the same cord to the computer—expecting the screen to just randomly appear one of these times—despite the fact that I'm not doing anything different.

Come on. One, two, three...work!

I lean forward and rub my head. I should have worn my hair up. Right now, my heavy locks are only making me hotter. I twist my hair into a knot at the base of my neck, jabbing a pencil through the middle of the bun to secure it in place. I go back to the stubborn computer and punch a few buttons. Here I want to cut into people's bodies for a living—and I can't even get a PowerPoint to show up.

"Hey, mind if I maybe…just…"

A pair of very large, very masculine hands reaches in front of me, and when I look up I'm greeted with startling-blue eyes on a chiseled face and just enough of a beard to make me want to touch it…just once.

No, no...don't touch it, Emma!

"Sorry, didn't mean to scare you, but I was in the back…over there?" He nods over his shoulder, to the doorway where two other equally handsome men are leaning, watching me flail. I've been flailing in front of them for nearly an hour. On my knees. I think maybe I swore a few times, too. *Oh my god!* "You're…kind of struggling, huh?" he says. I blink at him, twisting my lips before I look back at the computer in front of us both. I pull the cord out and plug it in again.

"This is my only move," I say with a shrug, looking back up at him again. "That's all I've got." Yep, those are definitely blue eyes. Not blue-gray like mine. His are a better blue, like…sky maybe?

His laugh comes from somewhere deep inside his chest, under the tight silvery gray shirt and slightly darker gray tie that he's wearing on his chest like a superhero emblem. I laugh internally at my observation: my hero in a suit and tie.

"I think you just need to put it in…display mode…which is right…" His speech comes out in pieces while he crouches down next to me and opens a few windows, punches a few buttons, and *holy shit, Miranda's presentation is on the screen!*

"You're amazing," I say, standing on my feet and staring at the screen with wide eyes and an open mouth, working every second to avoid looking back at him with the same awe and amazement. I can tell from my periphery that he's smiling. I can also tell that his smile—it's *really* nice.

He chuckles, and I give in. I look, and my body flushes instantly.

"No, I just do a lot of presentations. It's more of a matter of knowing how to push the right buttons, not really being amazing," he smirks, taking a few steps back until he reaches the edge of the stage I'm on—we're on.

This sexy, sexy man is talking about pushing buttons and I'm blushing in front of professors and doctors while on a stage.

"Oh...yeah, right," I say. My heart is beating the way it does when I chug uphill in a rollercoaster. I'm nervous, and my palms are sweating, and this hot guy with a beard just winked at me.

When he leaves the stage, I move my attention back to the computer—sorting through the slides to make sure they're in order and on the right one to start. I tug my purse out from under the table and pull the small note cards I've made out next. I sit against the back wall, in a seat in a line of chairs left there for the presenters for the night.

Dr. Miranda Wheaton saved my life.

Dr. Wheaton is more than a visionary.

It's an honor to study with her.

I mumble to myself the start of my few short paragraphs. I'm uncomfortable speaking in front of a crowd, but speaking about *this*...it amps up my anxiety about seven-thousand levels.

I understand why I need to, though. Or maybe not *need* to, but why people want to hear it. It's compelling. My story is the perfect illustration on why Dr. Wheaton is the best, why she deserves this award tonight, and why she'll continue to win hundreds more just as prestigious.

The crowd filters in, and after several minutes, the background is filled with nothing but non-stop chatter and the clanking of wine glasses. When I look up from my notes, I'm almost dizzied by the number of important people—sitting in chairs around tables with linens—looking at me.

I've never been nervous about the idea of cutting into someone. I'm not worried about the MCAT, and I'm actually looking forward to my first rotation through trauma. The idea of working in the moment—to save someone's life—it's the entire reason I made this my dream. But speaking to this room full of people?

I'm terrified.

"You look a little pale there, Emma. You feeling okay?" Miranda Wheaton's voice is somewhere between an angel and a sergeant in the military. Her tone is friendly and non-threatening, but there's a confidence underneath that is intimidating as hell. I wish more than anything I could mimic it. I'd like that ability in about six minutes when I step up to the mike.

"A lot of people here, huh?" I admit with a swallow as I look up at her and flip through the cards anxiously in my lap. She smiles and sits in the seat next to me, pulling her small pocketbook into her lap and flipping it open to check her lipstick in the mirror on the underside.

"They're all afraid they'll need me someday, so they figured they better show up," she jokes. I laugh lightly, mostly because she's probably right.

"I practiced a few times at home, and it's under a minute," I say, holding the cards up, hoping she doesn't want to see them. Christ, what would I do if she started editing them now?

She leans into me, her shoulder draped in a silk blouse, pressing against mine wrapped in polyester.

"You are going to do just fine. Honestly, you can get up there and tell four knock-knock jokes for all I care," she says. I smirk, but look back down at my cards, knowing the story on them is important to her, despite what she says. She claims she doesn't want the attention, but her office is immaculate, and the entire back wall is covered in awards, framed letters, and tokens from important people recognizing everything she gives.

Miranda does amazing things for people, and I was just one of them. But I'm the one…the one who has *the* story, and I've been urged by her, gently, enough times to share the story on her behalf to know she likes the credit that goes along with it. It's fine—she deserves it. I'm here because of her, and if it costs me a few uncomfortable minutes on a stage in front of Chicago's best doctors, then I can handle that.

As prepared as I am, I suddenly feel taken off guard when the dean of Tech's medical school begins to speak at the microphone. He doesn't share many details about me, just a teaser that I have a compelling story to tell—the whoosh of my pulse through my head drowning out the rest of what he says. I know it's my turn when he turns to face me, clapping, and I notice the rest of the crowd clapping as well.

I suddenly wish I had worn something prettier—something that would at least give them something to look at rather than the black pants and navy blue blouse with the thin gold necklace dangling between the pockets. I'm with it enough to remember the pencil in my hair, and I pull it out quickly, tucking my twist of hair to one side over my shoulder. I didn't even wear tall shoes. I'm in flats, because I was afraid I would have to walk up steps to the stage. Seems my youth and upbringing has worn off on me —always minimizing hazards.

I don't know why, but when I step to the podium, that thought rushes through me. That word—*hazards*. And then all I can think of is that day with Andrew, of skating, and the time I let go of his hand and stood on my own. The day I laughed at hazards, and begged my parents to let me just have this one thing—a day to be young on the ice with him. When I look back out over the crowd, my nerves feel in check. I place the cards flat in front of me, no longer feeling the urge to have to look at them. I know my story. I know it well.

"My name is Emma Burke, and I was born with a congenital heart defect. Usually," I pause, smiling at the thought I just had, "I have to really dumb it down for people when I explain it to them. But this isn't that kind of room, is it?"

I wait for a few seconds as the crowd gives in and laughs, a sense of comfort settling into my chest. I glance back at Miranda, who smiles in support, nodding—acknowledging all she and I have been through together.

"I was diagnosed with hypoplastic left heart syndrome. For those of you who are here with your medical-jargon-loving dates and aren't quite sure what that means—basically, I was born with half a heart. One side worked…and the other was more than just lazy."

I get a few more chuckles from making fun of my stupid infant diagnosis. It owes me a few laughs—it's stolen enough over the years.

"By the time I was eight, I had three surgeries. Yep…" I say, pausing, lips pulled together in an accepting smile. "All the big ones. You know… Norwood, Glenn, Fontan…Larry, Moe, Curley…"

The audience gives in completely now, their laughter the kind that people passing by outside could hear. I glance up and into the eyes of my new friend, the one with the sexy tie and touchable beard. He's smiling and laughing, too. For some reason, that makes me feel even more comfortable.

"Things were going well. I had a forever-good excuse to get out of running laps in PE. I had to get some exercise, but never anything like running. I could do less vigorous things, like simple tumbling or dancing. I'm horribly uncoordinated, so trust me—dancing was not too much for my young heart to handle."

Out of nowhere, my arm chills at the memory of Andrew's elbow looped through mine; my mind hums the sound of the fiddle that played over and over for that glorious week we had square dancing. Even as I stare back into the smiling eyes of my new friendly face across the room, my memory is pulling up the dimples and messy hair of the boy I met when I needed someone most. I don't think of the him I know now, but rather then—when he was…everything.

"For a long time, I was surviving and beating odds. Then the fatigue got worse," I say to a nodding audience. They don't know my story personally, but they all know how my story goes. Stories like mine—they have fuzzy endings, no spoilers that tell me exactly how my life's going to play out. I've always been of the mindset that my life is what I make of it—even if I have half a heart.

That's what got me here.

"I was a status two. Not sick enough to get the first heart out of the gate. Not even sick enough to get the tenth, really. And my parents, brother, and I spent a year getting called into Philadelphia, from our home in Delaware, for false hope and rejections. All for a surgery and post-op treatment that we couldn't afford in the first place."

"I got scared—plain and simple," I shrug. "I was fifteen at the time, almost sixteen, and looking at a black hole. I couldn't get excited for things like driving or prom or the Friday-night football game. My girlfriends were all growing up, getting boyfriends, figuring out who they were, but I *knew* who I was. I was too busy being both frightened and hopeful of moving from status two to status one. That fear consumed me, and it could have paralyzed me. Instead…I wrote a letter."

"I don't know how many letters Dr. Miranda Wheaton gets. All these years, I've never actually asked her," I say, turning to face my saving grace, my brow pinched as I shake my head at her in question.

She raises her shoulders as she smiles and whispers, "It's a lot." I laugh to myself, turning back to my podium.

"She says *a lot,*" I say, garnering a few chuckles from the crowd. "Well, I don't know what it was that convinced her to open mine, read it, and then fly all the way to Delaware to meet with me and my parents in person, but I'm sure I'll never be able to repeat the magic of those words in my letter again. I hope I never have to."

"I was Dr. Wheaton's twenty-first donated surgery. As she said when she met with my family months before it actually happened—the wait for a new heart would still be long. And there would still be false starts. But Chicago was where I needed to be.

"So we moved. And I homeschooled for the first few months in the city while my parents looked for work, and a suburb we could afford. I spent those early weeks waiting for the call—for a heart—at home. But part of being a status-twoer, is not being sick enough *not* to want to leave your house—or, if you're a teenager, to be somewhere with friends. So I went to school, and life…it went on—the safety net of hope that Dr. Wheaton swore would come there to catch me when I fell.

"On November first of my sophomore year of high school, that net…it worked," I smile, no longer registering the fact that I'm in front of anyone at all. "There was a heart, and it wasn't right for anyone above me. But it was perfect for *me*. I was pulled from school, and in surgery in less than three hours."

"Dr. Wheaton is sitting up here next to me tonight, thanks to her generosity. I don't take it lightly, and I hope one day I get to stand at the operating table with her, assisting and learning, as we give a gift like this," I say, my hand clutched against my heart—my second heart, "to someone else. It is an honor, distinguished guests, to present to you Miranda Wheaton…this year's recipient of the S. Holden Taft Award."

The applause erupts quickly as everyone gets to their feet. Dr. Wheaton hugs me as we exchange spots. When I get to my seat, the enormity of everything catches up to me, and breathing begins to feel difficult.

It's a panic attack. I know them. I don't have them often, only when I let myself really stop and think about…well…my life. Usually, I'm just working hard, studying, applying for something—pushing. Always pushing. It's when I stop that I realize—*holy shit, I'm alive.*

I'm sitting in a chair at the end of the row, so as Dr. Wheaton begins her talk, I excuse myself to the small curtained area to the side of the stage, and around to the wall behind the rows of dinner tables. There's a water station, and my hand is shaking as I guzzle cup after cup.

"You probably need to breathe more than you need to drink," he says. My IT guy is also my emergency medic. So far, he's getting all the hero roles, and I'm only technically-inept and skittish. I should be more embarrassed, but I'm to overwhelmed, so I nod in agreement, handing the small paper cup to him and raising my arms above my head to open up my lungs.

"Breathe in until she looks to the left," he whispers, now leaning against the wall next to me. I glance from him back up to Miranda, noticing that he's right—she has a pattern to her speech. She starts at one side of the room, then switches topics, takes a breath and moves to the other.

I breathe with her on every turn—in several seconds, out several more. Eventually, this routine becomes kind of funny, and it makes me giggle. I breathe through it though, still feeling flutters in my belly from nerves. Unless...the flutters are from something else.

"When I had to give my first dissertation...this is how she told me to deal with the room," he whispers next to me. "Divide it in half to make the crowd smaller. Thing is, I gave my dissertation to a table of seven people. Not a lot to divide, and frankly...I would have given anything for it to have been more crowded or noisier."

I look at him, still breathing, but now on my own.

"When it's a small room like that, you can totally hear when someone writes something down. Screws with your head," he smirks. He's playing it cool as if we're just two people who like to stand off to the side—as if this is where we're supposed to be.

I turn my head to watch the end of Miranda's speech. She touches on the topic of me once more—at the end—when she lets everyone know about how I wrote her a second letter, after my surgery, telling her I had every intention of walking in her footsteps. She makes a joke of it, of how I was right, and it didn't live up to the first one I wrote. But then she talks about how I beat out more than seven hundred other applicants for her mentorship, and my smile slips, because I'm sure everyone's thinking about how I probably didn't deserve the slot, that she picked me because she felt bad, or she thought I had a great story. Sometimes I let that doubt eat at me, and I feel a little inadequate. It gets a lot of applause today, though, and most of the room turns to look at me, so I plaster the smile back in place.

"Just keep breathing," my mystery friend whispers from behind his hand as he pretends to run it over his beard. When the dean takes over at the podium again and begins recognizing others in the audience, my friend nudges me to get my attention, then nods over his shoulder, toward the double doors to the right of us. I follow him out quietly, and allow myself to sigh loudly, my lips flapping and making a motorcycle sound.

"Wow, you were really holding a lot of that in, huh?" he chuckles.

"I guess I was," I say, feeling the threat of my chest tightening again now that we're out in the hallway alone. I look down at my hands, which are clutching my purse hard, my knuckles white. I breathe out a short laugh and relax my hold.

"I'm Graham, by the way," he says, his palm out, waiting for mine, which is clammy, and I'm embarrassed to touch him, but I do anyhow. When our hands meet, I notice more than I probably should just from shaking someone's hand—like the fact that there's a callus at the base of his fingers, and his nails are kept short, and his palms are unusually warm for the coldness of the room.

"Hi, Graham. I'm...Emma," I start, squinting my eyes as I cut myself off with a shake of my head. "You know that already though, I guess."

"Yeah, I got that from your speech," he chuckles, leaning into me enough that his arm brushes against mine. "Which...nice job, by the way. I think you might have stolen her thunder."

"Thanks," I say, my face flushing and my lips twitching with the pressure to smile. The doors next to us push open before I can say anything else, and the crowd begins to exit a few people at a time, many stopping to congratulate me along the way. I'm not sure why—I didn't win the award. I'm gracious anyhow, though, and Graham stands next to me the entire time.

"Well...what did you think?" Dr. Wheaton says as she steps through the doors last. Her eyes flit from me to Graham and back again. I open my mouth to speak, but before I can, Graham responds.

"It was better than your last speech. You still do the side-to-side thing, you know," he says, his hands comfortably hung from his thumbs in his pants pockets, his head tilted at her in a friendly way. Something in his eyes is off, though, like while they may be familiar with each other—he's also challenging her, maybe even baiting her a little.

"Graham, when you've been doing it one way as long as I have, you don't change," she answers, her mouth twisted, almost as if she's scolding him.

"Yet you can learn the latest surgical techniques and master them," he chuckles, nodding before turning his head away. "Funny what old dogs *can* learn."

There's a flash of displeasure that crosses her face, but the consummate professional, she quickly masks it, her deep red lips smiling.

"For now. Until I teach someone else," she says, directing the focus to me. I feel her eyes on me, and my head starts swimming with a little bit of fear and pride all at once.

"Better her than me," he says, tossing a laugh out, still looking away from her.

"So how do you two know each other?" Miranda asks. I feel my stomach drop, suddenly nervous as my brain slowly starts to put their relationship together. Standing next to one another, it's painfully clear—but apart, I guess my nerves blinded me.

"I just met her tonight, but..." Graham says, leaning toward me again, his elbow jutting out just enough to touch my arm. I catch Miranda's eyes as they see it, and I can't tell if the expression on her face is one that approves or not. "I was gonna see if I could convince her to meet me for coffee tomorrow."

My eyes grow wide, and I feel like I've been thrown into some sort of sick and twisted test. I look to Dr. Wheaton, thinking I probably need her approval, or that maybe she'll give me an out, telling him it's not appropriate.

"Just make sure my son picks up the tab," she says, bending toward my ear.

"Oh, yeah...right," I giggle. It's not a cool giggle, but a messy, nervous one, that turns into a choking kind of cough that leads me to have to excuse myself as she says goodbye to her son—her hot son...the one that just asked me out...in front of her...after having an awkward pissing match with her in front of me on top of it all. I'm really not sure if coffee with Graham is a good idea or not, but I'm not sure I have a choice in the matter now.

I spend longer than I need at the drinking fountain, until she's walking out the main door with the dean and a few of her colleagues, leaving me with Graham, who's somehow still calm and confident-looking. I don't think his hands left his pockets once.

"So…coffee?"

The way he sucks in his top lip and raises his eyebrows is, well—it's adorable, even if his clear need for dominance is a little off-putting. And it also seems to have rendered my tongue useless, because more than a few seconds have passed without an answer from me, and he's starting to bunch his brow. And now he's looking at me like maybe I'm a little off.

Maybe…maybe I am a little off?

"Oh, yeah. I mean, yes. Sure. I'd love to," I stammer. Graham slips his hand from his pocket with his phone, holding it up and ready to type.

"What's your number? I'll text you early in the afternoon, and we'll find a good time."

I pause awkwardly-long again due to the inner-dialogue I have with myself, trying to decide if this is a good idea or a bad one. Eventually, I rattle off my number, my pulse speeding up as he types into his phone.

"Well…Emma," he says, reaching for my hand again. I give it to him, and this time his touch is a little more familiar, and a little…more. His fingers wrap around my wrist, and when I look up at him, I notice the twitch in his lips as he watches his hold on me. "I'll see you tomorrow."

"Sounds gerd…I mean, good. *Gerd*…is just on my mind I guess…medical awards dinner and all. Oh god." I shut my eyes as he laughs. I open them as I start to take a step toward the door. "I swear, tomorrow I'll be back at the top of my game. Public speaking does a number on me."

"I look forward to seeing the top of your game," he chuckles.

I raise a hand and spin to face the double glass doors, actively thinking about pushing them open, not running into them, not tripping, and walking quickly, but not too quickly away. This is why I don't date. Thinking of all of this, trying not to look like a jackass for a solid minute—it's too hard. Give me advanced chem and bio, instead.

My giddiness lasts only a few minutes, and soon I'm walking back to my apartment, dreading the fact that I have a date with someone.

Handsome as he may be, Graham is not Andrew.

These butterflies are not the same.

* * *

ANDREW

I don't think I've ever spent the night in a girl's bed without getting something out of it. Even in Iowa, when I hooked up with girls my senior year or at junior college, I never stayed at a chick's place without at least a hand job.

I could have had anything I wanted last night—anything…but Emma. That's the problem. This whole thing—coming back to their apartment again, hooking up with Lindsey—it was always really about Emma.

Punishing Emma—*seeing* Emma.

I guess in a way, I'm getting something out of this, but it doesn't feel as good as I thought it would. There must be a shred of decency left inside me, because I made out with Lindsey until my lips were raw last night, and then we just went to sleep. In her bed. Fucking spooning like we were two kids sneaking off at camp. I bet she thinks I'm this big gentleman—either that, or an enormous pussy. She kept giving me these little signs, small tugs of her shirt, little exposures of her skin that signaled it was all clear for me to keep on moving.

But I couldn't do it.

I started stroking her hair, putting her to sleep. I panicked, like I was babysitting an infant, and just trying to put it to sleep, the whole time feeling sick as fuck to my stomach. I lay there awake holding her, wishing she were Emma. Emma—who I hate. I hate Emma. I can't even talk myself out of hating her. Yet…I keep fantasizing about touching her instead of Lindsey. That's the only way I can make my affection feel like it's real. My head gets cloudier with every minute that passes in this scenario I've trapped myself in.

I left their apartment when the sun came up, not able to take it any more. Lindsey woke up just enough to see I was leaving, but I kissed her back to bed and slipped out her door. I should have kept walking, but my eyes caught the sleeve of Emma's shirt hanging from the side of the trash-can. It's like she put it there to surrender—the only flag she has to wave.

It smelled like her. She still smells the same.

I should have left it in the trashcan where she put it. But I didn't want her to surrender. I wanted her to keep playing, to have to hold on to this stupid piece of material that I now know reminds us both of before. I want her to have to look at it, too—even if she never wears it again.

If she surrenders, I win.

Then what?

I'm kind of impressed that she sent her roommate to me wearing it. Up until now, she's been just taking my comments and dismissing them, even when I can tell they get to her. She's been going along with this pretense that we don't know each other. I have been giving her nothing but shit, and she's just been taking it.

Until now.

"Didn't your roommate wear that yesterday?" I say in an offhanded manner as I step out into the hallway from the locker room where Lindsey's been waiting for me. I saw her in the sweatshirt during the goddamned game, and it was the only thing I could concentrate on. I blew a major play. All I want in the world is for her to take it off, to get rid of it. I feel a little bad about my comment, though, because I see her face fall as she looks down and pulls the bottom of the sweatshirt out to look at it.

Shit…this part of my plan doesn't feel good. Lindsey isn't the one I mean to be provoking.

"Oh, I…yeah, I guess she did. I just like it, so she said I could borrow it," she says. I can tell she's lying because she's embarrassed. Emma probably fed her some bullshit to make her feel pretty in that sweatshirt just so she'd wear it here, and I just crapped all over her. She pulls it off and folds it over her arm, though, and I smile to myself at how easy it was to take away Emma's power.

Lindsey's still pouting a little when I turn around. I grab my equipment bag and jerk it up higher on my shoulder, then lean into her, kissing her neck. "I like you better in your things," I say, which makes her blush. She's already forgotten about the sweatshirt.

"Harper, you still have to talk with coach. He's pissed, dude," Trent says as he comes out of the locker room, his eyes quickly noticing my date. He smirks and winks at me in front of her, which irritates me. He's doing that eyebrow waggle too, which is only going to make Lindsey think I talk about her to Trent. I don't. In fact, Trent doesn't even know her name.

"I have a 4.0. There is literally nothing for me to study, so why should I waste time sitting there in the study lab," I sigh, ready to get back to the fact that I blew my study hall hours, which I don't need, and coach wants to bench me for it. Some system—the guy with the highest GPA gets the smack down, but Tony Agaluta, our goalie who's flunking basic algebra, gets stickers on his goddamned helmet because he shows up at four o'clock every day for tutoring—*and still fails!*

"I don't make the rules, Harp. And neither does coach," Trent says. Sometimes I want to punch my friend. He's like Dudley-Do-Right, even when he's being logical.

"Well, unless he's planning on sitting me tomorrow, which fuck it if he is, I'm pretty sure our talk can wait until then," I say, repositioning my heavy bag on my arm.

Trent rolls his eyes, but then turns his attention back to Lindsey. Lindsey is his type. I should just give her to him, rid myself of this entire dumb fucking idea I had.

"Hey, I'm Trent," he says, shaking her hand.

"Hey, I'm Trent," I repeat, mocking him. He doesn't turn to look at me when he reaches to the side and punches me in the right peck. "Ow…fuck nut!"

"You must be Emma?" Trent asks. Fucker did that on purpose.

I'd feel bad about the look on Lindsey's face right now except I'm pretty sure the look on mine is worse. He called her *Emma,* which means somewhere along the way he noticed that name. He saw her license once, briefly, but I didn't think he memorized it. And I get enough from the quick glance he shoots me to know that he's trying to make this a teachable moment.

Not in the mood, Trent. I'm so far in on a bad idea there's really no way to get out now. Quit making it worse.

"She's…my roommate," Lindsey says, her voice half of the volume it was before.

"He knows that. He's just a really shitty listener. This is Lindsey, Trent. And thanks for paying attention to me when I talk." I lay it on super thick, and Lindsey eats it up. Trent's eyes become slits, and I know I've only made him more curious. Just one more thing I'll think about atoning for…or not. Might as well embrace this piece-of-shit guy I've become.

"Right, my mistake," Trent says. What he really means is *"What are you up to, you asshole?"* I put my arm around Lindsey and lead her out ahead of him. This conversation between them—it's done.

Trent heads to his car, and probably to Majerle's, which is where I'd planned on going with Lindsey after the game, but now I just want to get her back to her apartment so I can go through with everything I chickened out on last night. She seems all right with it, too, her fingers hooked onto mine over her shoulder as we walk the six blocks to her apartment.

My back is killing me from carrying my gear. I normally dump it in Trent's car, or drop it off at home before we go out, but those weren't options tonight. Maybe I'll somehow work a back rub out of this.

I feel a charge when we get to her front door, and I know why it's there. It's there because I anticipated this—the look on Emma's face the second I walk in behind Lindsey. In a second, her eyes go from Lindsey's to mine, and down to the sweatshirt folded over her purse.

There's that disappointment I was banking on. I grin, and she catches it before quickly looking away.

Lindsey dumps her purse on the table as we walk in, and I take advantage of it, picking up the sweatshirt and twisting it in my hands to make it even smaller. Emma watches the entire time, her cheek caught between her teeth while she rethinks her decision to send her friend out in it in the first place.

That's right, Emma. This bothers you more than it bothers me.

"How was the awards dinner?" Lindsey asks from behind Emma as she opens the fridge to pull out a beer for each of us.

"It was good."

I don't think Emma even registered her answer. She's too busy staring at the sweatshirt—her eyes never blinking as she watches my hands work the fabric as I step closer to her.

"Here," I whisper, handing it to her. She takes the other side, and for a second we're both holding on, like a tug of war. Her eyes flash to mine, and I notice she stops breathing. I should stop here, but something happens when she looks at me, and I step in a little closer, close enough that I know she can feel my breath. "Are we done now?"

I let go of my grip, but I keep my eyes locked with hers. For a brief moment, she looks wounded, and I start to smile.

"I met someone," she says. She's speaking to Lindsey, but as the left side of her mouth starts to rise, her eyes haze, and something stronger steps in place of the girl who was letting me walk all over her a second ago.

You think I care that you met someone, Emma Burke? Go ahead—make me care.

"Oh yeah?" Lindsey moves into my side, handing me a beer. I put my arm around her and let my hand cup her shoulder. Emma's eyes move to it, so I loosen my grip and drag my fingers along her arm suggestively, just to see if Emma's gaze follows. It does, and I take a very satisfied, long drink, not bothering to hide the smile on my lips behind the bottle.

"Yeah," Emma says, her voice weak again. I almost feel like I'm putting her in a trance, her eyes are tracing every single stroke of my fingers along her friend's arm. "He's a grad student," she continues, telling her roommate about some boy who thought she was cute and asked her out on a date. I couldn't care less. She says something about how he saved her, came to her rescue and got the projector working. She's gushing over some guy who knew how to click a goddamned mouse, and she's calling *him* her savior. The more she talks, the more I feel every scar on my body all at once—the burn marks, the stab wounds, the broken bones that never healed quite right—abuse I took so Emma Burke didn't have to experience anything sad.

Something in me snaps.

I know it's crossing the line when I do it, and I know that it's going to start something that won't end in spooning tonight. That's why I came here, though…isn't it? Emma keeps talking, but her eyes are constantly checking my hands. Every pass of my fingers over Lindsey's shoulder and down her bicep moves closer to her breast, until finally, I let my thumb drag slowly along the curve of her tit, taking extra time when I feel the hard peak underneath her thin bra and shirt—and Lindsey, bless her fucking little heart, actually hums in pleasure.

"I'm seeing him tomorrow, so I'll let you know...you know...if it's something..." Emma cuts her story short, suddenly a lot less sure of herself. She sucks in her bottom lip as she flits her eyes to me quickly before looking down and then back up to her friend, who is now absolutely dying for me to touch her more.

That's right, Emma. Nobody cares that you met a boy and he's your fucking hero.

"Yeah, that's awesome. I'm so excited for you," Lindsey says, nothing about her focused on Emma. Lindsey is my puppet right now, and I'm pretty sure she didn't hear anything past the part where Emma said she met someone. Everything after that was about my hand on her breast, and how fast my dick will be inside her next.

"Anyhow, I think I'll turn in," Emma says, faking a yawn. "That speech, it's always hard, ya know..." I roll my eyes at her sad performance, then run my hand down Lindsey's arm to find her fingers waiting to tug my hand and body to her bed.

"Yeah, us too," Lindsey says at the feel of my grip. I follow her down the hall as we leave Emma alone in the kitchen behind us. I don't care that she's alone. I don't care that she knows where I'm going, and I don't care that she's met some guy who wants to buy her coffee.

I don't care about Emma Burke.

I step into Lindsey's room, and she pauses at the doorway, hanging out of it to look down the hallway to her friend. That's guilt she's feeling. She needs to let that go.

"She's okay," I say, coming up behind her, breathing into her, reminding her. My fingers find her stomach, and I tug her shirt from her jeans and let my hand find her bare skin.

"Yeah, you're probably right," she says, part of her giving into me, but part of her still out there in the hallway. I can tell. I kiss her neck, moving my hand through her hair, wrapping it around my fingers. She sighs, letting her weight fall into me. I turn her to face me and lift her into my arms, my hands grabbing her ass as I walk us backward. We just need to get to her bed. She'll forget everything there.

I'll forget everything there.

"Goodnight."

Lindsey's door is still open; Emma pauses on the other side of the hall and speaks, her profile outlined by the faint light spilling from her room, which means she can see just as much of us. I knew the door was open; I wanted her to see. I timed that kiss just right. I hoped she'd walk by, but another piece of me wants to take that last kiss back.

Lindsey's mouth tightens up and eventually falls away from mine.

"Goodnight," she says back to her friend, her forehead sliding along my shoulder until her face is tucked against my chest.

Fuck, I'm an asshole.

"I'm sorry."

Lindsey is apologizing to me. The irony.

"It's fine…really," I say, looking over her form as Emma's door closes behind her. Emma never looks back again. She's seen enough. Maybe I have, too.

"Something's with her, tonight. I think it was the speech. I…I probably should have talked to her more, or maybe gone with her. *Gah*…I'm so sorry, I just feel bad now. You probably think I'm nuts." Lindsey looks up at me with her mouth caught between an apology and a frown—waiting for me to tell her it's okay. I pull her in against me for a hug, mostly because I can't handle looking in her eyes anymore. I don't like the reflection in them.

"You know what? I'm gonna go ahead and go," I say, my lips tight now, too. I'm not looking at Lindsey though. I'm looking beyond her. I realize it a little late, and she catches me. When my eyes drift back down to hers, there's a hint of suspicion in them. "Why don't you and your roommate have a night—do that girl-talk thing, huh?"

Her misgivings about my motivation seem to melt, and her hands squeeze my arms in thanks. The puppy-dog grin she looks up at me with seals it. I hug her again, but my eyes stay on the shut door across the hallway.

Lindsey follows me through their kitchen and living room, where I grab my gear and pull it back up on my shoulder, leaving this apartment one more time without satisfaction.

"I'll call you tomorrow," she says as I back out of her door.

I hold up a few fingers and start my steps toward the elevator bank, but remember that tomorrow's Sunday, and Harley told me to keep my evening open in case he could line something up. I could really use the stars to align for a fight—financially and emotionally—I take a few quick paces back to her door, catching it before she closes it completely.

"You know what? Actually, I've got some family things tomorrow, and I'm not sure how late I'm going to be. I'll just text you when I get home?" She looks down, and I can tell she's trying to decide if she wants to believe the line of bullshit I'm giving her. Part of me wants her to call me on it, and part of me also thinks maybe that's what I need—a good fight to distract me, to let me feel something other than angry and alone.

"Sure," she says. It's a pained response, but for now, I'll take it. I'm tired; I'm also not in the mood for a breakup. And a breakup would mean no more Emma…and I'm not so sure I'm ready for that either.

"Great," I smile, leaning in to kiss her lips lightly, just to leave her feeling something better than how I'm sure my blow-off just did. I really do have family shit to deal with tomorrow; I really only stretched the truth some.

The doorman is starting to recognize me, and he smiles and waves as I pass by this time. It's the hockey gear, and my Tech sweatshirt and hat. It works on girls and doormen, it seems.

As long as everything felt like it took at Lindsey and Emma's, I end up walking through my apartment door forty-five minutes behind Trent. He didn't go to the bar, and I have a strange feeling that he was waiting for me—probably sitting here stewing in his own self-righteousness and whatever-the-fuck he thinks he has all figured out. He's sitting on the couch, his feet up, beer in his hand, and the TV on a replay of some NASCAR race. He hates racing, so I know he's just posturing.

I walk behind the sofa with my gear, hell bent on not stopping or taking his bait.

"You're in over your head, Harper. What are you doing?" he asks, and mother fuck! I stop. I stop because he knows more than I thought he did. And since he has the bad shit all figured out, maybe he can help me wrap my head around what the hell is wrong with me—and why I'm still so angry.

I reach over the sofa and take the half-empty beer from his hand, claiming it for my own. I drop my gear behind the sofa and walk the rest of the way around the couch, sitting on the corner of the coffee table across from him.

My eyes are on his chin for the longest time. It's like when you're a kid and you know you're wrong, and you're about to get your ass chewed, but you just don't want to give in to the adult and take your licks. I don't want to have to face his goddamned honest face, so I keep my eyes on his chin and take a long sip from the beer I commandeered, draining it almost completely.

"I don't know, Trent. She was there. It was her, and I don't know, but I can't fucking stop," I say.

"Drew…who the hell is Emma?" He says her name, and my chest flips inside out, my heart running through an irregular rhythm of several fast beats followed by nothing at all.

"I've told you," I lie.

"No, Drew. Not the drunken version you tell when you think you're being honest. I mean the *real* story," he says. I give in and look up the inch it takes to meet his eyes, and I hold his gaze while I wait for my heart to begin working again. I don't talk about Emma. It started as a promise I made to myself that night, and then it grew into a rule I made to protect myself. I'm not so sure what would happen if I broke it now.

"There was a girl," I say, letting my eyes wander over to the TV, which he's conveniently muted. There's a pile-up of cars in the race, one is on fire, and I can't help but find some kind of sick humor in the many ways that scene mirrors my own life. "I got screwed over by the law…" I start, my eyes moving back to his, the recognition in his expression already there. He knows the story. And now he's filling in the details.

"Harp…" He shakes his head, literally biting his tongue, his hand rubbing the back of his neck, as if this is somehow stressful for him. I'm about to tell him to drop the empathy act when there's a soft knock at our door.

It's probably one of the guys, wondering why we're not celebrating at

Majerle's. I use it as an excuse to get out of our conversation, and as Trent moves to the door, I walk into our kitchen to get each of us another beer. When I come out, she's standing in the doorway, and Trent is rubbing his chin.

"Over your head," he says under his breath as he trades spots with me near the door. He takes one of the beers from my hand and pauses to make sure my eyes meet his, get the warning in them, before he moves back to his spot on the couch.

"What are you doing here?" I don't even waste time with being nice. I'm so pissed she's at my door. It means she knows where I live, and she doesn't get to know things about me. That's not how this works.

"Why are you doing this, Andrew?"

I hear Trent scoff behind me, and it pisses me off that he's hearing any of this. I slide my beer on the small shelf nearby and grab my jacket from the hook on the back of the door, motioning for her to get the hell out of my way. She takes a step back as I move outside with her and hand her my jacket. She looks at it like I just handed her a slab of meat.

"It's forty degrees out here, and your teeth are chattering. Just put the damn thing on," I say, walking down the path toward the road. Our street is filled with cars nestled up next to meters, and graffiti mars the sidewalks. It's a far cry from the tree-lined cobblestone walkway that leads to Emma's front door. I live in the real world.

Emma joins me near the roadway, but she's still holding my jacket in her hands. I nod at her hands to put it on, and she scowls.

"Seriously, don't make this a thing. It's a twenty-dollar winter coat from Target. Just wear it for five minutes for fuck sake."

She takes in a sharp breath before shoving one arm into a sleeve. "I don't even know who the hell you are anymore," she mumbles.

"Isn't that the point? We pretend we don't know each other?" I move in close, and she takes a step back. She wants to keep distance between us, which only makes me want to shatter her comfort more. I advance again, this time a little aggressively as my chest rumbles with light laughter. She doesn't move this time, instead her shoulders sagging as she lets out a slow breath.

"Is that the point? Why is that the point, Andrew? What are you doing?

Do you *want* me to pretend I don't know you? I mean...I thought that's what you wanted. I thought you really liked Lindsey. But then you keep doing things and saying things and you're so—"

"So what, Emma?" I challenge her, waiting for her to say it. Her toes are matched with mine, and I feel her shoe against the tips of my own. My lip curls, unable to stop from grinning when I tap my foot against hers softly. Her eyes wince, just a little, but enough that I see it. She's drowning in the fog of my breath, and I exhale once hard just to erase her. She backs down, her eyes falling to both of our feet as she takes a step back.

"Go on, Emma," I say, moving toward her again. "What am I? Am I mean? Am I...angry? Am I the kind of guy who returns a girl's license to her so she doesn't have to worry? Does that make me your hero?"

She nods, but then shakes her head, bringing her hands up to the side of her face. Her eyes are threatening tears, and I know I have her on the brink.

"Or am I the guy who tells a lie for you, and then sits back while your life is perfect and mine is a fucking nightmare, and you can't even bother the common decency of saying *thanks*?"

Her body grows rigid at that last one, and her face finds mine, her eyes wide and red, the water pooling in them, ready to fall to the ground in front of her. My hands out to my sides, I shake my head at a loss. I tried to make sense of it so many nights I lay awake at Lake Crest. I even tried to understand why she didn't care after I moved to Iowa. I think about it every time my feet touch the ice, every time a fist lands on my face, and when I look at the scars I got for her.

"Come on, Emma. Tell me...what am I?"

Her breath falters, and the tears finally release down her cheeks as her bottom lip quivers with her cry and her gaze falls to the ground.

"You're different, Andrew," she says. I laugh her answer off, looking up at the sky, knowing she'd say something like that. I'm different. No shit, I'm different. You would be too.

"I..." she continues, stopping to sniffle once. I fold my arms and tilt my head to the side to watch her. I look at her with contempt, but I enjoy the view—of her struggling. I might as well enjoy the show.

"I used to just not know where you went..."

My brow pinches as she pauses to take a slow breath to steady herself.

Where I went? She pulls my jacket from her body, folding it in half and handing it back to me. I look down at it, no intention of taking it from her. She's being ridiculous. It's cold outside, and her body is shaking.

"Just keep the jacket, Emma," I protest. I'm not loud now.

"No. I don't want it," she says, her eyes meeting mine and leveling me with her temporary strength as she drops the coat at my feet. She swallows hard, as if this hurts. "You asked me who you are, Andrew. But I think maybe I never really knew. Whoever I met when I was a kid, that boy…he's gone. I don't know where he went. And I think maybe he never existed."

I look down at my jacket, then back up to Emma, her arms hugging her body, her long hair wild in the night wind. She's wearing a long-sleeved white shirt that's thin enough the wind forces it against her skin, showing every curve of her body. My eyes scan lower to her jeans and the Converse on her feet, so much of her still *that* girl, still trapped in the past.

"Why did you come here? Was it just to tell me some poetic shit that I already know?" I ask.

Her eyes soften into pity as she begins to take a step back in the direction of her apartment. It's late, and freezing, and I'm pretty sure she followed me here by foot. I shouldn't let her walk home alone. But then again, she shouldn't have come here in the first place, so kind of her fault.

"I hope you really like Lindsey…" she says. My mouth flinches because I don't want to accept her statement. I don't want to *deal* with her statement.

I bend down and grab my jacket, slinging it over one shoulder as I salute her with my other hand.

"Have a safe walk home, Emma. Maybe next time you drop by, you'll start being honest with yourself," I say over my shoulder, as angry with her as I was before her impromptu visit, but maybe now for other reasons.

"I won't be back," she says. "In fact, I plan on never seeing you again." She turns and walks away with purpose, back to where she came from, her stride fast, confident, and maybe…free.

"Fuck!" I yell when I'm sure she can no longer hear me. I tug on the sleeve of the jacket in my hands, ripping a seam in the middle.

When I come inside, Trent is just where I left him, but I'm no longer in the mood to deal with his psycho-babble-shit, so I throw my jacket onto the coffee table and walk right by him into my room, slamming the door behind me.

"This is one of those bad ideas, Harper," he says through my door a few seconds later. "We all have them, but you went ahead and put it into action. Just…stop now."

"Shut the fuck up, Trenton. I don't need you to tell me things I already know," I say, pulling my pillow up over my face and ears. It won't matter; I can't drown out the voice in my head. Turns out, I can't drown out Trent, either.

"I kinda think you do, Harp. Otherwise you wouldn't make such shitty decisions," he says.

I open my mouth to swear at him again, but I decide against it, sighing instead. I smack my hand on the base of the lamp next to my bed, turning out my light, then I flip to my side to plug my phone into it's charger—setting my alarm to make sure I'm up in time to drive to Woodstock and endure more criticism and advice from my family.

I used to just not know where you went.

It's that one thing she said that drums in my head when I close my eyes. It was in there, with all of those other things she said. But it's that one thing that hit my ears as if she were assaulting me with her words. That one phrase, it felt important, and I was too angry to stop and acknowledge it, to question it further.

One question, really.

Don't you know, Emma? Don't you know where I went?

CHAPTER 11

EMMA BURKE, AGE 16

"I'm scared," I say under the comfort of my mom's hand on my forehead. I won't admit this in front of my dad. As strong as he is, I'm his weakness. My mom—she's the one who can handle life's imperfect parts, but my dad, he doesn't like to know I have nightmares or misgivings or regrets.

"It's okay to be scared," she says, her smile soft. "But…" she scoots in closer to me on the bed, moving the long tubes and cords out of our way, "it's also okay to be hopeful. And excited. And driven, or curious, or the millions of other things you get to feel now."

Her eyes are teary, but I know it's not because she's scared. She's happy. We've all waited for this day for so long. I'm getting a new heart. In an hour, I will be taken through those doors I've envisioned in my head, put to sleep, cut open—and a miracle will happen.

I will be a miracle.

A few nurses come in to take vitals and check on me. My mom steps out of the way, but she keeps her hand on mine as they work around us. I'm glad. The moment she lets go, I know the trembling will start.

I'm scared. But I'm hopeful too.

I'll be able to do so many things—things I always dreamt of. I'll be able to skate again. Maybe...maybe I'll find Andrew?

"Hey, Mom?" I tug on her hand, and she leans down to give me attention while the nurses finish their prep work.

"Have you heard from Andrew's mom yet? Dad said he found her number and left her a message. Have you...did he...or did they ever call back?"

It's been six weeks since Andrew was taken away in the back of a squad car. The officers that drove me home after the accident told my parents very little. But they said enough. Andrew was taken in for possession and driving under the influence. None of what they said made sense with the Andrew I knew—or the Andrew I was with all night. He wasn't acting weird, and I didn't smell any alcohol or see any drugs or smell marijuana. But maybe you can't see those things?

I guess he couldn't see my problems either. My heart was broken, but in Andrew's mind, it pumped blood and beat just as his own.

I waited to hear from him. I waited for nearly a week, figuring he was probably in trouble for the accident and for the possession charge. From what I could figure out online, he likely got some community service. And he probably lost his license until he's eighteen. He's a minor, so I can't find his court-hearing record online. But he said he would be okay, and he knew what he was doing. He promised, and that's the only reason I let him do what he did.

Every night, I expected to hear him below my window. I'd sit there and look out at the long roadway leading up to my house, waiting to see him. Maybe he'd walk, or maybe he'd drive even though he wasn't supposed to.

He never came.

"Mom?" She's paying attention to a conversation with a group of nurses, but shakes her head and looks back at me.

"Sorry, I was trying to see when they were taking you," she smiles.

"Andrew?" I remind her.

Her smile stays in place, but even though her mouth doesn't move, the meaning of her smile—it changes.

"Did Dad talk to him? Is he okay?" I try to sit up, but my mom holds my arm and shakes her head and chuckles at me.

"Honey, no, nothing like that," she says. I liked it better when I was excited, when I thought my dad saw Andrew. "He heard from his mom. And he's going to live somewhere else for a while. With a relative, I think. He has some things he needs to work through. Drugs…Em, whatever he has going on, it's serious."

I swallow and watch her face for a clue that she has more to say. She brushes a few pieces of my hair back and straightens my eyebrow by running her finger along it—a doting thing she's done since I was a kid. And after a few seconds, I realize that's all the information she has.

Andrew left. No goodbye or letter or stone at my window. Just some secondhand hint that he has a drug problem and "things to work through," and I just can't quite buy the full story. There's something missing, something I'm not being told.

But if Andrew really wanted me to know, he'd tell me.

"Well hello, Emma," Dr. Wheaton says, practically glowing like an angel as she passes through my room door. She's in scrubs; I like this look even more than the white coat she wears normally or the business suits she has for our monthly meetings at her office in the city. Everything else goes silent the moment she arrives. The chaos stops—no more Andrew, or machines beeping, and the sound of privacy curtain rings dragging open and bed guardrails flipping up. It's all gone. All I see is Dr. Miranda Wheaton's smile, the same one that made me a promise six months ago that this day would come.

It's here.

My heart—it's here.

CHAPTER 12

ANDREW

The potatoes are good. If nothing else, my mother's garlic mashed potatoes are so goddamned good, I've been able to drown myself in helping after helping, which has somehow kept much of the conversation off me.

Not entirely—just *mostly.* There was that brief moment when I came in and Mom was finishing up in the kitchen where she went through the list of things I need to pay for this month; the bill for spring tuition is due, and my insurance is apparently going up…again. Not that I ever get to drive. My car has been sitting in the apartment storage garage since the accident, the damage to the wheel well just enough to throw the alignment to shit. It's fixable, but just like everything else in my life, it costs money.

"I hate you; I hope you know," Kensi whispers in my ear, leaning into me while my mom, Dwayne and Owen talk about Germany more. I stop eating, my fork stuck in my mouth as I turn my head sideways and look at her, taken off guard by those words.

"Wha?" I say, mouth stuffed full like a chipmunk.

Her serious face breaks slowly into a smile.

"If I ate like you did, my ass would be so fat. It's not fair, and I hate you for it," she says.

"Oh," I grin, laughing with my full mouth. I swallow my last bite, stand, and pick up my plate and hers to take them to the kitchen. She follows me, and I hear Owen's steps coming behind her. I'm too full to eat any more, so I guess I should take his last lecture before he leaves the country. I ready myself for a litany of reminders not to fuck up, be good to Mom, and never trust House, but the lecture doesn't come. Instead, he leans silent on the counter opposite me as I rinse the dishes and slip them into the dishwasher.

I pick up the towel, sensing he's still staring at me, and finally give in. "What is it?" I sigh.

He chuckles, his arms crossed over his chest, finally nodding his head to follow him outside. I narrow my eyes, but toss the towel on the counter behind me and move toward the door, pausing for Owen to slip on his jacket. Kensi follows us both out the door, and I notice she's shivering by the time we step down the stairs and begin to head toward the parking lot. Today's the coldest it's been this fall.

"Here," I say, pulling my sweatshirt from over my head and tossing it to her.

"Thanks," she smiles, putting it on without hesitating. I shove my hands in my pockets to keep warm in just my black T-shirt.

"Why do you always have to make me look like a dick in front of my girlfriend?" Owen says, pulling his jacket off and handing it to Kensi. She laughs and shrugs it away.

"I don't need it now. I'm good in Andrew's sweatshirt," she teases.

"Seriously? He's all skinny and shit. My jacket's warmer." I think he might actually have hurt feelings over this. He doesn't sound like he's joking, and I think...shit...I think he might be pissed. I look at Kensi, and we both purse our lips, trying to remain composed. It doesn't last long as I practically spit out the laugh I'm holding in.

"You're such a pussy, O. I haven't been skinny in four years. In fact, I'm pretty sure I could kick your ass without working up a sweat now—so don't distract from the fact that I'm a bigger gentleman to your girlfriend with some false illusion that I'm still just a kid. I haven't been a kid for a long time now. Maybe you're just an insensitive dick who needs to pay more attention to her," I say. My words somehow fell into bitterness. I'm not sure how or why, but it's too late now. Nobody quite knows how to respond, either. We're all standing in the parking lot caught in the cone-of-awkward-silence I just plopped on top of us.

Owen looks down at his jacket in his hand, then glances sideways to Kensi, who shrugs at him. He lets out a breath of a laugh, then looks back up to me, pointing at me while he puts his jacket back on.

"You are going to take that shit back in about fifteen seconds," he says, his mouth in a hard line.

I shake my head and whisper, "Whatever." It's easier than apologizing.

Owen walks to my mom and Dwayne's storage garage and punches in the code, and I step forward to stand next to Kensi while the door lifts. I feel better standing next to her, especially when I've done something wrong. And I did—do something wrong. My brother didn't deserve any of that. I'm just in a mood; one I can't shake. That's not an excuse to shit on him, though.

"Insensitive dick, huh?" he says, tossing a key at me as he gestures toward my car with his other hand. I let my eyes move from his to the keys in my hand, and it clicks with me instantly. I practically trip over myself as I step to the driver's side front tire—to the side of the car, the bumper, the front door, the paint—it's perfect.

"Shit, O!" I run my fingers along the side of the car as I kneel down. "Turns out *I'm* the insensitive dick. When…how? This must have cost a fortune!"

"It wasn't cheap," Owen says. Kensi moves to stand behind me, putting her hand on my shoulder as I stay crouched down, looking at my reflection in the black sheen of the paint. It looks better than it did before Emma and I wrecked it.

Before Emma wrecked it.

I force that thought away, instead wanting to focus on the good things happening right now. I look up at Kensi, and she nudges her head sideways toward my brother, raising her eyebrows. That selfless fucker did this for me.

Damn.

I stand slowly, leaving my gaze on what is probably my most prized possession for a little longer before turning my focus to my brother. Owen simply smiles, raising his shoulders, his hands never leaving the pockets of his jacket while he owns his good deed.

"O, I…I'm sorry," I say. There's quiet between us for a few long seconds, and I let it take us over so I can stand still for once in my life and appreciate what I have—appreciate my brother.

"It's no sweat. You deserve something nice; I'm still proud of you," he says. "Just as proud as I've always been. Maybe…maybe a little more, even."

I pinch my brow and gaze down at the keys, my keys, in my hand. I haven't held these keys with an intention of using them in years. Tonight, I'm driving home on my own. No cab for me.

"Why a *little more*?" I ask, curious how anyone could be proud of me lately.

"Because when shit got hard, you found another gear. It isn't easy," he says, his eyes zeroing in on mine. Owen and I never really talk about James. In fact, we never really *have* talked about our late brother—about what happened, about James's addiction and suicide. But we don't have to say words—the scar is there for both of us, different but the same, and we can see it in each other's eyes. James was hurting, in his own way, and Owen and I are hell bent on never letting each other feel that helpless. We lost James, and the loss is going to stop there.

I move to Owen and reach for his hand, gripping it when he puts his palm out for me to shake. When our hands meet, I move closer to hug him firmly, feeling the tightness I've been carrying around in my chest release just a little, simply from holding my brother close.

"Thanks, O. So much," I say over his shoulder, my voice hoarse. His hand on my back brings me peace. "I'm gonna miss you."

"Me too, bro. Me, too," he says, patting me hard on the back a few times before we both let go for good.

"I'll pay you back," I say, looking back to my keys again, still a little stunned that my car, my baby, is back and running and beautiful again. Owen starts to chuckle.

"I don't want you to pay me back, but there's one thing you can do," he says, pulling Kensi into his side, hugging her and moving his hand up and down her still-cold arms. I shrug at him with a questioning look. "You can quit hitting on my girlfriend with your *oh, I'm a gentleman, here take my shirt and...oh...did you see my abs?* move."

I smirk as he mocks me, then start to laugh hard when the words he just said finally hit me.

"Dude...my abs? Really? Jealous much?" I look to Kensi, who's laughing too. Owen's eyebrows are raised, but he's not laughing like we are—so we both try our best to stop. "Got it. Okay. No more abs or winter-wear for Kensi. Done. Kens?"

She looks at me.

"You're gonna need to start bringing your own jacket to things and opening your own car doors and junk, 'cuz...well...you know he's not going to do any of it," I say, laughing halfway through as I needle my brother for the last time until he comes back from Europe in a year. He steps forward and pushes me off balance, but his right cheek rises with his grin.

* * *

Today was the first in a long time that everything in me felt right. It was certainly the first in many trips home that I returned to my apartment without feeling like a failure. Mom was easy on me—minus the few reminders about financial responsibilities—and Dwayne was...Dwayne. He's always neutral, which I suppose I can't blame him for. He has to be on our mom's side, but Owen and I make difficult enemies. He really can't win.

I think what really made the world shift for me today though was the feeling of driving myself back home—in my car. I was careful, always right at the speed limit, several lengths away from the cars in front of or behind me. Nothing was going to touch my car. No scratches, no dings. Not even the threat of a hard break to throw the alignment out of whack.

She sang for me on the highway as I drove home in the late afternoon sun. The engine purred with every mile, the rumble of the road below me, and the angry tires still with plenty of tread, gripped the road. One day soon—when I'm comfortable again—I'm going to take her out in the country and open her up.

For now, though, I think I'll just enjoy driving her with the same amount of zeal that my grandfather would have behind the wheel.

Nice and easy.

Trent is leaving, locking up our front door as I pull up to park along the sidewalk, revving the engine until he can't help but turn around.

I leave the motor running and step out to look at him over the top of the car, my hands flat on the surface, loving it like it's a woman.

"Please say you did not steal that," he says, rolling a basketball from one hand to the other as he steps closer, admiring. This car demands attention, and I can tell it's won over Trent's heart just as it does every person with a penis.

"Ha ha, very funny. O fixed it up for me. Where you headed? I'll give you a ride," I say, twirling the keys like a teenager who just got his license. I might as well be.

Trent's mouth quirks into a half grin, his eyes still on the shape of the car.

"Yeah, a'right. I'm going to shoot at the rec center. You wanna come?" He opens the door, letting out a soft whistle as he feels the weight of it as it swings wide. The car still needs some fixes—the interior is still a little rough and it could use an upgrade on the air conditioning and stereo system, but the body and the engine are levels beyond what I ever thought I would get them to.

I slide in and shut my door as Trent climbs in.

"I'm not up for shooting, but I'll drive. I'll take us to practice tomorrow too," I say, pulling out slowly on our small side road.

"Fuck that shit, you'll drive us everywhere from now on," he says, looking in his side mirror. "Though…are you always going to drive like a fucking old woman?"

"Yes," I say quickly, glancing to him, but only for a second. Eyes back on the road. "Yes I am."

He chuckles, and I look both ways at the stop sign, checking my mirror for a sign of anyone behind us before I rev the engine once more and let the tires squeal just enough to give us a good jump off the line. I cut us off when I hit forty and back it down quickly to senior-citizen pace, but the thrill I feel from punching the gas, just a tiny bit, lets me know this careful habit—it won't last forever.

"Hey, so that Harley dude from the gym stopped by earlier, said he tried calling you, but couldn't get through," Trent says. I pull my phone out and slide it on my lap, not looking until we hit the red light before the main road to campus. My phone was low when I left for my mom's this morning; it must have died in the middle of the day.

"Did he say anything?"

My mind goes right to the list of bills I have due and the pathetic double-digit dollar amount I have in the bank right now. I don't get paid for the before-school program until Friday, and even then, five hours of morning coloring with five-year-olds isn't going to make a dent in my tuition bill. I'm not due to fight for him until later this month, but the thought that maybe he could use me a little earlier has me driving faster so I can say *yes* before he asks someone else.

"Nah. He just told me to tell you to stop by when you got home. He's a weird dude," Trent says. "He seems young to own a gym."

"Yeah, but it's not a very nice gym," I say.

Trent's never been. I'm pretty sure if he saw the sketchy warehouse set-up I spend time in, he'd start to question my sanity more than he does now. As scary as the gym is though, Harley is just the opposite. He comes off as a preppy young businessman from money, and that's because that's exactly what he is—on the outside. But he's also connected, with people who help him make things happen, people who make large bets with him, and sometimes, for him—and the money always flows. If there's ever a kink in the system, Harley makes sure it's taken care of. He might dress like a lawyer, but he's built like a fighter.

And when I do him a favor, I *always* get paid.

"Nice gym or not, junior Wall Street freaks me out a little," he says as I pull up to the drop-off for the rec center on campus. Trent steps out onto the lighted walkway, girls in yoga pants and tank tops walk along behind him with mats rolled under their arms. I laugh to myself at how different this gym is from the one I'm about to drive to.

"I'll be okay, *Mom*," I yell through the open window.

Trent rolls his eyes, then starts dribbling as he turns and heads toward the building. As a new group of girls passes the car, I wait to see if they notice, glance my direction, take in the ride, and wonder about the driver. Only one of them does though, and not for long. Their attention is focused on my roommate about twenty feet ahead of them. As nice as my car is, it's still nothing compared to the Captain America of hockey.

I leave Trent to be worshiped by sorority girls and head to the vacant row of buildings on the south side of town, circling Harley's gym twice until I find a spot that doesn't put my car right on the corner where some asshole could rear-end it. The sun is still up, but barely. I'm hoping Harley hasn't left yet. I don't know who he's rolling out for rounds tonight, but I'm sure he's leaving with someone soon.

The lights are on in the space, which gives me hope. I pound my palm on the rolling door when I hear voices, and after a few seconds, I see three pairs of feet appear underneath as it lifts. Music is playing in the background, the low thump of the stereo offset by the slapping sounds of gloves hitting hands.

"You finally check your damn messages?" Harley says. He's dressed in his dark gray suit, like he always does for fight nights, his hair slicked back and his glasses tinted. He says it makes him look older, and I think he thinks it makes him look tougher. I always thought it just made him look like a pansy asshole. Honestly, the version of him I see at the gym—the one that walks around with his shirt off and lifts fifty-pound dumbbells, tossing them around the joint like they're water bottles—is a shitload more intimidating. But Harley's also never been screwed out of money, so maybe he knows some shit I don't.

"Phone died, and I was at my ma's. Sorry," I answer, holding my phone up for proof. He slaps my hand.

"Put that shit away. I believe you," he says, turning to face the guy standing in the ring working out with Bill, one of Harley's head trainers. "Danny, he's here. You can go ahead and bail. I'll hit you with something in two weeks. Take care of that fuckin' hand."

The dude boxing in the ring is bald and looks a few years older than me, but we're about the same size. He pulls the tape from his hand, twisting it into a ball that he throws in the trash, and nods at Harley in response. Bill comes over to look at me, leaning on the ropes with both arms.

"I don't know, dude. You think we can roll him out there?" Bill asks.

Harley looks at him, his back to me still, and the silence means he must be making one of his faces at Bill, the kind that says *shut the fuck up* without the use of words. Bill leans forward and spits on the concrete floor, then looks at me.

"All right, boss. You know best," he says, his grin either crooked from getting punched by Danny a few minutes earlier or because he's snickering at me.

"Roll who out where?" I ask, ignoring Bill and hoping like hell this means payday for me.

"Pitch has a fight tonight. It's kind of a big one, and I need it to look good, but I need Pitch to *feel* good—like he can kill in his next fight, 'cuz that one will be real. He's been off, so I need to get him right again. Danny usually works with him, and he was going to go tonight, but that asshole hurt his hand doing some goddamned house project for his wife or whatever. You're close to the right weight, and you've handled Pitch before," he says, tossing a pair of shorts my way along with a backpack.

"If by handled you mean let him knock my front teeth loose and deviate my septum," I say. I need money, but fuck—Pitch could honestly kill me if he tried hard enough.

"Funny septum joke. I like it. Look, it's late and I just sent Danny home. Are you in or are you going to fuck me over? Because if you're going to fuck me over, you can just get out of here and find a new place to work out your juvenile-aggression shit or whatever it is you do when you come here."

I swallow hard, and I know he sees it. I can't cut myself loose from Harley—I need both the money and the pain, and I think he knows it. I nod and sit on the folding chair to pull out my gear from the backpack.

"Where's this thing at?" I ask, my tongue in my cheek as I check the gloves, tape and mouth guard to make sure everything looks ready, wishing there was armor buried in that bag, too, for the massive stomach shots Pitch always likes to land.

"It's by Cicero, just down the street from Union. You can ride with us," he says.

"I'm good. I got a car," I say, wrapping my wrists and hands early, cutting the tape with my teeth.

"Well look who finally grew up and got himself a license," Harley teases.

"I've had a license, asshole. My car's just back from the dead finally. And I have work and practice in the morning, so I wanna head home right after we're done," I say, looking up to notice Harley and Bill have already made it to the back door to leave, not bothering to listen to me—not really giving a shit, more likely.

"We'll pull around; you can follow us," Bill says as the door shuts behind them.

"Oh, you're welcome, Harley. Always happy to help out. I'm sure I'll love getting my ass kicked for thirty minutes in front of an angry, drunken crowd. This all sounds super," I whisper, chuckling to myself as I grab the rest of my things and walk back through the sliding door, pulling it down behind me and tugging up to make sure it's locked.

Actually, I'll probably like it more than I'm willing to admit. And I know if it's a Pitch fight, the pay is going to be pretty damn sweet too.

I toss my bag in the passenger seat and get in, pulling out as soon as I see Bill's black Tahoe in front of me. I follow them down Lakeshore for the twenty minutes it takes to get to our highway, then manage to find their car again on Roosevelt after losing them in traffic. We stop near sixteenth, where the roads are packed with BMWs and Porsches parked illegally. I'm not sure who else is on the card, but if Pitch is going, I have a feeling a lot of these people are here for him. I hope they've come to drop some cash, and I hope like hell I can make it four rounds.

I find a spot near the exit reserved for the crew and Bill holds up a badge when one of the club owners tries to give me grief for parking there. He nods and waves me forward to join them.

"Thanks," I say.

"Sweet ride. I'd park that shit somewhere close, too," Bill says.

The back rooms are swelling with people, half of them women all waiting to get with one of the fighters for the night. They drag their hands over my body as I pass through the narrow, crowded spaces behind Harley and Bill until we slip into a training room near the main hallway to the ring. Most of the fights I've done have been in front of dozens—maybe a hundred people at the most. The crowd I hear through the brick and concrete walls sounds like it reaches close to a thousand.

"All right, here's the deal," Harley says, already running through texts and numbers on his phone. "You need to make it to four. You understand? Four."

I nod. Shit, I hope I'm standing after four. My heart is pounding with the force of a boxer trying to break out from inside, and my body is drenched with sweat already. How ironic. I keep my game face on though and get to work, changing and prepping myself for whatever I'm about to step into.

"You go four, and we're looking at eight K for the night, you feel me?" I don't react on the outside much, just nodding that I hear him. Inside is a different story, because eight thousand dollars is about four times the amount I normally make at one of these. That also probably means my face is about to take four times the force from Pitch's fist.

Tuition. Paid.

Insurance for six months. Paid.

Three months rent. Paid.

Shit, maybe with the money I make from coloring with kindergarteners in the mornings, I can take Lindsey out for a real date, like dinner and a movie or something.

Or…not take Lindsey on a date.

Not take Lindsey anywhere, and just disappear because I can't take Emma somewhere. I don't want to take Emma anywhere, but I also can't let go now that I've found her. *Fuck!* I've managed to go the entire day without thinking about my problem—I'm stringing along a really nice girl I have absolutely no interest in. Of course, it all comes racing into my head now—minutes before I'm about to intentionally thrust myself into mayhem.

A good time for a distraction.

I pull my phone out and click it to check the time, but am greeted by nothing but a blank screen. Still dead. No music, nothing to read—only my fucked-up thoughts left to keep me company while I stand in a yellow-painted brick room that's big enough to house a training table and a locker, but nothing else. The room starts to feel smaller with every minute that passes, and my heart begins to race more, sweat threatening to drip from my brow as my eyes dart from corner to corner, my ears perked and waiting for the knock to come. I need out. This room—it looks like Lake Crest.

I need out. I need out now!

I lie back and hold a towel over my eyes, the weight of my arm closing over one ear and blocking out any other light.

"You like getting hit, boy?" he says. "You like the way it feels? I'll hit you again. I'll hit you so hard you'll fuckin' cry yourself to sleep for a month, wishing you had a mommy and a daddy who gave a shit and didn't send you to a place like this with a guy like me. I'll set you straight. I bet you'll never try shit like that with me again! When I give you a job, you do it!"

The voice in my head feels real, and I fling the towel away from my eyes and sit up swiftly, looking around at the bare walls. It's only a memory, but the fact that it was real once—that a man who was supposed to protect me did exactly the opposite—is enough to bring it back to life as I sit here waiting in this tiny yellow room.

The pound on the door comes seconds later, and I race to my feet, welcoming the escape.

"You ready?" Bill asks. His expression is worried, which isn't one he usually makes at me. I respect it, but I also can't let it get in my head, so I hold my gloves out for him to pound and then push them into my temples and chest a few times to prime myself for Pitch's worst.

I wait behind the crowd, behind Bill, while a blonde woman reads the cards in the center of the ring, announcing Pitch to a deafening sound of screams and the thunder of feet pounding bleachers. I tell myself the louder they are, the more money they'll drop, and I breathe deeply as she announces me, Pitch's opponent.

"And fighting in his sixteenth match, the Irish blood running restless through his veins, Andrew *Wicked Boy* Harper!" She lets the echo of my last name drag on loudly through the mike, and I focus on her lips and the noise they make rather than the heavy *boos* and threats from the crowd around me. *Wicked Boy* Harper was Harley's idea—he gave me that name the first time I fought for him. He said the word came to him the first time he saw me spar in the ring. I just kept getting up, asking for more.

Wicked. Poisoned. Empty.

My eyes meet Pitch's as I step into the ring, and his lip ticks up with the only hint of recognition I'm going to get for the night.

That's right. It's me. Go easy, but get us paid.

I move to the corner and let Bill shout things at me that won't matter. He makes me drink water, checks my tape and gloves, then stands with me and squeezes my head in his hands, bringing his head against mine, the foul smell of his breath only mildly better than the view of the nicotine-stained toothpick dangling from his cracked lips as he mutters a prayer.

Too late, Bill—I'm beyond salvation, and Pitch is the only one who can control how much pain I get tonight.

The bell sounds, and I turn to face my penance, to earn my stay and forget my life. Pitch swings hard, and I dodge. He swings again, and I dodge. And then we dance.

I spend most of the first round moving with him, faking and stepping at all the right times, working from my memory of our sparring last week. I catch the smirk on his lip more than a few times, and I also note the nodding approval from Harley in the crowd when I let a few jabs land in my side near the end of the round.

His punches come full force. There's nothing pretend about them, even if he's going easy. The announcer says he's toying with me—I'm the mouse. That's fine, as long as this mouse gets to eat some cheese later tonight with all of his teeth in his mouth.

We spend the second round doing much of the same, but this time his fists find new spots on my body, and when the first hook lands squarely on my right cheekbone—my body is instantly flooded with the chemistry I'm constantly seeking. The sting is immediate; the bruising deep, and the pain is so good. I smirk as my head slings to the side, my mouth guard slipping from my lips. I suck it back in place, spitting blood out on the mat before grinning back at my opponent.

"Come on, Pitch! Yeah, baby. Yeah!" I shout, my gloves pounding my chest then hitting together.

My feet feel lighter, yet my head feels heavier. Everything is turning on itself around me, but Pitch is still locked in. I swing at him a few times, landing blows to his right ribs, where I know he can take it.

The bell rings, and I move over to Bill in the corner. He holds something from a stick against my right cheek and eyebrow, slowing down the blood that wants to spill.

Let it spill! Let me bleed!

"Come on, hurry up! Get me back out there!" I shout at him. He shakes his head, ignoring me. I push at him to get out of my way, but he leans into me with all his weight, which is twice mine.

"You're a crazy little punk, and I get that you need this, but just do me a favor and let me save you from getting killed, huh?" he speaks through gritted teeth.

"Whatever," I say, looking past him to Pitch, who smiles at me. He wants more too. He's having fun with this, and I'm forgetting everything. It's exactly what I need.

The bell rings, and I brush Bill away and rush back to the center where I find Pitch waiting, his fist opening up the wounds Bill just spent seconds trying to secure. I laugh as I stumble back on my feet, losing my balance enough to catch a glimpse of Harley, whose lip is between his teeth under his angry eyes.

I gotcha, Harley. I know this is only three. I'll stay on my feet. I just want to feel it a little more. Let me go, let me spar.

I come at Pitch with everything I've got. My swings are sloppy; he blocks most of them, but I'm wild and aggressive. A few shots land on his chin and head with enough power that he stumbles back a step or two. The crowd actually turns for a second, cheering for me. My breath, as stuttered as it comes, is mixed with a rush of adrenaline and fear and pride.

I'm too lost in this feeling of glory to see his next swing, and soon I'm caught in the ropes, his fists taking turns moving from my right side to my left, my skin red from punches and my bones begging to break.

But I'm still breathing.

I'm still feeling.

The bell sounds, and I falter back to the stool, where Bill goes to work quickly, my view of him skewed now from the swelling happening around my eye.

"You've never been hit like this," he says. He won't make eye contact with me, and it pisses me off.

"I'm fine!" I shout, spitting in the bucket he is holding under my chin.

"Yeah…" he says, pulling my chin up with his monster hand, the roughness of his calluses scraping my face so I'm forced to look him in the eye. "You're fine, huh? Then go out there and you end this. This is it. No more rounds for you, no matter how fucked up you are and how much you think you can take, you got it?"

Four rounds. I knew the gig. I got it. I stare at him without answering, though, because he's pissing me off. He growls at me, pushing my face from his view with disgust.

The bell rings, and I find Pitch once again ready for me in the center, his feet still nimble, his arms still up at his sides, everything about him fresh. I'm a bloody mess, and it makes me start to laugh.

"You're a crazy motherfucker, you know that?" Pitch pushes back a step, bouncing, as he stares at me.

"Oh, I'm crazy. And I can take anything you've got. Bring it, big man," I slur, my smile big as his fist elevates then rushes forward, landing squarely on my nose.

Oh fuck! Oh yes!

His swings don't stop. The pain keeps coming. I feel every single shot, as if time slows down just so I can take in the sensation of the leather of his glove pushing deep inside my gut, my chest, my face. Nothing else matters. Nothing else exists. I bleed. I land. The ref counts, and Bill drags my torn and broken body to the corner amidst the roar of the crowd around me; they're celebrating my fall, my failure.

They love me for it, and I'm drunk on my self-loathing.

"I'll do my best, kid, but I think you're gonna need to make a trip to the emergency room for some of this," Bill says, his face somber. Bill's disappointed too.

"I'm fine," I growl.

He laughs once, but his face remains serious.

"I said I'm fine!" I repeat, my face square with his. His eyes stay on mine, and we both breathe while they announce Pitch as the winner and people rush the ring to congratulate him, to touch him. I'm lost in the corner with Bill and my pain and nothing else.

"Okay, kid. But I don't like putting you back together. If this were my call, this wouldn't have been you tonight," he says, pressing a wet towel on my face. I grab it from him and stand.

"Well it's not your call. It's mine. And Harley's. And we say I'm fine," I say, spitting once more at his feet as I climb through the ropes and out to the back rooms where Harley is waiting for me.

The envelope exchange is fast, and unlike Bill, Harley hardly spends time looking at my face. The bruising and blood disgusts him, and I think I scare him a little. It's fine; I scare myself.

I don't count the money until I get outside and to my car, but before the rest of the crowd starts to spill into the streets, I pull the envelope from my backpack and leaf through the hundred dollar bills, counting twice and getting eighty-four each time. My lips can't fight against smiling no matter how badly it hurts my face to do so. The laughter comes when I hit the highway, pressing the pedal down with ease, crawling the car up to ninety-five as I weave into the flow of traffic, passing anything in my way.

The rush will carry me home.

And when I come down, I'll be at my next destination. I'll be at *her* house, and she can bring the pain back all over again.

* * *

EMMA

Graham has been the perfect gentleman. His mother would be proud. Or, I think she would be. It's still hard to say—I'm not clear about their relationship.

I didn't let Lindsey know I was leaving to meet him. I didn't want to deal with expectations. I brushed her attempt to talk off last night, telling her I was just stressed after the awards dinner. I told her I was walking to the store and back—instead, going to Andrew's to confront him. I wanted to see him without the veil, to see if he would be the same if it were just us.

Turns out he was worse.

He's so broken, and I don't know why. I let that consume me, and it was starting to push me into depression when Graham called and asked if I wanted to meet for a quick dinner. I jumped at his offer, wanting to find something else—anything else—that would mesmerize me for a while.

Graham has been ideal, what women are supposed to want—at least what I *think* women are supposed to want, all beardy and strong and masculine—but my mind hasn't abandoned its thoughts of Andrew once all evening. His messy hair, pierced ears, half-shaven face with eyes that have this way of boxing me in and suffocating me.

"So what's it like studying with my mom?" he asks as we walk from the small café two blocks away from my apartment. He offered to walk me home, and I allowed it.

"She's…I don't know…kind of tough I guess?" I say, glancing to his smiling face then back down to the walkway in front of me.

"She's mean, huh?" he laughs. "It's okay; you can say it to me. I mean hell, the woman raised me. She tells my dad what to do, too. That's the whole reason I went into psychology. I wanted a practice and specialty she knew nothing about. I had eighteen years of that woman knowing what's best, telling me what to do, but never really caring enough to stick around and watch me succeed at her plan. She just laid out new orders for me to follow, new expectations. I'm done with it."

"I bet she still knows a few things about your world," I smile, not really comfortable complaining about Miranda to Graham, or hearing his complaints—which seem to be plentiful.

Graham chuckles, holding his hand out in front of me to stop me from stepping in the road as we reach the intersection. A delivery truck races by, kicking my pulse up as it passes.

"Thanks," I say, embarrassed and looking down.

He bends his elbow out to the side, nudging me until I look up at him again. "Don't mention it," he says, leaving his arm out for me to take. I slide my fingers under his bicep and let him lead. He layers his other hand over mine, and I notice that when I loosen my hold, he tightens his. I think it's because he's still worried about me stepping off the curb, but there's also something overly-possessive about the way his touch feels. If I weren't this close to home, I'm not sure how okay I would be with it. "And no, my mom doesn't do psychology," he continues, lowering his head, picking up my gaze and bringing my eyes back up to his. "My mom thinks it's a shit practice, actually. But we're past that argument. I'm too far in now anyhow."

"How many more years do you have?" All I can think of while we walk is how different his arm feels. There's heat that goes along with his skin, and his muscles are bigger than Andrew's. Or maybe they're not. I haven't touched Andrew in years, and the version of him in my life now is definitely not a teenaged boy.

"Probably four more if I want to really be something. Which I do. I want to be the doctor who solves things, with papers published in journals and all that. You see, Mom and I both have that in common," he says, and I squint at him, my brow pinched as I try to follow his suggestion. "You know, awards and accolades—Wheatons love the attention."

I smile as he chuckles, and I feel relief that he recognizes this about his mom as well.

"Well, at least you all earn it…the awards, I mean?" I say. He acknowledges with a quick nod and smile, but his expression quickly fades as he turns his head from me.

"I plan on earning it," he says, his focus on the long sidewalk in front of us, his mouth in a tight straight line. "Mom…she gets awards because people have just gotten used to giving them to her at this point."

I breathe in slowly through my nose, glancing at him carefully, turning away before he looks down at me. I don't respond to his criticism of the woman who saved my life. It's clear that he's privy to a side of her I don't know, though, and I'm pretty sure I don't want to delve into it—not now, anyhow.

My nerves make themselves present as we get closer to my apartment. Graham has been a gentleman, but I'm also not sure if that lasts all the way up to my front door. His hold on me is still rigid and unforgiving; the few tests I've tried to relax my muscles haven't induced the same response from him. I'm not inviting him in, and my extremely-limited dating experience hasn't taught me how to navigate this next step yet.

Karma seems to have sent me assistance, though, as the moment we get to the front of my building, a voice calls my name from the ground. Andrew is sitting with his back against the wall, his hood pulled forward over his head. He looks drunk on his feet as he slowly gets himself to a stand, but when I see his face I realize it's more than that making him shaky.

"Jesus, Andrew! What happened?" I pull away from Graham again, but he puts a hand over my chest, wanting to step in front of me. I wave him off, whispering that it's all right, then reach up to touch the side of Andrew's hoodie; he jerks away. I hold my palm flat, then move to touch the material again, pulling it back just enough so I can see the cuts and bruises on his face in the light. His eyes aren't on me at all, though. He's staring at Graham behind me.

"I got in a fight," he says, a low rumbling laugh brewing in his chest, but never fully escaping his lips. His smirk never pulls into anything more, and his gaze can't seem to leave Graham.

"Yeah, I can tell. Andrew, you need to see a doctor," I say.

"That's why I'm here," he says, shifting his eyes to me, but only for a second.

"Em, you need me to call someone?" Graham asks, his hand flat on my back as he lets me know he's right there behind me.

"She's fine. Who are you?" Andrew's voice is louder this time, but his face is just as hard. As beaten as he is, his eyes are still clear and threatening.

I look down, closing my eyes and wishing to rewind time. I'm just not sure how far back I should go. Maybe…maybe all the way before Andrew.

Graham reaches around me, his gesture protective, as he holds his hand out for Andrew. "I'm Graham Wheaton, a friend of Emma's," he says.

Andrew looks at his hand in front of me, his mouth seesawing back and forth as his eyebrows rise, then slowly his mouth slides into a smile. Never full, and never friendly.

"Graham," he repeats his name, finally closing the distance and shaking, his muscles flexing to show exactly how little Graham intimidates him. I'm shocked he's not pissing on him, just to really show what a man he is. "You're the guy with the PowerPoint. A real hero, I hear," he says, every word double-edged with meaning—he's being affable as far as Graham is concerned, but I know better. He's mocking me. His eyes move to mine, and my stomach sinks.

Graham chuckles. "Yeah, I guess that's me," he says.

I feel Andrew's gaze as he steps closer to me. The amount of testosterone radiating around starting to suffocate me, and I need to extradite myself from it all.

"Graham, I had a really nice time. I'm okay, really. I think I need to help Andrew out, until my roommate gets home, but I'll text you tomorrow. If that's okay?"

My face is in no way a reflection of how I'm feeling. On the outside, I smile and look grateful for his protection, not worried at all over the guy standing—*bleeding*—next to me. Inside, I'm repeating swear words and praying that my roommate comes home early from her spin class. Glancing at my watch, I realize her class has just started, so that chance—it's really slim.

Graham's holding his position, keeping his eyes on Andrew, his head cocked slightly to one side. When Andrew notices, he mimics him, just before he leans forward and spits a bloody mess at his feet on the sidewalk in front of us all.

"She's fine, Graham," Andrew says with a small nod of his head.

Graham still doesn't move, but he turns his face to look at me, his eyebrows raised. "You sure?"

I roll my eyes and sigh, glancing from Andrew and back again. "I'm fine. He isn't here for me. But I can't leave him out here waiting. *I'll text you,"* I say, repeating my words from earlier, maybe also wanting to rub in the fact that I'll be talking to Graham again, seeing him again, making more plans with him.

Graham is worth a second look. And maybe if I can go out with him without a mountain of anxiety dangling over me, I'll end up liking him more.

Leaving his eyes on Andrew, Graham reaches to my chin and tilts my cheek toward his lips, kissing the side of my face lightly, the whiskers of his beard tickling me and making me smile.

I watch Graham step backward, his hands pushed in the pockets of his gray jeans, his sweater curled up around his neck, everything about him right out of the pages of an Abercrombie catalogue. He even smelled nice all night. I should have told him that.

I should like Graham. I should *feel* something.

But I also feel like maybe, just then, he was marking me—laying claim on his territory. And that makes me feel uneasy.

"So guys with beards…that's what does it for you, huh?" Andrew says, not letting my mind stray too far. I turn back to him, Graham's image still in my mind, a comical contrast from the rough, beaten mess standing before me now.

"You're an asshole," I say, shaking my head and stepping past him, pushing the glass doors open and greeting Sam at the front desk.

"Good evening, Miss Burke. Saved a copy of the paper for you; thought you'd like to see it today," Sam says, as I stop to gather my mail and then pull the paper from him.

I smile politely and whisper, "Thanks," but I leave the paper rolled. It's a copy of the Tech Campus News, and I know why he saved it for me. I saw the reporters there last night, taking pictures. No need to see a reminder of what I look like when I'm being open and honest. I'll just put it in the box in my closet with the others.

"What's so special about the paper? More stories about how your PowerPoint hero came to the rescue?" Andrew says behind me as we both step into the elevator. The doors close on us, and instantly the space feels small. I don't answer him, but I feel him—I feel him watching me from four feet away, his arms folded over his chest, his hood draped over his face, his body smelling as if he's stumbled in from some alley.

We reach my floor, and I step out, not inviting him. If he wants my help, he'll just have to show himself in. I unlock my door, toss my mail and keys and purse on the table and walk down the hallway to our bathroom. I hear the door close a few seconds later, and soon Andrew steps into the frame, stopping with his hands gripping either side of the wall, his head slung forward. His knuckles are covered in blood, and his legs are spackled with red. He's wearing black shorts that drape below his knees.

"Why were you fighting?" I ask, pulling the alcohol from the cabinet and the bag of cotton and gauze from underneath our sink. I step to him, and notice his grip tighten on the wood as I move into his view, his lip twitches on one side—he sneers like a stray dog not ready to trust the hand about to feed it.

"I fight for money," he says, his mouth now a hard line, his brow still shadowed by his sweatshirt. I reach up to move it, but freeze the second his eyes meet mine, the swelling on his brow, the blood on his cheek nothing compared to the broken look in his eyes.

"So this wasn't like some pissing contest in a bar or you trying to act like a big shot on the ice?" I ask, dabbing the cotton again, ignoring what I saw in his eyes. I wish for that look to go away—it makes me weak.

"I fight to forget about things," he says, leaning forward just enough that his breath tickles my neck. I swear I feel his lips against my skin. Maybe I imagine it.

Maybe I want it to be real.

My breath hitches, but only once. I look down at the bottle in my hands, inhaling once more, deeply, the scent a mix of the alcohol fumes and him, then I pour some solution on one of the pads, moving it to his face. He's playing me, and I don't like it. I expect him to jerk when I touch him; his cuts are deep, and the alcohol is bound to burn at first. He doesn't flinch. My eyes move from his wounds to his gaze—off and on as I work to clean him up. His expression never changes. It's hard. His eyes hazed as he watches me. He's trying to intimidate me.

"What are you trying to forget about, Andrew?" I speak softly; something about him feels like I could set it off at any moment. I push his hood back just then, and my hand finds his hair as I do. The movement is natural, and I don't know why my fingers act as they do. It's muscle memory, from one night and years of dreams. I push a few strands back, letting my fingers touch his scalp—touch him. He's still so familiar. The feeling of him rushes through me, and it burns.

He doesn't answer me. His eyes watch me as I work to clean out the deep cuts on his face—one on his eyebrow definitely in need of sutures.

"I'm going to have to stitch this one," I say, touching it once more with the cloth. He shrugs with one shoulder. "Unless you'd rather wait and have someone else. Lindsey will be home in an hour."

"You can sew me up." His answer comes fast, the words crisp and short. His tongue lingers between his teeth as his mouth curves to smile, as if everything he says means something else, too.

"Where else are you hurt?" I ask, treating him like a patient. Andrew is no different from one of the people I talk to at the clinic when we volunteer and fill out charts. This…is just a clinic visit.

Andrew is just a patient.

Just a patient.

His face forms a response to my question, but slowly, his lips curl ever so slightly more on the side, and his eyes close just as slowly. He laughs, the kind of laugh that seems like it comes from somewhere else—from memories, from the past, from loss maybe. What begins as smug body language meant to dominate me gives way before my eyes to confession.

"Everywhere, Emma. I. Hurt. Everywhere."

My breath stops, and I wait as his eyes look down at his hands, as he turns them to see his palms, to look at the scrapes and cuts on his fingers. He snickers to himself again, but stops quickly, looking at me as he stands in front of me, our bodies maybe a foot apart, maybe less. He grabs the bottom of his sweatshirt and pulls it up over his head, all of him overshadowing me, his skin and muscles bare before me.

I don't look at first, but when I do I see the dark purple bruising that's taking over his sides and ribs. That's not what I'm supposed to see, though. That's not why he pulled his shirt from his body, why he's standing here with his sweatshirt lying on the floor at his feet. That's not why his breathing has changed, or why he sounds like a frightened boy, each exhale short and desperate. The largest scar is maybe three inches long, and it starts an inch to the right of his belly button. Others are smaller, but clustered, and they look like burns. The lines are faint enough I know they've been there for a while.

This is something that's been with him for years.

"How long have you been fighting?" I ask, my arms no longer able to hold the open alcohol still enough not to shake drops on the floor. I set it down on the sink, leaving my hand on the counter to brace myself, my arm shaking with my own weight and need for balance.

"You see my scars there, Emma?" he asks, stepping closer. I try to move back, but I'm in a corner, the bathroom small, and my back already against the sink.

"I do. Andrew, how long have you been fighting?"

I answer him and repeat my question fast, thinking it will make him pause. It doesn't. He keeps moving forward, his eyes down on his own skin, and the closer he comes, the faster my lungs fight for air. When he reaches for my right hand, the one now gripping the corner of the counter so hard that my knuckles are white, I refuse to let go. Andrew leaves his hands on mine, though, waiting for me to surrender. I eventually loosen my grip, and he picks my hand up in his, his touch tender, slow, sweet. My lip quivers at the memory, but I hold it in. He places it on the line of four small circles on his side, holding it there against his bare skin, his eyes unflinching as he watches his hand cover my hand as it covers his wounds.

"This isn't from fighting, Emma. These scars...they're from surviving," he says. His body shakes under my touch.

He never looks up. Several seconds pass in silence, and the tiny room begins to stink of the opened alcohol bottle. I look over his face, his arms and hands and body—so much of him covered in bruises. It's like he was stolen—taken by someone, tortured, and returned half the boy he was—only to grow into a man with holes and broken pieces.

"What happened to you?" My voice cracks when I ask, my eyes still on the look of his hand on mine.

His hand. On mine.

"You have no idea, do you?"

I feel my brow pull in tight, my stomach binding as my mind begins to run through the thousand of possible things that means. I shake my head, my eyes moving up his body, gazing along his long torso, his golden skin, his curved muscles and neck and chin—his face so much older, but still the same. His eyes the ones I waited for, the only ones that ever looked at me that way before a kiss. Even if I didn't realize it, I was waiting for him. I was in love with Andrew Harper the first time he held my hand. I've just been waiting to see him again to fully fall. I can't fall now. Not when he's...like this. But I fear I may not have control over any of that—over...*feeling.*

"I'm afraid, Andrew," I tell him. When his chest fills with a deep breath and his head drops to the side, I know he understands.

"You have no idea..." he says, this time not asking a question.

His hand lets go of its hold on me, but I leave my hold on him a little longer, noticing his eyes close again as I do. When he opens them, he keeps his gaze down and away, his thoughts lost somewhere else entirely.

I let my hand slip away carefully, like a child trying to balance two cards in a pyramid. I watch him for a sign, waiting for him to say something more. I don't know what to ask. I don't know what I don't know. But I'm starting to think it's a lot—and it might mean the difference between the man standing here in front of me, and the boy I once thought I loved.

"I should stitch you up," I say quietly, my lip pinned between my teeth to keep me from saying more. A shift happened just now—I hold the power. I can feel it. I'm not sure I want it, or am ready for it. Andrew only nods, his movement small, his eyes still at the corner of the room.

I slide the small drawer at the edge of the counter open and pull out the medic box from our hours at the clinic. Tech believes in teaching the basics early, so all pre-med students are trained medics before they begin their four years of med school. I've stitched maybe a dozen lacerations. I'm a better sewer than Lindsey. But I wish…oh how I wish it were her hands doing this now.

I flex my fingers, rubbing the tips against my palms, working the nerves through them. I pull the thread and needle out, readying it before preparing the alcohol and tape and gauze.

"I'll need you to sit," I say, expecting Andrew to use this, to take my request and turn it into a challenge, to defy me just for the sake of watching me suffer. Instead, he nods with the same lethargy he's had since I touched him, his legs moving to the edge of the bathtub where he sits, holding on to the side, his eyes still lost.

I'm careful with every movement at first. And when I finally puncture his skin, I move my hands swiftly, repeating to myself that this is only a patient, that this is just like the other times, and that I can move smoothly. My hands work fast, closing the wound on his brow before the shaking settles in. I don't feel it until I bring the scissors up to cut, and I have to pause before finally slicing the ends of the thread away.

"The place was called Lake Crest," he says. I wait for more, but his silence indicates that he wants a response from me. I don't know what Lake Crest is, where it is, what it means, but I want more—I think I *need* more. Even if it terrifies me.

"Okay," I say, my voice quiet, unthreatening. I cut a small square of padding and two strips of tape to cover Andrew's stitches. He remains on the tub, his hands still clutching—holding on. I'm delicate with my touch, but the tape doesn't stick, so I run my finger softly along each strip against his face. When I look to his eyes again, they capture mine.

"Lake Crest is a place they send boys who need to be broken…when they fuck up and do something wrong. It's run by the state, and a guy named Nick Meyers. The first time Nick choked me, it was because I refused to kiss his feet…*actually* kiss his feet. He held my windpipe in his hands while security stood behind me with a Taser, just in case I decided to fight back."

Oh my god!

"The second time, I decided to try. The volts sent me to my knees."

My eyes close involuntarily.

"Some of the boys did him favors. That's how it worked there. You were either on top, on the bottom, or invisible. Favors put you on top. I tried real hard to be invisible, but they wouldn't let me. The ones who did him favors would leave the campus late at night, coming back with large envelopes—sometimes coming back with stab wounds and beaten faces."

"Nick kept after me. He didn't like that I said *no,* that I wouldn't bend to his needs. I was a threat to his secrets, because I saw more than the others. I paid attention. Money passed through his hands like water, and I saw it all. I didn't want any part of it. I only wanted to survive. And there were so many things to endure. So many factions, gangs within gangs, groups you needed to be *in* with and *out* with. I only wanted to be left alone."

His eyes find mine again, but his words pause, his jaw working back and forth while he thinks. I think he's trying to protect me from knowing too much after knowing nothing at all.

"I wrote you letters. Dozens."

His eyes penetrate me. Mine grow wide, my stomach becomes sick as I clutch the sink again, letting my legs have their way this time as I slide down to sit on the floor, my world spinning.

"You never wrote back. Not once."

No!

His voice sounds angry, but only at first. It breaks quickly; the realization squelching years' worth of hate and doubt caused by some unknown force. I never knew. I would have written. I would have traded him, saved him—*loved him*. I needed him. My heart was broken.

And I needed him.

He needed me.

He needed me...*more!*

"One day, I said *yes.*" He looks down again, running his thumb over the long scar on his belly.

"He did that?" I ask, my words crackling from my chest, my eyes barely able to look at the long line that slices through him.

Andrew nods.

"I said *yes* just so I could get out, so I could find you. I had to know why you weren't writing, where you were...if you were okay. I never collected what was due to him that night. I never had any intention of meeting his people at all. He found out before I could make it to the bus station to buy a ticket with the money I'd hidden under a loose tile on my floor. You were a forty-minute bus ride away—but I never got to see you. At least not then. I had to continue to live off of your memory. He took me into his office as soon as we got back to campus, hitting me until I could no longer stand. And when the guard pulled my arm over his shoulder to carry me on my weak legs back to my room, he told them to wait for one more second so *he could give me something to make sure I'd never forget.* The knife was small, but sharp; more of a razor. I bled for days—just deep enough so it would heal on its own...*in time.*"

It's all too much. His story—*his life!*

"Andrew," I whisper, my lips dry, my mouth drier. My throat aches, and my heart hurts as it never has before.

"You didn't know," he says, his mouth half open, his eyes back to the lost place. I shake my head to confirm his assumption. He notices. "All this time...you...you didn't know."

"I would have come. I swear, Andrew...if I knew what had happened to you...I would have made them..." I'm breathless with my words, my plea cut short before I can tell him I would have made them stop, would have confessed the truth.

"Em? You home?"

Lindsey's shout and clamor through the front door rocks me like thunder, and I stumble to my feet, clearing the counter of the remains of my work on Andrew. I look to him, expecting him to be just as frozen, just as stunned and worried about what to say, what to do. Instead, he's already standing, pulling his sweatshirt back over his body as he moves toward the sink to wash his hands.

I watch him.

"Oh! Damn! You scared me—" Lindsey jumps when she sees me in the bathroom, stuttering when she sees Andrew in here, too. Her eyes dart between us.

"I was helping him. He needed…stitches," I say, looking for a sign from him, waiting for his eyes to look up to see me in the mirror. He turns the sink off, dries his hands then leans into her, never looking at me at all.

"I had a bit of a fight. Hockey thing. I'm okay. Emma stitched me up," he lies, kissing the top of her head.

My eyes sting with jealous tears as his mouth touches her hair.

"Oh my god, are you okay?" Lindsey says, quickly working her hands to appraise his wounds on her own. He flinches and steps away, but not far.

"Sorry, sore. But I'm okay. I promise. I just promised I'd come by. I didn't want you to worry. I'm going to go home, clean up, and maybe knock myself out for the night," he chuckles.

"Sure, yeah. I mean…you can stay…" She's still taking all of him in.

"Thanks, but I'll be better company tomorrow," he says, touching the side of her face gently. His touch is tender. His performance is flawless. His instant hold on me is painful—but it's real. And I hate Lindsey right now. I hate her so much.

She walks him to the door, and I start to follow behind, but my legs only carry me a few steps before they stop, like I've reached my limit—this is as far as I get to go on this journey.

They say a few things to one another, half whispering, and she begins to close the door as he leaves. His hand grabs the edge, though, and his gaze looks over her right to where I am, his eyes saying we have more to say—both of us.

We do. I do. *I have scars, too, Andrew. They aren't evil like yours. Mine are miracles. But you need to know.*

"Thanks for the stitches, Emma." His voice is calm, his mouth a faint smile—all of it…*fake.*

The door closes, and Lindsey begins speaking. I nod and respond, but I never once hear a single word. I pretend. I keep on pretending.

And when Graham sends me a text just to make sure everything is okay, I tell him it is, pretending for his sake too.

Because the lie is so much happier than the truth, and I only know a sliver of it.

CHAPTER 13

ANDREW

I got sent home from work this morning. Seems the school doesn't really want the people showing up to hang out with little kids in the morning to look like they just got the shit kicked out of them. I told them it was a hockey fight. It got me a pat on the back from the principal and a promise that he'd have to come watch me play sometime.

I still got sent home though. Whatever. I had eight grand in my pocket and could afford losing out on the ten dollars I'd get from coloring princess posters and playing kickball this morning.

Trent was asleep by the time I returned last night, and I always leave well before he's awake. So far, I've managed not to have to deal with any of the shit on my body or in my brain. But hooray for busted lip and swollen eye! I got sent home early, and Trent is sitting on the sofa slurping the milk from his cereal, eying me, ready to make me work.

"Dude. You look like hell," he says in between slurps. The bowl finally empty, he slides it in front of him on the coffee table. He's going to just leave it there. I know it. I stare at it until he rolls his eyes, stands, and carries the bowl into the kitchen.

"You're like a fuckin' chick sometimes, you know that?" He actually rinses it and puts it in the dishwasher, which makes me proud. If I'm like a chick, he's like a Labrador. Only, Labs learn faster.

"Let me get this straight: You're calling me a woman because I don't want to live like a homeless man in shit and filth?"

His sigh in response is overexaggerated, and it makes me laugh.

"You're trying to distract from the point…and hey…*shit and filth?* Come on, it's a dirty bowl. Hardly a crack house," he says, collapsing back into his spot on the sofa, staring up at me, hands folded on his chest.

The shrink is in.

I rub my hand over my chin, and it hurts like hell. Trent chuckles at me.

"Do you want me to ask questions? Or…do you just want to tell me why in the hell you look like this?"

I hold his stare for a few seconds, because shit…maybe I want the ease of just saying *yes* or *no* to his questions. I shrug, shaking my head, and take the chair opposite him, turning it backward and laying my arms over the back, my forehead resting on them so I can shut my eyes. I'm exhausted.

"Did Emma do this to you? Or that Harley dude?" he asks.

"Neither of them *did* anything to me, ass monkey," I say, not bothering to look up.

"Okay," he says, his pause long and quiet and…why isn't he talking? I glance up to find him staring at me, his brow pulled forward, his mouth a hard line.

"Coach isn't going to like this," he says.

"Whatever. It's not like I'm you," I shrug.

Dick thing for me to say, but it's true. I'm the guy people expect to show up looking like this. Trenton is the face of the team. I'm just the guy who the crowd loves seeing get thrown in the box.

"Look, I can sit here and play twenty questions and never get close to what's actually going on with you. How about you try this friendship thing out and maybe trust me with some shit, huh?" He leans forward, resting his elbows on his knees. I laugh and look away, but I can feel him looking. I turn back to see his face serious, so I lower my gaze, maybe a little ashamed.

Digging into my pocket, I pull out the envelope from my fight, holding it in front of me for a second before finally tossing it on the table between us. Trent watches it land in front of him, glances to me again, then looks back to it, pulling it in his hands. His eyes react when he opens the fold and sees how many hundreds are stuffed inside. He closes it quickly, tossing it back on the table before running his hands over his face. He can't seem to bring his eyes to me now, and I know it's because he's thinking the worst.

"I need to know. Did you do something…illegal to end up with this?" What he means—is *am I selling drugs.*

"No…not…not really," I shake my head. It's not really legal, but my end…well it gets sketchy. I'm just doing a job. I get offered a fight and a purse. I do my thing; I go home with money. I'm not hurting anyone.

"Not really…as in you are just like…what…a middle man?" Trent's voice grows louder, and he's rubbing his hands together nervously. I can sense his temper, his patience waning.

I pull my face up to really look at him, my hands gripping the back of the chair. "Do I *look* like a middle man?" I say, arms out, my beaten body as evidence. "I fight sometimes. For money. Harley…he pays me," I say.

Trent flinches, not expecting that answer.

"So you're, what…like a boxer? Are you any good?"

"I can take a punch," I say. "That's why he books me. I'm like a practice fight for his real guys."

"So you get paid to get the shit beat out of you?"

I nod slowly, letting my eyes drift back to the table, to the stack of cash peaking out from the yellow envelope.

"Yep," I say, chewing at the inside of my mouth.

"Wow," he says quietly. Slowly. He leans forward again and picks up the envelope, really flipping through this time. His eyes flash as the number he's counting grows higher. "So…the worse shape you're in, the bigger the payday? Is that how this works?"

He chuckles, handing me my money. I lean back and stuff it back into my pocket.

"Nah. Last night was sort of special. I fought a guy that's sort of a big deal. Paid my tuition," I say.

"That guy…he gave you that?" he asks, pointing to my crusty brow, the dark stitches sticking out. I touch it, and immediately think of Emma. I nod in response.

"Does Harley just stitch you up then?" he asks.

I purse my lips, tilting my head to the side.

"I...uh...I had *Emma* do this," I say, finger back on her handy work.

Trent starts to laugh slowly, standing as it grows to a full belly laugh, the kind that makes him start to cough. He walks into the kitchen and pulls a bottle of water from the fridge, guzzling half of it before finally calming himself down enough. My life is funny to him.

"Emma," he repeats. I just nod.

"Not...what was her name?" He's being an ass now.

"Her name is Lindsey. You know her name. Stop," I say, standing, done with my little session. I flip the chair around and walk toward my room.

"A'right, a'right. I'm sorry. You're right. I'm helping, listening—go on, give me the story behind that part. Emma...you said she's the girl. This is *the* girl? The one who you went to that group home for or whatever?"

"It wasn't a group home. It was more like a reform school. And yeah... same Emma," I say, folding my arms, protecting my heart. "Long story short, I took the fall for her, then I never heard from her again."

"Oh that shit ain't cool," Trent pipes in. At least he's on my side for this. I hold up a hand to spare him.

"Yeah, that's sort of what I always thought, except..." I pause, shutting my eyes for a beat, picturing her face as I told her, as she filled in the gaps, as her heart broke hearing my pain. "Turns out she never knew. She thought I was just gone. I don't know where, but just...gone. Not in some shit-hole wannabe prison getting the shit kicked out of me on a daily basis."

"Oh...damn, bro," Trent says, leaning forward to lean on the counter across from me.

"Yep," I say, mouth tight. "Damn. Or damned. Whatever."

I walk away and leave my friend with the synopsis of my hell. I toss my envelope on my bed along with my keys and whatever other crap I've collected in my pocket. I look around at the blankness of my room, the walls and dresser top void of anything personal. I don't have anything personal. I've kept my life sterile. I don't even have a favorite...*anything!*

Except my car. I have that back.

And maybe I sort of have Emma back too. If I want her…

Do I want her?

Can I forgive her?

Is there really something to forgive anymore?

Letting go is proving harder than it should be. Or maybe it's as difficult as I wanted it to be. I spent years building up the walls and anger—turning them into weapons against the *Emmas* of the world so I'd never fall victim to one again. To find out I did it all in vain—I just don't know if I'm ready to believe that either. I don't know what to believe. I've held on to that sourness, that poison, for so long that my insides aren't sure what to do without it there.

I could fill it, though. I could fill it with her, with what we were supposed to be before that night ruined everything.

But would she even have me? Like this. What I am now? A hollow version of the boy my brother and mom spent years trying to protect to keep me whole and light and hopeful. One night was all it took to make my heart dark. One night, and a year of having my bones broken, my skin burned, my spirit shattered by an evil man and a group of boys just as damaged as I am.

She didn't know. She said she didn't know. Then she said she would have…what? Stopped me? Would I have let her? It's easy to say that now. Sorry is a word. Actions…those are harder.

But maybe…maybe if she showed me something, a piece of who she was. Maybe if I knew she really cared.

"Hey. Let's go hit the ice," Trent says behind me, snapping me out of my self-pity and dangerous self-diagnosis. He's holding my stick and my gear bag. His face is erased of everything I just told him. I stare at the stick in his grip, laughing lightly to myself. I just got my face tore up in a boxing ring and I want to make everything better by crashing my teammates into glass.

"I'll drive," I say, grabbing my bag from him and passing him in the hallway, my keys pressed in my palm.

"Hey, maybe I can take it for a test run sometime? You know…just up to the arena or whatever…" I stop at the door and laugh, then look at him over my shoulder, my lip raised. He already feels stupid for asking.

"No fucking way in hell," I say, and I swing the door wide enough for him to follow me out, admiring my car on the road. In this mountain of shit I'm sinking in, that car makes me smile.

Maybe I'll get Emma in it just once…for old time's sake. Just to see how she looks here, in our past, in what we almost were. Maybe I can try *us* on.

I drive away a little faster, and I notice Trent's smirk as I peel out.

* * *

EMMA

I don't know how I knew he'd be here. I just knew. I had to find a way to see him alone—without Lindsey. I need to know more. He needs to know more. And this need—it isn't about my friend. Even though she's precisely the reason I shouldn't be here.

I've compounded this sham of Andrew and I not knowing one another to the point that there's no escaping losing her friendship if it blows up now. No matter how I look at it, I've lied.

I lied to the girl who helped me bury my mother.

I suck in a deep breath, letting the cold harden my lungs—maybe my heart a little, too, just so I can hide it from the guilt brought on by thinking of Lindsey.

The Tech arena is colder than the one back home. It's nicer here, too. The rink is surrounded by stands, different from the few bleachers that press up to the glass in Woodstock. I see his name on the marquee by the door. It isn't one of the ones up top. It isn't even in the middle. But it's the first one I see.

I hear him before I see him, his voice carrying across the ice, his laughter—*his laughter.* I pause and take a seat in the front row on the opposite end, just so I can watch as he slides back and forth effortlessly, his stick working against his teammates, the ease with which he steals the puck away, the speed he shows when he chases—when he leads.

That vision right there, the man I'm looking at out there on this ice—that's *my* Andrew. He rushes once more, the puck loose and coming toward me, and he stops hard right in front of me, his face looks up, his eyes finding mine at the last second. He's breathing hard, and at first, it's because he's out of breath. But then he stops and stares at me a while longer, still breathing rapidly. That…that's because of *us.*

"Hey, Trent! Give me a sec, 'kay?" he yells to his friend still skating on the other end with a few of the guys. Trent nods and begins lining up pucks on the ice to take shots over and over again.

I follow Andrew along the other side of the glass toward the opening. He's wearing a dark beanie and his team jersey with a dark knit shirt underneath. Even the way he's dressed reminds me of the boy he was, the man he should be.

"Hey," I say. All this time, the walk here, the time thinking about coming here this morning, the hours awake last night, and the best I can come up with is *hey.*

"Hey," he says back, making me laugh. He grins, dimples denting both cheeks as he lowers his head and looks down at his skates. He's a solid foot taller than me right now.

"How'd you know I'd be here?" he asks, looking at me sideways, his lip curled on one side of his mouth. I like him better like this—happy. Or at least *not* angry. He isn't being mean.

"You used to go to the rink at home…you know…when you were stressed, or whatever," I say, my bottom lip tucked in my teeth, my face flushing from his closeness. I'm assuming he's stressed. I'm stressed. Last night, what he told me—that was a hell of a lot of stress-inducing crap, surely.

"Yeah," he says, leaning against the opening from the ice. "Some things don't change, I guess."

His gaze lingers on me after he says this, his smile subtle…special. Different. I wish I knew what he was thinking.

"I was hoping…maybe…we could talk a little? I…I don't know. I just… last night? I have so many questions. And I thought…" I'm stammering, my stomach all twisted and my confidence suddenly nonexistent. I'm afraid he thinks I'm being silly, that I'm being a child. That I got all the answers I deserve and that's where it all ends.

"I'd like that," he breaks into my thoughts, dipping his head lower to force my gaze back up to his. "I would *really* like that," he repeats, and this time he's wearing a real smile, a full one.

"It doesn't have to be now. You have practice, and your friend is here..."

"Nonsense," he laughs, cutting me off. "Yo, Trent! You know Emma, right?"

His friend holds a hand up to wave. I wave back, still blushing.

"I'm gonna take off so we can go talk. You okay with that?" he yells over the ice.

"I think that's the first smart thing you've done in a week," his friend yells back.

"Real nice, Trent. Real nice," Andrew laughs, his hand finding the back of his neck as he shakes his head, but peers up at me. This is his version of embarrassed. I remember it, too.

"Give me a few minutes, and I'll meet you by the front doors," he says. His eyes stay on me, and his mouth is in this forever-quirked smile, small enough to erase, but there.

I nod and walk to the front lobby where I came in and spend a few minutes looking over the plaques and trophies and clippings in the case along the wall. There's only two photos of Andrew in the bunch—one the team photo, and another a clip of him from the school paper, the picture of his face looking busted and bruised, just like last night. The headline reads HARPER THE BRUIN'S BRUISER. It makes me smile.

"That was after the opener, against Southern. I spent a lot of time in the box," he shrugs.

"I bet it makes the other team think twice about being aggressive," I say, giving him an excuse for being rough on the ice. He seems embarrassed by it, but smiles sheepishly when I say that.

"Yeah, that's sort of my job. I'm like the guy they put in the basketball game just to foul out," he chuckles.

I don't look at him, but I catch his eyes in the reflection in the glass in front of us. It feels easier to look at him this way, even when he's looking back.

"So, you hungry? I skipped breakfast," he says.

"Uhm, yeah...I could eat," I say, my chest suddenly feeling tighter.

"Come on," he says, nodding toward the front door. I look away from his reflection, to the real him, and I follow him out, walking a few steps behind, watching his form. His body is still bruised, but the swelling in his face is gone. His shoulders are broader, his T-shirt clinging to his back, his jeans loose around his waist. His feet are in flip-flops, sliding along the ground.

"We can go somewhere close. I don't want you to have to carry your bag far," I say.

He chuckles.

"Nah, let's go get pancakes at Estos," he says. Estos is far, maybe a half an hour away, which means I'll be with him for most of the morning, alone, away from my roommate, who's sort of dating him, I think...

"Oh no, it's okay, close is fine," I say, fumbling to make an excuse, to stay near home base, to keep the option of backing out of this crazy idea if I want to. I stop talking, though, when I notice his car parked in the lot. Suddenly breathing becomes hard, and that night comes crashing over me—the lights flashing, the man on the road, my hands numb, my eyes burning, my future gone.

My lips open with a gasp, and I suck in a hard breath.

"My heart..." I say, my words almost a whisper, my voice cracking and stopping before I say too much.

"Huh?" he asks, turning and seeing me. He drops his bag and reaches for my hand when he fully takes me in. "Shit. Shit, shit, shit...I'm so sorry, Emma. I thought you'd like to see it, my car, all fixed up. I just got it back, and I was excited. I didn't even think about what...I...I just didn't think."

I look down, my fingertips in his palm, his other hand on my arm. It's a cautious touch, but he did it so fast—on instinct.

He's always acting on instinct...for me.

"I'm...I'm okay," I pant. "It's weird, I haven't panicked like that in a while. I'm fine, really," I stammer, my mind catching up to the words I said, the admission that I once panicked. Five years ago, the panic came often, hitting me when I least expected it—sparked by seeing a fire truck race by, from riding in a car through the woods or sometimes a nightmare. I'm not sure when it began to fade, but one look at his car brought those feelings screaming back to the surface.

Andrew keeps his fingers loosely tangled with mine, and his eyes move down to where our hands are touching as he peels his hold away one finger at a time. I feel sadder with each finger that leaves my hand. Everything gets colder. It feels like…loss.

"Okay, if you're sure." His voice is quiet, and his face is wearing a mix of disappointment and worry.

"Yeah, I'm good." I push my lips together and force a smile, begging my stomach to stop clenching.

I move to the passenger side and pause, looking to him before I tug on the handle.

"Owen…he had it fixed," he smiles.

I grin back, then glance down at the handle again, still swimming in memories. Some of them, though…are good.

"So you mean I don't get you opening the door for me like a gentleman anymore," I smirk. I'm flirting. I shouldn't be flirting. It's my nerves.

Andrew stops at his door, pulling it open but leaning over the top of the car, both hands flat on the surface as he stares at me, one eyebrow raised.

"I will open doors for you anytime, Emma Burke," he says, the left side of his lip raised as he chews at the inside of his cheek. His eyes are soft, and smiling with his lips, then he taps the roof of the car once and climbs in. I do as well.

Andrew is flirting back. I swallow hard.

Inside the car is almost worse than outside. While the gashes, poor paint and other exterior things are all gone from the outside, covered in a fresh coat of slick, racing black and polish, the inside is still the same—still packed with memories everywhere I look. I focus intently on my seatbelt, on pulling it tight, on the vents in front of me. I tuck my purse between my feet and squeeze, focusing on the feel of my muscles pushing against it. I focus on anything I can that isn't the feel of my legs on Andrew's lap, my lips on his, his hands around my waist—and the crash.

"Are you sure? We could walk," he says, the keys perched at the ignition, his hand gripping the wheel, his head tilted to the side, eyes bruised, but looking so full of hope.

"I'm okay," I exhale, letting my body relax a little. I glance to the side of his face, then smile bigger. "And you still have holes in your ears."

His head falls forward on the wheel, and he laughs hard as he turns the engine over. "Yes, Emma. Yes, I do," he says, continuing to laugh as he looks over his shoulder and pulls us out onto the road.

He drives slowly, always five miles slower than the limit, and he doesn't speak. He's being careful and cautious for me. He doesn't have to say so; I know he is. The first ten minutes in the car with him is nothing but silence, even the radio on a gentle hum. Looking at it, I doubt it can go any louder. I laugh to myself because I doubt Andrew even likes the slow rock music that's playing. My mind is racing with all of the questions I still have, but I don't know how to start them.

Every now and then, he glances to me, then back to the road. Each look is full of an *almost*—a question, an answer. Finally, one comes.

"Where..." he starts, but stops, his tongue held between his teeth as his eyes squint into the distance ahead. "Damn, I don't know why it's so hard to talk to you. It's hard, though. Is it hard for you?"

He glances at me, swallows once, then looks back to the road. I suck in my bottom lip, nodding. "Yeah, it is," I admit. "But maybe, now that we've said it, it won't be so hard?"

He chuckles, flexing his hands along the steering wheel, moving them to the top then around the sides, lengthening his arms into a stretch. I imagine his arms around me again, then just as quickly work to force that vision out of my head. "I'm pretty sure it's still hard to talk to you, Emma," he sighs.

I feel sad when he says this. We used to talk. That was our one thing—or at least it was on his end. He could talk to me, and I listened, never judging. He told me about his father, about James. I regret that I kept so much from him.

"You said *where.* Where what? Ask me, Andrew. Let's get through this... whatever it is," I say.

He smiles, glancing over his shoulder a few times as we merge onto the highway toward the next town over. "I'm not ready for *where.* That's a big question. I need to work up to it. How about...how about I start with a who," he says, the right corner of his mouth twisted with his pause, still unsure.

"Okay, who. Go for it," I say, just happy we're talking more easily.

"Who's the guy who walked you home the other day?" he asks. My chest constricts a little, like someone just jumped out from a corner to scare me.

I'm not sure why, because Graham isn't really anything…yet. He's my mentor's son, which I guess makes him…complicated.

"He's just a guy," I answer. The lamest reply possible, and it takes Andrew all of half a second to call me on it.

"Just. A. Guy." He laughs once, the sharp belly kind, then clicks the blinker to exit the highway, the sign for Estos standing above a hill. "Okay. We'll go with that for now. I'll let you have that one."

I sigh lightly, watching out the window as we pull in to a space near the door. Andrew cuts the engine, but sits still, watching families and old couples walk in and out of the restaurant.

"There really isn't much more to say," I say, feeling defensive. I can't really explain who Graham is without connecting him to how we met.

Andrew nods, then steps out of the car, leaving the door open, his feet on the pavement outside, but his body still inside with me.

"Where do you think I went?" he asks, his back to me. Everything about him is suddenly deflated, his shoulders lowered, his head sunken. "You said you didn't know where I went. You didn't know about Lake Crest. Where… where was I in your world?"

"Iowa," I answer quickly.

His body rises with a silent laugh, his shoulders raising once, but dropping back into sadness.

"Iowa," he repeats, standing slowly, turning and leaning into the car. "Come on. Let's go eat."

His door closes, and I take this small moment in his car alone to *gasp*, letting my body make a small sound, a short cry, so I don't do it in front of him. Then I get out and step around the car, joining him at the front door to the restaurant. He steps in front of me, pulling the door open, his head tilted to the side as I step through.

"Just a guy, huh?" He smirks. We look at each other, his hand finding my back as he guides me inside and I pass him, his touch gentle, but purposeful. I let him. I relish it. And I know I won't be able to let it go.

The hostess guides us to a booth in the back of the restaurant. It's away from the front windows, away from the view of his car. I'm glad. Looking at it is hard.

The waitress takes our order quickly. We both order a short stack and a coffee. When she walks away, Andrew sets his eyes on me squarely, his head leaning slightly to one side. I look back into his eyes, holding on as long as I can. It feels like a game of chicken, and eventually I lose, moving my attention to the rolled up silverware and napkin in front of me. I unravel it and move my knife and fork to the side, unfolding my napkin and spreading it on my lap. When I glance down at my hands, I realize just how badly they're shaking. Then Andrew's foot finds mine under the table, his shoe tapping into mine. It makes me laugh.

"There she is," he says. I let out one more breathy laugh, and it mixes with a cry. I choke it down quickly, before he can see.

I rub my hands on my cheeks, thankful when the waitress comes to quickly fill our coffee mugs. I thank her and go to work adding creams and sugars to my cup.

"Wow," Andrew chuckles. "That might be the unhealthiest cup of coffee I've ever seen."

I nod in agreement.

"I'm a little high strung," I shrug, blowing over the top of the liquid before attempting a sip. It's hot, so I set the cup in front of me to let it cool.

"Yeah, I'm sure the seven packs of sugar and liquid fat will totally help calm you down," he jokes.

"Feed the beast," I say with a shake of my head.

He chuckles at me, then pulls his arms up to rest his elbows on the table, leaning his face into one hand. His eyes haven't left me once in the last five minutes.

"I was in Iowa," he says finally. My eyes lower and my brow pinches as I try to understand. "Not at first, but after...when I got out of Lake Crest. I moved to Iowa with my uncle."

Every new piece he shares from his life fills these missing gaps in my world of Andrew Harper. Some of the things he says erase what I thought, strike out the story I'd believed and replace it with something sadder. He's careful when he shares, too—like he's testing me a little each time to see how I react. I think he's wondering if I care. He has no idea how much I do.

I care. I care, and it feels so dangerous to let myself, like caring about him could topple over so many other things that lay in the balance. This is how it's always been with us—our feelings on a teeter-totter.

"When did you move there? To Iowa?" I ask, hoping he says it was only a few weeks after the accident, that he wasn't at Lake Crest for long. I don't want my parents to have lied to me.

"Junior year," he says. His eyes are hard, almost stoic. His foot slides away, and I'm tempted to chase it. Instead, I bring my legs up to the booth, folding them under me.

A test.

"So you were at Lake Crest…for a year?" My eyes sting, but I hold in my cry. My mind races through memories of my mom, how she told me my dad went to look for Andrew, how they were told he was with family in another state. So. Many. Lies.

"Ten months, really. I came home at the end of spring, sophomore year," he says, pulling one of my empty sugar packets from the center of the table and folding the small paper into a fan pattern.

"Sophomore year," I repeat. He was home. And he never came to see me. My parents lied. And Andrew gave up too quickly. I shudder in the booth, and I know he sees it. His eyes flinch and his gaze lowers as he continues to study me; he's waiting to see if I'm pretending. "Why didn't you visit me? Before you left."

He shrugs quickly and pushes the small folded paper off to the side, running his palms over the table, clearing the few grains of sugar away that had spilled out.

"You'd moved on," he says, his eyes moving up to meet mine briefly. I gaze at him, my forehead low, not understanding. His teeth hold on to his top lip for a second. "You never wrote back," he finally adds.

I breathe in hard, holding my words while our waitress delivers our breakfasts. When she leaves, I let myself move beyond that silent barrier that's been making everything this morning so difficult, that wall that's been keeping us both from saying things.

"I never got your letters. Not once. I didn't know, Andrew. I didn't know. If I had known…"

He shakes his head, turning his attention to his pancakes, pouring syrup, cutting vigorously, stuffing a bite in his mouth. "It wouldn't have mattered," he shrugs.

How can he say that? It would have mattered. I wondered about him, worried about him, wanted to see his face for so long. I wanted his hand in mine when I was scared. I wanted him there—in the hospital when they cut me open.

Feeling brave, I reach over to his side of the table and put my hand on his, stopping him from lifting another bite.

"It would have," I say, staring at him, begging him to look back at me. He keeps his eyes trained on his plate in front of him, his muscles flexed and his arm still beneath the weight of my hand. I don't know why he's so against believing me.

"I drove by your house," he says, his lips paused open. His eyes finally move up to meet mine. "At the start of our junior year. You were getting ready for some dance, your parents were taking pictures. You were wearing this really nice dress. You had a date—some guy who looked like the kind of guy you *should* be going to a dance with. I'm just a fuck up."

"Don't say that," I swallow.

Our eyes remain on one another.

"Why not?" he asks.

"Because..." I start, not knowing how to explain everything Andrew has been in my life. He vanished, but the mark he left was a forever kind. His sacrifice for me so big, he has no idea how enormous. And now that I know what he went through...

"How many times did you write to me?" I ask instead.

He shakes his head and goes back to his breakfast, shrugging once.

"How many?" I repeat. My voice is more forceful the second time, and maybe a bit desperate.

His lips purse and he puts down his fork, pulling his napkin from the table to wipe his lips. "I don't know. Twenty maybe. Maybe more."

I gasp, pushing my plate away, holding my napkin to my mouth to hide my reaction from him.

He sighs, closing his eyes for a second, then he slides from the booth, stepping around to my side where he moves in next to me. My breathing stops with the feel of his body next to mine. And then his arm reaches around me, and everything strong inside collapses as I give in and lean into him to cry.

"I didn't know," I say again. It's all I have to give. I didn't know. He must hate me.

Andrew doesn't respond, but the feel of his hand as it cups my shoulder then slides up to reach into my hair, his fingers on the side of my head, threading my hair and sliding it from my instant-tear-strewn face, is enough.

"I didn't know," I whisper once more.

The waitress comes after a few minutes, and Andrew reaches into his pocket, pulling out his wallet and sliding a twenty on the table. His arm never leaves its hold around me.

"We're good. Keep the change," he says.

She walks away, and he remains in the spot next to me, his breathing slow and regular, his hand tender against me.

"Come on. Let me get you home," he finally says, his head leaning against mine as he speaks. I nod slowly. When his arm leaves from my body, the air rushes around me. The feel left behind can only be described as sickness.

I feel sick.

Andrew stands at the end of our table, waiting while I slide from the booth to follow behind him.

"Thanks for the breakfast," I say.

He laughs lightly.

"You didn't eat a thing. And you didn't even get to enjoy your fatty-ass coffee," he says. When I glance up at him, his crooked smile is waiting for me. "I think I owe you one."

I smirk back, but start to feel the sting of tears again. Andrew steps in to halt them.

"Come on," he says, running his hand down my arm until he finds my fingers, grasping them tightly. He squeezes just to let me know he's not letting go, then walks with me next to him, guiding me through the restaurant and back to his car, where he walks to my side to open the door.

"Thought maybe this was one of those times I should open the door for you," he says. My breath stutters from my body, almost feeling painful. I slide into my seat and let him close the door for me. I watch him rush around to his side, then wait while he starts the engine, buckles his belt and pulls away from the restaurant.

I'm lost in a world of *what-ifs* and other questions for most of the ride home, and I hardly realize how far we've travelled when Andrew wakes me from my trance.

"Who told you I was in Iowa?" he asks nervously. He's worried about upsetting me more. All this time—these years he must have thought the worst of me—and he's worried about how *I* feel now.

"My mom. She said my dad asked your family…" I drift off at the memory. I was in a hospital bed, terrified, wanting everything that ever made me feel secure to be in that room with me as doctors cracked open my chest. The realization of it all weighs on my shoulders, my head feels heavy and my body feels numb. "They lied…my parents…they lied."

I glance at Andrew, and his hands flex as they grip the steering wheel, his jaw tightening as he swallows. He looks to me, but only briefly before turning back to the road.

"Are your parents still there? In that house? I…haven't driven by since the last time I saw you." His eyes rake over me once again, and I wonder what he must have seen. I remember that day—it was homecoming our junior year. My mother had bought me a pink dress that showed my bare shoulders, but covered my chest completely. I had been worried about people seeing my scar. It was the most expensive dress I'd ever owned, but she didn't care about the price tag. She wanted me to experience something normal and not have to worry about what people saw. I found out about her cancer the day after the dance.

"My dad lives in Woodstock still. He put the house up for sale…after my mom died. But it's not an easy sale. He's still there," I say.

Andrew sinks deep into his seat, his hands running down the wheel to rest at the bottom. He glances out his side window and sighs. "I'm sorry," he says. "I didn't know."

"There's no way you could have," I say.

The bridge between us is so small and fragile. I hate to say anything more for fear that it will wash it all away. For so long, he was gone. And then he was only a wound—something that left me feeling hopeless. Maybe something I also tried to forget. I didn't mean to. I think I just *had* to forget him, or at least hide him from my heart. It wasn't right—and my heart, it knew he was there all along anyhow. The guilt over what he'd done for me, it was always tempting me, begging me to feel. All it took was seeing him to bring it back to life. And now that I know...*now that I know!* Right now, thanks to our words, secrets finding the surface—Andrew feels close; I can't lose him, even what little of him I have.

I'll take what little I have, whatever he'll give.

We pull up in front of my building, and my shoulders sag from the weight of everything else I wish I had the courage to say. I want more time—more mornings like this one. I want to travel back five years ago and fix things. I want to have known the truth then, to have gotten to decide for myself. And I want Lindsey not to be tangled in with our story. She is, and because she is, I'm slightly paralyzed. But my heart...it's still reeling after his words. And at the very least, there are some things he deserves to know...things he deserves to hear.

"Thank you for the ride," I say, grabbing my purse, clutching it to my chest. *Be brave, Emma. Be brave.* My heart is pounding underneath my grip. I close my eyes tightly, willing myself to get one thing out—to be raw and honest just once. "And thank you for what you did for me, Andrew—that night, for taking my place. You saved my life. You'll never know, and I'm so sorry that I didn't know, and I'm so angry right now that I can't even think clearly. But...just...you were always my angel. Just please know that. There hasn't been a night that's passed that I haven't wished for you to show up at my window just so I could tell you that," I say, my words falling out fast, my lips quivering, my hands shaking, my body sweating and flushed.

Somewhere in the middle of everything, I start to cry. My cheeks burn with embarrassment, and I blow air out through my lips, trying to regain my center, my world tilting just from the way he looks sitting there. I want him to look at me. I want him to tell me it's okay, that what he went through wasn't so bad. But he can't, because *that* would be a lie. Nothing is okay. None of what happened is all right—and Andrew is ruined because of it...because of me! My selfishness ruined him. My broken heart broke his—and I have to live with that.

"I just need you to know that one thing," I speak, my voice strained as I try to hold the meltdown that is seconds away at bay. "And I'm sorry if I didn't say it well or if I sound crazy right now. I think maybe I might be a little." I laugh and cry at the same time, my eyes falling closed. I'm losing it —cracking up. "I can't even look at you, I'm so embarrassed and scared, but...okay. Yeah. Just...you." I pause, breathing in deeply, looking down into my own hands that are clinging to each other. "Andrew, everything would have been different. I swear."

I glance up at him once before I pull the door handle and push the door open. His eyes are intent on his knuckles, and his grip in front of him is tight, his hands wringing on the leather of his steering wheel. He nods once slowly, but doesn't turn to face me.

I don't know if this is still him testing me, to see how far I'll go, how many speeches I'll make. I don't have anything left, though. This was all I had. And the fact that it might not be enough, that Andrew will still hate me, resent me—it feels so unbelievably unfair. Yet when I think of what he went through, it doesn't seem my punishment is harsh enough.

My feet are shaky on the ground as I step from his car, and I walk around the back because I can't bare the thought of him seeing me pass in front of him. I'm afraid I might fall. My face feels red, and the only thing I can think about is how I'm going to get the courage to ask my father why he lied to me, why Mom lied. My legs are tingling with energy, and I feel like I do when I dream—when my limbs want to run, but somehow they just can't.

One foot in front of the next, I watch the ground before me, not realizing that Andrew hasn't pulled away. I don't look back, and I don't see him coming, but his hand soon glides up my back, startling me. I gasp as I turn quickly, dropping my purse at my feet, my phone sliding from it, my lipstick rolling down the walkway into the dead grass, my medicine rolling next to it. I move on instinct to pick everything up, but Andrew's hands find my face quickly, his thumbs on my cheeks, his palms cupping my face. Soon his forehead is on mine, and he's breathing hard.

"Andrew," I whisper, my hands clutching the sides of his shirt. My eyes flutter closed as our heads rest together. He licks his lips once, grimacing from pain, his bruises still apparent and his wounds still fresh. His mouth opens in a hard breath.

"It was always you," he says, his body shuddering as he rocks us side to side, his thumbs tracing my cheeks softly until one finds my lips. I let out a sharp breath at his touch, as the pad of his thumb slides over my bottom lip. Surely he can feel it shaking. My entire body is pulsing, the sound of my heartbeat loud in my ears, filling my head, drowning all reason. "It was worth it…for you."

His head tilts up just enough that his lips graze mine, our touch almost a tickle as his bottom lip passes over mine, his breath slow against me as his forehead rests heavy. "Emma," he breathes, his whisper against my mouth. "So long…I wanted…I waited."

My eyes flutter open then drift closed again, something awakening in me from his touch. My body rushes with heat as he steps in closer to me, his hold on me firmer, his breathing more steady.

Years begin to dissolve, and my heartbeat feels strong and steady.

Then music begins to play at my feet. It's Lindsey's ringtone—alarms sounding off, calling off mistakes, stopping accidents. This is my chance to stop hurting people, to *not* make things worse. I step back and Andrew's grip tightens, his body feeling panicked. We both look down and see her name.

I kneel down, and Andrew steps back a pace, his hands falling to his sides, his eyes wide.

I hold my ringing phone in my hand, then look up at him, his sad eyes saying everything that's in mine.

"Hey," I answer the phone, never breaking my gaze at Andrew, who keeps his eyes on mine as well.

"Hey, I'm at the library. I need to finish up a research project, but I'm starving. Wanted to see if you wanted to grab lunch before our lab?" Lindsey's voice is in one world, and I'm in another. Those worlds are so far apart, and one will destroy the other if I let them collide.

"Sure," I say. My eyes stay on Andrew's, my hands wishing they could touch him again, but my head knows they can't. The dull ache starts to creep in slowly. "I'll meet you at the library in half an hour."

Lindsey and I say goodbye, and I push my phone into my purse quickly, no longer able to look up and see Andrew's face. I reach for my lipstick, but before I can grab the rest of my things, he kneels down and takes my pills into his hands. My initial instinct is to grab them back, but my fingers recoil before I do. A few seconds pass, and I know he's reading the long name, wondering what it's for. Eventually he passes the bottle to me, and I stuff it into my purse before zipping it closed.

"Thanks," I say without looking at him. I won't give any hint that that bottle is anything significant, even though when I finally stand and meet his stare, I know the question is just perched on his lips. He doesn't ask it though.

This is one secret I'm not ready to share today. There are too many things, and Andrew's heart has been broken enough without having to add the weight of my story—of what he missed while he was busy being tortured at Lake Crest—to his heavy load of things to bear.

"Lindsey…she's in my lab and wants to meet," I say quietly. He nods. He knows. "Andrew…I…"

He holds up a hand, shaking his head, his lips a deeply unhappy smile.

"It's okay. She's your friend, and I'm…" he pauses, chuckling to himself, "I'm not in the place I should be."

He pulls his keys from one pocket and his beanie from another, tugging his hat over his head and opening his palm for one more wave goodbye as he falls back on his heels, turning to leave. "I'll see you again soon, Emma. There's too much to talk about—me and you?"

I watch him go, wanting to race to him, wrap myself around him, kiss him like I really want to. But I stay in my place, remaining in the lie we've built on Lindsey's behalf, regretting every second of it, and now taking it as my punishment just as I'm sure Andrew is.

His engine fires up, the sound hitting that familiar nerve, but this time I'm able to stop the feeling before it numbs me. I wait to watch him pull away, and he lowers his window, looking ahead, breathing—thinking. Then he leans out the window, urging me to take a few steps closer so I can hear him.

"I said I wasn't in the place I should be," he says over the low idle of his car, licking his lips once, pulling his bottom lip in, chuckling to himself and looking down into his lap. He shakes his head slowly, then peers out the window again, his eyes square on mine, his heart talking to mine now. "What I meant to say was I'm not with the person I should be."

There's an emptiness and fullness that settles over us at the same time—

a feeling of hope and hopelessness. We wade in it, breathe it in together, and I want to run back to him, to tell him the rest of my story, to climb back into his car and let him drive us away, not caring if it hurts Lindsey. But my feet stay where they are, and Andrew's hand pats the side of his car, his fingers drumming along the shiny black surface and the gleam of the chrome stripe.

He drives away, and long after he's out of sight, I wait.

I wait for him to come back.

I think I've always been waiting.

CHAPTER 14

ANDREW

I should have kissed her anyway. I should have stayed. I should have picked her up in my arms and carried her into her goddamned apartment.

Instead, I drove away, headed right to Harley's gym, and convinced him I was fine, good enough to stand in the ring for an hour with some new guy. This time, though, I hit back. I hit back more than I normally do. I hit back with the force of all of the shit I was feeling. I took out my frustration with Emma, with her parents and the lies they clearly told, with her lack of trying to find out the truth sooner. Was it her job to find out the truth? Would I have if I were in her position?

There's still this part of me that can't help but feel like I was busy thinking about her while she forgot about me completely—while I lost a year of my life and most of my soul.

I took it all out in the middle of Harley's gym on some guy named Taylor. Some frat boy who cleaned up during the campus fight night and thought maybe he'd make a go of it, get himself some sponsors and really try and fight. I'm pretty sure I broke his nose.

Harley was pissed at first, and before I left, I thought he was walking over to tell me to quit showing my crazy face in his gym. Instead, he pulled up a stool and sat silently while I unwrapped my knuckles and packed up my bag, sliding his chair away right before I left, his back to me as he grumbled "that dude isn't ready. Good work, tonight."

Good work. Ha!

I left feeling just as confused and frustrated. I spent the night ignoring the three—*she sent three!*—texts from Lindsey. And then I laid awake, getting to my feet and moving to the door, with every intention of driving to Emma's apartment, before talking myself out of it and throwing my ass back in bed.

The problem is it's not just Emma's apartment. It's Lindsey's, too. I've made things messy. But I haven't slept with Lindsey. I mean…I've *slept* with Lindsey. But that hardly counts. That can't count. Not now that things with Emma are…well, they're different.

I didn't think my hate could give way so easily. I'd spent so many years harboring it, carving it into this delicate weapon to guard myself from ever dreaming again. It turned into vengeance when I saw her in the bar. There was only one thing that could have made a difference, and that was Emma not knowing where I'd been. I don't know why her parents lied to her, and I hold them accountable. My anger—it's shifted in their direction. And I'm a son-of-a-bitch for hating her mom now that she's gone. But I do. I don't know what their motives were, but I'm sure it had to do with everything they thought I was, and the one thing they thought I wasn't—good enough for their daughter.

Sleep might have helped me find reason today. Only, I didn't get any. I spent my morning workout just as pent-up, and now I'm laying here on this bench, rubbing my eyes raw, my cheekbones still bruised and tender from the beating they took two days ago, my heart bruised from the one it took yesterday.

"Better sit up, Harp. Coach is coming," Trent says, throwing his wet towel on my chest. I don't even fight back, letting it drench my shirt and make me feel as miserable on the outside as I do in.

"Your ass better not be hung over," Coach Bishop says, pushing my legs from the bench as he walks by, knocking me off balance. He's the only one on the team who can legitimately kick my ass, even at my scrappiest. I stumble from my resting place and follow him through the lockers to his office, throwing the towel over Trent's shoulders as I pass him.

"Fuck ass!" he yells, shrugging it from his now-wet shirt and shoulders.

"You started it," I chuckle.

"What are you, fucking twelve?" Coach grunts as I turn my attention back to him in his office. "Go on, close the goddamn door."

I do as he says and take my seat. Bishop is one of the country's best college hockey coaches. His NHL career was mediocre, a starter for the Stars and Sharks for a few years, but traded around the country year after year until he finally gave up. He slid into the job at Tech as a favor owed to him by a friend, but he's stayed for a decade thanks to his two hundred wins and forty-six losses.

"What's with your face?" he asks, pulling the toothpick from his lips and using it to point at me. He has this permanent scowl and crinkle around his eyes that makes him look like Popeye.

"Had a little fight. It won't happen again." I'm a fucking liar. Eight grand an hour, it sure as shit better happen again.

He stares at me for a few hard seconds, then leans back in his chair, slowly pulling his feet up on his desk. I'm holding my hands on my kneecaps, my posture straighter than it ever is anywhere else—I'm like a child waiting for my suspension from the principal.

"Don't get yourself hurt. I need your ass on the ice. You're starting," he says.

My shock is a little delayed because at first I start to stand, expecting to leave with my tail between my legs, but then his words register, and I fall back into my seat.

"Starting," I repeat. I don't ask. I know one thing—you don't ask Bishop questions. I just need clarification. I'm not questioning.

"You get punched in your goddamned ears? Yes. Starting," he says. "Your numbers are better than Gilbert, so I need you to spend more time out there on the puck. I need you to keep it out of Northwestern's control next week, and out of Penn's after that. You get that puck, and you get it to Metzger, and we will win it all this year. Now, you think you can do that? Or do you want to go back to spending your time in some stink-ass back alley with a mugger or whatever fuckin' piece-of-shit lie you told me about those bruises on your face?"

I blink for a second.

"No sir. I got it. Get the puck to Trent. Done," I say, standing before I say anything else stupid. "And you're right. I did lie. It was a *big* fight. But you should see the other guy."

I wait for him to laugh. He doesn't. I said something stupid, so I leave before I continue making it worse.

Trent's waiting for me by my locker, so I let him stew in curiosity while I throw my sweatshirt on and pack up my gear. I glance at him, but keep my face hard, letting him believe I got my ass chewed out as he follows me out of the rink, out to the parking lot and finally to the back of my car.

"Well, how bad? Did he suspend you? Please say he didn't suspend you," he asks. I unlock my trunk and throw my bag inside with a thud, closing the trunk and holding my excitement in for a few more seconds while I sigh and turn to face him.

"Do you prefer working a shot based on our offense or would you rather have more breakaways?" I ask. His face is blank at first, and his expression starts out as *what-the-fuck,* then suddenly it hits him.

"You asshole!" he punches my chest.

"Starting, at least through Penn," I smile.

"Hell yes, you are!" Trent slaps my hand, gripping it at our shoulders before he bumps into me. We both walk around our sides and get into the car. I pause before I start it, my mind flashing to Emma for a second, then back to the good news I got this morning. My heart feels lighter, and things suddenly seem clearer. I keep it to myself as I pull away, but in that instant, I decide that tonight's the night I'm honest with Lindsey and go after what I really want, what I've always wanted.

Emma Burke.

It takes Trent and me a few extra minutes to find a spot in the main student lot. I would have just driven back home and left my car there, but Trent's class starts soon, and I didn't want him to be late.

"Dude, why so many people today? Is there some event I don't know about?" I ask, wondering if I missed the memo that the President was on campus today or something.

"It's homecoming. There's a lot of stuff going on along the main mall, like a carnival or some crap. They're giving away free food—people show up for that," he says.

I finally find a spot near the very back of the lot, next to a dumpster, and I make Trent get out while I back in so he can guide me. No way am I scratching my car less than a week since I've had it back. Once I'm in, we both grab our backpacks and start the long walk to the heart of campus, the smell of barbecue pork and burgers overcoming us the closer we get and guiding us in.

"You weren't kidding," I say when we see the line of tents along the main walkway. Beyond the food vendors, there's a stage with some third-rate, campus rock band playing Blink 182. It's slightly appalling, however, the crap band is out-douched by the more pathetic groupies screaming for them along the stage.

"Why don't chicks do that for us?" Trent asks, handing me a pork sandwich from the tent just to the left of him. I bite into it, talking through my full mouth, wiping the small dab of sauce that starts to slip down my chin.

"They don't scream for you? Wow, I mean, I make girls scream all the time...I just figured you did too—"

"You make girls scream, hmmm?" Her voice cuts in, and I choke on my bite while Trent grins. Fucker saw her coming.

"I'm Emma, by the way. I don't think we've ever formally met," she says, shaking Trent's hand. He looks at me as he does, his tongue tucked in the corner of his mouth with his eyebrows raised. By some miracle, he keeps his mouth shut, but he knows I'm gone when it comes to her. He probably knew the second he put the *who* and *where* together over the driver's license I lifted at the bar.

"Emma, nice to meet you. I've heard..." I cough to interrupt him, a warning that he doesn't break the man code—we don't talk about when we talk about chicks. It doesn't work. "I've heard *way* too much about you."

Asshole.

I pinch the bridge of my nose as Trent excuses himself to grab more of the handouts. I open one eye to the vision of Emma sucking in her bottom lip, her cheeks red. I nod slowly, shrugging to admit my guilt.

"Yeah, Trent's my Lindsey," I say with instant regret. Her face falls as she takes a step away; she thinks we're too close now that I've uttered Lindsey's name. Unlike Trent, Lindsey doesn't know the details. They're really nothing alike at all. God, I wish I thought before I spoke. I wish I thought before I acted!

Fuck, I wish I thought before I *thought!*

Emma's wearing a dark gray hoodie and tight jeans tucked into boots at her feet, nothing remarkable, yet instantly memorable to me. Her hair is down in waves, the shorter layers up front blowing over her face as she pulls them away, tucking strands behind her ear.

"You know how I first recognized you?" I ask in my haze from looking at her. I'm definitely not thinking now. No…now, I'm feeling.

She shakes her head in tiny movements, her cheeks rounding with a slight smile, her lips closed tight as she works to hold in the effects of my attention. I love her blush. "It was your eyes."

Her lashes lift as her eyes widen when I say this, the silver shining.

"I was obsessed with those eyes when I was sixteen," I say. "I could never forget them."

God, that felt good to say!

We stare at each other for a long moment, and Emma relents to the small giggle building in her chest before looking down at her feet. "Thank you," she says, her voice meek and beautiful. That's the same, too—the timber, the inflections…all of it.

I kick at her toe with my shoe. She kicks back.

"I always liked your shoes," she says, her face falling to the side, her hand coming up to hide her embarrassed look.

My head falls forward, and I stare at my feet, my black Chucks, the same shoes I've owned for years, just a newer pair. Maybe a little bigger.

"They really are my best attribute," I nod, joking. She laughs, her voice a little raspy, maybe sleepy, too, and swings her arm at me, brushing against mine.

"No," she says. I look up at her. I want to kiss her. Her smile fades from a playful one to a serious one—an *honest* one. "That's not your best attribute," she says, her eyes looking as if they're about to cry.

I ache to reach for her, to touch her cheek to stop the sadness from taking over that space around her eyes, when she takes a sharp step back, lengthening the distance between us.

"Graham. Hi," she says nervously.

Just a guy is here.

"Hey, I was looking for you," he says, his eyes making a dominant glance in my direction. I laugh and roll mine.

"We were just checking out the free food," she says, squinting her eyes closed and shaking her head when he looks away. She does this move sometimes when she's uncomfortable—like she's a genie trying to wish the situation away.

"Were you?" he chuckles. This smug ass wipe thinks I'm intimidated by him.

"Yeah," I answer, surprising Emma, her eyes widening fast, caution lights firing behind them. I'm going to ignore that sign. "It's nice...you know...to be able to just *take what you want?"*

The moment that passes between Emma's friend and me is short, but it's filled with threats and lots and lots of *fuck yous.*

"Emma?" He's talking to her, but looking at me. I hate this *just some guy.* "There's this dinner my mom's hosting, her chief of staff and a bunch of other surgeon-types are going to be there. She's fairly insistent that I go, but it won't be any fun on my own. I thought maybe you'd like to join me?"

This guy is so fucking arrogant. He's flaunting his credentials like a peacock. No way Emma falls for this.

"I'd love to," she answers, slicing through the middle of my thoughts, cutting off my immediate assumption that *just some guy* is in fact nobody. She's just made him *somebody.*

"Great," he grins, pushing his hands in his pockets and pivoting on the heels of his shoes in my direction, just to make sure I get a glimpse at his triumphant smile. All I notice are his shoes, though. Shoes that are so irritatingly preppy—all I can visualize is the way they would look underneath the pressure of my Chucks, scuff marks left behind in the shapes of honeycombs.

"Great," Emma finally says in return, her *great* far less enthused. I stare at her. I'm a little baffled over the fact that this is all happening in front of me, especially after the things we've talked about, the progress we made… thought we made.

"So I'll see you tomorrow. I'll come by…around eight," he says, backing away slowly. I notice he never leans in to kiss her cheek. He's not cocky enough to do that. That's probably a good thing, because my hand is flexed at my side, and I think if he did, I'd punch his fucking face in. Then I'd step on his shoes.

I keep my stare on Emma, and when she turns from watching Captain Douchebag saunter away, she meets my gaze, then immediately drops her focus to the ground.

"*Just some guy*, huh?" I laugh.

"His name's Graham, Andrew," she sighs. "And it's not a thing with us, it's just…it's complicated to explain," she shrugs, glancing around me. She can't even make eye contact with me now.

"The dude's named after a cracker, Emma. Seriously?" I look beyond her where I can still see him walking down the main path where he's met up with two other guys that look just like him. He isn't small. In fact, we're probably roughly the same size. He's just covered in so much…douchebaggery…it makes him look smaller. His pants are pink. What the fuck? "I thought we were past this…or that you wanted…shit, I don't know…what I wanted? I thought we…"

"Lindsey's here," she cuts me off. The expression on her face is blank at first then it's instantly replaced by the fakest of smiles. I can tell her expression is a lie, though—her eyes give her away. They're full of regret and wishes. "Whatever you were about to say…don't. Lindsey is here, walking toward us. She's my best friend, Andrew. You started this, and I don't think I can lose Lindsey because of it. She's been through so much with me, and I can't—"

"Hey, I've been looking for you," Lindsey says from behind me. She slides her arm around me, her fingers running over my stomach and chest as she hugs me from behind. Emma turns away, but not before the look of pain flashes over her face. I shut my eyes and breathe deeply.

"Hi, yeah…sorry. I've been crazy busy with practice and classes." Lie, lie, lie. I've been ignoring you, not dealing with the beast I created, running away from my consequences, while I pine after the love of my past and drown in the truth.

"It's okay. I was just worried...you know, about your bruises. Your eye looks better," she says, reaching to touch my cheekbone lightly. It takes all of my willpower not to turn away—not because it hurts, but because I don't want Lindsey touching it. I don't want Emma seeing Lindsey touch it.

"Yeah...I heal quickly," I say, all of my attention on Emma. I'm not even sure I said that last part out loud.

My trance is broken when a yellow Velcro strap slides along the ground, sticking to my leg. I bend down to pick it up as some guy from our student government waves his hands emphatically on the nearby stage, the microphone in his hand.

"And we have our second team of players. You," he shouts, pointing at me. I glance around and look back at him, pointing to myself as he nods. "It's a hundred-dollar bookstore card if you win the three-legged race. Get on up here with your partner."

"I'm good, dude," I say, not wanting to be part of some stupid spirit week activity. But Lindsey changes my mind. Lindsey, of all people, changes everything.

"Oh my god, no...you have to do this. Trust me. You and Emma—she is the freaking master at this. Remember, Em? Last year, at the pre-med picnic? Seriously, it's like she was born for this race. Everyone who was her partner won." Lindsey waves her hand at the stage, buying us time while she urges her friend to join me. If Lindsey only knew.

"I don't really feel up to it, Linds," Emma starts.

"I really could use a hundred bucks credit," I say just for guilt. Suddenly, I'm desperate for her to do this race with me, to come with me, to give me five more minutes of her time. Her eyes slide up to meet mine, and I say something entirely different to her with my look. I beg her. *Please, do this one stupid thing with me. I can't explain it, but I feel like this might be the turn.*

Emma glances back to her friend, who is literally jumping up and down while clapping. She sighs and reaches for the Velcro strap, taking it from me and walking toward the stage. I trail behind, ignoring Lindsey's touch on my back, her encouragement and cheer for me. All I see is the wild strands of Emma's hair twisting in the wind like the fingers of temptation calling me to them.

It's going to storm tonight. I can smell it in the air.

* * *

EMMA

I hate spirit week. Whose idea was it to have field day anyhow? I'm finding out, then I'm going to sink their campaign when they run for student government again. I might run against them. My platform will be to do away with forced audience participation.

When I get to the chair at the starting line, I sit down, moving my leg as far away from the edge as I can so I don't have to feel him. I can't feel him. Why doesn't he get that? He started this—he's the one who decided to get to me through Lindsey. And she can't be hurt by whatever happens next. It doesn't matter what his reasons were, or what happened in our past.

It's hard to hold on to that promise to myself though when he's right here. I don't know what the scent is that he wears, but it's hypnotic, and it messes with my good sense. I'm convinced that's what makes me weak. It can't be my heart—I can't defeat it if that's the case.

"Okay, contestants, time to strap yourself to your partners," the guy orders through the microphone. Andrew chuckles from somewhere deep in his chest. I glance up and see Lindsey watching us from the other side of the main mall. She's waving and smiling.

Andrew bends down, his hand running down my jeans along my calf as he wraps the Velcro strap around both of our legs. The heat from his body rushes through me instantly followed by more of his scent, and I feel my stomach drop in a free fall. I shut my eyes and breathe out slowly, just trying to survive this, to make the right decision.

"Please…please stop," I breathe, my eyes closing as I slump back into my chair.

His hands freeze against me as his head falls forward.

"I haven't slept with her," he says, his hands moving again to fasten our strap. He remains leaning forward when he's done, not ready to look me in the eye. That's probably for the best because my eyes are wide—I was so *sure* they'd been intimate. Those thoughts, they're the ones that tortured me. To find out that they haven't been *as* intimate as I'd imagined...

"You have to know, Emma. If I'd only known you were in the dark...if you'd only known where I was. Things...they would have gone so differently. I won't even say *could have,* because damn Emma...I know they *would* have. I'm going to talk to Lindsey. I'll tell her everything. Just don't go to that dinner. Please."

His voice is broken. His spirit...broken. The sound of him is desperate, and I can't say it isn't anything different from the feelings within my own heart. But my best friend is staring at me, the smile on her face enormous. And it isn't even the fact that she thinks Andrew is her *one,* or that she has deep feelings for him. It's that she trusts this story we've given her, and if she finds out I was part of the lie, she will never smile at me like that again. And that smile—it's the one that kept my heart beating after I buried my mom.

"If you tell Lindsey the truth, I will never forgive you," I say, my chest burning as the words leave my mouth. How can the heart want two things that are so very far apart?

"Let's go, racers," the announcer calls.

Everyone stands but Andrew and me. I feel his stare burning the side of my face, but I keep my eyes fixed on my friend. I smile at her and raise my hand slowly, my fingers curling. She can't know anything is wrong.

"You have no idea how important she's been to me, Andrew. Do not betray me," I say, feeling his breath shudder from his body. His head slings forward and his hand comes to cup the back of his neck as he nods slowly. My lips hang open, the words right there, waiting to come out. I want to tell him *never mind.* I want to tell him it will be okay and Lindsey will understand. I want to tell him I'm wrong, that he wouldn't be betraying me at all. But I can't. Our time was a few short weeks when we were sixteen. That time—it's gone. And I have to let him go. He needs to let go too.

"Come on, let's go win a goddamned gift card," he says, placing his arm around my shoulder as we stand, our bodies tethered together, his fingers gentle along my shoulder.

We walk in sync to the starting line, and before the man blows the whistle to begin, Andrew's fingers curl just enough to scratch against the fabric of my sweatshirt until his hand clutches the material into his fist before finally letting go.

He let go.

And I've never hurt more.

CHAPTER 15

EMMA, AGE 19

The truth is I was waiting for the phone call. I'd been waiting for nearly three years. From the moment both of my parents sat me down and told me Mom had pancreatic cancer, I'd been waiting for this call.

She hadn't been well for months. Her body just couldn't fight anymore. The rounds of chemo, the trials, the naturopathy—the prayers; eventually, cancer wins. All we can ask for is comfort and time.

My mother got three years. I should take comfort in that. My father should, too. And maybe one day we will. But for now, I want to be angry with the world.

"Em? You have to eat something," Lindsey says from the other side of my bedroom door. I've lived with her for a year. I've known her for only a little more. The way she's held me up since my dad called three weeks ago with the news that my mother died feels like more years should have been shared between us. She never signed up for this, and I've kept most of it to myself. Until…until the phone call that opened up my heart, split my body in two and took away that feeling of safety that comes along with knowing both of your parents are alive and well.

"I did," I lie, my throat sore and dry. I can't cry any more—but my mouth hangs open, wanting to. I want to all of the time.

"Em, I have been out there on that sofa all day. I'm binge-watching hot superhero movies. I'm on my fourth one, and you haven't left this room. I would have known. I'm four feet away from the refrigerator. I would have *seen* you eat," she says.

"You missed it; you were in the bathroom when I came out and made a sandwich." I'm smiling a little. It hurts. This is the first time I've smiled in a week. It feels…unnatural.

"I haven't peed once," she says.

"Now *you're* the one who's lying," I laugh. The sound of that hurts my chest.

"Ha, see! I knew you were lying," she says, pointing a finger at me as she opens my door. I let my smile remain so she can see it; she's earned this one. Hers falls though when she sees me. I know I look bad. And I'm sure… oh man, I'm pretty sure I smell bad. I haven't really *moved* a lot lately. I've gotten most of my homework through home study and got a medical withdrawal from my language class. I picked German. I think I'm switching to Spanish the next time around. There's one silver lining to this cloud of shit —I was failing German. "And for the record, I *wasn't* lying," Lindsey continues. "I really haven't peed in eight hours—two Chris Evans movies in a row. You know how I feel about Captain America."

She sits on the bed next to me with a bounce. She's let me wallow for the last couple weeks, but last night she gave me one hell of a speech.

"You can be sad," she said. "You can carry that around somewhere inside all the time. It's human, and you deserve to. But your mom would be mad to see you waste even a single day not living. She'd want to see you giving each day your best, even if you have to carry your sadness through it the whole damn way. Drag that sadness around; make it your bitch. But don't waste the good ones."

She was right. She's still right. She doesn't say anything when she sits next to me now, only stares at me, like a blinking contest. I lose. My eyes hurt from crying. Everything is so…dry.

"I'm getting up," I say, dragging my arm up my body so my finger can cross my heart with a promise. This is a tactical error on my part, because Lindsey sees my hand and grabs it, pulling me from my bed, one leg sliding to the floor, the other following in desperate fashion to find my balance before she drags me on my ass. She would, too—she's very strong for a petite thing.

"I'm hungry. And now I'm sad that there are no real superheroes in the world, so you, my friend, are getting in the shower. You have exactly seven minutes to get yourself presentable, and then we are going to my favorite restaurant and sitting by the window to watch hot frat boys walk by," she orders.

"I don't know, Linds. I'll get up, but I don't think I'm quite ready to go out," I say, dragging my feet toward our bathroom. She shoves a folded towel at my chest.

"I told you last night—you're done wasting days. We're going out. I want a superhero," she says, holding one hand on her hip, looking a little like one herself.

I sigh, then stick my tongue out at her, backing into the bathroom and kicking the door shut. I stare at the blankness of it for a second or two and I think of my mother.

"You know I love you, right?" I say to my friend, my best friend. Lindsey doesn't know this, but she *is* a superhero. She's also the second best friend I've had in my life. I've been close to exactly two people not related to me—and the first one disappeared without a trace.

Andrew Harper, where are you?

"I know. And I love you too. Now hurry your ass up; you're down to six minutes, and you know all the cute ones come out when it gets dark outside," she says. I grin at her words, stepping into the shower and turning the water on. I can tell she's sitting by the door. I also know that if I don't make it out of here in six minutes, she'll come in after me.

For the first time since I answered the phone and heard my father cry, I breathe.

CHAPTER 16

ANDREW

I wonder if Emma would think I'm betraying her now?

The house still looks the same, only the yard is dead, weeds taking up most of the space along the stone walkway that leads to the door. The compact sedan out front is the same one her family owned when we were in high school. That was my only confirmation that her family still lived here.

Her family. It's…smaller now.

I didn't know her parents well, if at all. I never got the chance. For those first few weeks in Lake Crest, I daydreamed about getting to know them. I had these fantasies that her parents would surprise me with a visit while I was there. Once, I even thought I saw a couple that looked like them in the waiting room—at least, it looked like them from the back. I walked through, postured a little straighter, shirt tucked in so I would make a good impression. The couple turned out to be there to pick up their son.

Now I get to meet her father, to acquaint myself with him, like this. I turn off the engine and sit in my car for a few minutes, looking over the house, psyching myself up for this probably-horrible idea. I look down at my forearms and my eyes lock in on the burn mark on my right arm. It's five years old, but it burns just as it did when Nick Meyers pressed his cigar into me. It was also the hardest mark to hide from my mom. I roll the long sleeves of my plaid shirt down as I exit my car, wanting to hide my scars from Emma's dad. The bruising from my fight is fading, but he'll still notice. Not much I can do about that.

My heart thumps wildly as I step up her walkway, little doses of the familiar attacking me the closer I get to the door. I recognize the smell of the bushes that line her yard, even though many of them are dead. I'm overcome with the curve around her house, the way to her window, and the pebbles in the yard across the street that I used to get her attention. I can almost see *her* walking toward me.

I press the button before I can chicken out, and a small dog scurries toward the front door from the inside. The side window gives me a view of its paws against the windowsill on the other side. A light flicks *on* in the hallway, and I can see the shadow of a person walking toward the door.

I think I'm going to be sick. This…this was a bad idea.

"Can I help you?"

A boy stands in the now-open doorway in front of me. This must be Emma's brother, Cole. He's awkward and his face looks caught somewhere between youth and his teen years. Maybe he's ten?

"Hi," I say, allowing myself a deep breath and a pause before speaking. It's part of my new rule to think before I talk. I bring my hand up to scratch my face as the boy scrunches his eyes and closes his lips tight. He's thinking he just opened the door to a stranger. He kinda did—dumb shit.

"I'm a friend of your sister's," I say to relax him. It doesn't seem to help, though, and now he crosses his arms. "I was looking for your dad?" I'm not quite *ready* for his dad, but I think any more time alone with little brother, and he'll slam the door on my face.

"Hang on," he says, pursing his lips at me, and squinting for a second more. "Dad! Some guy's here. He's not selling anything!"

I chuckle to myself, but stay still at the doorway while Cole walks away leaving the door wide open. A few seconds later, his father steps around the corner. He recognizes me instantly—his feet almost skidding to a stop. His hair has grayed, and thinned. He has glasses on, pulled to the edge of his nose, and his body is thinner than I remember.

"Mr. Burke," I say. I work hard to keep my voice even, to keep my mouth in an almost smile, to keep my eyes non-threatening. He has to know why I'm here. And he has to think I'm pissed. I am pissed. But I also think the man in front of me has been through hell and back—he's wearing his depression like a coat.

"Why are you here?" he asks, his question more of a grumble really as he fumbles his glasses from his face, pushing them in his pocket. He steps outside, closing the door behind him, then guides me to an open chair next to a bench on the end of their wooden porch.

He picks up a pillow and slides it across the wood, clearing it of dirt and debris, then motions for me to sit. I'd rather stand. I feel stronger, more in charge when I stand. Nick Meyers always made me sit when I was called to his office. I give in to Emma's father, though, and he quickly sits across from me, his body heaving out a breath.

He's afraid.

"I'm sorry to just show up. Really...I...hmmmm," I pause, running my hand along my face with a small chuckle. "Look...Mr. Burke."

"You can call me Carl, Andrew," he says. His eyes are tired, maybe a little sad, too.

I acknowledge his attempt to be civil with a tight smile before I lean forward, my hands clasped in front of me as my elbows rest on my knees. I tried not to look like a punk today. Normal jeans, a gray shirt, plaid button-down and my black hat—I debated on the gauges, but I ultimately decided the big holes sagging in my ears would put him off more. He keeps glancing at them, though, so I'm not sure I was right.

"I came for some answers. Well...one answer, mainly," I say, my hands wringing in front of me. I twist the silver ring around my thumb nervously, and eventually it falls off, rolling along the crooked planks of wood between us, coming to rest against his work boot. He reaches down to pick it up, clasping it in his fist as he closes his eyes.

"You want to know why we lied," he says.

My lungs collapse, and I struggle to fill them again. I expected confrontation. I expected denial.

I didn't expect this!

I don't speak, but nod slowly, my eyes waiting for his to open. When they do, they seem even more lost than they were when he first spotted me at his doorway.

"Katherine, Emma's mother, had pancreatic cancer," he says. His eyes fall even more, but their color—the same gray in Emma's—begins to grow darker.

"I'm very sorry, sir. I heard," I say, bowing my head. It's hard to see his pain—it feels too familiar.

"Thank you. It's been a couple years, but losing Kate was hard," he says.

"I understand," I say back quickly. We both stare into each other's eyes for a moment, and I can tell he respects the connection we both share—for loss.

"I'm sorry about what you've been through, Andrew. With your father… and with James," he says. I can tell he means it.

"Thank you," I say.

Carl leans back, the wood of the bench creaking with his weight. He folds his hands at his chest as he studies me. I remain frozen, my thumbs locked together, folded over my clasped hands. I'm willing him to give me answers—I'm hoping it gives me some sort of clue.

"Come with me," he says, suddenly leaning forward and getting to his feet. I stand in response and follow him into his house, the screen door slamming closed behind us.

We wind through a formal living room and dining area that I doubt has been used since Emma's mother died. I doubt it's been cleaned since then, either, the rings of dust deep around coasters and lamps. I trail Carl to a small space in the back of the house that looks like a den, an old desk taking up the center, and boxes piled around the walls. The small dog comes into the room behind us, and when Carl sits in the chair, bending down to pull out a low drawer in the desk, the dog rushes over to him, jumping on his lap.

"Teddy, not now," he says, scooping him and dropping him on the floor. He glances up at me. "Hazard of the job," he smirks. I had forgotten—Emma's father is a dogcatcher.

I bend down, and Teddy scurries up to me, putting his front paws on my knees. I scratch at his chin.

"I always wanted a dog," I say, chuckling slightly.

"You want this one?" Carl says, I think only *half* kidding.

I rub my thumbs behind Teddy's ears, watching his tail wag, until Carl leans back again in his chair, a file folder in his hands. He lays it on the desk, flipping it open, nodding for me to look.

I move to his side as he rolls his chair out a little to make room for me. When I begin to slide out the clippings and photos, my stomach lurches. The first thing I notice is a photo that appears to have been printed out at home—Emma in a hospital gown. Her hair is just as it was the last time I saw her before Lake Crest, her eyes look happy—hopeful even—though maybe a little sunken in, and her mom is sitting on the edge of the hospital bed with her.

"Did Emma…donate bone marrow or something?" I feel insensitive asking the question, but I don't understand what I'm looking at, and the potential of what it might mean terrifies me to the point that I have to kneel next to the desk, no longer able to stand.

"No," Carl chuckles softly, picking the photo up and pulling his glasses out to study it closer. "No…this was the day Emma got her heart."

"Her…I'm sorry…" I stumble with my words.

"I didn't think she told you. She was funny like that. I think it was her age, wanting to prove how normal she was, what she could do. I get it…she just wanted people to treat her normal," he says.

"I'm sorry, Carl. I'm…I'm not following. Emma…she needed a heart? Was it the accident? Did something happen?" My mind is racing with dozens of questions. I understand getting cut and bleeding; I understand how burns and bruises heal. If this were mechanics, I would be able to get what Emma's father was saying, but this is Emma's world—medicine and biology and a broken body. I don't understand, and I can't help but feel like it's my fault, and that's why her parents never told her where I was.

My head is sweating, and I tug my hat off and run my hand through my hair, huffing for air. I fall back on my heels and land on my ass, bending my knees up and staring straight ahead.

"Andrew, it's okay. She's okay now, and no…this wasn't from the accident," he says. I barely register him, but nod in response.

"What…what was wrong with her?" I ask.

He sighs, sliding some photos around in the folder before pulling out a piece of paper and handing it to me. I read a few words along the top, something about New Hampshire Hospital, left ventricles, medications. It's dated the year before I met Emma.

"Emma was born with hypoplastic left heart syndrome. Basically, half of her heart worked, and the other half was broken. She had three surgeries before we turned to the transplant. That's when you met her—when she was waiting on the list. We moved here for a doctor. Dogcatchers and phone-bank workers—we're not exactly rolling in the dough," he says, his lip inching up on one side in a half smile. I reflect it with one of my own. I don't say it out loud, but turns out young men with juvenile records don't make a lot of dough either. I'm hopeful that will change, though.

"This doctor, Dr. Wheaton, she performed Emma's surgery for free. But we still had to wait for her to come up on the list," he says, his eyes wandering back to the folder. I slide the diagnosis sheet up, and he folds it in with the other papers. "Her heart finally came…about a month after that accident you two had."

He doesn't try to mask the disapproval in his voice, and I cower a little under it. I lower my gaze, but I don't acknowledge it any more. That accident has taken up too much of my life.

"While I was at Lake Crest," I say instead, wanting to talk about where *I* was, and why Emma couldn't know.

"Yes," he says, not even flinching.

His conviction causes me to look up, and our eyes lock again. We keep coming to the same civil standoff.

"I would have supported her…through that…her surgery? If I had known," I say, swallowing hard. "I wrote her letters. I would have written her every day, tried to call…"

I stop when I see his face fall, his lips pursed, a hint of regret perhaps shadowing his expression.

"You know I wrote her letters. You…you never gave them to her," I say, that sick feeling from when I stepped out of my car coming over me again in a wave. It's quiet for almost a full minute, the only sound the papers shuffling back into the folder, the drawer being pulled open and Carl's chair sliding back from the desk as he stands. I pull myself up to stand with him, following him back from the den toward the front of the house. He stops in the kitchen.

"Can I get you a water? I don't have much, but...I have water," he says.

I laugh once under my breath and look back to the room on one end of the hallway and the doorway to my car on the other. All of this—and I still don't have the answers I needed, the closure I needed—I'm still the fuck-up from that family everybody talks about.

"Sure, I'll take a water," I sigh. He reaches in and pulls out a small bottle, wiping the condensation away with a towel on the counter before handing it to me. I hold it up, clutched in my hand, and smile tightly before whispering a sarcastic "Thanks."

Carl pulls the top from his and guzzles about half down before setting the bottle on the counter behind him. I twist my cap off and move my bottle to my lips, my eyes meeting Carl's in between drinks. I shuffle my feet, readying myself for Carl to show me out.

"I couldn't lose them both," he says. I startle a little, not expecting any more answers from him. I lower my brow, but wait for him to give me more. "I knew Kate was sick when we moved here. We were hoping for a better prognosis, and had been seeing new doctors in the city. But their answers were all the same."

He relaxes into the counter behind him, his hands finding the edge and squeezing as he looks up to the ceiling. When his eyes fall back down to mine, they're red and glassy. "I couldn't lose them both, Andrew. And I was afraid if Emma stayed with you—"

"You were afraid I'd ruin her," I finish for him. My eyes shut with the realization, with my delivery of the sentence and final act of what went wrong between me and Emma Burke.

"It's not about your family, Andrew. I know what you're thinking, and don't. It isn't about that—it never was," he says.

My gut tells me he's lying.

"When we got the call to pick her up that night at the police station, our world was rocked. She was this close...*this close*...to having a fresh start, to having a chance," he says, his lips a hard line, the rest of what he wants to say only a breath away. I stare into his eyes and dare him. "You were drunk, and you were high, Andrew. Drunk…and high!"

I roll my shoulders and take his condemnation. I nod slowly, my lips forcing themselves into a defensive smile and eventually a chuckle. I look down to the side as I reach into my pocket for my keys.

"Says the Woodstock Town Police report," I seethe.

"They convicted you, Andrew. A year in detention…"

"Ah…reform school," I correct smugly, holding one finger up. I shake my head at him, my insides feeling as if I've just gone a round in the ring. I open my mouth, but I'm smart enough to know that whatever I say next, if I speak right now, it won't be nice. So I close my lips instead and hold up my water to him. "I'm gonna take this with me, for the road, if that's okay?"

I turn and move to the door, not expecting his steps behind me. He's several paces back, and I know he's relieved to know I'm leaving. My thoughts dart to so many possibilities—racing one minute to the lost opportunities I had with Emma then quickly to everything she was probably told. The questions boil fast, and before I reach for the latch on the screen, I stop.

"I just need to know…did you tell Emma that I was drunk and high? Or did you keep that to yourself, too?" His face is ghost white, a mix of shame and indignant self-righteousness. "You know what? Never mind…I'll ask her myself."

I see him lurch toward me just before I close the door behind me. I don't know if he followed me. My pace was swift back to my car, and I never once glanced back at the broken house and broken man I was leaving.

* * *

I CASHED in one more sick day for my trip to Emma's dad's this morning. But my face was already returning to normal. My only class today was mathematic theory, and I've already completed the practice work and reading, so I gave myself permission to skip that, too. I haven't missed one yet this semester, so it shouldn't raise any flags with coach. It's our off day, but I've been itching for the ice. Trent has a full schedule today, though, and he won't be home until well after five. My boiling blood won't wait that long, so after an hour pacing our apartment and throwing a racquetball against the wall to the point that one of our senior neighbors came over to ask me to "stop the partying," I head to Harley's gym.

The place is hopping for the middle of the day, so I work in with one of the regulars. I spend an hour not talking, only rushing my taped fists into another guy's gloves and chest. He pops me in the jaw a few times, but the familiar heat that usually accompanies it never comes. It seems I've been hit so much that I'm finally immune. Or maybe, I'm so angry that it's going to take more than what this featherweight can serve up to help me.

"Harp, I'm out," my partner says, slicing his glove in front of his face at his neck. He's calling it. I frown at him. "Dude, we've been going an hour. I come here for the workout, man. But I also have to get my ass to class."

I nod at him, my hard breathing catching up to me as I lean on the ropes. I pull the tape from one hand and reach my palm out to shake his, pulling the other hand free of tape as he grabs his bag and leaves the gym.

My heart rate feels faster than normal—spikes of adrenaline still pushing through it. I force myself to breathe long and deep, dropping my head into my hands so I can focus and really listen to my rhythm. What a simple thing—a heartbeat.

Emma's heart…it didn't do this. Or not…quite like this. I looked up her condition as soon as I got home. I read about the surgeries she probably had when she was young, and then I thought back to how her skin felt the only time I touched it. It was over her bra, and in a dark car—the stolen moments of two teens in lust. I never felt a scar.

My mind is lost in the past, and that's why I don't see him coming. But his words yank me right out of the puzzle I'm trying to solve, and they drop me into hostile territory.

"Nick Meyers said you were a fighter," he says. My head jerks up at the mention of his name, my hands forming fists instantly, my breathing picking up its pace, like an engine revving. Graham, Emma's *just some guy,* stands on the floor in front of me, two feet lower than the ring. He's wearing cut-off sweatpants and a tank top that squeezes his large frame.

"Nice to see you again, Graham," I practically choke on his name. "I didn't know they were letting assholes in here now."

He laughs at my response, but he doesn't think I'm funny. He doesn't think I'm funny at all. His eyes fall to his feet as he kicks at an old, dried piece of gum stuck to the floor.

"Harley, you're really letting this place fall to shit. You need to get an intern or something, someone to come through here and clean every once and a while," he shouts, then glances up at me, his eyes slits as they take me in. "Maybe this guy can be your intern."

Harley walks over slowly, and I study him, watching every nuance as I try to decide if he and Graham are friends. He never smiles, and when he stops in front of us both—equal distance between us—he folds his arms and frowns. I'm not sure what Graham is to Harley or how he knows him, but he isn't a friend. More than that—what does Graham have to do with Nick Meyers?

"I said I'd talk to him, Graham. Let the kid cool off. I'll catch up with you later, okay?" Harley grumbles.

Graham's smile slides wider as he nods.

"A'right," he says. I cough down a laugh when he speaks and Harley shoots me a look to keep my mouth shut. I can't help it—this dude sounds like a poser trying to talk all tough and shit. I'll give him this; he's bigger than me, and he looks like he knows how to throw a punch. But he also wore pink pants the last time I saw him.

"Hey, I'll say *hi* to Emma for you," he winks before walking away. My entire body flexes. Harley notices, and he holds his hand up to stop me.

Once Graham rounds the door, I turn my focus to Harley, who's staring back at me with equal intensity.

"You wanna tell me how you know Graham Wheaton?" he asks, chewing at the inside of his mouth. Harley looks like a Marine—what he lacks in height he makes up for in bulk. He's always been into fitness and boxing, and when you combine his build with his smarts, he's perfect for this business.

"I just met the guy. We don't...gel," I say.

"I can see that," he says, lifting the ropes for me to slide through. I climb out and turn a chair around, straddling it and resting my arms on the back.

"How do *you* know Graham Wheaton?" I ask, not liking the fact that this asshole has now ruined two things that make me happy—my gym, and Emma.

"He's my biggest investor. Well, his father is, at least. His dad's into real estate. We have a deal. He comes here to work out. He's got some skills," Harley says, downplaying that last part. I can tell he's not giving Graham the fighting credit he probably deserves, and I think it's because on a personal level, Harley likes me better.

"I see," I say, my insides still trying to process the name that Graham threw out to get at me. Could he really know Nick Meyers? Fuck me if that ghost from my past is an investor here, too.

"He wants to fight you," Harley says, and I spit out a spray of water as soon as his voice hits my ears.

"Shut the fuck up," I say.

"He's offering five grand. All you have to do is go down in four. That's five grand…just for you, Drew. This wouldn't be like Pitch. Graham's good, but he's not big like that—it would be fair, and you'd come out all right—and five grand richer. I won't be able to line something like that up for you again in months. He's looking at a small event in a week or two."

I stare at him while he speaks, trying to sort through the crazy shit coming out of his mouth.

"I don't know, Har," I say, looking down and kicking my foot. "That guy…I don't trust him."

"You don't have to," he says, holding up a check for me to see. "He gave me the deposit. I hold the money."

I breathe in slowly. Any other name on that check with that number and I'd be sold. But something about this feels *not* right. Even so, I would love to have an excuse to slam my fist through his face. I take the check in my hand, rub it between my fingers and look at it for several long seconds before I begin nodding.

"So, you're in?" Harley asks.

"Yeah, I'm in," I say, not liking the taste in my mouth.

Harley takes the check back with a nod. He never smiles. I don't think he has a good taste either. But he likes money, and I know that the five thousand that goes to my pocket isn't what he's in this for.

I leave the gym at three, knowing I have hours until Trent is home, and my feet carry me to Majerle's. I text him to join me, but I'm gone hours before he says he can make it. Chuck quit serving me after my fifth Jack, so I stumbled into the liquor store at the end of the block, leaving my car safe along the roadside outside the tavern.

And then I called Lindsey and told her I wanted to come over tonight so we could talk. I'm going to end the lies, and I'm going to punch *Graham cracker* in the face. And I'm also going to go home and drink. I'm going to drink a lot. In the middle of the day. Just like the fuck-up loser I am.

* * *

EMMA

"We haven't had a girl's night in forever," Lindsey says, pouting a little. She just got off the phone with Andrew. He told her he was coming over, and she got excited. They haven't spent much time together over the last couple days. I know why, and it's killing me to know so much.

It's also killing me that he's coming here, to be with her. He's only doing that to hurt me. I can't let it hurt me. I'll leave early, meet Graham at the restaurant—whatever it takes to avoid him.

"I know. I miss my Emma-Lindsey time," I say, sinking down next to her on the sofa. I'm half dressed, a long, silky black shirt hanging over my underwear.

"You better finish getting dressed. Unless you're trying to get something going with this Graham guy," Lindsey teases. I stand and sigh, looking down at my bare legs and feet.

"You think I can go in jeans?" I joke.

"Uhm…to Polo's? No," she laughs. "I am pretty sure when the restaurant quits putting prices on the menu that they require their guests come in something a grade fancier than flip-flops and leggings."

"Ugh," I sigh. "Fine."

I stomp my feet playfully back to my room, returning to my closet, to the rows of boring formal wear and pantsuits. I pull out the silk pants and decide those will be good enough.

"Hey, Em?" Lindsey calls down the hall. "I forgot to give you something.

Your dad…he came by. He left something for you. He said it was important."

"My dad came by? He knows my schedule," I say, my brow pulled in and my mouth twisted while I try to both figure out why my father came when I wasn't here and how to work the tight band of my pants over my hips. I haven't worn these in a year, and it seems my hips are not willing to work with me tonight. I discard them and reach for the cocktail dress I bought on sale over the summer and have never had a chance to wear.

"Yeah, I thought it was weird too. He said something about having to take your brother somewhere or something. I don't know. But he left this," she says as she enters my room. She tosses a large manila envelope on my bed as I spin to face her. I glance at it, but don't recognize it. It must be my mail from home. Sometimes I get magazines.

"What do you think?" I ask, bending down to pull on my silver strappy heals. These shoes make me taller than anyone in the room—always. I think the only person who could possibly stand taller than me in these shoes…is Andrew.

I huff and right my posture, shaking my curls from my shoulders, then spinning to one side so Lindsey can properly evaluate my outfit, a slender-fitting gray dress with a back that dips low. She smiles, but tilts her head to the side. She glances to my dresser top, her eyes lighting up when she spots a pin. "Here, let me just try something," she says, pulling the pin in her hand, opening it and taking a small strand of my hair between her fingers. She twists it into a tight line, pulling it to the back of my head where she fastens it in place. "There," she says, standing back with her arms crossed. "Now he can see your eyes."

My shoulders relax as I smile back at her. With a simple gesture, Lindsey has made me feel beautiful.

"Thanks," I say, taking one more deep breath.

"Relax," she says. "He already likes you."

I nod and keep my happy expression in place, never letting her know that what I'm really worried about is *me* liking *him.*

Lindsey retreats to her room, probably to get ready for Andrew's visit, and for a moment, I think about walking to her room and telling her everything. My feet never leave their comfortable roots in my carpet though. I tell myself that it's because I just don't want to ruin my friend's happiness. And that's definitely *part* of my reason. But I'm also scared. I'm afraid of how she'll react, afraid it will ruin something between us, and maybe... maybe a little afraid that it will solidify the path for Andrew and me. Lindsey and I wouldn't survive that. I'd have to pick. And my heart is so very selfish.

Graham will be here soon, so I look over my dress once more, making sure everything that *should* be hidden, is. This is a dinner with important people, so I decide to pull out the thin black sweater just to be safe. I look over myself once more in the mirror to see how the sweater lies in the back, and I catch a glimpse of the envelope on my bed behind me. I step over to it and lift it in one hand, a little surprised at how heavy it feels.

Sitting on my bed, I listen to the sound of our apartment. Nothing.

I pull the envelope into my lap and slide my finger along the poorly-sealed edge, reaching in. My fingers find a stack of thick-feeling paper, and when I pull what's inside out, my eyes catch up to what I think my soul already knew, and time stops. Even the handwriting cuts to the core, the way he took care to write my name, the look of his own name on paper. Every single envelope is sealed. Never opened.

"Your words went into oblivion," I whisper to myself, the tears pooling up quickly. I glance up to my door, my feet following my gaze to the lock on my door, and I click it, rushing back to the envelopes that were all meant for me—the words I should have read years ago.

These letters represent the gap in everything from my life before to now.

With a hard swallow, I tear into the one on top.

Emma,

I'm sorry that this has to be a letter. It's the only thing I'm allowed to do. I wanted to call you, but there really wasn't an opportunity. I didn't know where to call, either. All this time, and I still never asked you for your phone number. I'm such a jerk.

The past floods my insides, overtaking me completely. The envelopes still in my hand feel hot to touch, and I drop them on the bedspread beside me, spreading them out like a deck of cards, the one letter I began to read still on top.

He's sorry.

After what he did for me, the first thing he wrote me was *sorry.*

I slide one out from the middle, tugging the loosely-sealed edge open, and I pull the letter free. This one is only a single page. I notice that the letters are less thick the closer to the bottom of the spread-out stack I go.

Dear Emma,

Yeah. I'm writing again. I guess I'm a glutton for punishment. I wish I could tell you the things that I see here. I wish I could tell you the things I've been through. I'm so unbelievably alone. I thought I was lonely before I met you, but god what I wouldn't give to go back to that time. Not that I want to go back to life before you. Actually, I'd like to relive getting to know you again. Those few weeks were...well they meant a lot to me. I would probably skip the part where we get in the accident though—or at least I wouldn't go to my friend House's party. That was stupid.

I don't know what anyone's told you. But I'm counting on the fact that you know me—the real me. You know I'm not some drugged-out loser, right? I was at a party I shouldn't have gone to and tried some things that I shouldn't have tried. Everyone looks at me differently now, though. I'm afraid they look at me and see my brother James. I'm not James, Emma. I hope you know that.

I tear quickly into more letters, each one giving me another piece of Andrew's heart, a piece of his soul. He pours out feelings in some letters, talking about how afraid he is of Lake Crest, and in others he's almost resolved to what his life is there, offering me nothing at all, almost as if he's protecting me from what he's going through. The more I read, the sadder he becomes, and the less of Andrew I see. I pull one near the end, not ready —and maybe also not willing—to read his final letter.

Dear Emma,

I miss you.

I wanted to see what those words felt like. There are more words...other things to write, to say. Maybe one day I'll say them to you in person. Or maybe...I won't. I

hope I'm not freaking you out, it's just that this place is so dark and heartless that I wanted to remind myself what light was like. You...you're my light.
I talked with my brother's girlfriend Kensi for a while tonight. She came to visit. I wasn't very good company at first, but then she asked me questions about you. She's offered to visit you for me, to bring you something. I thought about letting her bring you one of my hats or my sweatshirt. I don't know...I thought girls liked that sort of thing. But I'm too afraid you won't want it.
I'm afraid you won't want me.
I want to see you so badly it hurts.
You don't know this, but I tried—I tried to see you. This place has a way of keeping people on leashes though. I'm okay. Don't worry, I can take it. I promise you this place won't defeat me entirely. I'll come back to you, Emma. We'll start over, and I'll take you on a proper date. I'll hold your hand and buy you popcorn and kiss you in a dark movie theater. And I'll be your date for prom. And I'll spend my summer trying to make you laugh.
I'll come back to you if you'll have me. It's all I'm living for.
Please write soon.
Completely yours,
Andrew

I can barely see through the tears that stream down my face. My breath is stuttering, and my chest hurts. On instinct, I hold my palm flat over the center, over my scar, counting as I breathe in and breathe out.

One. Two. Three. Four. Five.

The calm that usually follows is short—the mixture of anger, regret, and heartbreak flooding me again and again.

Andrew was mine. I was his reason for everything. And when he needed me most, I wasn't there—because I never knew. And now…now that he's here…all I'm doing is pushing him away more. My skin turns red, and my body feels hot. My fist clenched, I bring my other arm down on the bed, slamming it hard enough to make the letters jump from the force. I slam my fist down again, then swipe the letters in all directions, sending them to the floor as I collapse onto my bed, my face deep in my sheets. I open my mouth wanting to scream, but I'm aware enough to know that I can't. Not here, not where anyone can hear me.

I scream inside, to myself, wishing I could turn back time.

"Em?" Lindsey knocks at my door. I push myself up, rushing to the floor to gather my letters, to protect them and save them.

"Just a second. I'm fixing something...on my dress," I breathe out in a panic, scooping the letters back into the envelope and tucking it into my backpack on my desk to hide them.

"It's okay. I just wanted you to know Andrew's here," she says. My eyes grow wide, and my body freezes, my fingers about to clutch my door. I pull my hand away and hold it against me.

Andrew's here. Just on the other side of this door. I can't see him—not now. I'm not ready. I want him. I don't want him with Lindsey. I'm greedy and selfish and these letters...his letters, they've completely swept away all reason. And it's going to hurt my best friend. I don't know what to do.

"Oh," I say, my mouth holding the *O* as I wait to think of what comes next. Nothing does.

"Are you leaving soon?"

She wants to be alone with him. I get that. And I have to leave to meet Graham and Miranda for dinner. I need to be there in twenty minutes, with my mentor and her son—whom I feel nothing for, who if it weren't for timing and circumstance, I probably wouldn't even like. This isn't how any of this should be. How can I look Graham in the face after reading what's in Andrew's heart? How can I live this lie knowing he once felt so much for me. He still does. I know it...I believe it.

"Yeah, just...just a sec," I choke out. I turn to the side where my backpack rests next to my purse, and I pull my purse into my hands, my eyes staying on the letters I want to carry with me too. I never want to leave them alone. I need to memorize them, feel them—no matter how badly they hurt to read.

Instead, I pull my mirror from my purse and check my face, powdering my cheeks and wiping away the blurred eyeliner from my cry seconds before. I can paint myself as much as I want—it will never erase how I feel right now. My heart is a steady rhythm, a warning that I should stay in this room, feign an illness. I can't go out there, I can't see him, and I cannot be anything with Graham.

"Emma?"

Lindsey sounds desperate. I should pull her in here, tell her everything, take the lashing she will give me—that I will deserve. I should.

"I'm ready," I say with the last breath that leaves my body in this room.

I push my door open and immediately meet Lindsey's eyes. They're wide. Why are they wide?

"I think he's drunk," she winces, pursing her lips and nodding her head down the hallway. I see part of his body, his legs leaning out as he leans against a wall in our kitchen. His dark jeans gather around his feet, his black shoes, his hands hanging from his thumbs looped in his pockets. I see enough to know that seeing the rest will break me open again.

"Oh," I say, just as I said before. I'm weak.

"It's okay," she says, shaking her head. "You have to go; you're going to be late. I'll sober him up. Who knows, maybe this will break the ice that he's had surrounding him lately."

Ice. Andrew's had…ice. Because of me.

Lindsey walks back down the hall, and I notice Andrew push off from the wall and sway on his feet, his expression meaningless—blank. His eyes haze as he paints her body with his gaze, but on his way back up, his focus is solely on me, and suddenly his expression changes. We're the same. We are hurting the same. And the way he looks right now—it's as desperate as I feel. Those words he wrote years ago, they're still so very relevant now; I see it in his eyes. I see it in his soul.

He remains several feet away from me, his fingers reaching for Lindsey's hand while he watches me pull my coat from the hook near the door.

"Call me if you need anything. We'll be up late," Lindsey says. The smile on her face makes everything hurt worse. I notice it, but only briefly. For the rest of the time, my eyes stay on Andrew.

"That's some guy," he says, his voice monotone and his eyes flat. "He can't even come to your door to pick you up."

"Andrew!" Lindsey chides him, grimacing. I can tell she's right—he is a little drunk. But I also think he's more sober than she realizes, too. I think this Andrew is on the other side of a binge, on his way out, coming through the pain, but bringing it with him. It never leaves him, really.

"It's okay," I smile at my friend. My eyes find him again, and when Lindsey turns away, I mouth, "I'm so sorry."

His face falls the second my lips send the message. I don't know why I said it, other than I had to—I need to say so much more. I need to read those letters.

I pull the door open and step into the hall, breathing deeply to survive one more night, to be a pleasant dinner guest, to impress my mentor and not to offend her son. I just need a personality for a few more hours, and then I can figure things out.

When I turn to lock the door behind me, Andrew is holding it open, just enough for my face to be square with his. His eyes hold mine hostage, drifting to my mouth then down my entire body. My scar burns on my chest even though he can't see it, and I clutch my purse to me tightly to cover it up even more.

"I have to go," I say.

"I'm telling Lindsey," he says, his lips parted and open, his teeth holding his tongue. His breathing is deep, his chest rising with the pressure of everything. He's not telling me this to tease me. He's telling me because it's what he plans to do, because he's determined. Those words are the gate to a whole hell of a lot he has to say. I can tell. And I wish our time were different; I wish it were right for him to say it and me to hear it. But it's not…it's just…not.

"Don't," I say, a small shake of my head.

"I have to, Emma. You know I do," he says, closing the door behind him. I place my hand on it and will myself to open it again, to come up with an excuse, to protest what he's about to do—to stop him from hurting my friend. But I hurt her too. And carrying this on any longer, that's not right either.

I back away slowly until I turn to the elevator, and I never look back again, washing away the thoughts of what Andrew could possibly be saying right now and reminding myself to be pleasant and not to screw up my relationship with Miranda Wheaton.

CHAPTER 17

ANDREW

It seems that Lindsey was a high school all-star softball player. This would have been a good thing to know when she picked up the glass paperweight and hurled it at my face. I dodged it in time, but not fast enough for the follow-up of the metal photo frame. The sharp edge caught my chin, slicing it open deep enough that it bled huge droplets on her living room floor.

I deserved it.

I probably should have waited for Trent to show up at the bar, to help me work out my very loosely-planned plan. I also probably should have waited until I was *really* sober, not just the pretend *I think I'm sober* that I was when I told Lindsey "We need to talk."

My buzz was good, and it felt like my mind was clear finally—like I had the courage to do the difficult thing, the thing that Emma couldn't do. It was my fault that Lindsey was even involved in the first place.

However, she probably deserved a lucid version of me explaining things.

"I'm in love with Emma," was the first thing I said. I didn't open easy.

No. I'd thought this through at the bar—again, probably not the best idea—and every time I played this out in my head, just stating the truth, and getting it out quickly, always felt right.

It was probably wrong.

Lindsey's first reaction was to laugh. She thought this was a joke. But then she realized she was laughing, while I was leaning against the wall, my hands deep in my pockets, sweating, my heart throbbing, my head aching, my mind remembering the look on Emma's face as the door closed behind her. My past would always be tangled with Emma Burke, and so would my heart.

Lindsey slapped me then. Hard. I nodded *yes*, almost wishing for more.

"I'm sorry," I said. My face still somber—brutally honest. I was sorry. I am sorry.

She hit me again, this time her palm cupped as it came at me. The force jerked my head to the side, and I took a few steps back. As much as I like a good battle in the ring, I was always completely sober for it. And it wasn't a woman whom I'd lied to kicking my ass. As much as my instincts balled my fists to fight back, my head knew better. I'd let her have this—she could take all she wanted.

"You...*love her*?" she'd asked. She didn't understand. I knew there was no way to explain this simply. All that mattered was protecting Emma—protect *her* relationship with Lindsey.

I told her that I'd loved her since we were kids; something tragic had happened between us, her parents had kept us apart, but I didn't know—so I had always blamed Emma. I tried to explain why Emma went along with my deception, that she wanted Lindsey to have me—but I belonged with Emma.

Have me. As if I'm a prize.

Lindsey's mind clearly had the same thought, because that's when she hurled the heavy glass globe at me, shattering it into thousands of pieces. She was a little manic—and my eyes went wide in surprise, my entire body flinching from it. I wasn't ready for her next blow.

She was kind enough to stitch me up. She tugged hard, and I'm pretty sure I caught her lip curled in a devil's smirk every time she stuck the needle through me. I think she gave me more stitches than necessary, and I can tell it's a sloppy job—also sure she did *that* on purpose. It's fine. I have plenty of scars. At least I provoked this one.

Lindsey cut the threads on my chin, then told me to get out. She yelled it three more times, throwing my phone and keys into the hallway behind me, my stuff ricocheting off my back. I glanced at Sam on my way out, holding up a hand as he shook his head and chuckled. He mumbled something about karma catching up to me. He has no idea.

Lindsey passed me as she left her building with a duffle bag, pausing long enough to tell me I was pathetic and to ask me to tell Emma to move out.

I started to protest, to defend Emma, but she only held up a hand and seethed "Don't." Lindsey's angry and hurt, and I get that. But I won't give up on making things right between the two of them. That's a promise I'm making to Emma.

I've been sitting out here on the stoop of her building ever since her roommate left. I've been waiting for hours—my hangover already seeping into every cell in my body. I was clearly not sober for any of that.

Trent texted me an hour ago, saying he came to meet me at Majerle's, but it looked like I left. I told him he had "no idea." He sent a question mark, so I told him I can no longer be left unattended. He sent a string of smart-ass remarks after that, which I never answered back. He's going to be disappointed in me when I see him, as it is—no need to start the lecture on a text string.

The ice pack Sam tossed to me an hour ago has completely melted. I don't know why he took pity on me, but the notion that the old man likes me feels nice. I get the feeling he and I might be a little alike—or at least we were when he was my age.

Most of the lights in Emma's building have gone dark. It's well past midnight, and the longer I sit here, the more my mind runs rampant with thoughts of her and that Graham dude doing things. I've fucked my life up so badly, it's bordering on a Shakespearean tragedy. But I'm done losing out in life. I'm done not going for what I want, for being on the shit end of people's opinions and what everyone else thinks is best.

I want Emma Burke. I always have. And I'm going to fight like hell to make her mine. I know a thing or two about fighting.

The quiet night air and the rasp of the crickets forms a constant hum that almost lulls me to sleep. The sudden rumble of the taxi pulling along her street jolts me awake though. And when Emma steps through the back door, tears pouring from her eyes, her face red and upset, her body convulsing with emotion, I'm rushed with adrenaline.

I sprint to her, and the closer I get, the worse I realize it is. Her cheek is bruised, her dress is torn, the strap on her purse is dangling by a thread.

I want to kill someone.

"Emma!" A breathy shout leaves my chest, and my legs feel like they want to fold under me. Someone hurt her—someone hurt her badly. Her lip quivering, she finally collapses against me, completely falling to pieces against my chest. I hold one arm around her, dig into my pocket, and fish out a crumpled twenty that I throw at the cab driver.

"That's not enough," he says, leaning out the window. I flinch toward him, and Emma startles. Thankfully, that move and the look on my face is enough.

"Mother fucker," he grumbles, twisting his steering wheel and pulling away fast.

Emma's still shaking in my arms, and I take this short moment to survey the rest of her. Scratches line her bare arms, and I realize just now that she's also barefoot.

"Did he do this to you?" I ask.

She's quiet, her eyes barely open, her tears still coming down like rain.

"Emma, did that Graham guy touch you?" I repeat. I'm trying so hard to keep my voice calm, but I know I sound like a lunatic.

I open my mouth to ask her again, but she finally nods slightly, stuffing her knuckles into her teeth as she lets out an enormous scream that echoes down the street. Sam hears from inside and rushes out to us.

"Miss Burke? Are you all right?"

He eyes me like a protective father, and I like him even more because of it.

"She's hurt, Sam. We need to call nine-one-one..." I start, but Emma interrupts.

"No!" she screams, clutching my shirt and twisting her head to look at me, shaking her head *no.* She begs, and I feel like I'm free falling, my stomach sick and my head not sure what's right or wrong right now.

Emma is all that matters.

"Miss Burke?" Sam asks again, his eyes flitting from her to me.

"No," she coughs out. "No...please don't call. I'm...I'm all right. It's a misunderstanding, and that...that would make things worse. Please...take me inside."

I breathe in slow, painful air, my lungs burning against the motion because home is the one place Emma needs to go, and I've gone and ruined that, too.

"I'm taking you home with me," I say, her eyes wide on mine. She's so frightened and in shock. "I don't want you to be alone, and we can't...we can't stay here."

I swallow hard, not wanting to give her details right now, not wanting to pile on her nightmare with more. She doesn't ask, but instead lets her head fall forward, nodding in agreement. She's letting me take control.

"Let's go inside and get some of your things," I glance to Sam, silently asking him to let me help with this. Our eyes meet, and I know he's in my corner.

Sam holds the door open for us, and I walk with her weight against me, my eyes meeting his once more. We follow Sam to the elevator, and he calls a car down for us to step inside. I nod to him once more as the doors slam to a close between us. Emma's breathing is steady, but every breath is deep and labored, almost like she's trying to self-soothe, but failing miserably.

"Emma," I hum her name, cradling her to me. She shivers when I speak, and I shut my eyes wishing I could do more, wishing we were past so many things so I could give her the love she needs right now.

I follow her into her apartment, pausing at the door to her bedroom as her body slips away from mine long enough to grab a small bag. She stuffs handfuls of clothing in, not really paying much attention. I step inside her room finally and push her hands down, holding them still.

"Go get your things in the bathroom. Let me do this. I'll do it right. I swear," I say, looking at the stack of thin shirts she's packed while the weather outside is in the low fifties. She shakes her head *okay* then moves to the bathroom.

I work quickly, grabbing a few sweaters from her closet, pulling jeans from shelves and emptying her underwear drawer without looking. I don't know what she wants or needs to be comfortable, so I take a little bit of everything; I can give her my things to stay warm, too.

Knowing Emma, I also grab her backpack, pulling the zipper fully open to slide the books strewn about her desk inside. I stop suddenly though at a familiar sight. My letters are scattered in her bag, some of them in a large envelope, others pushed far into the bag, bent and folded as if she hid them in a hurry. I listen for her in the bathroom and decide to brave a glance at the large envelope containing most of them.

Emma,
From Dad

My body rushes with a wave of panic, but the sound of Emma shutting the medicine cabinet across the hallway jolts me from the numbness that I want to swim in. My letters. Carl—he brought them to her. Emma—she read them. At least...some of them. I stuff her books on top quickly, knowing that when she can, she'll realize that I saw them.

"Here, make sure I got what you need," I say, distracting her with the other bag. Her eyes widen at the sight of her backpack, but I turn my attention away so she doesn't give it more thought than she can afford to now. "I'm getting us a ride."

She nods once, then lowers herself to sit on her bed, her overnight bag in her lap so she can stare into it. I don't think she's really looking at anything, but I feel pretty sure that I put enough of everything inside for her to be all right for a few days.

My phone rings in my ear while I watch her.

"Yo, what-up with the cryptic texts you jerk?" Trent asks, his laughter light. I need him to be serious now, and I also can't work through his logic and reason and the million ways that this is a bad idea and how so much of it is probably my fault.

"Trent, I need you. It's Emma. She's—" I glance to her and step into the hallway. "That fucker did something to her, hurt her, Trent. She's here, and

Lindsey's gone. And I know I have a shit-ton to fill you in on, but Emma's hurt. I need you to come get us."

There's a brief silence.

"I'll be right there," he says. "Text me the address."

"Thank you, Trent. Jesus...just...thank you," I say, relaxing a little knowing he's coming. I hang up and send him the address to Emma's building then return my focus to Emma, who is still an ice statue on the edge of her bed.

"Trent's coming. Let's get you downstairs," I say, lowering enough to thread my arm around her and lift her gently along with me.

We take slow steps out of her apartment, and I take her key to lock up behind us. Sam greets us at the end of the hall, the elevator held open. I'm not sure if he did that to keep an eye on me or to help us move Emma smoothly downstairs. Right now, it doesn't really matter.

Trent pulls up outside within minutes, and one look at Emma stops any questions he's dying to ask me. He steps from the car, leaving the motor running, and opens the back door for Emma to step inside. I follow her, nodding *no* when he looks at me like it's a bad idea for me to be this close to her. Think what you want about me, dude—there's no way in hell I'm leaving her side tonight.

Trent pulls her two small bags into the front seat next to him, and minutes later we're unloading at our apartment. I tug Emma's arm gently as we exit the car, and she follows so I can guide her inside.

Her feet are still barefoot—*shit!* I forgot her shoes. I grimace to myself, but keep moving forward. My arm never leaves its cradle around her body. She fits against me so well, if only she weren't shivering. I guide her all the way into my room, and she doesn't protest. I pull out an extra-large Tech hockey shirt and lay it on the bed next to where she's sitting.

"Go ahead and change. I'll step outside and give you a minute," I say, my eyes studying her knees, too afraid to look up in her tear-filled eyes. She stopped sniffling during the drive, her eyes instead wide and stunned in one position. I'd give anything to read her thoughts so she wouldn't have to tell me what happened—I'd just know. My biggest fear is that what I'm imagining is exactly what happened—or not even close to as bad as it really was. Either way, when I get my shot, I'm going to hit that guy so hard that his tongue will choke him.

I shut the door behind me quietly, as if I'm trying not to wake her. I don't know why, but I just feel like too much noise will frighten her. She seems shell-shocked.

"She okay?" Trent whispers. He pulled a bottle of water from our fridge. I smile at him and nod *thanks.*

"I don't know," I say, shaking my head and looking back at the closed door behind me. "I don't know what he did, what happened, but this isn't my Emma…"

"Your Emma…" Trent repeats. His eyes are lecturing me subtly.

"She's always been mine," I say, my mouth working on automatic, primed to deliver nothing but the truth until I erase everything bad that's ever happened in Emma's life. My eyes dare Trent's. He turns his head a tick to the right, waiting for me to say more. When I don't, he nods once and holds up a single hand.

"All right then. I'll be awake for a bit taking care of some reading. If you need anything…"

"Thanks, man," I say, watching his door close with the same caution I shut mine. I smile at how much he understands without asking.

I knock lightly on my door and Emma's voice cracks out "Come in."

She's still wearing everything she was before, my shirt in her lap, her fingers kneading it like bread. Her eyes are lost in a trance. "My shoes…I…I don't know what happened to my shoes," she whispers. I look down to her feet as her toes curl.

I open my mouth to ask her if she needs more time alone, time to dress, but then I shut my lips, breathing slowly and silently through my nose.

"Here," I say, holding a hand out to her. She looks at it for several seconds before sliding her own into my grasp. I'm delicate with her fingers, but I can't help but let my thumb run over the top of her hand in a soothing way. That's all I do it for—I want to soothe her. I want to fix things for her. I want to avenge her.

I crack open my door and glance toward Trent's. When I confirm his is still closed, I walk with her to our bathroom and shut the door behind us. I don't lock it because I have a strong feeling that doing something like that would spike her panic—she can't feel trapped tonight. I turn the shower on and set the shirt I brought in with us down on the sink.

"We need to get you cleaned up," I say, pulling one of my large towels from the cabinet behind the door. I unravel it and hold it up, covering her body from my view. "Can you step out of your dress on your own?"

She nods slightly again.

I watch the dirtied garment fall to the floor by her feet, and I swallow down my rage. Her underwear fall next, and I close my eyes for a second—I hide my wince because I hate that she wasn't wearing more than this. That asshole had his hands on too much of her. Yet I'm relieved she's wearing what she is still, that he didn't...

I lean my head toward the shower, then move the towel so she can step inside, shielded from my view. I drape the top over the top of the glass door, then sit on the toilet next to the shower while the water cascades over her body. I focus on the sound of the rain falling from the faucet for several minutes, the entire time wondering what I'm going to do next, how I'm going to make her better, when she breaks the silence, choking out a small cry.

"Don't leave me, Andrew. Stay in here. Are you still here?"

I stand to my feet fast and raise a hand over the towel, clutching the top.

"I'm right here, Emma. I'll be right here, and I'll go anywhere you tell me to," I say.

"Will you help me?" she asks.

"Emma..." I shut my eyes, my head falling forward onto the towel-covered glass.

"I trust you, Andrew. I...I just...I can't seem to get myself to move. Everything feels not right. And my heart is beating so fast..."

It's that part that gets me—Emma's heart beating fast. I'd give anything to be the man who gets to protect that heart. I want to hold it in my hands. And the fact that she trusts me—that's the first time I've felt like maybe I deserve to hold it.

I deserve her.

"Okay," I whisper.

I slide the towel out of the way but keep my eyes trained on her head, her wet hair clinging to her cheeks and neck. I don't dare look any further.

Reaching down with one hand, I pour a generous amount of shampoo into one hand and hold it up for her to see. There can't be any surprises.

She nods slowly, so I move my hand over her head, lathering her hair and letting the soap run down her body. I want to look at her injuries, but nothing else.

"Where are you hurt?" I ask, my jaw tight with the question. What I really want to ask is *where did that asshole hurt you?*

Her eyes glance down at herself, holding her arms out slowly until she raises her hands up one at a time in front of her face and between us. Her eyes are trained on her fingers at first, but then her focus changes to my eyes.

"I. Hurt. Everywhere."

My breath falls short and my stomach twists tightly as she breathes out the same words I spoke to her.

Her bruises—those are small and will fade quickly. But the marks we can't see—the invisible things Graham left behind—those are things that are hurting her right now.

"Emma…" I say, moving my hands from her hair to her fingers, clutching them and bringing them forward to me until I rest them on my chest. Her body is soaking, and the water is trailing down her arms and soaking my shirt. I don't care in the least.

"I'm so sorry, Emma," I say. I know they seem like empty words, but they're all I've got, and for me, they aren't empty. They're so full she has no idea—so full of love and care and a need to protect this girl.

"I know," she says, her lashes falling with the dew from the shower spray.

I hold her hands there and just watch her with her eyes closed. I let her stand still, because I think she needs this more than she needs anything else. I let the water wash the rest of the soap from her hair, and when enough time has passed, I turn off the spray and pull the towel down from the top of the shower to wrap it around her body.

I guide her with the same care as before out of the shower, and when I'm certain she can stand all right on her own, I pull the shirt into my hands and bunch it up to slip it over her head. She lets me, and I work it down her body until the towel falls and she pushes her hands through the arms. She hugs herself in it, and somehow it gives me peace to see her do this with something of mine.

She's staring at me now, which I guess is better than staring into nothingness. I only wish I knew what was going on in her head—I hope she knows I didn't look while she was naked, that I kept my promise.

I tug open my sink drawer and pull out the small brush inside. I hold it up for her, then move to pass it through her hair slowly. I'm careful with the tangles, and I don't comb any longer than I think I need to. I don't want to hurt her, and I can see the purple on her cheek—I know her head has to hurt.

I've had a bruise just like that. Someone *hit* me to give it to me.

With her hair brushed and her body cleaned, I take her hand and walk with her back to my room, closing the door when she steps inside. I pull back my blankets and tear away the top one, laying it on the floor.

"You're not sleeping up here?" she chokes out her question, and her body is shivering. I pause, looking at the thin blanket on the floor. I know it will be miserable, but I also know that tonight is not the night to be taking advantage of anyone.

"You can have my bed," I explain.

"You're leaving me alone?" she asks, her voice growing more panicked.

"I'll be right here. I'll even sit with my back against the bed until you fall asleep," I say, patting the place where I intend to sit. She nods slowly, then lowers herself to my bed. I pull the remaining blankets up over her, and she wraps her arms around them just as she did my shirt. My heart rushes again.

"I'm going to turn the light off. Unless…unless you need it," I say.

She looks over at the switch, her mouth perched open for a few seconds, considering. "Is there…maybe…some other light? Not so bright?"

My eyes squint while I think, and I turn to my desk, to my laptop, which I plug in so the battery doesn't die and flip open to my streaming videos, leaving it on *mute* so the only thing left behind is a small, blue hue cast about my room. I flip the switch and look to her.

"Is this enough?" I ask.

She nods, then pulls the blankets up tight to her chin.

I know she isn't going to sleep, so I pull my phone into my lap as I nestle next to the bed on the floor, prepared to read until morning if I have to. I won't leave her side.

I open up my reading app and scroll to the book I started a few months ago, before the semester started, and before I knew Emma was here. It's an overly complicated sci-fi fantasy with so many characters that I have to scroll back to the beginning to remind myself what the hell is happening. I'm not sure why I bother, because my eyes are just reading words—I'm retaining nothing.

Several minutes pass, and the bed behind me is still silent. I know she isn't sleeping though. I know, because I wouldn't sleep either. I didn't—for weeks—the first time someone jumped me at Lake Crest. I'd shut my eyes for quick rests, but my body never fell away completely. I was quick to wake at the smallest sound.

That's where Emma is now.

"Emma?" I whisper finally, just wanting to reassure her that I'm here.

A few seconds pass, and I think maybe I'm wrong, maybe she's asleep after all. Then I feel her weight shift on the bed, and soon her breath at the side of my face, her body so close to mine.

"I trust you, Andrew," she breathes. I don't look at her, her eyes are so near, her mouth…so near. I shut my eyes to avoid any temptation.

"Thank you, Emma. I'm sorry you can't trust others…I…I shouldn't say that. I'm just…God, I'm so sorry…" I ramble.

"I trust you," she says again. "Please…please come up here. Please hold me."

My lip quivers with this situation I'm in. My arms twitch to hold her, my instincts taking over and wanting to be the man she needs. But this isn't how I wanted to hold Emma Burke at all—this isn't the reason.

But it's what she needs. So I crawl up into the bed, lifting the cover, and I pull her into me, my breath exhaling in time with hers as I feel so much of what she's suffering from escape, if only for this moment.

"I've got you, Emma," I say, my lips falling to her head. I sweep her hair behind her ear and kiss her head again, this time letting my lips stay there while I speak. "I've got you, and I won't let go. I won't let go now, okay?"

She nods one more time, and even though she never fully falls asleep, she lets her body rest. And I know what a triumph that is.

* * *

EMMA – EARLIER THAT EVENING

It's not like me to be afraid to talk. At least…not in small groups like this. That's one of the things Miranda likes about me—I speak my mind.

But there was a vibe at the table throughout our dinner. I felt it all night. Something's been…*off*. Miranda and Graham have traded snarky remarks, and from the small bits I have deciphered, I get the sense that she really doesn't approve of many of his choices, and that there's also a bit of resentment that runs rampant throughout their household. She's mentioned more than once that he shouldn't work so hard to take after his father, and there's a tone when she says that.

When the conversation veered toward Tech Med programs, Graham was completely cut out of the conversation, and that's when he started ordering drinks.

He's rowdy now, and I can feel my cheeks burning while he stands on the corner of Washburne and Racine shouting at cars that drive by, asking if anyone's an Uber Cab, his body teetering out into the roadway every so often, causing cars to honk. His mother left with the other deans and a man that seemed to be more than a friend, but clearly not her husband. She and Graham didn't bother to say goodbye to each other, and I can still feel the ice.

"I'll just call a cab," I say for the tenth time. He isn't listening to me.

Somehow, an actual cab drives by and responds to his waving. He grabs my hand firmly, the first time he's touched me all night, and his fingers feel rough and sweaty. I slide into the back seat next to him, and he lets go of my hand. I reach forward and touch his arm, trying to get his attention. I want to go home. But he ignores me, leaning forward, relaxing both arms over the front seat and talking to the driver.

When he sits back to rest next to me, he tugs his tie loose from his shirt, his right hand nervously tapping on his leg. He glances at me and does a double take. I think maybe my nervous look registers with him.

"Hey, I just wanted to stop by this place. A few of the guys invited us.

We won't stay long. That okay?" He's asking, but not really. I nod and smile, and he leaves his glare on me a little longer than comfortable.

"So how well do you know that Andrew guy?" he asks. My guard goes up, and inside, I start to rewind everything I said tonight. Andrew has been the only thing on my mind—his letters, what he whispered when I left my apartment, the last week I've experienced with him. I've been checking my phone obsessively to see if Lindsey's texted me about their talk, but so far she hasn't. I'm pretty sure I haven't said anything about him aloud.

"I don't know. That's hard to say. I mean, we were friends in high school," I say, my answer purposely vague, not wanting to lie, but not wanting to divulge. Graham keeps his stare on me, the same look as before —it makes me shiver. His lip quirks up on one side, and he pulls a cigarette from a silver case he slides out of his back pocket.

I watch him light it, then glance to the windows around us, all of them up. I roll mine down for the sheer need of fresh air. The driver does the same.

"I didn't know you smoked," I say. I work hard to keep my face from souring. I get the sense Graham has had his fill of disapproval for tonight—I think maybe that's what his brashness is about.

He takes a long drag from his cigarette, holding the smoke in for a second or two, letting it swirl out around his teeth, rushing around his beard and filling most of the cab. That beard seemed so sexy when I first saw it, but now...I don't know.

"You know he has a record?" Graham asks me, his eyes back on mine, studying me and watching carefully for me to give something more away. I shrug and look out the window, wishing I were headed home rather than somewhere deep into the city.

"I heard something about that. He was a kid, though, so that stuff doesn't stay on your permanent record or anything," I say, still averting my eyes. I can feel him looking at me, and several seconds pass before he reacts to my response.

"Guess so. But shit like that still gets out..." he trails off.

I shut my eyes, but keep my face toward the window, not indulging him any more in this topic. I'm saved when the cab pulls abruptly next to some club named Primal. There's a line out the door, and the light strobing from the open doorways makes me dizzy. I dig my heels in as we step from the car, not wanting to go inside, but Graham simply tugs my arm a little harder.

My head rattles with the thumping of the music, and it takes us several minutes to slide through the packed bodies grinding along the main floor. We finally make it to a small tabletop against the wall in the back where two guys raise their hands and bump fists with Graham, half hugging him as he steps up close enough. They eye me over his shoulder, and the one closest to me smiles.

"I'm Brody," he says, reaching out his hand. "I sort of met you a couple weeks ago. I went with Graham to that dinner for his mom."

He looks familiar, and I'm honestly just thankful that he's kind. It's going to make however long I have to be here bearable.

"Nice to see you again. Emma," I shout into his ear. He nods and gives me a thumbs up, but I'm pretty sure he didn't hear a word I said.

"Whatcha drinking?" he asks.

"Water's fine," I say, looking around at the table loaded with drinks. Graham already seems to have one in his hand, and he glances at me, the same suspicious look he was giving me in the car.

When the waitress comes, my new friend Brody orders me a water, but Graham steps in, putting his hand on his friend's chest, his fingers splayed as he pushes Brody a little off balance.

"She'll have one of those vanilla pineapple things," he says. The waitress darts her eyes to me, and Graham morphs into his suave self, sliding his arm around me affectionately and leaning his head down to look me in the eyes. "It's sweet. You'll like it, I promise."

I nod *okay*, even though I don't really want it, and my inside self screams at me. Graham leaves his arm around me as he begins talking with his friends, and I do my best to ignore the possessive feel of it. It's nothing like the way Andrew's touch feels—nothing gentle or seductive or special. It's barbaric feeling, his arm heavy and hot, and even though I haven't tried to step out of his grasp, I can tell he wouldn't let me.

A guy brings our drinks over on a platter, and when he hands Graham his, I notice that Graham spends several long seconds looking at it while the waiter hands out everyone else's. I take mine, and after a tiny sip, slide it onto the table in front of me. I'm going to do my best to turn it into something that's forgotten.

Just as the waiter turns to leave, Graham grabs hold of his forearm, stopping him from leaving. The waiter regards his hand, then looks over Graham, I think trying to decide who would hit the other harder in a stand-off.

"I ordered a *full* drink, and you brought me this," Graham says, a slight slur to his drunken speech. He's still very confident sounding, but sloppy around the edges.

The waiter looks down at the drink in Graham's hand. It's maybe an inch and a half from being full, a sip short at the most.

"I'm not sure what you want me to do," the waiter says. I notice Graham's jaw twitch and his neck tense as he shoves the drink into the waiter's hand.

"I want you to go get me the right fucking drink!" he seethes. The waiter stares at him, blinking, I think a little stunned and waiting for everyone to laugh like this is a big joke. Only nobody does. I notice Graham's friends have all moved on and are talking with each other, ignoring this display, which makes me think this is probably normal behavior. "I mean…am I wrong?"

He looks to me for support, and I shake my head slightly, my palms instantly sweating. I want to leave. I want to leave right now.

He turns to one of his friends, nudging him on the arm and motioning to the drink, now held out between them by the waiter.

"Dude, that's crap, right? I ordered a full fucking drink, and this asshole brings me this. I'm not paying for that. Am I wrong?" His voice is carrying over most of our corner of the bar now, and several people are looking at us. I notice the waiter straighten his posture, rolling his back muscles, gearing up for whatever's next.

Graham's friend chuckles and laughs out *yeah* in response before returning to the conversation he was in before.

"I'll bring you a new one," the waiter finally says, muttering to himself as he turns away.

Graham's eyes drift hazily over to me, and his stare is intense and instantly causes my body to heat up and my back to sweat.

"Did that embarrass you?" he asks.

It takes me a moment to catch up to what he said; I'm too busy wondering if it's a joke, or if he's teasing. His mouth never cracks a smile, though.

"A little," I admit.

He holds his stare on me, then lets his eyes trail down my body in a way that makes me clench my knees together and flex my leg muscles, ready to kick and scream and run.

"It shouldn't embarrass you," he says.

I don't make eye contact. As I step closer to the table and run my finger along my drink as a distraction, I shrug and whisper "Maybe."

I can feel his stare on me, and it makes me mindful of every movement I make. I pull my small purse up to the tabletop and take out my compact, looking in the mirror even though I have no need. I clip it shut again, then move my phone to a place I can view it inside my purse. I slide the screen on and check the time, not quite midnight. I groan inwardly at the thought that I might be stuck here for a while.

My finger is poised over the contacts button when I feel Graham's breath at my neck.

"You calling that Harper dick?" he questions. There's a bite to his tone.

"I was checking the time and just making sure my roommate didn't need anything," I smile.

I pretend.

His heavy stare lands on me again, and somehow he feels bigger. His shirt is opened at the top, his tie now loose on both sides. It's funny how this look can be both sexy and repulsive—depending on who and when.

"You know I'm going to fight him?" he asks.

I pinch my brow, wondering what he means. Is he seriously challenging Andrew to a duel? I'm not sure who I'd bet on if he was. I know who my heart would pick.

"I was the Sigma national champ, last year. I'm trying to stay in fighting shape. It's my hobby, and when I found out Harper liked to box, I thought… well…" he says, his lips slightly curled into a grin.

"I don't really care for boxing," I say, wishing the liquid in my glass were water so I could drink it.

Graham's stare lingers a moment or two longer, then he steps past me to join his circle of friends at the next table, putting an arm around one of the guys. I turn so my back is to him, and I breathe out slowly, clutching my purse in my hands again, convincing them not to tremble. I glance around the bar, to the dozens of plush seating areas with well-dressed couples nestled close to each other, groups of women taking shots and laughing loudly, men running fingers up girls' legs, teasing them, flirting—fondling.

My head feels fuller with every beat of the music, and it's making it hard to see. I trace the walls of the interior, searching for anything that might get me through the next thirty minutes, my gut sinking, knowing it will probably be an hour. When I finally spot an open sofa, I move to it, my purse in my hands, my drink on the table behind me. I tuck myself into the corner cushions, then look over the other women sitting near me so I can emulate their behavior. All I want to do is fit in long enough to leave.

I settle on curling one leg under the other, then I pull my purse close, next to me and remove my phone, opening the text box. I think about texting Lindsey for a rescue, but then I remember Andrew—he's telling her.

I can't call Lindsey. She might not even come after he tells her everything.

My eyes fall to my lap and I slip my phone back into my purse. Graham finds me a few minutes later, and my stomach sinks when I see him hold a finger up to a friend and weave through the people to get closer to me. The heat of him next to me as he sits down close on the sofa repulses me.

"You want me to take you home?" he asks.

Yes! Yes, this is what I want. He's not a bad guy, and he gets it. Oh thank god.

I nod and apologize. "I'm just not feeling very well," I say.

He smiles, but briefly, knocking back the rest of his drink—the new one brought to him a few seconds ago from the waiter he badgered and bullied —then plunks his glass down on the small metal table in front of us.

"I'll take you home," he says.

I move my purse in front of me, looping the strap over my neck, relieved and ready to go. As I uncross my legs, I feel the eerie tickle of his finger sliding up my left thigh, stopping at the hem of my dress. My leg jerks in response. Graham chuckles, the sound escaping his throat raspy and dirty.

"Come on," he nudges over his shoulder, standing and pulling out his wallet. I notice several hundred dollar bills unfold before he gets to two twenties. He steps over to his friend and hands them to him, then reaches for my hand, tugging it completely into his grip. My instincts are screaming at me to fight against it. But I desperately want to leave, and right now, this seems like my only way home.

We get out front and Graham practically drags me to the corner, stopping abruptly, looking both ways, then dragging me behind him across the street. My foot jerks and I feel one of my heels break off, so I hop a few steps, his hand still grasping mine.

"My shoe!" I scream.

He looks down at my feet behind him, sighing heavily as I take my shoes off. His hand reaches for my arm when I do, and as soon as I'm able to walk, he drags me to the other side of the street.

"Cabs are easier to get over here," he grumbles.

We rush to the corner, a closed art gallery and several dark office lobbies lining the sidewalk. We pause by a metal trashcan, and I lean against it to lift my feet one at a time and look at their bottoms, inspecting for cuts. The blacktop has already stained them, and there's a pebble lodged in the skin of one. I pull it out with my fingers, and as I'm leaning forward I feel the snaking sensation of Graham's hand on my bare back. I arch myself away from him, straightening up quickly as I take a step away, leaving my broken shoes on the ground near the trashcan.

Graham holds both of his hands up innocently, his eyes still hazy and his mouth in a hard line. His right leg leans a little too far and he falters, but regains his balance quickly, his eyes on me the entire time. I look to the road, looking for a cab to call on my own, and in that second, he reaches for me again, this time his hand grasping around my side, his fingers sliding around my ribs, to my back, pulling up the material gathered around my lower back and causing my skirt to hike up several inches as he pulls me to him.

I shove my hands into his chest, forcing space between us, but I'm no match for his strength as I struggle against him. I feel his hand slide around my back completely, into the scooped curve of my dress, his fingers clawing at my ass. I bring my knee up, but he anticipates me and blocks my blow, turning enough to the side.

"Isn't this how your man Andrew likes it?" he huffs. His hold is rough, bruising my body everywhere he grips it, and I start to cry.

"Let go! Graham, let go of me!" I scream, my words muffled against his mouth as he forces a kiss on me, his beard scratching at my face and his breath hot. I push so hard that the strap on my purse breaks, and I feel my things fall to the sidewalk below us. I also feel Graham's other hand reach around me to force me even tighter into him. He tastes of old whiskey and stale smoke.

He growls as I shove against him hard, breaking his hold enough to get a foot of space from him, enough room to scream.

"Help me! Somebody!" My voice echoes, and I notice a few people across the street turn their attention toward us, but they move in slow motion—everything does. I can't tell if they're ignoring us, or coming to help, and soon Graham's hand is cupping my mouth. He's intoxicated and his fingers are messy, one of them at the part of my lips, so I open my mouth and grip what I can with my teeth, biting hard and fast. He rips his hand away, but flings his fist at me in an instant, his blow landing on my right cheek and sending my body to the ground on my knees.

"You bitch!" he yells, and I see him lunge at me from the corner of my eye. Before he reaches me, a pair of arms scoop under me and push me toward an open cab, and I notice one of Graham's friends holding him, pushing him backward several steps as the door closes on me. My belongings are thrown in next to me, and the cab driver looks over the seat mouthing something. I can't hear him—every noise a siren blaring in my ears, until finally I'm able to read his lips.

What's your address?

I manage to give him my building, and as the car begins to roll into traffic and Graham's figure fades from view, I start to cry harder, not stopping until the cab slows in front of my building and an angel is waiting for me on the curb.

CHAPTER 18

EMMA

The light is dim, but it still feels too bright for my eyes. I hold my hand over my face, stretching my other arm and legs out, feeling the burn in my muscles and remembering the bruises on my skin. My fingers are cool over my eyes, and I leave them there until they warm.

I know where I am.

I'm glad I'm here.

I'm scared I'm here.

I wanted to be here, but never like this.

I pull my hand away and roll to the side. I felt Andrew leave the bed sometime early this morning. I thought about waking, but I didn't know what to say to him. I didn't want him to look at me—to see me like this. I feel weak and ashamed. And I feel alone.

Pulling in the heavy blue quilt to my body, I take in the scent on the material. It reminds me of young Andrew, and as I let my eyes look over the thinning fabric squares, I wonder to myself if he's had this blanket since high school. I smile at the thought of it—imagining him bringing pieces of home here to college with him. Then I wonder if he got to bring these same things to Lake Crest, and my smile fades.

There's a sound in the hallway, and I watch for movement under the door, wondering if Andrew's out there, if he'll come inside to check on me. Several minutes pass, though, so I finally leave the bed and shuffle slowly around his room to his dresser, pulling a few drawers open until I find one with a pair of sweatpants inside. I pull them on, rolling the top twice to keep them up on my waist. It feels good to dress in his things; it feels...safe. The clothes in my bag feel stiff—I don't want them.

I pause with my hand on his doorknob, closing my eyes and breathing in slowly as I twist and open his door out to the hallway. I see the bathroom across from me and wince at the thought of what Andrew did for me last night, what he could have seen. I know he didn't look though. As dazed as I was, I know because I watched him. I scoot across the hall to pee, then wash my hands and shut the light off behind me as I slide slowly down the rest of the hallway to the sound of the television blaring. There's a head leaning on the back of the sofa, and I recognize his roommate quickly, the crunch of the cereal as he scoops it from the bowl in his lap making me smile.

"Hi," I squeak. He jumps slightly, craning his neck to look at me, then moving fast to place his bowl onto the coffee table in front of him as his long legs maneuver around furniture into the kitchen.

"Emma, yeah. Hi...uh...Drew...he's...he's not back yet. Shit, uhm...you want breakfast?" he says, stumbling about the kitchen, opening cabinets and searching for something for me to eat. I'm not hungry. My stomach still feels sick.

"I'm okay. Thank you," I say.

He shuts all of the doors again, then leans against the counter, looking at me, his eyes scanning around the room.

"Can I get you something? I don't know, blanket maybe? Or...do you want to watch TV?" He rushes back into the living room and starts picking things up, turning the volume down on the program he was watching and glancing up at me every so often. It's sweet.

"Really, I'm okay. I...I was looking for Andrew," I say, my eyes falling, embarrassed about why I'm here, that I need someone—that I need *him*. I know I shouldn't be, but I feel so helpless.

"He's at work," he says.

"At...at that gym?" I ask, the thought of Andrew getting hit by someone squeezing my heart.

Trent chuckles lightly and looks at his feet, shaking his head. "No, his *real* job," he says. "He's at the elementary on Fourteenth. He's probably coloring right now."

My lips form a tight smile at the mental picture that paints.

"Coloring," I repeat.

Trent nods and laughs again. "Yep, Harper's one bad-ass colorer," he says.

Looking down, I let my smile grow slightly bigger. My feet are bare, and the chill hits them. I wiggle my toes.

"You need some shoes?" Trent asks. I laugh once to myself then look up at him, holding my arms out to show off my Andrew wardrobe.

"Andrew packed my bag, but he didn't include footwear," I shrug. "Seems I need a little of everything."

Trent nods, then holds up a finger and jogs back to his room. I wait in the middle of his living room, listening to the sounds of drawers sliding open and his closet door closing. He comes out with a pair of short socks and sport sandals.

"Here," he says, motioning to the sofa. "Have a seat."

I step around to the front, and he kneels in front of me, handing me the socks to put on. I slip them on quickly then put my feet on the floor so he can slide them into the sandals and adjust the Velcro so they don't come loose.

"You're like Prince Charming, only instead of a glass slipper, it's an old Adidas sandal," I laugh, holding my foot out and moving it to test to be sure the shoe doesn't fall away. Trent laughs with me.

"I guess so," he says. "Only, don't tell Drew that. He'll rip my head off if he hears you call *me* Prince Charming. That's his job."

I keep my eyes on him, and he glances up at me a few times, his lips in a tight smile, perhaps a little guilty for selling his friend's feelings out to me. I'm glad he did, though. And he's right—it is Andrew's job.

I head down the hall for a quick glance in the bathroom mirror then walk to Andrew's room to grab my broken purse and keys. Trent catches me before I leave completely, asking if I want a ride, but as much as I appreciate the gesture, I also want to go to Andrew alone. He seems okay with my "Thanks, but no thanks."

I leave their apartment, looking like a member of the Tech hockey team. It's still early, maybe not quite seven, and the traffic on the road is light. The fall weather is growing colder, and I notice my breath form a small cloud in front of me as I walk. I blow hard once just to test. I love it when the weather is like this.

I pass a few people walking their dogs, and I push my hair forward, wanting to hide the glaring bruise on my face. I don't know what drove me to leave the safety of his apartment this morning, only that I *had* to see him. I have to thank him, and it doesn't feel like it can wait. When I reach the school, I notice a few cars pull up to a main lot, parents stepping out and walking young kids up to a side building. I head to the open door, holding it as a woman walks out, her phone resting between her cheek and shoulder as she mouths *thanks* and passes me.

When I glance inside, I see Andrew's back to me; he's sitting on a long lunch-table bench with about a dozen six and seven-year-old girls gathered around him—all of them coloring. His hair is messy, tousled in varied directions, and he's wearing his black, long-sleeved shirt with gray jeans, the laces from his Converse shoes dangling off to the sides, waiting to trip him.

He looks like an innocent little boy in a man's body as his arm shakes from side to side with his coloring, his head leaning and his other hand twisting the paper in a slow circle so he can fill up something with the bright blue in his hand.

There's a tiny girl sitting next to him, her legs folded up as she sits sideways and watches him color. "Use pink next," she says, her voice high and precious. Her ponytails flop next to her face as she turns her head toward me and grins. She's missing two of her teeth on the top, but she's smiling like a supermodel. I hold a hand up and bunch my fingers in a wave. She waves back, then taps Andrew on the shoulder, scooting up on her heels to reach his ear. When she's done whispering, Andrew flips his body around quickly, his eyes wide on me.

"Sorry…Trent…he told me you were here," I say. His shocked look fades into a happy one, and he holds his crayon out for the young girl next to him to take.

"Kaitlyn, you mind finishing?" he asks. She pouts at first, but he brings both of his hands together in a begging motion and she finally sighs and begins coloring.

It takes him a few seconds to untangle his long legs from the bench that's clearly too small for him, then he looks over at the group of coloring girls until he reaches me.

"Just like you to have all the girls hovering around you," I tease.

He laughs, looking down and pushing his hands in his pockets, twisting one foot nervously as he nods in agreement, his eyes finally meeting mine. He squints the left one closed slightly, his right lip curling up—he's adorable. He's always been adorable.

"The boys all sleep in, so I don't get to play the boy things until the bell almost rings. They're lazy, I guess. The girls all get here right when I open up," he shrugs.

"I don't think they're lazy," I smile. "I think the girls just really like you."

He sucks in his bottom lip and nods to one side.

"Maybe," he grins. His gaze shifts from my eyes to the bruise on my right cheek, and I bring my hand up, sweeping hair back in the way to hide it. Andrew reaches to me slowly though, pausing to make sure it's okay that he approaches me. He's being cautious. He moves my hair back out of the way when I nod that it's okay, then leans his head to the side to look at my face, running the backs of his knuckles down my cheek slowly. It burns along my tender skin.

"It's not a very deep bruise," he says, tracing the skin one more time with his thumb. "I think it will start to fade quickly. It already looks better than it did."

His eyes come back to mine, and I notice the deep cut and stitches on his chin. This time it's my turn to assess the damage, and I run my finger along the rough edge of the threading then flit my eyes to his.

"You have another fight?" I ask, my gut twisting at the memory of what Graham said, that he plans on fighting Andrew. I wonder if that's true.

Andrew's brow lowers and he purses his lips.

"What?" I ask, worried that he may have done something else, that he might have hunted down Graham early this morning.

"Lindsey..." he starts, and I pinch my brow. "I...I told her the truth. And maybe I wasn't quite as...sensitive in my delivery as I should be?"

His face is bunched, not even hiding his shame, and my stomach sinks a little.

"So you did...tell her," I say. He said he would, and I had a feeling he would follow through. But that means Lindsey is probably angry with me.

"It's going to be okay, Emma. I promise," he says, cupping the side of my face with one hand. I stand there stiff, and I can see the hurt in his eyes as his hand slides away. "I told her it was all my fault, and I swear to god, I will make it right between you two."

"You don't have to. I'll...I'll talk to her," I say, looking down.

"Yeah...maybe not quite yet though?" he says, and when I look up, he's squinting one eye again. I exhale a deep breath and let my shoulders slump. "She wants you to move out."

I can't help the whimper that escapes me, and I bring my hands to cover my mouth. I stare at him, waiting for the part where he says he's kidding. But all I see is sympathy. He wears it well, and at least I have that —Andrew looking at me like he cares. Like he's deeply affected by my unhappiness.

"Emma...I'm sorry," Andrew says, shaking his head. He reaches for me, but pulls back again, instead putting his hands in his pockets. I hate that he's still so unsure with me. His touch—it would be so healing right now. But I understand his caution—it's out of respect. He's worried about what I've been through. "I'll fix this," he says, looking down at his feet. He repeats it again, this time more for himself.

I stare down along with him, not sure what to do now. I look at my hands, the way his shirt falls over my palms, and as upset as I am that I've lost Lindsey, my heart lurches that I have Andrew.

His foot kicks into mine, and I breathe out a small laugh before looking up at him, his lopsided grin saying he's sorry but he's happy he has me too.

"You look better in my things than I do," he smirks, unable to hold my gaze for long, his grin growing into an embarrassed one.

"I like the way you look in them," I say, biting my lip and flitting my eyes. This is the first time I've ever overtly flirted with him, and the thrill of it rushes my body. A few girls giggle behind him, and Andrew turns to look, chuckling when he faces me again. This—it's all such a wonderful distraction from the scenes I keep replaying in my head.

He grabs his neck and rubs before raising one eyebrow and looking at me. "I think you might be right about my *girl crew*, and I'm not so sure they like you—I'm sort of their territory," he teases.

There's a long, comfortable silence between us, and my fingers tingle, wanting to touch him. I leave them wrapped in the comfort of his cotton sleeves though, and instead let the flurry of butterflies run around the inside of my body. It's nice to feel something different—I think this is joy. It's definitely anticipation.

"Move in with me," Andrew says, and the butterflies inside me all start running into each other, my heart speeding up and my hands forming tight fists as my nails dig into my own palms. My eyes must have given me away, because Andrew kicks his foot into mine again. "No, no…I just mean…you need somewhere to go, and I know Trent won't mind. Just until I get things worked out with you and Lindsey. We're close to campus, and I'd like…" he swallows hard. "I'd like to have you there, to know you're safe."

Our eyes hold onto each other, and our breathing falls into sync.

"Okay," I whisper, my lips tingling, not sure if they should smile or cry a little. "Okay," I nod again, maybe reassuring myself. "I'll grab some things this morning, while she's in class. I have class today, so I won't be at your house until late this afternoon. Is that…is that okay?"

"That's fine. Here," he says, reaching into his pocket and sliding a key from his ring. "I'm heading right to practice from here, and I'll just get in with Trent later and make a copy for myself."

"Don't you have class?" I ask.

Andrew shakes his head, laughing through a shrug. "I'll go tomorrow. It's fine. I've already done most of my work for the semester," he says.

"Nerd," I tease.

"Among many other things," he says, his smile a little sad.

"Many *good* things," I say. I hope my words make him smile, but he only breathes in deeply, shaking off my compliment.

"Maybe someday. I'm working on it," he says.

I want to tell him he's already there, and to thank him for taking care of me, but the doors burst open behind me and several boys come running, two of them grabbing onto Andrew's right arm when they reach him, climbing him like a jungle gym. A few of the parents are standing behind me, waiting to talk to him, so I just hold up his key and suck in my lower lip as I smile.

I take the long route to my apartment—my *old* apartment—and Lindsey is gone by the time I get there. I pull a few bags from under my bed and fill them with most of my clothes, thankful Andrew seemed to grab many of my necessities last night. When I glance at my desk, I realize my letters and backpack are also gone, and my body jolts with a shot of adrenaline. I panic at first that something happened—that during their talk, Lindsey discovered them, destroyed them, that they're gone. But my backpack is gone, which means Andrew must have seen them and brought that to his apartment too.

Andrew saw them.

I pause at that thought, not sure if it's good or bad. He wrote them for me, but now that we're both aware of the words he wrote—or at least many of the words he wrote—something deeply personal feels like it's settled in between us.

Lindsey will be gone for several hours—today is one of her longest, and though I used to wait desperately for her to get home so we could have dinner together, I'm grateful for the time now. I sit on my bed and pull my phone out of my purse, dialing on rote and in a trance. When my father answers on the other end, I'm not ready to speak—my mind still caught between being angry over the letters he kept from me and wanting to run to his familiar embrace after what Graham did. He waits me out, though.

"You get my package?" he finally asks. I nod even though he can't hear me.

"I'm sorry I didn't give it to you sooner," he says, and I hear him swallow, hear him thinking of ways to explain.

"Why?" I ask, a tear forming in the tender corner of my right eye. I pull the bottom of Andrew's shirt up to dry it.

"Your mom wanted to give them to you," he says, and knowing that makes me feel both grateful and terrible at once. "She made me save them. I threw the first one away, and she went out to the trash by the curb and pulled it from the bag."

My dad laughs, but it's a sad sound that comes out—one made of memories and repentances. "She told me it was a federal offense," he laughs through a cry. I join him, wiping away another tear, this one for that memory of my mom. "She said that any boy who took the time to write a letter, to mail it, with a stamp and everything, was worth rescuing. But I was so afraid of what might happen if Andrew wasn't worthy of you. I was afraid he would take you away—and not that he'd make you run away, but pull you away from us. His home life was so..."

"His brothers and mother and step-father—they're all really close and amazing dad. That isn't fair. That *wasn't* fair!" I shout, glad to be alone, free to be angry and feel.

"I know that now. But your mom...she was sick, and I just couldn't risk it. Oh god, Em...I'm so sorry. I was so scared, and I didn't want to lose you too..." My dad's words end with his crying, and I hear him let out heavy sobs, miles away from me, nowhere near me so I could hug him and assure him I was still here, even if I was angry with him. I got it.

I get it.

"I'm glad you didn't throw them away," I whisper as he grows quieter. "I'm glad...I'm glad Mom told you to keep them."

I listen to my father breathe, and I lay back on my bed that isn't really mine and wait for him to speak again. A few minutes pass before he finally does.

"Did he tell you that he came?" My eyes pop open, and I sit up straight.

"After Lake Crest? Yes..." I say, wondering if there's more to the story, if there are parts Andrew didn't tell me.

"Oh, no...not then. I didn't know...I didn't know he came then. I meant a couple days ago. He visited me, wanted to know why his letters never made it. He...he could have hit me he was so angry. I could tell," my father says. "But he didn't. He took everything in, everything I had to say, and as much as it wrecked him to know the truth, he respected me, and my bad decisions. I was wrong, Emma. And I'm sorry you didn't know about the letters before."

"I know now," I say in a faint voice. "I know now."

My eyes close at the thought of Andrew, at how much he cared for me then, and how much he must care for me now—even after so many wrong turns.

"Did he tell you why he went to Lake Crest?" I say, my eyes still closed, picturing everything that happened that night—picturing the resolve on Andrew's face when he told me to trade him places.

"I know, Emma. And even if he wasn't drunk or high at the time, it still…it still sticks with me that he was driving you around that way—" I cut my father off, before I lose the courage to tell the truth—the first time I've done so to anyone but Andrew.

"He wasn't driving, Dad. Andrew traded me places. I was the one who wrecked the car, and he…" I start to choke as the tears rush my face. "He took the fall for me, Dad. Andrew didn't want me to face any repercussions—and even though he didn't know it was my heart I was afraid of losing, he knew I was afraid of something. So he gave up a year of his life for me. A *year*, Dad."

"Emma…" my dad's breathing stutters as he tries to catch up to the truth, to soak in everything I just told him. "Emma?"

"I was driving. And that man stepped out in front of me, in the dark. And all I could think about was how any kind of misdemeanor or indiscretion would make Dr. Wheaton change her mind, would take me off the list. I was selfish, Dad!"

"Stop it!" my father yells on the other end. "Don't you dare think that, Emma Jane. Don't you ever call yourself selfish. You were scared, and it's okay to be afraid when you're sixteen and looking at the possibility of—"

"He lost so much, Dad…" I cry to my father. "So much…"

"He did," my dad agrees. If only my father knew how much Andrew truly lost—how much of himself was gone.

Another long silence passes while we both sit together on the phone, both of our thoughts consumed with Andrew Harper I'm sure—both of us thinking of the good he has to offer, the good he gave, and how very ungrateful we were for it.

"Thank you for giving me the letters," I say finally, sitting and looking at my stuffed bags at my feet. I look around the room, and I think of my friend that I'm leaving behind, but when I look at the clothes I'm in, I think of the friend I'm running to, and I consider how my life seems to need to be in balance—to always give me something, but lose something else in return.

I will never give Andrew up again, though. But I want Lindsey, too.

I don't say it to my father aloud, but I think it: *I am selfish.*

* * *

ANDREW

Somehow, I was on point today at practice. I have no idea how with the mess swimming in my head right now. I'm too distracted by everything to attend class, which was the first thing Coach brought up as I passed his office in the locker room. My mouth almost made it worse when my argument for him was that I didn't really *need* my advanced calculus classes, because I could build a working rocket out of the parts from his car right now—and ensure it had enough power to reach the stratosphere. He told me I was a smart ass and better show my face to my professors tomorrow. He's right, on both counts.

I've been waiting for Trent to ask about Emma, to want the details. He's doing that thing where he talks about everything *but* the elephant in the room, though. He even asked me about laundry, and if I'd done my load for the week or not. He's pushing me to let all of my baggage out, without prying—*directly*—and it's working. His goddamned method is working.

"Emma's moving in," I sigh as we pull into the only open space along the street by our apartment.

"Aha!" he exclaims, as if that…*that* is the thing he honestly expected me to say. He remains still, his hands on his knees; he sits proudly, like a fucking peacock in the passenger seat, then the meaning of what I said sinks in. He jerks to the side to look at me again. "Wait, what?"

I lean back in the seat and pull my hat from my head, tossing it on the dash, then run my hand through my hair, holding it between my fingers. I nod as I speak.

"Emma's moving in. Just…just for a few days. Lindsey's pissed," I say.

"Yeah, saw that coming," Trent says with a short laugh.

"Okay, no need to be a righteous asshole about it. You were right, bad idea, I'm a dick, got it," I say, glancing sideways at him before opening the car and slamming the door behind me. Trent follows suit and walks behind me up to our apartment door.

"Good, glad we're on the same page with all of that," he says. "So where, might I ask, will Emma be *staying* in our apartment?"

I sigh and let my head fall on our door as I wait for Trent to push his key in the lock. I shrug because I really hadn't thought about that yet. I was assuming she'd just stay with me, in my room, but maybe that's a little too presumptuous.

"Your ass can have the couch. No way am I giving up my room," Trent says.

"I know," I sigh and push through the door the second he unlocks it. I head straight to the kitchen and grab a beer, twisting the cap and gulping half of it down like water.

Trent sits on one of the stools at the counter and studies me for a few seconds. "What else?" he finally asks.

"What do you mean *what else*? Emma's moving in because I fucked up her living situation. What else is there?" I say, pulling the bottle up to my mouth. Trent lowers his brow at me when I do. "What?" I ask.

"Nothin' man. Just…slow it down. You got sloppy last night, and that's how you fucked things up in the first place," he says. I nod and slide the beer to the middle of the counter, then pull myself up to sit on the seat opposite of my friend.

"I fucked things up a long time ago. Last night was nothing—trust me," I say. I let my eyes focus on the beer, on the label and the gray color of the paper, the way it matches Emma's eyes. I can literally see her everywhere. I retrain my gaze to Trent, and he's studying me. "I love her. And it's so fucking bad. And it's messed me up…damn. Trent, I'm so messed up over it, I don't even know what to do."

"You tell her," he answers quickly.

I laugh in response, but he shakes his head and simply repeats his answer.

"Tell her what? Hey, I'm sorry I'm a loser who doesn't know how to have a real relationship; so instead, I steal chick's wallets—and love them and leave them? But really I'm not *that* broken, so maybe try me out?"

"Uh...no. You don't say that," he says, getting to his feet and grabbing my beer in his hand, finishing it. I raise an eyebrow at him, and he points a finger at me. "Hey, I don't do dumb shit after a beer or two. That's your thing."

"That Graham dude wants to fight me," I say, catching Trent off guard as he's about to toss the empty bottle in our recycle box. He pauses, pursing his lips before finally throwing the bottle away and moving back to his seat.

"So he, what...like challenged you to a duel at dawn or something?" he jokes.

I shake my head and let my gaze fall to my lap.

"No, or maybe, yeah. I...I don't know. It was before this whole thing happened, before last night. He knows Harley, and he's got some major bank."

"So you want to fight him for the money," Trent says, and I can hear his disapproval loud and clear. I fill my lungs and hold my breath, letting the air seep out slowly before looking my friend in the eyes.

"At first, yeah. It's a lot of money," I say.

"At first," he repeats me.

I nod.

"Now, I just want to beat the shit out of him for free," I say, my mouth hard, my breathing stopping, my eyes angry as I imagine the feel of my fist landing on him. I want to destroy him.

Trent doesn't respond, and eventually he slides from his seat and moves into our living room, picking up the remote and putting on ESPN, going right to his routine. I watch him for a few seconds, and I try to find the courage to ask him what he thinks I should do. But I already know—he doesn't think I belong in the ring with that guy, and he knows I won't be able to control myself when I face him. And I don't want Trent to tell me not to do it.

After a few minutes, I leave the kitchen and kick my shoes off by the front door, then grab my backpack from the table and start to carry it to my room.

"You should take her out on a real date. That's what you do. Buy her flowers, give her chocolate, or a teddy bear. Hell…do all three. You need all the help you can get," he says, stopping me before I reach my room. I turn my head back to look at him, and at first he keeps his attention on the TV, but eventually he faces me, giving me a slight shrug. "You asked me what you should do, and if you really love her, you should make that absolutely clear to her."

I chew at the inside of my mouth for a few seconds, considering what Trent said. Eventually, I nod in agreement, then make my way to my room so I can come up with something perfect for Emma—something I can do tonight, because I cannot let one more day go by where I'm anything but in love with this girl.

CHAPTER 19

EMMA

I skipped Miranda's lecture today. I'm sure she'll text me. I've only missed once before, and it was because of a financial-aid meeting. She questioned my absence then, and it was easy to explain. Today's is a little more challenging. *"Oh, well, you see...your son got all grabby with me, then hit me when I fought back, and I want to hide this from you because I'm afraid you'll pick his side."*

Yeah—skipping was a good call.

I left my things at Andrew's this morning, and somehow, despite months of walking home in one direction, my legs managed to remember that today they lived somewhere else. The tickle in my tummy is constant the closer I get to his apartment, and I can't decide if it's because I'm excited, or because I'm anxious over Lindsey. I think maybe it's both.

I still feel selfish.

I'm about to push his key in the lock when the door suddenly opens in front of me, Andrew stepping through it and closing it behind his back. He's wearing a thin white T-shirt with skulls on the front over a black long-sleeved shirt, tight black jeans, and gray lace-up boots. His hair is combed back, and he smells almost edible. I swear his cologne is circling me for the kill. He pushes his hands into his pockets nervously, and shuffles his feet as he looks down at them while he talks.

"So I have plans. I mean, for me and you. I mean...shit. I'm already messing this up," he stammers. I suck in my bottom lip, trying not to smile or embarrass him. He looks me in the eyes and takes a deep breath, holding up a finger, stepping into his apartment and exiting it again just as he did before. "Let's try this again. Emma, I'd like to take you out tonight. On a date—a *real* date. And if this turns out to be corny or lame or if I gross you out or...whatever...then it's all Trent's fault. He told me I should show you how I feel. So, tonight, if you're willing to give me a shot, I'd like to start over. I'd like *us* to start over. And I'd like to treat you like you deserve to be treated...like I should have treated you all along. Whadaya say?"

My lip slides loose from my hold, and I can't stop the quick spread of my smile. Andrew smiles in return, nodding once and letting out a heavy breath. "Phew. Good. Okay then, before you go inside, I want you to know that I realize I might have gone a little overboard. But like I said—I didn't want there to be any question in your mind about my intentions here. I'm asking you on a date, and that date ends when you say goodnight. And then I will take my place on our *very* comfortable couch, giving you your privacy in my room for as long as you need it."

I open my mouth, my brow pinching with guilt; I hate the thought of pushing him out of his room, but Andrew holds a hand up quickly. "No questioning me. Not tonight. I'm too nervous about everything being perfect for you to question tonight, okay?"

"Okay," I say. Andrew closes his eyes, his smile once again relieved.

He pushes his door open, holding his arm out to direct me inside, where there are three gigantic boxes placed on the floor—wrapped in purple paper with white bows.

"Purple's my favorite color," I say.

"I know," he says in return. "Go on. Open them."

I look to him nervously, but move to the first box, excited to see what's inside. I tear away the tissue paper and pull off the lid to find two enormous Care Bears sitting inside. I lift them up and cradle each one on a hip, like they're children, and the silliness of them makes me giggle.

"Okay, so hear me out," Andrew starts, closing the door behind him and leaning against it. "That one there, the blue one? His name is Grumpy or Grouchy or…"

"Grumpy," I confirm for him, my mouth aching from my smile.

"Good, right. Well, Grumpy…that one's me. He's got this cloud that follows him around, and he's just generally blue and mopey and shit, and he doesn't really have any friends, other than this yellow bear here with the sunshine on it's stomach."

"Funshine Bear," I answer, looking over at the yellow bear on my other hip.

"Right…wait…Funshine? That's really his name?" Andrew asks. I nod *yes.*

"Wow, this is getting even lamer, and I'm really embarrassed," he says.

"Don't be," I say, catching his gaze before it falls. He squints one eye, questioning me. "So far, this is really sweet. Keep going."

He nods, his cheeks dented with the dimples of the smile he's trying to hide. The bashful boy from our youth is coming out to play, and it makes my heart soar to see.

"Okay, well *Funshine,* or as I called him, *Happiness...*this one's you. She's Grumpy's only friend in the world. And she's the only one that can make Grumpy forget about the damn cloud stuck on his body. He needs her. Without her, he's just not…well, without her there's just too much of the cloud," Andrew says, his mouth settling into a more serious smile. I notice how fast his chest is rising and falling, how hard he's breathing. He's scared.

I look at both of the bears and squeeze them to my body, then look back at him. "I love them. I'm keeping them with me all night," I say, and his lips slowly curl up again.

"Good," he nods, looking down. When he glances back up, he gestures to the second box. "Go on. Open it."

I tuck both bears under my left arm and move to the second box, working with one hand to unwrap it. I finally get the lid off the top and when I look down, I notice a pair of pink and white ice skates that look to be my size. I flash my eyes back to Andrew's, smiling.

"Holding your hand on the ice is the one memory I turned to when my cloud got really dark and heavy and hopeless. I'd like to take you skating tonight, at the rink, so I can hold your hand…if you'll let me?"

He's not breathing as hard as before, but he still sucks his bottom lip in, anxious for my answer. I nod *yes* quickly, then move to the third box. Before I can dig into the paper, though, Andrew places his hand on top, stopping me.

"This one comes at the end. It's…well…it's sort of important that I keep everything in order. When we get back from the rink, I'll let you open it up," he says, his head leaned to the side, his eyes pleading.

"Okay," I say.

He's close enough that he could kiss me. I want him to. He never does, though. Instead, his eyes dance over me, following the curve of my face and line along my shoulders. For class, I changed into one of my turtlenecks and jeans, but I crave the warm feeling of being in his clothes again.

"You look nice," I say to him, my eyes moving to the top of his head, to the hair that's usually stuffed under a hat or twisted in all directions. He runs his hands through it, smoothing it back again, but messing it up just enough that a few strands fall forward over his brow, somehow making him even sexier.

"This is the best I've got," he says, arms outstretched. "I'm not really a suit-and-tie kind of guy."

It's my turn to let my eyes roam down him, his wide chest and thin waist, his arms filling the fabric of his shirt, his jeans tight around his muscular legs. I bite my lip on one side and smile through the other.

"I like this look better anyhow," I say, peering up at him.

His lips fall open with a breath, and I hold mine, thinking that maybe now he'll kiss me. But he closes his mouth quickly, smiling and taking a step back.

"We should get to the rink. I managed to find a half an hour that it's not being used, and the guy doing me a favor will be pissed if we're late," he says.

"Okay," I say softly, holding my bears tightly.

Andrew picks my backpack up from the floor and slings it over his shoulder, then tugs at the bears in my hand. I resist at first.

"You can't skate with these," he chuckles. "But…I'll put them with your things. You can have them back the second we get home."

Home.

How strange that he feels like home. And yet, how very not strange at all.

"Okay," I say again. I'm unable to do anything but agree with him. It's not that I owe him. It's that I *want* to go along with him. I meant what I said last night—I trust Andrew Harper…with my life.

I let him guide me back outside after he deposits my things in his room, and when he opens the door of his car for me, I force myself to keep my thoughts ahead—to focus on the future and possibilities rather than the past. Andrew's careful with me, taking my hand as I sit in the low bucket seat. He leans forward through the door as I buckle the belt, his head cocked to one side, silently asking me if I'm all right—the last ride in this car flooded me with painful memories.

I smile at him when my belt clicks, and his eyes skim down my body, down my legs, then back to my lips, and they quiver under the heat of his stare. Nothing about the way he's looking at me feels threatening or possessive; it's adoring, and it makes my palms sweat. Adored is exactly how I always wanted to feel, and I haven't felt it since he left my life five years ago.

He exhales slowly, backing away from the door and nudging it closed with the tips of his fingers, bringing both of his hands up to his mouth and closing his eyes as he continues to back away, shaking his head and smirking underneath it all.

When he gets into his seat, sliding in, buckling, and starting the engine, I question the soft chuckle and grin he's still wearing. He looks into his rearview mirror, almost like he's working extra hard not to look at me again. The tension causes my heart to speed up.

"What is it? Come on, Andrew…don't tease," I say.

His eyes shut; he laughs once again, his head falling forward, then his eyes open as he leans to the side, resting his head on his steering wheel.

"You have no idea how you bewitch me, Emma Burke," he says, his teeth dragging his bottom lip, his tongue caught in their snare next. "No idea."

His eyes wander around my face, and in that instant I see it—Andrew

Harper is worshiping me. My heart drums louder, and I tuck my hands underneath my legs, holding my own breath.

The trip to the rink is short, and we spend those few minutes both blushing and taking small peeks at each other, like grade-schoolers who've passed notes back and forth and have just gotten thrown together in some playground tunnel. I don't know what to do or how to act—only that I know I want to leap onto his lap right now and never let go.

I stay put, and wait for Andrew to round the car to open my door for me on his insistence that I let him *play gentleman* for the night. He walks me up to the back door of the rink, and hands a guy a fifty-dollar bill before we slip inside. I wince at the amount of money, knowing how he earns it, and how little he has to throw away. But the slight smile he gives me keeps me from protesting. He's proud of this date—and I am going to love every second of it.

"Are we supposed to be here?" I ask, noticing most of the lights are off, minus three or four shining on the center of the ice.

"Define...*supposed to,*" Andrew says, rolling his neck and grimacing at me.

I stop and watch him take a few steps in front of me, his body older, his legs longer, his look so very much the Prince Charming I've cast in my dreams. He was the original—the only.

"I don't think I should define it. I have a feeling the answer's *no* either way, so I'm just gonna go with the flow," I say, a little nervous that we're breaking a rule—a little excited by it, too.

"Probably for the best," he winks.

We slip through a small opening in the bleachers, and Andrew reaches for my hand, linking a few of his fingers with mine to guide me to my seat. When he stops, he doesn't let go of his slight hold, but turns to the side, his chin toward me and his breath tickling against my neck.

"Do you..." He stops, swallowing hard. "Do you need help with your skates?" I get the immediate sense that's not what he really wanted to ask. I know it's not what I wanted him to say.

I shake my head in tepid movements and take my skates from his other hand and sit to lace them. Andrew sits across from me, and when his skates are done, he slides his toe forward, knocking his blade into mine.

We both look at it, then gaze up at each other, instantly breaking into laughter.

"I think you have a foot fetish," I tease as he reaches a hand out and helps me to stand.

Andrew shakes his head slightly as we scoot along the rubber floor out to the ice, his grip growing in strength. We switch to the icy floor and my skates begin to slide out from under me. His arm swiftly moves from my hand to around my body, steadying me on my wobbly legs, and he chuckles to himself.

"Emma, I don't have a foot obsession…I have a *you* obsession," he says, and my breath stops short, my ears working hard to make sure they heard that right, my heart secretly knowing they did.

Andrew leads me slowly to the other end of the rink, careful to keep us closer to the center of the ice, where the light reaches. We're far away from the wall, though, so my grip on him is a little more desperate, and I wonder if that, too, was maybe part of the plan.

"You're better on your feet this time," he smiles.

I giggle because just as he says it, my left leg sweeps out from under me, and I nearly fall on my ass. Andrew's hands are fast, though, and he saves me again, this time spinning me around so I'm facing him, his hands under my elbows and forehead against mine as we both stare at my awkward feet.

"Sorry," I say. It comes out in a breath, very little sound, because being in front of him like this brings me back to our last kiss—a feeling I want again so desperately.

I roll my head against him and shut my eyes, letting him guide me in a slow circle around the middle of the rink.

"Hey, it's our first dance," he says. I pull my head back a few inches and spare a glance at him, glad I did as the right side of his mouth is raised just enough to leave a dimple.

"It is," I say. "You would have been such a better date for prom."

His smile fades, and I kick myself for mentioning anything about those years that we missed.

"I would have taken you," he says, his words coming out a little somber. I feel his fingers move along my sides, almost as if they're grasping to hold onto me tighter—to keep me from going away. I dare myself to move in closer to him, to embrace him more, and his grasp tightens again to steady me. He wants me here, too.

"I didn't have a real prom date for my senior prom," I say.

"Liar," he challenges. I feel his body shake against me in quiet laughter. He thinks I pity him.

"No, really. I went with a few girlfriends. I don't even have a picture," I say, closing my eyes as I rest my head against his chest. "And that dance you saw me getting ready for—homecoming, junior year—was a guy who just wanted a date to make someone else jealous. He was the first guy I thought was really into me since you. He left with the other girl."

I feel the rhythm of his heart against my cheek, and I let myself imagine what our prom pictures would have looked like—what *Andrew* would have looked like, how he never would have let go of my hand the entire night.

"I'm really sorry, Emma," he says, his chin resting on top of my head now, all of him cradling me. "I really wish I was there."

We're moving in inches, my feet never leaving the ice, letting him do the work and gliding us in slow motion with no destination in mind. In his embrace, and out of his view, I let a single tear slide down my cheek, because I really wish he were there, too.

"You're here now," I say, my voice raspy and giving me away. He squeezes me tighter, and I shake with one more cry, bringing a hand up to wipe the tear from my cheek before he sees it.

"I am," he says softly. "I am."

I can feel him breathe, and I can feel the pause each time he opens his mouth, wanting to say something more.

"You can tell me anything," I say, finally. "Really. Anything, Andrew."

I feel him swallow hard.

"We don't have to talk about it…if you don't want to. But Graham…" My stomach revolts just hearing his name, and I clutch to Andrew a little harder. His hand finds the back of my head, stroking my hair and cradling me. "Did he…?"

I shake my head quickly, knowing what Andrew's worry is, and thankful that there was help and that I was able to fight just long enough, loud enough. "He only hit me. He tried—" I stop short before retelling everything.

Andrew whispers "*Shhh,*" above my head and adjusts me in his cradle once more. "I'm sorry I wasn't there to stop him from hitting you, Emma. So very sorry," he says.

"Like I said...you're here now..." I say against him.

We sway in our hold on each other for the next fifteen minutes, until a bright light clicks on near the exit, and Andrew sighs, waving a hand to his friend who let us in. He never lets go of me for long, though, guiding me safely back to the bench and swiftly finding my hand again once our skates are off and we're walking to the car.

We drive back to his apartment in a rush, and I notice Andrew's left leg bouncing with his nerves. He grinds the gear on his car as he pulls into a space along his street, and I hold my lips in a tight line to hide my smirk.

I start to step out from his car on my own, but he tells me to wait, rushing around the front so he can open it for me. He doesn't grab my hand this time, though, instead, both of his hands tugging at the Tech University tag on his key chain, his fingers wrestling with the apartment key I returned to him after Trent made me a copy of his. He's nervous as we approach the door, and he drops his keys once in his attempt to unlock his apartment, finally opening the door and gesturing for me to step inside before him. He sets his things on a small table near his door then runs his hands through his hair, completely destroying the combed shape, returning his hair to his normal messy look. I secretly like it better this way.

His hands in his pockets, he steps forward a few paces, his posture nearly perfect and his shoulders raised high as his feet move nervously.

"My plan was to have you open the last box now," he says, shrugging toward it. I step in that direction, but he begins to talk again, so I stop. "I want you to open it. I do. And I'll let you. It's just...when I thought this whole evening out, I was...I don't know...really..."

"Oh god, were you drunk date-planning?" I tease.

"No!" he says, rolling his eyes. "I was just...I don't know...overly romanticizing things maybe? And now that we're here, and I'm standing here, and you're all beautiful, and you smell good, and you feel good, and I've held you, and—"

"Andrew..." I sigh, stepping closer to him, placing a hand on his arm, tugging his hand free from his pocket. I lace my fingers with his, pulling his hand to my lips, and pressing a soft kiss against the back of his hand—leaving my lips there as he watches with his mouth hung open.

"*Gah*! Emma," he says, his eyes scanning down the rest of my body now, the heat there this time—the desire and greed mixing with the amber color of his eyes. "You can open the last box," he says. "Just…if this seems really silly or childish when you see what's inside, just know that the sentiment is maybe the most adult thing I've ever done in my whole goddamned life."

My heart starts to race, and I have a small panic over what *could* be in that box. I glance from him to the box and back again a few times, moving my hands slowly to the paper and the lid, checking with him constantly for reassurance. I tear the paper away completely, and lift the lid, still turning to watch Andrew, to watch his reaction. With the lid off, I lean over the large box to look inside, seeing only a small paper folded at the bottom. Andrew nods toward it, urging me to pick it up and open it. I reach in, unfolding it to reveal a simple word written inside.

Me.

My brow pinches as I struggle to understand, but soon Andrew's hands are around mine, gripping the paper with me.

"Me," he says, reciting the word. "If you want me—you have *me.* Or… more clearly…I'm yours."

I blink, staring at his hands, listening to him hand over his heart, and my own beats louder than it ever has, its strength growing by the second, the thump echoing in my chest.

"God, Emma. I'm yours. I've *always* been yours. From the moment I saw the dark silk of your hair and the storm in your eyes, I was a lost cause…lost to you. I've been through hell, and I would go again. I would go willingly, and would charge through the gates if it meant it would keep you safe."

My lips part open with a tiny gasp, and my chest shudders at the beautiful honesty of his words—of his promise that I in no possible way deserve.

"Andrew, I never should have let you go to that place. I never should have let them take you away. I should have told the truth, defended you, taken your place…" I say, my eyes burning from the tears building somewhere deep and buried within me.

Andrew moves to me quickly, his hands finding my face, his thumbs erasing the tears as they fall and his eyes searing through mine. "That's the thing, though," he says. "I never would have let *you*. You get to come first. I don't have a choice, Emma, the universe wants you to be my reason for living. I'm a slave to its demand. And I will lo..." Andrew stops his speech suddenly, his body rigid and his eyes scared as hell as they stare back into me.

He shuts them; one small tear escapes, leaving a wet trail along the rough stubble of his face. Such a soft moment on something so hardened and masculine—a face still lightly bruised and battered from aggression cries for *me* now. His eyes are clear when he reopens them, and I fall into him completely.

"I will love you for always," he says, his voice void of any fear or apprehension. The only sign left that he's scared at all is the hard swallow that follows the most beautiful thing he could have ever said. He doesn't ask to love me. He tells me. He claims me. And though he doesn't say it, I am his too whether I want to be or not—Andrew Harper will spend his last breath defending my honor. I'm lost to this man. I was lost to the boy years ago—happily lost, and so in love in return.

I take the small note still clutched in my hand and bring it to my lips, kissing it and smiling to him.

"You're mine," I say, wanting to hear how it sounds, wanting to feel the way the words run off my tongue.

Andrew laughs lightly, nodding just enough. "Yeah...I am."

"I'm yours," I say, his eyes widening ever so subtly, giving away his excitement and hunger. "And I will love you more."

Andrew's jaw twitches as his gaze remains on me, on my eyes and my mouth and my body. I'm his—and I want to be taken. The air between us is almost thick enough to drown in—our breath gone, and each the only thing the other needs to survive from this point forward.

His mouth mere inches from mine, his lips find mine within the second it takes me to blink. His hands again cradle my face, his body moving me in demanding steps backward through his living room and down the small hallway to his room until my back is flat against his closed door. The sudden stop gives him enough leverage to push the hardness of his body into me.

In one swift movement, his hands rush down my back, scooping me up and wrapping my legs around him as he maneuvers the door open behind me. He takes long, deliberate steps to his bed, his hands grabbing the bottom of my sweater and tugging it over my head as my body slides down his to sit at the end of his mattress.

He turns around, kicking the door closed, then faces me, pulling both of his shirts over his head quickly. My eyes take in his form, but they also gaze over his fading bruises and the few scars left on him from his time at Lake Crest. I slide toward him and run my hands along his hard chest and hot skin, my fingers grazing over every curve, contour, and mark left behind by those who tried to hurt him. I gaze up at him, my breath catching at the way he looks at me, at the love reflected in his eyes.

Leaning forward more, I keep my eyes on his as I kiss my way up his stomach and chest, taking care to be tender where I know he's still hurt. I trail kisses up the center of his chest, holding my lips longer over his heart as I climb to my knees to reach more of him.

Andrew moves two fingers to my chin, tilting my face toward his, then slides both of his hands deep into my hair, holding me there under the scrutiny of his gaze as I wrap my hands around his wrists.

"God, Emma, you have no idea how many nights I dreamt of looking at you just like this," he says, and for a moment, his smile seems lost—he seems worried.

"I'm yours," I repeat, needing to reassure him.

His eyes fall closed and he brings his forehead to rest against mine, his lips grazing lightly on mine with his breath until he sucks my bottom lip in between his and I feel the scratch of his teeth as he lets go.

"I will be the man who deserves you. I will, Emma. I promise," he says, his breaths shallow, almost panting. I nod *yes*, knowing he'll keep good on any promise to me—knowing he already deserves me, and I'm the one who has work to do.

Andrew slowly presses his weight into me, laying me back in his bed as he crawls over me with the grace of a tiger, his tongue licking his bottom lip and his hazed eyes raking over me with desire. When my head hits his pillow, his body cages me completely, his hands cupping my face gently at first, then growing stronger as he leans my head to one side, giving his mouth access to my neck and shoulder.

The sensation of his tongue drawing a line down my body makes me arch my back, and Andrew seizes the opportunity to sweep one arm behind me to hold me up, my breasts firm and barely concealed by the thin undershirt I'm wearing. Andrew's eyes find the hard peaks of my nipples quickly, and he bites through the fabric, his tongue soaking the material as he makes each of my breasts his, working them into painful submission through my clothes.

Lying me on my back again, he leans his head down and grabs the bottom of my undershirt with his teeth, and I hold my breath, bringing my knuckles to my mouth as he slowly drags the bottom of my shirt up and over my breasts. The cold air makes the ache in my nipples sweeter, but I'm also paralyzed over the display of my scar. My mark isn't subtle—there's no way around being cut open three times, and I notice the moment the evidence of my transplant hits Andrew's eyes. His breathing is steady, and as much as his body is still in a lustful trance, he's also seeing a glimpse of our past—of reasons why and excuses and selfish requests.

"Your father told me," he breathes, his eyes never leaving my scar. I can't tell if he's afraid of it or disgusted by it, and I part my lips with a worried breath as he speaks. Just as the sound leaves me, his eyes close and he leans down, kissing the dark pink of the center of my scar, the deep line that draws nearly the length of where my ribs meet. "I went to see him, to find out *why*..." Andrew swallows, his lips dusting against my body as he speaks, his strong arms holding him above me. "I just needed answers—why you didn't write, why they lied to you. He told me. And as much as I wish you were the one who told me, I also understand why you didn't. You were afraid of dying, Emma. And your father was afraid of you dying, too. I..." Andrew's voice breaks, and his eyes finally lift to mine. "I would have feared losing you, too. So I don't blame him, Em...for keeping my letters from you, for lying about where I was, for telling you to forget about me. I don't blame him. I would have done the same if I knew it meant you were safe."

I swallow hard, willing my eyes to keep their hold on his, not to break. I feel like looking at him, bare and all of my secrets before him, is the ultimate show of trust—this is me giving him my heart. I won't turn away, not now.

"I regret so much," I say, my voice hoarse with emotion.

"I know," he says, his lips grazing mine as he breathes the words again. "I know. But I'm begging you…no more regrets."

My eyes hold his a few seconds longer, and I nod *yes*. "No more regrets," I repeat, as if reciting my pledge. My arms around his neck, I pull him to me, the warmth of his chest crushing against mine, igniting something deeper inside of us both. Andrew's movements grow needier, his hands roaming my body more, gripping and clawing down my back as he kisses his way from my mouth down each of my breasts, sucking the peaks and pinching each between his teeth while I writhe beneath him.

He slides down my body, his lips pausing over my stomach, his mouth open and panting with a hungry need as he unhooks the button of my jeans and grips them around my waist, sliding them down my legs as he stands. My body shivers. He stands before me, slowly removing his jeans and boxers, letting himself spring free while I wait in nothing but my small, white cotton panties. I've never wanted to feel someone inside me more, to take someone completely, to give myself wholly. My legs part for him, and he groans, kneeling on the floor in front of me, and he slides his hands from the tips of my toes up the insides of each of my thighs, my core throbbing and my heart pounding.

"I…I waited," I say, biting my lip hard, my eyes intent on him as his long lashes lift and his eyes widen on mine. "For you. I…I haven't given this to anyone. I saved it. And I'm pretty sure I was saving it for you."

His breath catches once and he exhales slowly, leaving his gaze on me. He lowers his head to the inside of my knee, placing soft kisses all the way up my leg until he's at my very center.

"This," he says, running a finger slowly along the waistband of my panties, teasing me by slipping a finger underneath, but never far enough. His eyes boring into mine, he draws a soft line with a barely-there touch from my belly button, over the top of my panties and down to the wet center where he presses his thumb, easing my need and igniting it all at once. "This…is only mine?"

"Yes," I breathe.

His breathing ragged, his lips fall to my center, and he runs his tongue over the small strip of material, the only thing between us, and my body goes wild in response. The heat of his breath is almost too much to take. I feel his hand sliding along the inside of my leg, then pull aside the center strip, exposing me to him, and my body rushes with heat from blushing and desire. I grip at his pillow, pulling it over my face, biting the material hard as his tongue traces it's same path, this time no barrier there to stop it from dipping deeper inside me.

"Oh my god, Andrew..." I pant, arching against him. His hand tugs hard, tearing my panties until they're completely ripped away. Andrew's tongue caresses me as his thumb presses on the swollen center between my legs until finally his hand slides forward far enough for him to push a finger deep inside, leaving it there as he works me with his mouth. The pressure is so much that I pull my legs up, bending my knees, wanting to hold on, to make this last longer.

Andrew continues to suck and kiss me, letting his other hand find my breasts, running the rough pad of his thumb over each nipple and pulling them back to attention instantly until I cry out with the sensation of my first orgasm. The waves are almost too intense to take, and I pull away on instinct, but Andrew holds me to him, pressing his tongue into me hard, cupping my breasts and pushing his other fingers in and out at an intoxicating rhythm.

As I come down from my high, he kisses his way back up my stomach, worshiping my breasts until he's completely holding himself over me, his body matched up with mine, his hard cock hot against my skin. He takes himself in one hand, and runs the tip down through my wet and still-pulsing center in long, slow strokes that almost send me over the edge again. The sensation has me raising my hips, begging for him to penetrate me.

"Patience," he says, his mouth an arrogant grin as he dominates me. Andrew moves to his feet, stepping around to the side of his bed where he slides open his night table drawer to pull out a condom. I watch as he tears it open and slides it over himself, my mind a little worried over his size and how this is all going to feel. We've reached the limits of my sexual experience, but I'm also desperate for him to take me beyond them.

Andrew positions himself in front of me again, repeating the same teasing strokes along my center, his cock in his hand as he pauses and pushes just enough against me to have my body completely ready to accept him. Leaning forward, he runs his hand behind my neck, tilting my head back slightly as he kisses me hard, possessively, then drags his hand in a hard line down the side of my body, his thumb grazing my nipple as it passes. He reaches the inside of my thigh and pushes my right leg out, opening me to him more, my left leg following his lead as he guides himself to my entrance. His eyes concentrate on every movement, and I'm completely seduced by the vision of him looking at me like this, of him watching himself slide inside me, slowly.

His movement is slow at first, taking long seconds in one place to let me grow accustomed to his size before sliding back out and entering me again, each time falling deeper and deeper until he finally thrusts forward, filling me completely.

"Oh god!" I cry, arching again, his arms sweeping under me, holding me to him while his hips take over the work of pumping in and out in long, tortuous strokes.

"My dreams, Emma. This is better than my dreams," he says, his breath hot against my ear.

I wrap my legs around him, searching for ways to feel him even deeper inside, and Andrew responds, his hands moving to my ass, pulling me up into him with every pummel, our pressure meeting, the sweet ache growing and growing with every thrust.

I can feel the sweat beading on my body, and Andrew's back is moist as his muscles work to hold us together, to send us both over the edge.

"I'm so close, Andrew. Please…just a little more," I gasp, my teeth grazing his shoulder, my fingers digging into his skin as he rocks into me. The need to release builds until I can no longer breathe, and when I feel Andrew begin to push harder, I know he's with me, so I let everything go.

"Come for me, baby. Please…come for me," he growls into my neck. I cry out loud until all I have left in me are soft whimpers of pleasure as I feel Andrew thicken inside me, his breath held as he follows me into bliss.

"Emma! Fuck me, Emma," he grunts, pulling me into him harder and harder, exploding inside me until all that is left is exhaustion and two satiated souls in love.

Andrew doesn't still right away, sliding in and out in slow movements, wanting to drain every last moment of pleasure from my body. He finally pulls out of me completely, then kisses my scar softly before whispering against my skin. "For always, Emma Burke. For always," he breathes.

* * *

SHOWERED and now nestled deep in Andrew's sheets and arms and clothes, reality begins to settle in, and I grow still and quiet. For long minutes, Andrew doesn't ask why, instead content to have me here and hold me, to stroke my hair and press his lips to the back of my head every so often as I lay here in the safest place in the world.

"Do you know that the only time I ever smoked a joint was that one time?" Andrew says, breaking the silence. I swallow hard. "Once. Ha! I'm like the perfect anti-drug campaign. *Don't do drugs, kids. Even just once could ruin your whole life."*

His joke is the sad kind, and I squeeze his arms, pulling them tighter around me. "I'm sorry, Andrew," I say, kissing his hand and pressing it against my face.

"Don't be. I made my choices. I made every single one of them," he says. I'm not looking at him when he speaks, but there's something about the timber in his voice that lets me know he's smiling. Right now—with me—he's smiling.

"You still shouldn't have had to go through any of that," I say, shutting my eyes at the thought of his younger self at the hand of someone hurting him. "They shouldn't have punished you at all, let alone to that extent."

"I'm a Harper. We're *bad seeds,"* he chuckles.

"No. You're not," I whisper.

"How you see me," he says against my neck, leaving a soft kiss there before blowing it away. "That's what matters."

His hand moves back up to my hair, and he continues the gentle strokes, combing his fingers through my long waves and letting them fall against my bare arm, my body hugged in the soft cotton of one of his shirts.

"Are you going to tell someone?" Andrew asks, and I turn a little, my head shifting to look at him, not sure what he means. I'll tell the world about you, about how I love you, Andrew. Why wouldn't I?

"About Graham," he explains, my gut sinking the second he utters his name. "I know it's hard, and I know you want to just forget, but he hurt you, Emma. He can't get away with that."

"I know," I say, letting my face fall back to the pillow, away from him.

"I'll go with you…to tell someone. We can go together," he says, and I squeeze him again, so thankful for him, but sick knowing I'm going to disappoint him.

"I can't," I say, my eyes shuddering to a close as his arm pulls away from me and he pushes himself up to sit next to me. I suck in a long, painful breath, feeling the bruises on my ribs as I do, as if those injuries mock me. I sit up to face Andrew, but never lift my eyes to his. "He's Dr. Wheaton's son. She…she's my mentor, and she was the one who…" I move my fist slowly to my chest, letting my thumb scratch over the space in the middle where my scar resides.

Andrew understands in an instant, breathing in once, sharply. His head bows and he nods. Slowly leaning to the side, he slides his phone from his small night table, then holds it up to me, his lips pursed, his forehead wrinkled with question. "May I?" he asks, pointing to the camera lens. I pinch my brow, but offer a small nod *yes*. I let my expression fall to nothingness as he clicks a photo of me then lays by my side.

He turns the screen to face us both, sliding his finger over my image, zooming in, the purple around my eye still very much there. I close my eyes remembering the feel of Graham's hand crashing into me.

"I understand, Em. I swear I do. I just…I thought you needed to see what I see," he says.

I pull his phone into my hands, zooming the image back out, hoping from farther away the bruise is less noticeable, but it's not—it's all I see. I push the small button at the bottom to share the image with me, sending it to myself. Then I move to Andrew's contacts screen and enter my number, biting my lip as I hand the phone back to him.

"I thought it was about time we exchanged numbers," I say through a half-hearted laugh. Andrew makes the same sound, pulling his phone in his hands and typing me a message. I read along as he types I LOVE YOU, then slides his phone back onto his table, pulling me into his arms again.

I have him. He's mine, and I'm his. And we've left this wake of destruction, disaster, and remorse all about us to get here, yet I hold onto him tightly feeling somehow justified that it was still all worth everything.

"I don't want you to fight him," I exhale, tucking my face into his arms, burying myself into him even more. His body grows rigid—he didn't realize I knew.

He doesn't answer, but I feel his chin adjust above my head, his breathing slow, a silent apology.

"I don't want you to get hurt," I finally admit, and he holds me tighter, kissing my head, then whispering one more promise in my ear.

"I won't," he says. "I can't walk away, Emma, but I won't let him hurt me…or you. I swear."

I nod *okay,* but stay in my cocoon of his arms, not sure that he can keep this promise. Graham is two different people, and they are both manipulative, each possessing a different kind of charm. And now that I've seen both sides, I worry that there's yet another side I haven't seen—one that doesn't live in the rational, human world, and one that holds grudges and seeks revenge at any cost. The thought that Andrew's exactly that type doesn't warm my heart either—and I'm afraid when they're forced together, the destruction will be impossible to come back from.

CHAPTER 20

ANDREW

Well that went about as well as I expected.

I woke up early, leaving Emma a note, then rushed to her apartment before work so I could try and talk with Lindsey. She never unhooked the chain, only opening the door wide enough to gain some distance to slam it closed. I think if my fingers or face had been in the way, she would have used more muscle, too.

I slid the letter under her door anyhow, begging her to meet me after work this morning at the coffee shop on her corner. I figured it would be safe. I didn't think Emma would walk down this street until she knew it wouldn't result in a painful run-in with her roommate.

I glance through the window as I walk toward the entrance, and the café is nearly empty, minus one or two students holed up in a booth with their laptops and piles of books. I glance at my watch, which says I'm right on time, then take a deep breath as I walk through the door and prepare for my plan to crash and burn.

"I'll take a large iced coffee," I say to the guy behind the counter. He pulls out a cup and writes my order on the side of it, then rings me up on the register. I remove my wallet to pay.

"Add a non-fat soy latte to that," I hear over my shoulder. I don't startle, but I definitely breathe. I nod *yes* to the guy, then hand him my card, paying for both orders.

"Thanks for coming," I say, turning enough to the side to catch her profile. She's dressed in a business suit, her hair pinned back in a clip, and the look surprises me a little.

"I have an interview. It's for an internship at the clinic. You get fifteen minutes," she says through tight lips.

We both wait for our coffees in awkward silence, then I follow her to a small table near the corner windows. Might as well be on display for everyone that walks by; maybe it will keep her from hitting me again.

"Your chin looks like shit," she says, blowing on her coffee after removing the lid. I chuckle and run my finger along the rough stitches, then pull the lid from my coffee to take a drink.

"Look, I know you didn't want to come here this morning, so *thank you*. Thank you for coming," I say, setting my cup down and folding my hands together, my elbows resting on the table.

"I didn't come for you. I came because you said I needed to know about Emma," she says. Her tone is angry and clipped, but she admitted she came here for Emma, and that's all I need to hear.

"Right. Emma," I say, cracking my knuckles and looking at my hands.

"I swear to god, Drew, if you're here to tell me you made a mistake, and you're going to break up with her now, I will punch you again—right in those stitches," she says, pointing one of her perfectly polished nails right at my chin. I don't doubt her threat for a second, so I lean back in my seat to give me some distance, and inhale to calm myself and make sure I get through to her—about how much she means to Emma, and how much Emma needs her now.

"That Graham guy, the one she went out with a couple nights ago? He hit her, Linds. That douchebag hit her, and I...I don't know what else, but I know she fought, and it could have been worse," I say, my nostrils flaring as the anger boils inside. Lindsey holds her gaze on me, her brow lowering just a touch, her lips pursing tighter, and I can tell that she still loves Emma by the way her breathing turns into a charge of fury.

"What is she going to do?" she asks, her eyes not leaving mine.

I breathe in deeply and push my cup a few inches along the table, wiping away the cold, wet ring it leaves behind on the table. "Nothing," I say. I feel Lindsey lean forward with the urge to speak, so I keep going. "And I guess there isn't much she can do. He's that doctor's son, and it would make things complicated. Honestly, at this point? You probably know more about that part of her life than I do. I told her she should say something to someone, or at least talk to someone…other than me. She's just…she's just going to move on, though, I guess. But I think it would help a hell of a lot if you were around to help her."

I glance up at her, and she's still rigid, her mouth a firm line as she blinks and eventually looks down at her own drink. She pulls it to her lips, sipping slowly, and I can see there's part of her that wants to bend, but I also see the shattered trust and hurt, too.

"I know I'm a broken record, but I swear Lindsey—this entire thing—it's on me. And *you* were Emma's only priority. All she wanted was for you to be happy," I say.

"Then she should have told me the truth. The truth would have made me happy. Knowing my best friend trusted me enough to tell me everything…that's what would have made me happy," she says, her voice soft and distant.

"I get that. And I think if Emma could go back, she would. But she couldn't decide then what would hurt you less. And I didn't make it easy. I'm just asking for you to be open to the idea of forgiving her. She needs you, Linds. And I think maybe you miss her too," I say.

Her eyes meet mine for a few seconds before she pulls her wrist up, checking the time again, and tugging her purse close to her body. She takes a large final sip of her drink, plunking it on the table in front of me and dusting the corners of her mouth with a napkin she quickly folds and stuffs inside the empty cup.

"Thanks for the coffee, Andrew," she says, her mouth tight. "It's been… well, I'd say it's been real, but it never was…was it?"

"I'm sorry, Lindsey," I shrug. She nods once, then slides a pair of sunglasses on her face, turning, leaving, and never looking back.

With my failed attempt with Lindsey behind me, I jog into campus, making sure to make an appearance at my classes for the day. I've marked the dates for tests on my calendar, and I never miss those, but it seems I've missed a quiz or two in calculus. I'm still getting an A, but it's by the skin of my teeth, so I make a tentative promise to myself that I'll show for the rest of my classes this semester. Scholarships are like gold for me, and I have to piece them together—*B's* don't really help the cause.

I check my phone obsessively, waiting to hear from Emma, and by the time I'm in my last class for the day, I break, sliding my phone into my lap so I can send her a message. I glance at the photo I sent her first, and the purple around her eye sends a shock through my core, and my fists form on instinct.

I look up, checking the status of where we're at in my Neighborhood and Urban Poverty class, my last undergrad sociology credit, and a class I took in high school. Turns out they make you take a lot of shit again when you check out of honors college to do a stint in juvie.

Feeling confident that I know where the lesson is, I lean one arm over the small desktop in front of me to make it look like I'm listening, then glance down to type my text.

How are you today?

A few minutes pass, torturous seconds that feel like an hour before she writes back.

I'm good. I just bought my ticket for this hockey game tonight. Don't tell anyone, but I know one of the players.

I grin like a fool over the fact that Emma's coming to watch me, but then I think about the long walk she has from the rink back to my apartment—alone—and in a millisecond I've zipped up my bag and sprinted from the back door of the lecture hall.

It takes me about five minutes to catch up to where she is, and I see her standing at the stoplight on the busy corner, looking at her phone, waiting for me to write back.

You shouldn't text and walk that close to the road. You could get hit by a car.

I cross my arms and wait for her to read, and she immediately starts looking for me, her eyes finally finding me and her smile lighting up my world. She takes a few steps away from the curb then types me one more note.

Stalker.

I grin again and write back.

That's not what you called me last night.

I can see her blush from here. Rather than tease her any longer, I push my phone in my back pocket and jog over to where she's waiting, not giving her time to say another word as I pull her into me and kiss her so hard that it feels like I'm branding her with my affection.

"Wow," she says, stumbling back on her feet. "Do all ticketholders get one of those?"

I shrug and nod *yes.* "Trent makes out with the old ladies. I get the hot ones," I smile. She giggles before punching me lightly in the gut.

"You better not be giving those kisses out for free," she says.

"Not anymore, Em. Not anymore," I say, no laughter now.

I sling my arm around her shoulder and pull her into me tightly as we step into the intersection. We make idle chat at first, me asking her about her day, her mine. But I can tell there's something bigger on her mind, and part of me is worried it's me.

"Hey," I say, stopping our walk so she can face me as I lightly run my thumb over her chin. "What's buggin' you?"

She looks down, a faint laugh through a frown, then shrugs as she looks back up at me.

"Lindsey wasn't in class today. I know you said it would just take time, but I was kind of hoping I'd at least see her, ya know?" Her mouth twists into disappointment. I wish I had good news for her, a curtain I could pull back and her life would be perfect on the other side, just waiting for her to step right through. But I don't, and I *hate* that I can't cure her anxiety.

"She'll come back. I know it," I say, squeezing her close so I can kiss her head. It's not a lie. I saw it in Lindsey's eyes, and if I have to keep stalking her just to remind her of what she's missing, I will.

As we walk up the pathway to my apartment door, my phone buzzes in my back pocket. I pull it out to read, expecting an update from Trent on what time he wants to get to the rink for pregame. He likes to get there before everyone else, and I usually join him. I hold the door open for Emma and glance at my phone as she passes, my mind not understanding the message at first until I realize who it's from. It's Harley. And that fight he had scheduled for me for a few weeks from now—it's been moved up.

Rich boy wants to show off what he's got Sunday night. I can't get a venue, so it'll be here. The money line is trending big on your favorite round if you know what I'm sayin'.

My stomach rolls when I read his message, and I slow as I trail behind Emma toward my room. My eyes stay on my phone as I follow her through my door, closing it behind us, and my heartbeat is drumming out every other sound as I realize I'm going to have to tell her. I will never lie to Emma—ever.

"So can I wear one of your Tech Hockey shirts? I want to look like I fit in…" She stops talking the instant she turns to face me, the joy from moments ago sucked away into the black hole of doom that I can't seem to avoid when it comes to all things me-and-Emma-Burke.

She never asks. I don't wait for her to. She deserves to know, and my gut told me the second she asked me not to fight Graham that I would tell her the minute I got the call. There's also no way I'm letting her near him—she'll be safe, here, in my home with Trent, when I fight.

"That was my guy…at the gym. Graham set a date," I say, glancing back at my phone, sort of hoping that there's a follow-up saying everything's been cancelled. I won't back out—but I wouldn't exactly be upset if he did at this point.

"When?" she asks, falling to my bed, pulling her knees up and hiding her mouth behind the tops. Damn, I hate that she's stressed over this or worried. I hate that she's thinking about Graham. And I hate that bruise on her face. That's the one thing justifying what I'm going to do.

"Sunday," I say, my jaw flexing as I swallow. The part of me that wants to protect her hates to tell her any of this.

But I will never lie.

"That's in two days," she says, her eyes staring at her kneecaps, her fingers gripping her jean-covered shins.

I move closer, slowly, lifting one foot in my hand, pulling her leg from her grip and taking her shoe off. I rest that foot on the floor and do the same with her other leg. The entire time, her eyes never quite make it to mine. She's afraid to look at me, and I know it's because she's afraid to show me she's afraid.

I step in between her legs and kneel down, running my hands along her thighs and then around her, hugging her to me, my head resting on her lap.

"I will be okay, Emma. I won't let him hurt you, and he won't hurt me. I'm stronger than he is," I say, and deep down I know I am. He may have me in size, but my heart beats for this girl, and when I have that in my corner, there's nothing I can't defeat.

"I don't trust him, Andrew," she says, and I feel her body shake once beneath me, but she holds it in, not wanting to cry in front of me. I stand to my feet, taking her hands to pull her to hers, and the second she rises, I sweep her into my arms, sitting with her on my lap. She folds into me, her fit perfect, like everything I've ever been missing.

"I'm scared," she says, her eyes closed, her face pressed into my chest. Her breathing slows, but I feel every rise and fall.

"I'm so scared. I can't lie to you. I won't," she pauses, her voice trailing off. She rolls her head against me, her forehead pressed against my heart, her face still shielded from my view. "If you're going to stand in a ring with him...I want you to kill him."

I hold her tightly, and I feel her muscles tense. I feel her anger, and I feel her worry. I kiss her head and run my hands down her back, wanting nothing more than to make her worries disappear and her wishes come true. After a few minutes, I sway her playfully, but when it doesn't produce a smile, I stop. We are at a depth too deep for small gestures. What she needs now is love, protection, and a guarantee. I promise her the world, but the voice in the back of my head also reminds me who I am.

Good doesn't usually come to the Harpers.

* * *

EMMA

Andrew is amazing on the ice. He's always been beautiful to watch out there—the grace with which he skates, such a contrast to the force he can deliver when he wants something badly enough.

He wants to destroy Graham Wheaton. I can see it in his eyes. What scares me is I want him to destroy him too. I want Graham to pay, to repent, to disappear—I want him to vanish from all of my memories. But Andrew can't make that happen. Nobody can. And the risk that he might lose something bigger than the gamble he's making in that ring consumes my every thought.

Andrew was slow to return in the third period. He was missing from the bench, and I went absolutely insane as I sat here alone wondering where he could be. This is the trouble with having zero friends—no wing-woman of rationality, and all logic is lost.

He returned a few minutes into the third with the trainer, probably needing to be taped or iced for one of the blows he took on the ice. And as much relief that it gave me to see him there, where he should be, it wasn't enough to quell what was really worrying me. I'm afraid Graham Wheaton is going to play dirty and take out my rejection on him. I'm also afraid Graham is powerful enough to get away with it.

I'm in a haze for most of the final minutes, my mind on rapid-fire in search of a way to get Andrew out of this, something I could dangle as an incentive to deter him, a trick to keep him out of that ring and away from that gym Sunday night. But he wouldn't fall for it, and I don't want to trick him.

I wait as the crowd clears out, moving over to the small exit near the bench where Andrew told me to wait for him before the game. He and Trent are two of the first to leave. I notice a group of girls hovering above the bench waiting for the players to exit; they begin to maneuver their way closer. Andrew brushes by them, scooping me up against his side, his body warm from the shower he just took.

I kiss him hard, my hands grabbing at his face, and as I pull away, I stare down a pair of twins eyeing him. Andrew follows my gaze, then looks back to me, pressing his forehead against mine as he chuckles.

"They're not here for me," he says. "The chicks always swarm for Trent. They know which one of us is going to make NHL bank one day."

"I don't know, those twins were making googley eyes at you. I think you're selling yourself short," I say.

"Twins? Where?" he jokes, jerking away from me to look, but coming back quickly, leaning me back in his arms with a possessive kiss, the roughness of his stubble scratching sweetly against my cold cheeks and chin.

"Come on, let's get you home," he says, taking my hand in his, weaving his fingers through mine, his eyes watching our connection before dropping his hand between us. "That will never get old," he grins.

We walk to his car, dropping his gear in the trunk and waiting for Trent to take his compliments from his fan girls and catch up. Trent insists I take the front seat, and we make the short trip home, the conversation centered on their three-to-one win over Ohio State.

There's an actual skip to Andrew's step as he walks up to his apartment, and it makes me smile seeing it. He's happy, and his body can't help but reflect it. He keeps rehashing plays on the ice with Trent, and his friend gives Andrew credit where it's wholly deserved.

Their celebrating carries over as we get inside, and Trent walks into their kitchen, opening the fridge wide as he talks with his back to us, giving Andrew enough time to tug me to him, then lean me over and kiss me hard.

"Well shit! That's the problem with always going to Majerle's to celebrate our wins, we're never prepared with beer to celebrate at home. There's only one left," Trent says, twisting the cap and turning around just in time to catch us in a full-on make-out session. "Or maybe you don't *need* beer to celebrate," he chuckles, pressing the bottle to his mouth and drinking.

"Shut up," Andrew says, taking his keys back out of his pocket. "I'll run to the store. I'll be back in five minutes. You want anything...I don't know...girly?"

"I like beer," I blush.

His eyebrows lift in a teasing way, but he pulls my chin close and dusts my lips with a kiss, smiling and winking before he leaves. I watch the door close, then I shiver once at the realization he's gone. Even here in the safety of his home—with his roommate who I know won't hurt me—I immediately feel vulnerable. I never thought Graham would hurt me. But he did. And I hate that I feel so dependent on Andrew for safety.

I turn to Trent and hug my body, my lips in a tight smile. He sits on the back of the sofa, and I relax a little with the distance between us. I think

Trent senses my edginess, and I know he at least has an idea of what happened with Graham. I'm sure Andrew's talked to him, and my bruises are still very much on display. I've quit looking in mirrors. I don't like what I'm reminded of when I do.

"Andrew is crazy about you, you know," Trent says, light laughter coming out as he looks down at his feet before raising an eyebrow at me. "You in this as much as he is?"

I hold his stare, then nod *yes*. He begins to nod with me.

"Good," he says, looking back down. "That's good."

I move to the stool by their counter in the kitchen, sliding it out enough to sit on top and rest my head on my hands. As safe as I feel here, I'm still not okay—I'm *miles* from okay. When Andrew's gone, all I see are Graham's lips curl into an evil grin, smoke trailing around his whiskers. I feel my skin burn from everywhere he touched, and I try to replace it with the feel of Andrew.

What holds me hostage, though, is the knowledge that it isn't over—that Graham isn't over. Andrew is going to face him, and I want to be there to keep *him* safe. But I can't—my body and heart literally wouldn't survive being in Graham's presence. I'm afraid one more look at him and my nightmare would never leave.

"Did he tell you about his fight?" I ask, unable to fully look at him. I feel like I'm sharing secrets behind Andrew's back.

"He did," Trent says, and I glance up to see his mouth paused open, like he wants to protest the fight too. But he doesn't, instead biting at his bottom lip and shaking his head.

"Don't let him," I beg, my voice breaking when I ask, and my eyes burning from tears. The emotion hits me fast; I pull my sleeves up over my wrists and push them into my eyes, squeezing them shut tightly until I can speak again with composure, without my voice feeling weak and frantic. I clear my throat and look down. "He'll listen to you, Trent. Please," I whisper.

It's quiet between us for several seconds, and I work to regain control of my emotions, knowing Andrew will return home any minute. I focus on every breath, thinking of Andrew's smile, and forcing out the thoughts of Graham and his devil eyes.

"He doesn't listen to me, Emma. Andrew Harper listens to Andrew Harper," Trent says through a faint laugh. "But he's been a lot more reasonable since you showed up, so maybe...just maybe...he'll come around before he does something really stupid. I know that's what I'm hoping for..."

The sound of the key in the door has Trent on his feet, and his face is a full smile as Andrew walks inside—no sign of the worry I saw seconds before.

Andrew slides two six-packs of beer into the fridge, pulling out a bottle for him and me before peeling away the caps and placing a cold one in my hand. Trent finishes his first, then reaches into the fridge to grab a fresh one to catch up to us, tapping Andrew on the shoulder as he moves to stand next to him, holding the top of his beer out to tap into one another.

"To friendship, and finally getting what you deserve," Trent says, his eyes flitting to me. I smile, knowing that he's trying to give a subtle hint to Andrew that he has so much going for him right now. Unfortunately, I fear those words ring about revenge in Andrew's mind.

"To getting what you deserve," he says, an ominous smirk on his lips. "Soon enough."

I can feel his body growing hostile at the thought of Graham, and I can tell how much he wants to make him pay. Panicked, I push my beer bottle into his next, just before he can pull it away to take a sip. I'm not satisfied with this toast, and I want to throw out a Hail Mary.

"And to remembering what you have...what's here to come home to," I say, causing him to turn to me, his head falling to the side and his eyes meeting mine instantly.

"To you," he says. "The reason I do anything," he adds with a whisper. I close my eyes, holding my breath as he pulls my head into him and kisses the top, cradling me in his arm.

"I'm drinking to this, but just so we're clear here, Em, that last part of the deal is just you two," Trent says, motioning his beer between Andrew and me. I laugh, but it's a façade. Andrew's is genuine, and as he tilts his beer to drink, Trent and I exchange one last glance—and I can tell he's just as worried as I am.

CHAPTER 21

ANDREW

Saturday was a blur. We won our hockey game, and Emma came with me again. This time, we joined the team at Majerle's. Emma and I only stayed for an hour, anxious to race home to be alone. The newness of it all is part of it, along with the longing we've both endured—at least I know *I've* endured. But it's more than that, too. This all feels fleeting, like there are hurdles yet to clear. I know that's partly my fault.

She hasn't asked me not to go since we last talked about the fight. She won't ask—I can tell. But I also know she doesn't want me to. I know I could handle him. I think she knows it, too. She wants it. But she's afraid of the unexpected. The things we couldn't plan for have been our downfall so many times.

We've lain here the entire morning, her running her fingers up and down my arm and back while I press my face to the side in my pillow and stare at her. I like the way she looks at me—like I'm *someone.*

"You were really amazing last night," she hums.

I smirk, and bunch my shoulder. "That's not the first time I've heard that," I tease. Her hand stops moving and she brings it down on my shoulder with a quick *smack*. "Owwwww!"

I grab her, rolling her over so she's pinned beneath me, her eyes lit up with her laughter, her hair a chaotic storm of smoke around her.

"I meant at your hockey game, you cocky asshole," she says, rolling her eyes, but giving way to laughter again as I push my thumbs into the ticklish spots along her sides.

"I know," I say, my forehead against hers. Our laughter fades into a rhythmic breath and I close my eyes, feeling the tip of my nose brush against hers until I find my way to her lips. "I was just hoping I was amazing at other things, too," I speak against her mouth, biting my lip, then hers.

"You were," she says against me, her lips closing the slight distance until we're kissing so hard it feels as if it's for survival.

It feels as if it could be the last.

My phone buzzes with a text, and we both pause our movement until I lift myself enough to look into her eyes, neither of us happy.

"You should get that," she says, her face falling to the side, away from my phone.

Away from me.

I take a deep breath and lean to the edge of the bed, rolling away from her until I sit with my feet on the floor. It's nearly noon; we've slept most of the day away. I open my messages to find one from Harley. I knew it was him.

The fight is set for six at his gym. They're usually later, and it strikes me how rushed and unprofessional everything about this feels compared to the fights I've done for him before.

I text him back *OKAY,* then close my phone before turning to take in Emma, still lying in my bed with her back to me. I lay back down behind her, running my palm up the perfect line of her spine, sweeping her hair to the side and pressing my lips on the back of her hot neck.

"Was that about the fight?" she asks, her voice hoarse and quiet.

I press my head into the back of hers and breathe her in. "Yes," I say. I feel her nod against me, then eventually her hands find my arms and she pulls them around her tightly.

"When?" she asks, pulling my palm up to her chest, pressing it flat against her heart. It's beating so hard I can almost feel it working in and out.

"Six," I say. "But I need to leave in a couple hours to get ready."

She nods again, and her body quivers lightly. I know she's crying, but I also know she's trying to hide it from me. I let her think she has, and I run my thumbs over her knuckles as our hands caress each other.

"Hold me...like this...until you go?" Her voice is a whisper now.

"Okay," I say, snuggling into her more before pulling the blanket over us. I stroke her skin and hair until I can tell she's calm. She isn't asleep—she's too afraid of missing something. It takes me back to Lake Crest when I never let myself completely lose sense of where I was and what was happening around me. I learned early on that sleeping left me vulnerable—it's when others took advantage and stole away anything I had.

Nobody would be stealing anything from us today—not Emma's father, my history, or the ghosts of my past. I'd make sure of it. This small moment—it's Emma's and mine. And soon, when I'm about to face the sorry excuse for a man who marred her perfect face, I'll make sure he can't rob us of anything either.

* * *

Leaving her felt impossible. Emma has a paper due, so she buried herself in my bed, surrounded by books and her laptop. She played aloof as I packed my bag and left, as if it were just me getting ready to leave for practice, or class, or work. But her eyes were empty, and I know her thoughts were on where I'm really going.

I kissed her and promised her I'd call as soon as I was on my way back. She smiled, barely, nodding and pushing her ear buds in, her music turned so loud that I could hear it clearly on my end. I let her front. I know she needs this.

She never asked to come, which is good because I don't want to have to argue with her. I can't have her near him. I gave Trent orders to keep her home, too. He laughed at me at first, but quit when he took in my face—an understanding of how serious this is settling onto him.

I almost told Trent the truth—just so he would be able to stay calm, to do whatever he needed to do to keep her calm. But I stopped myself, still not one-hundred-percent committed to my midnight-hatched plan. I almost backed out at the bank when I withdrew every cent I had. I'm still not convinced I'll be able to follow through with it now as I step through the back door of Harley's gym—the street lined with expensive cars and the main warehouse filled with gambling men ready to spend their money on two twenty-something punk shits beating each other senseless for no title or ring.

I guess for some there's glory. For most of the guys I've fought, the prize has always been knowing they're ready for what's next, a gift of confidence as they head into the ring with someone real—someone who mattered. But today—there's not glory. There's grudge and hate and vengeance between two sick men. I'm well enough to admit I'm sick, to admit I like the feel of pain more than I should. I know the way I cope with what really hurts in my life is unhealthy. But now that I know how Emma feels, what it's like to have her completely fill the space inside my chest and heart, I'm not hungry for something to take me away anymore.

When life is good, I don't need the distraction of the rush. I've just never had *good* before, I guess.

Harley is still in his back office when I walk through the heavy metal door. It slams shut behind me, and Bill steps out from the office to see who's entering.

"Just me," I say, holding up a hand. He nods, then reaches his hand out to shake mine. His eyes glance around my body and his brow furrows when he realizes I don't have my usual training bag with me. All I have is a small envelope—nothing more. I nod and pat him on the back as I pass by, slipping into Harley's office.

"You're early. What, can't wait for that fix and need Bill to knock you in the head a few times now?" He snickers as he talks, amused at how predictable I am. Normally, he'd be right. But not today.

I plunk the heavy envelope on his desk then shove my hands in my pockets, staring at it, staring at *him* staring at it. He pokes it with a pen, turning it slightly, then tapping it.

"What's this?" he says, peering up at me, his hat turned backward so I can see the angry suspicion in his eyes.

"It's every cent I have to my name. Something like twenty-seven hundred. And I know I'll probably owe you more, and I'll get it to you, because I didn't want this to be a problem for you, to cost you anything," I say, my eyes meeting his. There's nothing Harley can do to me. I quit being afraid of people the day I stepped out of Lake Crest Academy.

He leans back in his chair, pulling the envelope in his hands and slicing it open on one end to look in at the small stack of money. He tosses it back on his desk, and folds his arms again, studying.

"What the fuck are you talking about?"

"I'm out, Harley," I say. I hear Bill chuckle softly behind me, and I glance at him, shaking my head. "No, I'm serious. I mean it. I'm out. I'm sorry, but I'm not fighting this guy today. I'm done fighting."

The air grows thick with quiet, the sound of chatter in the main gym faint in the background and the repeated thump of a speed bag working down the hall blurring into the rest of nothingness that fills Harley's hot office. He pulls his hat from his head, running his hand through his hair.

He leans forward, his palms flat on his desk on either side of the envelope, and he begins to shake his head, laughing to himself. I hold my breath, though, because I know better.

In a swift movement, he hurls the envelope at me. Money flies loose in all directions. He shoots his chair back against the wall, rounding his desk, slamming me into his door with enough force it closes behind me. His arm thrusts against my chest, knocking the wind from me. He slides it up my body until his forearm rests against my windpipe.

He. Can't. Hurt me.

"What the fuck do you mean, you're *done?* You are done when I say you're done, you crazy head-case motherfucker! I have a room full of high-dollar customers out there—with money they want to spend...*with me*... and that pathetic chunk of change you waltzed in here with is not even close to covering it—do you understand?"

I don't react. I simply hold his gaze, my mouth in a hard line and my breath working hard to pass through my nose and find a way into my limbs.

"You are going to get out there in an hour and stand in that goddamned ring and I don't give a shit if you raise your hand once. You can let him hit you until you go fucking blind! I don't care! All that matters is you go down in the fourth round, and then you can pack up all your shit and I never have to see your face again. Understood?"

His nostrils flaring, Harley leans into me, and my fingertips tingle from the lack of oxygen. I never let my eyes slip from his, and he loosens his hold on me just enough that I'm able to shake my head *no.*

He pushes into me again, this time rearing back and punching me in the gut and chest as his other arm brings renewed force against my neck.

"No," I choke out.

"Not an acceptable answer!" he rages.

"It's the only answer you're going to get," I say, my words cracked and hard to hear, but Harley hears them. His nose to mine, he's inches from my lips, and he reads them as I speak.

I watch his pupils dilate as the wave of realization comes over him. He's not going to win this battle. There's nothing he can say that's going to change my mind. Emma doesn't want me in the ring with Graham, so I'm not going.

"Fuck!" Harley says, punching a hole through the wall next to my head. His hand comes down three more times. I don't flinch.

"Harper, you better rethink this real quick! If you don't get your ass ready..."

"What are you going to do to me?" I interrupt. Harley flinches at my boldness, stumbling back a step or two, his brow lowering as his chest picks up speed, breathing in and out with more force. He opens his mouth, ready to lay into me again, but I ignore it all, talking right through him.

"This isn't about you, Harley. It's about me, and doing right by someone. And I never wanted to shit on everything you've done for me, have given me by letting me come here. You've given me an escape, so many times, man. And I am aware and grateful for you and your lack of judgment. Believe me...you've saved me from the brink more often than you'll ever know."

Harley looks up, his face still angry, his teeth gnashed.

"You could almost kill me and the answer would still be no," I say, and I watch as his chest stutters. "And that's only because I know *completely* killing me wouldn't do you any good either. You can't rule me, Harley. You never could."

I look over to Bill, standing, arms folded, against the wall across from us, his eyes switching from me to Harley and back again. Bill's doing his best to look armed and ready, but I can see the doubt and shock underneath it. He never thought I'd leave. I never thought I'd leave. Up until last night, I thought I'd be here today ready to pummel Graham, forgetting about the fourth-round rule, powering through until there was nothing left of him.

Then Emma cried in her sleep, her body cinching up on me, and her arms squeezing at her chest as if she were dying. That one vision—seeing her hurt when she wasn't awake and aware enough to hide the pain—was all it took.

I will never make her hurt like that again.

"Get the fuck out!" Harley yells. "Get your goddamned face away from me, get your car off my street, and leave."

His hand runs over his chin as his wide eyes look around his desk until he finds his chair, sitting in it and leaning back.

"I'm sorry, Harley. I really am grateful," I say, lifting my hand to shake his. He slaps it away, hard, then leans to the side, spitting on his floor and stomping the wetness into the ground with his heavy boot.

I look to Bill, my lips pursed, and I shake my head, perhaps a little in shame. I don't like leaving them in a position, but I weighed the pros and cons. Harley will be fine. Tomorrow, he'll have another me—another pawn to put in the ring. He'll get over today quickly, and Graham will live without the glory. And I will live without punishing him. As badly as I want to, I will live.

I step from the office and walk down the hallway slowly, letting my fingertips drag along the wood-paneled wall on my way out, remembering the feel of the tongue-and-groove pattern that I will never see again.

I don't know how I'm going to pay for next semester, and come three months from now, I'm not sure how I'm going to make my portion of the rent. But I'll figure it out. I'll take three jobs, beg coach to find more money for my scholarship portion, or hell—I'll sell my car. It doesn't matter as long as Emma's eyes are waiting for me, her arms waiting to hold me, her heart waiting to need me. I can live without so very many things. What I can't live without, though, is her.

Sliding into my car without a penny to my name, I turn my key, then adjust my mirror, looking at myself for the first time in maybe years. I stare into my own eyes and try to recognize something, and for once, I think I just might. My lip curls on one side, and I look back down, tugging my beanie on my head, my smile growing as I think about what I'm racing home to, shifting into drive and grinning all the way through the warehouse district.

I stop at the last light before I leave the shadows of the delivery bays—between two of the largest shipment buildings—and I think about calling Emma. I leave my phone in my pocket, deciding surprising her will be even sweeter. When I glance back into my review mirror, I see the swell of bright headlights racing toward me, and I don't have time to do anything but prepare my body for the blow.

The large SUV hauls through me, smashing my back-end, shattering glass, and pushing my car into the intersection—a passing car clips my front bumper, spinning me into the pole at the side of the road.

My arms are cut to shit, and my lip is bleeding badly, but my bones don't seem to be broken. I'm still whole. I kick at the door, the smell of gasoline rich. As I'm stepping out, I look toward the spot of the impact, the crushed SUV still revving, but the driver no longer inside. My head is ringing, and my body is tingling with adrenaline, but I somehow am aware enough to notice that both doors to the front seat are open. Two people were inside, and I have a strange sensation that they meant to hit me.

I wobble on my unsteady legs, and the faint sound of someone calling my name tries to force its way through the rush of blood passing over my eardrums. I spin in all directions, my head soon dizzy from my movement. I find the two people from the SUV—each grabbing one of my arms and kicking my legs out from under me, dragging me closer to the car that hit my front end.

"What the fuck, man!" I kick and jerk, but their hold is tight, and their size is nearly double mine. They stretch my body in opposite directions, kicking at my legs until they're able to drag me to the back end of the black Mercedes that hit me the second time.

"Always so unwilling, Harper. Always so quick to say *no*—to put up a fight. You never could just *do* what you were supposed to." His voice reaches down my throat and through my ears, strangling me…before seeping through the rest of my body and killing my spirit, one cell at a time.

I left Lake Crest when I was seventeen years old, never formally bidding farewell to the man who'd broken me more than any tragedy in my life had been able to before. I opted out of my exit interview, knowing nobody really cared to listen about my tales of corruption or reports of abuse. Instead, I let my last memory of that man be the beating he gave me and the round burn of his cigar on my wrist.

Standing before me, his hair grayed, but his body the same—his height somehow more than mine despite his age—I'm instantly filled with terror, and I fight to run, pulling and kicking against the beasts he's brought with him to hold me here for him to torture. I've been here, in this exact position with this man, so many times before.

"Graham was always such a good boy. He and I, we've had a great business relationship since he left my school. He saw the potential for our mutual gain—my…ability to persuade people for him, to make his indiscretions vanish. And we've made loads of money in return. I could hardly believe it when he mentioned your name a few weeks ago. What was it he called you? Oh yes, this *nuisance* that he wanted me to make disappear. But I don't do that anymore, Andrew. I don't make people disappear. I've…changed."

His grin is that of the devil, his mustache thin and his teeth yellow from nicotine. The acid in my stomach threatens to come up, so I will it down. I won't be weak in front of him. I'm weak for no one.

"So that's how Graham knew I went to Lake Crest," I say, spitting blood to the side, the spray of it hitting one of his beasts, who jerks me harder; I smirk, pleased that I've pissed him off.

"He was two years before you. Drugs…just like you," he says, and I jerk at the comparison. I'm nothing like Graham—not then, not now.

"I thought you would be another one I could trust, just like him. That's what I did at that shit-for-nothing school; I made apprentices, partners in my...*business.* But you were too stupid, weren't you?" His brow lowers, and he reaches into his side pocket, pulling out a lighter before moving to the breast pocket of his jacket for a cigar. I wince at the sight, my wrist burning from the memory.

"I'm not weak, like Graham. That's all," I say, the blood from my lip choking me again. I lean forward and spit, turning to the side and grinning at the guy I spit at before. "That better?" I say, an eyebrow raised.

"Oh, I don't think Graham's weak. After all, he isn't the one being held down and beaten by the light of the moon and headlights of my car, is he?" His laugh is soundless, and my body grows rigid on instinct, expecting to feel his hand on me, his fist through me; the need to protect myself, strong. "Look at that. I can still get to you, can't I?"

I twist as he steps closer, and the hold on me grows stronger.

"You're pathetic," I spit out. "You can't do anything to me. You have nothing to gain," I say, my eyes darting around him as he saunters close enough to blow a puff of his smoke into my face.

"Maybe I don't have anything to gain. But I sure as shit don't have anything to lose, either. I had a shitload of money invested on this fight happening tonight, and you just cost me. You...*you!* You were always costing me, and when Harley said the fight wasn't on because one guy dropped out, I knew who it was. I got into this on a whim, when Graham mentioned it was you. I thought it would be a quick-and-entertaining way to make some cash. I booked thousands, and some assholes even bet on you. Ha! Imagine that," he says, his face close enough that I can smell the sourness of his breath. "Someone actually thought you would win. But you're just the pathetic coward you always were, aren't you?"

"I'm no coward," I seethe, my mouth once again full of blood. "I'm just not your pawn. *You're* the one who has always been afraid. I was a child, and I stood up to you. You're nothing."

I swallow hard, then let my lids fall closed for a brief second as I think of Emma's face, my heart beating, my hands on her. There's nothing he can take from me, and I've survived him before. I found her in the end.

I open my eyes and stare at him, almost challenging him, begging for his worst, when something shifts—a flash that makes my world tilt, my head dizzy. His thugs drop their hold under my arms and take off running back to the smashed-up SUV that brought them here. Nick Meyers walks away just as quickly, his step not quite a run, but his clip urgent. Their tires squeal and they swerve back into the direction they came from, their lights darting around buildings and disappearing around corners—the sound of their engines vanishing just as fast.

"That's right, you fucker!" I yell, lifting my arm and swinging it over my hand, giving my ghosts a giant middle finger. "Run away, you fucking loser! I will never belong to you!"

My legs collapse under my weight, and my knees hit the gravel hard, the rocks digging into my skin as I fall forward, my hands catching me before my face hits the ground. I'm instantly heavy. The ground begins to swirl, and despite the fact that the sun has fallen below the horizon, my world is bright. Everything yellow. Everything slow. My mouth is overcome with the taste of metal, and I let myself fall to my back, my head to the side as I vomit blood. The feeling sends a searing burn through my stomach, and I curl my knees up into my body like a child, my hands moving to my belly, wanting to make the pain stop.

Wet—so wet. Everything wet! I pull my hand up in front of me and immediately lurch with the desire to vomit again. The blood is everywhere. I look down to see my shirt soaked through, and as I pull the fabric up, I see the gaping hole in my belly, the round wound spilling out blood faster than I can think. My mind races with what to do, putting together what happened, then I remember it—the sound. I shut it out, but it was there—the loud cap of the gun, the acrid stench from the fire of it.

My hand finds my pocket, and I slide my phone out, hitting the emergency icon and letting it ring. A woman answers, and I choke on my blood as I lay myself more to the side. More vomit. Moaning…I need to make noise so they hear me. I moan, and I slap at the pavement, and then eventually, there's nothing.

* * *

EMMA

I haven't written a single word. I've been sitting in here among the smell of Andrew, buried in his covers, my books all around me, and all I've done is blink. I haven't opened my laptop once, and the few times Trent has knocked lightly on the door, I've lied that I'm "fine" and "getting a lot done."

He doesn't believe me. I can tell. And his knocks have come more often as the day has shifted into evening, as six o'clock has passed and as nearly an hour after the time Andrew was set to fight has come and gone.

I'm giving him two more minutes. Two minutes, and then I'm calling. Two minutes, and then I'm dragging Trent out into the streets with me to find him. The soft knock comes again, and this time I invite him in.

"Nothing?" Trent asks, nodding to my phone, his own in his hand. I shake my head quickly, my eyes wide on my blank screen. Why is my screen blank? Why no ringing or message?

"I'm sure he's on his way," he says, sitting on the end of the bed near my feet. I nod *yes*, but I don't believe it. Something is wrong—I feel it in my gut.

The two minutes comes and goes, and as soon as my phone reads 7:01, I let the tear I've been holding in for hours fall down my cheek.

"We have to find him," I say.

"I know," Trent says, standing and walking from the room. "I'll get my keys."

I kick away the useless books on his bed, running to the restroom to pull my hair into a tie and shove my feet into my running shoes. I swallow my nightly round of meds with the feeling that I won't be home in time to take them, then I rush around the corner, still pulling my arms into the sleeves of one of Andrew's sweatshirts when I run into Trent. He's holding a hand up to me, his phone pressed to his ear with his other hand, and his face is completely blank.

"Yes, I'll call them. Yes, yes. Thank you. I'll be there soon, too," Trent says. I reach for his hand, grabbing onto his fingers, threading mine with his and holding his fist hostage. I have a sense that I'm going to need it to stand soon.

"Was that him?" I ask. He shakes his head *no*.

"Hospital," he says, his eyes wide, not looking at anything. "Someone... shot him, Emma. He's in critical..."

My lungs collapse and everything blurs. I fall down Trent's leg, my grasp on his hand too weak, and his the same as he stands limply, in shock.

"I...I have to call his mom. I...I don't think I can drive, Em. I..." Trent's eyes fall to mine, and we both look into each other. We should have tried harder. We could have stopped this. Andrew...I might lose Andrew!

"I'll call a cab. Where is he?" I fumble with my phone, dropping it on the floor and cracking a corner of the screen. Shit! I hope it still works. I click it *on*, and breathe out hard when it lights up.

"Mercy," Trent says, falling into one of the stools in his kitchen, his eyes forward on his phone as he chews at the inside of his mouth.

I manage to speak clearly enough to request our cab, and I listen as Trent delivers the painful news to a family that's had so much of it over the years. He ends his phone call, unable to give them many answers, just as our cab pulls up, and we both drag ourselves to it. As I close the door, I glance up and realize that we left the front door completely open, and I motion to Trent.

He shrugs, so I let the driver pull away. There's nothing worth anything in that apartment, anyhow. The only thing that matters is fighting for his life seventeen miles away.

"Hold on, Andrew," I murmur to myself. "Please, just...hold on."

CHAPTER 22

EMMA

The *beeping* sound haunts me. I wait for irregularities. Though, I've learned now that even those sounds are meaningless. Andrew is being kept alive by a tangled mess of tubes and wires and liquids all working together. His body repaired as best as doctors could, the worry now is how long until he wakes on his own, and what state his brain was in after he was left to die in some back lot only miles away from our home.

Our home.

His family showed up minutes behind Trent and me, and his brother came in this morning. He looks so much like Andrew; it's hard to look at him. He's been kind, but very quiet. He rarely leaves Andrew's side. He lets me stay, too. I told him who I was, that staying here was important, and he just nodded once, never questioning that my need to be present was just as great as his.

He stepped out to grab coffee and call his girlfriend. They weren't able to both make the flight from Germany. I don't think they could afford it. It must have cost thousands as it was. I can tell Owen misses her, though, and

I can tell she loves Andrew like her own flesh and blood. I heard her crying through the phone earlier.

She sounds like me.

"Here, I made it black, but brought a little of everything," Owen says, handing me a small cardboard box filled with sugars and creams along with a Styrofoam cup of steaming coffee. I nod *thanks,* then slide it onto the table next to me. He stares at it for a moment quietly.

"I'm not very hungry," I say.

"Yeah," he sighs, setting his cup down, no intention of drinking it either. "There's a girl here for you," he says, his eyes on his brother as he slides one of the tubes over Andrew's chest and away from his neck, wanting him to be comfortable even in this state. "She said her name's Nicole or Lesley or something like that."

"Lindsey," I whisper.

"Yeah, that was it," he says. "Anyhow, she's in the family room down the hall. I told her I'd come get you."

"Thanks," I say, my eyes zeroing in on Andrew's, willing them to open. "If anything changes..." I start to say as I stand. Owen raises a hand, acknowledging me.

I hate leaving his room. I'm so afraid I'll miss something. So afraid I'm what's helping him breathe—as self-centered as that sounds. The door closes lightly behind me, and I take small, sliding steps down the hall, my hand dragging along the cold metal of the railings until I get to the windows for the family room. Andrew's mom and stepdad took off for a nearby hotel to grab a room so they could shower and stay close for as long as Andrew would be here. The only one in the waiting room now is Lindsey. Her back is to me as I open the door, but she sits up fast and turns around, her eyes meeting mine as soon as I enter.

"Hi," I say, lifting my shoulders, not sure if I should hug her, or thank her, or apologize. Probably all three, but my body doesn't seem to want to leave the spot where it stopped walking.

"Hi," she says in return, standing, but not moving closer. We're both at the same impasse. Her head falls, and she laughs lightly with tears in her eyes. "Andrew said he'd find a way to get me and you together."

She bites her lip when she looks at me, her head shaking. I move to her, and the closer I get, the less worried I am over everything else. Her arms open to me, and she holds me tight as I cry into her. I cry hard and long, until my face is empty and my heart feels close to normal again. When I finally step away, I keep hold of her hand, and I shake it up and down as I speak, nervous to let her go and so happy to be touching my friend.

She's here. Of course, she's here.

"I'm so sorry, Lindsey. God, I'm so sorry," I say, my face puffy and my voice a pathetic rasp.

"I know," she says. She doesn't smile, and her eyes fall from mine quickly. "I was so hurt. I'm *still* hurt, and that's going to take time. It's not that I thought Andrew and I were going to run away and make a life together. Hell, I was starting to think he was gay because the boy never liked to make out for long, and it sure as hell never went anywhere. Though he was a good kisser. Moody as shit, but a good kisser."

She laughs at this, and I laugh, too. Hers fades, though, and she looks right into my eyes.

"I was hurt because you didn't tell me something important in your life. You can trust me, Emma. With anything. And the thought that you couldn't...with Andrew? It hurt."

I sit in a small chair next to her and look down at my hands. "I didn't want to hurt you," I say, not able to look at her when I speak. "It felt like I had to pick, you or him, and I'm so sorry I didn't have faith in how strong *we* were. That's on me, Linds. And I'm so...so deeply sorry."

I whisper an apology again, but I know its just words. And I know it's time, like she said, that's going to truly heal her and me. But she's here now, when I need her desperately. She's here. I sense her shadow as she sits next to me on the sofa, and I let myself go, catching her up on what I know—there's an investigation, they think it's some smalltime bookie who thought Andrew owed him money.

"So it wasn't Graham?" she asks. I shake my head *no*.

It grows quiet between us again for several minutes. I don't like the quiet. My mind gets carried away, starts imagining the whirling sounds of his machines and beeping and people rushing—Andrew leaving.

"You should try to go home, maybe shower?" Lindsey says, her mouth twisted on one side. "You can...you can come...*home*. It won't be easy, but

I've had time to think, and I don't want this to be the end of the *Emma and Lindsey show.* I'm probably going to say bitchy things sometimes, and be totally passive aggressive, but I want to try to...you know...move past it?"

I suck in a sharp breath, my cry surprising me almost as much as her gesture. I reach over and squeeze her hand again, my eyes fluttering as they close and I nod, accepting her offer.

"I missed my classes today. I missed...Miranda," I say, tucking my lip in, waiting for Lindsey's response. I'm hoping she'll give me a solution.

"Yeah, that's...that isn't good," she agrees. "But I think you need to talk to her, Em. You know you can switch mentors, if something's uncomfortable or if it gets awkward."

I nod again, grateful for her suggestion—one I'd thought about myself. It's hard to give up time with the person I admire because her son happens to be an awful human being. Then again, I'm not sure how wonderful Miranda is after all. She saved my life, but maybe that doesn't make her a hero—maybe it just makes her good at her job. I've seen glimpses of the cracks in her selfless façade, and they're discouraging.

"Just promise you'll think about it," Lindsey says, her hand on my knee. "You have options."

* * *

My conversation with Lindsey stuck with me, even now, hours after she left.

I have options.

I'm not so sure I do, but looking at Andrew...watching him lay here—so much working on his behalf just so he can breathe—I feel a little angry with myself for letting Graham off without any punishment for what he did. I know he's not the hand that put Andrew here today, but he's partly the reason. And he *is* the hand that struck me.

I wonder how many others he's abused?

My mind keeps replaying the switch flipping in him. I go to all of those moments where he wasn't quite a gentleman in the first place. He was short, or rude, or curt during a conversation. His hands were always just *a little too assuming* with me, crossing the line *a little too far*; his presumption that I was his property happened quickly, and without my consent.

"You should take a break," Owen says, kicking my foot from the chair he and I have both commandeered as our footstool. He smirks, spreading his enormous feet out on the surface of the seat in a teasing way, taking up all the space.

I sit up, rubbing my face and sliding my advanced bio book back in my bag on the floor. I haven't slept but for a few minutes here and there, and I can feel the knots in my hair around the base of my neck. I think...maybe... I also smell a little.

"Go home. Take a nap. Get some rest. I promise I'll text you if *anything* happens," he says, holding out a fist for me to pound. I laugh at it, then squeeze it between both of my hands. Twenty-four hours together in this situation has formed an instant bond between Owen and me. I get why Andrew loves him so much.

I pull my bag over my shoulders and head through the door, spinning around before leaving and pointing at him. "You promise. If *anything* happens," I say.

Owen crosses his heart, and I believe him. I've learned that's part of the deal with Harper boys—they don't swear on their hearts often, and when they do, they mean it.

I think about going to my old apartment, and when I hail a cab out front, that's the address I give the driver. But when I step out of the car, my legs carry me to Andrew's. The smell is comforting, and I *feel* him alive here. I need that—the image of him living, him just being. I shower quickly and leave a note for Trent asking him to text me when he gets home. He was taking care of alerting the school and the coach.

My hair dried and my clothes changed, I feel a small reserve of energy kick in my body. I brew myself a double cup of coffee and fill one of Trent's mugs so I can carry it with me to stave off sleepiness for a few hours longer. I lock up and begin to walk back to the hospital, but I notice the light outside, the glow of late afternoon, and I check the time on my phone. It's not quite four-thirty, and Miranda's office hours end at five.

I don't want to go. I stop walking at least a dozen times, a dozen more I turn around. But Lindsey is right. And Andrew was right. I need to tell someone—I need to tell Miranda first.

By the time I get to her door, I can hear the sounds of her on the other side powering down her computer and packing up her things. With a deep breath, I knock lightly, and her door slowly slides open with the force of my touch. Her body leans back in her chair, and soon our eyes meet.

"Emma, hi. I was just packing up. I missed you today," she says, no longer looking at me. She's checking out, moving on to her next thing. I step into her office and watch as she pulls her makeup bag from her purse, pulling out a mirror and lip gloss that she circles around her lips twice. I wonder who she's wearing that for?

"Yes, I know. I'm sorry I missed today. I...a friend of mine was in a terrible accident. I've been at the hospital with him," I say, sitting down as she stands. She glances as our bodies play opposite, her lips pursing and her brow furrowing with inconvenience. She sits anyhow, because she's not a rude person. She's just not as selfless as I always thought.

"I hope he's all right," she says, and I notice how rehearsed her sympathy sounds. I think she may be a sociopath—I read somewhere that most successful people are.

"He's at Mercy, and it's...well...we're waiting for him to wake up," I grimace. On cue, she bows her head—more rehearsed sympathy on its way.

"I see. Well, I'm very sorry," she says. "We can catch up later this week. I understand, Emma. And I have somewhere I need to leave for soon, so—"

"Right," I say, standing, my bag in my lap sliding to the floor. I awkwardly bend and pick it up, squeezing my eyes shut as my head is down. *Be strong, Emma. Be strong.* "I...I'll let you get going. I just...I only had one thing I wanted to talk to you about first. It...it won't take long."

Really, it should take hours. Maybe even days. There should be wake-up calls and interventions discussed, but I get the sense that I have about two minutes to make my case. I pull my phone from the front pocket of my bag, clicking it *on*, sliding it across her desk, the photo of my face filling the screen.

Miranda remains standing, her head down and looking at the girl on my phone—the one with a deep-purple bruise around her eye, with matching handprints around her arm where Graham dug his fingers in. Miranda only stares, waiting for me to say it.

"I respect you. So much. And it's more than my heart, though...yeah... my heart has a lot to do with it. But that's not why I came here. I came here to learn from you, because I believe in what you do, and I want to be like you—professionally," I say. Her lip twitches at my addendum. "It's out of that respect that I thought I should tell you first. I'm filing a police report. I'm leaving here and going to the student advocacy center first. And I'm not sleeping until I've documented my story. Graham...gave me that." I move my finger to the screen, pointing to it, then rolling my sleeve up on that same arm and turning it over, exposing the soft flesh of my forearm and the black, finger-sized marks left from his hold on me. "And this," I add.

Miranda's eyes dart around the evidence, her look almost analytical. I wait for tears. For an apology. For...something. But she only nods.

"If that's what you think is best, then do what you think is necessary," she says, her eyes rising to meet mine. I'm in shock at the complete lack of empathy in them, and I can't help my candor.

She doesn't believe me.

"Miranda," I say, and she straightens at my use of her first name. I've called her that before, but something tells me she'd rather show her dominance now. First names make us feel like equals. "Dr. Wheaton, your son needs help. I don't want *this* to happen to someone else...or worse," I say, swallowing hard at the thought of what could have happened. My nightmares play that version, even during catnaps at the hospital—it's nothing but a teeter-totter of Graham's anger and Andrew's pain.

"Like I said," she says, sliding her chair under her desk and walking to the door, encouraging me to follow. "You do what you feel is necessary. Now, I do need to make an obligation, so if we can talk more at our regular meeting later this week..."

Her lips are in a perfect smile, and I notice how her eyebrows are raised indignantly. I'm not sure what I expected from coming here, but I no longer feel beholden to her for what she's given me. A weight has been lifted.

I tug my bag over my shoulder and mimic her smile with a clenched-teeth version of my own. I step out of her office and she sends me away with one more condolence for my friend in the hospital, and I walk away, shaking my head and listening to the sound of her heels stamp along the floor in the other direction—all the way to the elevator on the other end.

I leave my sleeve rolled up as I take the stairs down two flights to the ground, and I look at the marks on my arm, renewed strength finding me that I'm right—that I owe nothing to anybody. I push through the main doors, out onto the campus mall, and move my own fingers to the marks on my arms, my hands not able to spread wide enough to meet every mark, and I think to myself how my bruises are like fingerprints—there's really only one, singular match.

I stop at the advocacy center first. I remember learning about it during orientation, thinking I would never need it. I'm so grateful for it now. It's after five in the afternoon, but there are people here at the front, waiting—with open arms. From the moment I step inside and utter the words "I was attacked," I'm surrounded by support. My advocate's name is Jane, and even her eyes on me while I'm talking let me know she's on my side. She believes me, and Jane and I—we've got this.

The forms with the advocacy center take an hour to complete, but I insist on filing my report with the police tonight. I don't want to wait—I'm afraid I'll change my mind, and I'm also afraid of closing my eyes at night. This act I'm doing right now, it feels like a much-needed antidote to the poison Graham left behind.

The officer who greets us at the campus police station is kind. Her last name is Rodriguez. She told me her first name, and I know it's on the card she handed me, but I can't take my eyes off of her tag. I'll remember her last name for now. I don't think she likes that I insist Jane comes with me. But I can't do this alone, and reluctantly the officer agrees, ushering me to a private room where I document every single moment of that night—what happened, and the people I know were there to see it. I give them Graham's phone number, and his friend Brody's name, the only friend of his I really spoke to. I'm sure his friends will stand up for him—*I'm sure they've seen a scene like mine before.* But I remembered other things from that night. The club's security guy was named Jax, and he helped me into a cab. I describe a few others, including the cab driver…he saw things, too.

I'm racking my brain, trying to dig out more details, things I can give

Officer Rodriguez that will help even more. The longer I speak, the angrier I get, and eventually, the emotion builds up to a boiling point and my hand forms a fist, punching hard against the table.

"It's okay, Miss Burke. What you gave us, it's enough for now," the officer says, her hands still from writing in her notepad and her head cocked to one side. She's almost being kind, but yet the whole thing feels sterile at the same time—emotionless. My breathing is a little rapid, and it takes me a few seconds to let the heat dissipate from my face.

"I'm sorry. I haven't really…I haven't really gone through *anger* yet," I say, grabbing the bottle of water she brought for me, twisting the top off and drinking nearly half of it down.

"It's all okay," Jane says, her hand moving forward to mine, which is once again balled in a fist on the table. She pats it once, causing me to look up, my lungs finally taking a deep breath. "What you feel—whatever you feel, whenever you feel it—it's okay."

I take in Jane's words, and I unfurl my fingers, flexing my hand and sliding it along the surface of the table outward from me, laying forward and stretching before pulling my body back in.

"It's okay," I repeat in a whisper.

"Yes," she says.

After two hours of rehashing, probing questions into my background, and conversation that almost makes me feel as if *I'm* the one being investigated, Officer Rodriguez pulls all of the paperwork into a file, then makes some notes on the top cover before stacking it on top of several other folders. I wonder how many of those are cases just like mine?

Jane walks out from the back offices with me, and I can't help myself—I hug her. She hands me a few of her cards, encouraging me to share them with others I think might need help, and she also urges me to call—whenever. I'm going to. A lot. Then she guides me back out to the front lobby where a homeless man is passed out across four seats. All of his earthly possessions are tucked in a black plastic bag clutched in his hand while he slumbers.

Jane and I part ways when I leave the police station. The air is crisp and cold. I stop at the steps and pull on Andrew's sweatshirt, then lift my bag over my back and make my way to the train stop near the edge of campus.

My fingers are tingling and my feet feel heavy, and in the middle of my walk I have to pause and hold my arms over my head, reminding myself to breathe so I don't fall over. My stomach kicks in its two cents, and I bend forward and throw up the little contents that are in my stomach. The panic attack comes and goes, but it leaves me feeling even more exhausted.

I buy a ticket to take me back to Mercy and climb aboard the next train to arrive, hugging my bag in my lap—clutching something personal, just like the homeless man from the police lobby. It's late. Hours have disappeared while I've told my story. Time well spent. Empowering, though emotionally draining. No matter how tired I may feel, I don't dare shut my eyes. I left my half-full coffee mug in Miranda's office, and as much as I could use the caffeine, I smirk at the thought of how irritated she's going to be with the smell of stale coffee and the reminder of me, and my visit, there to greet her in the morning. In the midst of so much that's awful, at least I have this one small win.

CHAPTER 23

EMMA

It's been sixty hours.

Six. Zero.

The doctors told us not even to consider worrying about things until we start to hit that seventy-two-hour mark.

Those numbers are arbitrary. I know they are, because they aren't in any of my books. Nothing is for certain, and throwing out hours is just a way for doctors to buy time to find consciousness. The cases run the gamut—some people waking up immediately, others taking weeks. Science points to medians, but medians are just clusters of numbers—they don't mean anything when the person you love is all that counts.

But I also know Andrew Harper, and I know if there is a number to beat, he's going to. I spent most of this morning talking to him. He doesn't talk back, which I jokingly told him was refreshing. Owen was in the room, and he just moved his phone low enough to raise a brow at me, then went back to texting his girlfriend.

When Owen stepped outside for a while, I whispered in Andrew's ear that I reported Graham. I needed to say it out loud, even in a whisper. I needed Andrew to hear it. I finally let myself exhale a little—the weight lifting for just a moment.

With every hour that's passed, I've watched him like a hawk, waiting... knowing any second I'd hear him. It's why I've ignored the raging growl building in my belly. The floor at my feet is lined with emptied cups, and my breath tastes foul, and the growling—it's getting harder to ignore, until finally one lingers so long I can actually feel the pang work around my intestines and climb up my esophagus.

"Okay, either you're shifting into a vampire and the sun coming in through that window is secretly melting away your skin, or you need to feed that monster in your gut," Owen says, his phone flat against his leg again.

"What?" I ask. My stomach betrays me, growling again—with a vengeance.

"It's gross. You sound like my grandfather. Seriously, go eat," Owen chuckles. I shrug and roll my eyes, standing, but stopping at the door. He raises a hand, never looking away from his phone screen. "I know, I know...text you the second something happens."

"The. Second," I point at him.

I've been very positive this morning. It's the first time I've felt this full of hope since my parents pulled me out of high school to head to the hospital for my surgery. Things feel brighter, and breathing feels easier.

Andrew is going to wake up today.

I have zero doubts.

I head down to the break room on the first floor where a few kids are lined up, all dressed in various costumes—ghosts, goblins, and superheroes with hospital gowns underneath. I'd lost track of time lately, and I realize it's Halloween.

I notice a line of doctors and nurses, all with pockets full of candy, positioned at tables around the cafeteria, and the scene paints a smile on my face. The girl closest to me is wearing wings, her bald head painted with beautiful designs and glitter. I'm amongst real fighters.

Andrew is right where he belongs.

I rush through the line at the gift shop across the hall, grabbing a granola bar for myself, and a row full of candy—the big bars—for the line of trick-or-treaters waiting in the hallway. I ask a nurse if it's okay if I help, too, and she smiles, nodding *yes*.

"The more we can do to remind them of life's good parts, the better," she grins.

I pause and watch as she moves to a table, placing her basket of small, crocheted angels in her lap, handing one along with a Hershey kiss to every kid that comes by.

"Hope and love," she says to me, laughing lightly. "I'm sure they just see the chocolate. But a few of them...they see the hope and love, too."

"I like that," I say. "Mind if I...take one? I know someone who could use it."

She nods, and pulls a blue angel from her stash, wrapping its soft arms around two kisses.

"You deserve something sweet, too," she says, winking at me.

"Thank you," I whisper, taking her gift and tucking it in the front pouch of Andrew's sweatshirt. I pull a chair out from the next table over and pour my candy bars on the table, loving the light in each child's eyes as they step up and whistle through missing teeth "trick-or-treat" and "thank you."

This is most definitely a good part.

* * *

ANDREW

It's Christmas, and I'm eight. My grandpa bought me a pedal car from the Goodwill, and Owen and he are in the garage fixing it so I can ride it. The pedals were bent, so they're taking the ones from Owen's bike and putting them on for me. Owen always gives me his things. I hope I have something for him one day.

I'm waiting at the back door, my feet dangling outside over the stoop, but my body inside where it's warm. Mom keeps yelling to shut the door. We have a fire going, and I'm letting out heat I guess. But I want to watch them work. My other brother, James, didn't come to Christmas. We all woke up in the morning, and he wasn't home.

Owen told me James is lost, but he seems to find his way home. I think he didn't want to come here because we don't make him very happy. There's a lot of yelling when James is home. And my mom cries a lot, too. I feel terrible, but I'm sort of glad he wasn't here for Christmas. It was a really nice day.

My grandfather just swore and threw that wrench thingy down on the ground. I giggle, and he and Owen both turn to look at me. I pull my feet inside and start to shut the door, hoping I didn't make them mad, but Owen catches the door before I can close it.

"You think you can do better, hot shot? Come on out; let's see you give it a try." Owen hands me his work gloves and a screwdriver. I stare at them, and the box of tools spread around the garage floor, then look up at Owen's face. He's smirking, so I know he isn't mad. And I *would* like to be in the garage—with the men, doing man things, like swearing and stuff.

I pull Owen's gloves on, my fingers barely making it halfway down the finger slots, and I grip the screwdriver in my right hand. My grandfather holds a flashlight up and begins walking me through the way my car works.

"The chain has to loop through these gears, but it's tricky, because those gears are bigger than the ones from Owen's bike, so we have to somehow make his parts work with the car parts, and all of those things need to turn the front tires when you pedal. Make sense?" My grandpa's hair tufts down in his eyes, and he reaches up, smoothing it back and pulling his glasses from his face, wiping away the smudges on his shirt before putting them back on.

"I think...I think I got it," I say, letting my eyes run through the process, what my grandfather said, over and over.

Owen moves to a chair, pulling up a water bottle and guzzling down half of it before handing the rest to our grandpa. I hear them whispering in the background, something about how they'll give me five minutes to play, then step back in and finish, but eventually their voices fade away, and all I hear is my own voice in my head.

My eyes lock in on individual parts, on grooves and patterns, and suddenly everything becomes clear. "I need both chains," I say.

My grandpa laughs and continues to talk with Owen.

"No, Grandpa. The old chain. I need it," I say, my voice serious. Owen stands up and moves over next to me, kneeling down and following the line of my sight, staring at the same gears and parts I am.

"He's right," he whispers, snapping to my grandpa to bring over the chain. Our grandpa does, and Owen hands it to me. I start snapping and unsnapping gears, blending both sizes into one, asking Owen for help when I'm not strong enough. My hands can't work fast enough, and it's like my mind is already riding the pedal car down the hill while my hands are still busy screwing and clipping metal pieces.

Within the hour, the three of us are rolling my new car down the driveway, already dusted with a fresh layer of snow. I don't care, though, because I deserve a test drive.

"How did you do that?" Owen says as he buckles the helmet to my head. It's an old motorcycle helmet that we bought from a garage sale, so one of Owen's shirts is stuffed inside to make it fit.

"I don't know. I just…I could *see* it. Is that…am I…weird?" I ask.

Owen presses on my head, making sure the helmet is snug enough.

"Yes," he grins. "You're very weird. But you might also be a genius. Now go kick some ass down that hill and don't crash your present."

The wind hits my face with Owen's push, and soon I'm soaring down the roadway, pulling on levers and leaning to veer from the right to the left. The road is empty. In fact, there aren't any houses near me anymore. I look up, and the sky is clear, and the sun is bright. When I look back, my house is gone, and so are Owen and my grandpa.

I'm going so fast, though, I can't stop. I keep pulling on the brake, but nothing is working. I didn't look at the brakes—I should have checked them!

"Andrew…Andrew, stop!"

I hear Owen. I can hear him, but he sounds different.

"Stop fighting, Andrew. Stop fighting!"

I'm not fighting. Why does he think I'm fighting? I'm scared. I'm lying down and the roadway is bumpy. I can't stop. But I'm not fighting.

"Andrew!"

I see him.

A dream.

Where am I?

My body. My arms. My head, legs, chest.

Owen is holding my right arm down against a bed, and my eyes are fighting to stay open long enough to see him. I see him. He's older. I'm older!

The fight. I didn't fight. I didn't fight! That's what this is. They think I was fighting, but I wasn't. I left, and then there was a crash. And Nick. The devil was there, and—

He shot me.

"I need Emma," I try to say, but when I hear my words, they're mumbles, nonsensical—something is stopping them, choking me. I try to speak again, but it's impossible, and it makes me start to cry in frustration. Owen's hands are on me again, and I flail just wanting to yell, to scream. He needs to understand me.

"Andrew. Stop fighting me," Owen says, his head close to mine.

Stop fighting.

Yes, that's it. I breathe deep, everything hurts, the sensation of wires and tubes intubating me and poking me everywhere, but I keep my arms still. I will my legs to lay still. And soon my eyes focus—I see Owen. He's smiling, and he's talking to doctors, my mom's voice coming from somewhere behind me.

I jerk with my arms, wanting to see, but so many people are over me now. My eyes find Owen, and grow wide. A man with glasses and a white coat is hovering over me, and my throat burns as I try to speak. He's telling me to stop, and I finally feel it—the tube in my throat.

I hold Owen in my sight while the man removes the tube, and everything hurts. The doctor is telling me not to speak yet, but I ignore him.

"You flew here from Germany," I say, my voice gravely and my throat raw. Owen laughs, sliding his hand down my arm to my hand, holding it like he did when I was a kid.

"Yeah, you shit head. I flew here from Germany," he says, running his sleeve over his eyes to blot away tears.

"Where…is…is Emma here?" I ask, my voice still barely audible.

Owen smiles, though, hearing me clearly. He nods.

"Yeah, she's here. She's barely left this room, and man is she going to be pissed at me when she finds out I told her to go eat and that's when you wake up. I'll go get her," he says, and I close my eyes, nodding *yes*.

Yes. Emma. I need Emma.

* * *

EMMA

I hand the last kid in line three candy bars, because that's all I had left.

"You should get a reward for being so patient," I wink. He smiles, reaching into his pillowcase to inspect the three chocolates I gave him.

I thank the nurse closest to me for letting me participate, then I tear a corner away from my granola bar, pushing part of it through and biting into the salty end. My stomach rolls in appreciation.

"Emma!"

Owen's voice startles me, and I jump, turning to see him racing toward me, his phone clutched in his hand.

"Andrew?" I ask, shoving the rest of my bar in my mouth, chewing manically. Owen nods, laughing and crying at the same time.

"I was going to text you, but I run faster than I type. Just now. He asked for you!"

I'm chasing behind him, trying to keep pace with his long strides as he takes the stairs three at a time.

"He asked for me," I repeat his words, smiling and pounding my feet as fast as they'll go. I toss my wrapper into a trash that we pass on our way down Andrew's hall after Owen buzzes us in through the large double doors. I see doctors and nurses all moving in and out of his room as I get closer, but I ignore them, weaving through and under until I'm at his bedside.

The instant I see his open eyes, I know—this is one of life's good parts, too, the kind of moment I will hold on to forever. My eyes swell with tears, and I lunge to his side, grabbing his hand and laying my torso across him, wanting to hug tighter but knowing he had so many open wounds underneath.

I feel his hand squeeze mine, his strength weak, but his movement very much alive and well.

"Oh my god I'm so happy to see you," I say, stepping back for a nurse to take vitals. I move around every person who needs him, but I never let go of my touch on him. His mom is sitting on the other side, her hands wrapped around his arm.

"How was your lunch?" he teases. His voice is scratchy, but I hear *him* underneath it all.

"You ass. I leave your room for five minutes, and *that's* when you decide to wake up?" I move my head to his shoulder, laying my face against his arm, feeling the beat of his heart with my hand. This entire time, his heart —it's been strong.

"You know me—flair for the dramatic," he says, swallowing hard.

"Andrew, I'm going to work on removing the tube in your nose, and it should make it a little easier to talk. But I'm going to need you to lie still and just be patient for a few minutes, okay?" the doctor says.

Andrew nods, and I squeeze his hand again, threading my fingers tightly with his. I roll his hand over in mine, opening his palm, and with the tip of my finger, I write *I love you* again and again. Andrew keeps his promise to the doctor, and we don't talk for almost an hour while they work around him, eventually removing many of the monitors and tubes attached to his body. My eyes never leave his the entire time, and even though he can't speak, I see the love in his eyes for me.

Eventually, the room clears, and for a small window of time, Andrew and I are alone.

"I didn't fight, Emma," he whispers, his voice still raw. I lay my head flat on his chest, the welcome stroke of his hand over my head and through my hair keeping time with the rhythm of his heart as I watch the lines zigzag up and down on the monitor.

"I know. Thank you," I weep against his chest. His hand stills as he leans forward as much as he can, his lips finding my head.

"That man…he would have found me eventually," he says, and I lift my head to look at him, my brow pinched.

"They said it was some bookie or something, and he thought you owed him money?" I stare deep into Andrew's eyes, and his mouth falls into a peaceful line.

"It was my demon," he says, rolling his arm over and motioning to the deep burn scar on his wrist. "He wanted to torture me one last time, I guess."

My eyes hover over his scar, and I pull his arm to my lips, pressing a soft kiss over the round mark, wanting to hide it all with my love. I rest my head back against him, knowing any moment his family will be back to break up our small bubble. They miss him too, but I'm selfish.

"Someone else took care of your demon for you," I sigh. "Owen can fill you in more, but I guess the investigators figured out where he lived, and when they got to his house to question him, they found him in the living room dead from a gunshot wound."

Andrew's chest pauses, and I tilt my head up to look at him. I don't like it when he's not breathing. Not breathing…it makes me nervous.

"Do they know who?" he asks.

I shake my head *no* and return my focus to the feel of his fingers in mine. Andrew does the same, and we both lay silently, our hands making long, methodic strokes along each other's skin. I can never get enough of the feel of him—life beating through his body, love pumping through his veins.

"My brother thinks you're cute," he teases after several minutes of quiet. I smile against him, turning my head just enough to press a kiss over his heart. "I mean, I'd understand if you want to jump ship and get on Team Owen. You could probably take Kensi in a fight."

"I like this Harper," I say, pulling my legs up onto his bed with me so I can lie next to him and snuggle in closer. Andrew leans his foot to the side, tapping his toe into the tip of my shoe. It makes me giggle.

"You always did have a thing for my shoes," he jokes.

I shove him lightly, then bury my face against his arm.

"Not true," I say, bringing my eyes to his, blushing and glancing to the side of his face. "It's the holes in your ears. I told you I liked them."

He laughs, moving his hand up to feel the small plastic circle tucked in his ear. The hospital took the metal gauges out, so Owen brought him new ones.

"Yeah, I'm a pretty sexy beast," he says, laughing and immediately wincing from the pain.

The chatter outside his door starts to build, and I know our time alone is done. There's so much I want to say, so many kisses I need to give and embraces that I need to savor. But I guess I have time now. Andrew Harper was a gift, a friend when I was scared and alone, a savior when I almost lost everything, and the love of my life that I got lucky enough to find a second time. He's all mine. And I'm his. And I am never letting go again.

His room fills with his family and Trent, Owen quickly putting a phone in his hand so he can talk to Kensi. Andrew tends to them all, hugging and talking and smiling for them—giving them light and hope—giving them the *good parts.* But he never lets go of my hand. And just when I think he's losing his grip, starting to move his attention from me to the other amazing and deserving people in his life, he turns my hand to the side, smoothing it flat and writing in it a letter at a time.

FOR ALWAYS.

EPILOGUE

CHRISTMAS DAY

ANDREW

Emma said I didn't need to bring a gift, but it felt wrong. The last time I was at her father's house, I noticed it was dark. That's half the reason we all used to pretend that house was haunted. When a home is built around the turn of the last century, the lighting is a little old.

It isn't much, but I carry the wrapped box in my arms, hoping her father will let me install the light in the foyer later today. I think it will make him happy—to have a little brightness in his house.

I know part of the reason I need a gift, though, is because of my nerves. I'm still consumed with wanting her father to like me. I've spent five years not giving a shit about others' opinions of me. Part of my own shelter, I just always assumed most people thought I was an asshole, so when they didn't, I was pleasantly surprised.

But Carl Burke—I care about his opinion. I care about his daughter, and that's the *only* reason I care about anything at all.

"Relax, he cooked all day, and he wanted you here," Emma says, dusting snowflakes from my arm. I wore the only nice jacket I have—it's black and wool…and hot as fuck!

I hold my arm out for her to take as we walk up the main path to the house. I'm driving a twenty-year-old Volvo. It's fast, and it sure as hell won't ever break. But it's not my Camaro.

When I got out of the hospital, my mom gave me a letter with a check inside. She said the man who delivered it was young, maybe mid-twenties, with blonde hair and a strong build. He told her he was from H and Sons, and they were handling the settlement from the insurance claim. But I know there was no claim, and I know it was just Harley's way of making sure the universe was right between us.

I always told you I take care of my business. Seems there were a few people who were bad *for business, and I wanted you to know, they won't be seeking you out anymore either. I'm sorry about your car; she was a beauty. This probably won't even come close to getting you in that kind of ride, but…I thought you deserved your money back. I never wanted a dime from you. You can't work for me anymore; I think you understand why. But, I'd be happy to give you a reference if you want to apply for a gym—a* real *gym, in the city. I know a guy who knows a guy, so maybe give this number a call.*

Glad to see you back on your feet.

H

My savings was just enough to buy a piece-of-shit from the auction, and Owen helped me tune it up a little before he left again for Germany. His season over there started a few weeks ago now, so I hope by the time he comes back, I can afford a Camaro again.

We spent the morning at my parents' house. Dwayne hooked me up with new gear and skates. Maybe I can break them in this winter so I can find my way back to the ice with the rest of the team. Coach was able to work my scholarship out with the financial aid department, diverting my money to next season since I was given a medical withdrawal from most of my classes this semester. I asked to take my finals anyhow, knowing I could pass, but they were rather insistent. Emma has about seven million years of school left, so I'm in no rush to leave.

My life took one enormous hiccup—everything about it thrown in all directions—yet somehow, when the dust settled, things looked brighter. I only hope that trend continues for one more hour, or at least through the second Carl opens the door and welcomes me inside.

"He knows I'm coming, right?" I ask Emma, my free hand now deeply rooted in my pocket, my other clutching my poorly wrapped box like a teddy bear.

"My god, Andrew. For such a bad-ass, you're pretty wussy right now," she laughs.

I mock her laugh, then let my mouth fall to a straight line. "I fail to see the humor in this. It's easy for you; you're the daughter. Last time I was here, I pretty much slammed the door in your father's face," I gulp.

Emma nods, pursing her lips in a tight smile, then reaches up to straighten my tie. For all that's holy, I'm wearing a tie. My jacket is a sweat-shop and I have a noose around my neck.

"That was before he really knew you," she says, her eyes wide and bright. I love the way she looks at me. I wish *everyone* saw me through her eyes.

Emma is so very strong. She calls me the fighter, but I don't know—I kind of think that's her. After she filed her police report, others came forward, and Graham was sentenced to two years of counseling. I could tell Emma was disappointed, but she never let it show. There was a plea bargain, with many—but Emma didn't want anything. She only wanted to be sure Graham couldn't do what he did to her again. Maybe, just this once, penance will work.

Graham's mother ended up taking a position at Northwestern...something she said was *already* in the works. I have my doubts, but I'm thankful that Emma doesn't have to face a reminder of her nightmares on a daily basis. Her heart was holding her hostage, but no more.

I'm not prepared, but the door opens anyway, and Carl and Cole stand side-by-side, both greeting us and ushering us in from the cold. They each take turns hugging Emma, and I step to the side, not wanting to be in the way.

"Well...we're here. We're...we're all here," Carl says, his voice sounding as nervous as I feel. He glances down, then back up to me. "Andrew...can I take your coat, son?"

"That'd be great," I say, probably a little too anxious. Emma ribs me with her elbow, and I roll my eyes at her. "It's so hot," I whisper, and her mouth quirks up on one side with a smile.

I set the package down on the side table and pull my arms from my sleeves slowly, my movements still not as sure and strong as they need to be. My entire front was opened up in surgery, and the healing is slow. Seems the only thing that heals slower than muscle is a broken heart; over the last few months, I've healed both.

I hand my coat to Carl, and he folds it over his arm, patting it and breathing in through his nose. "I'm...I'm really glad you're here, Andrew," he says, his eyes down at my jacket in his arms.

"Me, too, sir," I say, glancing to Emma then back to her father. He takes a slow step toward me, then raises his head to look into my eyes, his own delivering a heavy and honest message—an apology.

With one arm outstretched, Carl pulls me close, his heavy hand patting my back as he hugs me as if I'm his own. "I never thanked you, Andrew. What you did..." he starts, his voice clearly overrun with emotion. He's referring to my time at Lake Crest, to the trade I made with his daughter there on that highway—the lie I told to save her from the dark, and I know he's about to say more about it, but he doesn't need to. His simple thanks... that's enough.

"You don't have to," I say, hugging him in return, smiling at Emma over his shoulder before pulling away. "Really. I would do it all again."

He steps back, clearing his throat and running his hand under his eye. "Yes, I know you would," he says, pausing and lifting his gaze to mine. "I know you would, which is why I have peace."

Emma and Cole are walking down the hall, but I hear his words to me. He moves on quickly, hanging my coat before escorting me down the hallway to their simple dining room. I let him talk about things he needs to do to the house, and I eventually make him open my gift early, loving the smile on his ragged and tired face when he sees the small chandelier. I offer to stay late tonight, to help hang it and rewire a few things, and Emma sits back and watches as I form a bond with her father, as he trusts me with his most cherished possession, and I promise without words to never take her for granted.

On a day made for family and selflessness, I somehow become my brother—wanting to give all I have so others can feel joy. But it's not really selfless at all, because my heart is so full from it.

Full.

And beating.

And so very far away from *alone*.

THE END

ACKNOWLEDGMENTS

I first learned about Hypoplastic Left Heart Syndrome during a drive home through the Arizona desert from my parents' house on a late Sunday afternoon. I listen to a lot of NPR, and someone had done a story on one of the first long-term survivors of the Norwood procedure. I tuned in, my son napping in the backseat while we drove, and listened as I felt blessed that my son was born with a complete and working heart. The story was hopeful, inspirational and heartbreaking.

It left a mark.

I've wanted to weave this rare diagnosis into one of my stories for a while now. I just didn't know when the fit would feel right...until I began plotting out Emma Burke. Emma felt like so many of the stories I'd read on the condition, and as I dug deeper, learning all I could from friends in the medical profession (thanks, Robin Meyers Bull!) and organizations that research and support HLHS, I knew this was the book for this very important story.

As I began plotting, I started following a blog on the Children's Organ Transplant Association for Sadie Chapman. Sadie and Emma—they share the same diagnosis. And they're both dreamers. Sadie wants to be an actress, Emma, a surgeon. As I was writing, Sadie was on a waiting list for a new heart. On July 8, 2015, it came.

The costs associated with transplant surgeries are tremendous. Beyond the surgery itself, there are medications and biopsies and endless doctors visits to ward off organ rejection and other complications. But COTA does an amazing job of helping those like Sadie share their stories with the public. She is one of so many in need of support. For more information, visit cota.org. For more on Sadie, visit cotaforsadiec.com.

And Sadie: we have never met, but the reach of your heart is far, and the beat is strong. It kicks throughout Wicked Restless, and I thank you for that.

Please note that Wicked is most definitely fiction—and Emma's path is not necessarily that of the typical patient.

To say I love these Harper boys and the world they live in would be selling them short. Getting to dive back into their town, their family, this time through Andrew's eyes, was pure joy. I have the readers who were hungry for Andrew's take on life to thank for that. Thank you for loving the Harper boys as much as I do. It means the world to me.

I must also send thanks to Tracey Breeden, my go-to knowledge base on all things police procedure, protocol and general "but what if *this* happened—would he get arrested?" questions. I am so blessed to call you my friend.

While I'm an ESPN addict, when it comes to college hockey, there were some nuances I wasn't so sure on—practice routines, schedules, conferences, travel. Thank you to Scott Young, director of hockey operations and assistant coach of the Boston University men's hockey team, for taking the time out to chat up this tomboy and very girly romance writer! You filled in the gaps, and gained a forever fan for the Terriers (unless they ever face the Sun Devils).

As with every work, I would get nowhere if it were not for my team of amazing beta readers and editors. Thank you, Shelley, Bianca, Jen, Debbie, Ashley, Tina and Billi Joy Carson (Editing Addict) for steering me right. You ladies can drive me anywhere! And of course, thanks to the hubs and kiddo for putting up with the laptop at dinner, ballgames, practice, batting lessons, the trip to the East Coast (this list is endless). I love you both to the moon!

As with Wild Reckless, Wicked Restless tackles some very serious topics. I don't believe in shying away from things—the effects of mental health and the far-to-common instances for assault and rape among college students is unfortunately not fiction. Below are some resources that specialize in helping you when you need it most. If someone you know could use a helping hand to find healing and strength, please consider passing these websites along:

National Child Abuse Hotline
1.800.422.4453 www.childhelp.org

National Domestic Violence Hotline
1.800.799.7233 www.ndvh.org

Rape, Abuse & Incest National Network
1.800.656.4673 www.rainn.org

National Teen Dating Abuse Helpline
1.866.331.9474 www.loveisrespect.org

National Suicide Prevention Lifeline
1.800.273.8255 www.suicidepreventionlifeline.org

As always, thank you for spending time on my book. If you enjoyed Wicked Restless, please consider leaving a review and/or sharing your recommendation with a friend. I'm thankful for every kind word, and I promise to work hard to give you more to swoon over. Consider this my foot tap to you ;-).

With love,
Ginger

ALSO BY GINGER SCOTT

The Varsity Series

Varsity Heartbreaker

Varsity Tiebreaker

Varsity Rulebreaker

The Waiting Series

Waiting on the Sidelines

Going Long

The Hail Mary

Like Us Duet

A Boy Like You

A Girl Like Me

The Falling Series

This Is Falling

You And Everything After

The Girl I Was Before

In Your Dreams

The Harper Boys

Wild Reckless

Wicked Restless

Standalone Reads

Cowboy Villain Damsel Duel

Drummer Girl

BRED

Cry Baby

The Hard Count

Memphis

Hold My Breath

Blindness

How We Deal With Gravity

ABOUT GINGER SCOTT

Ginger Scott is an Amazon-bestselling and Goodreads Choice and Rita Award-nominated author from Peoria, Arizona. She is the author of several young and new adult romances, including bestsellers Cry Baby, The Hard Count, A Boy Like You, This Is Falling and Wild Reckless.

A sucker for a good romance, Ginger's other passion is sports, and she often blends the two in her stories. When she's not writing, the odds are high that she's somewhere near a baseball diamond, either watching her son swing for the fences or cheering on her favorite baseball team, the Arizona Diamondbacks. Ginger lives in Arizona and is married to her college sweetheart whom she met at ASU (fork 'em, Devils).

FIND GINGER ONLINE: www.littlemisswrite.com

www.ingramcontent.com/pod-product-compliance
Lightning Source LLC
Chambersburg PA
CBHW050118030726
47505CB00007B/1919

* 9 7 8 1 9 5 2 7 7 8 0 7 0 *